Only the best.

In this ambitious anthology you'll revel in the sardonic, overtly amoral plotting of Patricia Highsmith. You'll rediscover the strangely poignant turns of Stanley Ellin, and the profoundly underrated Margaret Millar, a genius who mixed savage social satire with brooding horror. You'll be treated to Stephen King at his chilling best. You'll find yourself on the violent urban streets of Ross Macdonald and Mickey Spillane, and steeped in the ominous regional flavor of Sharyn McCrumb and Tony Hillerman. You'll marvel at the cunning webs spun by Lawrence Block, Ruth Rendell, Anthony Boucher, and Sara Paretsky, all of whom defy expectations as they reinvent the genre. And you'll understand the awesome reputations of those authors who set the standard, such as the legendary Harlan Ellison, Fredric Brown, the master of the twist ending, and James M. Cain, uncannily skilled at knowing what went on between men and women behind closed doors.

Jeffery Deaver is the *New York Times* bestselling author of nineteen suspense novels, including *The Blue Nowhere* and *The Bone Collector*, which was made into a feature film starring Denzel Washington and Angelina Jolie. He has been nominated for three Edgar Awards from the Mystery Writers of America and is a two-time recipient of the Ellery Queen Readers Award for Best Short Story of the Year. A lawyer who quit practicing to write full-time, he lives in California and Virginia.

A CENTURY OF GREAT SUSPENSE STORIES

Edited by
Jeffery Deaver

BERKLEY PRIME CRIME, NEW YORK

A CENTURY OF GREAT SUSPENSE STORIES

A Berkley Prime Crime Book
Published by The Berkley Publishing Group,
a division of Penguin Group (USA) Inc.
375 Hudson Street, New York, New York 10014.

Visit our website at
www.penguinputnam.com

Anthology copyright © 2001 by Jeffery Deaver.
Text design by Kristin del Rosario.

First Edition: November 2001
This Edition: March 2003 / ISBN 0-425-19338-1

The Library of Congress Cataloging-in-Publication Data

A century of great suspense stories / edited by Jeffery Deaver.
p.   cm.
ISBN 0-425-18192-8 (alk. paper)
1. Detective and mystery stories, American.   2. American fiction—20th century.
3. Suspense fiction.   I. Deaver, Jeff.

PS648.D4 C43   2001
813'.087208—dc21
2001025881

PRINTED IN THE UNITED STATES OF AMERICA

10   9   8   7   6   5   4   3   2   1

Copyrights for *A Century of Great Suspense Stories*:

CONTENTS

Introduction

A T MY BOOK signings and at mystery conference seminars, I'm frequently approached by fans who ask for advice in getting started in the business of writing suspense fiction. Many times these folks tell me that their intention is to start along this career path by taking up short stories and, once they've learned that medium, graduating to novels.

I have to break the news to them that this would be like mastering Japanese to help them learn Russian. Yes, both short stories and novels are literary forms that convey a fictional story to readers, but that's about the end of the similarity. The skills used in writing a novel are very different from those required to write a short story. Crafting a story obviously takes less time than writing a novel but I'd venture to say that, word for word, the short story is a far more ambitious undertaking. Nuance and suggestion are the keys to successful stories; there is no room for needless atmosphere or characterization or for overwrought exposition. As the adage goes: I didn't have much time, so I wrote it long.

The responses a short-story writer seeks to elicit are different from a novelist's. Readers of short fiction have less opportunity to learn to love, or hate, the characters and to form attachments to the locale, so the emotional force in short stories derives from plotting. Twists and surprises are the readers' payoff and the best short stories are those that deliver a one-two punch. I find that in my novels my protagonists, while possibly flawed, are at their core decent, likable individuals who strive mightily against truly nasty evildoers. They more or less prevail. In the stories I write, on the other hand, that ain't necessarily so; my apparent heroes often emerge at the end of the story as heinous villains, while the innocent suffer like Job.

Short stories are, in other words, a unique literary form—and one that has remained remarkably consistent throughout this century. Slang, syntax, and fashion may have changed, but—adjusted for inflation, so to speak—the structure and dynamics of stories written in the early days of the century are virtually the same as those written today, as the selections in this volume attest.

It was an enviable job to compile these stories, though culling a handful from the thousands written over the past one hundred years and daring to label those the best was, well, an arduous task. Making the job even more difficult is the key defining word in the title: *suspense.* While all crime fiction—from whodunits to procedurals to cozies to hard-boiled detective stories—is about conflict and therefore should be suspenseful, I've focused on stories whose purpose is to unnerve readers and speed them to the end of the tale, where a twist or turn awaits, rather than to let them spend a pleasant twenty minutes or so with a favorite series character or puzzle about who a killer might be or laugh at the wry observations of a witty amateur sleuth. This has resulted in some glaring omissions, but I find comfort in the fact that the authors not represented here appear voluminously in other anthologies; their work is not neglected.

Apologies disposed of, let me then say what a delightful mix we have here.

While many writers of short fiction recount the exploits of public law enforcers and private detectives (here represented by Marcia Muller; Mickey Spillane; Ross Macdonald, and the mother of detective fiction, Anna Katharine Green), it is in the cobwebby attic of psychological suspense that the short story excels, and these are the tales that form the core of this anthology. Among the contributors who've mined this vein are Harlan Ellison, John Lutz, John D. MacDonald, Margaret Millar, Ed McBain, Sharyn McCrumb, Sara Paretsky, and James M. Cain. Some writers in the collection provide us with uncompromisingly grim stories while others take a more fanciful or ironic look at the workings of the criminal mind (Donald Westlake, Robert Bloch, Lawrence Block, and Ed Gorman).

The focus here is largely on American writers, but no collection of this sort would be complete without a sampling of the superb writers from across the Big Puddle, among them Robert Barnard, Ruth Rendell, and—we'll take a further jump, across the Big Channel—the prolific Frenchman George Simenon.

Every practitioner approaches the craft of writing differently, and short-story authors are no exception. Some of the stories here are lush, some are austere—in the best postmodern tradition. Length varies dramatically, points of view differ—even the methodology of creation varies significantly. We have represented here perhaps the two most polar opposite of craftsmen: Stanley Ellin would slowly rework and polish each *page* of his stories many times before proceeding to the next. Rex Stout, on the other hand, shunned revision at all costs and his fiction would explode, virtually unedited, from his mind.

Some of the writers here are specialists in a particular genre and never deviate from that category; others are comfortable with other genres. Contributor Fredric Brown wrote science fiction in addition to suspense. Stephen King is, of course, the master of the horror genre (not to mention any other category he might wish to write in). Robert Barnard, another of the British delegation here, is a well-respected critic and writer of nonfiction.

No anthology compiling suspense in the 1900s would be complete without a few legal thrillers (not as new a genre as youngsters who've recently discovered John Grisham would think—consider *Bleak House* and Dreiser's *An American Tragedy*). Here we have stories by masters Steve Martini; Lisa Scottoline; Jeremiah Healy; and Erle Stanley Gardner, the creator of the most popular fictional lawyer of all time—Perry Mason.

The settings of these stories vary widely and several I've included because, in addition to being excellent tales, locale is virtually another character: the Southwest (Tony Hillerman), the Carolinas (Michael Malone), the California/Nevada woods (Bill Pronzini), and Papua New Guinea (Janwillem van de Wetering).

A final note: Special mention should be made of several of our contributors, who might be called the linchpins of short suspense fiction in the past one hundred years: the cousins Manfred B. Lee and Frederic Dannay, known to the world as Ellery Queen, critic and reviewer Anthony Boucher, and Edward D. Hoch, who is perhaps the only person in the country whose full-time career has been writing short stories.

Enough of my rambling. Now it's time to do *your* part: Make a cup of tea or pour a glass of whisky, sit yourself down comfortably in your favorite chair, and enjoy the highlights of a hundred years of writing by men and women who love nothing more than to take their readers on a brief, but delightful, literary roller coaster ride.

JEFFERY DEAVER

THE GENTLEMAN IN THE LAKE

Robert Barnard

"Among the writers I admire most are Christie, Allingham, Rendell and Margaret Millar," Robert Barnard once noted. Perhaps this is why his own voice is that of a "pure" detective writer. Whatever else a given Barnard novel may offer (humor, keen social observation, place description that is genuinely poetic), his novels and stories always remain focused on the mystery. While one hates to speculate on which writers of our time will be read by future generations, Barnard, with his grace, intelligence, and enormous range of skills, is certainly a likely contender. *Death of an Old Goat* (1977), *Bodies* (1986), and *A City of Strangers* are among his many worthwhile novels, with his latest including *Unholy Dying*.

THERE HAD BEEN violent storms that night, but the body did not come to the surface until they had died down and a watery summer sun sent ripples of lemon and silver across the still-disturbed surface of Derwent Water. It was first seen by a little girl, clutching a plastic beaker of orange juice, who had strayed down from the small car park, over the pebbles, to the edge of the lake.

"What's that, Mummy?"

"What's what, dear?"

Her mother was wandering round, drinking in the calm, the silence, the magisterial beauty, the more potent for the absence of other tourists. She was a businesswoman, and holidays by the Lakes made her question uncomfortably what she was doing with her life. She strolled down to where the water lapped onto the stones.

"*There*, Mummy. *That.*"

She looked towards the lake. A sort of bundle bobbed on the surface a hundred yards or so away. She screwed up her eyes. A sort of *tweedy* bundle. Greeny-brown, like an old-fashioned gentleman's suit. As she watched she realised that she could make out, stretching out from the bundle, two lines . . . *Legs*. She put her hand firmly on her daughter's shoulder.

"Oh, it's just an old bundle of clothes, darling. Look, there's Patch wanting to play. He has to stretch his legs too, you know."

Patch barked obligingly, and the little girl trotted off to throw his ball for him. Without hurrying the woman made her way back to the car, picked up the car phone, and dialed 999.

———

IT WAS LATE on in the previous summer that Marcia Catchpole had sat beside Sir James Harrington at a dinner party in St. John's Wood. "Something immensely distinguished in Law," her hostess Serena Fisk had told her vaguely. "Not a judge, but a rather famous defending counsel, or prosecuting counsel, or *something* of that sort."

He had been rather quiet as they all sat down: urbane, courteous in a dated sort of way, but quiet. It was as if he was far away, reviewing the finer points of a case long ago.

"So nice to have *soup*," said Marcia, famous for "drawing people out," especially men. "Soup seems almost to have gone out these days."

"Really?" said Sir James, as if they were discussing the habits of Eskimos or Trobriand Islanders. "Yes, I suppose you don't often . . . *get it.*"

"No, it's all melons and ham, and pâté, and seafood cocktails."

"Is it? *Is it?*"

His concentration wavering, he returned to his soup, which he was consuming a good deal more expertly than Marcia, who, truth to tell, was more used to melons and suchlike.

"You don't eat out a great deal?"

"No. Not now. Once, when I was practising. . . . But not now. And not since my wife died."

"Of course you're right: People don't like singles, do they?"

"Singles?"

"People on their own. For dinner parties. They have to find another one—like me tonight."

"Yes . . . Yes," he said, as if only half-understanding what she said.

"And it's no fun eating in a restaurant on your own, is it?"

"No . . . None at all . . . I have a woman come in," he added, as if trying to make a contribution of his own.

"To cook and clean for you?"

"Yes . . . Perfectly capable woman. . . . It's not the same, though."

"No. Nothing is, is it, when you find yourself on your own?"

"No, it's not. . . ." He thought, as if thought was difficult. "You can't *do* so many things you used to do."

"Ah, you find that too, do you? What do you miss most?"

There was a moment's silence, as if he had forgotten what they were talking about. Then he said: "Travel. I'd like to go to the Lakes again."

"Oh, the Lakes! One of my favourite places. Don't you drive?"

"No. I've never had any need before."

"Do you have children?"

"Oh yes. Two sons. One in medicine, one in politics. Busy chaps with families of their own. Can't expect them to take me places. . . . Don't see much of them. . . ." His moment of animation seemed to fade; and he picked away at his entrée. "What *is* this fish, Molly?"

When, the next day, she phoned to thank her hostess, Marcia commented that Sir James was "such a sweetie."

"You and he seemed to get on like a house on fire, anyway."

"Oh, we did."

"Other people said he was awfully vague."

"Oh, it's the legal mind. Wrapped in grand generalities. His wife been dead long?"

"About two years. I believe he misses her frightfully. Molly used to arrange all the practicalities for him."

"I can believe that. I was supposed to ring him about a book I have that he wanted, but he forgot to give me his number."

"Oh, it's two-seven-one-eight-seven-six. A rather grand place in Chelsea."

But Marcia had already guessed the number after going through the telephone directory. She had also guessed at the name of Sir James's late wife.

"WE CAN'T DO much till we have the pathologist's report," said Superintendent Southern, fingering the still-damp material of a tweed suit. "Except perhaps about *this*."

Sergeant Potter looked down at it.

"I don't know a lot about such things," he said, "but I'd have said that suit was dear."

"So would I. A gentleman's suit, made to measure and beautifully sewn. I've had one of the secretaries in who knows about these things. A gentleman's suit for country wear. Made for a man who doesn't know the meaning of the word 'casual.' With a nametag sewn in by the tailor and crudely removed . . . with a razor blade probably."

"You don't *get* razor blades much these days."

"Perhaps he's also someone who doesn't know the meaning of the word 'throwaway.' A picture seems to be emerging."

"And the removal of the nametag almost inevitably means—"

"Murder. Yes, I'd say so."

MARCIA DECIDED AGAINST ringing Sir James up. She felt sure he would not remember who she was. Instead, she would call round with the book, which had indeed come up in conversation—because she had made sure it did. Marcia was very good at fostering acquaintanceships with men, and had had two moderately lucrative divorces to prove it.

She timed her visit for late afternoon, when she calculated that the lady who cooked and "did" for him would have gone home. When he opened the door he blinked, and his hand strayed towards his lips.

"I'm afraid I—"

"Marcia Catchpole. We met at Serena Fisk's. I brought the book on Wordsworth we were talking about."

She proffered Stephen Gill on Wordsworth, in paperback. She had thought as she bought it that Sir James was probably not used to paperbacks, but she decided that, as an investment, Sir James was not yet worth the price of a hardback.

"Oh, I don't . . . er . . . Won't you come in?"

"Lovely!"

She was taken into a rather grim sitting room, lined with legal books and Victorian first editions. Sir James began to make uncertain remarks about how he thought he could manage tea.

"Why don't you let me make it? You'll not be used to fending for yourself, let alone for visitors. It was different in your generation, wasn't it? Is that the kitchen?"

And she immediately showed an uncanny instinct for finding things and doing the necessary. Sir James watched her, bemused, for a minute or two, then shuffled back to the sitting room. When she came in with a tray, with tea things on it and a plate of biscuits, he looked as if he had forgotten who she was, and how she came to be there.

"There, that's nice, isn't it? Do you like it strong? Not too strong, right? I think you'll enjoy the Wordsworth book. Wordsworth really *is* the Lakes, don't you agree?"

She had formed the notion, when talking to him at Serena Fisk's dinner party, that his reading was remaining with him longer than his grip on real life. This was confirmed by the conversation on this visit. As long as the talk stayed with Wordsworth and his Lakeland circle it approached a normal chat; he would forget the names of poems, but he would sometimes quote several lines of the better-known ones verbatim. Marcia had been educated at a moderately good state school, and she managed to keep her end up.

Marcia got up to go just at the right time, when Sir James had got used to her being there and before he began wanting her to go. At the door she said: "I'm expecting to have to go to the Lakes on business in a couple of weeks. I'd be happy if you'd come along."

"Oh. I couldn't possibly—"

"No obligations either way: we pay for ourselves, separate rooms *of course*, quite independent of each other. I've got business in Cockermouth, and I thought of staying by Buttermere or Crummock Water."

A glint came into his eyes.

"It would be wonderful to see them again. But I really couldn't—"

"Of course you could. It would be my pleasure. It's always better in congenial company, isn't it? I'll be in touch about the arrangements."

Marcia was in no doubt she would have to make all the arrangements, down to doing his packing and contacting his cleaning woman. But she was confident she would bring it off.

"KILLED BY A blow to the head," said Superintendent Southern, when he had skimmed through the pathologist's report. "Some kind of accident, for example a boating accident, can't entirely be ruled out, but there was some time between his being killed and his going into the water."

"In which case, what happened to the boat? And why didn't whoever was with him simply go back to base and report it, rather than heaving him in?"

"Exactly. . . . From what remains, the pathologist suggests a smooth liver—a townee not a countryman, even of the upper crust kind."

"I think you suspected that from the suit, didn't you, sir?"

"I did. Where do you go for a first-rate suit for country holidays if you're a townee?"

"Same as for business suits? Savile Row, sir?"

"If you're a well-heeled Londoner that's exactly where you go. We'll start there."

MARCIA WENT ROUND to Sir James's two days before she had decided to set off North. Sir James remembered little or nothing about the proposed trip, still less whether he had agreed to go. Marcia got them a cup of tea, put maps on his lap, then began his packing for him. Before she went she cooked him his light supper (wondering how he had ever managed to cook it for himself) and got out of him the name of his daily. Later on she rang her and told her she was taking Sir James to the Lakes, and he'd be away for at most a week. The woman sounded sceptical but uncertain whether it was her place to say anything. Marcia, in any case, didn't give her the opportunity.

She also rang Serena Fisk to tell her. She had an ulterior motive for doing so. In the course of the conversation she casually asked: "How did he get to your dinner party?"

"Oh, I drove him. Homecooks were doing the food, so there was no problem. Those sons of his wouldn't lift a finger to help him. Then Bill drove him home later. Said he couldn't get a coherent word out of him."

"I expect he was tired: If you talk to him about literature you can see there's still a mind there."

"Literature was never my strong point, Marcia."

"Anyway, I'm taking him to the Lakes for a week on Friday."

"*Really*? Well, you are getting on well with him. Rather you than me."

"Oh, all he needs is a bit of stimulus," said Marcia. She felt confident now that she had little to fear from old friends or sons.

This first visit to the Lakes went off extremely well from Marcia's point of view. When she collected him, the idea that he was going somewhere seemed actually to have got through to him. She finished the packing with last-minute things, got him and his cases into the car, and in no time they were on the M1. During a pub lunch he called her "Molly" again, and when they at last reached the Lakes she saw that glint in his eyes, heard little grunts of pleasure.

She had booked them into Crummock Lodge, an unpretentious but spacious hotel which seemed to her just the sort of place Sir James would have been used to on his holidays in the Lakes. They had separate rooms, as she had promised. "He's an old friend who's been very ill," she told the manager. They ate well, went on drives and gentle walks. If anyone stopped and talked, Sir James managed a sort of distant benignity which carried them through. As before, he was best if he talked about literature. Once, after Marcia had had a conversation with a farmer over a dry stone wall, he said:

"Wordsworth always believed in the wisdom of simple country people."

It sounded like something a schoolmaster had once drummed into him. Marcia would have liked to say, "But when his brother married a servant he said it was an outrage." But she herself had risen by marriage, or marriages, and the point seemed to strike too close to home.

On the afternoon when she had her private business in Cockermouth she walked Sir James hard in the morning and left him tucked up in bed after lunch. Then she visited a friend who had retired to a small cottage on the outskirts of the town. He had been a private detective, and had been useful to her in her first divorce. The dicey method he had used to get dirt on her husband had convinced her that in his case private detection was very close to crime itself, and she had maintained the connection. She told him the outline of what she had in mind, and told him she might need him in the future.

When, after a week, they returned to London, Marcia was completely satisfied. She now had a secure place in Sir James's life. He no longer looked bewildered when she came round, even looked pleased, and often called her "Molly." She went to the Chelsea house often in the evenings, cooked his meal for him, and together they watched television like an old couple.

It would soon be time to make arrangements at a Registry Office.

———

IN THE PROCESS of walking from establishment to establishment in Savile Row, Southern came to feel he had had as much as he could stand of stiffness, professional discretion, and awed hush. They were only high-class tailors, he thought to himself, not the Church of bloody England. Still, when they heard that one of their clients could have ended up as an anonymous corpse in Derwent Water, they were willing to cooperate. The three establishments which offered that particular tweed handed him silently a list of those customers who had had suits made from it in the last ten years.

"Would you know if any of these are dead?" he asked one shop manager.

"Of course, sir. We make a note in our records when their obituary appears in the *Times*."

The man took the paper back and put a little crucifix sign against two of the four names. The two remaining were a well-known television newsreader and Sir James Harrington.

"Is Sir James still alive?"

"Oh certainly. There's been no obituary for him. But he's very old: We have had no order from him for some time."

It was Sir James that Southern decided to start with Scotland Yard knew all about him, and provided a picture, a review of the major trials in which he had featured, and his address. When Southern failed to get an answer from phone calls to the house, he went round to try the personal touch. There was a For Sale notice on it that looked to have been there for some time.

THE ARRANGEMENTS FOR the Registry Office wedding went without a hitch. A month after their trip, Marcia went to book it in a suburb where neither Sir James nor she was known. Then she began foreshadowing it to Sir James, to accustom him to the idea.

"Best make it legal," she said, in her slightly vulgar way.

"Legal?" he enquired, from a great distance.

"You and me. But we'll just go on as we are."

She thought about witnesses, foresaw various dangers, and decided to pay for her detective friend to come down. He was the one person who knew of her intentions, and he could study Sir James's manner.

"Got a lady friend you could bring with you?" she asked when she rang him.

" 'Course I have. Though nobody as desirable as you, Marcia love."

"Keep your desires to yourself Ben Brackett. This is business."

Sir James went through the ceremony with that generalized dignity which had characterised him in all his dealings with Marcia. He behaved to Ben Brackett and his lady friend as if they were somewhat dodgy witnesses who happened to be on his side in this particular trial. He spoke his words clearly, and almost seemed to mean them. Marcia told herself that in marrying her he was doing what he actually wanted to do. She didn't risk any celebration after the ceremony. She paid off Ben Brackett, drove Sir James home to change and pack again, then set off for the Lake District.

This time she had rented a cottage, as being more private. It was just outside Grange—a two bedroom stone cottage, very comfortable and rather expensive. She had taken it for six weeks in the name of Sir James and Lady Harrington. Once there and settled in, Sir James seemed, in his way, vaguely happy; he would potter off on his own down to the lakeside, or up the narrow abutting fields. He would raise his hat to villagers and tourists, and swap remarks about the weather.

He also signed, in a wavering hand, anything put in front of him.

Marcia wrote first to his sons, similar but not identical letters, telling them of his marriage and of his happiness with his dear wife. The letters also touched on business matters: "I wonder if you would object if I put the house on the market? After living up here I cannot imagine living in London again. Of course the money would come to you after my wife's death." At the foot of Marcia's typed script Sir James wrote at her direction: "Your loving Dad."

The letters brought two furious responses, as Marcia had known they would. Both were addressed to her, and both threatened legal action. Both said they knew their father was mentally incapable of deciding to marry again, and accused her of taking advantage of his senility.

"My dear boys," typed Marcia gleefully. "I am surprised that you apparently consider me senile, and wonder how you could have allowed me to live alone without proper care if you believed that to be the case."

Back and forth the letters flew. Gradually Marcia discerned a subtle difference between the two sets of letters. Those from the MP were slightly less shrill, slightly more accommodating. He fears a scandal, she thought. Nothing worse than a messy court case for an MP's reputation. It was to Sir Evelyn Harrington, MP for Flinchingford, that she made her proposal.

SOUTHERN FOUND THE estate agents quite obliging. Their dealings, they said, had been with Sir James himself. He had signed all the letters from Cumbria. They showed Southern the file; and he noted the shaky signature. Once they had spoken to Lady Harrington, they said. A low offer had been received, which demanded a quick decision. They had not recommended acceptance, since, though the property market was more dead than alive, a good house in Chelsea was bound to make a very handsome sum once it picked up. Lady Harrington had said that Sir James had a slight cold, but that he agreed with them that the offer was derisory and should be refused.

Southern's brow creased: Wasn't Lady Harrington dead?

There was clearly enough of interest about Sir James Harrington to stay with him for a bit. Southern consulted the file at Scotland Yard and set up a meeting with the man's son at the House of Commons.

Sir Evelyn was a man in his late forties, tall and well set up. He had been knighted, Southern had discovered, in the last mass knighting of Tory backbenchers who had always voted at their party's call. The impression Sir Evelyn made was not of a stupid man, but of an unoriginal one.

"My father? Oh yes, he's alive. Living up in the Lake District somewhere."

"You're sure of this?"

"Sure as one can be when there's no contact." Southern left a silence, so the man was forced to elaborate. "Never was much. He's a remote bugger . . . a remote sort of chap, my father. Stiff, always working, never had the sort of common touch you need with children. Too keen on being the world's greatest prosecuting counsel . . . He sent us away to school when we were seven."

Suddenly there was anger, pain, and real humanity in the voice.

"You resented that?"

"*Yes.* My brother had gone the year before and told me what that prep school was like. I pleaded with him. But he sent me just the same."

"Did your mother want you to go?"

"My mother did as she was told. Or else."

"That's not the present Lady Harrington?"

"Oh no. The present Lady Harrington is, I like to think, what my father deserves. . . . We'd been warned he was failing by his daily. Dinner burst in the oven, forgetting to change his clothes, that kind of thing. We didn't take too much notice. The difficulties of getting a stiff-necked old . . . man into residential care seemed insuperable. Then the next we heard he's married again and gone to live in the Lake District."

"Didn't you protest?"

"Of course we did. It was obvious she was after his money. And the letters he wrote, or she wrote for him, were all wrong. He would *never* have signed himself 'Dad,' let alone 'Your loving Dad.' But the kind of action that would have been necessary to annul the marriage can look ugly—for *both* sides of the case. So when she proposed an independent examination by a local doctor and psychiatrist, I persuaded my brother to agree."

"And what did they say?"

"Said he was vague, a little forgetful, but perfectly capable of understanding what he'd done when he married her, and apparently very happy. That was the end of the matter for us. The end of *him*."

MARCIA HAD DECIDED from the beginning that in the early months of her life as Lady Harrington she and Sir James would have to move round a lot. As long as he was merely an elderly gentleman pottering around the Lakes and exchanging meteorological banalities with the locals there was little to fear. But as they became used to him there was a danger that they would try to engage him in conversation of more substance. If that happened, his mental state might very quickly become apparent.

As negotiations with the two sons developed, Marcia began to see her way clear. Their six weeks at Grange were nearing an end, so she arranged to rent a cottage between Crummock Water and Cockermouth. When the sons agreed to an independent assessment of their father's mental condition and nominated a doctor and a psychiatrist from Keswick to undertake it, Marcia phoned them and arranged their visit for one of their first days in the new cottage. Then she booked Sir James and herself into Crummock Lodge for the relevant days. "I'll be busy getting the cottage ready," she told the manager. She felt distinctly pleased with herself. No danger of the independent team talking to locals.

"I don't see why we have to move," complained Sir James when she told him. "I like it here."

"Oh, we need to see a few places before we decide where we really want to settle," said Marcia soothingly. "I've booked us into Crummock Lodge, so I'll be able to get the new cottage looking nice before we move in."

"This is nice. I want to stay here."

There was no problem with money. On a drive to Cockermouth Marcia had arranged to have Sir James's bank account transferred there. He had signed the form without a qualm, together with one making the account a joint one. Everything in the London house was put into store, and the estate agents forwarded Sir James's mail, including his dividend cheques and his pension, regularly. There was no hurry about selling the house, but when it did finally go Marcia foresaw herself in clover. With Sir James, of course, and he was a bit of a bore. But very much worth putting up with.

As Marcia began discreetly packing for the move Sir James's agitation grew, his complaints became more insistent.

"I don't want to move. Why should we move, Molly? We're happy here. If we can't have this cottage we can buy a place. There are houses for sale."

To take his mind off it, Marcia borrowed their neighbour's rowing boat and took him for a little trip on the lake. It didn't take his mind off it. "This is lovely," he kept saying. "Derwent Water has always been my favourite. Why should we move on? I'm not moving, Molly."

He was beginning to get on her nerves. She had to tell herself that a few frazzled nerves were a small price to pay.

The night before they were due to move, the packing had to be done openly. Marcia brought all the suitcases into the living room and began methodically distributing to each one the belongings they had brought with them. Sir James had been dozing when she began, as he often did in the evening. She was halfway through her task when she realised he was awake and struggling to his feet.

"You haven't been listening to what I've been saying, have you, Molly? Well, have you, woman? I'm not moving!"

Marcia got to her feet.

"I know it's upsetting, dear—"

"It's not upsetting because we're staying here."

"Perhaps it will only be for a time. I've got it all organised, and you'll be quite comfy—"

"Don't treat me like a child, Molly!" Suddenly she realised with a shock that he had raised his arm. "Don't treat me like a child!" His hand came down with a feeble slap across her cheek. "Listen to what I say, woman!" Slap again. "I am not moving!" This time he punched her, and it hurt. "You'll do what I say, or it'll be the worse for you!" And he punched her again.

Marcia exploded with rage.

"You *bloody* old bully!" she screamed. "You brute! That's how you treated your wife, is it? Well, it's not how you're treating me!"

She brought up her stronger hands and gave him an almighty shove away from her even as he raised his fist for another punch. He lurched back, tried to regain his balance, then fell against the fireplace, hitting his head hard against the corner of the mantelpiece. Then he crumpled to the floor and lay still.

For a moment Marcia did nothing. Then she sat down and sobbed. She wasn't a sobbing woman, but she felt she had had a sudden revelation of what this man's—this old monster's—relations had been with his dead wife. She had never for a moment suspected it. She no longer felt pity for him, if she ever had. She felt contempt.

She dragged herself wearily to her feet. She'd put him to bed, and by morning he'd have forgotten. She bent down over him. Then, panic-stricken, she put her hand to his mouth, felt his chest, felt for his heart. It didn't take long to tell that he was dead. She sat down on the sofa and contemplated the wreck of her plans.

SOUTHERN AND POTTER found the woman in the general-store-cum-newsagent's at Grange chatty and informative.

"Oh, Sir James. Yes, they were here for several weeks. Nice enough couple, though I think he'd married beneath him."

"Was he in full possession of his faculties, do you think?"

The woman hesitated.

"Well, you'd have thought so. Always said, 'Nice day,' or 'Hope the rain keeps off,' if he came in for a tin of tobacco or a bottle of wine. But no more than that. Then one day I said, 'Shame about the Waleses, isn't it?'—you know, at the time of the split-up. He seemed bewildered, so I said, 'The Prince and Princess of Wales separating.' Even then it was obvious he didn't understand. It was embarrassing. I turned away and served somebody else. But there's others had the same experience."

AFTER SOME MINUTES Marcia found it intolerable to be in the same room as the body. Trying to look the other way, she dragged it through to the dining room. Even as she did so she realised that she had made a decision: She was not going to the police, and her plans were not at an end.

Because after all, she had her "Sir James" all lined up. In the operation planned for the next few days, the existence of the real one was anyway something of an embarrassment. Now that stumbling block had been removed. She rang Ben Brackett and told him there had been a slight change of plan, but it needn't affect his part in it. She rang Crummock Lodge and told them that Sir James had changed his mind and wanted to settle straight into the new cottage. While there was still some dim light, she went into the garden and out into the lonely land behind, collecting as many large stones as she could find. Then she slipped down and put them into the rowing boat she had borrowed from her neighbour the day before.

She had no illusions about the size—or more specifically the weight—of the problem she had in disposing of the body. She gave herself a stiff brandy, but no more than one. She found a razor blade and, shaking, removed the name from Sir James's suit. Then she finished her packing, so that everything was ready for departure. The farming people of the area were early to bed as a rule, but there were too many tourists staying there, she calculated, for it to be really safe before the early hours. At precisely one o'clock she began the long haul down to the shore. Sir James had been nearly six foot, so though his form was wasted, he was both heavy and difficult to lift. Marcia found, though, that carrying was easier than dragging, and quieter too. In three arduous stages she got him to the boat, then into it. The worst was over. She rowed out to the dark centre of the lake—the crescent moon was blessedly obscured by clouds—filled his pockets with stones, then carefully, gradually, eased the body out of the boat and into the water. She watched it sink, then made for the shore. Two large brandies later, she piled the cases into the car, locked up the cottage, and drove off in the direction of Cockermouth.

After the horror and difficulty of the night before, everything went beautifully. Marcia had barely settled into the new cottage when Ben Brackett arrived. He already had some of Sir James's characteristics off pat: his distant, condescending affability, for example. Marcia coached him in others, and they tried to marry them to qualities the real Sir James had no longer had: lucidity and purpose.

When the team of two arrived, the fake Sir James was working in the garden. "Got to get it in some sort of order," he explained, in his upper-class voice. "Haven't the strength I once had, though." When they were all inside, and over a splendid afternoon tea, he paid eloquent tribute to his new wife.

"She's made a new man of me," he explained. "I was letting myself go after Molly died. Marcia pulled me up in my tracks and brought me round. Oh, I know the boys are angry. I don't blame them. In fact, I blame myself. I was never a good father to them—too busy to be one. Got my priorities wrong. But it won't hurt them to wait a few years for the money."

The team was clearly impressed. They steered the talk round to politics, the international situation, changes in the law. "Sir James" kept his end up, all in that rather grand voice and distant manner. When the two men left, Marcia knew that her problems were over. She and Ben Brackett waited for the sound of the car leaving to go back to Keswick, then she poured very large whiskies for them. Over their third she told him what had happened to the real Sir James.

"You did superbly," said Ben Brackett when she had finished.

"It was bloody difficult."

"I bet it was. But it was worth it. Look how it went today. A piece of cake. We had them in the palms of our hands. We won, Marcia! Let's have another drink on that. We won!"

Even as she poured, Marcia registered disquiet at that "we."

SITTING IN HIS poky office in Kendal, Southern, with Potter, surveyed the reports and other pieces of evidence they had set out on the desk.

"It's becoming quite clear," said Southern thoughtfully. "In Grange we have an old man who hardly seems to know who the Prince and Princess of Wales are. In the cottage near Cockermouth we have an old man who can talk confidently about politics and the law. In Grange we have a feeble man, and a corpse which is that of a soft liver. In the other cottage we have a man who gardens—perhaps to justify the fact that his hands are *not* those of a soft-living lawyer. At some time between taking her husband on the lake—was that a rehearsal, I wonder?—and the departure in the night, she killed him. She must already have had someone lined up to take his place for the visit of the medical team."

"And they're there still," said Potter, pointing to the letter from the estate agents in London. "That's where all communications still go."

"And that's where we're going to go," said Southern, getting up.

They had got good information on the cottage from the Cockermouth police. They left their car in the car park of a roadside pub, and took the lane through fields and down towards the northern shore of Crummock Water. They soon saw the cottage, overlooking the lake, lonely . . .

But the cottage was not as quiet as its surroundings. As they walked towards the place they heard shouting. A minute or two later they heard two thick voices arguing. When they could distinguish words, it was in a voice far from upper-crust:

"Will you get that drink, you cow? . . . How can I when I can hardly stand? . . . Get me that drink or it'll be the worse for you tomorrow. . . . You'd better remember who stands between you and a long jail sentence, Marcia. You'd do well to think about that *all the time*. . . . Now get me that scotch or you'll feel my fist!"

When Southern banged on the door there was silence. The woman who opened the door was haggard-looking, with bleary eyes and a bruise on the side of her face. In the room behind her, slumped back in a chair, they saw a man whose expensive clothes were in disarray, whose face was red and puffy, and who most resembled a music hall comic's version of a gentleman.

"Lady Harrington? I'm Superintendent Southern and this is Sergeant Potter. I wonder if we could come in? We have to talk to you."

He raised his ID towards her clouded eyes. She looked down at it slowly. When she looked up again, Southern could have sworn that the expression on her face was one of relief.

LIFE IN OUR TIME

Robert Bloch

Psycho (book and film alike) is the dividing line separating old-style suspense fiction from new-style. After *Psycho*, all bets were off. Suspense fiction (as opposed to the straight mystery) could and did go anywhere. The man who started all this was an unassuming, friendly and very witty writer named Robert Bloch (1917–1994), a talented professional whose other novels included such dark suspense masterpieces as *The Scarf*, *The Kidnapper*, and *The Night of the Ripper*. Some insist that his short stories were even better than his novels. He published several volumes of his stories during his lifetime. You never quite knew what to expect from a Bloch story. He delighted in defying expectations, often by incorporating unexpected humor in his work. Even in the grim struggle of Norman Bates, Bloch managed to work in a laugh or two. His skills as a short-story craftsman *par excellence* are on full display here.

WHEN HARRY'S TIME capsule arrived, Jill made him put it in the guesthouse.

All it was, it turned out, was a big metal box with a cover that could be sealed tight and soldered so that the air couldn't get at what was inside. Jill was really quite disappointed with it.

But then she was quite disappointed with Harry, too—Professor Harrison Cramer, B.A., B.S., M.A., Ph.D. Half the alphabet wasted on a big nothing. At those flaky faculty cocktail parties, people were always telling her, "It must be wonderful to be married to a brilliant man like your husband." Brother, if they only knew!

It wasn't just that Harry was 15 years older than she was. After all, look at Rex Harrison and Richard Burton and Cary Grant and Lawrence Olivier. But Harry wasn't the movie-star type—definitely not! Not even the mad-scientist type, like Vincent Price in those crazy "campy" pictures. He was nothing—just a big nothing.

Of course, Jill got the message long before she married him. But he did have that imposing house and all that loot he'd inherited from his mother.

Jill figured on making a few changes, and she actually did manage to redo the house so that it looked halfway presentable, with the help of that *fagilleh* interior decorator. But she couldn't redo Harry. Maybe *he* needed an interior decorator to work on him, too; *she* certainly couldn't change him.

And outside of what she managed to squeeze out of him for the redecorating, Jill hadn't been able to get her hands on any of the loot, either. Harry wasn't interested in entertaining or going out or taking cruises, and whenever she mentioned a sable jacket he mumbled something under his breath about "conspicuous consumption"—whatever that was! He didn't like modern art or the theater, he didn't drink or smoke—why, he didn't even watch TV. And he wore flannel pajamas in bed. *All* the time.

After a couple of months Jill was ready to climb the walls. Then she began thinking about Reno, and that's where Rick came in. Rick was her attorney—at least, that's the way it started out to be, but Rick had other ideas. Particularly for those long afternoons when Harry was lecturing at seminars or whatever he did over there at the University.

Pretty soon Jill forgot about Reno; Rick was all for one of those quickie divorces you can get down in Mexico. He was sure he could make it stick and still see to it that she got her fifty-fifty share under the community property laws, and without any waiting. It could all be done in 24 hours, with no hassle; they'd take off together, just like eloping. Bang, you're divorced; bang, you're remarried; and then, bang, bang, bang—

So all Jill had to worry about was finding the right time. And even that was no problem, after Harry told her about the time capsule.

"I'm to be in full charge of the project," he said. "Complete authority to choose what will be representative of our present culture. Quite a responsibility, my dear—but I welcome the challenge."

"So what's a time capsule?" Jill wanted to know.

Harry went into a long routine and she didn't really listen, just enough to get the general idea. The thing was, Harry had to pick out all kinds of junk to be sealed up in this gizmo so that sometime—10,000 years from now, maybe—somebody would come along and dig it up and open it and be able to tell what kind of civilization we had. Big deal! But from the way Harry went on, you'd think he'd just won the Grand Prix or something.

"We're going to put the capsule in the foundation of the new Humanities Building," he told her.

"What are humanities?" Jill asked, but Harry just gave her one of those *Good-lord-how-can-you-be-so-stupid?* looks that always seemed to start their quarrels; and they would have had a fight then and there, too, only he added something about how the dedication ceremonies for the new building would take place on May 1st, and he'd have to hurry to get everything arranged for the big day. Including writing his dedicatory address.

May 1st was all Jill needed to hear. That was on a Friday, and if Harry was going to be tied up making a speech at the dedication, it would be an A-OK time to make that little flight across the border. So she managed to call Rick and tell him and he said yeah, sure, perfect.

"It's only ten days from now," Jill reminded Rick. "We've got a lot to do."

She didn't know it, but it turned out she wasn't kidding. She had more to do than she thought, because all at once Harry was *interested* in her. *Really* interested.

"You've got to help me," he said that night at dinner. "I want to rely on your taste. Of course, I've got some choices of my own in mind, but I want *you* to suggest items to go into the capsule."

At first Jill thought he was putting her on, but he really meant it. "This project is going to be honest. The usual ploy is pure exhibitionism—samples of the 'best' of everything, plus descriptive data which is really just a pat on the back for the *status quo ante*. Well, that's not for me. I'd like to include material that's self-explanatory, not self-congratulatory. Not art and facts—but artifacts."

Harry lost her there, until he said, "Everything preserved will be a clue to our contemporary social attitudes. Not what we *pretend* to admire, but what the majority actually *believes in* and *enjoys*. And that's where you come in, my dear. You represent the majority."

Jill began to dig it, then. "You mean like TV and pop records?"

"Exactly. What's that album you like so much? The one with the four hermaphrodites on the liner?"

"Who?"

"Excuse me—it's purportedly a singing group, isn't it?"

"Oh, you're talking about the Poodles!" Jill went and got the album, which was called *The Poodles Bark Again*. The sound really turned her on, but she had always thought Harry hated it. And now he was coming on all smiles.

"Great!" he said. "This definitely goes in."

"But—"

"Don't worry, I'll buy you another." He took the album and put it on his desk. "Now, you mentioned something about television. What's your favorite program?"

When she saw that he was really serious, she began telling him about "Anywhere, U.S.A." What it was, it was about life in a small town, just an ordinary suburb like, but the people were great. There was this couple with the two kids, one boy and one girl, sort of an average family, you might say, only he was kind of playing around with a divorcee who ran a *discothetique* or whatever they call them, and she had a yen for her psychiatrist—he wasn't really *her* psychiatrist, he was analyzing one of the kids, the one who had set fire to the high school gymnasium, not the girl—she was afraid her parents would find out about her affair with the vice-principal who was really an enemy agent only she didn't know it yet, and her real boy friend, the one who had the brain operation, had a "thing" about his mother, so—

It got kind of complicated, but Harry kept asking her to tell him more, and pretty soon he was smiling and nodding. "Wonderful! We'll have to see if we can get films of a typical week's episodes."

"You mean you really want something like that?"

"Of course. Wouldn't you say this show faithfully captured the lives of American citizens today?"

She had to agree he was right. Also about some of the things he was going to put into the capsule to show the way people lived nowadays—like tranquilizers and pep pills and income tax forms and a map of the freeway-expressway-turnpike system. He had a lot of numbers, too, for Zip Code and digit dialing, and Social Security, and the ones the computers punched out on insurance and charge-account and utility bills.

But what he really wanted was ideas for more stuff, and in the next couple of days he kept leaning on her. He got hold of her souvenir from Shady Lawn Cemetery—it was a plastic walnut that opened up, called "Shady Lawn in a Nutshell." Inside were twelve tiny color prints showing all the tourist attractions of the place, and you could mail the whole thing to your friends back home. Harry put this in the time capsule, wrapping it up in something he told her was an actuarial table on the incidence of coronary occlusion among middle-aged, middle-class males. Like heart attacks, that is.

"What's that you're reading?" he asked. And the next thing she knew, he had her copy of the latest Steve Slash paperback—the one where Steve is sent on this top-secret mission to keep peace in Port Said, and right after he kills these five guys with the portable flame thrower concealed in his judo belt, he's getting ready to play beddy-bye with Yasmina, who's really another secret agent with radioactive fingernails—

And that's as far as she'd got when he grabbed the book. It was getting so she couldn't keep anything out of his eager little hands.

"What's that you're cooking?" he wanted to know. And there went the TV dinner—frozen crêpes suzettes and all. To say nothing of the Plain Jane Instant Borscht.

"Where's that photo you had of your brother?" It was a real nothing picture of Stud, just him wearing that beatnik beard of his and standing by his motorcycle on the day he passed his initiation into the Hell's Angels. But Harry put *that* in, too. Jill didn't think it was very nice of Harry, seeing as how he clipped it to another photo of some guys taking the Ku Klux Klan oath.

But right now the main thing was to keep Harry happy. That's what Rick said when she clued him in on what was going on.

"Cooperate, baby," he told her. "It's a real kinky kick, but it keeps him out of our hair. We got plans to make, tickets to buy, packing and like that there."

The trouble was, Jill ran out of ideas. She explained this to Rick but he just laughed.

"I'll give you some," he said, "and you can feed 'em to him. He's a real way-out kid, that husband of yours—I know just what he wants."

The funny part of it was that Rick did know. He was really kind of a brain himself, but not in a kooky way like Harry. So she listened to what he suggested and told Harry when she got home.

"How about a sample of the Theater of the Absurd?" she asked. Harry looked at her over the top of his glasses, and for a minute she thought she'd really thrown him, but then he grinned and got excited.

"Perfect!" he said. "Any suggestions?"

"Well, I was reading a review about this new play everybody's talking about—it's about this guy who thinks he's having a baby so he goes to an abortionist, only I guess the abortionist is supposed to be somebody mystical or something, and it all takes place in a greenhouse—"

"Delightful!" Harry was off and running. "I'll pick up a copy of the book. Anything else?"

Thank God that Rick had coached her. So she said what about a recording of one of those concerts where they use a "prepared" piano that makes noises like screeching brakes, or sometimes no sound at all. And Harry liked that. He also liked the idea about a sample of Pop Art—maybe a big blowup of a newspaper ad about "That Tired Feeling" or maybe "Psoriasis."

The next day she suggested a tape of a "Happening" which was the real thing, because it took place in some private sanatorium for disturbed patients, and Harry got really enthusiastic about this idea.

And the next day she came up with that new foreign movie with the long title she couldn't pronounce. Rick gave her the dope on it—some far-out thing by a Yugoslavian director she never heard of, about a man making a movie about a man making a movie, only you never could be quite sure, in the movie, whether the scene was supposed to be a part of the movie or the movie was a part of what was really happening, *if* it did happen.

Harry went for this, too. In a big way.

"You're wonderful," he said. "Truthfully, I never expected this of you."

Jill just gave him her extra-special smile and went on her merry way. It wasn't hard, because he had to go running around town trying to dig up books and films and recordings of all the stuff he had on his list. Which was just how Rick said it would be, leaving everything clear for them to shop and set up their last-minute plans.

"I won't get our tickets until the day before we leave," Rick told her. "We don't want to tip off anything. The way I figure it, Harry'll be moving the capsule over to where they're holding the ceremonies the next morning, so you'll get a chance to pack while he's out of the way." Rick was really something, the way he had it all worked out.

And that's the way it went. The day before the ceremony, Harry was busy in the guest house all afternoon, packing his goodies in the time capsule. Just like a dopey squirrel burying nuts. Only even dopey squirrels don't put stuff away for another squirrel to dig up 10,000 years from now.

Harry hadn't even had time to look at her the past two days, but this didn't bother Jill any. Along about suppertime she went out to call him, but he said he wasn't hungry and besides he had to run over and arrange for the trucking company to come and haul the capsule over to the foundation site. They'd dug a big hole there for tomorrow morning, and he was going to take the capsule to it and stand guard over it until it was time for the dedication ceremonies.

That was even better news than Jill had hoped for, so as soon as Harry left for the trucking company she phoned Rick and gave him the word. He said he'd be right over with the tickets.

So of course Jill had to get dressed. She put on her girdle and the fancy bra and her high heels; then she went in the bathroom and used her depilatory and touched up her hair where the rinse was fading, and put on her eyelashes and brushed her teeth, and attached those new fingernails after she got her makeup on and the perfume.

When she looked at the results in the mirror she was really proud of herself; for the first time in months she felt like her real self again. And from now on it would always be this way—with Rick.

There was a good moment with Rick there in the bedroom after he came in, but of course Harry *would* drive up right then—she heard the car out front and broke the clinch just in time, telling Rick to sneak out the back way. Harry would be busy with the truckers for at least a couple of minutes.

Jill forced herself to wait in the bedroom until she was sure the coast was clear. She kept looking out the window but it was too dark now to see anything. Since there wasn't any noise, she figured Harry must have taken the truckers into the guest house.

And that's where she finally went.

Only the truckers weren't there. Just Harry.

"I told them to wait until first thing in the morning," he said. "Changed my mind when I realized how damp it was—no sense my spending the night shivering outside in the cold. Besides, I haven't sealed the capsule yet—remembered a couple of things I wanted to add."

He took a little bottle out of his pocket and carried it over to the time capsule. "This goes in too. Carefully labeled, of course, so they can analyze it."

"The bottle's empty," Jill said.

Harry shook his head. "Not at all. It contains smog. That's right—smog, from the freeway. I want posterity to know everything about us, right down to the poisonous air in which our contemporary culture breathed its last."

He dropped the bottle into the capsule, then picked up something else from the table next to it. Jill noticed he had a soldering outfit there to seal the lid, ready to plug in after he'd used a pump to suck all the air out. He'd explained about the capsule being airtight, soundproof, duralumin-sheathed, but that didn't interest her now. She kept looking at what he held in his hand.

It was one of those electric carving knives, complete with battery.

"Another Twentieth Century artifact," he said. "Another gadget symbol of our decadence. An electric knife—just the thing for Mom when she carves the fast-frozen, precooked Thanksgiving turkey while she and Dad count all their shiny, synthetic, plastic blessings."

He waved the knife.

"They'll understand," he told her. "Those people in the future will understand it all. They'll know what life was like in our time—how we drained Walden Pond and refilled it with blood, sweat, and tears."

Jill moved a little closer, staring at the knife. "The blade's rusty."

Harry shook his head. "That's not rust," he said.

Jill kept it cool. She kept it right up until the moment she looked over the edge of the big metal box, looked down into it, and saw Rick lying there. Rick was stretched out, and the red was oozing down over the books and records and photos and tapes.

"I was waiting for him when he sneaked out the back of the house," Harry said.

"Then you knew—all along—"

"For quite a while," Harry said. "Long enough to figure things out and make my plans."

"What plans?"

Harry just shrugged. And raised the knife.

A moment later the time capsule received the final specimen of life in the Twentieth Century.

Batman's Helpers

Lawrence Block

There are two kinds of stylists: the show-off who wants to be congratulated every time he turns a nice phrase, and the kind who quietly turns a nice phrase but just gets on with the story. Lawrence Block is one of the latter. Even at the outset of his career, when he was turning out books at a furious pace, he managed to bring elegance and taste to even minor assignments. His hard work paid off. He is one of the premier crime novelists of our time, with two best-selling series: the Matt Scudder novels (dark), including *Eight Million Ways to Die, The Devil Knows You're Dead*, and the Edgar-winning *A Dance at the Slaughterhouse*, and the Bernie Rhodenbarr mysteries (humorous), including *The Burglar Who Thought He Was Bogart*, and *The Burglar Who Traded Ted Williams*. Block is also one of our most accomplished short-story writers. No wonder the Mystery Writers of America hailed him as one of the Grand Masters. Recently he has turned to editing books and has three stellar anthologies: *Master's Choice*, Volumes 1 and 2, and *Opening Shots*.

RELIABLE'S OFFICES ARE in the Flatiron Building, at Broadway and Twenty-third. The receptionist, an elegant black girl with high cheekbones and processed hair, gave me a nod and a smile, and I went on down the hall to Wally Witt's office.

He was at his desk, a short stocky man with a bulldog jaw and gray hair cropped close to his head. Without rising he said, "Matt, good to see you, you're right on time. You know these guys? Matt Scudder, Jimmy diSalvo, Lee Trombauer." We shook hands all around. "We're waiting on Eddie Rankin. Then we can go out there and protect the integrity of the American merchandising system."

"Can't do that without Eddie," Jimmy diSalvo said.

"No, we need him," Wally said. "He's our pit bull. He's attack trained, Eddie is."

He came through the door a few minutes later and I saw what they meant. Without looking alike, Jimmy and Wally and Lee all looked like ex-cops—as, I suppose, do I. Eddie Rankin looked like the kind of guy we used to have to bring in on a bad Saturday night. He was a big man, broad in the shoulders, narrow in the waist. His hair was blond, almost white, and he wore it short at the sides but long in back. It lay on his neck like a mane. He had a broad forehead and a pug nose. His complexion was very fair and his full lips were intensely red, almost artificially so. He looked like a roughneck, and you sensed that his response to any sort of stress was likely to be physical, and abrupt.

Wally Witt introduced him to me. The others already knew him. Eddie Rankin shook my hand, and his left hand fastened on my shoulder and gave a squeeze. "Hey, Matt," he said. "Pleased to meetcha. Whattaya say, guys, we ready to come to the aid of the Caped Crusader?"

Jimmy diSalvo started whistling the theme from "Batman," the old television show. Wally said, "Okay, who's packing? Is everybody packing?"

Lee Trombauer drew back his suit jacket to show a revolver in a shoulder rig. Eddie Rankin took out a large automatic and laid it on Wally's desk. "Batman's gun," he announced.

"Batman don't carry a gun," Jimmy told him.

"Then he better stay outta New York," Eddie said. "Or he'll get his ass shot off. Those revolvers, I wouldn't carry one of them on a bet."

"This shoots as straight as what you got," Lee said. "And it won't jam."

"This baby don't jam," Eddie said. He picked up the automatic and held it out for display. "You got a revolver," he said, "a .38, whatever you got—"

"A .38."

"—and a guy takes it away from you, all he's gotta do is point it and shoot it. Even if he never saw a gun before, he knows how to do that much. This monster, though"—and he demonstrated, flicking the safety, working the slide—"all this shit you gotta go through, before he can figure it out I got the gun away from him and I'm making him eat it."

"Nobody's taking my gun away from me," Lee said.

"What everybody says, but look at all the times it happens. Cop gets shot with his own gun, nine times out of ten it's a revolver."

"That's because that's all they carry," Lee said.

"Well, there you go."

Jimmy and I weren't carrying guns. Wally offered to equip us but we both declined. "Not that anybody's likely to have to show a piece, let alone use one, God forbid," Wally said. "But it can get nasty out there, and it helps to have the feeling of authority. Well, let's go get 'em, huh? The Bat-mobile's waiting at the curb."

We rode down in the elevator, five grown men, three of us armed with handguns. Eddie Rankin had on a plaid sport jacket and khaki trousers. The rest of us wore suits and ties. We went out the Fifth Avenue exit and followed Wally to his car, a five-year-old Fleetwood Cadillac parked next to a hydrant. There were no tickets on the windshield; a PBA courtesy card had kept the traffic cops at bay.

Wally drove and Eddie Rankin sat in front with him. The rest of us rode in back. We cruised up to Fifty-fourth Street and turned right, and Wally parked next to a hydrant a few doors from Fifth. We walked to-gether to the corner of Fifth and turned downtown. Near the middle of the block a trio of black men had set up shop as sidewalk vendors. One had a display of women's handbags and silk scarves, all arranged neatly on top of a folding card table. The other two were offering tee-shirts and cassette tapes.

In an undertone Wally said, "Here we go. These three were here yes-terday. Matt, why don't you and Lee check down the block, make sure those two down at the corner don't have what we're looking for. Then double back and we'll take these dudes off. Meanwhile I'll let the man sell me a shirt."

Lee and I walked down to the corner. The two vendors in question were selling books. We established this and headed back. "Real police work," I said.

"Be grateful we don't have to fill out a report, list the titles of the books."

"The alleged books."

When we rejoined the others Wally was holding an oversize tee-shirt to his chest, modeling it for us. "What do you say?" he demanded. "Is it me? Do you think it's me?"

"I think it's the Joker," Jimmy diSalvo said.

"That's what I think," Wally said. He looked at the two Africans, who were smiling uncertainly. "I think it's a violation, is what I think. I think we got to confiscate all the Batman stuff. It's unauthorized, it's an il-legal violation of copyright protection, it's unlicensed, and we got to take it in."

The two vendors had stopped smiling, but they didn't seem to have a very clear idea of what was going on. Off to the side, the third man, the fel-low with the scarves and purses, was looking wary.

"You speak English?" Wally asked them.

"They speak numbers," Jimmy said. " 'Fi' dollah, ten dollah, please, t'ank you.' That's what they speak."

"Where you from?" Wally demanded. "Senegal, right? Dakar. You from Dakar?"

They nodded, brightening at words they recognized. "Dakar," one of them echoed. Both of them were wearing western clothes, but they looked faintly foreign—loose-fitting long-sleeved shirts with long pointed collars and a glossy finish, baggy pleated pants. Loafers with leather mesh tops.

"What do you speak?" Wally asked. "You speak French? Parley-voo français?" The one who'd spoken before replied now in a torrent of French; Wally backed away from him and shook his head. "I don't know why the hell I asked," he said. "Parley-voo's all I know of the fucking language." To the Africans he said, "Police. You parley-voo that? Police. *Policia*. You capeesh?" He opened his wallet and showed them some sort of badge. "No sell Batman," he said, waving one of the shirts at them. "Batman no good. It's unauthorized, it's not made under a licensing agreement, and you can't sell it."

"No Batman," one of them said.

"Jesus, don't tell me I'm getting through to them. Right, no Batman. No, put your money away, I can't take a bribe, I'm not with the Department no more. All I want's the Batman stuff. You can keep the rest."

All but a handful of their tee-shirts were unauthorized Batman items. The rest showed Walt Disney characters, almost certainly as unauthorized as the Batman merchandise, but Disney wasn't Reliable's client today so it was none of our concern. While we loaded up with Batman and the Joker, Eddie Rankin looked through the cassettes, then pawed through the silk scarves the third vendor had on display. He let the man keep the scarves, but he took a purse, snakeskin by the look of it. "No good," he told the man, who nodded, expressionless.

We trooped back to the Fleetwood and Wally popped the trunk. We deposited the confiscated tees between the spare tire and some loose fishing tackle. "Don't worry if the shit gets dirty," Wally said. "It's all gonna be destroyed anyway. Eddie, you start carrying a purse, people are gonna say things."

"Woman I know," he said. "She'll like this." He wrapped the purse in a Batman tee-shirt and placed it in the trunk.

"Okay," Wally said. "That went real smooth. What we'll do now, Lee, you and Matt take the east side of Fifth, and the rest of us'll stay on this side and we'll work our way down to Forty-second. I don't know if we'll get much, because even if they can't speak English they can sure get the word around fast, but we'll make sure there's no unlicensed Batcrap on the Avenue before we move on. We'll maintain eye contact back and forth across the street, and if you hit anything give the high sign and we'll converge and take 'em down. Everybody got it?"

Everybody seemed to. We left the car with its trunkful of contraband and returned to Fifth Avenue. The two tee-shirt vendors from Dakar had packed up and disappeared; they'd have to find something else to sell and someplace else to sell it. The man with the scarves and purses was still doing business. He froze when he caught sight of us.

"No Batman," Wally told him.

"No Batman," he echoed.

"I'll be a son-of-a-bitch," Wally said. "The guy's learning English."

Lee and I crossed the street and worked our way downtown. There were vendors all over the place, offering clothing and tapes and small appliances and books and fast food. Most of them didn't have the peddler's license the law required, and periodically the city would sweep the streets, especially the main commercial avenues, rounding them up and fining them and confiscating their stock. Then after a week or so the cops would stop trying to enforce a basically unenforceable law, and the peddlers would be back in business again.

It was an apparently endless cycle, but the booksellers were exempt from it. The courts had decided that the First Amendment embodied in its protection of freedom of the press the right of anyone to sell printed matter on the street, so if you had books for sale you never got hassled. As a result, a lot of scholarly antiquarian booksellers offered their wares on the city streets. So did any number of illiterates hawking remaindered art books and stolen bestsellers, along with homeless street people who rescued old magazines from people's garbage cans and spread them out on the pavement, living in hope that someone would want to buy them.

In front of St. Patrick's Cathedral we found a Pakistani with tee-shirts and sweatshirts. I asked him if he had any Batman merchandise and he went right through the piles himself and pulled out half a dozen items. We didn't bother signaling the Cavalry across the street. Lee just showed the man a badge—Special Officer, it said—and I explained that we had to confiscate Batman items.

"He is the big seller, Batman," the man said. "I get Batman, I sell him fast as I can."

"Well, you better not sell him anymore," I said, "because it's against the law."

"Excuse, please," he said. "What is law? Why is Batman against law? Is my understanding Batman is *for* law. He is good guy, is it not so?"

I explained about copyright and trademarks and licensing agreements. It was a little like explaining the internal combustion engine to a field mouse. He kept nodding his head, but I don't know how much of it he got. He understood the main point—that we were walking off with his stock and he was stuck for whatever it cost him. He didn't like that part, but there wasn't much he could do about it.

Lee tucked the shirts under his arm and we kept going. At Forty-seventh Street we crossed over in response to a signal from Wally. They'd found another pair of Senegalese with a big spread of Batman items—tees and sweatshirts and gimme caps and sun visors, some a direct knockoff of the copyrighted Bat signal, others a variation on the theme, but none of it authorized and all of it subject to confiscation. The two men—they looked like brothers and were dressed identically in baggy beige trousers and sky-blue nylon shirts—couldn't understand what was wrong with their merchandise and couldn't believe we intended to haul it all away with us. But there were five of us, and we were large intimidating white men with an authoritarian manner, and what could they do about it?

"I'll get the car," Wally said. "No way we're gonna shlep this crap seven blocks in this heat."

WITH THE TRUNK almost full, we drove to Thirty-fourth and broke for lunch at a place Wally liked. We sat at a large round table. Ornate beer steins hung from the beams overhead. We had a round of drinks, then ordered sandwiches and fries and half-liter steins of dark beer. I had a Coke to start, another Coke with the food, and coffee afterward.

"You're not drinking," Lee Trombauer said.

"Not today."

"Not on duty," Jimmy said, and everybody laughed.

"What I want to know," Eddie Rankin said, "is why everybody wants a fucking Batman shirt in the first place."

"Not just shirts," somebody said.

"Shirts, sweaters, caps, lunch boxes—if you could print it on Tampax they'd be shoving 'em up their twats. Why Batman, for Christ's sake?"

"It's hot," Wally said.

" 'It's hot.' What the fuck does that mean?"

"It means it's hot. That's what it means. It's hot means it's hot. Every-body wants it because everybody else wants it, and that means it's hot."

"I seen the movie," Eddie said. "You see it?"

Two of us had, two of us hadn't.

"It's okay," he said. "Basically, I'd say it's a kid's movie, but it's okay."

"So?"

"So how many tee-shirts in extra large do you sell to kids? Everybody's buying this shit, and all you can tell me is it's hot because it's hot. I don't get it."

"You don't have to," Wally said. "It's the same as the niggers. You want to try explaining to them why they can't sell Batman unless there's a little copyright notice printed under the design? While you're at it, you can explain to me why the assholes counterfeiting the crap don't counterfeit the copyright notice while they're at it. The thing is, nobody has to do any explaining because nobody has to understand. The only message they have to get on the street is 'Batman no good, no sell Batman.' If they learn that much we're doing our job right."

———

WALLY PAID FOR everybody's lunch. We stopped at the Flatiron Building long enough to empty the trunk and carry everything up-stairs, then drove down to the Village and worked the sidewalk market on Sixth Avenue below Eighth Street. We made a few confiscations without in-cident. Then, near the subway entrance at West Third, we were taking a dozen shirts and about as many visors from a West Indian when another vendor decided to get into the act. He was wearing a dashiki and had his hair in Rastafarian dreadlocks, and he said, "You can't take the brother's wares, man. You can't do that."

"It's unlicensed merchandise produced in contravention of interna-tional copyright protection," Wally told him.

"Maybe so," the man said, "but that don't empower you to seize it. Where's your due process? Where's your authority? You aren't police." Poe-lease, he said, bearing down on the first syllable. "You can't come into a man's store, seize his wares."

"Store?" Eddie Rankin moved toward him, his hands hovering at his sides. "You see a store here? All I see's a lot of fucking shit in the middle of a fucking blanket."

"This is the man's store. This is the man's place of business."

"And what's this?" Eddie demanded. He walked over to the right, where the man with the dreadlocks had stick incense displayed for sale on a pair of upended orange crates. "This your store?"

"That's right. It's my store."

"You know what it looks like to me? It looks like you're selling drug paraphernalia. That's what it looks like."

"It's incense," the Rasta said. "For bad smells."

"Bad smells," Eddie said. One of the sticks of incense was smoldering, and Eddie picked it up and sniffed at it. "Whew," he said. "That's a bad smell, I'll give you that. Smells like the catbox caught on fire."

The Rasta snatched the incense from him. "It's a good smell," he said. "Smells like your mama."

Eddie smiled at him, his red lips parting to show stained teeth. He looked happy, and very dangerous. "Say I kick your store into the middle of the street," he said, "and you with it. How's that sound to you?"

Smoothly, easily, Wally Witt moved between them. "Eddie," he said softly, and Eddie backed off and let the smile fade on his lips. To the incense seller Wally said, "Look, you and I got no quarrel with each other. I got a job to do and you got your own business to run."

"The brother here's got a business to run, too."

"Well, he's gonna have to run it without Batman, because that's how the law reads. But if you want to *be* Batman, playing the dozens with my man here and pushing into what doesn't concern you, then I got no choice. You follow me?"

"All I'm saying, I'm saying you want to confiscate the man's merchandise, you need you a policeman and a court order, something to make it official."

"Fine," Wally said. "You're saying it and I hear you saying it, but what I'm saying is all I need to do it is to do it, official or not. Now if you want to get a cop to stop me, fine, go ahead and do it, but as soon as you do I'm going to press charges for selling drug paraphernalia and operating without a peddler's license—"

"This here ain't drug paraphernalia, man. We both know that."

"We both know you're just trying to be a hard-on, and we both know what it'll get you. That what you want?"

The incense seller stood there for a moment, then dropped his eyes. "Don't matter what I want," he said.

"Well, you got that right," Wally told him. "It don't matter what you want."

W E TOSSED THE shirts and visors into the trunk and got out of there. On the way over to Astor Place Eddie said, "You didn't have to jump in there. I wasn't about to lose it."

"Never said you were."

"That mama stuff doesn't bother me. It's just nigger talk, they all talk that shit."

"I know."

"They'd talk about their fathers, but they don't know who the fuck they are, so they're stuck with their mothers. Bad smells—I shoulda stuck that shit up his ass, get right where the bad smells are. I hate a guy sticks his nose in like that."

"Your basic sidewalk lawyer."

"Basic asshole's what he is. Maybe I'll go back, talk with him later."

"On your own time."

"On my own time is right."

Astor Place hosts a more freewheeling street market, with a lot of Bowery types offering a mix of salvaged trash and stolen goods. There was something especially curious about our role as we passed over hot radios and typewriters and jewelry and sought only merchandise that had been legitimately purchased, albeit from illegitimate manufacturers. We didn't find much Batman ware on display, although a lot of people, buyers and sellers alike, were wearing the Caped Crusader. We weren't about to strip the shirt off anybody's person, nor did we look too hard for contraband merchandise; the place was teeming with crackheads and crazies, and it was no time to push our luck.

"Let's get out of here," Wally said. "I hate to leave the car in this neighborhood. We already gave the client his money's worth."

By four we were in Wally's office and his desk was heaped high with the fruits of our labors. "Look at all this shit," he said. "Today's trash and tomorrow's treasures. Twenty years and they'll be auctioning this crap at Christie's. Not this particular crap, because I'll messenger it over to the client and he'll chuck it in the incinerator. Gentlemen, you did a good day's work." He took out his wallet and gave each of the four of us a hundred-dollar bill. He said, "Same time tomorrow? Except I think we'll make lunch Chinese tomorrow. Eddie, don't forget your purse."

"Don't worry."

"Thing is, you don't want to carry it if you go back to see your Rastafarian friend. He might get the wrong idea."

"Fuck him," Eddie said. "I got no time for him. He wants that incense up his ass, he's gonna have to stick it there himself."

Lee and Jimmy and Eddie went out, laughing, joking, slapping backs. I started out after them, then doubled back and asked Wally if he had a minute.

"Sure," he said. "Jesus, I don't believe that. Look."

"It's a Batman shirt."

"No shit, Sherlock. And look what's printed right under the Bat signal."

"The copyright notice."

"Right, which makes it a legal shirt. We got any more of these? No, no, no, no. Wait a minute, here's one. Here's another. Jesus, this is amazing. There any more? I don't see any others, do you?"

We went through the pile without finding more of the shirts with the copyright notice.

"Three," he said. "Well, that's not so bad. A mere fraction." He balled up the three shirts, dropped them back on the pile. "You want one of these? It's legit; you can wear it without fear of confiscation."

"I don't think so."

"You got kids? Take something home for your kids."

"One's in college and the other's in the service. I don't think they'd be interested."

"Probably not." He stepped out from behind his desk. "Well, it went all right out there, don't you think? We had a good crew, worked well together."

"I guess."

"What's the matter, Matt?"

"Nothing, really. But I don't think I can make it tomorrow."

"No? Why's that?"

"Well, for openers, I've got a dentist appointment."

"Oh yeah? What time?"

"Nine-fifteen."

"So how long can that take? Half an hour, an hour tops? Meet us here ten-thirty, that's good enough. The client doesn't have to know what time we hit the street."

"It's not just the dentist appointment, Wally."

"Oh?"

"I don't think I want to do this stuff anymore."

"What stuff? Copyright and trademark protection?"

"Yeah."

"What's the matter? It's beneath you? Doesn't make full use of your talents as a detective?"

"It's not that."

"Because it's not a bad deal for the money, seems to me. Hundred bucks for a short day, ten to four, hour and a half off for lunch with the lunch all paid for. You're a cheap lunch date—you don't drink—but even so. Call it a ten-dollar lunch, that's a hundred and ten dollars for what, four and a half hours' work?" He punched numbers on a desktop calculator. "That's twenty-four forty-four an hour. That's not bad wages. You want to take home better than that, you need either burglar's tools or a law degree, seems to me."

"The money's fine, Wally."

"Then what's the problem?"

I shook my head. "I just haven't got the heart for it," I said. "Hassling people who don't even speak the language, taking their goods from them because we're stronger than they are and there's nothing they can do about it."

"They can quit selling contraband, that's what they can do."

"How? They don't even know what's contraband."

"Well, that's where we come in. We're giving them an education. How they gonna learn if nobody teaches 'em?"

I'd loosened my tie earlier. Now I took it off, folded it, put it in my pocket.

He said, "Company owns a copyright, they got a right to control who uses it. Somebody else enters into a licensing agreement, pays money for the right to produce a particular item, they got a right to the exclusivity they paid for."

"I don't have a problem with that."

"So?"

"They don't even speak the language," I said.

He stood up straight. "Then who told 'em to come here?" he wanted to know. "Who fucking invited them? You can't walk a block in midtown without tripping over another super salesman from Senegal. They swarm off that Air Afrique flight from Dakar, and first thing you know they got an open-air store on world-famous Fifth Avenue. They don't pay rent, they don't pay taxes, they just spread a blanket on the concrete and rake in the dollars."

"They didn't look as though they were getting rich."

"They must do all right. Pay two bucks for a scarf and sell it for ten, they must come out okay. They stay at hotels like the Bryant, pack together like sardines, six or eight to the room. Sleep in shifts, cook their food on hotplates. Two, three months of that and it's back to fucking Dakar. They drop off the money, take a few minutes to get another baby started, then they're winging back to JFK to start all over again. You think we need that? Haven't we got enough spades of our own can't make a living, we got to fly in more of them?"

I sifted through the pile on his desk, picked up a sun visor with the Joker depicted on it. I wondered why anybody would want something like that. I said, "What do you figure it adds up to, the stuff we confiscated? A couple of hundred?"

"Jesus, I don't know. Figure ten for a tee-shirt, and we got what, thirty or forty of them? Add in the sweatshirts, the rest of the shit, I bet it comes close to a grand. Why?"

"I was just thinking. You paid us a hundred a man, plus whatever lunch came to."

"Eighty with the tip. What's the point?"

"You must have billed us to the client at what, fifty dollars an hour?"

"I haven't billed anything to anybody yet—I just walked in the door— but yes, that's the rate."

"How will you figure it, four men at eight hours a man?"

"Seven hours. We don't bill for lunch time."

Seven hours seemed ample, considering that we'd worked four and a half. I said, "Seven times fifty times four of us is what? Fourteen hundred dollars? Plus your own time, of course, and you must bill yourself at more than regular operative's rates. A hundred an hour?"

"Seventy-five."

"For seven hours is what, five hundred?"

"Five and a quarter," he said evenly.

"Plus fourteen hundred is nineteen and a quarter. Call it two thousand dollars to the client. Is that about right?"

"What are you saying, Matt? The client pays too much or you're not getting a big enough piece of the pie?"

"Neither. But if he wants to load up on this garbage"—I waved a hand at the heap on the desk—"wouldn't he be better off buying retail? Get a lot more bang for the buck, wouldn't he?"

He just stared at me for a long moment. Then abruptly, his hard face cracked and he started to laugh. I was laughing, too, and it took all the tension out of the air. "Jesus, you're right," he said. "Guy's paying way too much."

"I mean, if you wanted to handle it for him, you wouldn't need to hire me and the other guys."

"I could just go around and pay cash."

"Right."

"I could even pass up the street guys altogether, go straight to the wholesaler."

"Save a dollar that way."

"I love it," he said. "You know what it sounds like? Sounds like something the federal government would do, get cocaine off the streets by buying it straight from the Colombians. Wait a minute, didn't they actually do something like that once?"

"I think so, but I don't think it was cocaine."

"No, it was opium. It was some years ago—they bought the entire Turkish opium crop because it was supposed to be the cheapest way to keep it out of the country. Bought it and burned it, and that, boys and girls, that was the end of heroin addiction in America."

"Worked like a charm, didn't it?"

"Nothing works," he said. "First principle of modern law enforcement. Nothing ever works. Funny thing is, in this case the client's not getting a bad deal. You own a copyright or a trademark, you got to defend it. Otherwise you risk losing it. You got to be able to say on such and such a date you paid so many dollars to defend your interests and investigators acting as your agents confiscated so many items from so many merchants. And it's worth what you budget for it. Believe me, these big companies, they wouldn't spend the money year in and year out if they didn't figure it was worth it."

"I believe it," I said. "Anyway, I wouldn't lose a whole lot of sleep over the client getting screwed a little."

"You just don't like the work."

"I'm afraid not."

He shrugged. "I don't blame you. It's chickenshit. But Jesus, Matt, most P.I. work is chickenshit. Was it that different in the Department? Or on any police force? Most of what we did was chickenshit."

"And paperwork."

"And paperwork—you're absolutely right. Do some chickenshit and then write it up. And make copies."

"I can put up with a certain amount of chickenshit," I said. "But I honestly don't have the heart for what we did today. I felt like a bully."

"Listen, I'd rather be kicking in doors, taking down bad guys. That what you want?"

"Not really."

"Be Batman, tooling around Gotham City, righting wrongs. Do the whole thing not even carrying a gun. You know what they didn't have in the movie?"

"I haven't seen it yet."

"Robin, they didn't have Robin. Robin the Boy Wonder. He's not in the comic book anymore, either. Somebody told me they took a poll, had their readers call a 900 number and vote, should they keep Robin or should they kill him. Like in ancient Rome, those fighters, what do you call them?"

"Gladiators."

"Right. Thumbs up or thumbs down, and Robin got thumbs down, so they killed him. Can you believe that?"

"I can believe anything."

"Yeah, you and me both. I always thought they were fags." I looked at him. "Batman and Robin, I mean. His *ward*, for Christ's sake. Playing dress-up, flying around, costumes, I figured it's gotta be some kind of fag S-and-M thing. Isn't that what you figured?"

"I never thought about it."

"Well, I never stayed up nights over it myself, but what else would it be? Anyway, he's dead now, Robin is. Died of AIDS, I suppose, but the family's denying it, like what's-his-name. You know who I mean."

I didn't, but I nodded.

"You gotta make a living, you know. Gotta turn a buck, whether it's hassling Africans or squatting out there on a blanket your own self, selling tapes and scarves. Fi' dollah, ten dollah." He looked at me. "No good, huh?"

"I don't think so, Wally."

"Don't want to be one of Batman's helpers. Well, you can't do what you can't do. What the fuck do I know about it, anyway? You don't drink. I don't have a problem with it myself. But if I couldn't put my feet up at the end of the day, have a few pops, who knows? Maybe I couldn't do it either. Matt, you're a good man. If you change your mind—"

"I know. Thanks, Wally."

"Hey," he said. "Don't mention it. We gotta look out for each other, you know what I mean? Here in Gotham City."

THE GIRL WHO MARRIED A MONSTER

Anthony Boucher

Anthony Boucher (1911–1968) was one of the most remarkable figures ever produced by the mystery genre. And the same could be said of him in the science fiction genre, too. Whether he was working as author, critic, or editor in these fields, his name on a story, novel, or magazine invariably meant that you were getting the best the field had to offer. Under the name H. H. Holmes, he wrote a number of memorable mystery novels; under his own name he created at least two dozen fantasy stories that are still being reprinted today. He touched virtually every writer of his time—by teaching them through the craft he brought to his fiction; or by buying and editing their stories for one of his magazines (he was co-founder of *The Magazine of Fantasy & Science Fiction*, for just one example); or as a critic: he wrote 850 weekly columns for the *New York Times Book Review*. And he was no snob. He was the first major critic to seriously review paperback originals. He died far too young, at age 57.

THERE SEEMED FROM the start to be an atmosphere of pressured haste about the whole affair. The wedding date was set even before the formal announcement of the engagement; Doreen was so *very* insistent that Marie must come at once to Hollywood to serve as maid of honor; the engagement party was already getting under way when Marie arrived at the house; and she had barely had time for the fastest of showers and a change of clothes when she was standing beside Cousin Doreen and being introduced to the murderer.

Not that she knew it for certain at that moment. Then—with one of Doreen's friends ad-libbing a bebop wedding march on the piano and another trying to fit limerick lyrics to it and all the others saying *"Da*rling . . . !" and "But *my* agent says . . ." and "The liquor flows like glue around here" and "*Live TV?* But my dear, how quaintly *historical!*"—then it was only a matter of some forgotten little-girl memory trying to stir at the back of her mind and some very active big-girl instincts stirring in front. Later, with the aid of the man in gray and his strange friend with the invisible fly, it was to be terrifyingly positive. Now, it was vague and indefinable, and perhaps all the more terrifying for being so.

Marie had been prepared to dislike him. Doreen was only a year older than she (which was 27) and looked a year younger; there was something obscene about the idea of her marrying a man in his fifties. Marie was pre-pared for something out of Peter Arno, and for a moment it was a relief to find him so ordinary-looking—just another man, like the corner grocer . . . or no, more like the druggist, the nice one that was a bishop in the Latter Day Saints. For a moment after that it was a pleasant surprise to find that he was easy, affable, even charming in a way you didn't expect of ordinary elderly men. He was asking all about her family (which was of course Doreen's, too) and about Utah and how was Salt Lake nowadays, and all the time he made you feel that he was asking about these subjects only be-cause they were connected with *you*.

In these first few moments the Hollywood party seemed to vanish and it was almost as if she was still back in Salt Lake and it was perfectly un-derstandable that Doreen should marry him no matter how old he was— and no matter how hard a little-girl memory tried to place the name LUTHER PEABODY (in very black type) and the photograph (much younger) that had gone with it.

At this point Doreen had said, "Luther, be nice to Marie, huh? I have to make like a hostess," and disappeared. Marie was alone with Luther Peabody, the party whirling around them like a montage gone mad. It wasn't quite what he said or where he touched her as he casually steered her toward the bar, though the words were deliberately suggestive and it was not a touch commonly bestowed by a bridegroom upon the maid of honor. It was more that the voice was too soft and the fingers were too soft and the eyes—the eyes that fixed her, and her alone, as if only they were in the room—the eyes were much too hard.

The little-girl memory was still a fragment; but whatever it was, it re-inforced this sudden adult recognition of peril. Without conscious thought Marie found that she had evaded Peabody, slipped behind two men argu-ing about guild jurisdiction in TV, and lost herself in a deep chair in an ob-scure corner.

Her whole body was trembling, as if it had been, in some curiously public way, outraged. And she was thinking that by contrast, a Peter Arno Lecher-of-Great-Wealth would make a clean and welcome cousin-in-law.

It was in the corner that the man in gray found her.

"You're Doreen's cousin Marie," he stated. "My name's MacDonald.

You don't have a drink. Or rather," he added, "you didn't have one." And he passed her one of the two martinis he was holding.

She managed, by an active miracle, not to spill any; but she still needed two sips before she could properly arrange her face into the right smile and say, "Thank you, sir."

"Good," he said. "I wasn't sure about plying you. One never knows with girls from Salt Lake."

"Oh, but I'm not a saint."

"Who is? Thank God."

"I mean" (the smile came more easily now) "I'm not a Mormon. Doreen isn't, either. Our fathers came to Salt Lake when they were both widowers, with us squalling on their hands. They married Utah girls, and all this enormous Mormon family you read about in Doreen's publicity is just step-family."

"Remind Doreen some time," he said dryly. "She's never disbelieved a word of her publicity. Including" (his eyes wandered about the brawling room) "the word 'starlet.' How long does one go on being a starlet? Is it semipermanent, like being a Young Democrat? They're still dunning me for dues when I should be putting the money into a hair-restorer."

"Oh, but *you* are young!" she reacted hastily. She'd never have said so ordinarily—he must be in his late thirties. But she had stopped shaking and he was comfortable and reassuring and not at all like a middle-aged fragment of memory with soft fingers and eyes from hell.

Mac-what'sit seemed almost to read her thoughts. He looked across to the bar, where Luther Peabody was being charming to some columnist's third assistant leg-woman. "You just got in, didn't you?" he asked.

"Yes," Marie said uneasily. "It's all been done in such a rush. . . ."

"And you'd just as soon get out again." It wasn't a question. "I have a car. . . ."

"**A**ND THAT," SAID MacDonald, "is Catalina."

They were parked on a bluff in Palos Verdes. It was almost sunset.

"There's something so wonderful," Marie said softly, "about being on a high place and looking at something new. The this-is-the-place feeling."

"Kingdoms of the world . . ." MacDonald muttered. "You see, I knew Doreen when she first came here. Met her through a radio-actress friend of mine." His voice hardened oddly.

"Were you . . . ?" But Marie didn't finish the sentence. They had come almost close enough for such a question, but not quite.

". . . in love with Doreen?" MacDonald laughed. "Good Lord, no. No, I was thinking of the girl who introduced us. One of my best friends killed her."

Suddenly the photograph and the black type were very clear, and Marie knew the story that went with them.

MacDonald did not miss her sudden start. He eyed her speculatively. "That's why I recognized you—because I knew Doreen way back when. You don't look anything alike now, but back before she got the starlet treatment . . . And she had the same this-is-the-place look."

"And now . . ." Marie said.

"And now," MacDonald repeated. After a moment of silence he said, "Look. You'd better tell me about it, hadn't you? It's something you can't say to Doreen, and it isn't doing you any good bottled up."

Marie, almost to her own surprise, nodded. "Another martini first."

THE SEASIDE BAR was small and almost deserted and exactly suited to letting one's hair down. "Not that it isn't as down as it can go, literally," Marie tried to smile.

"And very nice, too. Major difference between you and Doreen-that-was. Hers was always straight."

"I think she won't have it waved because she won't admit she's always been jealous of mine. No, that's catty and I shouldn't; but I think it *is* the only thing in me Doreen's ever envied. And it's your fault. I only said it because you're so easy to talk to."

"Occupational disease," said the man whose occupation she didn't know.

The drinks came and the waiter went and Marie tried to find the words for the thing that frightened her. "You see," she said, "I . . . know what it means to love the wrong man. Not just the wrong man, but a man who's *wrong*. I was a secretary at the radiation lab up at Berkeley and there was this research-worker. . . . You'd know his name; it's been in headlines. He was—it's a melodramatic word, but it's true—he was a traitor, and I was in love with him for months and never dreamed what he was like inside. I even wanted to defend him and stand by him, but then after he was convicted he took the mask off and for the first time . . . Anyway, that's why I went back to Utah. And why I know how Doreen can love this man and yet not know him . . . and why I have to *do* something.

"It isn't just 'woman's intuition,' or the fact that no man would ever see his eyes get like that or feel his fingers go softer than flesh. It's what I've remembered. It must be a long time ago, maybe fifteen years. I think I was in junior high. But there was this big case up in Portland or Seattle or some place. He was a . . . a Bluebeard, and this was the umpteenth wife he'd killed. It was all over the papers; everybody talked about it. And when you said something about a murder, I remembered it all and I could see the papers. It was the same name and the same face."

Now it was out, and she finished her martini in one gulp.

MacDonald showed no surprise. "That isn't," he said levelly, "the one I was thinking of. Maybe because we were obviously in junior high at different times. Funny how murder fascinates kids. I'll never forget Winnie Ruth Judd in 1931, even if I didn't understand half of it. And the one I'm remembering was a little before that, around '29. Right here in L.A. Same name, same face."

"But it can't be the same. Twice? He'd have been gassed the first time."

"Hanged, back then. But he must have been acquitted, both here and in Portland or wherever. Our innocent childish souls remember the grue, but not the trial."

"But they wouldn't acquit him twice, would they?"

"My dear girl, if you want statistics on the acquittal of murderers, even mass repeaters . . . You see, you came to a man in the right business."

Maybe it was the martini. Suddenly she felt that everything was going to be all right. This quiet man in gray would know what to do.

"Formally," he went on, "it's Lieutenant MacDonald, L.A.P.D., Homicide. I don't claim to bat a thousand, but that friend who killed the radio actress is in San Quentin now, doing life. All the information I can find on Luther Peabody, officially and unofficially, is yours to lay before Doreen. And no matter how much in love she is, it should be hard for her to keep her eyes shut."

"Lieutenant MacDonald, I love you," said Marie. "And you'll check your files right away and let me know?"

"Files?" said MacDonald. "Of course. And," he added with deliberate mystification, "I think I have another source that's even better."

"I'M DAMNED IF I see why," Doreen objected petulantly, "you had to run off from the party like that yesterday. It was one wingding of a party and after all as maid of honor you're part of the engagement. Besides, Luther was hurt. He liked you, and you didn't give him any chance to show it."

Marie pulled on a stocking and concentrated on straightening its seam. "Are you really in love with Luther?" she asked.

"I guess so. I like him. He's fun. Even on his feet. Oh—! Want to finish zipping this for me? It always sticks . . . What's the matter? Did I shock ums?"

"Well, I hadn't thought . . . I mean, he's so . . ."

"Old? Listen, darling, there's no substitute for experience. If you knew some of these young Hollywood glamor-boys . . ."

"Doreen . . ." The zipping task over, Marie was concentrating on the other stocking.

"Mmmm?"

"Maybe I shouldn't have as just a house guest, but I asked a friend to drop in for a cocktail."

"Oh? I was kind of hoping you and Luther and I could settle down for the afternoon and make up for yesterday. Who is he?"

"That nice MacDonald man I met at the party."

"Mac? Is that whom you ran away with? He's okay, I guess . . . if you like serious-minded cops. You two can have fun disapproving of me. Doreen Arlen, Girl Failure."

"Oh, Doreen, is it that bad?"

"No, don't mind me. I've got a deal cooking at CBS, and there's one of the independents that—Is that Luther already? How's my face? Quick!"

But it wasn't Luther Peabody. It was Lieutenant Donald MacDonald, and he said, "Hi, Doreen. I hope it isn't an imposition; I brought another guest."

Doreen shrugged. "Why doesn't somebody tell me—?" Then she broke off. She and Marie found themselves involuntarily staring at MacDonald's companion.

He was a small man, almost inhumanly thin. He might have been any age from 40 to 60, and he would probably go on looking much the same until he was 80. The first thing that struck Marie was the dead whiteness of his skin—almost like the skin of a subterranean cave-dweller, or of a corpse. Then she saw the brilliant blue of his eyes, and an odd hint of so much behind the blue that she knew—despite the abnormal pallor, despite the skeletal thinness—this man was, in some way of his own, intensely alive.

"Miss Doreen Arlen," MacDonald said, "Miss Marie Arlen, may I present Mr. Noble?"

"Any friend of Mac's and stuff," said Doreen. "Come on in. Luther isn't here yet; you want to tend bar, Mac?"

And somehow they were all in the living room and MacDonald was mixing drinks and it was a party and MacDonald's Mr. Noble still hadn't said a word. Not until MacDonald was arguing with Doreen about fetching another tray of ice cubes ("The key to a martini is a pitcher *full* of ice"), did Mr. Noble lean toward Marie and say, "Right."

"I beg your pardon?"

"You were." And Mr. Noble was silent again until MacDonald brought around the tray of drinks, when he shook his head and said, "Sherry?"

"Sure," said Doreen. "There's sherry in the kitchen. Nothing special, mostly for cooking, but—"

"Okay," said Mr. Noble.

MacDonald whispered to Doreen as she left, and she returned with a water glass, the sherry bottle, and a puzzled but resolute hostess look. Marie watched Mr. Noble's white hand fill the water glass. *"You were right."* What did he know? Why had MacDonald brought him?

The doorbell rang again, and this time it was Luther. He kissed Doreen, a little less casually than one usually kisses a fiancée before strangers, and then he was moving in on Marie with a cousinly gleam. *If he tries to kiss me . . .* , she thought in sudden terror.

And Mr. Noble looked up from his water glass of sherry to say flatly, "Peabody."

Luther Peabody looked expectantly at Doreen. He started to say "Introduce me, dar—" and then he looked at Mr. Noble again. Lieutenant MacDonald had retired to the bar. He was smiling. Peabody stared at the bony white face as if trying to clothe it with flesh and color.

"Lieutenant Noble," he said suddenly. It was not the voice with which he spoke to women.

"Ex," said Mr. Noble. "Out of the profession now. But not you, eh, Peabody? Still in the same line of work?"

"Doreen!" Luther Peabody's voice had regained its vigor, and a new dignity as well. "What is the meaning of this—this absurd confrontation scene? It's true that many years ago Lieutenant Noble, presumably in order to advance his own police career, chose to hound me as a murderer because of the accidental death of my first wife. It's a matter of public record that I was acquitted. I stand proved innocent by the courts. Why should this tragedy of my youth—?"

Marie could hardly believe it, but she would have sworn that Doreen was on the verge of laughter. Mr. Noble kept looking at Luther, but his bright blue eyes glazed over as though something was going on behind them. "Phoenix," he said. "1932. Same 'accident'—fall from stepladder. Same double-indemnity policy. Not enough evidence. No indictment."

"You see?" Peabody protested. "Another unfortunate—"

"Santa Fe. 1935. Same accident. Same policy. Acquitted. Seattle. 1938." He nodded toward Marie. "Same accident. No policy. Didn't need it; family fortune. Three trials. Three hung juries. State dropped the case. Long gap; Seattle very profitable. Butte. 1945. Same accident. Woman lived. Refused to prosecute, but got divorce. Las Vegas. 1949. Acquitted."

"You left out the funny one, Nick," MacDonald contributed. "Berkeley, 1947. Convicted, served 60 days for molesting. He went and clipped a hunk of hair off a woman he was a-courting, and she didn't like it."

"Fernandez," said Mr. Noble obscurely.

"I trust you appreciate the allusion, Mr. Peabody? Your colleague Raymond Fernandez, New York's 1949 Lonely Hearts killer, who also liked hair. He used it for sympathetic magic, but fetichism may have entered in. Which is it with you, incidentally? Some of the other victims showed signs of amateur barbering."

"Are you comparing *me*, sir, to such a brute as Fernandez?"

"On second thought," MacDonald mused quietly, "I withdraw the fetichism with him; brutes are more direct. Magic was undoubtedly his dominant motive. Now your true fetichist is usually to all appearances a fine plausible citizen. You'll agree, Nick, that we've insulted Mr. Peabody needlessly? He and Fernandez have markedly different attitudes toward hair, if not toward . . ." He left the sentence incomplete.

Marie held her breath, watching Doreen. Her cousin was still looking at Luther Peabody—not with fear and hatred, not with inextinguishable love, but now quite unmistakably with repressed laughter.

"Lieutenant MacDonald!" Luther exploded with seemly rage. "Your ex-colleague may well be irresponsible and I suspect that he is more than a little drunk" (Mr. Noble calmly refilled his water glass) "but you're an officer of the law. You know that the law has no charges to bring against me and that your imputations are slanderous. This is not my house. It's my fiancée's. I'll leave it to her to order you and your sherry-tippling friend from the premises."

Now Doreen's laughter burst out, clear and ringing. "*Dar*ling! You're so cute when you're stuffy."

She was the only unamazed person in the room.

"Look, Mac," she went on. "I've known this all along. I remember the news stories and the pictures. That's why I first went out with Luther. I thought it'd be fun to see what a real, live, unconvicted professional Blue-beard was like. Then I got to know him, and I like him, and he doesn't need to do any explaining to me. He's going to tell me they *were* all acci-dents and that he's a persecuted victim of fate—and he doesn't need to, be-cause I'm saying it first and I'm saying it to you, Mac, and to you, Mr. Noble. And I'm not ordering anybody out of any doors, but . . . do you re-ally think there's much point in staying?"

"BUT WHY, DOREEN? For heaven's sake, *why?*"
The girls were going to bed early. Even Luther Peabody had seemed disconcerted by Doreen's reaction and had left soon after. ("I want to be alone, my dear, with this precious trust you have placed in my hands.")

"I told you, darling. I like him. Maybe I even believe him."

"But you *can't!* It can't all be just innocent coincidence. It piles up too much. And that funny thing about the hair . . ."

"That," Doreen admitted, patting her long straight hair, "might give a girl to think. But honest, he hasn't made any passes at my hair. No fetichism about *him*."

Marie picked up the small book from the night table. It was a WAC textbook on judo for women. "So you believe him?"

"All right, so there's a five percent chance I'm wrong. A girl should be able to defend herself, I always say. If she wants to."

"Is that it? You *don't* want to? Are things so bad you're deliberately looking for . . . ?"

Doreen lit a cigarette. "I'm sorry. I don't need your wholesome Utah sympathy, thank you kindly. Doreen can look out for herself. And I'm *not* deliberately plunging to my death. Now will you go to sleep or am I going to have to go out and see what twenty-year-old wonders the TV's offering tonight?"

"May I ask you one question, Doreen?"

"Make it a bargain. One apiece. Something I want to say to you, too . . . You first."

"Has he . . . has he talked to you about insurance?"

"Of course. It's sensible, isn't it? He's better off than you seem to think, you know, and I'm young and healthy so the premiums are low. He's paid the first premium on a policy for me. One hundred grand. And now that your worst fears are confirmed—"

"Oh, Doreen! How *can* you?"

"I've a favor to ask of you. Don't go back to the seagulls and the Tabernacle yet. Stick around a while. We'll find you a job if you want; I've got contacts."

"Then you *do* think you need somebody to—"

"I said I believed him, didn't I? It's just . . . Well . . . Oh, skip it! Go home if you want to. Go marry a Fundamentalist and run off to the Arizona Strip. Luther marries 'em only one at a time—and when he marries me, he's going to stay married."

"I'll stay. Of course I'll stay, Doreen. But oh . . . You're not just my cousin. You've always been my best friend. And now . . . I just don't understand you at all."

"That is news?" Doreen asked, and switched off the light.

I T WAS A small tasteful wedding, held in the Sma' Kirk O' the Braes, and chiefly distinguished by the fact that the maid of honor never met the eyes of the bridegroom.

Throughout the service Marie could not help thinking of what marriage meant to her, or rather what she hoped it might mean. And here were Doreen and Luther . . .

"Why? *Why?*" She was almost in tears as MacDonald helped her into his car after the bridal couple had left for a Palm Springs weekend.

"We're going," MacDonald said, "to see the best man on *Whys* in L.A. You've met him, though it wasn't one of his more brilliant appearances. That's the second time Luther Peabody's bested him, and if I thought Nick was capable of such a human reaction, I'd say it rankles."

"Who *is* he, Mac? That whole scene was so strange . . ."

As they drove to downtown Los Angeles, MacDonald sketched a little of the career of Nicholas Joffe Noble, ex-Lieutenant, L.A.P.D. How the brightest Homicide man in Los Angeles had been framed to take the rap for a crooked Captain under investigation; how the sudden loss of job and reputation at the beginning of the depression had meant no money for an operation for his wife; how her death had broken him until he wound up on Skid Row living on sherry . . . and puzzles.

"Ten years ago," MacDonald said, "on my first case, one of the old-line Homicide boys steered me to him. Called him the Screwball Division, L.A.P.D. If a case makes no sense at all—and Lord knows that one didn't!—feed the facts to Nick Noble. His eyes sort of glaze over and something goes *tick* inside . . . and then the facts make a pattern.

"I've told him a lot about Doreen. He's been looking up some more stuff on Peabody, especially the Seattle case. Way I see it, we've got two problems here: Why is Doreen deliberately marrying a presumable mass murderer, and how in God's name are we going to prevent another 'accident'? And if those questions have an answer, we'll find it in the Chula Negra café, third booth on the left."

The little Mexican café was on North Main Street, near the new Federal Building, and the old Plaza and the medium-new Union Station, and the old Mexican Church and the new freeway which had brought them downtown. It had a new jukebox with some very old records and cheap new sherry in cracked old glasses.

In the third booth on the left the white little man sat, a half-full glass before him. He said "Mac" to MacDonald and "Miss Arlen" to Marie and then he brushed his white hand across his sharp-pointed white nose. "Fly," he said. "Stays there."

There was no fly. Marie looked down, embarrassed, and said, "Lieutenant MacDonald thought maybe you could—"

"Heard Mac's story," Mr. Noble interrupted. "Need yours. Talk."

And while MacDonald beckoned the plump young Mexican waitress and ordered more sherry, Marie talked. When she had finished, she watched the bright blue eyes expectantly. But they didn't glaze. Instead Mr. Noble shook his head, half in annoyance, half perhaps to dislodge the persistent if invisible fly.

"Not enough," he said. "No pattern."

"A whodunit's one thing," said MacDonald. "This is a *why*dunit. Why should a girl deliberately marry a Bluebeard? F. Tennyson Jesse works out quite an elaborate and convincing theory of murderees, people who deliberately invite being murdered."

"But Doreen isn't at all like that!" Marie protested.

"I know. Miss Jesse'd agree; Doreen doesn't fit the type. Some women want morbid sensation and pick out low, often strange kinds of men."

Marie said hesitantly: "You read about people being hypnotized. Luther does have such queer eyes—"

"Tabloid stuff," said Noble. "She knows what she's doing. Not enough. No pattern." He emptied his glass.

"And there's no official action we can take to protect her," said MacDonald. "That's the frustrating part. We can't go spending the taxpayers' money without a complaint. The insurance company's just as helpless. Dan Rafetti from Southwest National was in to see me today. He wanted some notes on Peabody to show Southwest's lawyers, but he wasn't hopeful. They can't dictate the policyholder's choice of beneficiary. All they can do is stop payment—when it's too late."

Slowly Marie rose from the table. "It was very nice of you to bring me here, Mr. MacDonald." She hoped her voice seemed under control. "And it was very silly of me to think you and your friend could pass a miracle. I did think you, at least, as an officer, might protect her."

"Wait a minute, Marie!" MacDonald was on his feet, too.

"It's all right, Mr. MacDonald. I can get home. At least if—*when* Doreen gets back from Palm Springs, I'll be there to—"

"You?" Noble's voice was sharp and dry. "You staying there with them? After marriage?"

"Why, yes. Doreen asked me to."

"Tell," he commanded.

Hesitantly she sat down and told. The blue eyes faded and thought seemed to recede behind them. Suddenly he nodded and said to MacDonald, "Recap M.O."

"Peabody's *modus operandi?* It's stayed the same as in your case. Apparently a mild dose of sleeping pills, then when the woman's unconscious a sharp blow to the base of the skull with the edge of the hand. Defense is always a broken neck by accident while under the influence of a slight self-administered overdose: Almost impossible to disprove."

The eyes glazed again. When their light returned it was almost painfully bright. "Pattern clear," he said. "Obvious *why*. But proof . . . Now listen. Both of you."

The cute plump waitress refilled the water glass uninstructed.

DOREEN AND LUTHER had been back from Palm Springs for two days now, and the honeymoon was figuratively as well as literally over.

How could she go on living here? Marie thought. Even to save Doreen. But Mac and Nick Noble said it would be only a matter of days . . . Marie squirmed back into the corner where Mac had first found her and tried to cut herself off from the quarrel that raged.

"But it's only plain damn common horse sense, Luther!" Doreen was screaming. "We have the good luck that Marie's going around with a cop and he lets slip that they're reopening that Seattle case. Are you just going to sit around and wait for them to extradite you?"

Luther Peabody's tone was too imperturbable to be called a shout, but it matched Doreen's in volume. "The Seattle D.A. would be an idiot to re-open the case. I was acquitted—"

"You weren't! They were hung juries. They can try you again and I won't let them!"

"Very well. I wasn't acquitted. But I was released three times. They can't convict me. I'm comfortable here, thank you, and I'm staying."

"I *won't* be the wife of a man on trial for murder! We'll go some place—any place—slip away—use another name for just a little while—just to let it get cold again—"

"My dear Doreen, I am staying."

"And I know why, too! That filthy-rich tin heiress from Bolivia we met at Palm Springs! I see myself getting you out of town while she's here. You'd sooner stay and be indicted or extradited or whatever it is and have all the scandal! What about my career?"

"You won't mind, my dear, if I ask, 'What career?' "

And after that, Marie thought wryly, it began to get nasty. And the plan wasn't working. The Seattle rumor was supposed to make Luther eager to get out, put time-pressure on him. Mac was taking a week's vacation, switching schedules with some other Lieutenant, so that he could act privately. He and a detective he'd hired were taking turns watching the house. And if Marie observed the faintest sign of anything wrong, she was to make a signal . . . What was the signal? She was so sleepy . . .

The newlyweds had stormed off to separate rooms. They had even stopped shouting across the house to each other. She was so sleepy, but it was so much trouble to get to her bed . . .

Marie managed to dig her fingers into her thigh so viciously that her eyes opened. "The faintest sign of anything wrong . . ." Of course. The first thing he'd do would be to drug the watchdog. He'd brought her the cup of cocoa Doreen had fixed. She had to make the signal . . . the signal . . .

She would be black-and-blue for weeks, but she kept digging into her thigh. Doreen insisted on keeping the Venetian blinds throughout the house with their slats slanted *up*, so sunlight couldn't come through to fade the carpeting. If MacDonald saw any window with the slats slanting *down* . . .

She heard the gratifying rattle of the shifting vanes as her hand slipped loosely from the cord and her eyes closed.

"YOU WAS SUPPOSED to relieve me an hour ago," said the man from the O'Breen Agency reproachfully.

"I know," MacDonald snapped. "I'm on vacation, but that doesn't stop a Homicide Captain from calling me down to Headquarters for more details on a report I filed last month.—What's that!"

"Yeah, I was just gonna tell you, Lieutenant. That blind switched damn near an hour ago. I didn't phone because I figured you was on your way here, and you don't see me risking my license trying to break in—"

But MacDonald was already at the door. He had no more authority to break in than the operative; but he had self-confidence, a marked lack of desire to warn the murderer by ringing a bell, and a lock-gun. The operative followed hesitantly at his heels. They both stopped short at the archway from hall to living room.

With the blinds as Doreen liked them, the room would have been dark, but the moon shone down through the reversed slats of the warning-blind onto the body. It was chicly dressed, as any starlet should be, in a fur-trimmed dressing gown. Its face was painted to starlet-mannequin perfection and the moon gleamed back from a starlet's overpainted fingernails. But one item differed from starlet standards: the coiffure.

The hair was so close-cropped that the head seemed almost bald.

MacDonald had switched the lights on and was bending over the body. "She's breathing!" he yelled. "We got a break! Phone—" And in a moment he was through to Homicide, arranging for official reinforcements, an immediate ambulance, and the nearest patrol car in the meantime.

He set back the phone and looked up at a strange tableau. In the front arch stood the private operative, gun drawn, face questioning. In the other arch, leading to the bedrooms, stood Luther Peabody, staring at the unconscious girl on the floor.

"All right, lover-boy," MacDonald began, not unglad that his position was, at the moment, unofficial. "My man has you covered. You're not trying a thing—not any more. And before the regulars get here, you're going to tell me a few fascinating items—starting with *'Where's Marie?'* "

"I don't understand," Peabody faltered. "I heard all this noise . . ." His eyes never left the body.

MacDonald hesitated. The man worried him. He *did* look as if he had just awakened from a sound sleep. And what was stranger: the gaze he fixed on the body seemed (unless he were the world's leading non-professional actor) to be one of absolute incredulous surprise.

Then a moan came from the floor that sounded almost like words, almost like "Did I . . ." MacDonald knelt and bent closer, still eying Peabody. "Did I . . . did I fix the slats right, Mac?" said the preposterous starlet-lips.

"Marie!" MacDonald gasped. "Then who—" Abruptly he rose as he saw a uniformed patrol-car man looming behind the operative. "MacDonald, Homicide," he said, moving forward with his open wallet extended. "The girl's alive—ambulance on the way."

The patrol-car man said, "We spotted a dame high-tailing it away from here, took a chance on picking her up. Bring her in, Clarence!"

And 200 pounds of Clarence brought in a scratching, biting fury who was unmistakably Doreen Arlen Peabody.

"DIDN'T MEAN TO be cryptic. Honest," said Nick Noble, brushing away the fly. "Thought you saw pattern. Seattle time-pressure wouldn't pressure Peabody. Be *less* apt to act when under observation. *Would* pressure Doreen. Had to act while she still had him around."

"The hospital says Marie'll be out tomorrow. Nothing serious. Doreen was a failure even at learning judo blows out of handbooks. But if I'm going to shine as Marie's savior, I'd better at least get completely straight what the devil happened. Want to help me sort it out?"

"No sorting. Straight pattern. Clear as soon as I knew Marie was staying on with them. Then all fell into place: Only possible *why*. Failure. Insurance. Family. Judo. Hair. Above all, hair."

"OK. Let *me* try. Doreen's not talking. We're going to have to release her anyway. You can't charge attempted murder when the victim won't make a complaint; and Marie says think what it'd do to the family in Utah."

"Step-family," said Nick Noble.

"Yes, that's a key point. With all Doreen's publicity, you think of this vast Family; but Marie's her only blood relative. That made the whole scheme possible. And the most cold-blooded—But let me try to reconstruct:

"Doreen meets Peabody. She remembers a little, checks up and learns more. Maybe she thinks, 'He can't get away with it forever'—and from that comes the thought: 'If any murder happens with him around, he's *it.*' "

"*Why,*" said Nick Noble.

"Exactly. The only possible *why* for deliberately marrying a mass murderer: to have the perfect scapegoat for the murder you're about to commit. She brings her cousin out here. They used to look a lot alike; really the main differences, speech and action aside, are Doreen's elaborate starlet makeup and Marie's wavy hair. So Doreen insures herself for an enormous amount, or maybe just lets Peabody do it, if that's what *he* has in mind. But Doreen's not worrying—She'll kill Marie, using Peabody's M.O. and putting her own clothes and makeup on the body. There's still the hair. Well, Peabody has a psychopathic quirk about hair. He's clipped tresses from his victims before. This time she'll make it seem he's gone hog-wild and cut off too much . . . too much to tell if it was straight or wavy. Meanwhile she'll scrub her face, use the lightest makeup, wear Marie's clothes, and wave her hair. She'll be the little cousin from Utah. It's her background, too; she was once very like Marie even in actions—it'll be a simple role.

"So Peabody is convicted of the murder of his wife. Maybe even as the Utah cousin she's going to be an eyewitness. It doesn't matter whether he's gassed or found insane. In any case the insurance company won't pay *him.* Policy reverts to the estate, which consists solely of the Utah cousin, who now has a hundred grand in cash and never goes back. Perfect!"

"She thinks."

MacDonald nodded. "She thinks. . . . You know, Nick, unofficial head that you are of the Screwball Division, L.A.P.D., this was the ideally screwball case for you. Exact illustration of the difference between a professional and an amateur. If Peabody had killed Doreen, the motive and what you call the *pattern* would have been completely obvious; and yet he'd probably have executed the details so well that the worst he'd get would be another hung jury. Now Doreen had worked out the damnedest most unlikely pattern conceivable; but if (God forbid!) she'd brought off her murder, I swear she'd have gone straight to the gas chamber. Doreen wasn't really good at anything, from acting to murder. Somewhere along the line, pure ordinary police routine would've caught up with the identification—"

"Radiation Lab," said Nick Noble.

"Of course. Marie's prints would be on file if she'd worked on such a security job. Then the hair: Doreen was giving herself a quicky fingerwave when she heard me rampaging around and panicked. I suppose later she'd have had a pro job done—and that'd be one more witness. Fake identity plus good old *cui bono?* and she's done for. All thought out in advance . . . except what happens next."

"Rouse," Nick Noble agreed.

"Exactly. The English 'blazing car' murderer back around the time of Peabody's debut. Everything brilliantly worked out up through the murder . . . then chaos. Arrested the day after the killing and executed four months later. Doreen would've gone that way too. But thanks to you—"

"What now?" Nick Noble asked as Rosario brought fresh glasses.

"Damned if I know. Maybe your pattern machine can figure it. She says she's going back to Peabody if he'll have her. Says she kind of likes him. Well, Marie didn't! Marie hated him from the start—"

"—and didn't hate you?" It was the first time MacDonald had ever seen a broad grin on that thin white face. "A little like Martha, Mac," said Nick Noble. "A little."

MacDonald remembered Martha Noble's tragic operation. "Luckier," he said. "Thanks to you." He rose, embarrassed. "I'll bring Marie around tomorrow. Want you to see her while she's still all shaven and shorn. She's lovely—it's an experience. Well," he concluded, "it's been a hell of a murder case, hasn't it? The murder case with no murder and no arrest. Files closed with nobody in prison and nobody dead."

"That's bad?" Nick Noble observed to his invisible insect.

THE WENCH IS DEAD

Fredric Brown

There is an awful lot of lonesomeness in the work of the late Fredric Brown (1906–1972). Though today he is mostly regarded as a master of the short, tart, wry surprise-ending tale, his best work, including *The Fabulous Clipjoint, The Screaming Mimi, The Far Cry*, and *Knock One-Two-Three*, deals with loss of some kind, and how the protagonist (or antagonist, Brown not being afraid to use anti-heroes upon occasion) is crushed by it. The story here was later expanded into a decent novel of the same name, which was a response of sorts to the glamor that the media had suddenly visited upon the Beats. You have to think of early Charles Willeford or George Orwell of *Down and Out in Paris and London* to fully appreciate Brown's social portraiture. One suspects that this was the life many of the Beats really led.

ONE

A FUZZ IS a fuzz is a fuzz when you awaken from a wino jag. God, I'd drunk three pints of muscatel that I know of and maybe more, maybe lots more, because that's when I drew a blank, that's when research stopped. I rolled over on the cot so I could look out through the dirty pane of the window at the clock in the hockshop across the way.

Ten o'clock said the clock.

Get up, Howard Perry, I told myself. Get up, you B.A.S. for bastard, rise and greet the day. Hit the floor and get moving if you want to keep that job, that all-important job that keeps you drinking and sometimes eating and sometimes sleeping with Billie the Kid when she hasn't got a sucker on the hook. That's your life, you B.A.S., you bastard. That's your life for a while. This is it, this is the McCoy, this is the way a wino meets the not-so-newborn day. You're learning, man.

Pull on a sock, another sock, pants, shirt, shoes, get the hell to Burke's and wash a dish, wash a thousand dishes for six bits an hour and a meal or two a day when you want it.

God, I thought, did I really have the habit? Nuts, not in three months. Not when you've been a normal drinker all your life. Not when, much as you've always enjoyed drinking, it's always been in moderation and you've always been able to handle the stuff. This was just temporary.

And I had only a few weeks to go. In a few weeks I'd be back in Chicago, back at my desk in my father's investment company, back wearing white shirts, and B.A.S. would stand for Bachelor of Arts in Sociology. That was a laugh right now, that degree. Three months ago it had meant something—but that was in Chicago, and this was LA, and now all it meant was bastard. That's all it had meant ever since I started drifting.

It's funny, the way those things can happen. You've got a good family and a good education, and then suddenly, for no reason you can define, you start drifting. You lose interest in your family and your job, and one day you find yourself headed for the Coast.

You sit down one day and ask yourself how it happened. But you can't answer. There are a thousand little answers, sure, but there's no *big* answer. It's easier to worry about where the next bottle of sweet wine is coming from.

And that's when you realize your own personal B.A.S. stands for bastard.

With me, LA had been the end of the line. I'd seen the *Dishwasher Wanted* sign in Burke's window, and suddenly I'd known what I had to do. At pearl-diver's wages, it would take a long time to get up the bus fare back to Chicago and family and respectability, but that was beside the point. The point was that after a hundred thousand dirty dishes there'd *be* a bus ticket to Chicago.

But it had been hard to remember the ticket and forget the dishes. Wine is cheap, but they're not giving it away. Since I'd started pearl-diving I'd had grub and six bits an hour for seven hours a day. Enough to drink on and to pay for this dirty, crumby little crackerbox of a room.

So here I was, still thinking about the bus ticket, and still on my uppers on East Fifth Street, LA. Main Street used to be the tenderloin street of Los Angeles and I'd headed for it when I jumped off the freight, but I'd found that the worst district, the real skid row, was now on Fifth Street in the few blocks east of Main. The worse the district, the cheaper the living, and that's what I'd been looking for.

Sure, by Fifth Street standards, I was being a pantywaist to hold down a steady job like that, but sleeping in doorways was a little too rugged and I'd found out quickly that panhandling wasn't for me. I lacked the knack.

I dipped water from the cracked basin and rubbed it on my face, and the feel of the stubble told me I could get by one more day without shaving. Or anyway I could wait till evening so the shave would be fresh in case I'd be sleeping with Billie.

Cold water helped a little but I still felt like hell. There were empty wine bottles in the corner and I checked to make sure they were completely empty, and they were. So were my pockets, except, thank God, for tobacco and cigarette papers. I rolled myself a cigarette and lighted it.

But I needed a drink to start the day.

What does a wino do when he wakes up broke (and how often does he wake otherwise?) and needs a drink? Well, I'd found several answers to that. The easiest one, right now, would be to hit Billie for a drink if she was awake yet, and alone.

I crossed the street to the building where Billie had a room. A somewhat newer building, a hell of a lot nicer room, but then she paid a hell of a lot more for it.

I rapped on her door softly, a little code knock we had. If she wasn't awake she wouldn't hear it and if she wasn't alone she wouldn't answer it.

But she called out, "It's not locked; come on in," and she said "Hi, Professor," as I closed the door behind me. "Professor" she called me, occasionally and banteringly. It was my way of talking, I guess. I'd tried at first to use poor diction, bad grammar, to fit in with the place, but I'd given it up as too tough a job. Besides, I'd learned Fifth Street already had quite a bit of good grammar. Some of its denizens had been newspapermen once, some had written poetry; one I knew was a defrocked clergyman.

I said, "Hi, Billie the Kid."

"Just woke up, Howie. What time is it?"

"A little after ten," I told her. "Is there a drink around?"

"Jeez, only ten? Oh well, I had seven hours. Guy came here when Mike closed at two, but he didn't stay long."

She sat up in bed and stretched, the covers falling away from her naked body. Beautiful breasts she had, size and shape of half grapefruits and firm. Nice arms and shoulders, and a lovely face. Hair black and sleek in a pageboy bob that fell into place as she shook her head. Twenty-five, she told me once; and I believed her, but she could have passed for several years less than that, even, now without make-up and her eyes still a little puffy from sleep. Certainly it didn't show that she'd spent three years as a B-girl, parttime hustler, heavy drinker. Before that she'd been married to a man who'd worked for a manufacturing jeweler; he'd suddenly left for parts unknown with a considerable portion of his employer's stock, leaving Billie in a jam and with a mess of debts.

Wilhelmina Kidder, Billie the Kid, my Billie. Any man's Billie if he flashed a roll, but oddly I'd found that I could love her a little and not let that bother me. Maybe because it had been that way when I'd first met her over a month ago; I'd come to love her knowing what she was, so why should it bother me? What she saw in me I don't know, and didn't care.

"About that drink," I said.

She laughed and threw down the covers, got out of bed and walked past me naked to the closet to get a robe. I wanted to reach for her but I didn't; I'd learned by now that Billie the Kid was never amorous early in the morning and resented any passes made before noon.

She shrugged into a quilted robe and padded barefoot over to the little refrigerator behind the screen that hid a tiny kitchenette. She opened the door and said, "God damn it."

"God damn what?" I wanted to know. "Out of liquor?"

She held up over the screen a Hiram Walker bottle with only half an inch of ready-mixed Manhattan in it. Almost the only thing Billie ever drank, Manhattans.

"As near out as matters. Honey, would you run upstairs and see if Mame's got some? She usually has."

Mame is a big blonde who works behind the bar at Mike Karas' joint, The Best Chance, where Billie works as B-girl. A tough number, Mame. I said, "If she's asleep she'll murder me for waking her. What's wrong with the store?"

"She's up by now. She was off early last night. And if you get it at the store it won't be on ice. Wait, I'll phone her, though, so if she *is* asleep it'll be me that wakes her and not you."

She made the call and then nodded. "Okay, honey. She's got a full bottle she'll lend me. Scram."

I scrammed, from the second floor rear to the third floor front. Mame's door was open; she was out in the hallway paying off a milkman and waiting for him to receipt the bill. She said, "Go on in. Take a load off." I went inside the room and sat down in the chair that was built to match Mame, overstuffed. I ran my fingers around under the edge of the cushion; one of Mame's men friends might have sat there with change in his pocket. It's surprising how much change you can pick up just by trying any over-stuffed chairs or sofas you sit on. No change this time, but I came up with a fountain pen, a cheap dime-store-looking one. Mame had just closed the door and I held it up. "In the chair. Yours, Mame?"

"Nope. Keep it, Howie, I got a pen."

"Maybe one of your friends'll miss it," I said. It was too cheap a pen to sell or hock so I might as well be honest about it.

"Nope, I know who lost it. Seen it in his pocket last night. It was Jesus, and the hell with him."

"Mame, you sound sacrilegious."

She laughed. "Hay-*soos*, then. Jesus Gonzales. A Mex. But when he told me that was his handle I called him Jesus. And Jesus was *he* like a cat on a hot stove!" She walked around me over to her refrigerator but her voice kept on. "Told me not to turn on the lights when he come in and went over to watch out the front window for a while like he was watching for the heat. Looks out my side window too, one with the fire escape. Pulls down all the shades before he says okay, turn on the lights." The refrigerator door closed and she came back with a bottle.

"Was he a hot one," she said. "Just got his coat off—he threw it on that chair, when there's a knock. Grabs his coat again and goes out my side window down the fire escape." She laughed again. "Was that a flip? It was only Dixie from the next room knocking, to bum cigarettes. So if I ever see Jesus again it's no dice, guy as jumpy as that. Keep his pen. Want a drink here?"

"If you'll have one with me."

"I don't drink, Howie. Just keep stuff around for friends and callers. Tell Billie to give me another bottle like this back. I got a friend likes Manhattans, like her."

When I got back to Billie's room, she'd put on a costume instead of the robe, but it wasn't much of a costume. A skimpy Bikini bathing suit. She pirouetted in it. "Like it, Howie? Just bought it yesterday."

"Nice," I said, "but I like you better without it."

"Pour us drinks, huh? For me, just a quickie."

"Speaking of quickies," I said.

She picked up a dress and started to pull it over her head. "If you're thinking that way, Professor, I'll hide the family treasures. Say, that's a good line; I'm getting to talk like you do sometimes."

I poured us drinks and we sat down with them. She'd stepped into sandals and was dressed. I said, "You've got lots of good lines, Billie the Kid. But correct me—was that lingerie instead of a bathing suit, or am I out of date on fashions?"

"I'm going to the beach today, Howie, for a sun-soak. Won't go near the water so why not just wear the suit under and save changing? Say, why don't you take a day off and come along?"

"Broke. The one thing to be said for Burke as an employer is that he pays every day. Otherwise there'd be some dry, dry evenings."

"What you make there? A fin, maybe. I'll lend you a fin."

"That way lies madness," I said. "Drinks I'll take from you, or more important things than drinks. But taking money would make me—" I stopped and wondered just what taking money from Billie would make me, just how consistent I was being. After all, I could always send it back to her from Chicago. What kept me from taking it, then? A gal named Honor, I guess. Corny as it sounds, I said it lightly. "I could not love thee, dear, so much, loved I not Honor more."

"You're a funny guy, Howie. I don't understand you."

Suddenly I wanted to change the subject. "Billie, how come Mame doesn't drink?"

"Don't you know hypes don't like to drink?"

"Sure, but I didn't spot Mame for one."

"Hype with a big H for heroin, Howie. Doesn't show it much, though. I'll give you that."

"I haven't known enough junkies to be any judge," I said. "The only one I know for sure is the cook at Burke's."

"Don't ever try it, Howie. It's bad stuff. I joy-popped once just to see what it was like, but never again. Too easy to get to like it. And Howie, it can make things rough."

I said, "I hear your words of wisdom and shall stick to drink. Speaking of which—" I poured myself another.

TWO

I GOT TO the restaurant—it's on Main a block from Fifth—at a quarter after eleven, only fifteen minutes late. Burke was at the stove—he does his own cooking until noon, when Ramon comes on—and turned to glare at me but didn't say anything.

Still feeling good from the drinks, I dived into my dishwashing.

The good feeling was mostly gone, though, by noon, when Ramon came on. He had a fresh bandage on his forehead; I wondered if there was a new knife wound under it. He already had two knife scars, old ones, on his cheek and on his chin. He looked mean, too, and I decided to stay out of his way. Ramon's got a nasty temper when he needs a jolt, and it was pretty obvious that he needed one. He looked like a man with a kingsize monkey, and he was. I'd often wondered how he fed it. Cooks draw good money compared to other restaurant help, but even a cook doesn't get enough to support a five or six cap a day habit, not at a joint like Burke's anyway. Ramon was tall for a Mexican, but he was thin and his face looked gaunt. It's an ugly face except when he grins and his teeth flash white. But he wouldn't be grinning this afternoon, not if he needed a jolt.

Burke went front to work the register and help at the counter for the noon rush, and Ramon took over at the stove. We worked in silence until the rush was over, about two o'clock.

He came over to me then. He was sniffling and his eyes were running. He said, "Howie, you do me a favor. I'm burning, Howie, I need a fix, quick. I got to sneak out, fifteen minutes."

"Okay, I'll try to watch things. What's working?"

"Two hamburg steak dinners on. Done one side, five more minutes other side. You know what else to put on."

"Sure, and if Burke comes back I'll tell him you're in the can. But you'd better hurry."

He rushed out, not even bothering to take off his apron or chef's hat. I timed five minutes on the clock and then I took up the steaks, added the trimmings and put them on the ledge, standing at an angle back of the window so Burke couldn't see that it was I and not Ramon who was putting them there. A few minutes later the waitress put in a call for stuffed peppers, a pair; they were already cooked and I didn't have any trouble dishing them.

Ramon came back before anything else happened. He looked like a different man—he would be for as long as the fix lasted. His teeth flashed. "Million thanks, Howie." He handed me a flat pint bottle of muscatel. "For you, my friend."

"Ramon," I said, "you are a gentleman and a scholar." He went back to his stove and started scraping it. I bent down out of sight to open the bottle. I took a good long drink and then hid it back out of sight under one of the tubs.

Two-thirty, and my half-hour lunch break. Only I wasn't hungry. I took another drink of the muskie and put it back. I could have killed it but the rest of the afternoon would go better if I rationed it and made it last until near quitting time.

I wandered over to the alley entrance, rolling a cigarette. A beautiful bright day out; it would have been wonderful to be at the beach with Billie the Kid.

Only Billie the Kid wasn't at the beach; she was coming toward me from the mouth of the alley. She was still wearing the dress she'd pulled on over the bathing suit but she wasn't at the beach. She was walking toward me, looking worried, looking frightened.

I walked to meet her. She grabbed my arm, tightly. "Howie. Howie, did you kill Mame?"

"Did I—*what?*"

Her eyes were big, looking up at me. "Howie, if you did, I don't care. I'll help you, give you money to get away. But—"

"Whoa," I said, "Whoa, Billie. I didn't kill Mame. I didn't even rape her. She was okay when I left. What happened? Or are you dreaming this up?"

"She's dead, Howie, murdered. And about the time you were there. They found her a little after noon and say she'd been dead somewhere around two hours. Let's go have a drink and I'll tell you what all happened."

"All right," I said. "I've got most of my lunch time left. Only I haven't been paid yet—"

"Come on, hurry." As we walked out of the alley she took a bill from her purse and stuffed it into my pocket. We took the nearest ginmill and ordered drinks at a booth at the back where we weren't near enough anyone to be heard. The bill she'd put in my pocket was a sawbuck. When the waitress brought our drinks and the change I shoved it toward Billie. She shook her head and pushed it back. "Keep it and owe me ten, Howie. You might need it in case—well, just in case." I said, "Okay, Billie, but I'll pay this back." I would, too, but it probably wouldn't be until I mailed it to her from Chicago and it would probably surprise the hell out of her to get it.

I said, "Now tell me, but quit looking so worried. I'm as innocent as new-fallen snow—and I don't mean cocaine. Let me reconstruct my end first, and then tell yours. I got to work at eleven-twenty. Walked straight there from your place, so it would have been ten after when I left you. And—let's see, from the other end, it was ten o'clock when I woke up, wouldn't have been over ten or fifteen minutes before I knocked on your door, another few minutes before I got to Mame's and I was up there only a few minutes. Say I saw her last around twenty after ten, and she was okay then. Over."

"Huh? Over what?"

"I mean, you take it. From when I left you, about ten minutes after eleven."

"Oh. Well, I straightened the room, did a couple things, and left, it must have been a little after twelve on account of the noon whistles had blown just a few minutes ago. I was going to the beach. I was going to walk over to the terminal and catch the Santa Monica bus, go to Ocean Park. Only first I stopped in the drugstore right on the corner for a cup of coffee. I was there maybe ten-fifteen minutes letting it cool enough to drink and drinking it. While I was there I heard a cop car stop near but I didn't think anything of it; they're always picking up drunks and all.

"But while I was there too I remembered I'd forgot to bring my sun glasses and sun-tan oil, so I went back to get them.

"Minute I got inside the cops were waiting and they asked if I lived there and then started asking questions, did I know Mame and when I saw her last and all."

"Did you tell them you'd talked to her on the phone?"

"Course not, Howie. I'm not a dope. I knew by then something had happened to her and if I told them about that call and what it was about, it would have brought you in and put you on the spot. I didn't even tell them you were with me, let alone going up to Mame's. I kept you out of it.

"They're really questioning everybody, Howie. They didn't pull me in but they kept me in *my* own room questioning me till just fifteen minutes ago. See, they really worked on me because I admitted I knew Mame—I had to admit that 'cause we work at the same place and they'd have found that out.

"And of course they knew she was a hype, her arms and all; they're checking everybody's arms and thank God mine are okay. They asked me mostly about where we worked, Mike's. I think they figure Mike Karas is a dealer, what with Mame working for him."

"Is he, Billie?"

"I don't know, honey. He's in some racket, but it isn't dope."

I said, "Well, I don't see what either of us has to worry about. It's not our—My God, I just remembered something."

"What, Howie?"

"A guy saw me going in her room, a milkman. Mame was in the hall paying him off when I went up. She told me to go on in and I did, right past him."

"Jesus, Howie, did she call you by name when she told you to go on in? If they get a name, even a first name, and you living right across the street—"

I thought hard. "Pretty sure she didn't, Billie. She told me to go in and take a load off, but I'm pretty sure she didn't add a Howie to it. Anyway, they may never find the milkman was there. He isn't likely to stick his neck out by coming to them. How was she killed, Billie?"

"Somebody said a shiv, but I don't know for sure."

"Who found her and how come?"

"I don't know. They were asking me questions, not me asking them. That part'll be in the papers, though."

"All right," I said. "Let's let it go till this evening, then. How's about this evening, Billie, are you going to The Best Chance anyway?"

"I *got* to, tonight, after that. If I don't show up, they'll want to know why and where I was and everything. And listen, don't you come around either, after hours tonight or in the morning. You stay away from that building, Howie. If they find that milkman they might even have him staked out watching for you. Don't even walk *past*. You better even stay off that block, go in and out the back way to your own room. And we better not even see each other till the heat's off or till we know what the score is."

I sighed.

I was ten minutes late reporting back and Burke glared at me again but still didn't say anything. I guess I was still relatively dependable for a dish-washer, but I was learning.

I made the rest of the wine last me till Baldy, the evening shift dish-washer, showed up to relieve me. Burke paid me off for the day then, and I was rich again.

THREE

SOMEONE WAS SHAKING me, shaking me hard. I woke to fuzz and fog and Billie the Kid was peering through it at me, looking really scared, more scared than when she'd asked me yesterday if I'd killed Mame.

"Howie, wake up." I was in my own little shoe-box of a room, Billie standing by my cot bending over me. I wasn't covered, but the extent of my undressing had been to kick off my shoes.

"Howie, listen, you're in trouble, honey. You got to get out of here, back way like I come in. Hurry."

I sat up and wanted to know the time.

"Only nine, Howie. But hurry. Here. This will help you." She screwed off the top of a half pint bottle of whisky. "Drink some quick. Help you wake up."

I took a drink and the whisky burned rawly down my throat. For a moment I thought it was going to make me sick to my stomach, but then it decided to stay down and it did clear my head a little. Not much, but a little.

"What's wrong, Billie?"

"Put on your shoes. I'll tell you, but not here."

Luckily my shoes were loafers and I could step into them. I went to the basin of water, rubbed some on my face. While I washed and dried and ran a comb through my hair Billie was going through the dresser; a towel on the bed, everything I owned piled on it. It didn't make much of a bundle.

She handed it to me and then was pulling me out into the hallway, me and everything I owned. Apparently I wasn't coming back here, or Billie didn't think I was.

Out into the alley, through to Sixth Street and over Sixth to Main, south on Main. A restaurant with booths, mostly empty. The waitress came over and I ordered coffee, black. Billie ordered ham and eggs and toast and when the waitress left she leaned across the table. "I didn't want to argue with her in front of you, Howie, but that food I ordered is for you; you're going to eat it all. You got to be sober."

I groaned, but knew it would be easier to eat than to argue with a Billie the Kid as vehement as this one.

"What is it, Billie? What's up?"

"Did you read the papers last night?"

I shook my head. I hadn't read any papers up to about nine o'clock and after that I didn't remember what I'd done or hadn't. But I wouldn't have read any papers. That reminded me to look in my pockets to see what money I had left, if any. No change, but thank God there were some crumpled bills. A five and two ones, when I pulled them out and looked under cover of the table. I'd had a little over nine out of the ten Billie had given me to buy us a drink with, a little under five I'd got from Burke. That made fourteen and I'd spent seven of it somehow—and God knows how since I couldn't possibly have drunk that much muskie or even that much whisky at Fifth Street prices. But at least I hadn't been rolled, so it could have been worse.

"They got that milkman, Howie," Billie was saying. "Right off. He'd given Mame a receipt and she'd dropped it on that little table by the door so they knew he'd been there and they found him and he says he'll know you if he sees you. He described you too. You thinking straight by now, Howie?"

"Sure I'm thinking straight. What if they *do* find me? Damn it, I didn't kill her. Didn't have any reason to. They can't do any more than question me."

"Howie, haven't you ever been in trouble with cops? Not on anything serious, I guess, or you wouldn't talk like that. That milkman would put you right on the scene at close to the right time and that's all they'd want. They got nobody else to work on.

"Sure they'll question you. With fists and rubber hoses they'll question you. They'll beat the hell out of you for days on end, tie you in a chair with five hundred watts in your eyes and slap you every time you close them. Sure they'll question you. They'll question you till you wish you *had* killed Mame so you could tell 'em and get it over with and get some sleep. Howie, cops are tough, mean bastards when they're trying to pin down a murder rap. This is a murder rap, Howie."

I smiled a little without meaning to. Not because what she'd been saying was funny, but because I was thinking of the headlines if they did beat the truth out of me, or if I had to tell all to beat the rap. *Chicago Scion in Heroin Murder Case*. Chicago papers please copy.

I saw the hurt look on Billie's face and straightened mine. "Sorry," I said. "I was laughing at something else. Go on."

But the waitress was coming and Billie waited till she'd left. She shoved the ham and eggs and toast in front of me. "Eat," she said. I ate.

"And that isn't all, Howie. They'll frame you on some other charge to hold you. Howie, they might even frame you on the murder rap itself if they don't find who else did it. They could do it easy, just take a few little things from her room—it had been searched—and claim you had 'em on you or they were in your room. How'd you prove they weren't? And what'd your word be against a cop's? They could put you in the little room and gas you, Howie. And there's something else, too."

"Something worse that *that?*"

"I don't mean that. I mean what they'd do to me, Howie. And that'd be for *sure*. A perjury rap, a nice long one. See, I signed a statement after they questioned me, and that'd make it perjury for me if you tell 'em the truth about why you went up to see Mame. And what else could you tell them?"

I put down my knife and fork and stared at her. I hadn't been *really* worried about the things she'd been telling me. Innocent men, I'd been telling myself, aren't framed by the cops on murder charges. Not if they're willing to tell the truth down the line. They might give me a bad time, I thought, but they wouldn't hold me long if I leveled with them. But if Billie had signed a statement, then telling them the truth was out. Billie was on the wrong side of the law already; they *would* take advantage of perjury to put her away, maybe for several years.

I said, "I'm sorry, Billie. I didn't realize I'd have to involve you if I had to tell them the truth."

"Eat, Howie. Eat all that grub. Don't worry about me; I just mentioned it. You're in worse trouble than *I* am. But I'm glad you're talking straight; you sound really awake now. Now you go on eating and I'll tell you what you've got to do.

"First, this milkman's description. Height, weight and age fairly close but not exact on any, and anyway you can't change that. But you got to change clothes, buy new ones, because Jesus, the guy got your clothes perfect. Blue denim shirt cut off above elbows, tan work pants, brown loafers. Now first thing when you leave here, buy different clothes, see?"

"All right," I said. "How else did he describe me?"

"Well, he thought you had blond hair and it's a little darker than that, not much. Said you needed a shave—you need one worse now—and said you looked like a Fifth Street bum, a wino maybe. That's all, except he's sure he could identify you if he ever saw you again. And that's bad, Howie."

"It is," I said.

"Howie, do you want to blow town? I can lend you—well, I'm a little low right now and on account of Karas' place being watched so close I won't be able to pick up any extra money for a while, but I can lend you fifty if you want to blow town. Do you?"

"No, Billie," I said. "I don't want to blow town. Not unless you want to go with me."

God, what had made me *say that?* What had I meant by it? What business had I taking Billie away from the district she knew, the place where she could make a living—if I couldn't—putting her further in a jam for disappearing when she was more or less a witness in a murder case? And when I wanted to be back in Chicago, back working for my father and being respectable, within a few weeks anyway.

What had I meant? I couldn't take Billie back with me, much as I liked—maybe loved—her. Billie the Kid as the wife of a respectable investment man? It wouldn't work, for either of us. But if I hadn't meant that, what the hell *had* I meant?

But Billie was shaking her head. "Howie, it wouldn't work. Not for us, not right now. If you could quit drinking, straighten out. But I know—I know you can't. It isn't your fault and—oh, honey, let's not talk about that now. Anyway, I'm *glad* you don't want to lam because—well, because I *am*. But listen—"

"Yes, Billie?"

"You've got to change the way you look—just a little. Buy a different colored shirt, see? And different pants, shoes instead of loafers. Get a hair-cut—you need one anyway so get a short one. Then get a hotel room—off Fifth Street. Main is okay if you stay away from Fifth. And shave—you had a stubble when that milkman saw you. How much money you got left?"

"Seven," I said. "But that ought to do it. I don't need *new* clothes; I can swap with uncle."

"You'll need more than that. Here." It was a twenty.

"Thanks, Billie. I owe you thirty." Owe her thirty? Hell, how much did I owe Billie the Kid already, outside of money, things money can't buy? I said, "And how'll we get in touch with one another? You say I shouldn't come to your place. Will you come to mine, tonight?"

"I—I guess they won't be suspicious if I take a night off, Howie, as long as it wasn't that first night. Right after the—after what happened to Mame. All right, Howie. You know a place called The Shoebox on Main up across from the court house?"

"I know where it is."

"I'll meet you there tonight at eight. And—and stay in your room, wherever you take one, till then. And—and try to stay sober, Howie."

FOUR

IT SHOULDN'T BE hard, I thought, to stay sober when you're scared. And I was scared, now.

I stayed on Main Street, away from Fifth, and I did the things Billie had suggested. I bought a tan work shirt, and changed it right in the store where I bought it for the blue one I'd been wearing. I stopped in the barber school place for a four-bit haircut and, while I was at it, a two-bit shave. I had one idea Billie hadn't thought of; I spent a buck on a used hat. I hadn't been wearing one and a hat makes a man look different. At a shoe repair shop that handled used shoes I traded in my loafers and a dollar fifty for a pair of used shoes. I decided not to worry about the trousers; their color wasn't distinctive.

I bought newspapers; I wanted to read for myself everything Billie had told me about the murder, and there might be other details she hadn't mentioned. Some wine too, but just a pint to sip on. I was going to stay sober, but it would be a long boring day waiting for my eight o'clock date with Billie the Kid.

I registered double at a little walk-up hotel on Market Street around the corner from Main, less than a block from the place of my evening date. She'd be coming with me, of course, since we wouldn't dare go to her place, and I didn't want there to be even a chance of trouble in bringing her back with me. Not that trouble would be likely in a place like that but I didn't want even the minor trouble of having to change the registration from single to double if the clerk saw us coming in, not for fifty cents difference in the price of the room.

I sipped at the wine slowly and read the papers. The *Mirror* gave it the best coverage, with pictures. A picture of Mame that must have been found in her room and that had been taken at least ten years ago—she looked to be in her late teens or early twenties—a flashlight shot of the interior of her room, but taken after her body had been removed, and an exterior of The Best Chance, where she'd worked. But, even from the *Mirror*, I didn't learn anything Billie hadn't told me, except Mame's full name and just how and when the body had been discovered. The time had been 12:05, just about the time Billie was leaving from her room on the floor below. The owner of the building had dropped around, with tools, to fix a dripping faucet Mame (Miss Mamie Gaynor, 29) had complained about the day before. When he'd knocked long enough to decide she wasn't home he'd let himself in with his duplicate key. The milkman's story and the description he'd given of me was exactly as Billie had given them.

I paced up and down the little room, walked the worn and shabby carpet, wondering. Was there—short of the sheer accident of my running into that milkman—any danger of my being picked up just from that description? No, surely not. It was accurate as far as it went, but it was too vague, could fit too many men in this district, for anyone to think of me in connection with it. And now, with a change of clothes, a shave, wearing a hat outdoors, I doubted if the milkman would recognize me. I couldn't remember his face; why would he remember mine? And there was no tie-in otherwise, except through Billie. Nobody but Billie knew that I'd even met Mame. The only two times I'd ever seen her had been in Billie's place when she'd dropped in while I was there, once for only a few minutes, once for an hour or so. And one other time I'd been up to her room, that time to borrow cigarettes for Billie; it had been very late, after stores and bars were closed.

The fact that I'd disappeared from my room in that block? That would mean nothing. Tomorrow a week's rent was due; the landlord would come to collect it, find me and my few possessions gone, and rent it again. He'd think nothing of it. Why should he?

No, now that I'd taken the few precautions Billie had suggested, I was safe enough as long as I stayed away from her building.

Why was I hiding here now, then?

The wine was gone and I wanted more. But I knew what shape I'd be in by eight o'clock if I kept on drinking it, starting at this hour of the morning.

But I'd go nuts if I stayed here, doing nothing. I picked up the papers, read the funny sheets, a few other things. Back in the middle of one of them a headline over a short item caught my eye, I don't know for what reason. *Victim in Alley Slaying Identified.*

Maybe my eye had first caught the name down in the body of the story, Jesus Gonzales. And Mame's jittery guest of the night before her death had been named Jesus Gonzales.

I read the story. Yesterday morning at dawn the body of a man had been found in an areaway off Winston Street near San Pedro Street. He had been killed with a blunt instrument, probably a blackjack. As he had been robbed of everything he was carrying, no identification had been made at first. Now he had been identified as Jesus Gonzales, 41, of Mexico City, DF. He had arrived in Los Angeles the day before on the SS Guadalajara, out of Tokyo. His passport, which had been left in his room at the Berengia Hotel, and other papers left with it, showed that he had been in the Orient on a buying trip for a Mexico City art object importing firm in which he was a partner, and that he was stopping in Los Angeles for a brief vacation on his return trip.

Mame's Jesus Gonzales? It certainly looked that way. The place and time fitted; less than two blocks from her room. So did the time, the morning after he'd been frightened by that knock at the door and had left unceremoniously via the fire escape.

But why would he have hooked up with Mame? The Berengia is a swank hotel, only people with well-lined pockets stay there. Mame was no prize; at the Berengia he could have done better through his own bellhop.

Or could it be a factor that Mame was a junkie and, stopping in at The Best Chance, he'd recognized her as one and picked her for that reason? He could have been a hype himself, in need of a jolt and in a city where he had no contacts, or—and this seemed even more likely because of his just having landed from Tokyo—he'd smuggled some dope in with him and was looking for a dealer to sell it. The simplest and safest way to find a dealer would be through an addict.

It was just a wild guess, of course, but it wasn't too wild to be possible. And damn it, Mame's Jesus Gonzales *had* acted suspiciously and he *had* been afraid of something. Maybe he'd thought somebody was following him, following him and Mame home from The Best Chance. If he was the same Jesus Gonzales who'd just been killed and robbed only two blocks from her place, then he'd been dead right in being careful. He'd made his mistake in assuming that the knocker on Mame's door was the man who'd followed him and in going down the fire escape. Maybe his *Nemesis* had still been outside the building, probably watching from across the street, and had seen him leave. And on Winston Street *Nemesis* had caught up with him.

Nice going, B.A.S., old boy, I thought. You're doing fine. It isn't every skid-row pearl-diver who can reconstruct a crime out of nothing. Sheer genius, B.A.S., sheer genius.

But it was something to pass the time, a lot better than staring at the wall and wishing I'd never left Chicago. Better than brooding.

All right, suppose it figured so far—then how did Mame's death tie in with it? I didn't see how. I made myself pace and concentrate, trying to work out an answer.

I felt sure Mame had been telling me the truth about Gonzales as far as she knew it, or else she would have had no reason for mentioning it at all. Whatever his ulterior motive in picking her up, whether to buy dope or to find a contact for selling it, he hadn't yet leveled with Mame before that knock came. Otherwise she wouldn't have told it casually, as she had, as something amusing.

But the killer wouldn't have known that. He couldn't have known that Mame was not an accomplice. If what he was looking for hadn't been on the person of the man he'd killed he could have figured that it had already changed hands. Why hadn't he gone back to Mame's the same night? I didn't know, but there could have been a reason. Perhaps he had and she'd gone out, locking the door and the fire escape window. Or maybe by that time she had other company; if he had knocked she might have opened the door on the chain—and I remembered now that there was a chain on her door—and told him so. I couldn't ask Mame now what she'd done the rest of the night after her jittery caller had left.

But if Gonzales was a stranger in town, just off the boat, how would the killer have known he had brought in heroin?—or opium or cocaine; it could have been any drug worth smuggling. And the killer must have known *something*; if it had been just a robbery kill, for whatever money Gonzales was carrying, then he wouldn't have gone back and killed Mame, searched her room. He'd have done that only if he'd known something about Gonzales that made him think Mame was his accomplice.

I killed a few more minutes worrying about that and I had the answer. Maybe not *the* answer, but at least an answer that made sense. Maybe I was just mildly cockeyed, but this off-the-cuff figuring I'd been doing *did* seem to be getting somewhere.

It was possible, I reasoned, that Mame hadn't been the first person through whom Gonzales had tried to make a contact. He could have approached another junkie on the same deal, but one who refused to tell him her contact. Her? It didn't have to be a woman, but Mame had been a woman and that made me think he'd been working that way. Say that he'd wandered around B-joints until he spotted a B-girl as an addict; he could get her in a booth and try to get information from her. She could have stalled him or turned him down. Stalled him, most likely, making a phone call or two to see if she could get hold of a dealer for him, but tipping off her boy friend instead. Killing time enough for her boy friend to be ready outside, then telling Gonzales she couldn't make a contact for him.

And if any of that had sounded suspicious to Gonzales he would have been more careful the second try, with Mame. He'd get her to her room on the obvious pretext, make sure they were alone and hadn't been followed before he opened up. Only, between The Best Chance and Mame's room, he must have discovered that they were being followed.

Sure, it all fitted. But what good did it do me?

Sure, it was logical. It made a complete and perfect picture, but it was all guesswork, nothing to go to the cops with. Even if they believed me eventually and could verify my guesses in the long run, I'd be getting myself and Billie the Kid into plenty of trouble in the short run. And like as not enough bad publicity—my relations with Billie would surely come out, and Billie's occupation—to have my father's clients in Chicago decide I wasn't fit to handle their business.

Well, was I? Worry about the fact that you want a drink so damned bad, I told myself, that soon you're going to weaken and go down and get another bottle. Well, why not? As long as I rationed it to myself so I would be drinking just enough to hold my own and not get drunk, not until after eight o'clock anyway . . .

What time was it? It seemed like I'd been in that damned room six or eight hours, but I'd checked in at around eleven and the sun was shining straight down in the dirty areaway my window opened on. Could it be only noon? I went out to the desk and past it, looking at the kitchen-type electric clock on the wall over it as I went by. It was a quarter after twelve.

I decided to walk a while before I went back to the room with a bottle, kill some time first. God, the time I had to kill before eight o'clock. I walked around the court house and over to Spring Street. I'd be safe there.

Hell, I'd be safe anywhere, I thought. Except maybe right in that one block of Fifth Street, just on the chance the police did have the milkman staked out in or near that building. And with different clothes, wearing a hat, he probably wouldn't recognize me anyway. Billie the Kid had panicked, and had panicked me. I didn't have anything to worry about. Oh, moving out of that block, changing out of the clothes I'd been wearing, those things had been sensible. But I didn't have to quit my job at Burke's—if it was still open to me. Burke's was safe for me. Nobody at Burke's knew where I'd lived and nobody in the building I'd lived in knew where I worked.

I thought, why not go to Burke's? He'd have the sign out in the window, now that I was an hour and a half late, but if nobody had taken the job, I could give him a story why I was so late and get it back. I'd gotten pretty good at washing dishes; I was probably the best dishwasher he'd ever had and I'd been steadier than the average one. Sure, I could go back there unless he'd managed to hire a new one already.

And otherwise, what? I'd either have to look for a new job of the same kind or keep on taking money from Billie for however long I stayed here. And taking money from Billie, except in emergency, was out. That gal named Honor back in Chicago was getting to be a pretty dim memory, but I still had some self-respect.

I cut back to Main Street and headed for Burke's. The back way, so I could see if anyone was working yet in my place, and maybe ask Ramon what the score was before I saw Burke.

From the alley doorway I could see my spot was empty, dishes piling high. Ramon was busy at the stove. He turned as I walked up to him, and his teeth flashed white in that grin. He said, "Howie! Thank God you're here. No dishwasher, everybody's going nuts."

The bandage was gone from his forehead. Under where it had been were four long scratches, downward, about an inch apart.

I stared at the scratches and thought about Ramon and his monkey and Mame and *her* monkey, and all of a sudden I had a crazy hunch. I thought about how a monkey like Ramon's could make a man do anything to get a fix. I moistened my lips. Ramon's monkey might claw the hell out of his guts, but it hadn't put those four scratches on his face. Not directly.

I didn't say it, I'd have had more sense; my mouth said it. "Mame had sharp fingernails, huh?"

FIVE

D EATH CAN BE a sudden thing. Only luck or accident kept me from dying suddenly in the next second or two. I'd never seen a face change as suddenly as Ramon's did. And before I could move, his hand had hold of the front of my shirt and his other hand had reached behind him and come up with and raised a cleaver. To step back as it started down would have put me in even better position for it to hit, so I did the only thing possible; I stepped in and pushed him backward and he stumbled and fell. I'd jerked my head but the cleaver went too wild even to scrape my shoulders. And there was a thunking sound as Ramon's head hit a sharp corner of the big stove. Yes, death can be a sudden thing.

I breathed hard a second and then—well, I don't know why I cared whether he was alive or not, but I bent forward and reached inside his shirt, held my hand over where his heart should be beating. It wasn't.

From the other side of the window Burke's voice sang out, "Two burgers, with."

I got out of there fast. Nobody had seen me there, nobody was *going* to see me there. I got out of the alley without being seen, that I knew of, and back to Main Street. I walked three blocks before I stopped into a tavern for the drink I really needed *now*. Not wine, whisky. Wine's an anodyne but it dulls the mind. Whisky sharpens it, at least temporarily. I ordered whisky, a double, straight.

I took half of it in one swallow and got over the worst of it. I sipped the rest slowly, and thought.

Damn it, Howie, I told myself, you've *got* to think.

I thought, and there was only one answer. I was in over my head now. If the police got me I was sunk. B.A.S. or not, I'd have a hell of a time convincing them I hadn't committed two murders—maybe three; if they'd tied in Jesus Gonzales, they'd pin that on me, too.

Sure, *I* knew what had really happened, but what proof did I have? Mame was dead; she wouldn't tell again what she'd told me about her little episode with Jesus. Ramon was dead; he wouldn't back up my otherwise unsupported word that I'd killed him accidentally in defending myself.

Out of this while I had a whole skin, that was the only answer. Back in

Chicago, back to respectability, back to my right name—Howard Perry, B.A.S., not Howard Perry, bastard, wino, suspected soon of being a psychopathic killer. Back to Chicago, and not by freight. Too easy to get arrested that way, vagged, and maybe by that time flyers would be out with my description. Too risky.

So was waiting till eight o'clock when it was only one o'clock now. I'd have to risk getting in touch with Billie the Kid sooner. I couldn't go to her place, but I could phone. Surely they wouldn't have all the phones in that building tapped.

Just the same I was careful when I got her number. "Billie," I said, "this is the Professor." That nickname wouldn't mean anything to anybody else.

I heard her draw in her breath sharply. She must have realized I wouldn't risk calling her unless something important had come up. But she made her voice calm when she answered, "Yes, Professor?"

"Something has come up," I said. "I'm afraid I won't be able to make our eight o'clock date. Is there any chance that you can meet me now instead—same place?"

"Sure, soon as I can get there."

Click of the receiver. She'd be there. Billie the Kid, my Billie. She'd be there, and she'd make sure first that no one was following her. She'd bring money, knowing that I'd decided I had to lam after all. Money that she'd get back, damn it, if it was the last thing I ever did. Whatever money she'd lend me now, plus the other two sums and enough over to cover every drink and every cigarette I'd bummed from her. But not for the love and the trust she'd given me; you can't pay for that in money. In my case, I couldn't ever pay for it, period. The nearest I could come would be by being honest with her, leveling down the line. That much she had coming. More than that she had coming but more than that I couldn't give her.

The Shoebox is a shoebox-sized place. Not good for talking, but that didn't matter because we weren't going to talk there.

She got there fifteen minutes after I did; I was on my second drink. I ordered a Manhattan when I saw her coming in the door.

"Hello, Billie," I said.

Hello, Billie. Goodbye, Billie. This is the end for us, today. It's got to be the end. I knew she'd understand when I told her, when I told her everything.

"Howie, are you in—"

"In funds?" I cut her off. "Sure, just ordered you a drink." I dropped my voice, but not far enough to make it conspicuous. "Not here, Billie. Let's drink our drink and then I've got a room around the corner. I registered double so it'll be safe for us to go there and talk a while."

The bartender had mixed her Manhattan and was pouring it. I ordered a refill on my whisky-high. Why not? It was going to be my last drink for a long while. The wagon from here on in, even after I got back to Chicago for at least a few weeks, until I was sure the stuff couldn't get me, until I was sure I could do normal occasional social drinking without letting it start me off.

We drank our drinks and went out. Out into the sun, the warm sunny afternoon. Just before we got to the corner, Billie stopped me. "Just a minute, Howie."

She ducked into a store, a liquor store, before I could stop her. I waited. She came out with a wrapped bottle and a cardboard carton. "The ready-mixed wasn't on ice, Howie, but it's all right. I bought some ice cubes too. Are there two glasses in the room?"

I nodded; we went on. There were two glasses in the room. The wagon not yet. But it wouldn't have been right not to have a last drink or two, a stirrup cup or two, with Billie the Kid.

She took charge of the two tumblers, the drinks. Poured the drinks over ice cubes, stirred them around a while and then fished the ice cubes out when the drinks were chilled.

While I talked. While I told her about Chicago, about me in Chicago, about my family and the investment company. She handed me my drink then. She said quietly, "Go on, Howie."

I went on. I told her what Mame had told me about her guest Jesus the night before she was killed. I told her of the death of Jesus Gonzales as I'd read it in the *Mirror*. I added the two up for her.

She made us another drink while I told her about Ramon, about what had happened, about how I'd just killed him.

"Ramon," she said. "He has knife scars, Howie?" I nodded. She said, "Knife scars, a hype, a chef. I didn't know his name, but I know who his woman was, a red-headed junkie named Bess, I think it's Bess, in a place just down the block from Karas' joint. It's what happened, Howie, just like you guessed it. It must have been." She sipped her drink. "Yes, Howie, you'd better go back to Chicago, right away. It could be bad trouble for you if you don't. I brought money. Sixty. It's all I have except a little to last me till I can get more. Here."

A little roll of bills, she tucked into my shirt pocket.

"Billie," I said. "I wish—"

"Don't say it, honey. I know you can't. Take me with you, I mean. I wouldn't fit, not with the people you know there. And I'd be bad for you."

"I'd be bad for you, Billie. I'd be a square, a wet blanket. I'll have to be to get back in that rut, to hold down—" I didn't want to think about it. I said, "Billie, I'm going to send you what I owe you. Can I count on your being at the same address for another week or so?"

She sighed. "I guess so, Howie. But I'll give you my sister's name and address, what I use for a permanent address, in case you ever—in case you might not be able to send the money right away."

"I'll write it down," I said. I tore a corner off the paper the bottle had been wrapped in, looked around for something to write with; I remembered the fountain pen I'd stuck in my trousers pocket at Mame's. It was still there.

I screwed off the cap. Something glittered, falling to the carpet, a lot of somethings. Shiny little somethings that looked like diamonds. Billie gasped. Then she was scrabbling on the floor, picking them up. I stared at the pen, the hollow pen without even a point, in my hand. Hollow and empty now. But there was still something in the cap, which I'd been holding so it hadn't spilled. I emptied the cap out into my hand. Bigger diamonds, six of them, big and deep and beautifully cut.

My guess had been wrong. It hadn't been heroin Gonzales had been smuggling. Diamonds. And when he'd found himself followed to Mame's, he'd stashed them there for safety. The pen hadn't fallen from his coat pocket; he'd hidden it there deliberately.

They were in two piles on the table, Billie's hands trembling a little as she handled them one at a time. "Matched," she said reverently. "My husband taught me stones, Howie. Those six big ones—over five carats each, cut for depth, not shallow, and they're blue-white and I'll bet they're flawless, all of them, because they're matched. And the fifteen smaller ones—they're matched too, and they're almost three carats apiece. You know what Karas would give us for them, Howie?"

"Karas?"

"Fifteen grand, Howie, at least. Maybe more. These aren't ordinary; they're something special. Sure, Karas—I didn't tell you everything, because it didn't matter then, when I said I thought maybe he had some racket—not dope. He handles stones, only stones. Gonzales might have heard of him, might have been trying to contact him through Mame."

I thought about fifteen thousand dollars, and I thought about going back to Chicago. Billie said, "Mexico, Howie. In Mexico we can live like kings—like a king and queen—for five years for that much."

And stop drinking, straighten out? Billie said, "Howie, shall I take these to Karas right now so we can leave quick?" She was flushed, breathing hard, staring at me pleadingly.

"Yes," I said. She kissed me, hard, and gathered them up.

At the doorway, hand on the knob. "Howie, were you kidding when you said you were in love with a girl named Honor in Chicago? I mean, is there a real girl named that, or did you just mean—?"

"I was kidding, Billie the Kid."

The door closed.

Her heels clicked down the wooden hall. I poured myself a drink, a long one, and didn't bother to chill it with ice cubes. Yes, I'd known a girl named Honor in Chicago, once, but— . . . *but that was in another country, and besides, the wench is dead.*

I drank my drink and waited.

Twenty minutes later, I heard Billie's returning footsteps in the hall.

CIGARETTE GIRL

James M. Cain

James M. Cain (1892–1977) wrote two indisputable masterpieces, *The Postman Always Rings Twice* and *Double Indemnity*. Some would add his novel *Mildred Pierce* to the list as well. He was always controversial because he wrote openly about sex, but what his critics never seemed to understand is that it was sex that became love of many different kinds. Nobody in the crime genre ever came to close to writing about man-woman relationships the way Cain did. And not even Cain could duplicate his own success in the second part of his career. While he wrote a variety of other novels, none matched his early ones. But then that doesn't really matter, does it? As the man who wrote both *Postman* and *Indemnity*, he was already immortal.

I'D NEVER SO much as laid eyes on her before going in this place, the *Here's How*, a night-club on Route 1, a few miles north of Washington, on business that was 99 percent silly, but that I had to keep myself. It was around 8 at night, with hardly anyone there, and I'd just taken a table, ordered a drink, and started to unwrap a cigar, when a whiff of perfume hit me, and she swept by with cigarettes. As to what she looked like, I had only a rear view, but the taffeta skirt, crepe blouse, and silver earrings were quiet, and the chassis was choice, call it fancy, a little smaller than medium. So far, a cigarette girl, nothing to rate any cheers, but not bad either, for a guy unattached who'd like an excuse to linger.

But then she made a pitch, or what I took for a pitch. Her middle-aged customer was trying to tell her some joke, and taking so long about it the proprietor got in the act. He was a big, blond guy, with kind of a decent face, but he went and whispered to her as though to hustle her up, for some reason apparently. I couldn't quite figure it out. She didn't much seem to like it, until her eye caught mine. She gave a little pout, a little shrug, a little wink, and then just stood there, smiling.

Now I know this pitch and it's nice, because of course I smiled back, and with that I was on the hook. A smile is nature's freeway: it has lanes, and you can go any speed you like, except you can't go back. Not that I wanted to, as I suddenly changed my mind about the cigar I had in my hand, stuck it back in my pocket, and wigwagged for cigarettes. She nodded, and when she came over said: "You stop laughing at me."

"Who's laughing? Looking."

"Oh, of course. That's different."

I picked out a pack, put down my buck, and got the surprise of my life: she gave me change. As she started to leave, I said "You forgot something, maybe?"

"That's not necessary."

"For all this I get, I should pay."

"All what, sir, for instance?"

"I told you: the beauty that fills my eye."

"The best things in life are free."

"On that basis, fair lady, some of them, here, are tops. Would you care to sit down?"

"Can't."

"Why not?"

"Not allowed. We got rules."

With that she went out toward the rear somewhere, and I noticed the proprietor again, just a short distance away, and realized he'd been edging in. I called him over and said: "What's the big idea? I was talking to her."

"Mister, she's paid to work."

"Yeah, she mentioned about rules, but now they got other things too. Four Freedoms, all kinds of stuff. Didn't anyone ever tell you?"

"I heard of it, yes."

"You're Mr. *Here's How?*"

"Jack Conner, to my friends."

I took a V from my wallet, folded it, creased it, pushed it toward him. I said: "Jack, little note of introduction I generally carry around. I'd like you to ease these rules. She's cute, and I crave to buy her a drink."

He didn't see any money, and stood for a minute thinking. Then: "Mister, you're off on the wrong foot. In the first place, she's not a cigarette girl. Tonight, yes, when the other girl is off. But not regular, no. In the second place, she's not any chiselly-wink, that orders rye, drinks tea, takes the four bits you slip her, the four I charge for the drink—and is open to propositions. She's class. She's used to class—out West, with people that have it, and that brought her East when they came. In the third place she's a friend, and before I eased any rules I'd have to know more about you, a whole lot more, than this note tells me.

"Pleased to meet you and all that, but as to who you are, Mr. Cameron, and what you are, I still don't know—"

"I'm a musician."

"Yeah? What instrument?"

"Any of them. Guitar, mainly."

Which brings me to what I was doing there. I do play the guitar, play it all day long, for the help I get from it, as it gives me certain chords, the big ones that people go for, and heads me off from some others, the fancy ones on the piano, that other musicians go for. I'm an arranger, based in Baltimore, and had driven down on a little tune detecting. The guy who takes most of my work, Art Lomak, the band leader, writes a few tunes himself, and had gone clean off his rocker about one he said had been stolen, or thefted as they call it. It was one he'd been playing a little, to try it and work out faults, with lyric and title to come, soon as the idea hit him. And then he rang me, with screams. It had already gone on the air, as 20 people had told him, from this same little honky-tonk, as part of a 10 o'clock spot on the Washington FM pick-up. He begged me to be here tonight, when the trio started their broadcast, pick up such dope as I could, and tomorrow give him the low-down.

That much was right on the beam, stuff that goes on every day, a routine I knew by heart. But his tune had angles, all of them slightly peculiar. One was, it had already been written, though it was never a hit and was almost forgotten, in the days when states were hot, under the title *Nevada*. Another was, it had been written even before that, by a gent named Giuseppe Verdi, as part of the *Sicilian Vespers*, under the title *O Tu Palermo*. Still another was, Art was really burned, and seemed to have no idea where the thing had come from. They just can't get it, those big schmalzburgers like him, that what leaks out of their head might, just once, have leaked in. But the twist, the reason I had to come, and couldn't just play it for laughs, was: Art could have been right. Maybe the lilt *was* from him, not from the original opera, or from the first theft, *Nevada*. It's a natural for a 3/4 beat, and that's how Art had been playing it. So if that's how they were doing it here, instead of with *Nevada*'s 4/4, which followed the Verdi signature, there might still be plenty of work for the lawyers Art had put on it, with screams, same like to me.

Silly, almost.

Spooky.

But maybe, just possibly, right.

So Jack, this boss character, by now had smelled something fishy, and suddenly took a powder, to the stand where the fiddlers were parked, as of course the boys weren't there yet, and came back with a Spanish guitar. I took it, thanked him, and tuned. To kind of work it around, in the direction of Art's little problem, and at the same time make like there was nothing at all to conceal, I said I'd come on account of his band, to catch it during the broadcast, as I'd heard it was pretty good. He didn't react, which left me nowhere, but I thought it well to get going.

I played him *Night and Day*, no Segovia job, but plenty good, for free. On "Day and Night," where it really opens up, I knew things to do, and talk suddenly stopped among the scattering of people that were in there. When I finished there was some little clapping, but still he didn't react, and I gave thought to mayhem. But then a buzzer sounded, and he took another powder, out toward the rear this time, where she had disappeared. I began a little beguine, but he was back. He bowed, picked up his B, bowed again, said: "Mr. Cameron, the guitar did it. She heard you, and you're in."

"Will you set me up for two?"

"Hold on, there's a catch."

He said until midnight, when one of his men would take over, she was checking his orders. "That means she handles the money, and if she's not there, I could just as well close down. You're invited back with her, but she can't come out with you."

"Oh. Fine."

"Sir, you asked for it."

It wasn't quite the way I'd have picked to do it, but the main thing was the girl, and I followed him through the OUT door, the one his waiters were using, still with my Spanish guitar. But then, all of a sudden, I loved it, and felt even nearer to her.

This was the works of the joint, with a little office at one side, service bar on the other, range rear and center, the crew in white all around, getting the late stuff ready. But high on a stool, off by herself, on a little railed-in platform where waiters would have to pass, she was waving at me, treating it all as a joke. She called down: "Isn't this a balcony scene for you? You have to play me some music!"

I rattled into it quickly, and when I told her it was *Romeo and Juliet*, she said it was just what she'd wanted. By then Jack had a stool he put next to hers, so I could sit beside her, back of her little desk. He introduced us, and it turned out her name was Stark. I climbed up and there we were, out in the middle of the air, and yet in a way private, as the crew played it funny, to the extent they played it at all, but mostly were too busy even to look. I put the guitar on the desk and kept on with the music. By the time I'd done some *Showboat* she was calling me Bill and to me she was Lydia.

I remarked on her eyes, which were green, and showed up bright against her creamy skin and ashy blonde hair. She remarked on mine, which are light, watery blue, and I wished I was something besides tall, thin, and red-haired. But it was kind of cute when she gave a little pinch and nipped one of my freckles, on my hand back of the thumb.

Then Jack was back, with champagne iced in a bucket, which I hadn't ordered. When I remembered my drink, the one I *had* ordered, he said Scotch was no good, and this would be on him. I thanked him, but after he'd opened and poured, and I'd leaned the guitar in a corner and raised my glass to her, I said: "What's made him so friendly?"

"Oh, Jack's always friendly."

"Not to me. Oh, no."

"He may have thought I had it coming. Some little thing to cheer me. My last night in the place."

"You going away?"

"M'm-h'm."

"When?"

"Tonight."

"That's why you're off at 12?"

"Jack tell you that?"

"He told me quite a lot."

"Plane leaves at 1. Bag's gone already. It's at the airport, all checked and ready to be weighed."

She clinked her glass to mine, took a little sip, and drew a deep, trembly breath. As for me, I felt downright sick, just why I couldn't say, as it had all to be strictly allegro, with nobody taking it serious. It stuck in my throat a little when I said: "Well—happy landings. Is it permitted to ask which way that plane is taking you?"

"Home."

"And where's that?"

"It's—not important."

"The West, I know that much."

"What else did Jack tell you?"

I took it, improvised, and made up a little stuff, about her high-toned friends, her being a society brat, spoiled as usual, and the heavy dough she was used to—a light rib, as I thought. But it hadn't gone very far when I saw it was missing bad. When I cut it off, she took it. She said: "Some of that's true, in a way. I was—fortunate, we'll call it. But—you still have no idea, have you, Bill, what I really am?"

"I've been playing by ear."

"I wonder if you want to know?"

"If you don't want to, I'd rather you didn't say."

None of it was turning out quite as I wanted, and I guess maybe I showed it. She studied me a little and asked: "The silver I wear, that didn't tell you anything? Or my giving you change for your dollar? It didn't mean anything to you, that a girl would run a straight game?"

"She's not human."

"It means she's a gambler."

And then: "Bill, does that shock you?"

"No, not at all."

"I'm not ashamed of it. Our home, it's legal. You know where that is now?"

"Oh! *Oh!*"

"Why oh? And *oh*?"

"Nothing. It's—Nevada, isn't it?"

"Something wrong with Nevada?"

"No! I just woke up, that's all."

I guess that's what I said, but whatever it was, she could hardly miss the upbeat in my voice. Because, of course, that wrapped it all up pretty, not only the tune, which the band would naturally play for her, but her too, and who she was. Society dame, to tell the truth, hadn't pleased me much, and maybe that was one reason my rib was slightly off key. But gambler I could go for, a little cold, a little dangerous, a little brave. When she was sure I had really bought it, we were close again, and after a nip on the freckle her fingers slid over my hand. She said play her *Smoke*—the smoke she had in her eyes. But I didn't, and we just sat there some little time.

And then, a little bit at a time, she began to spill it: "Bill, it was just plain cock-eyed. I worked in a club, the Paddock, in Reno, a regular institution. Tony Rocco—Rock—owned it, and was the squarest bookie ever—why he was a Senator, and civic, and everything. And I worked for him, running his wires, practically being his manager, with a beautiful salary, a bonus at Christmas, and everything. And then wham, it struck. This federal thing. This 10 percent tax on gross. And we were out of business. It just didn't make sense. Everything else was exempted. Wheels and boards and slots, whatever you could think of, but us. Us and the numbers racket, in Harlem and Florida and Washington."

"Take it easy."

"That's right, Bill. Thanks."

"Have some wine?"

". . . Rock, of course, was fixed. He had property, and for the building, where the Paddock was, he got $250,000—or so I heard. But then came the tip on Maryland."

That crossed me up, and instead of switching her off, I asked her what she meant. She said: "That Maryland would legalize wheels."

"What do you smoke in Nevada?"

"Oh, I didn't believe it. And Rock didn't. But Mrs. Rock went nuts about it. Oh well, she had a reason."

"Dark, handsome reason?"

"I don't want to talk about it, but that reason took the Rocks for a ride, for every cent they got for the place, and tried to take me too, for other things beside money. When they went off to Italy, they thought they had it fixed, he was to keep me at my salary, in case Maryland *would* legalize, and if not, to send me home, with severance pay, as it's called. And instead of that—"

"I'm listening."

"I've said too much."

"What's this guy to you?"

"Nothing! I never even saw him until the three of us stepped off the plane—with our hopes. In a way it seemed reasonable. Maryland has tracks, and they help with the taxes. Why not wheels?"

"And *who* is this guy?"

"I'd be ashamed to say, but I'll say this much: I won't be a kept floozy. I don't care who he thinks he is, or—"

She bit her lip, started to cry, and really shut up then. To switch off, I asked why she was working for Jack, and she said: "Why not? You can't go home in a barrel. But he's been swell to me."

Saying people were swell seemed to be what she liked, and she calmed down, letting her hand stay when I pressed it in both of mine. Then we were really close, and I meditated if we were close enough that I'd be warranted in laying it on the line, she should let that plane fly away, and not go to Nevada at all. But while I was working on that, business was picking up, with waiters stopping by to let her look at their trays, and I hadn't much chance to say it, whatever I wanted to say. Then, through the IN door, a waiter came through with a tray that had a wine bottle on it. A guy followed him in, a little noisy guy, who said the bottle was full and grabbed it off the tray. He had hardly gone out again, when Jack was in the door, watching him as he staggered back to the table. The waiter swore the bottle was empty, but all Jack did was nod.

Then Jack came over to her, took another little peep through the window in the OUT door, which was just under her balcony, and said: "Lydia, what did you make of him?"

"Why—he's drunk, that's all."

"You notice him, Mr. Cameron?"

"No—except it crossed my mind he wasn't as tight as the act he was putting on."

"Just what crossed *my* mind! How could he get that drunk on a split of Napa red? What did he want back here?"

By now, the waiter had gone out on the floor and came back, saying the guy wanted his check. But as he started to shuffle it out of the bunch he had tucked in his vest, Jack stopped him and said: "He don't get any check—not till I give the word. Tell Joe I said stand by and see he don't get out. *Move!*"

The waiter had looked kind of blank, but hustled out as told, and then Jack looked at her. He said: "Lady, I'll be back. I'm taking a look around."

He went, and she drew another of her long, trembly breaths. I cut my eye around, but no one had noticed a thing, and yet it seemed kind of funny they'd all be slicing bread, wiping glass, or fixing cocktail setups, with Jack mumbling it low out of the side of his mouth. I had a creepy feeling of things going on, and my mind took it a little, fitting it together, what she had said about the bag checked at the airport, the guy trying to make her, and most of all, the way Jack had acted, the second she showed with her cigarettes, shooing her off the floor, getting her out of sight. She kept staring through the window, at the drunk where he sat with his bottle, and seemed to ease when a captain I took to be Joe planted himself pretty solid in a spot that would block off a runout.

Then Jack was back, marching around, snapping his fingers, giving orders for the night. But as he pressed the back door, I noticed his hand touched the lock, as though putting the catch on. He started back to the floor, but stopped as he passed her desk, and shot it quick in a whisper: "He's out there, Lydia, parked in back. This drunk, like I thought, is a finger he sent in to stop you, but he won't be getting out for the airport, right now."

"Will you call me a cab, Jack?"

"Cab? I'm taking you."

He stepped near me and whispered: "Mr. Cameron, I'm sorry, this little lady has to leave, for—"

"I know about that."

"She's in danger—"

"I've also caught on to that."

"From a no-good imitation goon that's been trying to get to her here, which is why I'm shipping her out. I hate to break this up, but if you'll ride with us, Mr. Cameron—"

"I'll follow you down."

"That's right, you have your car. It's Friendship Airport just down the road."

He told her to get ready, while he was having his car brought up, and the boy who would take her place on the desk was changing his clothes. Step on it, he said, but wait until he came back. He went out on the floor and marched past the drunk without even turning his head. But she sat watching me. She said: "You're not coming, are you?"

"Friendship's a little cold."

"But not mine, Bill, no."

She got off her stool, stood near me and touched my hair. She said: "Ships that pass in the night pass so close, so close." And then: "I'm ashamed, Bill. I'd have to go for this reason. I wonder, for the first time gambling's really much good." She pulled the chain of the light, so we were half in the dark. Then she kissed me. She said: "God bless and keep you, Bill."

"And you, Lydia."

I felt her tears on my cheek, and then she pulled away and stepped to the little office, where she began putting a coat on and tying a scarf on her head. She looked so pretty it came to me I still hadn't given her the one little bouquet I'd been saving for the last. I picked up the guitar and started *Nevada*.

She wheeled, but what stared at me were eyes as hard as glass. I was so startled I stopped, but she kept right on staring. Outside a car door slammed, and she listened at the window beside her. Then at last she looked away, to peep through the Venetian blind. Jack popped in, wearing his coat and hat, and motioned her to hurry. But he caught something and said, low yet so I could hear him: "Lydia! What's the matter?"

She stalked over to me, with him following along, pointed her finger, and then didn't say it, but spat it: "He's the finger—that's what's the matter, that's all. He played *Nevada*, as though we hadn't had enough trouble with it already. And Vanny heard it. He hopped out of his car and he's under the window right now."

"Then OK, let's go."

I was a little too burned to make with the explanations, and took my time, parking the guitar, sliding off, and climbing down, to give them a chance to blow. But she still had something to say, and to me, not to him.

She pushed her face up to mine, and mocking how I had spoken, yipped. "Oh! . . . *Oh!* OH!" Then she went, with Jack. Then I went, clumping after.

Then it broke wide open.

The drunk, who was supposed to sit there, conveniently boxed in, while she went slipping out, turned out more of a hog-calling type, and instead of playing his part, jumped up and yelled: "Vanny! *Vanny!* Here she comes! She's leaving! VANNY!"

He kept it up, while women screamed all over, then pulled a gun from his pocket, and let go at the ceiling, so it sounded like the field artillery. Jack jumped for him and hit the deck, as his feet shot from under him on the slippery wood of the dance floor. Joe swung, missed, swung again, and landed, so Mr. Drunk went down. But when Joe scrambled for the gun, there came this voice through the smoke: "Hold it! As you were—and leave that gun alone."

Then hulking in came this short-necked, thick-shouldered thing, in Homburg hat, double-breasted coat, and white muffler, one hand in his pocket, the other giving an imitation of a movie gangster. He said keep still and nobody would get hurt, but "I won't stand for tricks." He helped Jack up, asked how he'd been. Jack said: "Young man, let me tell you something—"

"How you been? I asked."

"Fine, Mr. Rocco."

"Any telling, Jack—I'll do it."

Then, to her: "Lydia, how've *you* been?"

"That doesn't concern you."

Then she burst out about what he had done to his mother, the gyp he'd handed his father, and his propositions to her, and I got it, at last, who this idiot was. He listened, but right in the middle of it, he waved his hand toward me and asked: "Who's this guy?"

"Vanny, I think you know."

"Guy, are you the boy friend?"

"If so I don't tell you."

I sounded tough, but my stomach didn't feel that way. They had it some more, and he connected me with the tune, and seemed to enjoy it a lot, that it had told him where to find her, on the broadcast and here now tonight. But he kept creeping closer, to where we were all lined up, with the drunk stretched on the floor, the gun under his hand, and I suddenly felt the prickle, that Vanny was really nuts, and in a minute meant to kill her. It also crossed my mind, that a guy who plays the guitar has a left hand made of steel, from squeezing down on the strings, and is a dead sure judge of distance, to the last eighth of an inch.

I grabbed for my chord and got it.

I choked down on his hand, the one he held in his pocket, while hell broke loose in the place, with women screaming, men running, and fists trying to help. I had the gun hand all right, but when I reached for the other he twisted, butted, and bit, and for that long I thought he'd get loose, and that I was a gone pigeon. The gun barked, and a piledriver hit my leg. I went down. Another gun spoke and he went down beside me. Then there was Jack, the drunk's gun in his hand, stepping in close, and firing again.

I blacked out.

I came to, and then she was there, a knife in her hand, ripping the cloth away from the outside of my leg, grabbing napkins, stanching blood, while somewhere ten miles off I could hear Jack's voice, as he yelled into a phone. On the floor right beside me was something under a tablecloth.

That went on for some time, with Joe calming things down and some people sliding out. The band came in, and I heard a boy ask for his guitar. Somebody brought it to him, and then, at last, came the screech of sirens, and she whispered some thanks to God.

Then, while the cops were catching up, with me, with Jack, and what was under the cloth, we both went kind of haywire, me laughing, she crying, and both in each other's arms. I said: "Lydia, Lydia, you're not taking that plane. They legalize things in Maryland, one thing specially, except that instead of wheels, they generally use a ring."

A MATTER OF PRINCIPAL

Max Allan Collins

Rare is the writer who makes an entire subgenre his own. But that's just what Max Allan Collins has done with his Nate Heller historical private eye novels. From Bugsy Siegel to Amelia Earhart, from Al Capone to the Lindbergh infant, Collins has brought brilliant entertainment to the worldwide reading public, making him a major writer of his generation. A *New York Times* best-selling author, he has also written the *Dick Tracy* comic strip, produced at least four other series, become a legend in the world of comic book writing, and even managed to head up a very busy rock-and-roll band while keeping up his mystery career. He has also, if that is not enough, written screenplays for Hollywood and written and produced three films of his own, most notably *Mommy* and *Mommy 2: Mommy's Day*, both of which were praised highly by esteemed critic Leonard Maltin. Both are available on home video.

IT HAD BEEN a long time since I'd had any trouble sleeping. Probably Vietnam, and that was gunfire that kept me awake. I've never been an insomniac. You might think killing people for a living would give you restless nights. Truth is, those that go into that business simply aren't the kind who are bothered by it much.

I was no exception. I hadn't gone into retirement because my conscience was bothering me. I retired because the man I got my contracts through got killed—well, actually I killed him, but that's another story—and I had enough money put away to live comfortably without working, so I did.

The A-frame cottage on Paradise Lake was secluded enough for privacy, but close enough to nearby Lake Geneva to put me in contact with human beings, if I was so inclined, which I rarely was, with the exception of getting laid now and then. I'm human.

There was also a restaurant nearby, called Wilma's Welcome Inn, a rambling two-story affair that included a gas station, modest hotel accommodations and a convenience store. I'd been toying with the idea of buying the place, which had been slipping since the death of Wilma; I'd been getting a little bored lately and needed something to do. Before I started putting people to sleep, I worked in a garage as a mechanic, so the gas station angle appealed to me.

Anyway, boredom had started to itch at me, and for the past few nights I'd had trouble sleeping. I sat up all night watching satellite TV and reading paperback westerns; then I'd drag around the next day, maybe drifting to sleep in the afternoon just long enough to fuck up my sleep cycle again that night.

It was getting irritating.

At about three-thirty in the morning on the fourth night of this shit, I decided eating might do the trick. Fill my gut with junk food and the blood could rush down from my head and warm my belly and I'd get the fuck sleepy, finally. I hadn't tried this before because I'd been getting a trifle paunchy, since I quit working, and since winter kicked in.

In the summer I'd swim in the lake every day and get exercise and keep the spare tire off. But in the winter I'd just let my beard go and belt-size, too. Winters made me fat and lazy and, now, fucking sleepless.

The cupboard was bare so I threw on my thermal jacket and headed over to the Welcome Inn. At this time of night the convenience store was the only thing open, that and one self-serve gas pump.

The clerk was a heavy-set brunette named Cindy from nearby Twin Lakes. She was maybe twenty years old and a little surly, but she worked all night, so who could blame her.

"Mr. Ryan," she said, flatly, as I came in, the bell over the door jingling.

"Cindy," I said, with a nod, and began prowling the place, three narrow aisles parallel to the front of the building. None of the snacks appealed to me—chips and crackers and Twinkies and other preservative-packed delights—and the frozen food case ran mostly to ice-cream sandwiches and popsicles. In this weather, that was a joke.

I was giving a box of Chef Boyardee lasagna an intent once-over, like it was a car I was considering buying, when the bell over the door jingled again. I glanced up and saw a heavy-set man—heavy-set enough to make Cindy look svelte—with a pockmarked face and black-rimmed glasses that fogged up as he stepped in.

He wore an expensive topcoat—tan, a camel's hair number you could make payments on for a year and still owe—and his shoes had a bright black city shine, barely flecked with ice and snow. His name was Harry Something, and he was from Chicago. I knew him, in another life.

I turned my back. If he saw me, I'd have to kill him, and I was bored, but not that bored.

Predictably, Harry Something went straight for the potato chips; he also rustled around the area where cookies were shelved. I risked a glimpse and saw him, not two minutes after he entered, with his arms full of junk food, heading for the front counter.

"Excuse me, miss," Harry Something said, depositing his groceries before Cindy. His voice was nasal and high-pitched; a funny, childish voice for a man his size. "Could you direct me to the sanitary napkins?"

"You mean Kotex?"

"Whatever."

"The toiletries is just over there."

Now this was curious, and I'll tell you why. I had met Harry Something around ten years before, when I was doing a job for the Outfit boys. I was never a mob guy, mind you, strictly a freelancer, but their money was as good as anybody's. What that job was isn't important, but Harry and his partner Louis were the locals who had fucked up, making my outsider's presence necessary. Harry and Louis had not been friendly toward me. They had threatened me, in fact. They had beaten the hell out of me in my hotel room, when the job was over, for making them look bad.

I had never taken any sort of revenge out on them. I occasionally do take revenge, but at my convenience, and when a score strikes me as worth settling. Harry and Louis had really just pushed me around a little, bloodied my nose, tried to earn back a little self-respect. So I didn't hold a grudge. Not a major grudge. Fuck it.

As to why Harry Something purchasing Kotex in the middle of the night at some backwoods convenience store was curious, well, Harry and Louis were gay. They were queens of crime. Mob muscle who worked as a pair, and played as a pair.

I don't mean to be critical. To each his own. I'd rather cut my dick off than insert it in any orifice of a repulsive fat slob like Harry Something. But that's just me.

And me, I'm naturally curious. I'm not nosy, not even inquisitive. But when a faggot buys Kotex, I have to wonder why.

"Excuse me," Harry Something said, brushing by me.

He hadn't seen my face—he might not recognize me, in any case. Ten years and a beard and twenty pounds later, I wasn't as easy to peg as Harry was, who had changed goddamn little.

Harry, having stocked up on cookies and chips and Kotex, was now buying milk and packaged macaroni and cheese and provisions in general. He was shopping. Stocking up.

And now I knew what he was up to.

I nodded to surly Cindy, who bid me goodbye by flickering her eyelids in casual contempt, and went out to my car, a blue sporty Mazda I'd purchased recently. I wished I'd had the four-wheel drive, or anything less conspicuous, but I didn't. I sat in the car, scooched down low; I did not turn on the engine. I just sat in the cold car in the cold night and waited.

Harry Something came out with two armloads of groceries—Kotex included, I presumed—and he put them in the front seat of a brown rental Ford. Louis was not waiting for him. Harry was alone.

Which further confirmed my suspicions.

I waited for him to pull out onto the road, waited for him to take the road's curve, then started up my Mazda and glided out after him. He had turned left, toward Twin Lakes and Lake Geneva. That made sense, only I figured he wouldn't wind up either place. I figured he'd be out in the boonies somewhere.

I knew what Harry was up to. I knew he wasn't exactly here to ski. That lardass couldn't stand up on a pair of skis. And he wasn't here to go ice-fishing, either. A city boy like Harry Something had no business in a touristy area like this, in the off-season—unless Harry was hiding out, holing up somewhere.

This would be the perfect area for that.

Only Harry didn't use Kotex.

He turned off on a side road, into a heavily wooded area that wound back toward Paradise Lake. Good. That was very good.

I went on by. I drove a mile, turned into a farmhouse gravel drive and headed back without lights. I slowed as I reached the mouth of the side road, and could see Harry's tail lights wink off.

I knew the cabin at the end of that road. There was only one, and its owner only used it during the summer; Harry was either a renter, or a squatter.

I glided on by and went back home. I left the Mazda next to the deck and walked up the steps and into my A-frame. The nine millimeter was in the nightstand drawer. The gun hadn't been shot in months—Christ, maybe over a year. But I cleaned and oiled it regularly. It would do fine.

So would my black turtle-neck, black jeans, black leather bomber jacket, and this black moonless night. I slipped a .38 revolver in the bomber jacket right side pocket, and clipped a hunting knife to my belt.

The knife was razor sharp with a sword point; I sent for it out of the back of one of those dumb-ass ninja magazines—which are worthless except for mail-ordering weapons.

I walked along the edge of the lake, my running shoes crunching the brittle ground, layered as it was with snow and ice and leaves. The only light came from a gentle scattering of stars, a handful of diamonds flung on black velvet; the frozen lake was a dark presence that you could sense but not really see. The surrounding trees were even darker. The occasional cabin or cottage or house I passed was empty. I was one of only a handful of residents on Paradise Lake who lived year-round.

But the lights were on in one cabin. Not many lights, but lights. And its chimney was trailing smoke.

The cabin was small, a traditional log cabin like Abe Lincoln and syrup, only with a satellite dish. Probably two bedrooms, a living room, kitchenette and a can or two. Only one car—the brown rental Ford.

My footsteps were lighter now; I was staying on the balls of my feet and the crunching under them was faint. I approached with caution and gun in hand and peeked in a window on the right front side.

Harry Something was sitting on the couch, eating barbecue potato chips, giving himself an orange-mustache in the process. His feet were up on a coffee table. More food and a sawed-off double-barrel shotgun were on the couch next to him. He wore a colorful Hawaiian shirt; he looked like Don Ho puked on him, actually.

Hovering nervously nearby, was Louis, a small, skinny, bald ferret of a man, who wore jeans and a black shirt and a white tie. I couldn't tell whether he was trying for trendy or gangster, and frankly didn't give a shit, either way.

Physically, all the two men had in common was pockmarks and a desire for the other's ugly body.

And neither one of them seemed to need a sanitary napkin, though a towelette would've come in handy for Harry Something. Jesus.

I huddled beneath the window, wondering what I was doing here. Boredom. Curiosity. I shrugged. Time to look in another window or two.

Because they clearly had a captive. That's what they were doing in the boonies. That's why they were stocking up on supplies at a convenience store in the middle of night and nowhere. That's why they were in the market for Kotex. That's what I'd instinctively, immediately known back at the Welcome Inn.

And in a back window, I saw her. She was naked on a bed in the rustic room, naked but for white panties. She was sitting on the edge of the bed and she was crying, a black-haired, creamy-fleshed beauty in her early twenties.

Obviously, Harry and Louis had nothing sexual in mind for this girl; the reason for her nudity was to help prevent her fleeing. The bed was heavy with blankets, and she'd obviously been keeping under the covers, but right now she was sitting and crying. That time of the month.

I stood in the dark in my dark clothes with a gun in my hand and my back to the log cabin and smiled. When I'd come out into the night, armed like this, it wasn't to effect a rescue. Whatever else they were, Harry and Louis were dangerous men. If I was going to spend my sleepless night satisfying my curiosity and assuaging my boredom by poking into their business, I had to be ready to pay for my thrills.

But the thing was, I recognized this young woman. Like Harry, I spent a lot of hours during cold nights like this with my eyes frozen to a TV screen. And that's where I'd seen her: on the tube.

Not an actress, no—an heiress. The daughter of a Chicago media magnate whose name you'd recognize, a guy who inherited money and wheeled-and-dealed his way into more, including one of the satellite superstations I'd been wasting my eyes on lately. The Windy City's answer to Ted Turner, right down to boating and womanizing.

His daughter was a little wild, frequently seen in the company of rock stars (she had a tattoo of a star—not Mick Jagger, a five-pointed *star* star—on her white left breast, which I could see from the window) and was a Betty Ford clinic drop-out. Nonetheless, she was said to be the apple of her daddy's eye, even if that apple was a tad wormy.

So Harry and Louis had put the snatch on the snatch; fair enough. Question was, was it their own idea, or something the Outfit put them up to?

I sat in the cold and dark and decided, finally, that it just didn't matter who or what was behind it. My options were to go home, and forget about it, and try (probably without any luck) to get some sleep; or to rescue this somewhat soiled damsel in distress.

What the hell. I had nothing better to do.

I went to the front door and knocked.

No answer.

Shit, I knew somebody was home, so I knocked again.

Louis cracked open the door and peered out and said, "What is it?" and I shot him in the eye.

There was the harsh, shrill sound of a scream—not Louis, who hadn't had time for that, but the girl in the next room, scared shitless at hearing a gunshot, one would suppose.

I paid no attention to her and pushed the door open—there was no night latch or anything—and stepped over Louis, and pointed the nine millimeter at Harry, whose orange-ringed mouth was frozen open and whose bag of barbecue potato chips dropped to the floor, much as Louis had.

"Don't, Harry," I said.

I could see in Harry's tiny dark eyes behind his thick black-rimmed glasses that he was thinking about the sawed-off shotgun on the couch next to him.

"Who the fuck . . ."

I walked slowly across the rustic living room toward the couch; in the background, an old colorized movie was playing on their captive's daddy's super-station. I plucked the shotgun off the couch with my left hand and tucked it under my arm.

"Hi, Harry," I said. "Been a while."

His orange-ringed mouth slowly began to work and his eyes began to blink and he said, "Quarry?"

That was the name he'd known me by.

"Taking the girl your idea, or are you still working for the boys?"

"We . . . we retired, couple years ago. God. You killed Louis. Louis. You killed Louis . . ."

"Right. What were you going to put the girl's body in?"

"Huh?"

"She's obviously seen you. You were obviously going to kill her, once you got the money. So. What was the plan?"

Harry wiped off his orange barbecue ring. "Got a roll of plastic in the closet. Gonna roll her up in it and dump her in one of the gravel pits around here."

"I see. Do that number with the plastic right now, for Louis, why don't you? Okay?"

Tears were rolling down Harry's stubbly pockmarked cheeks. I didn't know whether he was crying for Louis or himself or the pair of them, and I wasn't interested enough to ask.

"Okay," he said thickly.

I watched him roll his partner up in the sheet of plastic, using duct tape to secure the package; he sobbed as he did it, but he did it. He got blood on his Hawaiian shirt; it didn't particularly show, though.

"Now I want you to clean up the mess. Go on. You'll find what you need in the kitchen."

Dutifully, Harry shuffled over, got a pan of warm water and some rags, and got on his knees and cleaned up the brains and blood. He wasn't crying anymore. He moved slow but steady, a fat zombie in a colorful shirt.

"Stick the rags in the end of Louis' plastic home, would you? Thank you."

Harry did that, then the big man lumbered to his feet, hands in the air, and said, "Now me, huh?"

"I might let you go, Harry. I got nothing against you."

"Not . . . not how I remember it."

I laughed. "You girls leaned on me once. You think I'd kill a person over something that trivial? What kind of guy do you think I am, Harry?"

Harry had sense enough not to answer.

"Come with me," I said, and with the nine millimeter's nose to Harry's temple, I walked him to the door of the bedroom.

"Open it," I said.

He did.

We went in, Harry first.

The girl was under the covers, holding the blankets and sheets up around her in a combination of illogical modesty and legitimate fear.

Her expression melted into one of confusion mingled with the beginnings of hope and relief, when she saw me.

"I've already taken care of the skinny one," I said. "Now Harry and me are going for a walk. You stay here. I'm going to get you back to your father."

Her confusion didn't leave, but she began to smile, wide, like a kid Christmas morning seeing her gifts. Her gift to me was dropping the blankets and sheets to her waist.

"Remember," I said. "Stay right there."

I walked Harry out, pulling the bedroom door shut behind me.

"Where are her clothes?"

He nodded to a closet. Same one he'd gotten the plastic out of.

"Good," I said. "Now let's go for a walk. Just you and me and Louis."

"Loo . . . Louis?"

"Better give Louis a hand, Harry."

Harry held the plastic-wrapped corpse in his arms like a B-movie monster carrying a starlet. The plastic was spattered with blood, but on the inside. Harry looked like he was going to cry again.

I still had the sawed-off shotgun under my arm, so it was awkward, getting the front door open, but I managed.

"Out on the lake," I said.

Harry looked at me, his eyes behind the glasses wary, glancing from me to his plastic-wrapped burden and back again.

"We're going to bury Louis at sea," I said.

"Huh?"

"Just walk, Harry. Okay? Just walk."

He walked. I followed behind, nine millimeter in one hand, sawed-off in the other. Harry in his Hawaiian shirt was an oddly comic sight, but I was too busy to be amused. Our feet crunched slightly on the ice. No danger of falling in. Frozen solid. Kids ice-skated out here. But not right now.

We walked a long way. We said not a word, until I halted him about mid-way. The black starry sky was our only witness.

"Put him down, Harry," I said. The nine millimeter was in my waistband; the shotgun was pointed right at him.

He set his cargo gently down. He stood looking gloomily down at the plastic shroud, like a bear contemplating its own foot caught in a trap.

I blasted both barrels of the shotgun; they blew the quiet night apart and echoed across the frozen lake and rattled the world.

Harry looked at me, stunned.

"What the fuck . . . ?"

"Now unroll Louis and toss him in," I said, standing near the gaping hole in the ice. "I'm afraid that plastic might float."

Horrified, the big man did as he was told. Louis slipped down the hole in the ice and into watery nothingness like a turd down the crapper.

"Slick," I said, admiringly.

"Oh Jesus," he said.

"Now you," I said.

"What?"

I had the nine millimeter out again.

"Jump in," I said. "Water's fine."

"Fuck you!"

I went over quickly and pushed the big son of a bitch in. He was flailing, splashing icy water up on me, as I put six bullets in his head, which came apart in pieces, like a rotten melon.

And then he was gone.

Nothing left but the hole in the ice, the water within it making some frothy reddish waves that would die down soon enough.

I gathered the weapons and the plastic and, folding the plastic sheet as I walked, went back to the cabin.

This was reckless, I knew. I shouldn't be killing people who lived on the same goddamn lake I did. But it was winter, and the bodies wouldn't turn up for a long time, if ever, and the Outfit had used this part of the world to dump its corpses since Capone was just a mean street kid. Very little chance any of this would come back at me.

Nonetheless, I had taken a risk or two. I ought to get something out of it, other than killing a sleepless night.

I got the girl's clothes and went in and gave them to her. A heavy-metal t-shirt and designer jeans and Reeboks.

"Did you kill those men?" she said, breathlessly, her eyes dark and glittering. She had her clothes in her lap.

"That's not important. Get dressed."

"You're wonderful. You're goddamn fucking wonderful."

"I know," I said. "Everybody says the same thing. Get dressed."

She got dressed. I watched her. She was a beautiful piece of ass, no question. The way she was looking at me made it clear she was grateful.

"What can I do for you?" she said, hands on her hips.

"Nothing," I said. "You're on the rag."

That made her laugh. "Other ports in a storm."

"Maybe later," I said, and smiled. She looked like AIDS-bait to me. I could be reckless, but not that reckless.

I put her in my car. I hadn't decided yet whether or not to dump the brown rental Ford. Probably would. I could worry about that later. Right now, I needed to get her to a motel.

She slept in the car. I envied her, and nudged her awake when we reached the motel just inside the Illinois state line.

I'd already checked in. I ushered her in to the shabby little room, its floor space all but taken up by two twin beds, and she sat on the bed and yawned.

"What now?" she said. "You want your reward?"

"Actually, yes," I said, sitting next to her. "What's your father's number?"

"Hey, there's time for that later . . ."

"First things first," I said, and she wrote the number out on the pad by the phone.

I heard the ring, and a male voice said, "Hello?"

I gave her the receiver. "Make sure it's your father, and tell him you're all right."

"Daddy?" she said. She smiled, then she made a face. "I'm fine, I'm fine . . . the man you sent . . . what?"

She covered the receiver, eyes confused again. "He says he didn't send anybody."

I took the phone. "Good evening, sir. I have your daughter. As you can hear, she's just fine. Get together one hundred thousand dollars in unmarked, nonsequential tens, twenties and fifties, and wait for the next call."

I hung up.

She looked at me with wide eyes and wide-open mouth.

"I'm not going to kill you," I said. "I'm just turning a buck."

"You bastard!"

I put the duct tape over her mouth, taped her wrists behind her and taped her ankles too, and went over and curled up on the other bed, nine millimeter in my waistband.

And slept like a baby.

THE WEEKENDER

Jeffery Deaver

Jeffery Deaver has had a rapid and much-deserved rise to the top of the best-seller lists. While his early novels were perhaps less ambitious than those he writes today, they have always been riveting reads, especially those he wrote about Rune, a female police detective living and working in New York City. Seen through her eyes, the urban landscape is a wondrous—and sometimes frightening—place indeed. *Manhattan Is My Beat* is especially good. These days, he writes such bestsellers as *Praying for Sleep; The Bone Collector*, which was the basis for the successful movie of the same name; and *A Maiden's Grave*. His readership expands with each new novel and with each new short story he writes.

THE NIGHT WENT bad fast.

I looked in the rearview mirror and didn't see any lights but I knew they were after us and it was only a matter of time till I'd see the cops.

Toth started to talk but I told him to shut up and got the Buick up to eighty. The road was empty, nothing but pine trees for miles around.

"Oh, brother," Toth muttered. I felt his eyes on me but I didn't even want to look at him, I was so mad.

They were never easy, drugstores.

Because, just watch sometime, when cops make their rounds they cruise drugstores more often than anyplace else. Because of the prescription drugs.

You'd think they'd stake out convenience stores. But those're a joke and with the closed-circuit TV you're going to get your picture took, you just are. So nobody who knows the business, I mean really *knows* it, hits them. And banks, forget banks. Even ATMs. I mean, how much can you clear? Three, four hundred tops? And around here the Fast Cash button gives you twenty bucks. Which tells you something. So why even bother?

No. We wanted cash and that meant a drugstore, even though they can be tricky. Ardmore Drugs. Which is a big store in a little town. Liggett

Falls. Sixty miles from Albany and a hundred or so from where Toth and me lived, further west into the mountains. Liggett Falls's a poor place. You'd think it wouldn't make sense to hit a store there. But that's exactly why—because like everywhere else people there need medicine and hair spray and makeup, only they don't have credit cards. Except maybe a Sears or Penney's. So they pay cash.

"Oh, brother," Toth whispered again. "Look."

And he made me even madder, him saying that. I wanted to shout look at what, you son of a bitch? But then I could see what he was talking about and I didn't say anything. Up ahead. It was like just before dawn, light on the horizon. Only this was red and the light wasn't steady. It was like it was pulsing and I knew that they'd got the roadblock up already. This was the only road to the interstate from Liggett Falls. So I should've guessed.

"I got an idea," Toth said. Which I didn't want to hear but I also wasn't going to go through another shootout. Sure not at a roadblock, where they was ready for us.

"What?" I snapped.

"There's a town over there. See those lights? I know a road'll take us there."

Toth's a big guy and he looks calm. Only he isn't really. He gets shook easy and he now kept turning around, skittish, looking in the back seat. I wanted to slap him and tell him to chill.

"Where's it?" I asked. "This town?"

"About four, five miles. The turnoff, it ain't marked. But I know it."

This was that lousy upstate area where everything's green. But dirty green, you know. And all the buildings're gray. These gross little shacks, pickups on blocks. Little towns without even a 7-Eleven. And full of hills they called mountains but weren't.

Toth cranked down the window and let the cold air in and looked up at the sky. "They can find us with those, you know, satellite things."

"What're you talking about?"

"You know, they can see you from miles up. I saw it in a movie."

"You think the state cops do that? Are you nuts?"

This guy, I don't know why I work with him. And after what happened at the drugstore, I won't again.

He pointed out where to turn and I did. He said the town was at the base of The Lookout. Well, I remembered passing that on the way to Liggett Falls this afternoon. It was this huge rock a couple hundred feet high. Which if you looked at it right looked like a man's head, like a profile, squinting. It'd been some kind of big deal to the Indians around here.

Blah, blah, blah. He told me but I didn't pay no attention. It was spooky, that weird face, and I looked once and kept on driving. I didn't like it. I'm not really superstitious but sometimes I am.

"Winchester," he said now, meaning what the name of the town was. Five, six thousand people. We could find an empty house, stash the car in a garage and just wait out the search. Wait till tomorrow afternoon—Sunday—when all the weekenders were driving back to Boston and New York and we'd be lost in the crowd.

I could see The Lookout up ahead, not really a shape, mostly this blackness where the stars weren't. And then the guy on the floor in the back started to moan all of a sudden and just about give me a heart attack.

"You. Shut up back there." I slapped the seat and the guy in the back went quiet.

What a night.

We'd got to the drugstore fifteen minutes before it closed. Like you ought to do. 'Cause mosta the customers're gone and a lot of the clerks've left and people're tired and when you push a Glock or Smitty into their faces they'll do just about anything you ask.

Except tonight.

We had our masks down and walked in slow, Toth getting the manager out of his little office; a fat guy started crying and that made me mad, a grown man doing that. He kept a gun on the customers and the clerks and I was telling the cashier, this kid, to open the tills and, Jesus, he had an attitude. Like he'd seen all of those Steven Seagal movies or something. A little kiss on the cheek with the Smitty and he changed his mind and started moving. Cussing me out but he was moving. I was counting the bucks as we were going along from one till to the next and sure enough we were up to about three thousand when I heard this noise and turned around and what it was, Toth was knocking over a rack of chips. I mean, Jesus. He's getting Doritos!

I look away from the kid for just a second and what's he do? He pitches this bottle. Only not at me. Out the window. Bang, it breaks. There's no alarm I can hear but half of them are silent anyway and I'm really pissed. I could've killed him. Right there. Only I didn't. Toth did.

He shoots the kid, *blam, blam, blam.* And everybody else is scattering and he turns around and shoots another one of the clerks and a customer, just *bang*, not thinking or nothing. Just for no reason. Hit this girl clerk in the leg but this guy, this customer, well, he was dead. You could see. And I'm going, *What're you doing, what're you doing?* And he's going, *Shut up, shut up, shut up.* . . . And we're like we're swearing at each other when we figured out we hadta get outa there.

So we left. Only what happens is, there's a cop outside. That's why the kid threw the bottle. And he's outa his car. So we grab another customer, this guy by the door, and we use him like a shield and get outside. And there's the cop, he's holding his gun up, looking at the customer we've got, and the cop, he's saying, *It's okay, it's okay, just take it easy.*

And I couldn't believe it, Toth shot him too. I don't know whether he killed him but there was blood so he wasn't wearing a vest, it didn't look like, and I could've killed Toth there on the spot. Because why'd he do that? He didn't have to.

We threw the guy, the customer, into the back seat and tied him up with tape. I kicked out the taillights and burned rubber outa there. We made it out of Liggett Falls.

That was all just a half hour ago but it seems like weeks.

And now we were driving down this highway through a million pine trees. Heading right for The Lookout.

WINCHESTER WAS DARK.
I don't get why weekenders come to places like this. I mean, my old man took me hunting a long time ago. A couple times and I liked it. But coming to places like this just to look at leaves and buy furniture they call antiques but's really just busted-up crap . . . I don't know.

We found a house a block off Main Street with a bunch of newspapers in front and I pulled into the drive and put the Buick behind it just in time. Two state police cars went shooting by. They'd been behind us not more than a half mile, without the lightbars going. Only they hadn't seen us 'causa the broke taillights and they went by in a flash and were gone, going into town.

Toth got into the house and he wasn't very clean about it, breaking a window in the back. It was a vacation place, pretty empty and the refrigerator shut off and the phone too which was a good sign—there wasn't anybody coming back soon. Also, it smelled pretty musty and had stacks of old books and magazines from the summer.

We brought the guy inside and Toth started to take the hood off this guy's head and I said, "What the hell're you doing?"

"He hasn't said anything. Maybe he can't breathe."

This was a man talking who'd just laid a cap on three people back there and he was worried about this guy *breathing?* Man. I just laughed. Disgusted, I mean. "Like maybe we don't want him to see us?" I said, "You think of that?" See, we weren't wearing our ski masks anymore.

It's scary when you have to remind people of stuff like that. I was thinking Toth knew better. But you never know.

I went to the window and saw another squad car go past. They were going slower now. They do that. After like the first shock, after the rush, they get smart and start cruising slow, really looking for what's funny— what's *different,* you know? That's why I didn't take the papers up from the front yard. Which would've been different than how the yard looked that morning. Cops really do that Columbo stuff. I could write a book about cops.

"Why'd you do it?"

It was the guy we took.

"Why?" he whispered again.

The customer. He had a low voice and it sounded pretty calm, I mean considering. I'll tell you, the first time I was in a shootout I was totally freaked for a day afterwards. And *I* had a gun.

I looked him over. He was wearing a plaid shirt and jeans. But he wasn't a local. I could tell because of the shoes. They were rich-boy shoes, the kind you see all the yuppies wear in TV shows about Connecticut. I couldn't see his face because of the mask but I pretty much remembered it. He wasn't young. Maybe in his forties. Kind of wrinkled skin. And he was skinny too. Skinnier'n me and I'm one of those people can eat what I want and I don't get fat. I don't know why. It just works that way.

"Quiet," I said. There was another car going by.

He laughed. Soft. Like he was saying, What? So they can't hear me all the way outside?

Kind of laughing *at* me, you know? I didn't like that at all. And, sure, I guess you *couldn't* hear anything out there but I didn't like him giving me any crap so I said, "Just shut up. I don't want to hear your voice."

He did for a minute and just sat back in the chair where Toth put him. But then he said again, "Why'd you shoot them? You didn't have to."

"Quiet!"

"Just tell me why."

I took out my knife and snapped that sucker open then threw it down so it stuck in a tabletop. Sort of a *thunk* sound. "You hear that? That was a eight-inch Buck knife. Carbon-tempered. With a locking blade. It'd cut clean through a metal bolt. So you be quiet. Or I'll use it on you."

And he gave this laugh again. Maybe. Or it was just a snort of air. But

I was thinking it was a laugh. I wanted to ask him what he meant by that but I didn't.

"You got any money on you?" Toth asked and pulled the wallet out of the guy's back pocket. "Lookit," Toth said and pulled out what must've been five or six hundred. Man.

Another squad car went past, moving slow. It had a spotlight and the cop turned it on the driveway but he just kept going. I heard a siren across town. And another one too. It was a weird feeling, knowing those people were out there looking for us.

I took the wallet from Toth and looked through it.

Randall C. Weller, Jr. He lived in Boston. A weekender. Just like I thought. He had a bunch of business cards that said he was vice-president of this big computer company. One that was in the news, trying to take over IBM or something. All of a sudden I had this thought. We could hold him for ransom. I mean, why not? Make a half million. Maybe more.

"My wife and kids'll be sick, worrying," Weller said. It spooked me, hearing that. First, cause you don't expect somebody with a hood over his head to say anything. But mostly 'cause there I was, looking right at a picture in his wallet. And what was it of? His wife and kids.

"I ain't letting you go. Now, just shut up. I may need you."

"Like a hostage, you mean? That's only in the movies. They'll shoot you when you walk out and they'll shoot me too if they have to. That's the way they do it. Just give yourself up. At least you'll save your life."

"Shut up!" I shouted.

"Let me go and I'll tell them you treated me fine. That the shooting was a mistake. It wasn't your fault."

I leaned forward and pushed the knife against his throat, not the blade 'cause that's real sharp but the blunt edge and I told him to be quiet.

Another car went past, no light this time but it was going slower and all of a sudden I got to thinking what if they do a door-to-door search?

"Why did he do it? Why'd he kill them?"

And funny, the way he said *he* made me feel a little better 'cause it was like he didn't blame me for it. I mean, it *was* Toth's fault. Not mine.

Weller kept going. "I don't get it. That man by the counter? The tall one. He was just standing there. He didn't do anything. He just shot him down."

But neither of us said nothing. Probably Toth, because he didn't know why he'd shot them. And me, because I didn't owe this guy any answers. I had him in my hand. Completely, and I had to let him know that. I didn't have to talk to him.

But the guy, Weller, he didn't say anything else. And I got this weird sense. Like this pressure building up. You know, because nobody was answering his damn, stupid question. I felt this urge to say something. Anything. And that was the last thing I wanted to do. So I said, "I'm gonna move the car into the garage." And I went outside to do it.

I was a little spooked after the shootout. And I went through the garage pretty good. Just to make sure. But there wasn't nothing inside except tools and an old Snapper lawn mower. So I drove the Buick inside and closed the door. And went back into the house.

And then I couldn't believe what happened. I mean, Jesus . . .

When I walked into the living room the first thing I heard was Toth saying, "No, way, man. I'm not snitching on Jack Prescot."

I just stood there. And you should've seen the look on his face. He knew he'd blown it big.

Now this Weller guy knew my name.

I didn't say anything. I didn't have to. Toth started talking real fast and nervous. "He said he'd pay me some big bucks to let him go." Trying to turn it around, make it Weller's fault. "I mean, I wasn't going to. I wasn't even thinking 'bout it, man. I told him forget it."

"I figured that," I said. "So? What's that got to do with tellin' him my name?"

"I don't know, man. He confused me. I wasn't thinking."

I'll say he wasn't. He hadn't been thinking all night.

I sighed to let him know I wasn't happy but I just clapped him on the shoulder. "Okay," I said. "S'been a long night. These things happen."

"I'm sorry, man. Really."

"Yeah. Maybe you better go spend the night in the garage or something. Or upstairs. I don't want to see you around for a while."

"Sure."

And the funny thing was, it was that Weller gave this little snicker or something. Like he knew what was coming. How'd he know that? I wondered.

Toth went to pick up a couple magazines and the knapsack with his gun in it and extra rounds.

Normally, killing somebody with a knife is a hard thing to do. I say "normally" even though I've only done it one other time. But I remember it and it was messy and hard work. But tonight, I don't know, I was all filled up with this . . . feeling from the drugstore. Mad. I mean, really. Crazy too a little. And as soon as Toth turned his back I went to work and it wasn't three minutes later it was over. I drug his body behind the couch and then—why not—I pulled Weller's hood off. He already knew my name. He might as well see my face.

He was a dead man. We both knew it.

———

"YOU WERE THINKING of holding me for ransom, right?"

I stood at the window and looked out. Another cop car went past and there were more flashing lights bouncing off the low clouds and off the face of The Lookout, right over our heads.

Weller had a thin face and short hair, cut real neat. He looked like every ass-kissing businessman I'd ever met. His eyes were dark and calm and it made me even madder he wasn't shook up looking at that big blood-stain on the rug and floor.

"No," I told him.

He looked at the pile of all the stuff I'd taken from his wallet and kept going like I hadn't said anything. "It won't work. A kidnapping. I don't have a lot of money and if you saw my business card and're thinking I'm an executive at the company they have about five hundred vice-presidents. They won't pay diddly for me. And you see those kids in the picture? It was taken twelve years ago. They're both in college now."

"Where," I asked, sneering. "Harvard?"

"One's at Harvard," he said, like he was snapping at me. "And one's at Northwestern. So the house's mortgaged to the hilt. Besides, kidnapping somebody by yourself? No, you couldn't bring that off."

He saw the way I looked at him and he said, "I don't mean you personally. I mean somebody by himself. You'd need partners."

And I figured he was right. The ransom thing was looking, I don't know, tricky.

That silence again. Nobody saying nothing and it was like the room was filling up with cold water. I walked to the window and the floors creaked under my feet and that only made things worse. I remember one time my dad said that a house had a voice of its own and some houses were laughing houses and some were forlorn. Well, this was a forlorn house. Yeah, it was modern and clean and the *National Geographics* were all in order but it was still forlorn.

Just when I felt like shouting because of the tension, Weller said, "I don't want you to kill me."

"Who said I was going to kill you?"

He gave me his funny little smile. "I've been a salesman for twenty-five

years. I've sold pets and Cadillacs and typesetters and lately I've been selling mainframe computers. I know when I'm being handed a line. You're
going to kill me. It was the first thing you thought of when you heard
him—" Nodding toward Toth. "—say your name."

I just laughed at him. "Well, that's a damn handy thing to be, sorta a
walking lie detector," I said and I was being sarcastic.

But he just said, "Damn handy," like he was agreeing with me.

"I don't want to kill you."

"Oh, I know you don't *want* to. You didn't want your friend to kill
anybody back there at the drugstore either. I could see that. But people *got*
killed and that ups the stakes. Right?"

And those eyes of his, they just dug into me, and I couldn't say anything.

"But," he said, "I'm going to talk you out of it."

He sounded real certain and that made me feel better. 'Cause I'd ruther
kill a cocky son-of-a-bitch than a pathetic one. And so I laughed. "Talk me
out of it?"

"I'm going to try."

"Yeah? How you gonna do that?"

Weller cleared his throat a little. "First, let's get everything on the
table. I've seen your face and I know your name. Jack Prescot. Right?
You're what, about five-nine, a hundred fifty pounds, black hair. So you've
got to assume I can identify you. I'm not going to play any games and say
I didn't see you clearly or hear who you were. Or anything like that. We all
squared away on that, Jack?"

I nodded, rolling my eyes like this was all a load of crap. But I gotta admit I was kinda curious what he had to say.

"My promise," he said, "is that I won't turn you in. Not under any circumstances. The police'll never learn your name from me. Or your description. I'll never testify against you." Sounding honest as a priest. Real
slick delivery. Well, he *was* a salesman and I wasn't going to buy it. But he
didn't know I was on to him. Let him give me his pitch, let him think I was
going along. When it came down to it, after we'd got away and were
somewhere in the woods upstate, I'd want him relaxed. Thinking he was
going to get away. No screaming, no hassles. Just two fast cuts and that'd
be it.

"You understand what I'm saying?"

I tried to look serious and said, "Sure. You're thinking you can talk me
out of killing you. Which I'm not inclined to do anyway. Kill you I mean."

And there was that weird little smile again.

I said, "You think you can talk me out of it. You've got reasons?"

"Oh, I've got reasons, you bet. One in particular. One that you can't argue with."

"Yeah? What's that?"

"I'll get to it in a minute. Let me tell you some of the practical reasons you should let me go. First, you think you've got to kill me because I know who you are, right? Well, how long you think your identity's going to be a secret? Your buddy shot a cop back there. I don't know police stuff except what I see in the movies. But they're going to be looking at tire tracks and witnesses who saw plates and makes of cars and gas stations you might've stopped at on the way here."

He was just blowing smoke. The Buick was stolen. I mean, I'm not stupid.

But he went on, looking at me real coy, "Even if your car was stolen they're going to check down every lead. Every shoe print around where you or your friend found it, talk to everybody in the area around the time it vanished."

I kept smiling like it was nuts what he was saying. But this was true, shooting the cop part. You do that and you're in big trouble. Trouble that sticks with you. They don't stop looking till they find you.

"And when they identify your buddy—" He nodded toward the couch where Toth's body was lying. "They're going to make some connection to you."

"I don't know him that good. We just hung around together the past few months."

Weller jumped on this. "Where? A bar? A restaurant? Anybody ever see you in public?"

I got mad and I shouted, "So? What're you saying? They gonna bust me anyway, then I'll just take you out with me. How's *that* for an argument?"

Calm as could be he said, "I'm simply telling you that one of the reasons you want to kill me doesn't make sense. And think about this—the shooting at the drugstore? It wasn't premeditated. It was, what do they call it? Heat of passion. But you kill me, that'll be first degree. You'll get the death penalty when they find you."

When they find you. Right. I laughed to myself. Oh, what he said made sense but the fact is killing isn't a making-sense kind of thing. Hell, it *never* makes sense but sometimes you just have to do it. But I was kind of having fun now. I wanted to argue back. "Yeah, well, I killed Toth. That wasn't heat of passion. I'm going to get the needle anyway for that."

"But nobody gives a damn about him," he came right back. "They don't care if he killed *himself* or got hit by a car accidentally. You can take that piece of garbage out of the equation altogether. They care if you kill *me*. I'm the 'innocent bystander' in the headlines. I'm the 'father of two.' You kill me, you're as good as dead."

I started to say something but he kept going.

"Now here's another reason I'm not going to say anything about you. Because you know my name and you know where I live. You know I have a family and you know how important they are to me. If I turn you in you could come after us. I'd never jeopardize my family that way. Now, let me ask you something. What's the worst thing that could happen to you?"

"Keep listening to you spout on and on."

Weller laughed hard at that. I could see he was surprised I had a sense of humor. After a minute he said, "Seriously. The worst thing."

"I don't know. I never thought about it."

"Lose a leg? Go deaf? Lose all your money? Go blind . . . Hey, that looked like it hit a nerve. Going blind?"

"Yeah, I guess. That'd be the worst thing I could think of."

That *was* a pretty damn scary thing and I'd thought on it before. 'Cause that was what happened to my old man. And it wasn't not seeing anymore that got to me. No, it was that I'd have to depend on somebody else for, Christ, for everything, I guess.

"Okay, think about this," he said. "The way you feel about going blind's the way my family'd feel if they lost me. It'd be that bad for them. You don't want to cause them that kind of pain, do you?"

I didn't want to, no. But I knew I *had* to. I didn't want to think about it anymore. I asked him, "So what's this last reason you're telling me about?"

"The last reason," he said, kind of whispering. But he didn't go on. He looked around the room, you know, like his mind was wandering.

"Yeah?" I asked. I was pretty curious. "Tell me."

But he just asked, "You think these people, they have a bar?"

And I'd just been thinking I could use a drink too. I went into the kitchen and of course they didn't have any beer in the fridge on account of the house being all closed up and the power off. But they did have Scotch and that'd be my first choice anyway.

I got a couple glasses and took the bottle back to the living room. Thinking this was a good idea. When it came time to do it it'd be easier for him and for me both if we were kinda tanked. I shoved my Smitty into his neck and cut the tape his hands were tied with, then taped them in front of him. I sat back and kept my knife near, ready to go, in case he tried something. But it didn't look like he was going to be a hero or anything. He read over the Scotch bottle, kind of disappointed it was cheap. And I agreed with him there. One thing I learned a long time ago—you going to rob, rob rich.

I sat back where I could keep an eye on him.

"The last reason. Okay, I'll tell you. I'm going to *prove* to you that you should let me go."

"You are?"

"All those other reasons—the practical ones, the humanitarian ones . . . I'll concede you don't care much about those—you don't look very convinced. All right? Then let's look at the one reason you should let me go."

I figured this was going to be more crap. But what he said was something I never would've expected and it made me laugh.

"For your own sake."

"For me? What're you talking about?"

"See, Jack, I don't think you're lost."

"Whatta you mean, lost?"

"I don't think your soul's beyond redemption."

I laughed at this, laughed out loud, because I just *had* to. I expected a hell of a lot better from a hotshot vice-president salesman like him. "Soul? You think I got a soul?"

"Well, everybody has a soul," he said and what was crazy was he said it like he was surprised that I didn't think so. It was like I'd said wait a minute you mean the earth ain't flat? or something.

"Well, if I got a soul it's taken the fast lane to hell." Which was this line I heard in this movie and I tried to laugh but it sounded flat. Like Weller was saying something deep and I was just kidding around. It made me feel cheap. I stopped smiling and looked down at Toth, lying there in the corner, those dead eyes of his just staring, staring, and I wanted to stab him again I was so mad.

"We're talking about your soul."

I snickered and sipped the liquor. "Oh, yeah, I'll bet you, you're the sort that reads those angel books they got all over the place now."

"I go to church but, no, I'm not talking about all that silly stuff. I don't mean magic. I mean your conscience. What Jack Prescot's all about."

I could tell him about social workers and youth counselors and all those guys who don't know nothing about the way life works. They think they do. But it's the words they use. You can tell they don't know a thing. Some counselors or somebody'll talk to me and they say, *Oh, you're maladjusted, you're denying your anger,* things like that. When I hear that, I know they don't know nothing about souls or spirits.

"Not the afterlife," Weller was going on. "Not morality. I'm talking about life here on earth that's important. Oh, sure, you look skeptical. But listen to me. I really believe if you have a connection with somebody, if you trust them, if you have faith in them, then there's hope for you."

"Hope? What does that mean? Hope for what?"

"That you'll become a real human being. Lead a real life."

Real . . . I didn't know what he meant but he said it like what he was saying was so clear that I'd have to be an idiot to miss it. So I didn't say nothing.

He kept going. "Oh, there're reasons to steal and there're reasons to kill. But on the whole, don't you really think it's better not to? Just think about it: Why do we put people in jail if it's all right for them to murder? Not just us but all societies."

"So, what? I'm gonna give up my evil ways?" I laughed at him.

And he just lifted his eyebrow and said, "Maybe. Tell me, Jack, how'd you feel when your buddy—what's his name?"

"Joe Roy Toth."

"Toth, when he shot that guy by the counter? How'd you feel?"

"I don't know."

"He just turned around and shot him. For no reason. You knew that wasn't right, didn't you?" And I started to say something. But he said, "No, don't answer me. You'd be inclined to lie. And that's all right. It's an instinct in your line of work. But I don't want you *believing* any lies you tell me. Okay? I want you to look into your heart and tell me if you didn't think something was real wrong about what Toth did. Think about that, Jack. You knew something wasn't right."

All right, I did. But who wouldn't? Toth screwed everything up. Everything went sour. And it was all his fault.

"It dug at you, right, Jack? You wished he hadn't done it."

I didn't say nothing but just drank some more Scotch and looked out the window and watched the flashing lights around the town. Sometimes they seemed close and sometimes they seemed far away.

"If I let you go you'll tell 'em."

Like everybody else. They all betrayed me. My father—even after he went blind, the son-of-a-bitch turned me in. My first P.O., the judges. Sandra . . . My boss, the one I knifed.

"No, I won't," Weller said. "We're talking about an agreement. I don't break deals. I promised I won't tell a soul about you, Jack. Not even my wife." He leaned forward, cupping the booze between his hands. "You let me go, it'll mean all the difference in the world to you. It'll mean that you're not hopeless. I guarantee your life'll be different. That one act—letting me go—it'll change you forever. Oh, maybe not this year. Or for five years. But you'll come around. You'll give up all this, everything that happened back there in Liggett Falls. All the crime, the killing. You'll come around. I know you will."

"You just expect me to believe you won't tell anybody?"

"Ah," Weller said and lifted his tied-up hands to drink more Scotch. "Now we get down to the big issue."

Again, that silence and finally I said, "And what's that?"

"Faith."

There was this burst of siren outside and I told him to shut up and pushed the gun against his head. His hands were shaking but he didn't do anything stupid and a few minutes later, after I sat back, he started talking again. "Faith. That's what I'm talking about. A man who has faith is somebody who can be saved."

"Well, I don't have any goddamn faith," I told him.

But he kept right on talking. "If you believe in another human being you have faith."

"Why the hell do you care whether I'm saved or not?"

"Because life's hard and people're cruel. I told you I'm a churchgoer. A lot of the Bible's crazy. But some of it I believe. And one of the things I believe is that sometimes we're put in these situations to make a difference. I think that's what happened tonight. That's why you and I both happened to be at the drugstore at the same time. You've felt that, haven't you? Like an omen? Like something happens and is telling you you ought do this or shouldn't do that."

Which was weird 'cause the whole time we were driving up to Liggett Falls, I kept thinking, *Something's funny going on. I don't know what it is but this job's gonna be different.*

"What if," he said, "everything tonight happened for a purpose? My wife had a cold so I went to buy Nyquil. I went to that drugstore instead of 7-Eleven to save a buck or two. You happened to hit that store at just that time. You happened to have your buddy—" He nodded toward Toth's body. "—with you. The cop car just happened by at that particular moment. And the clerk behind the counter just happened to see him. That's a lot of coincidences. Don't you think?"

And then—this sent a damn chill right down my spine—he said, "Here we are in the shadow of that big rock, that face."

Which is one hundred percent what I was thinking. Exactly the same—about The Lookout, I mean. I don't know why I was. But I happened to be looking out the window and thinking about it at that exact same instant. I tossed back the Scotch and had another and, oh, man, I was pretty freaked out.

"Like he's looking at us, waiting for you to make a decision. Oh, don't think it was just you though. Maybe the purpose was to affect everybody's life there. That customer at the counter Toth shot. Maybe it was just his time to go—fast, you know, before he got cancer or had a stroke. Maybe that girl, the clerk, had to get shot in the leg so she'd get her life together, maybe get off drugs or give up drinking."

"And you? What about you?"

"Well, I'll tell you about me. Maybe you're the good deed in *my* life. I've spent years thinking only about making money. Take a look at my wallet. There. In the back."

I pulled it open. There were a half-dozen of these little cards, like certificates. *Randall Weller—Salesman of the Year. Exceeded Target Two Years Straight. Best Salesman of 1992.*

Weller kept going. "There are plenty of others back in my office. And trophies too. And in order for me to win those I've had to neglect people. My family and friends. People who could maybe use my help. And that's not right. Maybe you kidnapping me, it's one of those signs to make me turn my life around."

The funny thing was, this made sense. Oh, it was hard to imagine not doing heists. And I couldn't see myself, if it came down to a fight, not going for my Buck or my Smitty to take the other guy out. That turning-the-other-cheek stuff, that's only for cowards. But maybe I *could* see a day when my life'd be just straight time. Living with some woman, maybe a wife, living in a house. Doing what my father and mother, whatever she was like, never did.

"If I was to let you go," I said, "you'd have to tell 'em something."

He shrugged. "I'll say you locked me in the trunk and then tossed me out somewhere near here. I wandered around, looking for a house or something and got lost. It could take me a day to find somebody. That's believable."

"Or you could flag down a car in an hour."

"I could. But I won't."

"You keep saying that. But how do I *know*?"

"That's the faith part. You don't know. No guarantees."

"Well, I guess I don't have any faith."

"Then *I'm* dead. And *your* life's never gonna change. End of story." He sat back and it was crazy but he looked calm, smiling a little.

That silence again but it was like it was really this roar all around us and it kept going till the whole room was filled up with the sound of a siren.

"You just want . . . What do you want?"

He drank more Scotch. "Here's a proposal. Let me walk outside."

"Oh, right. Just let you stroll out for some fresh air or something?"

"Let me walk outside and I promise you I'll walk right back again."

"Like a test?"

He thought about this for a second. "Yeah. A test."

"Where's this faith you're talking about? You walk outside, you try to run and I'd shoot you in the back."

"No, what you do is you put the gun someplace in the house. The kitchen or someplace. Somewhere you couldn't get it if I ran. You stand at the window, where we can see each other. And I'll tell you up front. I can run like the wind. I lettered in track and field in college and I still jog every day of the year."

"You know if you run and bring the cops back everything's gonna get bloody. I'll kill the first five troopers come through that door. Nothing'll stop me and that blood'll be on your hands."

"Of course I know that," he said. "But if this's going to work you can't think that way. You've got to assume the worst is going to happen. That if I run I'll tell the cops everything. Where you are and that there're no hostages here and that you've only got one or two guns. And they're going to come in and blow you to hell. And you're not going to take a single one down with you. You're going to die and die painfully 'cause of a few lousy hundred bucks . . . But, but, but . . ." He held up his hand and stopped me from saying anything. "You gotta understand, faith means risk."

"That's stupid."

"I think it's just the opposite. It'd be the smartest thing you ever did in your life."

"What'll it prove?" I asked. But I was just stalling. And he knew it. He said patiently. "That I'm a man of my word. That you can trust me."

"And what do I get out of it?"

And then this son-of-a-bitch smiled that weird little smile of his. "I think you'll be surprised."

I tossed back another Scotch and had to think about this.

Weller said, "I can see it there already. Some of that faith. It's there. Not a lot. But some."

And yeah, maybe there was a little. 'Cause I was thinking about how mad I got at Toth and the way he ruined everything. I didn't want anybody to get killed tonight. I *was* sick of it. Sick of the way my life had gone. Sometimes it was good, being alone and all. Not answering to anybody. But sometimes it was real bad. And this guy, Weller, it was like he was showing me something different.

"So," I said. "You just want me to put the gun down?"

He looked around. "Put it in the kitchen. You stand in the doorway or window. All I'm gonna do is walk down to the street and walk back."

I looked out the window. It was maybe fifty feet down the driveway. There were these bushes on either side of it. He could just take off and I'd never find him.

All through the sky I could see lights flickering.

"Naw, I ain't gonna. You're nuts."

And I expected begging or something. Or getting pissed off, more likely—which is what happens to me when people don't do what I tell them. Or don't do it fast enough. But, naw, he just nodded. "Okay, Jack. You thought about it. That's a good thing. You're not ready yet. I respect that." He sipped a little more Scotch, looking at the glass. And that was the end of it.

Then all of a sudden these searchlights started up. They was some ways away but I still got spooked and backed away from the window. Pulled my gun out. Only then I saw that it wasn't nothing to do with the robbery. It was just a couple big spotlights shining on The Lookout. They must've gone on every night, this time.

I looked up at it. From here it didn't look like a face at all. It was just a rock. Gray and brown and these funny pine trees growing sideways out of cracks.

Watching it for a minute or two. Looking out over the town, and something that guy was saying went into my head. Not the words, really. Just the *thought*. And I was thinking about everybody in that town. Leading normal lives. There was a church steeple and the roofs of small houses. A lot of little yellow lights in town. You could just make out the hills in the distance. And I wished for a minute I was in one of them houses. Sitting there. Watching TV with a wife next to me. Like Sandy or somebody.

I turned back from the window and I said, "You'd just walk down to the road and back? That's it?"

"That's all. I won't run off, you don't go get your gun. We trust each other. What could be simpler?"

Listening to the wind. Not strong but a steady hiss that was comforting in a funny way even though any other time I'da thought it sounded cold and raw. It was like I heard a voice. I don't know from where. Something in me said I ought to do this.

I didn't say nothing else cause I was right on the edge and I was afraid he'd say something that'd make me change my mind. I just took the Smith & Wesson and looked at it for a minute, then put it on the kitchen table. I came back with the Buck and cut his feet free. Then I figured if I was going to do it I ought go all the way. So I cut his hands free too. Weller seemed surprised I did that. But he smiled like he knew I was playing the game. I pulled him to his feet and held the blade to his neck and took him to the door.

"You're doing a good thing," he said.

I was thinking: Oh, man. I can't believe this. It's crazy.

I opened the door and smelled cold fall air and wood smoke and pine and I heard the wind in the rocks and trees above our head.

"Go on," I told him.

Weller didn't look back to check up on me . . . Faith, I guess. He kept walking real slow down toward the road.

I felt funny, I'll tell you, and a couple times when he went past some real shadowy places in the driveway and could disappear I was like, *Oh, man, this is all messed up. I'm crazy.*

I almost panicked a few times and bolted for the Smitty but I didn't. When Weller got down near the sidewalk I was actually holding my breath. I expected him to go, I really did. I was looking for that moment—when people tense up, when they're gonna swing or draw down on you or bolt. It's like their bodies're shouting what they're going to be doing before they do it. Only Weller wasn't doing none of that. He walked down to the sidewalk real casual. And he turned and looked up at the face of The Lookout, like he was just another weekender.

Then he turned around. He nodded at me.

Which is when the car came by.

It was a state trooper. Those're the dark cars and he didn't have the light bar going. So he was almost on us before I knew it. I guess I was looking at Weller so hard I didn't see nothing else.

There it was, two doors away and Weller saw it the same time I did.

And I thought: *That's it. Oh, hell.*

But when I was turning to get the gun I saw this like flash of motion down by the road. And I stopped cold.

Could you believe it? Weller'd dropped onto the ground and rolled underneath a tree. I closed the door real fast and watched from the window. The trooper stopped and turned his light on the driveway. The beam—it was real bright—it moved up and down and hit all the bushes and the front of the house then back to the road. But it was like Weller was digging down into the pine needles to keep from being seen. I mean, he was *hiding* from those sons-of-bitches. Doing whatever he could to stay out of the way of the light.

Then the car moved on and I saw the lights checking out the house next door and then it was gone. I kept my eyes on Weller the whole time and he didn't do nothing stupid. I seen him climb out from under the trees and dust himself off. Then he came walking back to the house. Easy, like he was walking to a bar to meet some buddies.

He came inside and shook his head. Gave this little sigh, like relief. And laughed. Then he held his hands out. I didn't even ask him to.

I taped 'em up again with adhesive tape and he sat down in the chair, picked up his Scotch and sipped it.

And, damn, I'll tell you something. The God's truth. I felt good. Naw, naw, it wasn't like I'd seen the light or anything like that. But I was thinking that of all the people in my life—my dad or Sandy or Toth or anybody else—I never did really trust them. I'd never let myself go all the way. And here, tonight, I did. With a stranger and somebody who had the power to do me some harm. It was a pretty scary feeling but it was also a good feeling.

It was a little thing, real little. But maybe that's where stuff like this starts. I realized then that I'd been wrong. I could let him go. Oh, I'd keep him tied up here. Gagged. It'd be a day or so before he'd get out. But he'd agree to that. I knew he would. And I'd write his name and address down, let him know I knew where him and his family lived. But that was only part of why I was thinking I'd let him go. I wasn't sure what the rest of it was. But it was something about what'd just happened, something between me and him.

"How you feel?" he asked.

I wasn't going to give too much away. No sir. But I couldn't help saying, "I thought I was gone then. But you did right by me."

"And you did right too, Jack." And when he said, "Pour us another round."

I filled the glasses to the top. We tapped 'em.

"Here's to you, Jack. And to faith."

"To faith."

I tossed back the whisky and when I lowered my head, sniffing air through my nose to clear my head, well, that was when he got me. Right in the face.

He was good, that son-of-a-bitch. Tossed the glass low so that even when I ducked, automatically, the booze caught me in the eyes, and man, that stung like nobody's business. I couldn't believe it. I was howling in pain and going for the knife. But it was too late. He had it all planned out, exactly what I was going to do. How I was gonna move. He brought his knee up into my chin and knocked a couple teeth out and I went over onto my back before I could get the knife outa my pocket. Then he dropped down on my belly with his knee—I remembered I'd never bothered to tape his feet up again—and he knocked the wind out and there I was lying, like I was paralyzed, trying to breathe and all. Only I couldn't. And the pain was incredible but what was worse was the feeling that he didn't trust me.

I was whispering, "No, no, no. I was going to, man. You don't understand. I was going to let you go."

I couldn't see nothing and couldn't really hear nothing either, my ears were roaring so much. I was gasping, "You don't understand you don't understand."

Man, the pain was so bad. So bad . . .

Weller must've got the tape off his hands, chewed through it, I guess, 'cause he was rolling me over. I felt him tape my hands together then grab me and drag me over to a chair, taped my feet to the legs. He got some water and threw it in my face to wash the whisky out of my eyes.

He sat down in a chair in front of me. And he just stared at me for a long time while I caught my breath. He picked up his glass, poured more Scotch. I shied away, thinking he was going to throw it in my face again but he just sat there, sipping it and staring at me.

"You . . . I was going to let you go. I *was.*"

"I know," he said. Still calm.

"You know?"

"I could see it in your face. I've been a salesman for twenty years, remember? I know when I've closed a deal."

I'm a pretty strong guy, 'specially when I'm mad, and I tried real hard to break through that tape but there was no doing it. "Goddamn you!" I shouted. "You said you weren't going to turn me in. You, all your goddamn talk about faith . . ."

"Shhhh," Weller whispered. And he sat back, crossed his legs. Easy as could be. Looking me up and down. "That fellow your friend shot back at the drugstore. The customer at the counter?"

I nodded slowly.

"He was my friend. It's his place my wife and I're staying at this weekend. With all our kids."

I just stared at him. His friend? What was he saying?

"I didn't know—"

"Be quiet," he said, real soft. "I've known him for years. Gerry was one of my best friends."

"I didn't want nobody to die. I—"

"But somebody did die. And it was your fault."

"Toth . . ."

He whispered, "It was your fault."

"All right, you tricked me. Call the cops. Get it over with, you goddamn liar."

"You really don't understand, do you?" He shook his head. Why was he so calm? His hands weren't shaking. He wasn't looking around, nervous and all. Nothing like that. He said, "If I'd wanted to turn you in I would just've flagged down that squad car a few minutes ago. But I said I wouldn't do that. And I won't. I gave you my word I wouldn't tell the cops a thing about you. And I won't."

"Then what do you want?" I shouted. "Tell me." Trying to bust through that tape. And as he unfolded my Buck knife with a click I was thinking of something I told him.

Oh, man, no . . . Oh, no.

Yeah, being blind, I guess. That'd be the worst thing I could think of.

"What're you going to do?"

"What'm I going to do, Jack?" Weller said. He cut the last bit of tape off his wrists with the Buck then looked up at me. "Well, I'll tell you. I spent a good bit of time tonight proving to you that you shouldn't kill me. And now . . ."

"What, man? *What?*"

"Now I'm going to spend a good bit of time proving to you that you should've."

Then, real slow, Weller finished his Scotch and stood up. And he walked toward me, that weird little smile on his face.

REASONS UNKNOWN

Stanley Ellin

Every generation produces one writer who stands a given genre on its head. The late Stanley Ellin (1936–1986) certainly did that with crime fiction. There was his style, as pithy and poignant as any literary writer's; there were his ideas, ever the equal of such great idea men as Roald Dahl and Saki; and there was his world view, which was every bit as complex as some of his darker protagonists. For all this, though, he had a sense of everyday life and everyday people that few in the genre ever came close to matching. Perhaps this was because, early in his life, he was a steelworker, a dairy farmer, and a teacher. While he is primarily thought of as a short-story writer, he wrote a number of excellent novels, among them *The Eighth Circle* and *Mirror, Mirror, on the Wall*.

THIS IS WHAT happened, starting that Saturday in October.

That morning Morrison's wife needed the station wagon for the kids, so Morrison took the interstate bus into downtown Manhattan. At the terminal there, hating to travel by subway, he got into a cab. When the cabbie turned around and asked, "Where to, mister?" Morrison did a double take. "Slade?" he said. "Bill Slade?"

"You better believe it," said the cabbie. "So it's Larry Morrison. Well, what do you know."

Now, what Morrison knew was that up to two or three years ago, Slade had been—as he himself still was—one of the several thousand comfortably fixed bees hiving in the glass-and-aluminum Majestico complex in Greenbush, New Jersey. There were 80,000 Majestico employees around the world, but the Greenbush complex was the flagship of the works, the executive division. And Slade had been there a long, long time, moving up to an assistant managership on the departmental level.

Then the department was wiped out in a reorganizational crunch, and Slade, along with some others in it, had been handed his severance money and his hat. No word had come back from him after he finally sold his house and pulled out of town with his wife and kid to line up, as he put it, something good elsewhere. It was a shock to Morrison to find that the something good elsewhere meant tooling a cab around Manhattan.

He said in distress, "Jeez, I didn't know, Bill—none of the Hillcrest Road bunch had any idea—"

"That's what I was hoping for," said Slade. "It's all right, man. I always had a feeling I'd sooner or later meet up with one of the old bunch. Now that it happened, I'm just as glad it's you." A horn sounding behind the cab prompted Slade to get it moving. "Where to, Larry?"

"Columbus Circle. The Coliseum."

"Don't tell me, let me guess. The Majestico Trade Exposition. It's that time of the year, right?"

"Right," said Morrison.

"And it's good politics to show up, right? Maybe one of the brass'll take notice."

"You know how it is, Bill."

"I sure do." Slade pulled up at a red light and looked around at Morrison. "Say, you're not in any tearing hurry, are you? You could have time for a cup of coffee?"

There was a day-old stubble on Slade's face. The cap perched on the back of his graying hair was grimy and sweatstained. Morrison felt unsettled by the sight. Besides, Slade hadn't been any real friend, just a casual acquaintance living a few blocks farther up Hillcrest Road. One of the crowd on those occasional weekend hunting trips of the Hillcrest Maybe Gun and Rod Club. The "Maybe" had been inserted in jest to cover those bad hunting and fishing weekends when it temporarily became a poker club.

"Well," Morrison said, "this happens to be one of those heavy Saturdays when—"

"Look, I'll treat you to the best Danish in town. Believe me, Larry, there's some things I'd like to get off my chest."

"Oh, in that case," said Morrison.

There was a line of driverless cabs in front of a cafeteria on Eighth Avenue. Slade pulled up behind them and led the way into the cafeteria which was obviously a cabbies' hangout. They had a little wrestling match about the check at the counter, a match Slade won, and, carrying the tray with the coffee and Danish, he picked out a corner table for them.

The coffee was pretty bad, the Danish, as advertised, pretty good. Slade said through a mouthful of it, "And how is Amy?" Amy was Morrison's wife.

"Fine, fine," Morrison said heartily. "And how is Gertrude?"

"Gretchen."

"That's right. Gretchen. Stupid of me. But it's been so long, Bill—"

"It has. Almost three years. Anyhow, last I heard of her Gretchen's doing all right."

"Last you heard of her?"

"We separated a few months ago. She just couldn't hack it any more." Slade shrugged. "My fault mostly. Getting turned down for one worthwhile job after another didn't sweeten the disposition. And jockeying a cab ten, twelve hours a day doesn't add sugar to it. So she and the kid have their own little flat out in Queens, and she got herself some kind of cockamamie receptionist job with a doctor there. Helps eke out what I can give her. How's your pair, by the way? Scott and Morgan, isn't it? Big fellows now, I'll bet."

"Thirteen and ten," Morrison said. "They're fine. Fine."

"Glad to hear it. And the old neighborhood? Any changes?"

"Not really. Well, we did lose a couple of the old-timers. Mike Costanzo and Gordie McKechnie. Remember them?"

"Who could forget Mike, the world's worst poker player? But McKechnie?"

"That split-level, corner of Hillcrest and Maple. He's the one got himself so smashed that time in the duck blind that he went overboard."

"Now I remember. And that fancy shotgun of his, six feet underwater in the mud. Man, that sobered him up fast. What happened to him and Costanzo?"

"Well," Morrison said uncomfortably, "they were both in Regional Customer Services. Then somebody on the top floor got the idea that Regional and National should be tied together, and some people in both offices had to be let go. I think Mike's in Frisco now, he's got a lot of family there. Nobody's heard from Gordie. I mean—" Morrison cut it short in embarrassment.

"I know what you mean. No reason to get red in the face about it, Larry." Slade eyed Morrison steadily over his coffee cup. "Wondering what happened to me?"

"Well, to be frank—"

"Nothing like being frank. I put in two years making the rounds, lining up employment agencies, sending out enough résumés to make a ten-foot pile of paper. No dice. Ran out of unemployment insurance, cash, and credit. There it is, short and sweet."

"But why? With the record you piled up at Majestico—"

"Middle level. Not top echelon. Not decision-making stuff. Middle level, now and forever. Just like everybody else on Hillcrest Road. That's why we're on Hillcrest Road. Notice how the ones who make it to the top echelon always wind up on Greenbush Heights? And always after only three or four years? But after you're middle level fifteen years the way I was—"

Up to now Morrison had been content with his twelve years in Sales Analysis. Admittedly no ball of fire, he had put in some rough years after graduation from college—mostly as salesman on commission for some product or other—until he had landed the job at Majestico. Now he felt disoriented by what Slade was saying. And he wondered irritably why Slade had to wear that cap while he was eating. Trying to prove he was just another one of these cabbies here? He wasn't. He was a college man, had owned one of the handsomest small properties on Hillcrest Road, had been a respected member of the Majestico executive team.

Morrison said, "I still don't understand. Are you telling me there's no company around needs highly qualified people outside decision-making level? Ninety percent of what goes on anyplace is our kind of job, Bill. You know that."

"I do. But I'm forty-five years old, Larry. And you want to know what I found out? By corporation standards I died five years ago on my fortieth birthday. Died, and didn't even know it. Believe me, it wasn't easy to realize that at first. It got a lot easier after a couple of years' useless job-hunting."

Morrison was 46 and was liking this less and less. "But the spot you're in is only temporary, Bill. There's still—"

"No, no. Don't do that, Larry. None of that somewhere-over-the-rainbow line. I finally looked my situation square in the eye, I accepted it, I made the adjustment. With luck, what's in the cards for me is maybe some day owning my own cab. I buy lottery tickets, too, because after all somebody's got to win that million, right? And the odds there are just as good as my chances of ever getting behind a desk again at the kind of money Majestico was paying me." Again he was looking steadily at Morrison over his coffee cup. "That was the catch, Larry. That money they were paying me."

"They pay well, Bill. Say, is that what happened? You didn't think you were getting your price and made a fuss about it? So when the department went under you were one of the—"

"Hell, no," Slade cut in sharply. "You've got it backwards, man. They do pay well. But did it ever strike you that maybe they pay too well?"

"Too well?"

"For the kind of nine-to-five paperwork I was doing? The donkey work?"

"You were an assistant head of department, Bill."

"One of the smarter donkeys, that's all. Look, what I was delivering to the company had to be worth just so much to them. But when every year—every first week in January—there's an automatic cost-of-living increase handed me I am slowly and steadily becoming a luxury item. Consider that after fourteen-fifteen years of those jumps every year, I am making more than some of those young hotshot executives in the International Division. I am a very expensive proposition for Majestico, Larry. And replaceable by somebody fifteen years younger who'll start for a hell of a lot less."

"Now hold it. Just hold it. With the inflation the way it is, you can't really object to those cost-of-living raises."

Slade smiled thinly. "Not while I was getting them, pal. It would have meant a real scramble without them. But suppose I wanted to turn them down just to protect my job? You know that can't be done. Those raises are right there in the computer for every outfit like Majestico. But nobody in management has to like living with it. And what came to me after I was canned was that they were actually doing something about it."

"Ah, look," Morrison said heatedly. "You weren't terminated because you weren't earning your keep. There was a departmental reorganization. You were just a victim of it."

"I was. The way those Incas or Aztecs or whatever used to lay out the living sacrifice and stick the knife into him. Don't keep shaking your head, Larry. I have thought this out long and hard. There's always a reorganization going on in one of the divisions. Stick a couple of departments together, change their names, dump a few personnel who don't fit into the new table of organization.

"But the funny thing, Larry, is that the ones who usually seem to get dumped are the middle-aged, middle-level characters with a lot of seniority. The ones whose take-home pay put them right up there in the high-income brackets. Like me. My secretary lost out in that reorganization too, after eighteen years on the job. No complaints about her work. But she ran into what I did when I told them I'd be glad to take a transfer to any other department. No dice. After all, they could hire two fresh young secretaries for what they were now paying her."

"And you think this is company policy?" Morrison demanded.

"I think so. I mean, what the hell are they going to do? Come to me and say, 'Well, Slade, after fifteen years on the job you've priced yourself right out of the market, so good-bye, baby?' But those reorganizations?

Beautiful. 'Too bad, Slade, but under the new structure we're going to have to lose some good men.' That's the way it was told to me, Larry. And that's what I believed until I woke up to the facts of life."

The piece of Danish in Morrison's mouth was suddenly dry and tasteless. He managed to get it down with an effort. "Bill, I don't want to say it—I hate to say it—but that whole line sounds paranoid."

"Does it? Then think it over, Larry. You still in Sales Analysis?"

"Yes."

"I figured. Now just close your eyes and make a head count of your department. Then tell me how many guys forty-five or over are in it."

Morrison did some unpalatable calculation. "Well, there's six of us. Including me."

"Out of how many?"

"Twenty-four."

"Uh-huh. Funny how the grass manages to stay so green, isn't it?"

It was funny, come to think of it. No, funny wasn't the word. Morrison said weakly, "Well, a couple of the guys wanted to move out to the Coast, and you know there's departmental transfers in and out—"

"Sure there are. But the real weeding comes when there's one of those little reorganizations. You've seen it yourself in your own department more than once. Juggle around some of those room dividers. Move some desks here and there. Change a few descriptions in the company directory. The smokescreen. But behind that smoke there's some high-priced old faithfuls getting called upstairs to be told that, well, somebody's got to go, Jack, now that things are all different, and guess whose turn it is."

Slade's voice had got loud enough to be an embarrassment. Morrison pleaded: "Can't we keep it down, Bill? Anyhow, to make villains out of everybody on the top floor—"

Slade lowered his voice, but the intensity was still there. "Who said they were villains? Hell, in their place I'd be doing the same thing. For that matter, if I was head of personnel for any big outfit, I wouldn't take anybody my age on the payroll either. Not if I wanted to keep my cushy job in personnel, I wouldn't." The wind suddenly seemed to go out of him. "Sorry, Larry. I thought I had everything under control, but when I saw you—when I saw it was one of the old Hillcrest bunch—it was too much to keep corked up. But one thing—"

"Yes?"

"I don't want anybody else back there in on this. Know what I mean?"

"Oh, sure."

"Don't just toss off the 'oh, sure' like that. This is the biggest favor you could do me—not to let anybody else in the old crowd hear about me, not even Amy. No post-mortems up and down Hillcrest for good old Bill Slade. One reason I let myself cut loose right now was because you always were a guy who liked to keep his mouth tight shut. I'm counting on you to do that for me, Larry. I want your solemn word on it."

"You've got it, Bill. You know that."

"I do. And what the hell"—Slade reached across the table and punched Morrison on the upper arm—"any time they call you in to tell you there's a reorganization of Sales Analysis coming, it could turn out you're the guy elected to be department head of the new layout. Right?"

Morrison tried to smile. "No chance of that, Bill."

"Well, always look on the bright side, Larry. As long as there is one."

Outside the Coliseum there was another of those little wrestling matches about paying the tab—Slade refusing to take anything at all for the ride, Morrison wondering, as he eyed the meter, whether sensitivity here called for a standard tip, a huge tip, or none at all—and again Slade won.

Morrison was relieved to get away from him, but, as he soon found, the relief was only temporary. It was a fine Indian summer day, but somehow the weather now seemed bleak and threatening. And doing the Majestico show, looking over the displays, passing the time of day with recognizable co-workers turned out to be a strain. It struck him that it hadn't been that atrocious cap on Slade's head that had thrown him, it had been the gray hair showing under the cap. And there was very little gray hair to be seen on those recognizable ones here at the Majestico show.

Morrison took a long time at the full-length mirror in the men's room, trying to get an objective view of himself against the background of the others thronging the place. The view he got was depressing. As far as he could see, in this company he looked every minute of his 46 years.

Back home he stuck to his word and told Amy nothing about his encounter with Slade. Any temptation to was readily suppressed by his feeling that once he told her that much he'd also find himself exposing his morbid reaction to Slade's line of thinking. And that would only lead to her being terribly understanding and sympathetic while, at the same time, she'd be moved to some heavy humor about his being such a born worrier. He was a born worrier, he was the first to acknowledge it, but he always chafed under that combination of sympathy and teasing she offered him when he confided his worries to her. They really made quite a list, renewable each morning on rising. The family's health, the condition of the house, the car, the lawn, the bank balance—the list started there and seemed to extend to infinity.

Yet, as he was also the first to acknowledge, this was largely a quirk of personality—he was, as his father had been, somewhat sobersided and humorless—and, quirks aside, life was a generally all-right proposition. As it should be when a man can lay claim to a pretty and affectionate wife, and a couple of healthy young sons, and a sound home in a well-tended neighborhood. And a good steady job to provide the wherewithal.

At least, up to now.

Morrison took a long time falling asleep that night, and at three in the morning came bolt awake with a sense of foreboding. The more he lay there trying to get back to sleep, the more oppressive grew the foreboding. At four o'clock he padded into his den and sat down at his desk to work out a precise statement of the family's balance sheet.

No surprises there, just confirmation of the foreboding. For a long time now, he and Amy had been living about one month ahead of income which, he suspected, was true of most families along Hillcrest Road. The few it wasn't true of were most likely at least a year ahead of income and sweating out the kind of indebtedness he had always carefully avoided.

But considering that his assets consisted of a home with ten years of mortgage payments yet due on it and a car with two years of payments still due, everything depended on income. The family savings account was, of course, a joke. And the other two savings accounts—one in trust for each boy to cover the necessary college educations—had become a joke as college tuition skyrocketed. And, unfortunately, neither boy showed any signs of being scholarship material.

In a nutshell, everything depended on income. This month's income. Going by Slade's experience in the job market—and Slade had been the kind of competent, hardworking nine-to-five man any company should have been glad to take on—this meant that everything depended on the job with Majestico. Everything. Morrison had always felt that landing the job in the first place was the best break of his life. Whatever vague ambitions he had in his youth were dissolved very soon after he finished college and learned that out here in the real world he rated just about average in all departments, and that his self-effacing, dogged application to his daily work was not going to have him climbing any ladders to glory.

Sitting there with those pages of arithmetic scattered around the desk, Morrison, his stomach churning, struggled with the idea that the job with Majestico was suddenly no longer a comfortable, predictable way of life but for someone his age, and with his makeup and qualifications, a dire necessity. At five o'clock, exhausted but more wide-awake than ever, he went down to the kitchen for a bottle of beer. Pills were not for him. He had always refused to take even an aspirin tablet except under extreme duress, but beer did make him sleepy, and a bottle of it on an empty stomach, he estimated, was the prescription called for in this case. It turned out that he was right about it.

In the days and weeks that followed, this became a ritual: the abrupt waking in the darkest hours of the morning, the time at his desk auditing his accounts and coming up with the same dismal results, and the bottle of beer which, more often than not, allowed for another couple of hours of troubled sleep before the alarm clock went off.

Amy, the soundest of sleepers, took no notice of this, so that was all right. And by exercising a rigid self-control he managed to keep her unaware of those ragged nerves through the daylight hours as well, although it was sometimes unbearably hard not to confide in her. Out of a strange sense of pity, he found himself more sensitive and affectionate to her than ever. High-spirited, a little scatterbrained, leading a full life of her own what with the boys, the Parent-Teachers Club, and half a dozen community activities, she took this as no less than her due.

Along the way, as an added problem, Morrison developed some physical tics which would show up when least expected. A sudden tremor of the hands, a fluttering of one eyelid which he had to learn to quickly cover up. The most grotesque tic of all, however—it really unnerved him the few times he experienced it—was a violent, uncontrollable chattering of the teeth when he had sunk to a certain point of absolute depression. This only struck him when he was at his desk during the sleepless times considering the future. At such times he had a feeling that those teeth were diabolically possessed by a will of their own, chattering away furiously as if he had just been plunged into icy water.

In the office he took refuge in the lowest of low profiles. Here the temptation was to check on what had become of various colleagues who had over the years departed from the company, but this, Morrison knew, might raise the question of why he had, out of a clear sky, brought up the subject. The subject was not a usual part of the day's conversational currency in the department. The trouble was that Greenbush was, of course, a company town, although in the most modern and pleasant way. Majestico had moved there from New York 20 years before; the town had grown around the company complex. And isolated as it was in the green heartland of New Jersey, it had only Majestico to offer. Anyone leaving the company would therefore have to sell his home, like it or not, and relocate far away. Too far, at least, to maintain old ties. It might have been a comfort, Morrison thought, to drop in on someone in his category who had been terminated by Majestico and who could give him a line on what had followed. Someone other than Slade. But there was no one like this in his book.

The one time he came near bringing his desperation to the surface was at the Thanksgiving entertainment given by the student body of the school his sons attended. The entertainment was a well-deserved success, and after it, at the buffet in the school gym, Morrison was driven to corner Frank Lassman, assistant principal of the school and master of ceremonies at the entertainment, and to come out with a thought that had been encouragingly flickering through his mind during the last few insomniac sessions.

"Great show," he told Lassman. "Fine school altogether. It showed tonight. It must be gratifying doing your kind of work."

"At times like this it is," Lassman said cheerfully. "But there are times—"

"Even so. You know, I once had ideas about going into teaching."

"Financially," said Lassman, "I suspect you did better by not going into it. It has its rewards, but the big money isn't one of them."

"Well," Morrison said very carefully, "suppose I was prepared to settle for the rewards it did offer? A man my age, say. Would there be any possibilities of getting into the school system?"

"What's your particular line? Your subject?"

"Oh, numbers. Call it arithmetic and math."

Lassman shook his head in mock reproach. "And where were you when we really needed you? Four or five years ago we were sending out search parties for anyone who could get math across to these kids. The last couple of years, what with the falling school population, we're firing, not hiring. It's the same everywhere, not that I ever thought I'd live to see the day. Empty school buildings all over the country."

"I see," said Morrison.

So the insomnia, tensions, and tics continued to worsen until suddenly one day—as if having hit bottom, there was no place for him to go but up—Morrison realized that he was coming back to normal. He began to sleep through the night, was increasingly at ease during the day, found himself cautiously looking on the bright side. He still had his job and all that went with it, that was the objective fact. He could only marvel that he had been thrown so far off balance by that chance meeting with Slade.

He had been giving himself his own bad time, letting his imagination take over as it had. The one thing he could be proud of was that where someone else might have broken down under the strain, he had battled it out all by himself and had won. He was not a man to hand himself trophies, but in this case he felt he had certainly earned one.

A few minutes before five on the first Monday in December, just when he was getting ready to pack it in for the day, Pettengill, departmental head of Sales Analysis, stopped at his desk. Pettengill, a transfer from the Cleveland office a couple of years before, was rated as a comer, slated sooner or later for the top floor. A pleasant-mannered, somewhat humorless man, he and Morrison had always got along well.

"Just had a session with the brass upstairs," he confided. "A round table with Cobb presiding." Cobb was the executive vice president in charge of Planning and Structure for the Greenbush complex. "Looks like our department faces a little reorganization. We tie in with Service Analysis and that'll make it Sales and Service Evaluation. What's the matter? Don't you feel well?"

"No, I'm all right," said Morrison.

"Looks like you could stand some fresh air. Anyhow, probably because you're senior man here, Cobb wants to see you in his office first thing tomorrow morning. Nine sharp. You know how he is about punctuality, Larry. Make sure you're on time."

"Yes," said Morrison.

He didn't sleep at all that night. The next morning, a few minutes before nine, still wearing his overcoat and with dark glasses concealing his reddened and swollen eyes, he took the elevator directly to the top floor. There, out of sight on the landing of the emergency staircase, he drew the barrel and stock of his shotgun from beneath the overcoat and assembled the gun. His pockets bulged with 12-gauge shells. He loaded one into each of the gun's twin barrels. Then concealing the assembled gun beneath the coat as well as he could, he walked across the hall into Cobb's office.

Miss Bernstein, Cobb's private secretary, acted out of sheer blind, unthinking instinct when she caught sight of the gun. She half-rose from her desk as if to bar the way to the inner office. She took the first charge square in the chest. Cobb, at his desk, caught the next in the face. Reloading, Morrison exited through the door to the executive suite where Cobb's assistants had been getting ready for the morning's work and were now in a panic at the sound of the shots.

Morrison fired both barrels one after another, hitting one man in the throat and jaw, grazing another. Reloading again, he moved like an automaton out into the corridor where a couple of security men, pistols at the ready, were coming from the staircase on the run. Morrison cut down the first one, but the other, firing wildly, managed to plant one bullet in his forehead. Morrison must have been dead, the medical examiner later reported, before he even hit the floor.

The police, faced with five dead and one wounded, put in two months on the case and could come up with absolutely no answers, no explanations at all. The best they could do in their final report was record that "the perpetrator, for reasons unknown, etc., etc."

Management, however, could and did take action. They learned that the Personnel Department psychologist who had put Morrison through the battery of personality-evaluation tests given every applicant for a job was still there with the company. Since he had transparently failed in those tests to sound out the potentially aberrant behavior of the subject, he was, despite sixteen years of otherwise acceptable service, terminated immediately.

Two weeks later, his place in Personnel was filled by a young fellow named McIntyre who, although the starting pay was a bit low, liked the looks of Greenbush and, with his wife in complete agreement, saw it as just the kind of quiet, pleasant community in which to settle down permanently.

KILLING BERNSTEIN

Harlan Ellison

There is no more overused word in our contemporary lexicon than *legendary*. Yet how else does one describe fiction writer, opinion-shaper, tilter-at-windmills, and social critic Harlan Ellison? Not that his "legend" is always a good thing. Too often it gets in the way of his accomplishments as a short-story writer and novelist. He first came to prominence in the early 1960s with a first-rate collection of stories called *Gentleman Junkie*. Dorothy Parker was nice enough to give it a much-deserved rave in *Esquire* magazine. He has since spent time as a TV scriptwriter, newspaper columnist, speaker, and occasional anthology editor. But most important of all, he has continued to write fiction that is singular of voice, aspiration, and accomplishment. At his best, he is one of the two or three best short story writers on our blue-green little world, and this is true whether he is writing science fiction, fantasy, or—as here—suspense.

IF GOD (OR Whoever's in charge) had wanted Dr. Netta Bernstein to continue living, He (or She) wouldn't have made it so easy for me to kill her.

The night before, she had said again, do it again, we can do it once more, can't we; and her thick, auburn hair smelled fresh and clean and it flowed across the pillows like the sunsets we get these days. The kind that burn the eyes they're so beautiful. Our grandparents never saw such wonders of melting copper, flickering at the edges, sliding into darkness at the horizon. Exquisite beyond belief, created by pollution. Smog produces that kind of gorgeous sunset. Grandeur, created by imminent destruction. Her hair burned and slid into darkness and I buried my face in it and we made love and I didn't make any mistakes.

And the next day she acted as if she didn't know me.

Talked to me as though I were one of the test children she had in for her perception analyses. I felt waves of actual dislike coming from her. "Netta," I said, "what's the matter? Did I say something?"

She looked back at me with the expression of someone who has been asked for her driver's license or other identification at a bank where she has had an account for sixteen years. I was a troublesome new teller, a trainee, an upstart stealing her time, impertinent and callow. "Duncaster," she said, calling me by my last name, "I have work to do. Why don't you go on about your business." The night before she had called me Jimmy a hundred times in a minute.

She pretended not to know what I was talking about. I tried to be polite referring to what had happened between us. I didn't want to use the wrong words, but there were *no words* she responded to. It was as if that bed, and the two of us on it, had never existed. I couldn't believe she could be that brutal. I left the office early that day.

And the next day she hung me out to dry. It was even more brutal than the day before. The day before, it had only been obvious dislike, go on about your business, Duncaster. But the next day we were mortal enemies. Like ancient antagonists from some primordial swamp, she was after me, and I knew it. I can't explain *how* I knew, I simply understood somewhere deep in the blood and bones that this woman was determined to rip out my throat.

Or perhaps I *can* explain it.

Take the film they made of *Jaws*. That is a terrifying film. It collapses entire audiences, and not merely because of the cinematic tricks. People in the middle of Kansas, people who've never even *seen* an ocean or a shark, go into cardiac arrest. Why should that be? There are terrors much closer to us—muggers on the streets, a positive biopsy report, being smashed to pudding in a freeway accident—terrors that *can* reach us; why should we be so petrified by that shark? I reject abstractions: the *vagina dentatus*, that paranoid hobgoblin of Freudian shadow-myth; the simplicity of our recoiling from something filled with teeth, an eating machine. I have another theory.

The shark is one of the few life forms that has come down to the present virtually unchanged from the Devonian. So few: the cockroach, the horseshoe crab, the nautilus, the coelacanth—probably older than the dinosaurs. The shark.

When we were still aquatic creatures . . . there was the shark. And even today, in the blood that boils through us, the blood whose constituency is the same as sea water, in the blood and somewhere deep in our racial memory, there is still the remembrance of the shark. Of swimming away from that inexorable eating machine, of crawling up onto the land to be safe from it, of vowing never to return to the warm seas where the teeth can reach us.

When we see the shark, we understand that *that* is one of the dreadful furies that drove us to become human beings. Natural enemy from beyond the curtain of time, from beneath the killing darkness. Natural enemies.

Perhaps I *can* explain how I knew, that next day, that Netta Bernstein and I were blood enemies.

The moment I walked into the conference room and saw her sitting next to Sloan—a clipboard fat with charts lying on the table in front of her—I knew she was lying in wait for me. The teeth, the warm seas, the eating machines that had followed us onto the land. And in that instant, I now realize, I first decided to kill her.

You have to understand how it is with a major toy company, how it works in the corporate way; otherwise it doesn't make sense . . . the killing of Netta Bernstein.

Fighting my way to the top at the MyToy Corporation had been the commitment of ten years of my life. It wouldn't have been any different at Mattel or Marx or Fisher-Price or Ideal or Hasbro or Kenner or Mego or Playskool or even Creative Playthings. The race is always to make The Big Breakthrough, to come up with the new toy that sweeps the field before the competition can work up a knockoff imitation. Barbie, G.I. Joe, Hot Wheels, they made millions for one man and one company because they were The Big Breakthroughs. In an industry where sixty percent of each year's product is brand-new, *has to be* brand-new because the kids have a saturation/boredom threshold that is not to be believed, it is the guy with The Big Breakthrough who gets to be Vice President of Product Planning, at $50,000 a year.

I was Director of Marketing Research. Gumball, Destruction Derby, Change-A-Face, those had been my weapons in the fight toward the $50,000 plateau. MyToy was one of the big five and I'd been on the rise for ten years.

But the last four ideas I'd hawked to top management had either been rejected or been put into production and bombed. The fashion-doll line had been too sophisticated—and the recession had hit; there was backlash against opulence, conspicuous consumption; and the feminist movement had come out strong against what they called "training little girls to be empty-headed clotheshorses." Dinosaur had been too impractical to pro-duce at a reasonable per-unit cost. Pretesting had shown that kids rejected Peggy Puffin as being "ugly," even though parents found the packaging attractive; they'd buy it, but the kids wouldn't play with it. And the lousy sales reports on Mother's Helper had verified a negative transference; old learning habits had generally inhibited learning new techniques. It was what the president of MyToy, Sloan, had called "disastrously counterproductive." And I'd begun to smell the ambivalence about me. Then the doubts. Then the veiled antagonisms. The dismissals, the offhand rejections of trial balloons I'd floated. And now there was even open hostility. I was at the crunch point.

Everything was tied up in the two new projects I'd worked out with R&D. The Can-Do Chipper and the Little Miss Goodie Two-Shoes doll. Research & Development had gotten the approval to put them into preliminary design, both aimed at pre-school development markets, and Netta Bernstein had tested them in the MyToy play therapy facilities.

MyToy was the only major toy company in America to maintain a full-time staff of child and research psychologists. Netta headed the team. The prototypes had been sent to her for live evaluation with test kids. The reports filled that clipboard. Fifty thou filled that clipboard. And I knew she was out to get me.

Sloan wouldn't look at me. I went down the length of the conference table, took an empty seat between Dixon and Schwann; I was bracketed by cost accountants, a pair of minor sales potential vassals. The seat on the right hand of Brian Sloan, God of MyToy, the seat I'd held for almost ten years, was occupied by Ostlander, the hungry little turncoat from Ideal who'd come over, bringing with him design secrets worth a fortune. Not The Big Breakthrough, but enough knockoff data to pay his way to the other side.

And on the left hand of God sat Netta Bernstein.

My future lay before her fastened tight in the clipboard. Her tests with the kids would make or break me. And the night before last she had said she loved me. And the day before she had told me to go away. And today I smelled the killing darkness of the Devonian seas.

The first hour was marking time. Sales reports, prospectus for third-quarter production, a presentation about the proposed Lexington, Kentucky, plant site, odds and ends. Then Sloan said we'd hear Netta's test results on the new designs. She never looked at me.

"I'll begin with the big dolls for preschoolers," she said, releasing the clip and removing the first batch of reports. "They all reach or exceed the expectations projected by prelim. They have the 'kid appeal' Mr. Sloan discussed last Thursday, with one small modification on the shopper doll. The mother model. I found, in giving the dolls to six selected groups of test children—eight in each group—that the pocket on the apron was ignored completely. The children had no use for it, and I think it can be eliminated to the advantage of the item."

Sloan looked at me. "Jimmy," he said, "what would that mean in terms of lowering the per-unit cost of the mother shopper?"

I already had my calculator out and was running the figures. "Uh, that would be . . . three cents per unit on a projected run of—" I looked at Schwann; he scribbled *3 mil* on his pad. "A run of three million units: ninety thousand dollars." It had been a most ordinary question, and an ordinary answer.

Netta Bernstein, without looking at me, said to Sloan, "I believe that figure is incorrect. The per-unit saving would be closer to 4.6 cents, for a total of one hundred and thirty-eight thousand dollars."

Sloan didn't answer. He just looked at Schwann and Dixon. They both nodded rapidly, like a pair of those Woolworth's cork birds that dip their beaks into a glass of water and then sit upright again. It would have been pointless to say the three-cents-per-unit figure had been given to me by prelim the week before and that Netta had obviously gotten more up-to-date stats on the project. It would have been pointless, not only because Sloan didn't like to hear excuses, but because Netta had clearly set out to mousetrap me. Cost stats were not her area, never had been, never should be; yet she had them. Chance? I doubted it. Either way, I looked like a doughnut.

There was a hefty chunk of silence, and then Netta went on to the test results of three other proposals, none of them mine. On one of them the changes would have been impractical, on the second the kids simply didn't like the toy, and on the third the changes would have been too expensive.

Then she was down to the last two sheaves of notes, and I smelled the warm Devonian seas again.

How I killed her was slovenly, sloppily, untidily, random, and rumpled.

As she reached into the clothes closet for her bathrobe I pushed her inside and tried to strangle her. She fought me off and started to come out and I pushed her back. The clothes rack bar fell out of its brackets and we were lying in a heap on the floor. I hit her a couple of times and she hit me back, even harder than I'd hit her. Finally, I grabbed the plastic clothing bag from a dress fresh from the dry cleaners, and suffocated her with it. Then I went into her bathroom and vomited up the prime rib and spinach.

I could feel Sloan's eyes on me as she launched into the recitation of the problems inherent in producing the Can-Do Chipper. The toy was a preschool game that flipped a group of colored chips into the air when the child stomped on a foot pedal. The chips came in four distinct shapes and colors, four of each, with decals on them of bees, birds, fishes, and flowers. The object was for the child to grab as many of his designated decal chips as possible. Some of the squares were yellow with bees, some of the circles were red with flowers, some of the triangles were blue with birds, some of the stars were green with fishes. But some stars had bees on them, some circles had birds on them . . . and so forth. So a child had to identify in that instant the chips were in the air not only its proper decal, but its shape and its color as well.

Netta had given the game to ten groups of four kids each, for "can-do" testing. She had left them alone in the big playroom on the third floor of the Research & Development wing. One needed a yellow color-coded badge to get *onto* the third floor, and a top-clearance red dot in the center of the yellow badge to get into that *wing*.

The children had not responded to the game as I'd indicated they would. They ignored the decals entirely, set up the rules the way *they* wanted to play it, and simply caught shapes or colors. The cost analysis people said we'd save twenty-five thousand dollars by omitting the decals, and I thought I was home free; but Netta added what I thought was a gratuitous observation: "I think the sales potential of this item is drastically reduced by the loss of the decals. There won't be any ready-to-hand advertising lures. In fact, when we gave each child a list of toys they could have for participating in the tests, and this was when we first brought them in, the Can-Do Chipper was in the lowest percentile of choice. And after we observed them through the one-way mirrors playing with the game, and after we showed them the cartoons and the commercials and then told them we'd made an error on the forms and they should *now* pick their prizes, it was the least wanted item on the list."

They scrubbed the project. I was two down for the day.

She went on to the Little Miss Goodie Two-Shoes doll, my Big Breakthrough. It was the last sheaf of test notes, and I harbored the foolish hope that Netta had been playing some kind of deadly stupid lovers' game with me, that she had saved my hottest project for last, so she could recommend it highly. She hung me out to dry.

"This is one of the most dangerous toys I've ever tested," she began. "To refresh your memory, it is a baby doll that contains a voice-activated tape loop. When you say to the doll, 'Good dolly, you're a good dolly,' or similar affectionate phrase, the doll goes *mmmmmm*. When you say, 'Bad dolly, you've been a bad dolly,' or similar hostile phrase, the dolly whimpers. Unfortunately, my tests with a large group of children—" and she looked directly at me, "—which I've cross-checked through our independent testing group at Harvard, clearly show that not only the tape loop is activated by hostile phrases. This toy activates aggression in children, triggering the worst in them and *feeding* it. They were brutal with the dolls, tormenting them, savaging them, tearing them apart when merely spanking them and throwing them against the walls failed to satisfy their need to hear the whimpering."

I was, on the spot, in an instant, a pariah.

I was the despoiler of the children's crusade.

I was the lurking child molester.

I was the lizard piper of Hamelin.

I was, with the good offices of Netta Bernstein, at the end of an auspicious career with the MyToy Corporation.

And the next day she kissed me, surreptitiously, in the elevator; and asked me if I was free to have dinner at her apartment that night.

I left the body in the clothes closet, shoved back in a fetal position under the mound of wrinkled dresses and pants suits. I went out and wandered around the marina till morning, playing the messy murder of Netta Bernstein over and over again. Then I went to work.

I walked past Sloan's office, toward my own, expecting the door to burst open and Sloan to be standing there with a couple of cops. "That's him, officers. The one who wanted us to sell a demon doll. And he killed our research psychologist, a beautiful woman named Netta Bernstein. Take his yellow color-coded badge with the red dot in the center, and get him the hell out of here."

But nothing of the kind happened. Sloan's door stayed closed, I walked past and headed for my office. As I came abreast of Netta's glass-walled office, I glanced in as casually as I had every day and saw Netta poring over a large graph on her desk.

I once visited the Olympic peninsula of Washington state. I thought it was very beautiful, very peaceful. Up beyond the Seattle-Tacoma vicinity. Virgin wilderness. Douglas fir and alder with whitish bark and brownish-red at the tops of the leaves. It's flat, but you can see the Olympic range and the Cascades and Mr. Rainier when the mist and fog and rain aren't obscuring the view. And even the mist and fog and rain seem peaceful, comfortable; cold, but somehow sanctified. A person could live there, fast and hard away from Los Angeles and the freeway stranglehold. But there was no $50,000 plateau on the Olympic peninsula.

I couldn't accept it. I don't think I even broke stride. I just walked past, well down the corridor, leaned against the wall for a moment, and breathed deeply. Staff walked past and Nisbett stopped to ask me if I was all right; I said I was fine, just heartburn, and he said, "Ain't it the truth," and he walked away. I could feel my heart turning to anthracite in my chest. I thought I would die. And then I realized I'd been hallucinating, projecting my guilt, having a delayed reaction to what had happened the night before, to what lay huddled in that clothes closet till I could figure out how to dispose of it.

I got myself under control, swallowing several times to force down the lump, breathing through my mouth to clear the dark fog that had begun to swirl in like the fog of the Olympic peninsula.

And then I turned back, walked slowly to Netta's office, and looked through the window-wall. She was talking to one of her assistants, a young woman who had worked with Madeline Hunter at UCLA, or had it been Iris Mink at UCLA Neuropsychiatric . . . *what the hell was I thinking!*

I had killed Bernstein the night before, had seen her eyes start from her head and her tongue go fat in her mouth and her skin turn dark blue with cyanosis when the strangling failed and the suffocation succeeded. She was meat, dead meat, lying under a pile of coat hangers. She could not possibly be in there talking to her assistant.

I opened the door and walked in.

They both looked up and the assistant stopped talking. Netta looked at me with annoyance and said, "Yes?"

"I, uh, the report, I, uh . . ."

She waited. They both waited. I moved my hands in random patterns. The assistant said, "I'll check it again, Netta, and show it to you after lunch; will that be all right?"

Netta Bernstein nodded it would be all right, and the assistant took the graph and slipped past me, giving me a security guard's look; when was the last time I'd seen a look like that?

When she was gone, Netta turned to me and said, "Well, what is it, Duncaster?"

Netta Bernstein was thirty-seven. I had checked. Her dossier in personnel said she had attended the University of Washington, had obtained her degree in psychology, and had majored in child therapy. She had been married at the age of eighteen, while still an undergraduate to one of her professors, who had soon after their marriage left the academy for a job with Merck Sharp & Dohme, the drug company, in New Jersey. She had remained with him until he had received a federal grant for a research project (unspecified, probably defense-oriented), and they had moved to a remote part of the Olympic peninsula of Washington state, where they had remained for the next sixteen years. Grays Harbor County. The husband had died three years before, and Netta Bernstein had gone to work in Houston, at the Baylor Medical School, department of biochemistry. Research on the RNA messenger molecules; something related to autistic children. She had left Baylor and come to MyToy, for a startling salary, only thirteen months before. She was beautiful, with thick auburn hair and the most penetrating cobalt-colored eyes I had ever seen. Eyes that were wide and dead in a clothes closet near the marina. Before I had killed her, she looked no more than nineteen years old, still as young and beautiful as she must have been when she was an undergraduate at the University of Washington. When I left her she looked like nothing human, certainly nothing living.

I stared at her. She looked nineteen again. There were no black bruises on her throat, her color was fresh and youthful, her cobalt-colored eyes staring at me.

"*Well*, Duncaster?"

I ran away. I hid in my office, waiting for the cops to come. But they never did. I went crazy, waiting. I had all the terrors and the guilt of knowing she would turn me in, that she was playing cobra-at-the-mongoose-rally with me. She hadn't died. Somehow she had still been breathing. I'd *thought* she was dead, but she wasn't dead; she was alive. Down the hall, waiting for me to throw myself out a window or run shrieking through the corridors screaming my confession. Well, I wouldn't do it! I'd outsmart her, I'd make sure she never told anyone about the night before.

I left the building by the service elevator, went to her apartment, and used the key I'd stolen the night before in anticipation of returning to dispose of the body. The first thing I did was check the clothes closet.

It was empty. The clothes were hung neatly. The dress with the plastic clothing bag from the dry cleaner was hanging among the others. There was no sign I'd even been there, that we had had dinner together, that we'd made love, that we'd argued over her performance in the conference room, that she'd denied meaning me any harm, that she had professed her love . . . and no sign I had killed her.

The apartment was silent and had never been the scene of a battlefield engagement for possession of the $50,000 plateau. I thought I might, indeed, be going crazy.

But when she got home, I killed Bernstein. Again.

I used a wooden cooking mallet intended to soften meat. I crushed her skull and wrapped her in the shower curtain and tied up her feet and torso with baling twine from under the sink. I attached a typewriter to the end of the cord, an IBM Selectric, and I carried her out to the marina at three a.m. had threw her in.

And the next day, Netta Bernstein was in her office, and she paid no attention to me, and I thought I'd go crazy, perhaps I'd *already* gone crazy. And that night I killed her with a tire iron and buried her body in the remotest part of Topanga Canyon. And the next day . . .

She didn't come to work.

They told me she had taken a leave of absence, had gone to Washington state on family business.

I ransacked the dossier and found the location. I flew up from LA International to the Sea-Tac Airport and rented a car. West from Olympia toward Aberdeen. North on Highway 101. Twenty miles north. I turned west and drove for fifteen miles, and came to the high wire fence.

I could see the long, low structure of the research facility where Netta Bernstein had lived with her husband for sixteen years. I got in. I don't remember how. I got in, that's all.

I circled the building, looking for a way inside, and when a crack of lightning flashed down the slate of the sky I saw my reflection in a window, wild-eyed and more than a little crazy. It was terribly cold, and I could smell the rain coming.

I found a set of doors and they were open. I went into the building. I went looking, wanting only one thing: to find Netta Bernstein, to kill her once again, finally, completely, thoroughly, without room for argument or return.

There was music coming from somewhere far off in the building. Electronic music. I followed the sound and passed through research facilities, laboratories whose purpose I could not identify, and came, at last, to the living quarters at the rear of the building.

They were waiting for me.

Seven of them.

Netta times seven.

The husband had been a geneticist. Fallen in love with an eighteen-year-old, auburn-haired, cobalt-colored-eyed undergraduate he met at a lecture. He had cloned her. Had taken the cutting and run off nine copies that had been raised from infancy, that had grown up quickly as she aged so slowly, so beautifully. Netta times ten. And when they had raised their children, there, far away from all eyes and all interference, he had died and left the mother with her offspring; left the woman with her sisters; left the thirty-four-year-old original with her sixteen-year-old duplicates. And

Netta had had to go out into the world to make a living, to the drug company, to Baylor, to MyToy.

But when she wanted to return to see herself in the mirrors of their lives, she would call one or two or another of the Nettas to come do her work at MyToy.

And one of them had fallen in love with me.

Killing Bernstein was impossible. Killing Netta, because love had made me crazy, was beyond anyone's power, beyond even madness and hatred.

And one of them had fallen in love with me.

I sat down and they watched me. They had removed the body of their sister from the closet, and they had brought her back home for burial. And soon they would return to Los Angeles and drive up into wild Topanga Canyon and dig up another. And the third they would never see again.

And one of them had fallen in love with me.

Here on the Olympic peninsula, the fog and the mist and the rain are cool and almost sanctified. There is music, and they don't harm me, and some day they may let me leave. They don't bind me, they don't keep me from going out into the night; but this is where I'll stay.

And perhaps some day, when they clone again, perhaps I'll get lucky again.

And perhaps one of them will fall in love with me.

LEG MAN

Erle Stanley Gardner

Erle Stanley Gardner (1889–1970) was one of the best-selling writers of all time—and one of the most prolific. When you put together his pulp magazine work with his novels, you have to add him to any list that includes Simenon and at least two members of the Dumas family for being mind-numbingly prolific. He did it all as far as mystery fiction was concerned—puzzles, noir, light comedy, howdunits, whydunits, and on and on—and he did it all competently and some of it much better than that. His comic novels under the pseudonym A. A. Faire are probably his best, with *The Bigger They Come* and *Bats Fly at Dusk* fetching as hell. His great successes were the Perry Mason novels and the long-running TV series of the same name. Gardner was a lawyer before turning to writing fiction, and he knew how to make trials exciting. He is easy, too easy, to undervalue.

MAE DEVERS CAME into my office with the mail. She stood by my chair for a moment putting envelopes on the desk, pausing to make little adjustments of the inkwell and paper weights, tidying things up a bit.

There was a patent-leather belt around her waist, and below that belt I could see the play of muscles as her supple figure moved from side to side. I slid my arm around the belt and started to draw her close to me.

"Don't get fresh!" she said, trying to pull my hand away, but not trying too hard.

"Listen, I have work to do," she said. "Let me loose, Pete."

"Holding you for ransom, smile-eyes," I told her.

She suddenly bent down. Her lips formed a hot circle against mine—and Cedric L. Boniface had to choose that moment to come busting into my office without knocking.

Mae heard the preliminary rattle of the door-knob, and scooped up a bunch of papers from the desk. I ran fingers through my hair, and Boniface cleared his throat in his best professional manner.

I couldn't be certain whether I had any lipstick on my mouth, so I put my elbow on my desk, covered my mouth with the fingers of my hand and stared intently at an open law book.

Mae Devers said, "Very well, Mr. Wennick, I'll see that it gets in the mail," and started for the door. As she passed Boniface, she turned and gave me a roguish glance, as much as to say, "Now, smartie, see what you've got yourself into."

Boniface stared at me, hard. His yellowish eyes, with the bluish-white eyeballs, reminded me of hard-boiled eggs which had been peeled and cut in two lengthwise. He was in a vile humor.

"What was all the commotion about?" he asked.

"Commotion?" I inquired raising my eyes, but keeping my hand to my mouth. "Where?"

"In here," he said.

Mae Devers was just closing the door. "Did you hear anything, Miss Devers?" I asked in my most dignified manner.

"No, sir," she said demurely, and slipped out into the corridor.

I frowned down at the open law book on the desk. "I can't seem to make any sense out of the distinction between a bailment of the first class and a bailment of the second class."

That mollified Boniface somewhat. He loved to discourse on the academic legal points which no one else ever gave a damn about.

"The distinction," he said, "is relatively simple, if you can keep from becoming confused by the terminology. Primarily, the matter of consideration is the determining factor in the classification of all bailments."

"Yes, sir," I said, my voice muffled behind my hand.

Boniface stared at me. "Wennick," he said, "there's something queer about your connection with this firm. You're supposed to be studying law. You're supposed to make investigations. You're a cross between a sublimated law clerk and a detective. It just happens, however, that in checking over our income tax, I find that the emoluments which have been paid you during the past three months would fix your salary at something over fifteen thousand dollars a year."

There was nothing I could say to that, so I kept quiet.

Mae Devers opened the door and said, "Mr. Jonathan wants to see you at once, Mr. Wennick."

I got out of the chair as though it had been filled with tacks and said, "I'm coming at once. Excuse me, Mr. Boniface."

Mae Devers stood in the doorway which led to the general offices and laughed at me as I jerked out a handkerchief and wiped lipstick from my mouth. "That," she told me, "is what you get for playing around."

I didn't have time to say anything. When old E. B. Jonathan sent word that he wanted to see me at once, it meant that he wanted to see me at once. Cedric L. Boniface followed me to the door of my office and stared meditatively down the corridor as though debating with himself whether or not to invade the sanctity of E. B.'s office to pursue the subject further. I popped into E. B's private office like a rabbit making its burrow two jumps ahead of a fox.

Old E. B. looked worse than ever this morning. His face was the color of skimmed milk. There were pouches underneath his tired eyes as big as my fist. His face was puckered up into the acrimonious expression of one who has just bit into a sour lemon.

"Lock the door, Wennick," he said.

I locked the door.

"Take a seat."

I sat down.

"Wennick," he said, "we're in a devil of a mess."

I sat there, waiting for him to go on.

"There was some question over certain deductions in my income tax statement," he said. "Without thinking, I told Mr. Boniface to brief the point. That made it necessary for him to consult the income tax return, and he saw how much you'd been paid for the last three months."

"So he was just telling me," I said.

"Well," E. B. said, "it's embarrassing. I need Boniface in this business. He can spout more academic law than a college professor, and he's so damn dumb he doesn't know that I'm using him for a stuffed shirt. No one would ever suspect him of being implicated in the—er, more spectacular methods which you use to clean up the cases on which he's working."

"Yes," I conceded, "the man's a veritable talking encyclopedia of law."

E. B. said, "We'll have to handle it some way. If he asks you any questions, tell him it's a matter you'd prefer to have him discuss with me. Wennick! Is that lipstick on the corner of your mouth?"

Mechanically, I jerked a handkerchief out of my pocket to the corner of my mouth. "No, sir," I said, "just a bit of red crayon I was using to mark up that brief and . . ."

I stopped as I saw E. B.'s eyes on the handkerchief. It was a red smear. There was no use lying to the old buzzard now. I stuck the handkerchief back in my pocket and said, "Hell, yes, it's lipstick."

"Miss Devers, I presume," he said dryly.

I didn't say anything.

"I'm afraid," he said, "it's going to be necessary to dispense with her services. At the time I hired her, I thought she was just a bit too—er, voluptuous. However, she was so highly recommended by the employment agency that—"

"It's all right," I said. "Go ahead and fire her."

"You won't mind?"

"Certainly not," I told him. "I can get a job some other place and get one for her at the same time."

"Now, wait a minute, Wennick," he said, "don't misunderstand me. I'm very well satisfied with your services, if you could only learn to leave women alone."

I decided I might as well give him both barrels. "Listen," I said, "you think women are poison. I think they're damned interesting. The only reason I'm not going to ask you whether the rumor is true that you're paying simultaneous alimony to two wives is that I don't think I have any business inquiring into your private life, and the only reason I'm not going to sit here and talk about my love life is that I know damned well you haven't any business prying into mine."

His long, bony fingers twisted restlessly, one over the other, as he wrapped his fists together. Then he started cracking his knuckles, one at a time.

"Wennick," he said at length, "I have great hopes for your future. I hate to see you throw yourself away on the fleeting urge of a biological whim."

"All right," I told him, "I won't."

He finished his ten-knuckle salute and shook his head lugubriously. "They'll get you in the long run, Wennick," he said.

"I'm not interested in long runs," I told him. "I like the sprints."

He sighed, unlaced his fingers and got down to business. "The reason I'm particularly concerned about this, Wennick, is that the case I'm going to send you out on involves a woman, a very attractive woman. Unless I'm sadly mistaken, she is a very vital woman, very much alive, very—er, amorous."

"Who is she?" I asked.

"Her name is Pemberton, Mrs. Olive Pemberton. Her husband's Harvey C. Pemberton, of the firm of Bass & Pemberton, Brokers, in Culverton."

"What does she want?" I asked.

"Her husband's being taken for a ride."

"What sort of a ride?"

He let his cold eyes regard me in a solemn warning. "A joy ride, Pete."

"Who's the woman?"

Old E. B. consulted a memo. "Her name is Diane Locke—and she's redheaded."

"What do I do?"

"You find some way to spike her guns. Apparently she has an ironclad case against Pemberton. I'll start Boniface working on it. He'll puzzle out some legal technicality on which he'll hang a defense. But you beat him to it by spiking her guns."

"Has the redhead filed suit?" I asked.

"Not yet," E. B. said. "At present it's in the milk-and-honey stage. She's getting ready to tighten the screws, and Mrs. Pemberton has employed us to see that this other woman doesn't drain her husband's pocketbook with this threatened suit. Incidentally, you're to stay at the Pemberton house, and remember, Mr. Pemberton doesn't know his wife is wise to all this and is trying to stop it."

"Just how," I asked, "do I account for my presence to Mr. Harvey C. Pemberton?"

"You're to be Mrs. Pemberton's brother."

"How do you figure that?"

"Mrs. Pemberton has a brother living in the West. Her husband has never seen him. Fortunately, his name also is Peter, so you won't have any difficulty over names."

"Suppose," I asked, "the real brother shows up while I'm there at the house?"

"He won't," E. B. said. "All you have to do is to go to the door at seven-thirty this evening. She'll be waiting for your ring. She'll come to the door and put on all the act that's necessary. You'll wear a red carnation in your left coat lapel so there'll be no mistake. Her maiden name, by the way, was Crowe. You'll be Peter Crowe, sort of a wandering ne'er-do-well brother. The husband knows all about you by reputation."

"And hasn't seen any pictures or anything?" I asked.

"Apparently not," E. B. said.

"It sounds like a plant to me," I told him dubiously.

"I'm quite certain it's all right," he said. "I have collected a substantial retainer."

"O.K.," I told him, "I'm on my way."

"Pete," he called, as I placed my hand on the door.

"What is it?"

"You'll be discreet," he warned.

I turned to give him a parting shot. "I certainly hope I'll be able to," I said, "but I doubt it," and pulled the door shut behind me.

ILOOKED AT my wrist watch, saw I had three minutes to go, and put the red carnation in the left lapel of my coat. I'd already spotted the house. It was a big, rambling affair which oozed an atmosphere of suburban prosperity. I took it that Bass & Pemberton, Brokers, had an income which ran into the upper brackets.

I jerked down my vest, adjusted the knot in my tie, smoothed the point of my collar, and marched up the front steps promptly at seven-thirty. I jabbed the bell. I heard slow, dignified masculine steps in the corridor. That wasn't what E. B. had led me to expect. I wondered for a moment if there'd been a hitch in plans and I was going to have to face the husband. The door opened. I took one look at the sour puss on the guy standing in the doorway and knew he was the butler. He was looking at me as a judge looks at a murderer when I heard a feminine squeal and caught a flying glimpse of a woman with jet-black hair, dusky olive complexion and a figure that would get by anywhere. She gave a squeal of delight and flung her arms around my neck.

"Pete!" she screamed. "Oh, Pete, you darling. You dear! I knew you'd look me up if you ever came near here."

The butler stepped back and coughed. The woman hugged me, jumped up and down in an ecstasy of glee, then said, "Let me look at you." She stepped back, her hands on my shoulders, her eyes studying me.

Up to that point, it had been rehearsed, but the rest of it wasn't. I saw approval in her eyes, a certain trump-this-ace expression, and she tilted her head to offer me her lips.

I don't know just what E. B. referred to as being discreet. I heard the butler cough more violently. I guess he didn't know she had a brother. I let her lead. She led with an ace. I came up for air, to see a short-coupled chap with a tight vest regarding me from brown, mildly surprised eyes. Back of him was a tall guy fifteen years older, with fringes of what had once been red hair around his ears. The rest of his dome was bald. He had a horse face, and the march of time had done things to it. It was a face which showed character.

Mrs. Pemberton said, "Pete, you've never met my husband."

The chunky chap stepped forward and I shoved out my hand. "Well, well, well," I said, "so this is Harvey. How are you, Harvey?"

"And Mr. Bass, my husband's partner," she said.

I shook hands with the tall guy. "Pete Crowe, my rolling-stone brother," Mrs. Pemberton observed. "Where's your baggage, Pete?"

"I left it down at the station," I told her.

She laughed nervously and said, "It's just like you to come without sending a wire. We'll drive down and pick up your baggage."

"Got room for me?" I asked.

"Have we!" she exclaimed. "I've just been dying to see you. Harvey is so busy with his mergers and his horrid old business that I don't ever get a chance to see him any more. You're a God-send."

Harvey put his arm around his wife's waist. "There, there, little girl," he said, "it won't be much longer, and then we'll take a vacation. We can go for a cruise somewhere. How about the South Seas?"

"Is that a promise?" she asked.

"That's a promise," he told her so solemnly I felt certain he was lying.

"You've made promises before," she pouted, "but something new always came up in the business."

"Well, it won't come up this time. I'll even sell the business before I get in another spell of work like this."

I caught him glancing significantly at his partner.

"We've just finished dinner," Mrs. Pemberton explained to me, "and Mr. Bass and my husband are going back to their stuffy old office. How about going down and picking up your baggage now?"

"Anything you say," I told her, leaving it up to her to take the lead.

"Come on then," she invited. "Harvey's car is out front. Mine's in the garage. We'll go get it out. Oh, you darling! I'm so glad to see you!" And she went into another clinch.

Harvey Pemberton regarded me with a patronizing smile. "Olive's told me a lot about you, Pete," he said. "I'm looking forward to a chance to talk with you."

Bass took a cigar from his pocket. "Is Pete the one who did all the big game hunting down in Mexico?" he asked.

"That's the one," Mrs. Pemberton told him.

Bass said, "You and I must have a good long chat some time, young man. I used to be a forest ranger when I was just out of school. I was located up in the Upper Sespe, and the Pine Mountain country. I suppose you know the section."

"I've hunted all over it," I said.

He nodded. "I was ranger there for three years. Well, come on, Harvey, let's go down and go over those figures."

"We go out the back way," Olive Pemberton told me, grabbing my hand and hurrying me out a side door. She skipped on ahead toward the garage. "Hurry," she said. "They have a conference on at their office and I want to hear what it's about."

She jerked open the garage door. I helped her into the car and she smiled her thanks as she adjusted herself in the seat. "I like my feet free when I'm driving," she said, pulling her skirt up to her knees.

She had pretty legs.

I climbed in beside her and she started the motor. We went out of there like a fire wagon charging down the main stem of a hick town. Her husband and Bass were just getting into their car as we hit the incline to the street. The car flattened down on its springs, then shot up in the air. I hung on. I heard rubber scream as she spun the wheel, waved her hand to her husband, and went streaking down the street.

"You always drive like that?" I asked.

"Most of the time," she said. "Sometimes I go faster."

"No wonder you want your feet free," I told her.

She glanced down at her legs, then her eyes were back on the road. "I want to beat them there," she explained. "I've bribed the janitor and I have an office next to theirs." She stepped harder on the gas, angrily.

"Hope I didn't scare you with my greeting," she said, with a sidelong glance. "I had to act cordial, you know."

"I like cordiality," I told her. "It becomes you."

She gave attention to her driving. It was the sort of driving which needed lots of attention. She reached the business section of town, hogged the traffic, crowded the signals at the intersections, and whipped the car into a parking lot. She said, "Come on, Pete," and led the way toward a seven-story building which apparently was the town's best in the way of office buildings.

"It's fortunate your name's really Pete," she commented as we entered the building.

I nodded and let it go at that. I was sizing her up out of the corner of my eye. She was one of these supple women who seem to be just about half panther. She must have been around thirty-two or three, but her figure and walk were what you'd expect to find on a woman in the early twenties. There was a peculiar husky note to her voice, and her eyes were just a little bit more than provocative.

The night elevators were on. The janitor came up in response to her ring. His face lit up like a Christmas tree when he saw her. He looked over at me and looked dubious.

"It's all right, Olaf," she said. "This man's helping me. Hurry up because my husband's coming."

We got in the cage. Olaf slammed the door and sent us rattling upward, his eyes feasting on Olive's profile. I've seen dogs look at people with exactly that same expression—inarticulate love and a dumb, blind loyalty.

He let us out at the sixth floor. "This way," she said, and walked on ahead of me down the corridor.

I noticed the swing of her hips as she walked. I think she wanted me to—not that she gave a particular damn about me, she was simply one of those women who like to tease the animals—or was she making a play for me?

"No chance of the janitor selling you out?" I asked as she fitted a key in the lock.

"No," she said.

"You seem to have a lot of faith in human nature," I told her, as she clicked back the lock and snapped on lights in the office.

"I have," she told me, "in masculine nature. Men always play fair with me. It's women who double-cross me. I hate women."

THE OFFICE WAS bare of furnishings, save for a battered stenographer's desk, a couple of straightback chairs, an ash-tray and waste basket. Wires ran down from a hole in the plaster, to terminate in an electrical gadget. She opened a drawer in the desk, took out two head pieces and handed me one. "When you hear my husband come in the next office," she said, "plug that in, and remember what you hear. I think things are coming to a show-down tonight."

I sat across from her and nursed the last of my cigarette. "Anything in particular I'm supposed to do about it?" I asked.

"Of course," she said.

"What?" I asked.

"That's up to you."

"Want me to bust things up with a club?" I asked.

She studied me with her dark, seductive eyes. "I may as well be frank with you," she said in that rich, throaty voice. "I don't care a thing in the world about my husband. I don't think he cares any more about me. A separation is inevitable. When it happens I want my share of the property."

"What's the property?" I asked her.

"Mostly a partnership interest," she said. "He's a free spender and he's been stepping around high, wide and handsome. After a man gets to be forty-three and starts stepping around, it takes money.

"So far, he's been just a mild sugar daddy. I haven't cared particularly just so there was plenty for me to spend. But now he's put his neck in a noose. This Diane Locke is shrewd. She's too damn shrewd, or maybe somebody with brains is back of her. I think it must be a lawyer somewhere. Anyway, they have Harvey over a barrel. He needs money, lots of money. The only way he can get it is to sell his partnership interest. You heard that crack he made about selling out so he could take me on a cruise."

I nodded.

"Well," she said, "if that's what's in the wind, I'm going to throw a lot of monkey wrenches in that machinery."

I did a little thinking. "The redhead," I said, "might open her bag, take out a nice, pearl-handled gun, and go rat-a-tat-tat. They have been known to do that, you know."

It was just a feeler. I wanted to see what she'd say. She said it. "That's all right, too. There's a big life insurance policy in my favor. But what I don't want is to have him stripped. He—Here they come now."

I heard the elevator door clang. There were steps in the corridor, then I heard keys rattling and the door in the adjoining office creaked back and I heard the click of the light switch. Mrs. Pemberton nodded to me, and I plugged in the jack and put the ear pieces over my head. She snapped a switch, and I could hear faint humming noises in the ear pieces. Then I heard a voice that I recognized as Bass' saying, "But, Harvey, why the devil do you want to sell out?"

"I want to play a little bit," Harvey Pemberton said. "I want to have a real honeymoon with my wife before I'm too old to enjoy it. We've never traveled. I married her four years ago, when we were putting through that big hotel deal. And I've had my nose pushed against the grindstone ever since. We never had a honeymoon."

"What are you going to do after you get back?"

"I don't know."

"You could arrange things so you could take a honeymoon without selling out," Bass said. "I hate to lose you as a partner, Harvey."

"No, I wouldn't leave a business behind in which I had all my money tied up," Pemberton said. "I'd worry about it so I'd be rotten companion. I want to step out footloose and fancy-free."

"One of the reasons I don't want you to do it right now," Bass said, "is that I'm rather short of money myself. I couldn't offer you anywhere near what your interest in the business is worth."

"What could you offer?" Pemberton said, an edge to his voice.

"I don't know," I heard Bass say.

"Oh, come," Pemberton told him impatiently. "You can't pull that stuff with me, Arthur. I told you this afternoon that I wanted to figure on some sort of a deal. You've had all afternoon to think it over."

There was silence for several seconds, and I gathered that Bass was, perhaps, making figures on paper. I heard Harvey Pemberton say, "I'm going to have an accountant work up a statement showing the status of the business and—"

"That doesn't have anything to do with it," Bass said. "It's not a question of what the business is worth, it's a question of what I can afford to pay without jeopardizing my working capital. I'll tell you frankly, Harvey, that I don't want you to sell. I don't want to lose you as a partner and you can't get anything like a fair value for your holdings at the present time. There's no one else you can sell them to. Under our articles of partnership, one partner has to give the other six months' notice before—"

"I understand all that," Pemberton said impatiently. "What's the price?"

"Ten thousand," Bass said.

"Ten thousand!" Pemberton shouted. "My God, you're crazy! The business is worth fifty thousand. I'm going to have an audit made in order to determine a fair figure. But I know my share's worth twenty-five. I'll take twenty for it, and that's the lowest price I'll even consider."

There was relief in Bass' voice. "That settles it then and I'm glad to hear it! You know, Pemberton, I was afraid you were in a jam over money matters and might have considered ten thousand dollars. It would be an awful mistake. I don't want you to sell."

Pemberton started to swear. Bass said, "Well, I'm glad we have an understanding on that, Harvey. Of course, I wouldn't try to exert any pressure to hold you here. In some ways it would be a good business deal for me to buy you out now. But I don't want to do it, either for my sake or yours. I'd have paid you every cent I could have scraped up, but—well, I'm glad you're staying. The business needs you, and I need you, and you need the business. Well, I'll be going. See you later. Good night."

Over the electrical gadget came the sound of a slamming door. Pemberton yelled, "Come back here, Arthur! I want to talk with you," but there was no other sound. I exchanged glances with our client.

"You see," she said, "he's trying to sell the business. That vamp would get most of the money. He'd probably run away with her. I want you to stop that."

"What's the program now?" I asked.

"I think he has an appointment with her," she said. "The janitor told me that he'd left instructions to pass a young woman to his office."

Pretty soon I heard the clang of the elevator door, and light, quick steps in the corridor past our door, then a gentle tapping on the panels of the adjoining office. I put the head phones back on, and heard the sound of a door opening and closing.

"Did you bring the letters?" Harvey Pemberton asked.

A woman's voice said, "Don't be such an old granny. Kiss me, and quit worrying about the letters. They're in a safe place."

"You said you could put your hand on them any time," Pemberton charged, "and were going to bring them here to show me just what I'd written."

"I brought you copies instead," she said. "My lawyer wouldn't let me take the originals."

"Why not?"

"I don't know. I guess he doesn't trust me. Harvey, I don't want you to think that I'm utterly mercenary, but you broke my heart. It isn't money I'm after, dear, I want you. But you hurt me, and I went to that horrid lawyer, and he had me sign some papers, and now it seems I have to go through with it, unless you go away with me. That's what I want."

"*My* lawyer tells me you can't sue a married man for breach of promise," Pemberton interrupted. "I think your lawyer is a shyster who's trying to stir up trouble and turn you into a blackmailer."

"No, he isn't, Harvey. There's some wrinkle in the law. If a girl doesn't know a man's married and he conceals that fact from her, why then he can be sued for breach of promise, just the same as though he hadn't been married. Oh, Harvey, I don't want to deal with all these lawyers! I want you. Can't you divorce that woman and come with me?"

"Apparently not," Harvey Pemberton said. "Since you've been such a little fool and signed your life away to this lawyer, he isn't going to let me get free. There's enough stuff in those letters to keep me from getting a divorce from my wife, and she won't get a divorce from me unless I turn over everything in the world to her. She wants to strip me clean. You want to do almost that."

For a moment there was silence, then the sound of a woman sobbing.

Pemberton started speaking again. His voice rose and fell at regular intervals, and I gathered he was walking the floor and talking as he walked. "Go ahead and sob," he said. "Sit there and bawl into your handkerchief! And if you want to know it, it looks fishy as hell to me. When I first met you on that steamboat, you didn't have any of this bawling complex. You wanted to play around."

"You w-w-wanted to m-m-marry me!" she wailed.

"All right," he told her, "I was on the up-and-up on that, too. I thought my wife was going to get a divorce. Hell's fire, I didn't *have* to use marriage for bait. You know that. That came afterward. Then, when I break a date with you because of a business deal, you rush up to see this lawyer."

"I went to him as a friend," she said in a wailing, helpless voice. "I'd known him for years. He told me you'd been t-t-trifling with me and I should get r-revenge. After all, all I want is just enough to get me b-b-back on my feet once more."

Pemberton said, "Add that to what your lawyer wants, and see where that leaves me. Why the hell don't you ditch the lawyer?"

"I c-can't. He made me sign papers."

Once more there was silence, then Pemberton said, "How the hell do I know you're on the level? You could have engineered this whole business."

"You know me better than that," she sobbed.

"I'm not so certain I do," Pemberton told her. "You were a pushover for me and now—"

Her voice came in good and strong then. "All right, then," she said, "if you don't want the pill sugar-coated we'll make it bitter. I'm getting tired of putting on this sob-sister act for you. I never saw a sucker who was so damn dumb in my life. You seem to think a middle-aged old gander is going to get a sweet, innocent girl to fall for just your own sweet self. Bunk! If you'd been a good spender, taken what you wanted and left me with a few knick-knacks, I'd have thought you were swell. But you thought I was an innocent little kid who'd fall for this Model T line of yours. All right, get a load of this: You're being stood up. And what're you going to do about it? I have your letters. They show the kind of game you were trying to play. So quit stalling."

"So that's it, is it?" he said. "You've been a dirty double-crosser all along."

"Oh, I'm a double-crosser, am I? Just a minute, Mr. Harvey Pemberton, and I'll read from one of your letters. Figure how it will sound to the jury.

" 'Remember, sweetheart, that except for the silly conventions of civilization, we are already man and wife. There is, of course, a ceremony to be performed, but I'll attend to that just as soon as I can arrange certain business details. It would hurt certain business plans which are rapidly coming to maturity if I should announce I was going to marry you right now. I ask you to have confidence in me, sweetheart, and to know that I cherish you. I could no more harm you than I could crush a beautiful rose. I love you, my sweetheart—' " She broke off and said, "God knows how much more of that drivel there is."

"You dirty, double-crossing tramp," he said.

Her voice sounded less loud. I gathered she'd moved over toward the door. "Now then," she said, "quit stalling. You have twenty-four hours. Either put up or shut up."

I heard the door slam, then the click of heels in the hall, and, after a moment, the clang of an elevator door.

All was silent in the other office.

I SLIPPED THE head piece off my head.

"Well," Mrs. Pemberton said, "there it is in a nutshell. I suppose he'll sell out to Bass for about half what his interest is worth and that little redhead will get it all."

"How do you know she's redheaded?" I asked.

"I've seen her and I've had detectives on her tail turning up her past and trying to get something on her. I can't uncover a thing on her, though. She dressed the window for this play."

"All right," I told her, "let your husband go ahead and fight. Even if he can't prove anything, a jury isn't going to give her so much in the line of damages."

"It isn't that alone," she said, "it's a question of the letters. He writes foolish letters. Whenever he loses his head, he goes all the way. He can't learn to keep his fountain pen in his pocket. Remember that Bass & Pemberton have some rather influential clients. They can't carry out business unless those clients believe in the business acumen of the members of the partnership."

"Those things blow over," I told her. "Your husband could take a trip to Europe."

"You don't understand," she said. "He made a fool of himself once before. That's why Bass had a clause in the partnership contract. Each of them put in two thousand dollars when they started the partnership. The articles of partnership provide that neither can sell his interest without first giving six months' notice to his partner. And then there's some provision in the contract by which Bass can buy Harvey out by returning the original two thousand dollars to him if Harvey gets in any more trouble with women. I don't know the exact provision. Now then, I want you to nip this thing in the bud. Harvey's desperate. Something's got to be done within twenty-four hours."

"All right," I told her, "I'll see what I can do. What's the girl's address?"

"Diane Locke, apartment 3A, forty-two fifteen Center Street. And it won't do you any good to try and frame her, because she's wise to all the tricks. I think she's a professional; but try and prove it."

"One thing more," I told her. "I want the name of the lawyer."

"You mean Diane Locke's lawyer?"

"Yes."

"I can't give it to you."

"Why not?"

"I don't know it," she said. "He's keeping very much in the background. He's some friend of the girl's. Probably he's afraid, he might be disbarred for participating in a blackmail action."

"How long has this thing been going on?" I asked.

"You mean the affair with that redhead? It started—"

"No," I said, "I mean this," indicating the office with a sweep of my hand.

"Since I couldn't get anywhere with the detective agency," she said. "Olaf, the janitor, is an electrician. He helped me rig things up. He got some old parts—"

"Think you can trust him?"

"With my life," she said.

I lit a cigarette and said, "How about the wash-room? Is it open?"

"I'll have to give you my key," she told me, opening her handbag. Then she hesitated a second and said, "I think it's in another purse. But the lock's mostly ornamental. Any key will work it. Or you can use the tip of a penknife."

I looked down into her handbag. "What's the idea of the gun?"

"For protection," she said, closing the bag.

"All right," I told her, "pass it over. I'm your protection now. You'll get in trouble with that gun."

She hesitated a moment while I held my hand out, then reluctantly took the gun from her purse and hesitated with it in her hand.

"But suppose you're not with me, and something should happen? Suppose he should find the wires and follow them in here and catch me?"

"Keep with me all the time," I told her.

The business end of the gun waved around in a half-circle. "Want me to go with you now?" she asked.

"Don't be a sap," I told her. "I'm going to the wash-room. I'll be right back."

"And if my husband comes in while you're gone, I suppose I'm to tell him it's no fair, that you're seeing a man about a dog, and he mustn't choke me until you get back."

I strode over to the door. "Keep your plaything until I come back," I said. "When we go out, you either get rid of the gun, or get rid of me. You're the one who's paying the money, so you can take your choice."

I crossed the office to the door, opened it, and pushed the catch so I could open the door from the outside. I wondered what would happen if Harvey Pemberton should make up his mind to go to the wash-room while I was in there, or should meet me in the corridor. I'd kill that chance by going to the floor below. I saw stairs to the right of the elevator, and went down.

The men's room was at the far end of the corridor. The first key on my ring did the trick.

Five minutes later, when I got back to Mrs. Pemberton, I saw that she was nervous and upset.

"What's the matter?" I asked. "Did something happen?"

She said in a nervous, strained voice, "I was just thinking of what would happen if my husband ran into you in the corridor."

I said, "Well, he didn't."

"You shouldn't take chances like that," she told me.

I grinned. "I didn't. I ran down the stairs for a couple of flights and used the room on the fourth floor."

Her face showed relief. "All right," I told her, "let's go. We'll pick up my baggage and then I'm going to take you home. Then, if you don't mind, I'll borrow your car. I have work to do."

"Have you any plan?" she asked.

"I'm an opportunist."

"All right," she said, "let's go. We'd better run down the stairs and ring the elevator from the lower floor."

We started for the door. She clicked out the light.

"Just a minute," I told her. "You're forgetting something."

"What?"

"The gun."

"It's all right. I thought it over. I decided you were right about it, so I ditched the gun."

"Where?"

"In the desk drawer."

I switched the lights back on and went over to look.

"The upper right-hand drawer," she said, her voice showing amusement.

I opened the drawer. The gun was there. I picked it up, started to put it in my pocket, then changed my mind and dropped it back in the drawer. "Come on," I told her, closing the drawer and switching off the lights.

We sneaked across the hall and down the flight of stairs to the lower floor. I rang for the elevator. Olaf brought the cage up and I took another look at him. He was a big raw-boned Swede with a bony nose, a drooping blond mustache, and dog eyes. His eyes never left Mrs. Pemberton all the way down to the ground floor.

Mrs. Pemberton kept her head turned away from him, toward the side of the elevator shaft, watching the doors creep by. When we got to the ground floor, she turned and looked at him. It was some look. His eyes glowed back at her like a couple of coals. Olaf opened the door, I took Mrs. Pemberton's arm and we crossed over to the parking station.

"I'll drive," I told her. "I want to get accustomed to the car."

I drove down to the station, got my baggage and drove Mrs. Pemberton back out to the house. The butler carried my things up and showed me my room.

After he left, I opened my suit-case. There were two guns in it. I selected one with a shiny leather shoulder holster. I put it on under my coat and knocked on the door of Mrs. Pemberton's room.

She opened the door and stood in the doorway. The light was behind her, throwing shadows of seductive curves through billowy, gossamer silk. I resolutely kept my eyes on her face. "I'm going out," I told her. "Will you hear me when I come in?"

"Yes," she said. "I'll wait up."

"If I cough when I pass your door, it means I have good news for you. If I don't cough, it means things aren't going so well."

She nodded, stepped toward me so that her lithe body was very close to mine. She put her hand on my arm and said in that peculiar, throaty voice of hers, "Please be careful."

I nodded and turned away. My eyes hadn't strayed once. Walking down the corridor and tiptoeing down the stairs, I reflected that I never had known a woman with that peculiar husky note in her voice who didn't like to tease the animals.

FORTY-TWO FIFTEEN CENTER Street was a three-story frame apartment house, the lower floor given over to stores. A doorway from the street opened on a flight of stairs. I tried the door, and it was unlocked.

I went back to sit in the car and think. It was queer the lawyer had never appeared in the picture except as a shadowy figure. No one knew his name. He was quoted freely, but he left it up to his client to do all the negotiating. Therefore, if the racket turned out to be successful, the client would be the one to collect the money. Then it would be up to her to pay the lawyer. That didn't sound right to me. It was like adding two and two and getting two as the answer.

I looked the block over. There was a little jewelry store in the first floor of the apartment house. It was closed up now, with a night light in the window, showing a few cheap wrist watches and some costume jewelry.

I drove around the corner and parked the car. A catch-all drugstore was open. I went in, bought some adhesive tape, a small bottle of benzine, a package of cotton, a writing pad and a police whistle. "Got any cheap imitation pearls?" I asked the clerk.

He had some strings at forty-nine cents. I took one of those. Then I went out to the car, cut the string of pearls and threw all but four of them away. I pulled a wad of cotton out of the box, put the four pearls in the cotton and stuffed the wad in my pocket. I popped the pasteboard off the back of the writing pad, cut two eyeholes in it and a place for my nose. I reinforced it with adhesive tape and left ends of adhesive tape on it so I could put it on at a moment's notice. Then I climbed the stairs of the apartment house and located apartment 3A.

There was a light inside the apartment. I could hear the sound of a radio, and gathered the door wasn't very thick. I took a small multiple-tool holder from my pocket and fitted a gimlet into the handle. I put a little grease on the point of the gimlet, bent over and went to work.

The best place to bore a hole in a paneled door is in the upper right- or left-hand corner of the lower panel. The wood is almost paper-thin there and doesn't take much of a hole to give a complete view of a room. Detectives have used it from time immemorial, but it's still a good trick. After the hole is bored, a little chewing gum keeps light from coming through the inside of the door and attracting the attention of a casual passer-by.

Making certain the corridor was deserted, I dropped to one knee and peeked through the hole I'd made. The girl was redheaded, all right. She was listening to the radio and reading a newspaper.

Watching through one hole to make certain that she didn't move in case my gimlet made any noise, I bored two more holes. That gave me a chance to see all of the apartment there was. I put a thin coating of chewing gum over each of the holes, went downstairs and waited for a moment when the sidewalk was deserted and there were no cars in sight on the street. Then I took the police whistle from my pocket and blew three shrill blasts. By the time the windows in the apartments commenced to come up, I'd ducked into the doorway and started up the stairs.

I held my pasteboard mask in my left hand. All I had to do was to raise it to my face, and the adhesive tape would clamp it into position. I backed up against the door of apartment 3A and knocked with my knuckles. When I heard steps coming toward the door, I slapped my left hand up to my face, putting the mask in position, and jerked the gun out of my shoulder holster. The redhead opened the door and I backed in, the gun menacing the corridor. Once inside of the door, I made a quick whirl, kicked the door shut and covered her with the gun.

"Not a peep out of you," I said.

She'd put on a negligée and was holding it tightly about her throat. Her face was white.

"All right, sister," I told her, "get a load of this. If any copper comes wandering down the hallway, you go to the door to see what he wants. If he asks you if anyone's in here or if you've seen anyone in the corridor, tell him no. The reason you'll tell him no, is that I'm going to be standing just behind the door with this gun. They're never going to take me alive. I'd just as soon go out fighting as to be led up thirteen steps and dropped through a hole in the floor. Get it?"

She was white to the lips, but she nodded, her eyes large, round and dilated with fright.

"I stuck up that jewelry store downstairs," I told her, "and I've got some swag that's worth money. Now, I want some wrapping paper and some string. I'm going to drop that swag in the first mailbox I come to and let Uncle Sam take the responsibility of the delivery. Get me?"

She swallowed a couple of times and said, "Y-yes."

"And I'll tell you something else: Don't hold that filmy stuff so tight around you. I'm not going to bite you, but if a cop comes to the door and sees you all bundled up that way, he'll figure out what's happened. If there's a knock. I want you to open the door a crack and have that thing pretty well open in front, when you do. Then you can pull it shut when you see there's a man at the door and give a little squeal and say, 'Oh, I thought it was Mamie!' Do you get that?"

"You're asking a lot of me," she said.

I made motions with the business end of the gun. "You've got a nice figure," I said. "It would be a shame to blow it in two. These are soft-nosed bullets. You'd have splinters from your spinal cord all mixed into your hip bone if I pulled this trigger. The cop in the doorway would get the next shot. Then I'd take a chance on the fire-escape."

She didn't say anything and I jabbed at her with the gun. "Come on, how about the wrapping paper?"

She opened a door into a little kitchenette, pulled out a drawer. There was brown paper and string in there. I said, "Get over there away from the window; stand over there in the corner."

I crossed over to the little card table. There was an ash-tray there with four or five cigarette ends in it and some burnt matches. I noticed that a couple of the matches had been broken in two. I pushed the tray to one side, spread the paper out, and took the cotton from my pocket.

When I opened the cotton, she saw the four big pearls nested in it and gave a little gasp. Standing eight or ten feet away as she was and seeing those pearls on the cotton, she felt she was looking at ready money.

"That all you took?" she asked in a voice that had a can't-we-be-friends note in it.

"Is that all I took?" I asked, and laughed, a nasty, sarcastic laugh. "That jeweler," I told her, "has been trying to get those four pearls for a client for more than two years. They're perfectly matched pearls that came in from the South Seas, and, in case you want to know it, they didn't pay any duty. I know what I'm after before I heist a joint."

I put the cotton around the pearls again, wrapped them in the paper, tied the paper with string and ostentatiously set my gun on the corner of the table while I took a fountain pen from my pocket to write an address on the package. I printed the first name which popped into my head, and a Los Angeles address. Then I reached in my pocket, took out my wallet and from it extracted a strip of postage stamps.

"What—what are they worth?" she asked.

"Singly," I told her, "they aren't worth over five thousand apiece, but the four of them taken together, with that perfect matching and luster, are worth forty grand in any man's dough." I shot her a look to see if she thought there was anything phony about my appraisal. She didn't. Her eyes were commencing to narrow now as ideas raced through her head.

"I suppose," she told me, "you'll peddle them to a fence and only get about a tenth of what they're worth."

"Well, a tenth of forty grand buys a lot of hamburgers," I told her.

She moved over toward a small table, slid one hip up on that, and let the negligée slide carelessly open, apparently too much interested in the pearls to remember that she wasn't clothed for the street. She had plenty to look at, that girl.

"You make a working girl dizzy," she said wistfully. "Think how hard I'd have to work to make four thousand dollars."

"Not with that shape."

Indignantly she pulled the robe around her. Then she leaned forward, let the silk slip from her fingers and slide right back along the smooth line of her leg.

"I suppose it's wicked of me," she said, "but I can't help thinking what an awful shame it is to sell anything as valuable as that for a fraction of what it's worth. I should think you'd get yourself some good-looking female accomplice, someone who could really wear clothes. You could doll her up with some glad rags and show up in Santa Barbara or Hollywood, or perhaps in New Orleans. She could stay at a swell hotel, make friends, and finally confide to one of her gentlemen friends that she was temporarily embarrassed and wanted to leave some security with him and get a really good loan. Gosh, you know, there are lots of ways of playing a game like that."

I frowned contemplatively. "You've got something there, baby," I told her. "But it would take a girl who could wear clothes; it'd take a baby who'd be able to knock 'em dead and keep her head while she was doing it; it'd take a fast thinker, and it would take someone who'd be one hundred per cent loyal. Where are you going to find a moll like that?"

She got up off the table, gave a little shrug with her shoulders, and the negligée slipped down to the floor. She turned slowly around as though she'd been modeling the peach-colored underwear. "I can wear clothes," she said.

I let my eyes show suspicion. "Yeah," I told her. "You sure got what it takes on that end, but how do I know you wouldn't cross me to the bulls if anybody came along and offered a reward?"

Her eyes were starry now. She came toward me. "I don't double-cross people I like," she said. "I liked you from the minute I saw you—something in your voice, something in the way you look. I don't know what it is. When I fall, I fall fast and I fall hard. And I play the game all the way. You and I could go places together. I could put you up right here until the excitement's over. Then we could go places and—"

I said suspiciously, "You aren't handing me a line?"

"Handing you a line!" she said scornfully. "Do I look like the sort of girl who'd have to hand anyone a line? I'm not so dumb. I know I have a figure. But you don't see me living in a swell apartment with some guy footing the bills, do you? I'm just a working girl, plugging along and trying to be on the up-and-up. I'm not saying that I like it. I'm not even saying that I'm not sick of it. But I am telling you that you and I could go places together. You could use me and I'd stick."

"Now, wait a minute, baby," I temporized. "Let me get this package stamped and think this thing over a minute. You sure have got me going. Cripes! I've been in stir where I didn't see a frail for months on end, and now you come along and dazzle me with a shape like that. Listen, baby, I—"

I raised the stamps to my tongue, licked them and started to put them on the package. The wet mucilage touched my thumb and the stamps stuck. I tried to shake my thumb loose and the stamps fell to the floor, windmilling around as they dropped. I swooped after the stamps, and sensed motion over on the other side of the table.

I straightened, to find myself staring into the business end of my gun, which she'd snatched up from the table.

"Now then, sucker," she said, "start reaching."

I stood, muscles tensed, hands slowly coming up. "Now, take it easy, baby. You wouldn't shoot me."

"Don't think I wouldn't," she told me. "I'd shoot you in a minute. I'd tell the cops you'd busted in here after your stick-up and I distracted your attention long enough to grab your gun; that you made a grab for me and I acted in self-defense."

"Now listen, baby," I told her, keeping my hands up, "let's be reasonable about this thing. I thought you and I were going away together. I'd show you London and Paris and—"

She laughed scornfully and said, "What a sap I'd be to start traveling with a boob like you. A pair of pretty legs, and you forget all about your gun and leave it on the table while you chase postage stamps to the floor."

"You going to call the cops?" I asked.

She laughed. "Do I look dumb? I'm going to give you a chance to escape."

"Why?"

"Because," she said, "I haven't got the heart to see a nice-looking young man like you go to jail. I'm going to call the cops and tell them I saw you in the corridor. I'll give you ten seconds start. That ten seconds will keep you from hanging around here, and calling the cops will put me in the clear in case anybody sees you."

"Oh, I see," I said sarcastically. "You mean you're going to grab off the gravy."

"Ideas don't circulate through that dome of yours very fast, do they?" she asked.

I made a lunge toward the paper parcel I'd wrapped up, but the gun snapped up to a level with my chest. Her eyes glittered. "Don't crowd me, you fool!" she said. "Of all the dumbhead plays you've made, that's the worst. I'll do it, and don't think I don't know how to shoot a gun, because I do."

I backed slowly away.

"There's the door," she said. "Get going." She started toward the telephone and said, "I'm going to call the cops. You have ten seconds."

I spilled a lot of cuss words, to make the act look good, unlocked the door, jerked it open and jumped out into the corridor. I made pounding noises with my feet in the direction of the fire-escape and then tiptoed back. I heard a metallic click as she shot the bolt home in the door.

AFTER WAITING A couple of minutes, I dropped to one knee and peeked through the hole in the door. She was over at the table, ripping the wrappings from the parcel. I straightened, and pounded with my knuckles on the door.

"Police call," I said in a deep gruff voice. "Open up."

Her voice sounded thick with sleep. "What is it?"

"Police," I said, and dropped again, to put an eye to the peep hole in the door.

She ran to a corner of the carpet, raised it, did something to the floor and then snatched up a kimona.

I pounded with my knuckles again.

"Coming," she said drowsily.

She twisted back the bolt, opened the door about the width of a newspaper and asked, "What do you want?"

I stood aside so she couldn't see me.

"We're looking for a man who robbed the jewelry store downstairs," I growled in my throat. "We think he came up here."

"Well, he didn't."

"Would you mind letting me in?"

She hesitated a moment, then said, "Oh, very well, if you have to come in, I guess you have to. Just a minute. I'll put something on. . . . All right."

She pulled the door back. I pushed my way into the room and kicked the door shut. She looked at me with wide, terror-stricken eyes, then jumped back and said, "Listen, you can't pull this. I'll have the police here! I'll—"

I walked directly to the corner of the carpet. She flung herself at me. I pushed her off. I pulled back the corner of the carpet and saw nothing except floor. But I knew it was there and kept looking, pressing with my fingers. Suddenly I found it—a little cunningly joined section in the hardwood floor. I opened it. My package had been shoved in there, and down below it was a package of letters.

Bending down so that my body concealed just what I was doing, I pulled out pearls and letters and stuffed them in my inside coat pocket.

When I straightened, I found myself facing the gun.

"I told you you couldn't get away with this," she warned. "I'll claim you held up the jewelry store and then crashed the gate here. What're you going to do about that?"

"Nothing," I told her, smiling. "I have everything I came for."

"I can kill you," she said, "and the police would give me a vote of thanks."

"You could," I told her, "but nice girls don't go around killing men."

I saw her face contort in a spasm of emotion. "The hell they don't!" she said, and pulled the trigger.

The hammer clicked on an empty cylinder. She reinforced the index finger of her right hand with the index finger of her left. Her eyes were blazing. She clicked the empty cylinder six times and then threw the gun at me. I caught it by the barrel and side-stepped her rush. She tripped over a chair and fell on the couch.

"Take it easy," I told her.

She raised her voice then and started to call me names. At the end of the first twenty seconds, I came to the conclusion I didn't know any words she didn't. I started for the door. She made a dash for the telephone and was yelling: "Police headquarters!" into the transmitter as I closed the door and drifted noiselessly down the corridor.

In the hallway I pulled off the pasteboard mask, moistened a piece of cotton in the benzine and scrubbed off the bits of adhesive which had stuck to my face and forehead. I wadded the mask into a ball, walked around to my car and drove away.

I heard the siren of a police radio car when I was three blocks away. The machine roared by me, doing a good sixty miles an hour.

WALKING DOWN THE corridor of the Pemberton home, I coughed as I passed Mrs. Pemberton's door. I walked into my bedroom and waited. Nothing happened. I took out the letters and looked at them. They were plenty torrid. Some men like to put themselves on paper. Harvey Pemberton had indulged himself to the limit.

I heard a scratching noise on my door, then it slowly opened. Mrs. Pemberton, walking as though she'd carefully rehearsed her entrance, came into the light of the room and pulled lacy things around her. "My husband hasn't come in yet," she said. "But he may come in any minute."

I looked her over. "Even supposing that I'm your brother," I said, "don't you think he'd like it a lot better if you had on something a little more tangible?"

She said, "I wear what I want. After all, you're my brother."

"Well, go put on a bathrobe over that," I told her, "so I won't be so apt to forget it."

She moved a step or two toward the door, then paused. "You don't need to be so conventional," she said.

"That's what you think."

"I want to know what you've found out."

"You're out in the clear," I told her. "All we need now is to—" I broke off as I heard the sound of an automobile outside. There was a business-like snarl to the motor which I didn't like, and somebody wore off a lot of rubber as the car was slammed to a stop.

"That's Harvey now," she said.

"Harvey wouldn't park his car at the curb in front, would he?" I asked.

"No," she admitted.

"Get back to your room," I told her.

"But I don't see what you're so—"

"Get started!" I said.

"Very well, Sir Galahad," she told me.

She started down the corridor toward her room. I heard the pound of feet as someone ran around the house toward the back door. Then I heard feet on the stairs, crossing the porch, and the doorbell rang four or five times, long, insistent rings.

I slipped some shells into the empty chambers of my gun, switched off the lights, opened my door, picked up my bag and waited.

I heard Mrs. Pemberton go to the head of the stairs, stand there, listening. After a moment I heard the rustle of her clothes as she started down. I stepped out to the hallway and stood still.

I heard her say, "Who is it?" and a voice boom an answer through the closed door. "Police," it said. "Open up."

"But I—I don't understand."

"Open up!"

She unlocked the door. I heard men coming into the corridor, then a man's voice say, "I'm Lieutenant Sylvester. I want to talk with you. You're Mrs. Pemberton?"

"Yes, but I can't understand what could bring you here at this hour. After all, Lieutenant, I'm—"

"I'm sorry," the lieutenant interrupted, "this is about your husband. When did you see him last?"

"Why, just this evening."

"What time this evening?"

"Why, I don't know exactly."

"Where did you see him last?"

"Will you please tell me the reason for these questions?"

"Where," he repeated, "did you see your husband last?"

"Well, if you insist on knowing, he was here for dinner and then left for the office about seven-thirty."

"And you haven't seen him since?"

"No."

The officer said, "I'm sorry, Mrs. Pemberton, but your husband's body was found on the floor of his office by the janitor about half an hour ago."

"My husband's body!" she screamed.

"Yes, ma'am," the lieutenant said. "He'd been killed by two bullets fired from a thirty-two caliber automatic. The ejected shells were on the floor of his office. In an adjoining office, furnished with a dilapidated desk and a couple of chairs, we found a home-rigged microphone arrangement which would work as a dictograph. In the drawer of that desk we found the gun with which the murder had been committed. Now, Mrs. Pemberton, what do you know about it?"

There was silence for a second or two, then she said in a thin, frightened voice, "Why, I don't know anything about it."

"What do you know about that office next to your husband's?"

"Nothing."

"You've never been in there?"

This time she didn't hesitate. "No," she said, "never. I don't know what makes you think I would be spying on my husband. Perhaps someone has hired detectives. *I* wouldn't know."

I tiptoed back to my room, picked up my bag and started silently down the corridor toward the back stairs. I could hear the rumble of a man's voice from the front room, and, at intervals, the thin, shrill sound of Mrs. Pemberton's half-hysterical answers.

I felt my way down the back stairs. There was a glass window in the back door, with a shade drawn over it. I raised a corner of the shade and peered through the glass. I could see the bulky figure of a man silhouetted against the lights which filtered in from the back yard. He was holding a sawed-off police riot gun in his hands.

I took a flash-light from my pocket and started exploring the kitchen. I found the door to the cellar, and went down. From the floor above came the scrape of chairs, then the noise of feet moving about the house.

There was a little window in the cellar. I scraped cobwebs away and shook off a couple of spiders I could feel crawling on my hand. I worked the catch on the sash and pulled it open. It dropped down on hinges and hung down on the inside. I pushed my bag out, breathed a prayer to Lady Luck, and gave a jump. My elbows caught on the cement. I wiggled and twisted, pulling myself up, and fighting to keep the side of the window from catching on my knees and coming up with me. I scrambled out to the lawn.

No one was watching this side of the house. I picked up my bag, tiptoed across the lawn and pushed my way through a hedge. In the next yard a dog commenced to bark. I turned back to the sidewalk and started walking fast. I looked back over my shoulder and saw lights coming on in the second story of the Pemberton house.

I walked faster.

FROM A PAY station, I put in a long distance call for old E. B. Jonathan. E. B. didn't appreciate being called out of his slumber, but I didn't give him a chance to do any crabbing.

"Your client down here," I told him, "is having trouble."

"Well," he said, "it can keep until morning."

"No," I told him, "I don't think it can."

"Why can't it?"

"She's going to jail."

"What's she going to jail for?"

"Taking a couple of pot shots at her husband with a thirty-two automatic."

"Did she hit him?"

"Dead center."

"Where does that leave you?" Jonathan asked.

"As a fugitive from justice, talking from a pay station," I told him. "The janitor will testify that I was with her when she went up to the place, where the shooting occurred. The janitor is her dog. He lies down and rolls over when she snaps her fingers. She thinks it'd be nice to make me the goat."

"You mean by blaming the shooting on you?"

"Exactly."

"What makes you think so?"

"I'd trust some women a hell of a lot more than you do, and some women a hell of a lot less. This one I trust a lot less."

"She's a client," E. B. said testily. "She wouldn't do that."

"I know she's a client," I told him. "That may put whitewash all over her as far as you're concerned, but it doesn't as far as I'm concerned. I made her ditch the gun out of her handbag so she wouldn't be tempted to use it. I got my finger-prints on the gun doing it. When the going gets rough, she'll think of that, and the janitor in the building will swear to anything she suggests."

He made clucking noises with his tongue against the roof of his mouth. "I'll have Boniface drive down there right away," he said. "Where can Boniface find you?"

"Nowhere," I said and hung up.

There was an all-night hamburger stand down by the depot. I ordered six hamburgers with plenty of onions and had them put in a bag to take out. I'd noticed there was a rooming-house across from the apartment where Diane Locke lived. I went there.

The landlady grumbled about the lateness of the hour, but I paid two days' rent in advance and she showed me a front room.

I said to her "I work nights, and will be sleeping daytimes. Please don't let anyone disturb me."

I told her I was Peter J. Gibbens from Seattle. She digested this sleepily and ambled away. I found a "Do not Disturb" sign in the room which I hung on the door. I locked the door and went to bed.

About three o'clock in the afternoon, I sneaked out in the hallway for a reconnaissance. There were newspapers on the desk. I picked up one, left a nickel, and went back to the room.

My own picture stared at me from the front page. "Peter Wennick, connected with prominent law firm in the metropolis, being sought for questioning by local police in connection with Pemberton murder." This was in bold, black type.

It was quite an account: Mrs. Pemberton had "told all." She had consulted the law firm in connection with some blackmail letters. The law firm had said I was a "leg man and detective." I had been sent down to investigate the situation and report on the evidence. She had taken me to the office, where, with a friendly janitor, she had rigged up a dictaphone. I had listened to a conversation between her husband and "the woman in the case."

On the pretext of leaving for the wash-room, I had thrown the night latch on the door of the office so I could return at any time. She had forgotten to put the night latch back on when we left. Therefore, I had left myself an opportunity to return and gain access to the room.

The janitor remembered when we had left. Something like an hour later, he had heard muffled sounds which could have been the two shots which were fired. He thought they had been the sounds of backfire from a truck. He'd been in the basement, reading. The sounds had apparently come from the alley, but might have been shots echoed back from the walls of an adjoining building. The medical authorities fixed the time of death as being probably half an hour to an hour and a half after we'd left the building.

Mrs. Pemberton had insisted she'd gone home, and that I had immediately gone out. She didn't know where. I had returned, to tell her that I had good news for her, but before I could report, police had come to the house to question her in connection with her husband's death. I had made my escape through a cellar window while police were searching the house.

Arthur H. Bass, Pemberton's partner, had stated that Pemberton had been very much worried for the past few days, that he had announced it was necessary for him to raise immediate funds and had offered to sell his interest in the partnership business for much less than its value. Bass had reluctantly made a nominal offer, but had advised Pemberton not to accept it, and when Pemberton had refused to consider such a nominal amount, Bass had been jubilant because he didn't want to lose Pemberton as a partner. He had met Pemberton at Pemberton's request, to discuss the matter.

The district attorney announced that he had interviewed "the woman in the case." Inasmuch as she seemed to have been "wronged" by Pemberton, and, inasmuch as a Peeping Tom who had tried to crash the gate of her apartment had caused her to place a call for the police at approximately the time Pemberton must have been killed, the police absolved her of all responsibility.

It seemed that this Peeping Tom, evidently trying to make a mash, had knocked at her door and advised her he had held up the jewelry store downstairs. She had promptly reported to the police, who had visited her apartment, to find her very much undressed, very much excited and shaken, and apparently sincere. Police records of the call showed that the police were actually in her apartment at the time the janitor had heard the sounds of what were undoubtedly the shots which took Pemberton's life.

Mrs. Pemberton, the news account went on to say, could give no evidence in support of her alibi, but police were inclined to absolve her of blame, concentrating for the moment on a search for Pete Wennick, the leg man for the law firm.

Cedric L. Boniface, a member of the law firm, very much shocked at developments, had made a rush trip to the city and was staying at the Palace Hotel. So far, authorities had not let him talk to Mrs. Pemberton, but they would probably do so at an early hour in the afternoon. Mr. Boniface said he "hoped Mr. Wennick would be able to absolve himself."

That was that.

Just for the fun of the thing, I turned to the Personals. It's a habit with me. I always read them in any paper. Under the heading: "Too late to classify," I came on one which interested me. It read simply: "P. W. Can I help? Call on me for anything. M.D."

Now there was a girl! Old E. B. Jonathan, with his warped, distorted, jaundiced idea of the sex, suspected all women except clients. Clients to him were sacred. I took women as I found them. Mae Devers would stick through thick and thin.

Mrs. Pemberton had paraded around in revealing silks and had called me Sir Galahad when I'd told her to go put on a bathrobe. The minute the going got rough, she'd tossed me to the wolves. The question was whether she either killed her husband while I was in the washroom or had gone back and killed him afterwards and deliberately imported me as the fall guy for the police. If she had, she'd made a damn good job of it.

Supper consisted of a couple of cold hamburgers. About five o'clock, I drew up a chair in front of the window and started watching. The redhead had accused me of being a Peeping Tom and now I was going to be one.

I didn't see Diane Locke come in or go out, and I didn't see anyone else I knew. After it got dark, a light came on in Diane's apartment. I sat there and waited. About nine o'clock I had another hamburger. I got tired of waiting and decided I'd force the play. I looked up the telephone number of Bass & Pemberton's office and memorized it. It was Temple 491. I shaved, combed my hair, put on a suit none of my new playmates had seen me wear, crossed the street, climbed the stairs of the apartment house and knocked on the door of apartment 3A.

Nothing happened at once. I dropped to one knee, scooped dried chewing gum out of the hole in the door and looked through. She was coming toward the door. And she had her clothes on.

I straightened as she came to the door, opened it, and asked, "What is it?"

"I'm from the police," I said in a thin, high, nasal voice this time. "I'm trying to check up on that call you put through to police headquarters last night."

"Yes?" she asked. She'd never seen me without a mask. "What is it you wanted to know?"

"I'm trying to check your call," I told her. "If you don't mind, I'll come in." I came in before she had a chance to mind. I walked over to the chair and sat down. She sat down in the other chair.

The chair I was sitting in was warm. "Pardon me," I said, "was this your chair?"

"No. I was sitting in this one," she told me.

She looked at me and said, "I've seen you before. There's something vaguely familiar about your face. And I think I've heard your voice somewhere."

I grinned across at her and said, "I never contradict a lady, but if I'd ever met you, I'd remember it until I was a hundred and ten."

She smiled at that and crossed her knees. I looked over at the ashtray. There were two cigarette stubs on it. Both were smoldering. There was only one match in the tray. It was broken in two.

She followed the direction of my eyes, laughed, and pinched out the stubs. "I'm always leaving cigarette stubs burning," she said. "What was it you wanted?"

I slid my hand under the lapel of my coat and loosened the gun. "Miss Locke," I said, "you understand that the time element here is important. It's a question of when you placed that call to the police, as well as when the police got here. We want to check carefully on all those times. Now, in order to do that, I've been checking your calls with the telephone company. It seems that you put through a call to Temple 491 very shortly after you called the police. Can you tell me about that call?"

She studied her tinted fingernails for a minute, then raised her eyes and said, "Yes, frankly, I can. I called Mr. Pemberton."

"Why did you call him?"

She said, "I think you'll understand that I felt very close to Mr. Pemberton in many ways. He had—well, he'd tricked me and betrayed me, but, nevertheless. . . . Oh, I just hated to make trouble for him. I called him to tell him I was sorry."

"Did you talk with him?" My throat was getting irritated from straining my voice high.

Once more she hesitated, then said, "No, he didn't answer the telephone."

"The telephone company has you on a limited call basis," I said. "They report that the call was completed."

Once more she studied her fingernails.

"Someone answered the phone," she said, "but said he was the janitor cleaning up the offices. So I hung up on him."

That gave me all I wanted to know. I said, and I spoke in my own voice now, "You know, it was a dirty trick they played on you, Diane. I don't think Bass cared whether you got anything out of it or not. He wanted Pemberton's interest in the partnership. In fact he had to have it because he'd been juggling funds. He was the mythical 'lawyer' behind you. You're his woman and he put you up to playing Pemberton for a sucker, hoping Pemberton would be involved enough so he could put into effect that trick clause in the partnership agreement and buy him out for two thousand dollars. When Pemberton said he was going to have an auditor make a complete analysis of the books for the purpose of finding out what a half interest was worth, Bass went into a panic."

She went white to her lips, but said nothing.

I went on: "As soon as your 'burglar' left and you found you'd lost the letters, you called Bass up and told him what had happened. He was in his private office, waiting for a call, waiting also for Pemberton to come back and accept his offer as a final last resort.

"But Bass was pretty smooth. He probably knew I wasn't Olive Pemberton's brother. He guessed I was a detective. That meant Olive was wise to the Diane business, and he was shrewd enough to figure there might be a dictograph running into Pemberton's office. He did a little exploring. The door to the adjoining office was unlocked, and he stepped in, looked the plant over, and found the gun. Obviously either Olive or I had left the gun there. It could be traced to one of us. It looked like a set-up. Bass took the gun with him, did the job and returned it.

"Killing Pemberton was his only out. Without the letters, his little blackmail scheme had fallen through. There'd be no money coming in to cover the shortage the audit would turn up. That meant he'd go to prison. Well, he'll go anyway, and he'll stay just long enough to be made ready for a pine box."

By this time the redhead had recognized me, of course. "You and your pearls," she sneered, but the sneer was only a camouflage for the growing fright in her eyes.

"Now," I went on, "you're in Bass' way. Bass can't have the police knowing he was behind the blackmail business, and you can show he was. He'll have to try to get rid of both of us."

"Arthur would never do anything like that," she cried.

The closet door was in front of me. The bathroom door was behind me. But a mirror in the closet door enabled me to see the bathroom one. I kept my eyes on these doors.

"He will, though," I told her, "and you know it. He's already killed once. Otherwise why did he come here tonight to tell you that under no circumstances were you to admit you'd talked with him over the telephone?"

She moistened her lips with her tongue. "How do you know all these things?" she asked.

"I know them," I told her, "because I know that persons who have ever worked as forest rangers in the dry country make it an invariable habit to break their matches in two before they throw them away. I know that he was here the other night because there were broken matches in your ash-tray. He'd sent you up to put the screws on Harvey Pemberton. I know that he's here tonight. I know he was in the office last night. Just before you came in he'd been talking with Harvey Pemberton. I didn't hear him take the elevator, so I know he went in to his private office after he'd finished that talk. He was still there when I left. I'm Wennick."

"But he wouldn't have done anything like that," she said. "Arthur couldn't."

"But you did telephone right after those letters had been stolen, and told him about it, didn't you?"

"Yes," she said, "I—"

The door behind me opened a half inch. I saw the muzzle of the gun slowly creep out, but it wasn't until I had my fingers on the butt of my own gun that I realized the barrel wasn't pointing at me, but at her.

"Duck!" I yelled.

I think it was the sudden yell which frightened her half out of her wits. She didn't duck, but she recoiled from me as though I'd thrown a brick at her instead of my voice. The gun went off. The bullet whizzed through the air right where her head had been, and buried itself in the plaster. I whirled and shot, through the door. I saw the gun barrel waver. I shot again, and then an arm came into sight, drooping toward the floor. The gun fell from nerveless fingers, and Arthur Bass crashed full length into the room.

OLD E. B. GLOWERED at me with little, malevolent eyes which glittered from above the bluish-white pouches which puffed out from under his eyeballs. "Wennick," he said, "you look like the devil!"

"I'm sorry," I told him.

"You look dissipated."

"I haven't shaved yet."

"From all reports," he said, "you cleaned up this Pemberton murder case and were released by the police at Culverton with a vote of thanks, some time before ten o'clock yesterday evening. Cedric Boniface was in the law library, briefing the question of premeditation in connection with murder. He didn't know what had happened until after the police had obtained Bass' dying statement and you had left."

I nodded.

"Now then," E. B. said, "why the hell is it that you didn't report to me?"

"I'm sorry," I told him, "but, after all, I have social engagements."

"Social engagements!" he stormed. "You were out with some woman!"

I nodded. "I was out with a young lady," I admitted, "celebrating her birthday."

He started cracking his knuckles. "Out with a young lady!" he snorted. "I had your apartment watched so I could be notified the minute you got in. You didn't get in until six o'clock this morning."

I listened to the dull cracking of his knuckles, then grinned at him. "The young lady," I said, "happens to have been born at five o'clock in the morning, so I had to wait until then to help her celebrate her birthday. If you doubt me, you might ask Mae Devers."

ONE OF THOSE DAYS, ONE OF THOSE NIGHTS

Ed Gorman

If versatility is a virtue, then Ed Gorman is virtuous indeed. He has written steadily in three different genres—mystery, horror, and westerns—for almost twenty years. He has also written a large number of short stories, with six of his collections of wry, poignant, unsettling fiction in print in the United States and United Kingdom. *Kirkus* said, "Gorman is one of the most original crime writers around," taking particular note of his Sam McCain–Judge Whitney series, which is set in small-town Iowa in the 1950s and has won rave reviews from coast to coast. It is no surprise that he captures the essence of life in the Midwest, since he lives in Cedar Rapids, Iowa. As for the wealth of detail he brings to every novel and story he writes, well, he's been there and back again, and the observations he shares about life, love, and loss make his books all the richer. His most recent novel is *Will You Still Love Me Tomorrow?*, the third Sam McCain book.

THE THING YOU have to understand is that I found it by accident. I was looking for a place to hide the birthday gift I'd bought Laura—a string of pearls she'd been wanting to wear with the new black dress she'd bought for herself—and all I was going to do was lay the gift-wrapped box in the second drawer of her bureau . . .

. . . and there it was.

A plain number-ten envelope with her name written across the middle in a big manly scrawl and a canceled Elvis Presley stamp up in the corner. Postmarked two days ago.

Just as I spotted it, Laura called from the living room, "Bye, honey, see you at six." The last two years we've been saving to buy a house so we have only the one car. Laura goes an hour earlier than I do, so she rides with a woman who lives a few blocks over. Then I pick her up at six after somebody relieves me at the computer store where I work. For what it's worth, I have an M.A. in English Literature but with the economy being what it is, it hasn't done me much good.

I saw a sci-fi movie once where a guy could set something on fire simply by staring at it intently enough. That's what I was trying to do with this letter my wife got. Burn it so that I wouldn't have to read what it said inside and get my heart broken.

I closed the drawer.

Could be completely harmless. Her fifteenth high-school reunion was coming up this spring. Maybe it was from one of her old classmates. And maybe the manly scrawl wasn't so manly after all. Maybe it was from a woman who wrote in a rolling dramatic hand.

Laura always said that I was the jealous type and this was certainly proof. A harmless letter tucked harmlessly in a bureau drawer. And here my heart was pounding, and fine cold sweat slicked my face, and my fingers were trembling.

God, wasn't I a pitiful guy? Shouldn't I be ashamed of myself?

I went into the bathroom and lathered up and did my usual relentless fifteen-minute morning regimen of shaving, showering, and shining up my apple-cheeked Irish face and my thinning Irish hair, if hair follicles can have a nationality, that is.

Then I went back into our bedroom and took down a white shirt, blue necktie, navy blazer, and tan slacks. All dressed, I looked just like seventy or eighty million other men getting ready for work this particular sunny April morning.

Then I stood very still in the middle of the bedroom and stared at Laura's bureau. Maybe I wasn't simply going to set the letter on fire. Maybe I was going to ignite the entire bureau.

The grandfather clock in the living room tolled eight-thirty. If I didn't leave now I would be late, and if you were late you inevitably got a chewing-out from Ms. Sanders, the boss. Anybody who believes that women would run a more benign world than men needs only to spend five minutes with Ms. Sanders. Hitler would have used her as a pin-up girl.

The bureau. The letter. The manly scrawl.

What was I going to do?

Only one thing I could think of, since I hadn't made a decision about reading the letter or not. I'd simply take it with me to work. If I decided to read it, I'd give it a quick scan over my lunch hour.

But probably I wouldn't read it at all. I had a lot of faith where Laura was concerned. And I didn't like to think of myself as the sort of possessive guy who snuck around reading his wife's mail.

I reached into the bureau drawer.

My fingers touched the letter.

I was almost certain I wasn't going to read it. Hell, I'd probably get so busy at work that I'd forget all about it.

But just in case I decided to . . .

I grabbed the letter and stuffed it into my blazer pocket, and closed the drawer. In the kitchen I had a final cup of coffee and read my newspaper horoscope. Bad news, as always. I should never read the damn things. . . . Then I hurried out of the apartment to the little Toyota parked at the curb.

Six blocks away, it stalled. Our friendly mechanic said that moisture seemed to get in the fuel pump a lot. He's not sure why. We've run it in three times but it still stalls several times a week.

A ROUND TEN O'CLOCK, hurrying into a sales meeting that Ms. Sanders had decided to call, I dropped my pen. And when I bent over to pick it up, my glasses fell out of my pocket, and when I moved to pick them up, I took one step too many and put all 175 pounds of my body directly onto them. I heard something snap.

By the time I retrieved both pen and glasses, Ms. Sanders was closing the door and calling the meeting to order. I hurried down the hall, trying to see how much damage I'd done. I held the glasses up to the light. A major fissure snaked down the center of the right lens. I slipped them on. The crack was even more difficult to see through than I'd thought.

Ms. Sanders, a very attractive fiftyish woman given to sleek gray suits and burning blue gazes, warned us as usual that if sales of our computers didn't pick up, two or three people in this room would likely be looking for jobs. Soon. And just as she finished saying this, her eyes met mine. "For instance, Donaldson, what kind of month are you having?"

"What kind of month am I having?"

"Do I hear a parrot in here?" Ms. Sanders said, and several of the salespeople laughed.

"I'm not having too bad a month."

Ms. Sanders nodded wearily and looked around the room. "Do we have to ask Donaldson here any more questions? Isn't he telling us everything we need to know when he says, 'I'm not having too bad a month'? What're we hearing when Donaldson says that?"

I hadn't noticed till this morning how much Ms. Sanders reminded me of Miss Hutchison, my fourth-grade teacher. Her favorite weapon had also been humiliation.

Dick Weybright raised his hand. Dick Weybright always raises his hand, especially when he gets to help Ms. Sanders humiliate somebody.

"We hear defeatism when he says that," Dick said. "We hear defeatism and a serious lack of self-esteem."

Twice a week, Ms. Sanders made us listen to motivational tapes. You know, "I upped my income, up yours," that sort of thing. And nobody took those tapes more seriously than Dick Weybright.

"Very good, Dick," Ms. Sanders said. "Defeatism and lack of self-esteem. That tells us all we need to know about Donaldson here. Just as the fact that he's got a crack in his glasses tells us something else about him, doesn't it?"

Dick Weybright waggled his hand again. "Lack of self-respect."

"Exactly," Ms. Sanders said, smiling coldly at me. "Lack of self-respect."

She didn't address me again until I was leaving the sales room. I'd knocked some of my papers on the floor. By the time I got them picked up, I was alone with Ms. Sanders. I heard her come up behind me as I pointed myself toward the door.

"You missed something, Donaldson."

I turned. "Oh?"

She waved Laura's envelope in the air. Then her blue eyes showed curiosity as they read the name on the envelope. "You're not one of those, are you, Donaldson?"

"One of those?"

"Men who read their wives' mail?"

"Oh. One of those. I see."

"Are you?"

"No."

"Then what're you doing with this?"

"What am I doing with that?"

"That parrot's in here again."

"I must've picked it up off the table by mistake."

"The table?"

"The little Edwardian table under the mirror in the foyer. Where we always set the mail."

She shook her head again. She shook her head a lot. "You are one of those, aren't you, Donaldson? So were my first three husbands, the bastards."

She handed me the envelope, brushed past me, and disappeared down the hall.

THERE'S A PARK near the river where I usually eat lunch when I'm downtown for the day. I spend most of the time feeding the pigeons.

Today I spent most of my time staring at the envelope laid next to me on the park bench. There was a warm spring breeze and I half-hoped it would lift up the envelope and carry it away.

Now I wished I'd left the number-ten with the manly scrawl right where I'd found it because it was getting harder and harder to resist lifting the letter from inside and giving it a quick read.

I checked my watch. Twenty minutes to go before I needed to be back at work. Twenty minutes to stare at the letter. Twenty minutes to resist temptation.

Twenty minutes—and how's this for cheap symbolism?—during which the sky went from cloudless blue to dark and ominous.

By now, I'd pretty much decided that the letter had to be from a man. Otherwise, why would Laura have hidden it in her drawer? I'd also decided that it must contain something pretty incriminating.

Had she been having an affair with somebody? Was she thinking of running away with somebody?

On the way back to the office, I carefully slipped the letter from the envelope and read it. Read it four times, as a matter of fact. And felt worse every time I did.

So Chris Tomlin, her ridiculously handsome, ridiculously wealthy, ridiculously slick college boyfriend was back in her life.

I can't tell you much about the rest of the afternoon. It's all very vague: Voices spoke to me, phones rang at me, computer printers spat things at me—but I didn't respond. I felt as if I were scuttling across the floor of an ocean so deep that neither light nor sound could penetrate it.

Chris Tomlin. My God.

I kept reading the letter, stopping only when I'd memorized it entirely and could keep rerunning it in my mind without any visual aid.

Dear Laura,

I still haven't forgotten you—or forgiven you for choosing you-know-who over me.

I'm going to be in your fair city this Friday. How about meeting me at the Fairmont right at noon for lunch?

Of course, you could contact me the evening before if you're interested. I'll be staying at the Wallingham. I did a little checking and found that you work nearby.

I can't wait to see you.

Love,
Chris Tomlin

Not even good old Ms. Sanders could penetrate my stupor. I know she charged into my office a few times and made some nasty threats—something about my not returning the call of one of our most important customers—but I honestly couldn't tell you who she wanted me to call or what she wanted me to say.

About all I can remember is that it got very dark and cold suddenly. The lights blinked on and off a few times. We were having a terrible rainstorm. Somebody came in soaked and said that the storm sewers were backing up and that downtown was a mess.

Not that I paid this information any particular heed.

I was wondering if she'd call him Thursday night. I took it as a foregone conclusion that she would have lunch with him on Friday. But how about Thursday night?

Would she visit him in his hotel room?

And come to think of it, why *had* she chosen me over Chris Tomlin? I mean, while I may not be a nerd, I'm not exactly a movie star, either. And with Chris Tomlin, there wouldn't have been any penny-pinching for a down payment on a house, either.

With his daddy's millions in pharmaceuticals, good ol' Chris would have bought her a manse as a wedding present.

The workday ended. The usual number of people peeked into my office to say the usual number of good nights. The usual cleaning crew, high-school kids in gray uniforms, appeared to start hauling out trash and run roaring vacuum cleaners. And I went through my usual process of staying at my desk until it was time to pick up Laura.

I was just about to walk out the front door when I noticed in the gloom that Ms. Sanders's light was still on.

She had good ears. Even above the vacuum cleaner roaring its way down the hall to her left, she heard me leaving and looked up.

She waved me into her office.

When I reached her desk, she handed me a slip of paper with some typing on it.

"How does that read to you, Donaldson?"

"Uh, what is it?"

"A Help Wanted ad I may be running tomorrow."

That was another thing Miss Hutchison, my fourth-grade teacher, had been good at—indirect torture.

Ms. Sanders wanted me to read the ad she'd be running for my replacement.

I scanned it and handed it back.

"Nice."

"Is that all you have to say? Nice?"

"I guess so."

"You realize that this means I'm going to fire you?"

"That's what I took it to mean."

"What the hell's wrong with you, Donaldson? Usually you'd be groveling and sniveling by now."

"I've got some—personal problems."

A smirk. "That's what you get for reading your wife's mail." Then a scowl. "When you come in tomorrow morning, you come straight to my office, you understand?"

I nodded. "All right."

"And be prepared to do some groveling and sniveling. You're going to need it."

W HY DON'T I just make a list of the things I found wrong with my Toyota after I slammed the door and belted myself in.

A) The motor wouldn't turn over. Remember what I said about moisture and the fuel pump?

B) The roof had sprung a new leak. This was different from the old leak, which dribbled rain down onto the passenger seat. The new one dribbled rain down onto the driver's seat.

C) The turn-signal arm had come loose again and was hanging down from naked wires like a half-amputated limb. Apparently, after finding the letter this morning, I was in so much of a fog I hadn't noticed that it was broken again.

I can't tell you how dark and cold and lonely I felt just then. Bereft of wife. Bereft of automobile. Bereft of—dare I say it?—self-esteem and self-respect. And, on top of it, I was a disciple of defeatism. Just ask my co-worker Dick Weybright.

The goddamned car finally started and I drove off to pick up my god-damned wife.

The city was a mess.

Lashing winds and lashing rains—both of which were still lashing mer-rily along—had uprooted trees in the park, smashed out store windows here and there, and had apparently caused a power outage that shut down all the automatic traffic signals.

I wanted to be home and I wanted to be dry and I wanted to be in my jammies. But most of all I wanted to be loved by the one woman I had ever really and truly loved.

If only I hadn't opened her bureau drawer to hide her pearls. . . .

She was standing behind the glass door in the entrance to the art-deco building where she works as a market researcher for a mutual-fund com-pany. When I saw her, I felt all sorts of things at once—love, anger, shame, terror—and all I wanted to do was park the car and run up to her and take her in my arms and give her the tenderest kiss I was capable of.

But then I remembered the letter and . . .

Well, I'm sure I don't have to tell you about jealousy. There's nothing worse to carry around in your stony little heart. All that rage and self-righteousness and self-pity. It begins to smother you and . . .

By the time Laura climbed into the car, it was smothering me. She smelled of rain and perfume and her sweet tender body.

"Hi," she said. "I was worried about you."

"Yeah. I'll bet."

Then, closing the door, she gave me a long, long look. "Are you all right?"

"Fine."

"Then why did you say, 'Yeah. I'll bet'?"

"Just being funny."

She gave me another stare. I tried to look regular and normal. You know, not on the verge of whipping the letter out and shoving it in her face.

"Boy, this is really leaking."

I just drove. There was a burly traffic cop out in the middle of a busy intersection directing traffic with two flashlights in the rain and gloom.

"Did you hear me, Rich? I said this is really leaking."

"I know it's really leaking."

"What's up with you, anyway? What're you so mad about? Did Sanders give you a hard time today?"

"No—other than telling me that she may fire me."

"You're kidding."

"No."

"But why?"

Because while I was going through your bureau, I found a letter from your ex-lover and I know all about the tryst you're planning to set up.

That's what I wanted to say.

What I said was: "I guess I wasn't paying proper attention during another one of her goddamned sales meetings."

"But Rich, if you get fired—"

She didn't have to finish her sentence. If I got fired, we'd never get the house we'd been saving for.

"She told me that when I came in tomorrow morning, I should be prepared to grovel and snivel. And she wasn't kidding."

"She actually said that?"

"She actually said that."

"What a bitch."

"Boss's daughter. You know how this city is. The last frontier for hardcore nepotism."

We drove on several more blocks, stopping every quarter-block or so to pull out around somebody whose car had stalled in the dirty water backing up from the sewers.

"So is that why you're so down?"

"Yeah," I said. "Isn't that reason enough?"

"Usually, about Sanders, I mean, you get mad. You don't get depressed."

"Well, Sanders chews me out but she doesn't usually threaten to fire me."

"That's true. But—"

"But what?"

"It just seems that there's—something else." Then, "Where're you going?"

My mind had been on the letter tucked inside my blazer. In the meantime, the Toyota had been guiding itself into the most violent neighborhood in the city. Not even the cops wanted to come here.

"God, can you turn around?" Laura said. "I'd sure hate to get stuck here."

"We'll be all right. I'll hang a left at the next corner and then we'll drive back to Marymount Avenue."

"I wondered where you were going. I should have said something."

She leaned over and kissed me on the cheek.

That boil of feelings, of profound tenderness and profound rage, churned up inside of me again.

"Things'll work out with Sanders," she said, and then smiled. "Maybe she just hasn't been sleeping well lately. You know her and her insomniac jags."

I looked over at her and I couldn't help it. The rage was gone, replaced by pure and total love. This was my friend, my bride, my lover. There had to be a reasonable and innocent explanation for the letter. There had to.

I started hanging the left and that's when it happened. The fuel pump. Rain.

The Toyota stopped dead.

"Oh no," she said, glancing out the windshield at the forbidding blocks of falling-down houses and dark, condemned buildings.

Beyond the wind, beyond the rain, you could hear sirens. There were always sirens in neighborhoods like these.

"Maybe I can fix it," I said.

"But honey, you don't know anything about cars."

"Well, I watched him make that adjustment last time."

"I don't know," she said skeptically. "Besides, you'll just get wet."

"I'll be fine."

I knew why I was doing this, of course. In addition to being rich, powerful, and handsome, Chris Tomlin was also one of those men who could fix practically anything. I remembered her telling me how he'd fixed a refrigerator at an old cabin they'd once stayed in.

I opened the door. A wave of rain washed over me. But I was determined to act like the kind of guy who could walk through a meteor storm and laugh it off. Maybe that's why Laura was considering a rendezvous with Chris. Maybe she was sick of my whining. A macho man, I'm not.

"Just be careful," she said.

"Be right back."

I eased out of the car and then realized I hadn't used the hood latch inside. I leaned in and popped the latch and gave Laura a quick smile.

And then I went back outside into the storm.

I WAS SOAKED completely in less than a minute, my shoes soggy, my clothes drenched and cold and clinging. Even my raincoat.

But I figured this would help my image as a take-charge sort of guy. I even gave Laura a little half-salute before I raised the hood. She smiled at me. God, I wanted to forget all about the letter and be happily in love again.

Any vague hopes I'd had of starting the car were soon forgotten as I gaped at the motor and realized that I had absolutely no idea what I was looking at.

The mechanic in the shop had made it look very simple. You raised the hood, you leaned in and snatched off the oil filter and then did a couple of quick things to it and put it back. And *voilà*, your car was running again.

I got the hood open all right, and I leaned in just fine, and I even took the oil filter off with no problem.

But when it came to doing a couple of quick things to it, my brain was as dead as the motor. That was the part I hadn't picked up from the mechanic. Those couple of quick things.

I started shaking the oil filter. Don't ask me why. I had it under the protection of the hood to keep it dry and shook it left and shook it right and shook it high and shook it low. I figured that maybe some kind of invisible cosmic forces would come into play here and the engine would start as soon as I gave the ignition key a little turn.

I closed the hood and ran back through the slashing rain, opened the door, and crawled inside.

"God, it's incredible out there."

Only then did I get a real good look at Laura and only then did I see that she looked sick, like the time we both picked up a slight case of ptomaine poisoning at her friend Susan's wedding.

Except now she looked a lot sicker.

And then I saw the guy.

In the backseat.

"Who the hell are you?"

But he had questions of his own. "Your wife won't tell me if you've got an ATM card."

So it had finally happened. Our little city turned violent about fifteen years ago, during which time most honest working folks had to take their turns getting mugged, sort of like a rite of passage. But as time wore on, the muggers weren't satisfied with simply robbing their victims. Now they beat them up. And sometimes, for no reason at all, they killed them.

This guy was white, chunky, with a ragged scar on his left cheek, stupid dark eyes, a dark turtleneck sweater, and a large and formidable gun. He smelled of sweat, cigarette smoke, beer, and a high, sweet, unclean tang.

"How much can you get with your card?"

"Couple hundred."

"Yeah. Right."

"Couple hundred. I mean, we're not exactly rich people. Look at this car."

He turned to Laura. "How much can he get, babe?"

"He told you. A couple of hundred." She sounded surprisingly calm.

"One more time." He had turned back to me. "How much can you get with that card of yours?"

"I told you," I said.

You know how movie thugs are always slugging people with gun butts? Well, let me tell you something. It hurts. He hit me hard enough to draw blood, hard enough to fill my sight with darkness and blinking stars, like a planetarium ceiling, and hard enough to lay my forehead against the steering wheel.

Laura didn't scream.

She just leaned over and touched my head with her long, gentle fingers. And you know what? Even then, even suffering from what might be a concussion, I had this image of Laura's fingers touching Chris Tomlin's head this way. Ain't jealousy grand?

"Now," said the voice in the backseat, "let's talk."

Neither of us paid him much attention for a minute or so. Laura helped me sit back in the seat. She took her handkerchief and daubed it against the back of my head.

"You didn't have to hit him."

"Now maybe he'll tell me the truth."

"Four or five hundred," she said. "That's how much we can get. And don't hit him again. Don't lay a finger on him."

"The mama lion fights for her little cub. That's nice." He leaned forward and put the end of the gun directly against my ear. "You're gonna have to go back out in that nasty ol' rain. There's an ATM machine down at the west end of this block and around the corner. You go down there and get me five hundred dollars and then you haul your ass right back. I'll be waiting right here with your exceedingly good-looking wife. And with my gun."

"Where did you ever learn a word like exceedingly?" I said.

"What the hell's that supposed to mean?"

"I was just curious."

"If it's any of your goddamned business, my cellmate had one of them improve-your-vocabulary books."

I glanced at Laura. She still looked scared but she also looked a little bit angry. For us, five hundred dollars was a lot of money.

And now a robber who used the word "exceedingly" was going to take every last dime of it.

"Go get it," he said.

I reached over to touch Laura's hand as reassuringly as possible, and that was when I noticed it.

The white number-ten envelope.

The one Chris had sent her.

I stared at it a long moment and then raised my eyes to meet hers.

"I was going to tell you about it."

I shook my head. "I shouldn't have looked in your drawer."

"No, you shouldn't have. But I still owe you an explanation."

"What the hell are you two talking about?"

"Nothing that's exceedingly interesting," I said, and opened the door and dangled a leg out and then had the rest of my body follow the leg.

"You got five minutes, you understand?" the man said.

I nodded and glanced at Laura. "I love you."

"I'm sorry about the letter."

"You know the funny thing? I was hiding your present, that's how I found it. I was going to tuck it in your underwear drawer and have you find them. You know, the pearls."

"You got me the pearl necklace?"

"Uh-huh."

"Oh, honey, that's so sweet."

"Go get the goddamned money," the man said, "and get it fast."

"I'll be right back," I said to Laura and blew her a little kiss.

IF I HADN'T been sodden before, I certainly was now.

There were two brick buildings facing each other across a narrow alley. Most people drove up to this particular ATM machine because it was housed in a deep indentation that faced the alley. It could also accommodate foot traffic.

What it didn't do was give you much protection from the storm.

By now, I was sneezing and feeling a scratchiness in my throat. Bad sinuses. My whole family.

I walked up to the oasis of light and technology in this ancient and wild neighborhood, took out my wallet, and inserted my ATM card.

It was all very casual, especially considering the fact that Laura was being held hostage.

The card would go in. The money would come out. The thief would get his loot. Laura and I would dash to the nearest phone and call the police.

Except I couldn't remember my secret pin number.

If I had to estimate how many times I'd used this card, I'd put it at probably a thousand or so.

So how, after all those times, could I now forget the pin number?

Panic. That's what was wrong. I was so scared that Laura would be hurt that I couldn't think clearly.

Deep breaths. There.

Now. Think. Clearly.

Just relax and your pin number will come back to you. No problem.

That was when I noticed the slight black man in the rain parka standing just to the left of me. In the rain. With a gun in his hand.

"You wanna die?"

"Oh, shit. You've got to be kidding. You're a goddamned thief?"

"Yes, and I ain't ashamed of it either, man."

I thought of explaining it to him, explaining that another thief already had first dibs on the proceeds of my bank account—that is, if I could ever remember the pin number—but he didn't seem to be the understanding type at all. In fact, he looked even more desperate and crazy than the man who was holding Laura.

"How much can you take out?"

"I can't give it to you."

"You see this gun, man?"

"Yeah. I see it."

"You know what happens if you don't crank some serious money out for me?"

I had to explain after all. ". . . so, you see, I can't give it to you."

"What the hell's that supposed to mean?"

"Somebody's already got dibs on it."

"Dibs? What the hell does 'dibs' mean?"

"It means another robber has already spoken for this money."

He looked at me carefully. "You're crazy, man. You really are. But that don't mean I won't shoot you."

"And there's one more thing."

"What?"

"I can't remember my pin number."

"Bullshit."

"It's true. That's why I've been standing here. My mind's a blank."

"You gotta relax, man."

"I know that. But it's kind of hard. You've got a gun and so does the other guy."

"There's really some other dude holdin' your old lady?"

"Right."

He grinned with exceedingly bad teeth. "You got yourself a real problem, dude."

I closed my eyes.

I must have spent my five minutes already.

Would he really kill Laura?

"You tried deep breathin'?"

"Yeah."

"And that didn't work?"

"Huh-uh."

"You tried makin' your mind go blank for a little bit?"

"That didn't work, either."

He pushed the gun right into my face. "I ain't got much time, man."

"I can't give you the money, anyway."

"You ain't gonna be much use to your old lady if you got six or seven bullet holes in you."

"God!"

"What's wrong?"

My pin number had popped into my head.

Nothing like a gun in your face to jog your memory.

I dove for the ATM machine.

And started punching buttons.

The right buttons.

"Listen," I said as I cranked away, "I really can't give you this money."

"Right."

"I mean, I would if I could but the guy would never believe me if I told him some other crook had taken it. No offense, 'crook,' I mean."

"Here it comes."

"I'm serious. You can't have it."

"Pretty, pretty Yankee dollars. Praise the Lord."

The plastic cover opened and the machine began spitting out green Yankee dollars.

And that's when he slugged me on the back of the head.

The guy back in the car had hit me but it had been nothing like this.

This time, the field of black floating in front of my eyes didn't even have stars. This time, hot shooting pain traveled from the point of impact near the top of my skull all the way down into my neck and shoulders. This time, my knees gave out immediately.

Pavement. Hard. Wet. Smelling of cold rain. And still the darkness. Total darkness. I had a moment of panic. Had I been blinded for life? I wanted to be angry but I was too disoriented. Pain. Cold. Darkness.

And then I felt his hands tearing the money from mine.

I had to hold on to it. Had to. Otherwise Laura would be injured. Or killed.

The kick landed hard just above my sternum. Stars suddenly appeared in the field of black. His foot seemed to have jarred them loose.

More pain. But now there was anger. I blindly lashed out and grabbed his trouser leg, clung to it, forcing him to drag me down the sidewalk as he tried to get away. I don't know how many names I called him, some of them probably didn't even make sense, I just clung to his leg, exulting in his rage, in his inability to get rid of me.

Then he leaned down and grabbed a handful of my hair and pulled so hard I screamed. And inadvertently let go of his leg.

And then I heard his footsteps, retreating, retreating, and felt the rain start slashing at me again. He had dragged me out from beneath the protection of the ATM overhang.

I struggled to get up. It wasn't easy. I still couldn't see. And every time I tried to stand, I was overcome by dizziness and a faint nausea.

But I kept thinking of Laura. And kept pushing myself to my feet, no matter how much pain pounded in my head, no matter how I started to pitch forward and collapse again.

By the time I got to my feet, and fell against the rough brick of the building for support, my eyesight was back. Funny how much you take it for granted. It's terrifying when it's gone.

I looked at the oasis of light in the gloom. At the foot of the ATM was my bank card. I wobbled over and picked it up. I knew that I'd taken out my allotted amount for the day but I decided to try and see if the cosmic forces were with me for once.

They weren't.

The only thing I got from the machine was a snotty little note saying that I'd have to contact my personal banker if I wanted to receive more money.

A) I had no idea who this personal banker was, and

B) I doubted that he would be happy if I called him at home on such a rainy night even if I did have his name and number.

Then I did what any red-blooded American would do. I started kicking the machine. Kicking hard. Kicking obsessively. Until my toes started to hurt.

I stood for a long moment in the rain, letting it pour down on me, feeling as if I were melting like a wax statue in the hot sun. I became one with the drumming and thrumming and pounding of it all.

There was only one thing I could do now.

I took off running back to the car. To Laura. And the man with the gun.

I broke into a crazy grin when I saw the car. I could see Laura's profile in the gloom. She was still alive.

I reached the driver's door, opened it up, and pitched myself inside.

"My God, what happened to you?" Laura said. "Did somebody beat you up?"

The man with the gun was a little less sympathetic. "Where the hell's the money?"

I decided to answer both questions at once. "I couldn't remember my pin number so I had to stand there for a while. And then this guy—this black guy—he came out of nowhere and he had a gun and then he made me give him the money." I looked back at the man with the gun. "I couldn't help it. I told him that you had first dibs on the money but he didn't care."

"You expect me to believe that crap?"

"Honest to God. That's what happened."

He looked at me and smiled. And then put the gun right up against Laura's head. "You want me to show you what's gonna happen here if you're not back in five minutes with the money?"

I looked at Laura. "God, honey, I'm telling the truth. About the guy with the gun."

"I know."

"I'm sorry." I glanced forlornly out the window at the rain filling the curbs. "I'll get the money. Somehow."

I opened the door again. And then noticed the white envelope still sitting on her lap. "I'm sorry I didn't trust you, sweetheart."

She was scared, that was easy enough to see, but she forced herself to focus and smile at me. "I love you, honey."

"Get out of here and get that money," said the man with the gun.

"I knew you wouldn't believe me."

"You heard what I said. Get going."

I reached over and took Laura's hand gently. "I'll get the money, sweetheart. I promise."

I got out of the car and started walking again. Then trotting. Then flat-out running. My head was still pounding with pain but I didn't care. I had to get the money. Somehow. Somewhere.

I didn't even know where I was going. I was just—running. It was better than standing still and contemplating what the guy with the gun might do.

I reached the corner and looked down the block where the ATM was located.

A car came from behind me, its headlights stabbing through the silver sheets of night rain. It moved on past me. When it came even with the lights of the ATM machine, it turned an abrupt left and headed for the machine.

Guy inside his car. Nice and warm and dry. Inserts his card, gets all the money he wants, and then drives on to do a lot of fun things with his nice and warm and dry evening.

While I stood out here in the soaking rain and—

Of course, I thought.

Of course.

There was only one thing I could do.

I started running, really running, splashing through puddles and tripping and nearly falling down. But nothing could stop me.

The bald man had parked too far away from the ATM to do his banking from the car. He backed up and gave it another try. He was concentrating on backing up so I didn't have much trouble opening the passenger door and slipping in.

"What the—" he started to say as he became aware of me.

"Stickup."

"What?"

"I'm robbing you."

"Oh, man, that's all I need. I've had a really crummy day today, mister," he said. "I knew I never should've come in this neighborhood but I was in a hurry and—"

"You want to hear about my bad day, mister? Huh?"

I raised the pocket of my raincoat, hoping he would think that I was pointing a gun at him.

He looked down at my coat-draped fist and said, "You can't get a whole hell of a lotta money out of these ATM machines."

"You can get three hundred and that's good enough."

"What if I don't have three hundred?"

"New car. Nice new suit. Maybe twenty CDs in that box there. You've got three hundred. Easy."

"I work hard for my money."

"So do I."

"What if I told you I don't believe you've got a gun in there?"

"Then I'd say fine. And then I'd kill you."

"You don't look like a stickup guy."

"And you don't look like a guy who's stupid enough to get himself shot over three hundred dollars."

"I have to back up again. So I can get close."

"Back up. But go easy."

"Some birthday this is."

"It's your birthday?"

"Yeah. Ain't that a bitch?"

He backed up, pulled forward again, got right up next to the ATM, pulled out his card, and went to work.

The money came out with no problem. He handed it over to me.

"You have a pencil and paper?"

"What?"

"Something you can write with?"

"Oh. Yeah. Why?"

"I want you to write down your name and address."

"For what?"

"Because tomorrow morning I'm going to put three hundred dollars in an envelope and mail it to you."

"Are you some kind of crazy drug addict or what?"

"Just write down your name and address."

He shook his head. "Not only do I get robbed, I get robbed by some goddamned fruitcake."

But he wrote down his name and address, probably thinking I'd shoot him if he didn't.

"I appreciate the loan," I said, getting out of his car.

"Loan? You tell the cops it was a 'loan' and see what they say."

"Hope the rest of your day goes better," I said, and slammed the door.

And I hope the rest of my day goes better, too, I thought.

"GOOD THING YOU got back here when you did," the man with the gun said. "I was just about to waste her."

"Spare me the macho crap, all right?" I said. I was getting cranky. The rain. The cold. The fear. And then having to commit a felony to get the cash I needed—and putting fear into a perfectly decent citizen who'd been having a very bad day himself.

I handed the money over to him. "Now you can go," I said.

He counted it in hard, harsh grunts, like a pig rutting in the mud.

"Three hundred. It was supposed to be four. Or five."

"I guess you'll just have to shoot us, then, huh?"

Laura gave me a frantic look and then dug her nails into my hands. Obviously, like the man I'd just left at the ATM, she thought I had lost what little of my senses I had left.

"I wouldn't push it, punk," the man with the gun said. "Because I just might shoot you yet."

He leaned forward from the backseat and said, "Lemme see your purse, babe."

Laura looked at me. I nodded. She handed him her purse.

More rutting sounds as he went through it.

"Twenty-six bucks?"

"I'm sorry," Laura said.

"Where're your credit cards?"

"We don't have credit cards. It's too tempting to use them. We're saving for a house."

"Ain't that sweet!"

He pitched the purse over the front seat and opened the back door.

Chill. Fog. Rain.

"You got a jerk for a husband, babe, I mean, just in case you haven't figured that out already."

Then he slammed the door and was gone.

"YOU WERE REALLY going to tear it up?"

"Or let you tear it up. Whichever you preferred. I mean, I know you think I still have this thing for Chris but I really don't. I was going to prove it to you by showing you the letter tonight and letting you do whatever you wanted with it."

We were in bed, three hours after getting our car towed to a station, the tow truck giving us a ride home.

The rain had quit an hour ago. Now there were just icy winds. But it was snug and warm in the bed of my one true love and icy winds didn't bother me at all.

"I'm sorry," I said, "about being so jealous."

"And I'm sorry about hiding the letter. It made you think I was going to take him up on his offer. But I really don't have any desire to see him at all."

Then we kind of just laid back and listened to the wind for a time.

And she started getting affectionate, her foot rubbing my foot, her hand taking my hand.

And then in the darkness, she said, "Would you like to make love?"

"Would I?" I laughed. "Would I?"

And then I rolled over and we began kissing and then I began running my fingers through her long dark hair and then I suddenly realized that—

"What's wrong?" she said, as I rolled away from her, flat on my back, staring at the ceiling.

"Let's just go to sleep."

"God, honey, I want to know what's going on. Here we are making out and then all of a sudden you stop."

"Oh God," I said. "What a day this has been." I sighed and prepared myself for the ultimate in manly humiliation. "Remember that time when Rick's sister got married?"

"Uh-huh."

"And I got real drunk?"

"Uh-huh."

"And that night we tried—well, we tried to make love but I couldn't?"

"Uh-huh." She was silent a long moment. Then, "Oh God, you mean, the same thing happened to you just now?"

"Uh-huh," I said.

"Oh, honey, I'm sorry."

"The perfect ending to the perfect day," I said.

"First you find that letter from Chris—"

"And then I can't concentrate on my job—"

"And then Ms. Sanders threatens to fire you—"

"And then a man sticks us up—"

"And then you have to stick up another man—"

"And then we come home and go to bed and—" I sighed. "I think I'll just roll over and go to sleep."

"Good idea, honey. That's what we both need. A good night's sleep."

"I love you, sweetheart," I said. "I'm sorry I wasn't able to . . . well, you know."

"It's fine, sweetie. It happens to every man once in a while."
"It's just one of those days," I said.
"And one of those nights," she said.

———

BUT YOU KNOW what? Some time later the grandfather clock in the living room woke me as it tolled twelve midnight, and when I rolled over to see how Laura was doing, she was wide awake and took me in her sweet warm arms, and I didn't have any trouble at all showing her how grateful I was.

It was a brand-new day . . . and when I finally got around to breakfast, the first thing I did was lift the horoscope section from the paper . . . and drop it, unread, into the wastebasket.

No more snooping in drawers . . . and no more bad-luck horoscopes.

MISSING: PAGE THIRTEEN

Anna Katharine Green

Anna Katharine Green (1846–1935) is often referred to as "the mother of detective fiction," a sobriquet she earned by refining many of the conventions of the mystery genre that we enjoy today. Besides creating the first female detective, she also wrote the first mystery novel that was published under a woman's name. Writing at about the same time that Sir Arthur Conan Doyle was developing Sherlock Holmes, she concentrated on the official law enforment agencies instead, writing the police procedural *The Leavenworth Case: A Lawyer's Story* in 1878. The book, her first, was phenomenally successful, selling over a million copies, and was picked up by the Yale Law School as required reading. The main character of the novel, Ebenezer Gryce, would appear in more than a dozen other books during her career. Her other sleuths included spinster detective Amelia Butterworth and private detective Violet Strange, who appears in this story.

ONE

"ONE MORE! JUST one more well paying affair, and I promise to stop; really and truly to stop."

"But, Puss, why one more? You have earned the amount you set for yourself,—or very nearly,—and though my help is not great, in three months I can add enough—"

"No, you cannot, Arthur. You are doing well; I appreciate it; in fact, I am just delighted to have you work for me in the way you do, but you cannot, in your present position, make enough in three months, or in six, to meet the situation as I see it. Enough does not satisfy me. The measure must be full, heaped up, and running over. Possible failure following promise must be provided for. Never must I feel myself called upon to do this kind of thing again. Besides, I have never got over the Zabriskie tragedy. It haunts me continually. Something new may help to put it out of my head. I feel guilty. I was responsible—"

"No, Puss. I will not have it that you were responsible. Some such end was bound to follow a complication like that. Sooner or later he would have been driven to shoot himself—"

"But not her."

"No, not her. But do you think she would have given those few minutes of perfect understanding with her blind husband for a few years more of miserable life?"

Violet made no answer; she was too absorbed in her surprise. Was this Arthur? Had a few weeks' work and a close connection with the really serious things of life made this change in him? Her face beamed at the thought, which seeing, but not understanding what underlay this evidence of joy, he bent and kissed her, saying with some of his old nonchalance:

"Forget it, Violet; only don't let any one or anything lead you to interest yourself in another affair of the kind. If you do, I shall have to consult a certain friend of yours as to the best way of stopping this folly. I mention no names. Oh! you need not look so frightened. Only behave; that's all."

"He's right," she acknowledged to herself, as he sauntered away; "altogether right."

Yet because she wanted the extra money—

THE SCENE INVITED alarm—that is, for so young a girl as Violet, surveying it from an automobile some time after the stroke of midnight. An unknown house at the end of a heavily shaded walk, in the open doorway of which could be seen the silhouette of a woman's form leaning eagerly forward with arms outstretched in an appeal for help! It vanished while she looked, but the effect remained, holding her to her seat for one startled moment. This seemed strange, for she had anticipated adventure. One is not summoned from a private ball to ride a dozen miles into the country on an errand of investigation, without some expectation of encountering the mysterious and the tragic. But Violet Strange, for all her many experiences, was of a most susceptible nature, and for the instant in which that door stood open, with only the memory of that expectant figure to disturb the faintly lit vista of the hall beyond, she felt that grip upon the throat which comes from an indefinable fear which no words can explain and no plummet sound.

But this soon passed. With the setting of her foot to ground, conditions changed and her emotions took on a more normal character. The figure of a man now stood in the place held by the vanished woman, and it was not only that of one she knew but that of one whom she trusted—a friend whose very presence gave her courage. With this recognition came a better understanding of the situation, and it was with a beaming eye and unclouded features that she tripped up the walk to meet the expectant figure and outstretched hand of Roger Upjohn.

"You here!" she exclaimed, amid smiles and blushes, as he drew her into the hall.

He at once launched forth into explanations mingled with apologies for the presumption he had shown in putting her to this inconvenience. There was trouble in the house—great trouble. Something had occurred for which an explanation must be found before morning, or the happiness and honour of more than one person now under this unhappy roof would be wrecked. He knew it was late—that she had been obliged to take a long and dreary ride alone, but her success with the problem which had once come near wrecking his own life had emboldened him to telephone to the office and—"But you are in ball-dress," he cried in amazement. "Did you think—"

"I came from a ball. Word reached me between the dances. I did not go home. I had been bidden to hurry."

He looked his appreciation, but when he spoke it was to say:

"This is the situation. Miss Digby—"

"The lady who is to be married to-morrow?"

"Who *hopes* to be married to-morrow."

"How, *hopes?*"

"Who *will* be married to-morrow, if a certain article lost in this house to-night can be found before any of the persons who have been dining here leave for their homes."

Violet uttered an exclamation.

"Then, Mr. Cornell," she began—

"Mr. Cornell has our utmost confidence," Roger hastened to interpose. "But the article missing is one which he might reasonably desire to possess and which he alone of all present had the opportunity of securing. You can therefore see why he, with his pride—the pride of a man not rich, engaged to marry a woman who is—should declare that unless his innocence is established before daybreak, the doors of St. Bartholomew will remain shut to-morrow."

"But the article lost—what is it?"

"Miss Digby will give you the particulars. She is waiting to receive you," he added with a gesture towards a half-open door at their right.

Violet glanced that way, then cast her looks up and down the hall in which they stood.

"Do you know that you have not told me in whose house I am? Not hers, I know. She lives in the city."

"And you are twelve miles from Harlem. Miss Strange, you are in the Van Broecklyn mansion, famous enough you will acknowledge. Have you never been here before?"

"I have been by here, but I recognized nothing in the dark. What an exciting place for an investigation!"

"And Mr. Van Broecklyn? Have you never met him?"

"Once, when a child. He frightened me *then*."

"And may frighten you now; though I doubt it. Time has mellowed him. Besides, I have prepared him for what might otherwise occasion him some astonishment. Naturally he would not look for just the sort of lady investigator I am about to introduce to him."

She smiled. Violet Strange was a very charming young woman, as well as a keen prober of odd mysteries.

The meeting between herself and Miss Digby was a sympathetic one. After the first inevitable shock which the latter felt at sight of the beauty and fashionable appearance of the mysterious little being who was to solve her difficulties, her glance, which, under other circumstances, might have lingered unduly upon the piquant features and exquisite dressing of the fairy-like figure before her, passed at once to Violet's eyes in whose steady depths beamed an intelligence quite at odds with the coquettish dimples which so often misled the casual observer in his estimation of a character singularly subtle and well-poised.

As for the impression she herself made upon Violet, it was the same she made upon everyone. No one could look long at Florence Digby and not recognize the loftiness of her spirit and the generous nature of her impulses. In person she was tall, and as she leaned to take Violet's hand, the difference between them brought out the salient points in each, to the great admiration of the one onlooker.

Meantime, for all her interest in the case in hand, Violet could not help casting a hurried look about her, in gratification of the curiosity incited by her entrance into a house signalized from its foundation by such a series of tragic events. The result was disappointing. The walls were plain, the furniture simple. Nothing suggestive in either, unless it was the fact that nothing was new, nothing modern. As it looked in the days of Burr and Hamilton so it looked to-day, even to the rather startling detail of candles which did duty on every side in place of gas.

As Violet recalled the reason for this, the fascination of the past seized upon her imagination. There was no knowing where this might have carried her, had not the feverish gleam in Miss Digby's eyes warned her that the present held its own excitement. Instantly, she was all attention and listening with undivided mind to that lady's disclosures.

They were brief and to the following effect:

The dinner which had brought some half-dozen people together in this house had been given in celebration of her impending marriage. But it was also in a way meant as a compliment to one of the other guests, a Mr. Spielhagen, who, during the week, had succeeded in demonstrating to a few experts the value of a discovery he had made which would transform a great industry.

In speaking of this discovery, Miss Digby did not go into particulars, the whole matter being far beyond her understanding; but in stating its value she openly acknowledged that it was in the line of Mr. Cornell's own work, and one which involved calculations and a formula which, if prematurely disclosed, would invalidate the contract Mr. Spielhagen hoped to make, and thus destroy his present hopes.

Of this formula but two copies existed. One was locked up in a safe deposit vault in Boston, the other he had brought into the house on his person, and it was the latter which was now missing, it having been abstracted during the evening from a manuscript of sixteen or more sheets, under circumstances which she would now endeavour to relate.

Mr. Van Broecklyn, their host, had in his melancholy life but one interest which could be called at all absorbing. This was for explosives. As a consequence, much of the talk at the dinner-table had been on Mr. Spielhagen's discovery, and the possible changes it might introduce into this especial industry. As these, worked out from a formula kept secret from the trade, could not but affect greatly Mr. Cornell's interests, she found herself listening intently, when Mr. Van Broecklyn, with an apology for his interference, ventured to remark that if Mr. Spielhagen had made a valuable discovery in this line, so had he, and one which he had substantiated by many experiments. It was not a marketable one, such as Mr. Spielhagen's was, but in his work upon the same, and in the tests which he had been led to make, he had discovered certain instances he would gladly name, which demanded exceptional procedure to be successful. If Mr. Spielhagen's method did not allow for these exceptions, nor make suitable provision for them, then Mr. Spielhagen's method would fail more times than it would succeed. Did it so allow and so provide? It would relieve him greatly to learn that it did.

The answer came quickly. Yes, it did. But later and after some further conversation, Mr. Spielhagen's confidence seemed to wane, and before they left the dinner-table, he openly declared his intention of looking over his manuscript again that very night, in order to be sure that the formula therein contained duly covered all the exceptions mentioned by Mr. Van Broecklyn.

If Mr. Cornell's countenance showed any change at this moment, she for one had not noticed it; but the bitterness with which he remarked upon the other's good fortune in having discovered this formula of whose entire success he had no doubt, was apparent to everybody, and naturally gave point to the circumstances which a short time afterward associated him with the disappearance of the same.

The ladies (there were two others besides herself) having withdrawn in a body to the music-room, the gentlemen all proceeded to the library to smoke. Here, conversation, loosed from the one topic which had hitherto engrossed it, was proceeding briskly, when Mr. Spielhagen, with a nervous gesture, impulsively looked about him and said:

"I cannot rest till I have run through my thesis again. Where can I find a quiet spot? I won't be long; I read very rapidly."

It was for Mr. Van Broecklyn to answer, but no word coming from him, every eye turned his way, only to find him sunk in one of those fits of abstraction so well known to his friends, and from which no one who has this strange man's peace of mind at heart ever presumes to rouse him.

What was to be done? These moods of their singular host sometimes lasted half an hour, and Mr. Spielhagen had not the appearance of a man of patience. Indeed he presently gave proof of the great uneasiness he was labouring under, for noticing a door standing ajar on the other side of the room, he remarked to those around him:

"A den! and lighted! Do you see any objection to my shutting myself in there for a few minutes?"

No one venturing to reply, he rose, and giving a slight push to the door, disclosed a small room exquisitely panelled and brightly lighted, but without one article of furniture in it, not even a chair.

"The very place," quoth Mr. Spielhagen, and lifting a light cane-bottomed chair from the many standing about, he carried it inside and shut the door behind him.

Several minutes passed during which the man who had served at table entered with a tray on which were several small glasses evidently containing some choice liqueur. Finding his master fixed in one of his strange moods, he set the tray down and, pointing to one of the glasses, said:

"That is for Mr. Van Broecklyn. It contains his usual quieting powder." And urging the gentlemen to help themselves, he quietly left the room.

Mr. Upjohn lifted the glass nearest him, and Mr. Cornell seemed about to do the same when he suddenly reached forward and catching up one farther off started for the room in which Mr. Spielhagen had so deliberately secluded himself.

Why he did all this—why, above all things, he should reach across the tray for a glass instead of taking the one under his hand, he can no more explain than why he has followed many another unhappy impulse. Nor did he understand the nervous start given by Mr. Spielhagen at his entrance, or the stare with which that gentleman took the glass from his hand and mechanically drank its contents, till he saw how his hand had stretched itself across the sheet of paper he was reading, in an open attempt to hide the lines visible between his fingers. Then indeed the intruder flushed and withdrew in great embarrassment, fully conscious of his indiscretion but not deeply disturbed till Mr. Van Broecklyn, suddenly arousing and glancing down at the tray placed very near his hand, remarked in some surprise: "Dobbs seems to have forgotten me." Then indeed, the unfortunate Mr. Cornell realized what he had done. It was the glass intended for his host which he had caught up and carried into the other room—the glass which he had been told contained a drug. Of what folly he had been guilty, and how tame would be any effort at excuse!

Attempting none, he rose and with a hurried glance at Mr. Upjohn who flushed in sympathy at his distress, he crossed to the door he had so lately closed upon Mr. Spielhagen. But feeling his shoulder touched as his hand pressed the knob, he turned to meet the eye of Mr. Van Broecklyn fixed upon him with an expression which utterly confounded him.

"Where are you going?" that gentleman asked.

The questioning tone, the severe look, expressive at once of displeasure and astonishment, were most disconcerting, but Mr. Cornell managed to stammer forth:

"Mr. Spielhagen is in here consulting his thesis. When your man brought in the cordial, I was awkward enough to catch up your glass and carry it in to Mr. Spielhagen. He drank it and I—I am anxious to see if it did him any harm."

As he uttered the last word he felt Mr. Van Broecklyn's hand slip from his shoulder, but no word accompanied the action, nor did his host make the least move to follow him into the room.

This was a matter of great regret to him later, as it left him for a moment out of the range of every eye, during which he says he simply stood in a state of shock at seeing Mr. Spielhagen still sitting there, manuscript in hand, but with head fallen forward and eyes closed; dead, asleep or—he hardly knew what; the sight so paralysed him.

Whether or not this was the exact truth and the whole truth, Mr. Cornell certainly looked very unlike himself as he stepped back into Mr. Van Broecklyn's presence; and he was only partially reassured when that gentleman protested that there was no real harm in the drug, and that Mr. Spielhagen would be all right if left to wake naturally and without shock. However, as his present attitude was one of great discomfort, they decided to carry him back and lay him on the library lounge. But before doing this, Mr. Upjohn drew from his flaccid grasp, the precious manuscript, and carrying it into the larger room placed it on a remote table, where it remained undisturbed till Mr. Spielhagen, suddenly coming to himself at the end of some fifteen minutes, missed the sheets from his hand, and bounding up, crossed the room to repossess himself of them.

His face, as he lifted them up and rapidly ran through them with ever-accumulating anxiety, told them what they had to expect.

The page containing the formula was gone!

Violet now saw her problem.

TWO

THERE WAS NO doubt about the loss I have mentioned; all could see that page 13 was not there. In vain a second handling of every sheet, the one so numbered was not to be found. Page 14 met the eye on the top of the pile, and page 12 finished it off at the bottom, but no page 13 in between, or anywhere else.

Where had it vanished, and through whose agency had this misadventure occurred? No one could say, or, at least, no one there made any attempt to do so, though everybody started to look for it.

But where look? The adjoining small room offered no facilities for hiding a cigar-end, much less a square of shining white paper. Bare walls, a bare floor, and a single chair for furniture, comprised all that was to be seen in this direction. Nor could the room in which they then stood be thought to hold it, unless it was on the person of some one of them. Could this be the explanation of the mystery? No man looked his doubts; but Mr. Cornell, possibly divining the general feeling, stepped up to Mr. Van Broecklyn and in a cool voice, but with the red burning hotly on either cheek, said, so as to be heard by everyone present:

"I demand to be searched—at once and thoroughly."

A moment's silence, then the common cry:

"We will all be searched."

"Is Mr. Spielhagen sure that the missing page was with the others when he sat down in the adjoining room to read his thesis?" asked their perturbed host.

"Very sure," came the emphatic reply. "Indeed, I was just going through the formula itself when I fell asleep."

"You are ready to assert this?"

"I am ready to swear it."

Mr. Cornell repeated his request.

"I demand that you make a thorough search of my person. I must be cleared, and instantly, of every suspicion," he gravely asserted, "or how can I marry Miss Digby to-morrow."

After that there was no further hesitation. One and all subjected themselves to the ordeal suggested; even Mr. Spielhagen. But this effort was as futile as the rest. The lost page was not found.

What were they to think? What were they to do?

There seemed to be nothing left to do, and yet some further attempt must be made towards the recovery of this important formula. Mr. Cornell's marriage and Mr. Spielhagen's business success both depended upon its being in the latter's hands before six in the morning, when he was engaged to hand it over to a certain manufacturer sailing for Europe on an early steamer.

Five hours!

Had Mr. Van Broecklyn a suggestion to offer? No, he was as much at sea as the rest.

Simultaneously look crossed look. Blankness was on every face.

"Let us call the ladies," suggested one.

It was done, and however great the tension had been before, it was even greater when Miss Digby stepped upon the scene. But she was not a woman to be shaken from her poise even by a crisis of this importance.

When the dilemma had been presented to her and the full situation grasped, she looked first at Mr. Cornell and then at Mr. Spielhagen, and quietly said:

"There is but one explanation possible of this matter. Mr. Spielhagen will excuse me, but he is evidently mistaken in thinking that he saw the lost page among the rest. The condition into which he was thrown by the un-accustomed drug he had drank, made him liable to hallucinations. I have not the least doubt he thought he had been studying the formula at the time he dropped off to sleep. I have every confidence in the gentleman's candour. But so have I in that of Mr. Cornell," she supplemented, with a smile.

An exclamation from Mr. Van Broecklyn and a subdued murmur from all but Mr. Spielhagen testified to the effect of this suggestion, and there is no saying what might have been the result if Mr. Cornell had not hurriedly put in this extraordinary and most unexpected protest:

"Miss Digby has my gratitude," said he, "for a confidence which I hope to prove to be deserved. But I must say this for Mr. Spielhagen. He was correct in stating that he was engaged in looking over his formula when I stepped into his presence with the glass of cordial. If you were not in a position to see the hurried way in which his hand instinctively spread itself over the page he was reading, I was; and if that does not seem con-clusive to you, then I feel bound to state that in unconsciously following this movement of his, I plainly saw the number written on the top of the page, and that number was—13."

A loud exclamation, this time from Spielhagen himself, announced his gratitude and corresponding change of attitude toward the speaker.

"Wherever that damned page has gone," he protested, advancing to-wards Cornell with outstretched hand, "you have nothing to do with its disappearance."

Instantly all constraint fled, and every countenance took on a relieved expression. *But the problem remained.*

Suddenly those very words passed some one's lips, and with their ut-terance Mr. Upjohn remembered how at an extraordinary crisis in his own life, he had been helped and an equally difficult problem settled, by a little lady secretly attached to a private detective agency. If she could only be found and hurried here before morning, all might yet be well. He would make the effort. Such wild schemes sometimes work. He telephoned to the office and—

Was there anything else Miss Strange would like to know?

THREE

M ISS STRANGE, THUS appealed to, asked where the gentlemen were now.

She was told that they were still all together in the library; the ladies had been sent home.

"Then let us go to them," said Violet, hiding under a smile her great fear that here was an affair which might very easily spell for her that dismal word, *failure*.

So great was that fear that under all ordinary circumstances she would have had no thought for anything else in the short interim between this stating of the problem and her speedy entrance among the persons involved. But the circumstances of this case were so far from ordinary, or rather let me put it in this way, the setting of the case was so very extraordinary, that she scarcely thought of the problem before her, in her great interest in the house through whose rambling halls she was being so carefully guided. So much that was tragic and heartrending had occurred here. The Van Broecklyn name, the Van Broecklyn history, above all the Van Broecklyn tradition, which made the house unique in the country's annals (of which more hereafter), all made an appeal to her imagination, and centred her thoughts on what she saw about her. There was a door which no man ever opened—had never opened since Revolutionary times—should she see it? Should she know it if she did see it? Then Mr. Van Broecklyn himself! Just to meet him, under any conditions and in any place, was an event. But to meet him here, under the pall of his own mystery! No wonder she had no words for her companions, or that her thoughts clung to this anticipation in wonder and almost fearsome delight.

His story was a well-known one. A bachelor and a misanthrope, he lived absolutely alone save for a large entourage of servants, all men and elderly ones at that. He never visited. Though he now and then, as on this occasion, entertained certain persons under his roof, he declined every invitation for himself, avoiding even, with equal strictness, all evening amusements of whatever kind, which would detain him in the city after ten at night. Perhaps this was to ensure no break in his rule of life never to sleep out of his own bed. Though he was a man well over fifty he had not spent, according to his own statement, but two nights out of his own bed since his return from Europe in early boyhood, and those were in obedience to a judicial summons which took him to Boston.

This was his main eccentricity, but he had another which is apparent enough from what has already been said. He avoided women. If thrown in with them during his short visits into town, he was invariably polite and at times companionable, but he never sought them out, nor had gossip, contrary to its usual habit, ever linked his name with one of the sex.

Yet he was a man of more than ordinary attraction. His features were fine and his figure impressive. He might have been the cynosure of all eyes had he chosen to enter crowded drawing-rooms, or even to frequent public assemblages, but having turned his back upon everything of the kind in his youth, he had found it impossible to alter his habits with advancing years; nor was he now expected to. The position he had taken was respected. Leonard Van Broecklyn was no longer criticized.

Was there any explanation for this strangely self-centred life? Those who knew him best seemed to think so. In the first place he had sprung from an unfortunate stock. Events of an unusual and tragic nature had marked the family of both parents. Nor had his parents themselves been exempt from this seeming fatality. Antagonistic in tastes and temperament, they had dragged on an unhappy existence in the old home, till both natures rebelled, and a separation ensued which not only disunited their lives but sent them to opposite sides of the globe never to return again. At least, that was the inference drawn from the peculiar circumstances attending the event. On the morning of one never-to-be-forgotten day, John Van Broecklyn, the grandfather of the present representative of the family, found the following note from his son lying on the library table:

Father:

> *Life in this house, or any house, with* her *is no longer endurable. One of us must go. The mother should not be separated from her child. Therefore it is I whom you will never see again. Forget me, but be considerate of her and the boy.*

> *William*

Six hours later another note was found, this time from the wife:

Father:

> *Tied to a rotting corpse what does one do? Lop off one's arm if necessary to rid one of the contact. As all love between your son and myself is dead, I can no longer live within the sound of his*

voice. As this is his home, he is the one to remain in it. May our child reap the benefit of his mother's loss and his father's affection.

Rhoda

Both were gone, and gone forever. Simultaneous in their departure, they preserved each his own silence and sent no word back. If the one went east and the other west, they may have met on the other side of the globe, but never again in the home which sheltered their boy. For him and for his grandfather they had sunk from sight in the great sea of humanity, leaving them stranded on an isolated and mournful shore. The grandfather steeled himself to the double loss, for the child's sake; but the boy of eleven succumbed. Few of the world's great sufferers, of whatever age or condition, have mourned as this child mourned, or shown the effects of his grief so deeply or so long. Not till he had passed his majority did the line, carved in one day in his baby forehead, lose any of its intensity; and there are those who declare that even later than that, the midnight stillness of the house was disturbed from time to time by his muffled shriek of "Mother! Mother!" sending the servants from the house, and adding one more horror to the many which clung about this accursed mansion.

Of this cry Violet had heard, and it was that and the door—But I have already told you about the door which she was still looking for, when her two companions suddenly halted, and she found herself on the threshold of the library, in full view of Mr. Van Broecklyn and his two guests.

Slight and fairy-like in figure, with an air of modest reserve more in keeping with her youth and dainty dimpling beauty than with her errand, her appearance produced an astonishment which none of the gentlemen were able to disguise. This the clever detective, with a genius for social problems and odd elusive cases! This darling of the ball-room in satin and pearls! Mr. Spielhagen glanced at Mr. Cornell, and Mr. Cornell at Mr. Spielhagen, and both at Mr. Upjohn, in very evident distrust. As for Violet, she had eyes only for Mr. Van Broecklyn, who stood before her in a surprise equal to that of the others but with more restraint in its expression.

She was not disappointed in him. She had expected to see a man, reserved almost to the point of austerity. And she found his first look even more awe-compelling than her imagination had pictured; so much so indeed, that her resolution faltered, and she took a quick step backward; which seeing, he smiled and her heart and hopes grew warm again. That he could smile, and smile with absolute sweetness, was her great comfort when later— But I am introducing you too hurriedly to the catastrophe. There is much to be told first.

I pass over the preliminaries, and come at once to the moment when Violet, having listened to a repetition of the full facts, stood with downcast eyes before these gentlemen, complaining in some alarm to herself:

"They expect me to tell them now and without further search or parley just where this missing page is. I shall have to balk that expectation without losing their confidence. But how?"

Summoning up her courage and meeting each inquiring eye with a look which seemed to carry a different message to each, she remarked very quietly:

"This is not a matter to guess at. I must have time and I must look a little deeper into the facts just given me. I presume that the table I see over there is the one upon which Mr. Upjohn laid the manuscript during Mr. Spielhagen's unconsciousness."

All nodded.

"Is it—I mean the table—in the same condition it was then? Has nothing been taken from it except the manuscript?"

"Nothing."

"Then the missing page is not there," she smiled, pointing to its bare top. A pause, during which she stood with her gaze fixed on the floor before her. She was thinking and thinking hard.

Suddenly she came to a decision. Addressing Mr. Upjohn, she asked if he were quite sure that in taking the manuscript from Mr. Spielhagen's hand he had neither disarranged nor dropped one of its pages.

The answer was unequivocal.

"Then," she declared, with quiet assurance and a steady meeting with her own of every eye, "as the thirteenth page was not found among the others when they were taken from this table, nor on the persons of either Mr. Cornell or Mr. Spielhagen, it is still in that inner room."

"Impossible!" came from every lip, each in a different tone. "That room is absolutely empty."

"May I have a look at its emptiness?" she asked, with a naïve glance at Mr. Van Broecklyn.

"There is positively nothing in the room but the chair Mr. Spielhagen sat on," objected that gentleman with a noticeable air of reluctance.

"Still, may I not have a look at it?" she persisted, with that disarming smile she kept for great occasions.

Mr. Van Broecklyn bowed. He could not refuse a request so urged, but his step was slow and his manner next to ungracious as he led the way to the door of the adjoining room and threw it open.

Just what she had been told to expect! Bare walls and floors and an empty chair! Yet she did not instantly withdraw, but stood silently contemplating the panelled wainscoting surrounding her, as though she suspected it of containing some secret hiding-place not apparent to the eye.

Mr. Van Broecklyn, noting this, hastened to say:

"The walls are sound, Miss Strange. They contain no hidden cupboards."

"And that door?" she asked, pointing to a portion of the wainscoting so exactly like the rest that only the most experienced eye could detect the line of deeper colour which marked an opening.

For an instant Mr. Van Broecklyn stood rigid, then the immovable pallor, which was one of his chief characteristics, gave way to a deep flush, as he explained:

"There was a door there once; but it has been permanently closed. With cement," he forced himself to add, his countenance losing its evanescent colour till it shone ghastly again in the strong light.

With difficulty Violet preserved her show of composure. "*The* door!" she murmured to herself. "I have found it. The great historic door!" But her tone was light as she ventured to say:

"Then it can no longer be opened by your hand or any other?"

"It could not be opened with an axe."

Violet sighed in the midst of her triumph. Her curiosity had been satisfied, but the problem she had been set to solve looked inexplicable. But she was not one to yield easily to discouragement. Marking the disappointment approaching to disdain in every eye but Mr. Upjohn's, she drew herself up—(she had not far to draw) and made this final proposal.

"A sheet of paper," she remarked, "of the size of this one cannot be spirited away, or dissolved into thin air. It exists; it is here; and all we want is some happy thought in order to find it. I acknowledge that that happy thought has not come to me yet, but sometimes I get it in what may seem to you a very odd way. Forgetting myself, I try to assume the individuality of the person who has worked the mystery. If I can think with his thoughts, I possibly may follow him in his actions. In this case I should like to make believe for a few moments that I am Mr. Spielhagen" (with what a delicious smile she said this) "I should like to hold his thesis in my hand and be interrupted in my reading by Mr. Cornell offering his glass of cordial; then I should like to nod and slip off mentally into a deep sleep. Possibly in that sleep the dream may come which will clarify the whole situation. Will you humour me so far?"

A ridiculous concession, but finally she had her way; the farce was enacted and they left her as she had requested them to do, alone with her dreams in the small room.

Suddenly they heard her cry out, and in another moment she appeared before them, the picture of excitement.

"Is this chair standing exactly as it did when Mr. Spielhagen occupied it?" she asked.

"No," said Mr. Upjohn, "it faced the other way."

She stepped back and twirled the chair about with her disengaged hand.

"So?"

Mr. Upjohn and Mr. Spielhagen both nodded, so did the others when she glanced at them.

With a sign of ill-concealed satisfaction, she drew their attention to herself; then eagerly cried:

"Gentlemen, look here!"

Seating herself, she allowed her whole body to relax till she presented the picture of one calmly asleep. Then, as they continued to gaze at her with fascinated eyes, not knowing what to expect, they saw something white escape from her lap and slide across the floor till it touched and was stayed by the wainscot. It was the top page of the manuscript she held, and as some inkling of the truth reached their astonished minds, she sprang impetuously to her feet and, pointing to the fallen sheet, cried:

"Do you understand now? Look where it lies, and then look here!"

She had bounded towards the wall and was now on her knees pointing to the bottom of the wainscot, just a few inches to the left of the fallen page.

"A crack!" she cried, "under what was once the door. It's a very thin one, hardly perceptible to the eye. But see!" Here she laid her finger on the fallen paper and drawing it towards her, pushed it carefully against the lower edge of the wainscot. Half of it at once disappeared.

"I could easily slip it all through," she assured them, withdrawing the sheet and leaping to her feet in triumph. "You know now where the missing page lies, Mr. Spielhagen. All that remains is for Mr. Van Broecklyn to get it for you."

FOUR

THE CRIES OF mingled astonishment and relief which greeted this simple elucidation of the mystery were broken by a curiously choked, almost unintelligible, cry. It came from the man thus appealed to, who, unnoticed by them all, had started at her first word and gradually, as action followed action, withdrawn himself till he now stood alone and in an attitude almost of defiance behind the large table in the centre of the library.

"I am sorry," he began, with a brusqueness which gradually toned down into a forced urbanity as he beheld every eye fixed upon him in amazement, "that circumstances forbid my being of assistance to you in this unfortunate matter. If the paper lies where you say, and I see no other explanation of its loss, I am afraid it will have to remain there for this night at least. The cement in which that door is embedded is thick as any wall; it would take men with pickaxes, possibly with dynamite, to make a breach there wide enough for any one to reach in. And we are far from any such help."

In the midst of the consternation caused by these words, the clock on the mantel behind his back rang out the hour. It was but a double stroke, but that meant two hours after midnight and had the effect of a knell in the hearts of those most interested.

"But I am expected to give that formula into the hands of our manager before six o'clock in the morning. The steamer sails at a quarter after."

"Can't you reproduce a copy of it from memory?" some one asked; "and insert it in its proper place among the pages you hold there?"

"The paper would not be the same. That would lead to questions and the truth would come out. As the chief value of the process contained in that formula lies in its secrecy, no explanation I could give would relieve me from the suspicions which an acknowledgment of the existence of a third copy, however well hidden, would entail. I should lose my great opportunity."

Mr. Cornell's state of mind can be imagined. In an access of mingled regret and despair, he cast a glance at Violet, who, with a nod of understanding, left the little room in which they still stood, and approached Mr. Van Broecklyn.

Lifting up her head,—for he was very tall,—and instinctively rising on her toes the nearer to reach his ear, she asked in a cautious whisper:

"Is there no other way of reaching that place?"

She acknowledged afterwards, that for one moment her heart stood still from fear, such a change took place in his face, though she says he did not move a muscle. Then, just when she was expecting from him some harsh or forbidding word, he wheeled abruptly away from her and crossing to a window at his side, lifted the shade and looked out. When he returned, he was his usual self so far as she could see.

"There is a way," he now confided to her in a tone as low as her own, "but it can only be taken by a child."

"Not by me?" she asked, smiling down at her own childish proportions.

For an instant he seemed taken aback, then she saw his hand begin to tremble and his lips twitch. Somehow—she knew not why—she began to pity him, and asked herself as she felt rather than saw the struggle in his mind, that here was a trouble which if once understood would greatly dwarf that of the two men in the room behind them.

"I am discreet," she whisperingly declared. "I have heard the history of that door—how it was against the tradition of the family to have it opened. There must have been some dreadful reason. But old superstitions do not affect me, and if you will allow me to take the way you mention, I will follow your bidding exactly, and will not trouble myself about anything but the recovery of this paper, which must lie only a little way inside that blocked-up door."

Was his look one of rebuke at her presumption, or just the constrained expression of a perturbed mind? Probably, the latter, for while she watched him for some understanding of his mood, he reached out his hand and touched one of the satin folds crossing her shoulder.

"You would soil this irretrievably," said he.

"There is stuff in the stores for another," she smiled. Slowly his touch deepened into pressure. Watching him she saw the rust of some old fear or dominant superstition melt under her eyes, and was quite prepared, when he remarked, with what for him was a lightsome air:

"I will buy the stuff, if you will dare the darkness and intricacies of our old cellar. I can give you no light. You will have to feel your way according to my direction."

"I am ready to dare anything."

He left her abruptly.

"I will warn Miss Digby," he called back. "She shall go with you as far as the cellar."

FIVE

V IOLET IN HER short career as an investigator of mysteries had been in many a situation calling for more than womanly nerve and courage. But never—or so it seemed to her at the time—had she experienced a greater depression of spirit than when she stood with Miss Digby before a small door at the extreme end of the cellar, and understood that here was her road—a road which once entered, she must take alone.

First, it was such a small door! No child older than eleven could possibly squeeze through it. But she was of the size of a child of eleven and might possibly manage that difficulty.

Secondly: there are always some unforeseen possibilities in every situation, and though she had listened carefully to Mr. Van Broecklyn's directions and was sure that she knew them by heart, she wished she had kissed her father more tenderly in leaving him that night for the ball, and that she had not pouted so undutifully at some harsh stricture he had made. Did this mean fear? She despised the feeling if it did.

Thirdly: she hated darkness. She knew this when she offered herself for this undertaking; but she was in a bright room at the moment and only imagined what she must now face as a reality. But one jet had been lit in the cellar and that near the entrance. Mr. Van Broecklyn seemed not to need light, even in his unfastening of the small door which Violet was sure had been protected by more than one lock.

Doubt, shadow, and a solitary climb between unknown walls, with only a streak of light for her goal, and the clinging pressure of Florence Digby's hand on her own for solace—surely the prospect was one to tax the courage of her young heart to its limit. But she had promised, and she would fulfil. So with a brave smile she stooped to the little door, and in another moment had started on her journey.

For journey the shortest distance may seem when every inch means a heart-throb and one grows old in traversing a foot. At first the way was easy; she had but to crawl up a slight incline with the comforting consciousness that two people were within reach of her voice, almost within sound of her beating heart. But presently she came to a turn, beyond which her fingers failed to reach any wall on her left. Then came a step up which she stumbled, and farther on a short flight, each tread of which she had been told to test before she ventured to climb it, lest the decay of innumerable years should have weakened the wood too much to bear her weight.

One, two, three, four, five steps! Then a landing with an open space beyond. Half of her journey was done. Here she felt she could give a minute to drawing her breath naturally, if the air, unchanged in years, would allow her to do so. Besides, here she had been enjoined to do a certain thing and to do it according to instructions. Three matches had been given her and a little night candle. Denied all light up to now, it was at this point she was to light her candle and place it on the floor, so that in returning she should not miss the staircase and get a fall. She had promised to do this, and was only too happy to see a spark of light scintillate into life in the immeasurable darkness.

She was now in a great room long closed to the world, where once officers in Colonial wars had feasted, and more than one council had been held. A room, too, which had seen more than one tragic happening, as its almost unparalleled isolation proclaimed. So much Mr. Van Broecklyn had told her; but she was warned to be careful in traversing it and not upon any pretext to swerve aside from the right-hand wall till she came to a huge mantelpiece. This passed, and a sharp corner turned, she ought to see somewhere in the dim spaces before her a streak of vivid light shining through the crack at the bottom of the blocked-up door. The paper should be somewhere near this streak.

All simple, all easy of accomplishment, if only that streak of light were all she was likely to see or think of. If the horror which was gripping her throat should not take shape! If things would remain shrouded in impenetrable darkness, and not force themselves in shadowy suggestion upon her excited fancy! But the blackness of the passage-way through which she had just struggled, was not to be found here. Whether it was the effect of that small flame flickering at the top of the staircase behind her, or of some change in her own powers of seeing, surely there was a difference in her present outlook. Tall shapes were becoming visible—the air was no longer blank—she could see—Then suddenly she saw why. In the wall high up on her right was a window. It was small and all but invisible, being covered on the outside with vines, and on the inside with the cobwebs of a century. But some small gleams from the starlight night came through, making phantasms out of ordinary things, which unseen were horrible enough, and half seen choked her heart with terror.

"I cannot bear it," she whispered to herself even while creeping forward, her hand upon the wall. "I will close my eyes" was her next thought. "I will make my own darkness," and with a spasmodic forcing of her lids together, she continued to creep on, passing the mantelpiece, where she knocked against something which fell with an awful clatter.

This sound, followed as it was by that of smothered voices from the excited group awaiting the result of her experiment from behind the impenetrable wall she should be nearing now if she had followed her instructions aright, freed her instantly from her fancies; and opening her eyes once more, she cast a look ahead, and to her delight, saw but a few steps away, the thin streak of bright light which marked the end of her journey.

It took her but a moment after that to find the missing page, and picking it up in haste from the dusty floor, she turned herself quickly about and joyfully began to retrace her steps. Why then, was it that in the course of a few minutes more her voice suddenly broke into a wild, unearthly shriek, which ringing with terror burst the bounds of that dungeon-like room, and sank, a barbed shaft, into the breasts of those awaiting the result of her doubtful adventure, at either end of this dread no-thoroughfare.

What had happened?

If they had thought to look out, they would have seen that the moon—held in check by a bank of cloud occupying half the heavens—had suddenly burst its bounds and was sending long bars of revealing light into every uncurtained window.

SIX

FLORENCE DIGBY, IN her short and sheltered life, had possibly never known any very great or deep emotion. But she touched the bottom of extreme terror at that moment, as with her ears still thrilling with Violet's piercing cry, she turned to look at Mr. Van Broecklyn, and beheld the instantaneous wreck it had made of this seemingly strong man. Not till he came to lie in his coffin would he show a more ghastly countenance; and trembling herself almost to the point of falling, she caught him by the arm and sought to read in his face what had happened. Something disastrous she was sure: something which he had feared and was partially prepared for, yet which in happening had crushed him. Was it a pitfall into which the poor little lady had fallen? If so—But he is speaking—mumbling low words to himself. Some of them she can hear. He is reproaching himself—repeating over and over that he should never have taken such a chance; that he should have remembered her youth—the weakness of a young girl's nerve. He had been mad, and now—and now—

With the repetition of this word his murmuring ceased. All his energies were now absorbed in listening at the low door separating him from what he was agonizing to know—a door impossible to enter, impossible to enlarge—a barrier to all help—an opening whereby sound might pass but nothing else, save her own small body, now lying—where?

"Is she hurt?" faltered Florence, stooping, herself, to listen. "Can you hear anything—anything?"

For an instant he did not answer; every faculty was absorbed in the one sense; then slowly and in gasps he began to mutter:

"I think—I hear—*something*. Her step—no, no, no step. All is as quiet as death; not a sound,—not a breath—she has fainted. O God! O God! Why this calamity on top of all!"

He had sprung to his feet at the utterance of this invocation, but next moment was down on his knees again, listening—listening.

Never was silence more profound; they were hearkening for murmurs from a tomb. Florence began to sense the full horror of it all, and was swaying helplessly when Mr. Van Broecklyn impulsively lifted his hand in an admonitory Hush! and through the daze of her faculties a small far sound began to make itself heard, growing louder as she waited, then becoming faint again, then altogether ceasing only to renew itself once more, till it resolved into an approaching step, faltering in its course, but coming ever nearer and nearer.

"She's safe! She's not hurt!" sprang from Florence's lips in inexpressible relief; and expecting Mr. Van Broecklyn to show an equal joy, she turned towards him, with the cheerful cry:

"Now if she has been so fortunate as to find that missing page, we shall all be repaid for our fright."

A movement on his part, a shifting of position which brought him finally to his feet, but he gave no other proof of having heard her, nor did his countenance mirror her relief. "It is as if he dreaded, instead of hailed, her return," was Florence's inward comment as she watched him involuntarily recoil at each fresh token of Violet's advance.

Yet because this seemed so very unnatural, she persisted in her efforts to lighten the situation, and when he made no attempt to encourage Violet in her approach, she herself stooped and called out a cheerful welcome which must have rung sweetly in the poor little detective's ears.

A sorry sight was Violet, when, helped by Florence, she finally crawled into view through the narrow opening and stood once again on the cellar floor. Pale, trembling, and soiled with the dust of years, she presented a helpless figure enough, till the joy in Florence's face recalled some of her spirit, and, glancing down at her hand in which a sheet of paper was visible, she asked for Mr. Spielhagen.

"I've got the formula," she said. "If you will bring him, I will hand it over to him here."

Not a word of her adventure; nor so much as one glance at Mr. Van Broecklyn, standing far back in the shadows.

NOR WAS SHE more communicative, when, the formula restored and everything made right with Mr. Spielhagen, they all came together again in the library for a final word.

"I was frightened by the silence and the darkness, and so cried out," she explained in answer to their questions. "Any one would have done so who found himself alone in so musty a place," she added, with an attempt at lightsomeness which deepened the pallor on Mr. Van Broecklyn's cheek, already sufficiently noticeable to have been remarked upon by more than one.

"No ghosts?" laughed Mr. Cornell, too happy in the return of his hopes to be fully sensible of the feelings of those about him. "No whispers from impalpable lips or touches from spectre hands? Nothing to explain the mystery of that room so long shut up that even Mr. Van Broecklyn declares himself ignorant of its secret?"

"Nothing," returned Violet, showing her dimples in full force now.

"If Miss Strange had any such experiences—if she has anything to tell worthy of so marked a curiosity, she will tell it now," came from the gentleman just alluded to, in tones so stern and strange that all show of frivolity ceased on the instant. "Have you anything to tell, Miss Strange?"

Greatly startled, she regarded him with widening eyes for a moment, then with a move towards the door, remarked, with a general look about her:

"Mr. Van Broecklyn knows his own house, and doubtless can relate its histories if he will. I am a busy little body who having finished my work am now ready to return home, there to wait for the next problem which an indulgent fate may offer me."

She was near the threshold—she was about to take her leave, when suddenly she felt two hands fall on her shoulder, and turning, met the eyes of Mr. Van Broecklyn burning into her own.

"*You saw!*" dropped in an almost inaudible whisper from his lips.

The shiver which shook her answered him better than any word.

With an exclamation of despair, he withdrew his hands, and facing the others now standing together in a startled group, he said, as soon as he could recover some of his self-possession:

"I must ask for another hour of your company. I can no longer keep my sorrow to myself. A dividing line has just been drawn across my life, and I must have the sympathy of someone who knows my past, or I shall go mad in my self-imposed solitude. Come back, Miss Strange. You of all others have the prior right to hear."

SEVEN

"I SHALL HAVE to begin," said he, when they were all seated and ready to listen, "by giving you some idea, not so much of the family tradition, as of the effect of this tradition upon all who bore the name of Van Broecklyn. This is not the only house, even in America, which contains a room shut away from intrusion. In England there are many. But there is this difference between most of them and ours. No bars or locks forcibly held shut the door we were forbidden to open. The command was enough; that and the superstitious fear which such a command, attended by a long and unquestioning obedience, was likely to engender.

"I know no more than you do why some early ancestor laid his ban upon this room. But from my earliest years I was given to understand that there was one latch in the house which was never to be lifted; that any fault would be forgiven sooner than that; that the honour of the whole family stood in the way of disobedience, and that I was to preserve that honour to my dying day. You will say that all this is fantastic, and wonder that sane people in these modern times should subject themselves to such a ridiculous restriction, especially when no good reason was alleged, and the very source of the tradition from which it sprung forgotten. You are right; but if you look long into human nature, you will see that the bonds which hold the firmest are not material ones—that an idea will make a man and mould a character—that it lies at the source of all heroisms and is to be courted or feared as the case may be.

"For me it possessed a power proportionate to my loneliness. I don't think there was ever a more lonely child. My father and mother were so unhappy in each other's companionship that one or other of them was almost always away. But I saw little of either even when they were at home. The constraint in their attitude towards each other affected their conduct towards me. I have asked myself more than once if either of them had any real affection for me. To my father I spoke of her; to her of him; and never pleasurably. This I am forced to say, or you cannot understand my story. Would to God I could tell another tale! Would to God I had such memories as other men have of a father's clasp, a mother's kiss—but no! my grief, already profound, might have become abysmal. Perhaps it is best as it is; only, I might have been a different child, and made for myself a different fate—who knows.

"As it was, I was thrown almost entirely upon my own resources for any amusement. This led me to a discovery I made one day. In a far part of the cellar behind some heavy casks, I found a little door. It was so low—so exactly fitted to my small body, that I had the greatest desire to enter it. But I could not get around the casks. At last an expedient occurred to me. We had an old servant who came nearer loving me than any one else. One day when I chanced to be alone in the cellar, I took out my ball and began throwing it about. Finally it landed behind the casks, and I ran with a beseeching cry to Michael, to move them.

"It was a task requiring no little strength and address, but he managed, after a few herculean efforts, to shift them aside and I saw with delight my way opened to that mysterious little door. But I did not approach it then; some instinct deterred me. But when the opportunity came for me to venture there alone, I did so, in the most adventurous spirit, and began my operations by sliding behind the casks and testing the handle of the little door. It turned, and after a pull or two the door yielded. With my heart in my mouth, I stooped and peered in. I could see nothing—a black hole and nothing more. This caused me a moment's hesitation. I was afraid of the dark—had always been. But curiosity and the spirit of adventure triumphed. Saying to myself that I was Robinson Crusoe exploring the cave, I crawled in, only to find that I had gained nothing. It was as dark inside as it had looked to be from without.

"There is no fun in this, so I crawled back, and when I tried the experiment again, it was with a bit of candle in my hand, and a surreptitious match or two. What I saw, when with a very trembling little hand I had lighted one of the matches, would have been disappointing to most boys, but not to me. The litter and old boards I saw in odd corners about me were full of possibilities, while in the dimness beyond I seemed to perceive a sort of staircase which might lead—I do not think I made any attempt to answer that question even in my own mind, but when, after some hesitation and a sense of great daring, I finally crept up those steps, I remember very well my sensation at finding myself in front of a narrow closed door. It suggested too vividly the one in Grandfather's little room—the door in the wainscot which we were never to open. I had my first real trembling fit here, and at once fascinated and repelled by this obstruction I stumbled and lost my candle, which, going out in the fall, left me in total darkness and a very frightened state of mind. For my imagination which had been greatly stirred by my own vague thoughts of the forbidden room, immediately began to people the space about me with ghoulish figures. How should I escape them, how ever reach my own little room again undetected and in safety?

"But these terrors, deep as they were, were nothing to the real fright which seized me when, the darkness finally braved, and the way found back into the bright, wide-open halls of the house, I became conscious of having dropped something besides the candle. My match-box was gone— not *my* match-box, but my grandfather's which I had found lying on his table and carried off on this adventure, in all the confidence of irresponsible youth. To make use of it for a little while, trusting to his not missing it in the confusion I had noticed about the house that morning, was one thing; to lose it was another. It was no common box. Made of gold and cherished for some special reason well known to himself, I had often heard him say that some day I would appreciate its value and be glad to own it. And I had left it in that hole and at any minute he might miss it—possibly ask for it! The day was one of torment. My mother was away or shut up in her room. My father—I don't know just what thoughts I had about him. He was not to be seen either, and the servants cast strange looks at me when I spoke his name. But I little realized the blow which had just fallen upon the house in his definite departure, and only thought of my own trouble, and of how I should meet my grandfather's eye when the hour came for him to draw me to his knee for his usual good-night.

"That I was spared this ordeal for the first time this very night first comforted me, then added to my distress. He had discovered his loss and was angry. On the morrow he would ask me for the box and I would have to lie, for never could I find the courage to tell him where I had been. Such an act of presumption he would never forgive, or so I thought as I lay and shivered in my little bed. That his coldness, his neglect, sprang from the discovery just made that my mother as well as my father had just fled the house forever was as little known to me as the morning calamity. I had been given my usual tendance and was tucked safely into bed; but the gloom, the silence which presently settled upon the house had a very different explanation in my mind from the real one. My sin (for such it loomed large in my mind by this time) coloured the whole situation and accounted for every event.

"At what hour I slipped from my bed on to the cold floor, I shall never know. To me it seemed to be in the dead of night; but I doubt if it were more than ten. So slowly creep away the moments to a wakeful child. I had made a great resolve. Awful as the prospect seemed to me,—frightened as I was by the very thought,—I had determined in my small mind to go down into the cellar, and into that midnight hole again, in search of the lost box. I would take a candle and matches, this time from my own mantel-shelf, and if everyone was asleep, as appeared from the deathly quiet of the house, I would be able to go and come without anybody ever being the wiser.

"Dressing in the dark, I found my matches and my candle and, putting them in one of my pockets, softly opened my door and looked out. Nobody was stirring; every light was out except a solitary one in the lower hall. That this still burned conveyed no meaning to my mind. How could I know that the house was so still and the rooms so dark because everyone was out searching for some clue to my mother's flight? If I had looked at the clock—but I did not; I was too intent upon my errand, too filled with the fever of my desperate undertaking, to be affected by anything not bearing directly upon it.

"Of the terror caused by my own shadow on the wall as I made the turn in the hall below, I have as keen a recollection to-day as though it happened yesterday. But that did not deter me; nothing deterred me, till safe in the cellar I crouched down behind the casks to get my breath again before entering the hole beyond.

"I had made some noise in feeling my way around these casks, and I trembled lest these sounds had been heard upstairs! But this fear soon gave place to one far greater. Other sounds were making themselves heard. A din of small skurrying feet above, below, on every side of me! Rats! rats in the wall! rats on the cellar bottom! How I ever stirred from the spot I do not know, but when I did stir, it was to go forward, and enter the uncanny hole.

"I had intended to light my candle when I got inside; but for some reason I went stumbling along in the dark, following the wall till I got to the steps where I had dropped the box. Here a light was necessary, but my hand did not go to my pocket. I thought it better to climb the steps first, and softly one foot found the tread and then another. I had only three more to climb and then my right hand, now feeling its way along the wall, would be free to strike a match. I climbed the three steps and was steadying myself against the door for a final plunge, when something happened—something so strange, so unexpected, and so incredible that I wonder I did not shriek aloud in my terror. The door was moving under my hand. It was slowly opening inward. I could feel the chill made by the widening crack. Moment by moment this chill increased; the gap was growing—a presence was there—a presence before which I sank in a small heap upon the landing. Would it advance? Had it feet—hands? Was it a presence which could be felt?

"Whatever it was, it made no attempt to pass, and presently I lifted my head only to quake anew at the sound of a voice—a human voice—my mother's voice—so near me that by putting out my arms I might have touched her.

"She was speaking to my father. I knew it from the tone. She was saying words which, little understood as they were, made such a havoc in my youthful mind that I have never forgotten them.

" 'I have come!' she said. 'They think I have fled the house and are looking far and wide for me. We shall not be disturbed. Who would think of looking here for either you or me.'

"*Here!* The word sank like a plummet in my breast. I had known for some few minutes that I was on the threshold of the forbidden room; but they were in it. I can scarcely make you understand the tumult which this awoke in my brain. Somehow, I had never thought that any such braving of the house's law would be possible.

"I heard my father's answer, but it conveyed no meaning to me. I also realized that he spoke from a distance,—that he was at one end of the room while we were at the other. I was presently to have this idea confirmed, for while I was striving with all my might and main to subdue my very heart-throbs so that she would not hear me or suspect my presence, the darkness—I should rather say the blackness of the place yielded to a flash of lightning—heat lightning, all glare and no sound—and I caught an instantaneous vision of my father's figure standing with gleaming things about him, which affected me at the moment as supernatural, but which, in later years, I decided to have been weapons hanging on a wall.

"She saw him too, for she gave a quick laugh and said they would not need any candles; and then, there was another flash and I saw something in his hand and something in hers, and though I did not yet understand, I felt myself turning deathly sick and gave a choking gasp which was lost in the rush she made into the centre of the room, and the keenness of her swift low cry.

" '*Garde-toi!* for only one of us will ever leave this room alive!'

"A duel! a duel to the death between this husband and wife—this father and mother—in this hole of dead tragedies and within the sight and hearing of their child! Has Satan ever devised a scheme more hideous for ruining the life of an eleven-year-old boy!

"Not that I took it all in at once. I was too innocent and much too dazed to comprehend such hatred, much less the passions which engendered it. I only knew that something horrible—something beyond the conception of my childish mind—was going to take place in the darkness before me; and the terror of it made me speechless; would to God it had made me deaf and blind and dead!

"She had dashed from her corner and he had slid away from his, as the next fantastic gleam which lit up the room showed me. It also showed the weapons in their hands, and for a moment I felt reassured when I saw that these were swords, for I had seen them before with foils in their hands practising for exercise, as they said, in the great garret. But the swords had buttons on them, and this time the tips were sharp and shone in the keen light.

"An exclamation from her and a growl of rage from him were followed by movements I could scarcely hear, but which were terrifying from their very quiet. Then the sound of a clash. The swords had crossed.

"Had the lightning flashed forth then, the end of one of them might have occurred. But the darkness remained undisturbed, and when the glare relit the great room again, they were already far apart. This called out a word from him; the one sentence he spoke—I can never forget it:

" 'Rhoda, there is blood on your sleeve; I have wounded you. Shall we call it off and fly, as the poor creatures in there think we have, to the opposite ends of the earth?'

"I almost spoke; I almost added my childish plea to his for them to stop—to remember me and stop. But not a muscle in my throat responded to my agonized effort. Her cold, clear 'No!' fell before my tongue was loosed or my heart freed from the ponderous weight crushing it.

" 'I have vowed and *I* keep my promises,' she went on in a tone quite strange to me. 'What would either's life be worth with the other alive and happy in this world.'

"He made no answer; and those subtle movements—shadows of movements I might almost call them—recommenced. Then there came a sudden cry, shrill and poignant—had Grandfather been in his room he would surely have heard it—and the flash coming almost simultaneously with its utterance, I saw what has haunted my sleep from that day to this, my father pinned against the wall, sword still in hand, and before him my mother, fiercely triumphant, her staring eyes fixed on his and—

"Nature could bear no more; the band loosened from my throat; the oppression lifted from my breast long enough for me to give one wild wail and she turned, saw (heaven sent its flashes quickly at this moment) and recognizing my childish form, all the horror of her deed (or so I have fondly hoped) rose within her, and she gave a start and fell full upon the point upturned to receive her.

"A groan; then a gasping sigh from him, and silence settled upon the room and upon my heart, and so far as I knew upon the whole created world.

"THAT IS MY story, friends. Do you wonder that I have never been or lived like other men?"

After a few moments of sympathetic silence, Mr. Van Broecklyn went on to say:

"I don't think I ever had a moment's doubt that my parents both lay dead on the floor of that great room. When I came to myself—which may have been soon, and may not have been for a long while—the lightning had ceased to flash, leaving the darkness stretching like a blank pall between me and that spot in which were concentrated all the terrors of which my imagination was capable. I dared not enter it. I dared not take one step that way. My instinct was to fly and hide my trembling body again in my own bed; and associated with this, in fact dominating it and making me old before my time, was another—never to tell; never to let any one, least of all my grandfather—know what that forbidden room now contained. I felt in an irresistible sort of way that my father's and mother's honour was at stake. Besides, terror held me back; I felt that I should die if I spoke. Childhood has such terrors and such heroisms. Silence often covers in such, abysses of thought and feeling which astonish us in later years. There is no suffering like a child's, terrified by a secret which it dare not for some reason disclose.

"Events aided me. When, in desperation to see once more the light and all the things which linked me to life—my little bed, the toys on the window-sill, my squirrel in its cage—I forced myself to retraverse the empty house, expecting at every turn to hear my father's voice or come upon the image of my mother—yes, such was the confusion of my mind, though I knew well enough even then that they were dead and that I should never hear the one or see the other. I was so be-numbed with the cold in my half-dressed condition, that I woke in a fever next morning after a terrible dream which forced from my lips the cry of 'Mother! Mother!'—only that.

"I was cautious even in delirium. This delirium and my flushed cheeks and shining eyes led them to be very careful of me. I was told that my mother was away from home; and when after two days of search they were quite sure that all efforts to find either her or my father were likely to prove fruitless, that she had gone to Europe where we would follow her as soon as I was well. This promise, offering as it did, a prospect of immediate release from the terrors which were consuming me, had an extraordinary effect upon me. I got up out of my bed saying that I was well now and ready to start on the instant. The doctor, finding my pulse equable, and my whole condition wonderfully improved, and attributing it, as was natural, to my hope of soon joining my mother, advised my whim to be humoured and this hope kept active till travel and intercourse with children should give me strength and prepare me for the bitter truth ultimately awaiting me. They listened to him and in twenty-four hours our preparations were made. We saw the house closed—with what emotions surging in one small breast, I leave you to imagine—and then started on our long tour. For five years we wandered over the continent of Europe, my grandfather finding distraction, as well as myself, in foreign scenes and associations.

"But return was inevitable. What I suffered on re-entering this house, God and my sleepless pillow alone know. Had any discovery been made in our absence; or would it be made now that renovation and repairs of all kinds were necessary? Time finally answered me. My secret was safe and likely to continue so, and this fact once settled, life became endurable, if not cheerful. Since then I have spent only two nights out of this house, and they were unavoidable. When my grandfather died I had the wainscot door cemented in. It was done from this side and the cement painted to match the wood. No one opened the door nor have I ever crossed its threshold. Sometimes I think I have been foolish; and sometimes I know that I have been very wise. My reason has stood firm; how do I know that it would have done so if I had subjected myself to the possible discovery that one or both of them might have been saved if I had disclosed instead of concealed my adventure."

A PAUSE DURING which white horror had shone on every face; then with a final glance at Violet, he said:

"What sequel do you see to this story, Miss Strange? I can tell the past, I leave you to picture the future."

Rising, she let her eye travel from face to face till it rested on the one awaiting it, when she answered dreamily:

"If some morning in the news column there should appear an account of the ancient and historic home of the Van Broecklyns having burned to the ground in the night, the whole country would mourn, and the city feel defrauded of one of its treasures. But there are five persons who would see in it the sequel which you ask for."

When this happened, as it did happen, some few weeks later, the astonishing discovery was made that no insurance had been put upon this house. Why was it that after such a loss Mr. Van Broecklyn seemed to renew his youth? It was a constant source of comment among his friends.

VOIR DIRE

Jeremiah Healy

Jeremiah Healy is one of the private-eye writers who helped change a moribund mystery field in the eighties. His debut novel about Private Detective John Francis Cuddy, *Blunt Darts*, announced that here was a wise new kid on the block. Since then he has written more than a dozen novels featuring his melancholy P.I. His books and stories since then have done nothing but enhance his reputation as an important and sage writer whose work has taken the private-eye form to an exciting new level. He is one of those writers who packs the poise and depth of a good mainstream novel into an even better genre novel. Recent books include *The Stalking of Sheilah Quinn*, and the latest Cuddy mystery *The Only Good Lawyer*.

ONE

BERNARD WELLINGTON, ESQUIRE, had that mournful look of an old dog betrayed by incontinence.

I watched Bernie ease himself into the high-backed swivel chair behind his desk, a muzzy twilight through the wide bay window silhouetting both man and furniture. An inch taller than my six-two-plus, you'd have pegged him an inch shorter, almost four decades spent bent over legal tomes stooping his shoulders and spoiling his posture. A widow's peak of black hair coexisted peacefully with the fringe of snow at sideburns and temple. Wellington's head and hands were disproportionately large, his voice a baritone burred by the long-term effects of good scotch. Descended from a Boston Brahmin family, he'd betrayed his corporate-law heritage in choosing criminal-defense work coming out of Harvard, lo, those many years ago.

That fine October Monday, though, Bernie had left a message with my answering service around lunchtime, asking me to meet him in his office at 5:00 P.M. Meaning after court.

As I took a client chair, the nail on Wellington's right middle finger began picking at some leather piping on the arm of his high-back. "John Francis Cuddy, it's been a while."

I hadn't seen him since doing the preliminary investigation for one of his armed robbery defendants five months earlier. "What've you got, Bernie?"

"What I've got is Michael Monetti."

The *Globe* and the *Herald* both had run third-page stories when Monetti, a career hood, was indicted some months back for the attempted murder of a "business associate."

I said, "His trial ought to be coming up soon."

"We impaneled the jury last Friday afternoon."

"A little late in the game to be calling for a private investigator."

"Ordinarily, yes. But . . ." Something was obviously bothering Bernie. "John, indulge me a moment?"

"Sure."

Wellington cleared his throat, the way I'd seen him do in the courtroom to focus attention on himself without having to raise his voice. "As I believe you know, the Commonwealth of Massachusetts has been one of the few states in the Union not permitting attorney voir dire of prospective jurors."

I reached back to my one year of law school for the French phrase meaning to *speak the truth*. "But the judge does ask them preliminary questions, right?"

"Right. However, an attorney who can't confront jurors individually before they're impaneled doesn't get much information or guidance toward exercising peremptory challenges. The typical juror questionnaire provides just generic data such as occupation, marital status, and children's ages. That's the reason for this new experiment."

"Experiment?"

"Our esteemed legislature passed a bill establishing a pilot project in three counties. Under the project, each attorney has a total of thirty minutes to question the entire jury panel on bias, temperament, etcetera, etcetera."

I thought about it. "Not much time, but still fairly helpful when you're representing somebody as mobbed up as Monetti."

Wellington seemed hurt. "My client is not 'mobbed up,' John."

"I don't recall any 'esteemed' judge letting him out on bail."

"And a travesty, that, especially when his extended family has been clustered in the front row of the audience every minute of the trial. The proud father is a former brick mason, the doting mother a retired schoolteacher. Michael's older sister prospers as a registered beautician, and he once bragged about the career of a second cousin who does standup comedy, like that chap Rich—"

"Bernie?"

A pause before, "What?"

"Maybe you should save the 'he comes from a good family' argument for the sentencing phase of the case."

A stony look. Wellington always had been better in the courtroom than in his office. Finally, though, a grudging "All right."

"And—no offense, Bern—I still don't see why you want to bring me in now."

The stony look softened, and Wellington leaned back into his chair's headrest, the leather bustle depressed and cracked from the countless times he must have pondered knotty problems of strategy and tactics. "I'm troubled by one of the jurors, John."

"How do you mean?"

"Our case falls under this new pilot project, and I had a truly splendid sequence of questions to include in my voir dire. But, for all the prospective male jurors called to the box from the pool, Michael insisted I use his questions instead."

"His questions?"

"Correct. My client wanted to know if those jurors had ever been in the armed forces, or arrested, or even if they'd worked in a 'strategically sensitive' industry."

Didn't make sense to me. "I can maybe see the 'arrested' part, Bernie, but what would Monetti's other questions have to do with his attempted-murder charge?"

"Nothing, John. And worse, Michael's approach undermined my opportunity to use the individual voir dire as a way of warming up the jury for him."

"So what happened with them?"

"The male jurors, you mean?"

"Yes."

"Two had in fact been arrested, and the prosecution used peremptory challenges on both."

"Meaning Monetti's questions actually helped the other side decide who it should ding?"

"Correct again." Wellington seemed to sour at the memory. "Of the remaining males called from the pool, one had been in the army, another the navy. Michael had me challenge both."

"Why?"

"He didn't say."

And I still didn't see Monetti's strategy. "What about the rest of the jurors?"

Wellington closed his eyes for a moment. "One had worked at a defense think tank on Route 128, and my client wanted him off, too. However, the three males who answered negatively to all of Michael's questions were eventually seated."

"Because neither the prosecutor nor you challenged them."

"That's right," said Wellington. "But believe me, I wanted to knock off one of the trio, a Mr. Arthur Durand."

I thought about it. "I'm guessing he's the juror who's 'troubling' you."

A nod. "I didn't like him from the get-go, John. The juror questionnaire said Mr. Durand was unemployed, never married, no kids. In person, he also wore old clothes and had this tendency of scratching his nose and squirming in his seat." Wellington caricatured both. "Plus, the man's hair and beard were longish and unkempt, and he had rather a dopey cast to his eyes."

"I don't know, Bern. That last part makes this Durand sound like perfect juror material for Monetti."

Another hurt look. "Except for Michael's hundred-dollar razor cut and thousand-dollar suits. In any case, though, while I just didn't like Mr. Durand, my client insisted on keeping him."

"And?"

Wellington sighed. "And we finished impaneling Friday afternoon, Mr. Durand being the last one from the pool to be seated. Then the jury was excused for the weekend and went home."

"No sequestration order?"

"Not for 'just' attempted murder, John." A deeper sigh. "So, we reconvene this morning, and guess what?"

"I'm drawing a blank, Bernie."

"All the jurors show up, including our Mr. Durand. However, it being just the first day of testimony, I didn't really know them very well yet."

"Know them?"

"Yes. After a few days of trial—even without attorney voir dire at the beginning—the jurors become burned into your brain by face and seat number."

"Because you're looking at them while the prosecutor is at bat with a witness?"

"Or while I'm cross-examining. But the first morning of a new case, I probably couldn't pick five of the jurors out of a lineup."

"Except for this Durand."

Wellington came forward in his chair. "Yes and no. I look over at him, and he's both gotten a haircut and shaved off the beard. The clothes are about the same, but when I move around the courtroom, his eyes are following me, like Mr. Durand is now actually paying attention. Oh, he still fidgets in his chair and scratches his nose, but something . . . I don't know, bothers me."

I shook my head. "Bern?"

"Yes?"

"Could there also be something you're not telling me?"

Wellington leaned back again, now swinging his chair in a slow, twenty-degree arc. "I've represented Michael on and off for the better part of two decades, John. Despite my Herculean efforts on those earlier occasions, his past record combined with another felony conviction this time around would carry a life sentence."

"And?"

A nearly glacial sigh now. "And once before—years ago—Michael had two of his loyal employees seek to 'influence' someone in the Commonwealth's witness-protection program."

Christ. "That was bright of him."

"Michael thought a change of testimony might result in at worst a hung jury, with the prosecutor maybe not pursuing a second trial or the second jury coming back 'not guilty.' "

"And did Monetti's ploy work?"

"No, but I'm afraid my client learns a lesson hard, John."

I chewed on that. "Meaning you're afraid he may have had his muscle pay a visit to the nonsequestered Arthur Durand."

Wellington closed his eyes. "That other time Michael tried it, the whole case nearly blew sky-high. Fortunately, the witness called me instead of the prosecutor."

"Called you?"

"To request a 'cash consolation' for his 'mental anguish.' "

I thought I knew Bernie better than that. "You didn't pony up the money."

A shocked expression. "Of course not. But as a result, we had to take a plea bargain thirty-percent worse than the deal originally offered by the prosecution. I told Michael, 'Never again,' or I was through representing him."

I didn't envy Wellington his ethical stand. "So, what do you want me to do?"

He leaned back into the cracked headrest, his fingernail picking at the leather piping some more. "I don't know, John. Perhaps you could come to court tomorrow, watch Mr. Durand for a while in the jury box, and then follow him afterward. That might give me some sense of whether Michael's stepped over the line again."

"Bernie, you want a private investigator shadowing a current juror?"

"Unless you've got a better plan."

Frankly, I was thinking about turning down the assignment altogether. But the return of the mournful, hangdog look to Bernie's face kind of took that option off the board.

I said, "Would tomorrow after lunch be alright?"

"You can't make it any earlier?"

"There's somebody I want to visit in the morning."

Bernard Wellington, Esquire, started to ask me who, but remembered just in time to catch himself.

TWO

THERE REALLY AREN'T any trees on her hillside to turn yellow or orange in the autumn, but the grass does what it can by exchanging summer's green for a salt-bleached brown. And the breeze off the harbor water is bracing enough, the gulls shrieking as they scavenge in that part of South Boston where Beth and I grew up, got married, and still spend time together.

In a manner of speaking.

I drew even with her row, opening the little campstool I carry now to spare my bad knee too much standing. The headstone reads as it always has. ELIZABETH MARY DEVLIN CUDDY. No easier to look at, though.

John, why aren't you working?

Smiling, I squared my butt on the stool. "What, you don't think your enterprising husband could have a cemetery for a client?"

Beth paused. *Something's troubling you.*

"No man could ever fool a good wife."

Never kept you from trying. Want to talk about it?

I found that I did.

As always, she listened patiently. Then, *So what's really the problem for you, the client or the case?*

"A little of both, I guess. Bernie Wellington's just fine. I even admire him for that stubborn way he clings to his ethics. But I don't like working for Michael Monetti, and I really don't like risking my license by following a current juror in a felony case."

But you're working for Wellington, not Monetti, right?

"Technically."

Literally. And whatever you find out might make the system work better, not worse. So, you really aren't doing anything wrong.

I didn't have a counterargument. "Will you represent me should the system disagree?"

Another pause, but this one more like the time it takes to force a smile. *Would that I could, John Cuddy. Would that I could.*

As a gull wheeled overhead, somebody said, "Amen."

BACK IN MY office on Tremont Street across from the Boston Common, I called a friend named Claire who has the computer access of a Microsoft billionaire. She answered on the third ring, and I asked her to run "Durand, Arthur" through what she calls her "databases." Claire said she'd have to get back to me, and I told her to leave a message with my service. Then I locked up, went downstairs, and headed over to the Park Street Under subway.

MICHAEL MONETTI HAD attempted the killing of his associate in Cambridge rather than Boston, so the trial was being held at the relatively modern Middlesex Superior Courthouse across the Charles River rather than our dilapidated Suffolk County one. A Green Line trolley carried me to Lechmere Station in East Cambridge, and I walked three blocks to the tall, gray-stoned building. After clearing metal detectors at the lobby level, I rode an elevator to the sixth floor.

The courtroom itself had hush-colored carpeting, polished oak benches, and a domed ceiling. From earlier experiences, I knew that dome gave the space the acoustics of a concert hall, ostensibly so no one in the audience outside the bar enclosure would have to strain in order to hear testimony from the witness stand. In reality, though, so much as a whisper from anywhere—including counsel tables—could be heard clearly everywhere.

Given the lunch hour, I was able to get an aisle seat in a row on the prosecution side of the audience. On the first bench across the aisle sat the people I took to be the Monetti family. An older man with scarred hands and an older woman with a stern demeanor were sandwiched around a fiftyish woman whose face shared characteristics of each apparent parent. Other people in the second row comforted them by nodding in unison or squeezing a shoulder.

Suddenly, a side door near the front of the bar enclosure opened, and Bernie Wellington came through it. He was followed by a slick, well-dressed guy in his late thirties, two bailiffs—one male, one female—leading him into the courtroom. I recognized Michael Monetti from the media coverage of his indictment. He shared the family features, but whereas the other members looked stalwart, Mikey resembled a killer whale somebody had shoehorned into a double-breasted suit.

As Bernie Wellington made eye contact with me, Monetti turned his chair at the defense table toward his cheering section. Smiling, he told them not to worry. The jail food wasn't so bad, he'd had worse, how was their lunch, and so on. The dome's acoustics carried every syllable back to me.

After the stenographer moved toward her seat and the court clerk toward his kangaroo pouch in front of the bench, the judge appeared from her chambers door, everyone rising. She was African-American and fairly young. When we were all settled again, the female bailiff who'd escorted Michael Monetti into the courtroom went to another side door and knocked. Seconds later, the jurors began filing through and into their rectangular box against the wall. Once they, too, were seated, the bailiff took a chair near the telephone table at our audience end of the jury.

Then Wellington stood and asked the judge if he could have a moment. She granted his request, and he came through the gate of the bar enclosure, walking down the aisle toward me.

Leaning over, Bernie brought his lips to within an inch of my ear, his voice as delicate as a lover's kiss. "Thanks, John. Durand is in seat number twelve, closest to you and that court officer."

I nodded, but waited until Wellington arrived back at the defense table, Monetti writing something on a pad and tugging on Bernie's sleeve. After that decent interval, I looked over to the bailiff seated at our end of the jury box. Just past her in the last chair of the front row was a skinny man scratching his nose with his left index finger. He had dark hair which indeed looked freshly cut, a suit jacket with lapels ten years old, and a collared shirt without benefit of tie. Suddenly, the skinny man shifted a little in his seat before cupping the scratching hand over his mouth and whispering to the young female juror on his right. She rushed one of her own hands toward her teeth, stifling a laugh.

The judge glared at the two of them in a way that told me it wasn't the first time she'd done so. Then the prosecutor—a red-haired and freckled-faced lad who looked all of sixteen—recalled one of his witnesses to the stand.

A police lab tech, she waxed eloquent about various fibers found at the scene of the crime. I tuned her out and glanced occasionally toward the jury. To the naked eye, Arthur Durand was paying attention, alright.

After the lab tech, the prosecutor put on a male ballistics expert, who testified that the three bullets removed from the victim's soft tissue came from the nine-millimeter Sig Sauer carried by Michael Monetti in violation of this statute and that. I left the courtroom just as the ballistics witness stepped down off the stand, because I wanted to be outside the building and in position to follow juror Durand on foot, by cab, or via public transportation.

AT A LITTLE after five, Durand wended his way through the crowd at the courthouse door, his shoes making the clacking noise of a cheap computer keyboard as he walked to Lechmere Station. Instead of the subway, though, he hopped an Arlington Heights bus, and I climbed on very casually with a bunch of "other" transferring commuters. The bus made stops through East Cambridge and then Somerville, Durand getting off in a decaying neighborhood about half a mile before the Arlington town line.

I followed him down the bus's steps and out the door, crossing the street so as to parallel his route of march. He passed a couple of alley mouths with Dumpsters slightly overflowing. At a wider side street, Durand turned. When I reached the intersection, I saw a block of wooden three-story houses.

I waited until he stopped at a house painted that hardware-sale shade of lavender. If Durand hadn't nodded his head toward the car parked diagonally across and up the street, though, I'm not sure I would have spotted them.

Two men, sitting in the front seat of a beige Ford, the Crown Victoria model with white-walled tires. At that distance, I couldn't make out faces, but the guy at the wheel was sipping through a straw from a big fast-food cup. His partner on the passenger side was motionless except for a single tug on his earlobe, the way Carol Burnett used to end her monologue.

Then Arthur Durand went up the stoop and into the lavender three-decker. I kept walking, but only around the block.

The Crown Vic was now halfway down the street from me. Unfortunately, I couldn't see its rear license plate because of a truck between us. On the other hand, I'd certainly known a lot of vehicles like it over the years.

The favorite unmarked car of plainclothes police everywhere in the state, though usually with only black-walled tires.

I didn't understand why Arthur Durand would be getting special protection as a juror unless Michael Monetti's stupid ploy involving the earlier-case witness had gotten around. However, best to invest some time and be sure.

I moved to the other side of the street, which gave me an unobstructed view of the two men's heads but still not their registration tag. The driver stopped sipping his drink and turned to his partner, saying something. The wheelman had straight sandy hair, the other dark curly hair, which was about the extent of description I could get without becoming obvious enough to be made by them.

I found a quiet doorway and waited.

It was nearly midnight—and me nearly starving—when the driver turned to his partner again, the other nodding and tugging on his ear some more. Then finally the Crown Victoria started up and pulled away.

But not so fast I couldn't get their plate number.

THREE

A GROGGY "WHO the . . . ?"

Into my end of the phone, I said, "Claire, this is John Cuddy."

"What time is it?"

"By my watch, seven A.M."

Her voice grew an edge. "Seven? You call fucking farmers at seven, Cuddy. Cyber-wizards, we like to sleep a little more toward noon."

"Sorry, Claire, but I've got a lot to do today, and I didn't pick up your message until after twelve last night."

"Yeah, well, hold on a minute."

A bonking noise came across the wire along with a distant, muffled "Shit."

Then Claire's voice was closer and clearer again. "Goddam phone. I should get a speaker thing, one of you guys ever paid me half what I'm worth for finding all this stuff for you."

"Your weight in gold, Claire."

"That some kind of crack?"

"No, it—"

"I mean, I lost five pounds in the last month, and I don't take kindly to—"

"A compliment, Claire."

"What?"

"It wasn't a crack, it was a compliment. As in, 'You're worth your weight in gold.' "

"Yeah, well, remember that when you're writing my check." A rustle of paper. "Let's see . . . let's see . . . 'Durand, Arthur,' right?"

"Right."

"Okay, with no middle initial, I wasn't sure how many I'd turn, but I've got three out by Springfield, two north of Worcester—probably a father-and-son thing—and just the one in our own Slummerville."

"Unkind, Claire. Give me the Somerville listing."

"That's Durand, Arthur 'G.' as in 'George.' " More rustling. "Let's see . . . No service record, no arrest record."

So, Durand had told the truth answering those questions.

Claire said, "He does have a driver's license, but no current car registration. Social Security is—you want the number and all?"

"Not necessary. Has there been any activity on the account?"

"Nothing from job withholding. Just a . . . yeah. Yeah, he's been collecting unemployment for about three months now."

Making the man someone who, as a juror, might be vulnerable to a bribe offer. "And before that?"

"Worked in a video store."

"Any time in 'sensitive industries'?"

"What, you mean defense contractors, that kind of thing?"

"Yes."

"Cuddy, I think you overestimate our Durand, Arthur G."

"How about bank records?"

"Simple savings and checking," said Claire. "No real activity beyond depositing his unemployment and writing his rent checks."

"You have a payee on those?"

"Yeah. 'Stralick,' that's S-T-R-A-L-I-C-K, Rhonda M."

"Address?"

"Same as your guy shows in Somerville."

So, maybe a resident landlady. "Any credit cards?"

"Negative."

"Bank loans?"

"Also *nega-tivo*, though I gotta tell you, Cuddy, I can't see how this Durand could qualify to finance anything beyond a tattoo."

"You turn up much else, Claire?"

"No records of marriage, divorce, or birth of child. The guy's your basic loner/loser."

"I can ask if he's available?"

"I'm not that fucking desperate, thank you very much. Let me just total your tab here."

"Hold it."

"Why?"

"I've got a license plate I'd like you to run."

"Jesus, Cuddy, you have any idea how much of an uproar the Registry of Motor Vehicles is in about this new federal law?"

"Which law's that, Claire?"

"The one's supposed to keep 'stalkers' from getting computer access to the home addresses of any sweeties they see driving by. But, if the Commonwealth doesn't pass its own statute, we're—"

"Claire?"

"What?"

"Just this one tag, please? And today, if possible."

A grunt. "Why not? You got me up at the crack of dawn, I'll have plenty of time to fucking *carpe diem* and get the registration for you too."

I WAITED UNTIL after court would resume at nine before leaving my apartment and walking downstairs to my old Honda Prelude behind the building. Going to Arthur Durand's place by car would be a lot more direct than trolley-and-bus, and in seven hours the night before I'd seen all of two cabs cruising the drag at the foot of his street.

I made my way to Somerville using the Western Avenue bridge and Central Square in Cambridge. Turning at Durand's corner, I did a drive-by of the lavender three-decker but didn't see any Crown Victoria staking out the block. There was a parking space near the next intersection, though, and I took it.

Walking back to Durand's building, I studied its exterior. If you could forgive the color, the clapboard facade was fairly well maintained, especially when compared to its neighbors. I climbed the stoop; three bells mounted next to the door had just unit numbers rather than names below them.

Figuring that an owner would live on the first floor to enjoy the back-yard, I started with "1." After thirty seconds, I tried it again. Same lapse of time, same lack of result.

I was about to press the button once more when the door huffed open, a piece of rubber insulation making for a pretty tight fit against the jamb. The woman on the other side struggled to still look forty. Her platinum-blonde hair was spun around her head like cotton candy, biggish ears not quite hiding under it. The facial features pushed through makeup applied in layers, and even a nice manicure couldn't hide the veins bulging on top of her hands. She wore a sweatsuit the color of the clapboards and fuzzy bedroom slippers.

"And who might you be, luv?"

A slight English accent. "John Cuddy."

"Well, now, John." Hooding her eyes, she canted her head. "You're the cute one, aren't you?"

"Ms. Stralick?"

A wariness now crossed her eyes. "You know my name?"

" 'Stralick, Rhonda M.' " I took out my identification holder.

Reading, she said, "Private investigator?"

"That's right."

"I don't know nothing about anything."

"That's okay." I closed the holder. "I'm just here for an employer who's thinking of hiring one of your tenants."

Wary became surprised. "Arthur?"

"Probably. I have 'Durand, Arthur G.' "

Stralick didn't seem convinced. "Who wants to hire him?"

"I'm afraid that's confidential. But what I have to do won't take very long."

Another change of expression. "Good. That'll give us more time to get acquainted, won't it?"

Said the spider to the fly. "Could I come in?"

Stralick made a sweeping gesture with her right arm.

After closing the front door, she led me along a short corridor to an apartment entrance past the base of a staircase that would serve the upper two floors of her house. "Please excuse the mess, John."

That would take some doing. In the living room, television trays functioned poorly as magazine racks, supermarket tabloids scattered like giant playing cards across one of those sculpted carpets popular twenty years ago. Opposite the flower-print couch was a widescreen Sony, the video on but the audio muted. Three teenaged girls—one white, one black, one

Latina—sat awkwardly on a stage, an older man sporting evangelist hair roaming the audience with a handheld mike. The brightly printed caption at the low left of the screen read, STEP-DAUGHTERS PREGNANT BY THEIR STEP-FATHERS.

I thought, And the mothers who love them both.

"What was that, John?" said Stralick, behind me.

Must have thought out-loud. "Nothing."

Next to the TV was an armchair with the bulbous design of a '52 Chevy. I went to it as my hostess took the couch, near enough to me that our knees almost touched.

Then she trotted out the hooded-eyes trick again. "So, what do you want to talk about?"

"Mr. Durand indicated on his job application that he was currently un-employed."

"Three months' worth," said Stralick.

"I'm sorry."

"No need to be sorry, luv." She licked her lips. "What I meant was, Arthur hasn't come up with the rent for the last little while."

"I see. Before that, though, was he prompt in his obligations to you?"

"Moneywise, yes."

"How about 'otherwise'?"

A shrug. "Arthur helps me out with the storm windows, the snow shoveling, that sort of thing." A coy smile. "But for real 'otherwise,' he's not exactly the life of the party."

"Sober, responsible types make better employees."

"You don't understand, John. After I divorced the bloody mound of shit who lured me to your country, I got a little lonely. But Arthur, he's quiet as a churchmouse, he is."

Stralick paused, maybe to give me a chance to jump in. When I didn't, she made a face before saying, "Weeks can go by, and I won't even hear him, much less see him. No taste for fun, Arthur." Another wetting of the lips. "If you get my drift."

"Fine with my client."

Stralick's eyes narrowed to slits. "I hope you're not as dull as your 'client,' luv."

I gave her an ingratiating smile. "Any reason you can think of why Mr. Durand shouldn't be hired?"

"Only if it'd mean you'll visit with me longer."

A proper bulldog, Ms. Stralick. "I wonder, then, could I get a look at his apartment?"

Now wary again. "Why?"

"I just like to see the place where a prospective employee lives. Helps me put some flavor into my report, maybe even make it a full-blown recommendation."

"God knows that'd be a help, what with Arthur in arrears on his rent the way he is."

"And it would also be good if my visit today could stay our little secret, okay?"

"I like 'secrets' as much as the next girl, luv, but I do have a question first."

"What's that?"

Back to coy. "If you know Arthur's unemployed, what makes you think he's not up there now?"

"Because Mr. Durand advised my client he'd be on jury duty for a while."

Stralick finally seemed convinced. "Right, then. Only I have to go with you, of course."

"Of course," I said, neutrally.

"KIND OF CAPTURES him, if you get my drift."
Rhonda Stralick had managed to rub or bump against me three times during our trip up the staircase. Arthur Durand's apartment consisted of a living room with bay window in front, bedroom next, bath and kitchen at the back. The worn, faded furniture seemed to be the only furnishings, and the rooms gave off a spic-'n'-span shine. Which didn't tell me much.

What wasn't there told me something, though. No knick-knacks, keepsakes, or even photos. More like a large, spartan motel room.

At least until you got to the kitchen.

"Damn him!" Stralick went to the sink, using a paper towel from a cylindrical dispenser to crush three or four cockroaches scurrying over a dead pizza box. "Arthur's usually neat as a pin, he is."

There were beer cans and other takeout trash on the flanking counters. "Maybe Mr. Durand had somebody over last night and forgot to clean up."

"Not bloody likely. No family, no visitors, no personality." She began to lift the box by its edges.

"You might want to leave that where it is."

Stralick looked at me. "Why?"

"So Mr. Durand won't know you let somebody in to see his apartment."

"Oh. Right you are, luv." She let the box drop back into the sink, then made a sensual ritual of wiping her hands across the thighs of her sweatsuit. "I hope this business with the bugs doesn't ruin our nice little mood."

Seeing an out, I took it. "Afraid so. Delicate stomach."

"Just my luck." Rhonda Stralick tried to put on a happy face. "Well, then. Next time you're in the neighborhood, you'll stop and visit awhile, won't you?" Now the hooded eyes again. "If you get my drift."

More like her tidal wave.

———

OUTSIDE, I'D JUST put the key in my Prelude's door-lock when I noticed the beige Crown Vic, parked beyond the intersection this time. I ducked my head a little, but I couldn't do much about having been seen leaving the lavender three-decker.

I executed a three-point turn to avoid driving by them and glanced in my rearview mirror. Instead of following me, the sandy-haired driver seemed to be squinting in my direction and talking to the dark-haired eartugger, who himself was writing something down.

Probably the letters and numbers on the Prelude's license plate, but there wasn't much I could do about that either.

FOUR

BACK IN THE office, I dialed Bernie Wellington's number. His secretary told me that, not surprisingly, he was still in court on the Monetti case. I asked her to have him return my call as soon as possible.

I considered trying Claire again, too, but twice in one day seemed to be skating over the edge of her good will. Paperwork on other cases occupied me until almost three, when the phone rang.

A sound nearly as shrill as her voice.

"John Cuddy."

"You own a pencil?"

"Ready, Claire."

"Alright, let's see . . . let's see . . . Yeah, the tag belongs to a rental agency."

That felt wrong, though it explained the white-walled tires. "You sure?"

"I'm insulted. But not as much as if I was the one actually running the plate."

"Give me that again?"

"I told you about this new federal crackdown on computer access, right?"

"Right."

"Okay, so I had this friend of mine over at the Registry do the search for me. He says the tag's from a Ford Crown Vic—some ridiculous color that amounts to 'beige'—and the car belongs to, and I quote, 'Best-Ride Car Rentals, Inc.,' over by the airport. Here's their address."

The name and location—almost five miles from Arthur Durand's apartment—meant nothing to me. "Claire, you ever hear of this outfit?"

"No, but my friend at the Registry has."

"In what context?"

"The 'connected' context."

Uh-oh. "A mob launderette?"

"Or maybe just a captive business the wiseguys turn to when their own wheels ought not to be involved. Help you any?"

"Maybe, maybe not. But thanks, Claire."

"Hey, Cuddy, do me a favor, huh?"

"What's that?"

"Mail my check before you pay these 'Best-Ride' people a visit, okay?"

Couldn't blame her for asking.

AFTER LEAVING TWO more messages for Bernie Wellington and not getting a return call, I decided to postpone the rent-a-car agency till the next morning. Locking up for the night at five-fifteen, I went downstairs to the parking space behind my office's building. In the Prelude, I crawled with the rush-hour traffic over to South Boston and the Jack O' Lantern tavern.

That part of Broadway near L Street in Southie is undergoing a general—if not quite gentle—gentrification. A lot of the old blue-collar, shot-and-a-beer joints are being squeezed out, their liquor licenses bought up by fern-and-butcher-block places for the new condo crowd. With orangy lights shining through tooth-gap windows, and an oval bar inside a walking moat before the tables start, "the Jack" is sort of a compromise: a good place for dinner with the wife and kids after work, then a watering hole for serious barflies from nine or so onward.

Maybe the early hour was what lulled me.

I'd been sitting on a stool at the bar, just finishing a steak platter with two Harp lagers, expertly drawn by Eddie Kiernan behind the taps. About five-eight and skinny as a rail, Eddie had played shortstop in the high minor leagues before coming back to the neighborhood and opening the Jack. In fact, I spent most of my dinner that evening listening to him grouse about the competition from his chi-chi new neighbors—"the wormy bastards"—and the skyrocketing rates for liability insurance they'd brought like a plague along with them.

Checking my watch, I saw it was nearly seven-thirty, so I got up to use the men's room and try Bernie Wellington one last time before driving home. As I made my way between the bar and the tables, a guy leaving his own stool slammed into me, then staggered back. A little theatrically, I remember thinking at the time.

Maybe six feet tall and solid, with sandy straight hair and an oft-broken nose, he flared. "The fuck is wrong with you, asshole?"

I took in half a breath. "I believe you're the one who bumped into me."

"The fuck he is," said a different man, standing at the bar.

I turned. Same size and build, but black curly hair and standard nose. He tugged on his left ear once, and I began to get the picture.

Sandy stepped up first, throwing a right cross at the left side of my face as I stayed turned toward his partner. I parried the sucker-punch, looping my left arm over Sandy's right and catching his fist under my armpit. With the heel of my left hand braced under his elbow, I lifted up, hard. I could feel more than hear the joint dislocate, but I heard more than felt Sandy's scream of pain as I released the hold.

Curly had swung his left just as I hunched my right shoulder up to protect my head and neck, but he'd had the time to realize that his first had better count. It rocked me into a table of four, who'd pushed back and stood up as the fighting began. Sandy was on the floor now, cradling a floppy forearm, facial features squinched up, voice down to a keening moan. When Curly stepped in to follow with his right, I used the table to support my own bad left knee. Then I side-kicked out with my right foot aimed at his left shin, all his weight having transferred forward onto that leg.

This time I did hear the cracking sound, Curly toppling like a felled tree with about as much noise. By now, Eddie had come out from behind the bar, a Louisville slugger in his hands. I was about to initiate appropriate inquiries of the two on the deck when instead Eddie jabbed me in the solar plexus with his bat as though he were doing bayonet drill.

I joined the hamburger plates on the party of four's table.

By the time my breath started returning to me, Sandy had struggled to his feet and gotten Curly up as well, the combined three good arms and three good legs carrying both of them through the Jack O' Lantern's door and into the October night.

Eddie was standing near my left thigh, his bat at half-mast.

I said, "Why . . . me?"

"I was scared shitless you were going to maim the wormy bastards. My liability premiums would shoot out of sight."

I forced some air down into the lungs. "Then how come . . . you didn't . . . hit them first?"

He gave me a jaundiced look. "I said I was insured, John, not insane."

As Eddie Kiernan promised the table of four he'd bring them new meals, I decided I couldn't blame him either.

WHEN I WAS able to breathe in for a count of eight without cramping, I left the tavern and made my way to the Prelude. Nobody had touched it. I got in, drove home, and climbed the stairs slowly, thankful for not having worse wounds to lick.

Once in the apartment, I checked with my answering service for the office. A message from Bernie Wellington, asking that I reach him the next day before court.

I went to the CD player, choosing some soft and soothing soprano sax, courtesy of the late Art Porter. Then I lowered myself onto the couch and stretched out, trying to make sense of a situation that was anything but soft and soothing.

Then I tried some more.

I STARTED AWAKE in the dark, the pain above my gut keeping me from sitting straight up. I'd been having a dream—about Rhonda Stralick, I'm embarrassed to admit—when a throwaway line of hers during my "visit" that day clicked into place. And suddenly something Bernie Wellington had mentioned joined it.

If I was right, Michael Monetti's oddball voir dire questions made perfect sense. I could even understand why the two guys staking out the lavender three-decker had rousted me at the Jack.

But I needed to confirm one more piece of the puzzle to be certain, and I came up with a way of doing it I thought might work.

FIVE

THAT NEXT THURSDAY morning, I took considerable care leaving the apartment building for two reasons. First, my solar plexus was still a tad ginger, thanks to Eddie's bat. Second, if Sandy and Curly also had a friend at the Registry to run my plate, then they—or their replacement—could have a home address for me as well.

In the parking lot, I got down on hands and knees, examining the Prelude's undercarriage to be sure no "aftermarket" options had been added to the ignition system. Starting up, I decided to avoid my office, since that was for sure where the muscle boys had been waiting before following me to the Jack O' Lantern.

It could have made for a long day, but our Museum of Fine arts on Huntington Avenue had a great photographic exhibit by Herb Ritts to go with its other, usual wonders. About 11 A.M.—and knowing Bernie Wellington would be in court—I used a pay phone to call his secretary. I left only a blind message with her for him to try me at the office after lunch.

No sense in risking Bernie's license, too.

LATER THAT SAME Thursday, I drove from the museum across the Charles to East Cambridge. Parking the Prelude a few blocks west of the Middlesex County Courthouse, I loitered discreetly outside the main entrance. At four-forty, Arthur Durand appeared in a stream of people too randomly dressed to be lawyers and too jaded to be anything but "citizens summoned to serve." That same young woman from the jury box was walking beside Durand, and he seemed to exaggerate some mannerisms of head and hands as he said something to her. She laughed again, this time not covering her mouth as in the courtroom, and they waved a casual goodbye, Durand scratching his nose with his left index finger.

I watched him move off toward Lechmere Station. When the woman turned north, I fell in behind her, half a block away and across the street.

SOMETIMES YOU GET lucky.

At the corner, she got into the passenger side of an idling station wagon, one of those Subarus you see Australia's Paul Hogan hucking on TV. There was a man about her age behind the wheel and a toddler strapped into a plastic restraint bucket against the rear seat.

The lucky part was that a taxi had just slewed to the curb in front of me, dropping off an elderly couple who'd already given the driver their fare.

The young family's car entered the traffic flow, my cab trailing it.

"MARJORIE, COME ON, huh? You want this family package or that one?"

"Hey, Phil, give me a break, okay? I've been listening to witnesses and lawyers since Monday. It doesn't look like we're anywhere near finished, and this Monetti guy isn't exactly O. J. material, you know?"

Phil wouldn't let go of his bone. "Yeah? Well, try picking up Troy each afternoon from day care."

"Like every other week of our lives I *don't?*"

I eavesdropped on them silently as we all shuffled our way along the cafeteria line of a Boston Market franchise, the operation that was lucky to survive changing from the successful marquee name of "Boston Chicken." The charming Marjorie and Phil couldn't make up their minds on which of the many dinner options—including roasted turkey and baked ham—to choose. Their toddler, Troy, was between them, his head following their argument like a rapt tennis fan watching an important match.

Marjorie finally went for the turkey combo, and Phil paid at the cashier before carrying the trays of food and drink to a nearby booth for four. I took my own ham platter to an empty table across from them.

After we all had settled in, husband wisely said to wife, "Let's change the subject, okay?"

"Okay," replied Marjorie, a relenting tone in her voice as she cut up a side dish of broccoli for Troy-boy.

Phil forked some turkey off his plate. "You still can't talk about the case?"

"Not until the judge says so, like after we vote and everything. But I'll tell you this. If it wasn't for Arthur, I'd be stir-crazy by now."

"He's that other juror you sit next to?"

"Right." Marjorie turned to her own meal. "The judge already had to tell him twice to stop saying things during dead spots in the testimony or whatever, account of how he was, like, breaking me up."

I again thought back to Rhonda Stralick's evaluation of her tenant as Phil said, "Jokes? During a murder trial?"

"Attempted murder." Marjorie took a slug of her cola. "But really, without Arthur and his impressions keeping all us jurors loose, I don't know where we'd be."

Phil pushed more turkey into his mouth. "Impressions of what?"

"Not of 'what.' Of 'who.' Arthur can do Sylvester Stallone and Arnold Schwarzenegger—"

"From the TV, Mommy?" said boy Troy, until now content to while away the meal smearing mashed potatoes across his face.

"That's right, honey. From the movies on TV." Then back to Phil with, "And Arthur has this wicked Johnny Carson, too, even better than that guy used to do."

"What guy?"

"Oh, you know. Rich-somebody-or-other."

"Rich who?"

"The one who did that great President Nixon. C'mon, Phil, you have to know who I mean."

Her husband claimed he didn't, but I was pretty sure I did.

"WELLINGTON."

"Bernie, it's John Cuddy."

"Good Lord, John," came the voice from the other end of the line. "Where have you been?"

"Kind of busy, Bern."

"*You're* busy? The Commonwealth expects to rest tomorrow, which means I'm supposed to open the defense case Monday, and I've been trying to reach—"

"It's a long story, and you might be better off not hearing all of it."

A hesitation. "How bad, John?"

"Let me ask you something first."

"What?"

"When you were impaneling the jury for Michael Monetti, did anything odd happen?"

"Odd? You mean, other than those questions he had me ask?"

"Right. Specifically with Arthur Durand."

"Well, yes." Another hesitation. "Not odd, so much, though. More co-incidental."

"Tell me what you mean."

On the other end of the line, Wellington seemed to gather his thoughts. "After I asked Mr. Durand the last of Michael's voir dire questions, I came back to our defense table to confer with my client about challenging him. Just then, one of Michael's family in the audience behind us sneezed rather loudly, and the entire courtroom laughed." Bernie's voice grew weary. "Trust me, John, that's been my only comic relief in the whole process."

"Was that also when Monetti told you to keep Durand on the jury?"

"When Michael said not to challenge him, right. And I don't mind sharing with you that it still feels wrong to have that chap in the box. Defense attorneys are being sued all the time now for 'ineffective assistance of counsel' if they fail to use all their peremptories and the jury returns a verdict of 'guilty,' and here's my own client basically ordering me not to—"

"Bern?"

"What?"

"I'll get back to you."

"John—"

S I X

THE NEXT MORNING, Friday, I got up at 6 A.M., my solar plexus barely twinging anymore. After dressing in old clothes, I drove the Prelude across the Western Ave bridge and through Central Square again, eventually reaching the foot of Arthur Durand's street. No sign of anybody surveilling the lavender three-decker today, but that didn't mean their overall plan wasn't still on.

I left my car and walked into the mouth of the nearest alley. Taking ten more steps, I hunkered down behind its Dumpster.

To wait.

At seven-forty, I heard the distinctive keyboard clacking of a certain person's dress shoes coming from the direction of Rhonda Stralick's house. I moved back to the mouth of the alley again. When the thin man who scratched his nose and shifted in his chair crossed the opening in front of me, I clotheslined him with my left forearm.

He went down hard, but not quite out.

I grabbed the collar of his jacket and dragged him quickly behind the Dumpster before he was focusing well again. After propping his butt and torso into a sitting position against the brick wall of the alley, I squatted onto my haunches. His eyes slowly registered me in front of him.

"What the . . . the fuck is going on?"

"My friend, we need to have a little chat before court resumes this morning."

He tried to make his hands work, palms pushing at the ground to scrabble back up.

I laid my own hands on his shoulders to calm him down. "You find yourself in deep weeds, boyo. Very deep weeds."

"The fuck are you—"

"First I talk, and then maybe you talk. Understand?"

He didn't say anything to that.

"Michael Monetti's criminal career is going south on him. One more felony conviction, and he never sees the sun again outside of exercise time in a prison yard. However, he's also about to be tried for attempted murder, and so something has to be done. Mikey once had his muscle tap a state-protected witness, but that didn't work out so well for him. Then he has a brainstorm about the current situation."

I looked down into the man's eyes and thought back to Bernie Wellington's "good family" speech. "Specifically, you. The accused's gifted second cousin."

"I don't know what—"

"Be patient, I'm not done yet. Mikey made it easy for you. Sit with the rest of the family at the front of the courtroom's audience that first afternoon of trial last week, sort of 'hide in plain sight.' Then watch as the jury's selected. If one of the males answered Mikey's voir dire questions the right way, you'd study the guy, see if he was also 'right' in other ways. Your approximate height and weight, hopefully some telltale mannerisms that would be easy to mimic."

I had my subject's undivided attention now.

"A man named 'Arthur Durand' turns out to fit the bill nearly perfectly, especially since his unkempt hair and beard would kind of haze anybody's memory of his facial features. So, when it comes time to maybe knock the guy off the jury, you send Mikey a little 'keep him' signal in the courtroom. A cough, maybe. Or a sneeze?"

The second cousin's eyes jumped.

"Now move on to that night—a week ago today. Your cousin's enforcers follow Durand home to Rhonda Stralick's three-decker around the corner. Meanwhile Mikey's sister the beautician gives you a haircut, so nobody would think it odd that 'Durand' had shaved off his beard, too. Your rough resemblance to the guy and considerable talent can do the rest, particularly for people like the other jurors, who'd never seen Durand before that afternoon."

"I'm . . . *I'm* Arthur Durand."

"You're not listening, my friend. The enforcers take Durand out of the three-decker, remove any photos of him there, and put you in his place. Bingo. The next day of trial—Monday morning, now—there's a juror among the twelve who's eventually going to create a 'hung' jury by voting his cousin 'not guilty' for sure. Maybe you'd even make a few friends in the box during the course of trial, what with some snappy patter and a knack for impressions of famous people. Like that great comic, Rich Little, used to do. It wasn't the real Durand's personality, but you might get a couple of other votes to swing your way, especially if you paid close attention to the evidence and raised good arguments during deliberation. The district attorney would think twice before pursuing a second trial if there were enough 'not guilty' votes the first time around. Hell, even an acquittal wouldn't be out of the question if most of your fellow jurors took a shine to you."

"I'm telling you. I'm Arthur Durand."

I shook my head. "You're a bit nervous now, right?"

No answer.

"Right?" I repeated.

A grudging "Right."

"Okay. Only problem is, you've been forgetting to scratch your nose the way Durand does. Or—more accurately—did."

A glimmer of something beyond nervous. "What are you talking about?"

"Let me guess. Mikey told you they were just going to snatch Durand for the course of the trial, then put him back into his life and you into yours, right?"

"I'm not saying."

"Fine. Just listen, then. The juror questionnaire covers things like job, family, and so on. Guess what? Durand had nobody. On the surface, great for your cousin's plan, because there'd be no one to miss Durand while he's 'gone' during the trial. Mikey even camped his enforcers each day outside the three-decker, probably as babysitters so your winning personality didn't go off romping at night and maybe piss in the stew somehow. But why would your cousin want you living in Durand's apartment this last week?"

No response.

"Mikey gave you an answer to that one, didn't he? 'Hey, cuz, we need to have somebody moving around up there, make some noise so the land-lady hears her tenant.' Again, on the surface it seems plausible. But there's a real risk, too. What if Rhonda Stralick should run into you on the stairs? Or come a-knocking on Durand's door, looking for the rent money? She knows her tenant pretty well, wouldn't be fooled into thinking you were him. And that seems to me a bigger risk than her not hearing 'Durand' walking around up there for a few days."

The second cousin was thinking about it, because his eyes started mov-ing left-right-left, kind of jittery.

I said, "So let's explore things a bit more. Mikey tells you he's just keeping Durand on ice for a while. Only thing is, how could your cousin be sure Durand wouldn't talk later about his little 'interlude'?"

Still no response.

"And if Durand wasn't going to talk—because he'd been handsomely bribed or was just rationally terrified—why bother to substitute you for him in the first place? Why not simply intimidate the real Arthur Durand into being the juror who'll definitely vote 'not guilty' and therefore at worst buy Mikey a second trial?"

Nothing except for those eyes flicking, like lightning bugs caught in a jar.

"Don't feel stupid, my friend. It took me a while to figure it out, too. Start by remembering that your cousin got burned when he approached that witness in the earlier case. Then think about those questions Mikey had his lawyer ask the male jurors for this go-around. Armed forces, ar-rest, sensitive employment. Durand answered 'no' to all the above. So tell me, what do those experiences carry with them?"

The second cousin shook his head.

"Okay, time's up, anyway. They all require the person involved to be fingerprinted, boyo, meaning Durand never had been. I'm guessing the same is true for you."

He swallowed hard, maybe seeing where I was heading.

"Now, here's the stumper: if Mikey's enforcers have been parked out-side the three-decker, and—"

"But they never showed up yesterday."

The first real admission. "I'm not surprised. They spotted me nosing around Wednesday, found out who I was, then set me up for a barroom beating that night."

The second cousin shook his head some more. "But . . . you don't look like—"

"I was able to discourage them."

He just stared at me.

"Now let's get back to my question, okay? If your cousin's enforcers have been babysitting you since they snatched the real Mr. Durand, and the rest of the Monetti clan—including even you—has been sitting dutifully in the courtroom, who does that leave to look after the poor kidnap victim, shut up in a room somewhere?"

The eyes did jumping jacks in the man's head. "Jesus fucking Christ."

"I'm afraid so, my friend. Arthur Durand is dead, probably killed by Mikey's enforcers that first night a week ago. However, when the trial ends—say another week from now—any evident 'disappearance' of a juror who'd just sat on a major case is going to be investigated fairly carefully by the police, something your cousin would not exactly welcome. Especially since Durand's landlady will maintain that her tenant is 'quiet as a church-mouse' while the other jurors would call him more the 'class clown.' So, better if Durand's body itself turns up simply and quickly, the result of some tragic 'accident,' maybe. Only problem? A roughly two-week-old corpse would be a tough sell to any medical examiner told that 'Arthur Durand' was alive and well through the end of jury deliberations. Therefore, I'm thinking Mikey will need a fresher body to stand in for the real Durand."

"But . . . but . . ."

"Which brings us back to why your cousin wanted you in that third-floor apartment this past week. You're probably about Durand's height and weight, but you wouldn't have had his dental work. So—after a disfiguring collision, say—the M.E. will be asked to match up the unlucky corpse with the missing Arthur Durand, and guess what? The fingerprints on the body will match those found in Durand's apartment."

"You're saying . . . you're saying Michael's gonna kill me?"

"Look at it from his standpoint. When the trial is over, you're kind of a loose thread, and potentially very embarrassing. What happens if your career as a standup comic starts to take off, and one of the jurors who sat with 'Arthur Durand' for two weeks recognizes you? Maybe he or she would go to the authorities with this odd piece of information."

"But Michael's . . . I'm his own *blood*."

"I'd bet your cousin sees it more as his own *future*. On the other hand, you know him better than I do. Which way do you think he'll flip on this one?"

Not much doubt from the eyes now, but no reason to leave any in his mind, either.

I said, "On the third hand, let's assume I'm wrong about Mikey's views regarding the bond of family. Even then, my friend, I blow the whistle on your little masquerade here, and you're up for at least conspiracy in the murder of the real Arthur Durand."

He looked down, eyes flicking left-right-left some more, then back up to me. "The fuck am I gonna do?"

"We go to the courthouse together this morning, and you have a frank talk with the judge and the district attorney."

His eyes got wide enough to see white all around the pupils. "What're you, nuts? If I wanted to fucking die, ratting out Michael would do it."

"You tell the authorities about what he's pulled here, and they'll place you with their witness-protection program."

"Yeah, and how safe am I gonna be in that? Michael's guys already broke the thing once."

"That's not all they broke."

"What?"

"The barroom, night before last. The both of them are in body casts by now."

"So Michael sends two more after me. What're my chances then?"

"Better than they are now."

The second cousin looked down again. "Basically . . ." He coughed twice, tears trickling along that nose he was no longer scratching. "Basically, what you're saying is, I gotta go in and tell the truth."

"The system calls it 'voir dire.' "

His face came back up. "Huh?"

"Never mind," I said.

CHEE'S WITCH

Tony Hillerman

Tony Hillerman created a whole new subgenre of crime fiction with the appearance of his novel *The Blessing Way* in 1970, that of mysteries exploring Native American culture. Though Native Americans had appeared in crime stories
before, Hillerman gave his Navajos depth as well as breadth. Having been
raised among them, and sent to a Native American boarding school, Hillerman
has also spent most of his later life with them. This gives his novels a purity of
intent and a true kinship with his characters that other writers simply can't
match. It's hard to pick a favorite among the Hillerman novels—they're all that
good—but two of the best are *Listening Woman* and *Skinwalkers*. He also edited *The Best American Mystery Stories of the Century*, a retrospective look at the
evolution of the genre in the twentieth century.

SNOW IS SO important to the Eskimos they have nine nouns to describe its variations. Corporal Jimmy Chee of the Navajo Tribal Police
had heard that as an anthropology student at the University of New Mexico. He remembered it now because he was thinking of all the words you
need in Navajo to account for the many forms of witchcraft. The word
Old Woman Tso had used was "anti'l," which is the ultimate sort, the absolute worst. And so, in fact, was the deed which seemed to have been
done. Murder, apparently. Mutilation, certainly, if Old Woman Tso had
her facts right. And then, if one believed all the mythology of witchery told
among the fifty clans who comprised The People, there must also be canni-
balism, incest, even necrophilia.

On the radio in Chee's pickup truck, the voice of the young Navajo
reading a Gallup used-car commercial was replaced by Willie Nelson
singing of trouble and a worried mind. The ballad fit Chee's mood. He was
tired. He was thirsty. He was sticky with sweat. He was worried. His
pickup jolted along the ruts in a windless heat, leaving a white fog of dust
to mark its winding passage across the Rainbow Plateau. The truck was
gray with it. So was Jimmy Chee. Since sunrise he had covered maybe two

hundred miles of half-graded gravel and unmarked wagon tracks of the Arizona–Utah–New Mexico border country. Routine at first–a check into a witch story at the Tsossie hogan north of Teec Nos Pos to stop trouble before it started. Routine and logical. A bitter winter, a sand storm spring, a summer of rainless, desiccating heat. Hopes dying, things going wrong, anger growing, and then the witch gossip. The logical. A bitter winter, a sand storm spring, a summer awry. The trouble at the summer hogan of the Tsossies was a sick child and a water well that had turned alkaline—nothing unexpected. But you didn't expect such a specific witch. The skin-walker, the Tsossies agreed, was the City Navajo, the man who had come to live in one of the government houses at Kayenta. Why the City Navajo? Because everybody knew he was a witch. Where had they heard that, the first time? The People who came to the trading post at Mexican Water said it. And so Chee had driven westward over Tohache Wash, past Red Mesa and Rabbit Ears to Mexican Water. He had spent hours on the shady porch giving those who came to buy, and to fill their water barrels, and to visit, a chance to know who he was until finally they might risk talking about witchcraft to a stranger. They were Mud Clan, and Many Goats People, and Standing Rock Clan—foreign to Chee's own Slow Talking People—but finally some of them talked a little.

A witch was at work on the Rainbow Plateau. Adeline Etcitty's mare had foaled a two-headed colt. Hosteen Musket had seen the witch. He'd seen a man walk into a grove of cottonwoods, but when he got there an owl flew away. Rudolph Bisti's boys lost three rams while driving their flocks up into the Chuska high pastures, and when they found the bodies, the huge tracks of a werewolf were all around them. The daughter of Rose-mary Nashibitti had seen a big dog bothering her horses and had shot at it with her .22 and the dog had turned into a man wearing a wolfskin and had fled, half running, half flying. The old man they called Afraid of His Horses had heard the sound of the witch on the roof of his winter hogan, and saw the dirt falling through the smoke hole as the skinwalker tried to throw in his corpse powder. The next morning the old man had followed the tracks of the Navajo Wolf for a mile, hoping to kill him. But the tracks had faded away. There was nothing very unusual in the stories, except their number and the recurring hints that the City Navajo was the witch. But then came what Chee hadn't expected. The witch had killed a man.

The police dispatcher at Window Rock had been interrupting Willie Nelson with an occasional blurted message. Now she spoke directly to Chee. He acknowledged. She asked his location.

"About fifteen miles south of Dennehotso," Chee said. "Homeward bound for Tuba City. Dirty, thirsty, hungry, and tired."

"I have a message."

"Tuba City," Chee repeated, "which I hope to reach in about two hours, just in time to avoid running up a lot of overtime for which I never get paid."

"The message is FBI Agent Wells needs to contact you. Can you make a meeting at Kayenta Holiday Inn at eight P.M.?"

"What's it about?" Chee asked. The dispatcher's name was Virgie Endecheenie, and she had a very pretty voice and the first time Chee had met her at the Window Rock headquarters of the Navajo Tribal Police he had been instantly smitten. Unfortunately, Virgie was a born-into Salt Cedar Clan, which was the clan of Chee's father, which put an instant end to that. Even thinking about it would violate the complex incest taboo of the Navajos.

"Nothing on what it's about," Virgie said, her voice strictly business. "It just says confirm meeting time and place with Chee or obtain alternate time."

"Any first name on Wells?" Chee asked. The only FBI Wells he knew was Jake Wells. He hoped it wouldn't be Jake.

"Negative on the first name," Virgie said.

"All right," Chee said. "I'll be there."

The road tilted downward now into the vast barrens of erosion which the Navajos call Beautiful Valley. Far to the west, the edge of the sun dipped behind a cloud—one of the line of thunderheads forming in the evening heat over the San Francisco Peaks and the Cococino Rim. The Hopis had been holding their Niman Kachina dances, calling the clouds to come and bless them.

Chee reached Kayenta just a little late. It was early twilight and the clouds had risen black against the sunset. The breeze brought the faint smells that rising humidity carries across desert country—the perfume of sage, creosote brush, and dust. The desk clerk said that Wells was in room 284 and the first name was Jake. Chee no longer cared. Jake Wells was abrasive but he was also smart. He had the best record in the special FBI Academy class Chee had attended, a quick, tough intelligence. Chee could tolerate the man's personality for a while to learn what Wells could make of his witchcraft puzzle.

"It's unlocked," Wells said. "Come on in." He was propped against the padded headboard of the bed, shirt off, shoes on, glass in hand. He glanced at Chee and then back at the television set. He was as tall as Chee remembered, and the eyes were just as blue. He waved the glass at Chee without looking away from the set. "Mix yourself one," he said, nodding toward a bottle beside the sink in the dressing alcove.

"How you doing, Jake?" Chee asked.

Now the blue eyes reexamined Chee. The question in them abruptly went away. "Yeah," Wells said. "You were the one at the Academy." He eased himself on his left elbow and extended a hand. "Jake Wells," he said.

Chee shook the hand. "Chee," he said.

Wells shifted his weight again and handed Chee his glass. "Pour me a little more while you're at it," he said, "and turn down the sound."

Chee turned down the sound.

"About thirty percent booze," Wells demonstrated the proportion with his hands. "This is your district then. You're in charge around Kayenta? Window Rock said I should talk to you. They said you were out chasing around in the desert today. What are you working on?"

"Nothing much," Chee said. He ran a glass of water, drinking it thirstily. His face in the mirror was dirty—the lines around mouth and eyes whitish with dust. The sticker on the glass reminded guests that the laws of the Navajo Tribal Council prohibited possession of alcoholic beverages on the reservation. He refilled his own glass with water and mixed Wells's drink. "As a matter of fact, I'm working on a witchcraft case."

"Witchcraft?" Wells laughed. "Really?" He took the drink from Chee and examined it. "How does it work? Spells and like that?"

"Not exactly," Chee said. "It depends. A few years ago a little girl got sick down near Burnt Water. Her dad killed three people with a shotgun. He said they blew corpse powder on his daughter and made her sick."

Wells was watching him. "The kind of crime where you have the insanity plea."

"Sometimes," Chee said. "Whatever you have, witch talk makes you nervous. It happens more when you have a bad year like this. You hear it and you try to find out what's starting it before things get worse."

"So you're not really expecting to find a witch?"

"Usually not," Chee said.

"Usually?"

"Judge for yourself," Chee said. "I'll tell you what I've picked up today. You tell me what to make of it. Have time?"

Wells shrugged. "What I really want to talk about is a guy named Simon Begay." He looked quizzically at Chee. "You heard the name?"

"Yes," Chee said.

"Well, shit," Wells said. "You shouldn't have. What do you know about him?"

"Showed up maybe three months ago. Moved into one of those U.S. Public Health Service houses over by the Kayenta clinic. Stranger. Keeps to himself. From off the reservation somewhere. I figured you federals put him here to keep him out of sight."

Wells frowned. "How long you known about him?"

"Quite a while," Chee said. He'd known about Begay within a week after his arrival.

"He's a witness," Wells said. "They broke a car-theft operation in Los Angeles. Big deal. National connections. One of those where they have hired hands picking up expensive models and they drive 'em right on the ship and off-load in South America. This Begay is one of the hired hands. Nobody much. Criminal record going all the way back to juvenile, but all nickel-and-dime stuff. I gather he saw some things that help tie some big boys into the crime, so Justice made a deal with him."

"And they hide him out here until the trial?"

Something apparently showed in the tone of the question. "If you want to hide an apple, you drop it in with the other apples," Wells said. "What better place?"

Chee had been looking at Wells's shoes, which were glossy with polish. Now he examined his own boots, which were not. But he was thinking of Justice Department stupidity. The appearance of any new human in a country as empty as the Navajo Reservation provoked instant interest. If the stranger was a Navajo, there were instant questions. What was his clan? Who was his mother? What was his father's clan? Who were his relatives? The City Navajo had no answers to any of these crucial questions. He was (as Chee had been repeatedly told) unfriendly. It was quickly guessed that he was a "relocation Navajo," born to one of those hundreds of Navajo families which the federal government had tried to reestablish forty years ago in Chicago, Los Angeles, and other urban centers. He was a stranger. In a year of witches, he would certainly be suspected. Chee sat looking at his boots, wondering if that was the only basis for the charge that City Navajo was a skinwalker. Or had someone seen something? Had someone seen the murder?

"The thing about apples is they don't gossip," Chee said.

"You hear gossip about Begay?" Wells was sitting up now, his feet on the floor.

"Sure," Chee said. "I hear he's a witch."

Wells produced a pro-forma chuckle. "Tell me about it," he said.

Chee knew exactly how he wanted to tell it. Wells would have to wait awhile before he came to the part about Begay. "The Eskimos have nine nouns for snow," Chee began. He told Wells about the variety of witchcraft on the reservations and its environs: about frenzy witchcraft, used for sexual conquests, of witchery distortions, of curing ceremonials, of the exotic two-heart witchcraft of the Hope Fog Clan, of the Zuñi Sorcery Fraternity, of the Navajo "chindi," which is more like a ghost than a witch, and finally of the Navajo Wolf, the anti'l witchcraft, the werewolves who pervert every taboo of the Navajo Way and use corpse powder to kill their victims.

Wells rattled the ice in his glass and glanced at his watch.

"To get to the part about your Begay," Chee said, "about two months ago we started picking up witch gossip. Nothing much, and you expect it during a drought. Lately it got to be more than usual." He described some of the tales and how uneasiness and dread had spread across the plateau. He described what he had learned today, the Tsossies' naming City Navajo as the witch, his trip to Mexican Water, of learning there that the witch had killed a man.

"They said it happened in the spring—couple of months ago. They told me the ones who knew about it were the Tso outfit." The talk of murder, Chee noticed, had revived Wells's interest. "I went up there," he continued, "and found the old woman who runs the outfit. Emma Tso. She told me her son-in-law had been out looking for some sheep, and smelled something, and found the body under some chamiso brush in a dry wash. A witch had killed him."

"How—"

Chee cut off the question. "I asked her how he knew it was a witch killing. She said the hands were stretched out like this." Chee extended his hands, palms up. "They were flayed. The skin was cut off the palms and fingers."

Wells raised his eyebrows.

"That's what the witch uses to make corpse powder," Chee explained. "They take the skin that has the whorls and ridges of the individual personality—the skin from the palms and the finger pads, and the soles of the feet. They take that, and the skin from the glans of the penis, and the small bones where the neck joins the skull, and they dry it, and pulverize it, and use it as poison."

"You're going to get to Begay any minute now," Wells said. "That right?"

"We got to him," Chee said. "He's the one they think is the witch. He's the City Navajo."

"I thought you were going to say that," Wells said. He rubbed the back of his hand across one blue eye. "City Navajo. Is it that obvious?"

"Yes," Chee said. "And then he's a stranger. People suspect strangers."

"Were they coming around him? Accusing him? Any threats? Anything like that, you think?"

"It wouldn't work that way—not unless somebody had someone in their family killed. The way you deal with a witch is hire a singer and hold a special kind of curing ceremony. That turns the witchcraft around and kills the witch."

Wells made an impatient gesture. "Whatever," he said. "I think something has made this Begay spooky." He stared into his glass, communing with the bourbon. "I don't know."

"Something unusual about the way he's acting?"

"Hell of it is I don't know how he usually acts. This wasn't my case. The agent who worked him retired or some damn thing, so I got stuck with being the delivery man." He shifted his eyes from glass to Chee. "But if it was me, and I was holed up here waiting, and the guy came along who was going to take me home again, then I'd be glad to see him. Happy to have it over with. All that."

"He wasn't?"

Wells shook his head. "Seemed edgy. Maybe that's natural, though. He's going to make trouble for some hard people."

"I'd be nervous," Chee said.

"I guess it doesn't matter much anyway," Wells said. "He's small potatoes. The guy who's handling it now in the U.S. Attorney's Office said it must have been a toss-up whether to fool with him at all. He said the assistant who handled it decided to hide him out just to be on the safe side."

"Begay doesn't know much?"

"I guess not. That, and they've got better witnesses."

"So why worry?"

Wells laughed. "I bring this sucker back and they put him on the witness stand and he answers all the questions with I don't know and it makes the USDA look like a horse's ass. When a U.S. Attorney looks like that, he finds an FBI agent to blame it on." He yawned. "Therefore," he said through the yawn, "I want to ask you what you think. This is your territory. You are the officer in charge. Is it your opinion that someone got to my witness?"

Chee let the question hang. He spent a fraction of a second reaching the answer, which was they could have if they wanted to try. Then he thought about the real reason Wells had kept him working late without a meal or a shower. Two sentences in Wells's report. One would note that the possibility the witness had been approached had been checked with local Navajo Police. The next would report whatever Chee said next. Wells would have followed Federal Rule One—Protect Your Ass.

Chee shrugged. "You want to hear the rest of my witchcraft business?"

Wells put his drink on the lamp table and untied his shoe. "Does it bear on this?"

"Who knows? Anyway there's not much left. I'll let you decide. The point is we had already picked up this corpse Emma Tso's son-in-law found. Somebody had reported it weeks ago. It had been collected, and taken in for an autopsy. The word we got on the body was Navajo male in his thirties probably. No identification on him."

"How was this bird killed?"

"No sign of foul play," Chee said. "By the time the body was brought in, decay and the scavengers hadn't left a lot. Mostly bone and gristle, I guess. This was a long time after Emma Tso's son-in-law saw him."

"So why do they think Begay killed him?" Wells removed his second shoe and headed for the bathroom.

Chee picked up the telephone and dialed the Kayenta clinic. He got the night supervisor and waited while the supervisor dug out the file. Wells came out of the bathroom with his toothbrush. Chee covered the mouthpiece. "I'm having them read me the autopsy report," Chee explained. Wilson began brushing his teeth at the sink in the dressing alcove. The voice of the night supervisor droned into Chee's ear.

"That all?" Chee asked. "Nothing added on? No identity yet? Still no cause?"

"That's him," the voice said.

"How about shoes?" Chee asked. "He have shoes on?"

"Just a sec," the voice said. "Yep. Size ten D. And a hat, and . . ."

"No mention of the neck or skull, right? I didn't miss that? No bones missing?"

Silence. "Nothing about neck or skull bones."

"Ah," Chee said. "Fine. I thank you." He felt great. He felt wonderful. Finally things had clicked into place. The witch was exorcised. "Jake," he said. "Let me tell you a little more about my witch case."

Wells was rinsing his mouth. He spit out the water and looked at Chee, amused. "I didn't think of this before," Wells said, "but you really don't have a witch problem. If you leave that corpse a death by natural causes, there's no case to work. If you decide it's a homicide, you don't have jurisdiction anyway. Homicide on an Indian reservation, FBI has jurisdiction." Wells grinned. "We'll come in and find your witch for you."

Chee looked at his boots, which were still dusty. His appetite had left him, as it usually did an hour or so after he missed a meal. He still hungered for a bath. He picked up his hat and pushed himself to his feet.

"I'll go home now," he said. "The only thing you don't know about the witch case is what I just got from the autopsy report. The corpse had his shoes on and no bones were missing from the base of the skull."

Chee opened the door and stood in it, looking back. Wells was taking his pajamas out of his suitcase. "So what advice do you have for me? What can you tell me about my witch case?"

"To tell the absolute truth, Chee, I'm not into witches," Wells said. "Haven't been since I was a boy."

"But we don't really have a witch case now," Chee said. He spoke earnestly. "The shoes were still on, so the skin wasn't taken from the soles of his feet. No bones missing from the neck. You need those to make corpse powder."

Wells was pulling his undershirt over his head. Chee hurried.

"What we have now is another little puzzle," Chee said. "If you're not collecting stuff for corpse powder, why cut the skin off this guy's hands?"

"I'm going to take a shower," Wells said. "Got to get my Begay back to L.A. tomorrow."

Outside the temperature had dropped. The air moved softly from the west, carrying the smell of rain. Over the Utah border, over the Cococino Rim, over the Rainbow Plateau, lightning flickered and glowed. The storm had formed. The storm was moving. The sky was black with it. Chee stood in the darkness, listening to the mutter of thunder, inhaling the perfume, exulting in it.

He climbed into the truck and started it. How had they set it up, and why? Perhaps the FBI agent who knew Begay had been ready to retire. Perhaps an accident had been arranged. Getting rid of the assistant prosecutor who knew the witness would have been even simpler—a matter of hiring him away from the government job. That left no one who knew this minor witness was not Simon Begay. And who was he? Probably they had other Navajos from the Los Angeles community stealing cars for them. Perhaps that's what had suggested the scheme. To most white men all Navajos looked pretty much alike, just as in his first years at college all Chee had seen in white men was pink skin, freckles, and light-colored eyes. And what would the imposter say? Chee grinned. He'd say whatever was necessary to cast doubt on the prosecution, to cast the fatal "reasonable doubt," to make—as Wells had put it—the U.S. District Attorney look like a horse's ass.

Chee drove into the rain twenty miles west of Kayenta. Huge, cold drops drummed on the pickup roof and turned the highway into a ribbon of water. Tomorrow the backcountry roads would be impassable. As soon as they dried and the washouts had been repaired, he'd go back to the Tsossie hogan, and the Tso place, and to all the other places from which the word would quickly spread. He'd tell the people that the witch was in custody of the FBI and was gone forever from the Rainbow Plateau.

INTERPOL: THE CASE OF THE MODERN MEDUSA

Edward D. Hoch

Edward D. Hoch is a marvel among mystery writers, a man who has made his living during the past three decades from working nearly entirely in the short story. He has published nearly 850 crime, mystery, and suspense tales, many of them in *Ellery Queen Mystery Magazine*, where he has been a very familiar author since the mid-1970s. He has served as the past president of Mystery Writers of America, and was the winner of its 2001 Grand Master award and its Edgar award for best short story of 1968. He has also edited distinguished anthologies, collections and even found time to write a novel or two. He has been Guest of Honor at the annual Bouchercon mystery convention and received its Anthony Award for best short story. In 2001 he will receive the convention's Lifetime Achievement Award. In 2000 he received The Eye, the life achievement award of the Private Eye Writers of America. In everything he does, he is the soul of graciousness, intelligence, and wit. He resides in Rochester, New York, with his wife, Patricia.

SHE WAS TOO beautiful to make a convincing Medusa, even with the terrible wig and its writhing plastic serpents. Gazing at herself in the mirror, Gretchen could only wonder at the chain of events that had caused Dolliman to hire her in the first place. Then the buzzer sounded and it was time to make her entrance.

She rose through a trap door in the floor, effectively masked by a cloud of chemically produced mist. As the mist cleared enough for the audience to see her, there were the usual startled exclamations. Then Toby, playing the part of Perseus, came forward with his sword and shield to slay her. It wasn't exactly according to mythology, but it seemed to please the audience of tourists.

As Toby lifted his sword to strike, her mind was on other things. She was remembering the charter flights to the Far East, the parties and the fun. But most of all she was remembering the gold. It was a great deal to give up, but she'd made her decision.

Toby, following the script they'd played a hundred times before, pushed her down into the swirling mists and grabbed the dummy head of Medusa that was hidden there. The sight of the bloody head always brought a gasp from the crowd, and this day was no exception. Gretchen felt for the trap door and opened it. While the crowd applauded and Toby took his bows, she made her way down the ladder to the lower level.

That was where they found her, an hour later. She was crumpled at the foot of the ladder, her Medusa wig a few feet away. Her throat had been cut with a savage blow, as if by a sword.

THE ADVERTISEMENT, IN the Paris edition of the English-language *Herald-Tribune,* read simply: *New Medusa wanted for Mythology Fair. Apply Box X-45.*

Laura Charme read it twice and asked, "Sebastian, what's a Mythology Fair?"

Turned around in his chair, Sebastian Blue replied, "An interesting question. The Secretary-General would like an answer, too. A Swiss citizen named Otto Dolliman started it in Geneva about two years ago. On the surface it's merely a tourist attraction, but it might be a bit more underneath."

They were in Sebastian's office on the top floor of Interpol headquarters in Saint-Cloud, a suburb of Paris. It was the sort of day when the girls in the translating department ignored the calendar and wore their summer dresses one last time. Laura had started out in the translating department herself, before the Secretary-General teamed her with Sebastian, a middle-aged Englishman formerly of Scotland Yard, and set them to investigating airline crimes around the globe.

"What happened to the old Medusa?" she asked Sebastian.

"She was a West German airline stewardess named Gretchen Spengler. It seems she was murdered two weeks ago."

"Oh, great, and I'll bet I'm supposed to take her place! I've been through this sort of thing before!"

Sebastian smiled across the desk at her. "Blame the Secretary-General. It was his idea. Seems Miss Spengler was believed to be a key link in a gold-smuggling operation which in turn is part of the world-wide narcotics network."

"You'd better explain that to me," Laura said, tossing her long reddish-blonde hair. "Especially if I'm supposed to take her place at this Mythology Fair."

"It seems that a good deal of Mob money—skimmed off the receipts of gambling casinos—finds its way into Swiss banks. It's used to make purchases on the international gold market, and the gold in turn is smuggled from Switzerland to the Far East, where it's then used to buy morphine base and raw opium for the making of heroin. The heroin is then smuggled into the United States, completing the world-wide circle."

"And how was Gretchen Spengler smuggling the gold?"

"Interpol's suspicion is that it traveled in the large metal food containers along with the hot meals for the passengers. Such a hiding place would need the cooperation of a stewardess, of course, so the gold wouldn't be accidentally discovered. Gretchen worked at Otto Dolliman's Mythology Fair in Geneva during her spare time, between flights, and Interpol believes Dolliman or someone else connected with the Fair recruited her for the gold smuggling. Chances are she was murdered because we were getting too close to her."

Laura nodded. "I can imagine how they'll welcome me if they discover I work for Interpol. And what are you going to be doing while I'm shaking my serpents?"

"I won't be far away," Sebastian promised. "I never am, you know."

G ENEVA IS A city of contrasts—small in size even by Swiss standards, yet still an important world crossroads and headquarters for a half-dozen specialized agencies of the United Nations, plus the International Red Cross and the World Council of Churches. The bustle at the airport reflected this cosmopolitan atmosphere, and Laura Charme was all but swallowed up in a delegation of arriving ministers.

Finally she fought her way to a taxi and gave the address of the Mythology Fair. "I take a great many tourists there," the driver informed her, speaking French. "Are you with a tour?"

"No. I'm looking for a job."

His eyes met hers in the mirror. "French?"

"French-English. Why do you ask?"

"I just wondered. The other girl was German."

"What happened to her?"

The driver shrugged. "She was killed. Such a shame—she was a lovely girl. Like you."

"Who killed her?"

"The police don't know. Some madman, certainly."

He was silent then, until at last he deposited her in front of a large old house overlooking Lake Geneva. Much of the front yard had been paved over and marked off for parking, and a big green tour bus sat empty near the entrance. Laura paid the driver and went up the steps to the open door.

The first person she saw was a gray-haired woman of slender build who seemed to be selling tickets. "Four francs, please," she said in French.

"I answered the advertisement for a new Medusa. I was told to come here for an interview."

"Oh, you must be Laura Charme. Very well, come this way." The woman led her past the ticket table and down a long corridor past framed portraits of various mythic heroes. She recognized Zeus and Jason and even the winged horse, Pegasus, but was stumped when it came to the women.

The gray-haired woman turned to her and said, in belated introduction, "I'm Helen Dolliman. My husband owns this." She gestured with her hand to include, apparently, the house and entire countryside.

"It's a beautiful place," Laura said. "I do hope I'll be able to work here."

The woman smiled slightly. "Otto liked the picture you sent. And it's difficult to get just the girl we want. I think you'll get the job." She paused before a closed door of heavy oak. "This is his office."

She knocked once and opened the door. The room itself was quite small, with only a single window covered by heavy wire mesh. The furnishings, too, were small and ordinary. But what set the room apart at once was the eight-foot-tall statue of King Neptune that completely dominated the far wall, crowding even the desk behind which a thin-haired middle-aged man was working.

"Otto," his wife announced, "this is Miss Charme, from Paris."

The man put down his pen and looked up, smiling. His face was drawn and his skin chalky-white, but the smile helped. "Ah, so good of you to come all this distance, Miss Charme! I do think you'll make a perfect Medusa."

"Thank you, I guess." Her eyes left his face and returned to the statue.

"You're admiring my Neptune."

"It's certainly . . . large."

He got up and stood beside it. "This is one of a series of the Roman gods, sculptured in the style of Michelangelo's Moses by the Italian Compoli in the last century. The trident that Neptune holds is very real, and quite sharp."

He lifted it from the statue's grasp and held it out to Laura. She saw the three spear-points aimed at her stomach and shuddered inwardly. "Very nice," she managed as he returned the weapon to its resting place with Neptune. "But tell me, just what is the Mythology Fair?"

"It is an exhibit, my dear girl—a live-action exhibit, if you will. All the gods and heroes and demons of myth are represented here—Greek, Roman, even Norse and Oriental. Our workrooms and dressing rooms are on the lower level. This level and the one above are open to the public for a small admission charge. They view paintings and statues representing the figures of myth—but more than that, they are entertained by live-action tableaux of famous scenes from mythology. Thus we have Ulysses returning to slay the suitors, the wooden horse at the walls of Troy, Perseus slaying Medusa, Cupid and Psyche, King Midas, Venus and Adonis, the labors of Hercules, and many others."

"Quite a bit of violence in some of those."

Otto Dolliman shrugged. "The public buys violence. And if some of our goddesses show a bit of bosom, the public buys that, too."

"I was wondering how someone like me could land the job of Medusa. I always thought she was quite ugly."

"It was the snakes in her hair that turned men to stone, my dear girl. And we will furnish those." He reached into the bottom drawer of his desk and produced a dark wig with a dozen plastic serpents hanging from it. As he held it out to Laura, the snakes began to move, seeming to take on a life of their own. Laura gasped and jumped back.

"They're alive!" she screeched.

"Not really," Mrs. Dolliman said, stepping forward to take the wig from her husband's hand. "We have little magnets in the snakes' heads, positioned so that the heads repel one another. They produce some quite realistic effects at times. See?"

Laura took a deep breath and accepted the wig. It seemed to fit her head well, though the weight of the magnetized serpents was uncomfortably heavy. "How long do I have to wear this thing?" she asked.

"Not more than a few minutes at a time," Dolliman assured her. "You come up through a trap door, hidden by some chemical mist, and Toby kills you with his sword. You fall back into the mist clouds, Toby reaches down, and holds a fake papier-mâché head aloft for the spectators to gasp at. I know it isn't exactly according to the myth—Medusa was asleep at the time of her death, for one thing—but the public enjoys it this way."

"Who's Toby?"

"What?"

"Who's Toby?" Laura repeated. "This fellow with the sword."

"Toby Merchant," Dolliman explained. "He's English, a nice fellow, really. He plays Perseus, and quite well, too. Come on, you might as well meet him."

Laura followed Otto and his wife out of the office and down the corridor to a wing of the great house. They passed a group of tourists, probably from the green bus out front, being guided through the place by a handsome young man, dressed in a black blazer, who bowed slightly as they passed.

"That's Frederick, one of our guides," Helen Dolliman explained. "With the guides and the actors, and a few workmen, we employ a staff of thirty-four people here. Of course many of the actors in the tableaux work only part time, between other jobs."

They paused before one stage, standing behind a dozen or so customers before a curtained stage. As the curtains parted Laura saw a bare-chested man who seemed to have the legs and body of a horse. She could tell it was a fake, but a clever one. "The centaur," Dolliman said. "Very popular with the tours. Ah, here is Toby."

A muscular young man about Laura's age, with shaggy black hair and a beard, came through a service door in the wall. He smiled at Laura, looking her up and down. "Would this be my new Medusa?"

"We have just hired her," Dolliman confirmed. "Laura Charme, meet Toby Marchant."

"A pleasure," she replied, accepting his hand. "But tell me, what have you been doing for a Medusa all these weeks?"

Toby Marchant shook his head sadly. "Venus has been filling in, but it's not the same. She has to run back and forth between the two stages. But she was doing it while Gretchen was flying, so she was the logical one to fill in." He glanced at Dolliman and brought his hand out from behind his back, revealing a paper bag. "Speaking of Gretchen—"

"Yes" Dolliman asked.

Toby opened the bag reluctantly and brought out the head of a young girl, covered with blood. Laura took one look and screamed.

Helen Dolliman motioned her to silence, glancing around to see who had heard the outburst. "It's only the papier-mâché head we told you about," she explained quickly. "You'll have to learn to control yourself better!"

"What is this place—a chamber of horrors?" Laura asked.

"No, no," Toby said, embarrassed and trying to calm her. "I shouldn't have pulled it out like that. It's just that the head was made to look like Gretchen and now she's dead. We can't use Venus' head. We'll need a new one made for Laura here, or the illusion will be ruined."

"I'll take care of it," Dolliman assured him. "Give me the bag."

Laura took a deep breath. "The taxi driver told me Gretchen was murdered. Did the police find her killer?"

"Not yet," Toby admitted. "But it must have been some sex fiend with one of the tours. Apparently he slipped downstairs and was waiting when she came through the trap door. I was right above her, but I never heard a thing."

"Toby was busy taking bows," Helen Dolliman snorted. "He wouldn't have heard a thing."

They went downstairs, showing Laura the dressing room that would be hers, the ladder leading to the trap door, the stage where she'd be beheaded five or six times daily, depending on the crowds. "Think you can do it?" Toby asked at the conclusion of a quick run-through.

"Sure," Laura said bravely. "Why not?"

A tall redhead wearing too much makeup came by, glancing up at the stage. "Better close that. Another bus just pulled up."

"This is our Venus and part-time Medusa," Toby said, making introductions. "Hilda Aarons."

Hilda grunted something meant to be a greeting and sauntered off. Laura was rapidly deciding that the Mythology Fair wasn't the friendliest place to work.

Sebastian Blue arrived two days after Laura started her chores as Medusa. He came with a group of touring Italians, but managed to separate himself from them, wandering off by himself down one of the side corridors.

"Can I help you?" a pleasant young man in a black blazer asked.

"Just looking around," Sebastian told him.

"I'm Frederick Braun, one of the tour guides. If you've become separated from your group I'd be glad to show you around."

Sebastian thought his blond good looks were strongly Germanic. He was a Hitler Youth, born thirty years too late. "I was looking for the director. I believe his name is Dolliman."

"Certainly. Right this way."

Otto Dolliman greeted Sebastian with a limp handshake and said, "No complaints, I hope."

"Not exactly. I represent the International Criminal Police Organization in Paris."

If possible, Dolliman's face grew even whiter. "Interpol? Is it about that girl's murder?"

"Yes, it is," Sebastian admitted. "We've had her under limited surveillance in connection with some gold-smuggling activities."

"Gretchen a gold smuggler? I can't believe that!"

"Nevertheless it seems to have been true. Didn't it ever strike you as strange that she continued working as an airline stewardess even after you hired her for your Mythology Fair?"

"Not at all, Mr. Blue. Both positions were essentially part-time. She worked charter flights and nonscheduled trips to the Far East mainly. And of course the bulk of her work here was during the vacation season and on weekends."

"Have you replaced her in the Fair?"

Dolliman nodded. "I hired a French girl just the other day. It's almost time for the next performance. Would you like to see it?"

"Very much."

Sebastian followed him down a hallway to the exhibit proper, where a string of little stages featured recreations of the more spectacular events of mythology. After watching a bearded Zeus hurl a cardboard thunderbolt, they moved on to the Medusa exhibit.

"That's Toby Marchant. He plays Perseus," Dolliman explained. The young man in a brief toga carried a sword and shield in proper Medusa-slaying tradition. He moved carefully through the artificial mist that rose from unseen pipes and acted out his search for the serpent-headed monster. Presently she appeared through the mist, up from the trap door. Sebastian thought Laura looked especially lovely in her brief costume. The snakes in her hair writhed with some realism, but otherwise she was hardly a convincing monster.

Toby Marchant, holding the shield protectively in front of him, swung out wildly with his sword. It was obvious he came nowhere near her, but Laura fell back into the mist with a convincing gasp. Toby reached down and lifted a bloody head for the spectators to gasp at.

"It was after this that Gretchen was killed," Dolliman explained in a whisper. "She slipped down through the trap door, and somebody was waiting at the foot of the ladder. Hilda found her about an hour later."

"Is it possible that Toby might have actually killed her in full view of the spectators?"

Dolliman shook his head. "The police have been all through this. The throat wound would have killed her almost instantly. She could never have gone through that trap door and down the ladder. Besides, the people would have seen it. There'd have been blood on the stage. She bled a great deal. Besides, his sword is a fake."

"That mist could have washed the blood away."

"No. Whoever killed her, it wasn't Toby. It was someone waiting for her below."

"The police report says the weapon was probably a sword."

"Unfortunately there are nearly fifty swords of various shapes and sizes on the premises. Some are fakes, like Toby's, but some are the real thing."

"I'd like to speak to your new Medusa if I could," Sebastian said.

"Certainly. I'll call her."

After a few moments Laura appeared, devoid of snakes and wearing a robe over her Medusa costume. Sebastian motioned her down the corridor, where they could talk in privacy. "How's it going?"

"Terrible," she confessed. "I've had to do that silly stunt five times a day. Yesterday when I came through the trap door that guide, Frederick, was waiting down below to grab my leg. I thought for a minute I was going to be the next victim."

"Oh?"

"He seems fairly harmless, though. I chased him away and he went. How much longer do I have to be here?"

"Till we find out something. Has anyone approached you about smuggling gold?"

She shook her head. "And I even mentioned over breakfast yesterday that I'd once been an airline stewardess. I think the gold smugglers have switched to a different gimmick, but I don't know what it is."

They'd almost reached Otto Dolliman's office, and suddenly Toby Marchant hurried out. "Have you seen Otto?" he asked Laura. "He's not in his office and I can't find him anywhere."

"We left him not five minutes ago, down by the tableaux."

"Thanks," Toby said, and hurried off in that direction.

"He seemed quite excited," Sebastian remarked.

"He usually is," Laura said. "But he's a good sort."

They paused by the open door of Dolliman's office, and he asked, "Do you think Dolliman is the gold smuggler? Is there any way all this could be going on without his knowledge?"

"It seems unlikely," she admitted. "But if he's behind it, would he kill Gretchen right on the premises and risk all the bad publicity?"

"These days bad publicity can be good publicity. I'll wager the crowds have picked up since the killing."

At that moment Otto Dolliman himself came into view, hurrying along the corridor. "Excuse me," he said. "I have to place an important call."

Toby came along behind him and seemed about to follow him into the office, but Dolliman slammed the big oak door. Toby glanced at Sebastian and Laura, shrugged, and went on his way.

"Now what was that all about?" Laura wondered aloud.

"It's your job to find out, my dear," Sebastian reminded her.

They were just moving away from the closed office door when they heard a sound from inside. It was like a gasp, followed by the beginning of a scream.

"What's that?" Laura asked.

"Come on, something's happening in there!" Sebastian reached the office door and opened it.

Otto Dolliman was sprawled in the center of the little office, his eyes open and staring at the ceiling. The trident from King Neptune's statue had been driven into his stomach. There was little doubt that he was dead.

"My God, Sebastian!" Laura gasped.

He'd drawn the gun from his belt holster. "Stay here in the doorway," he cautioned. "Whoever killed him must be still in the room."

His eyes went from the partly open window with its wire-mesh grille to the cluttered desk and the statue of Neptune beside it. Then he stepped carefully back and peered behind the door, but there was no one.

The room was empty except for Otto Dolliman's body . . .

"The thing is impossible," Sebastian Blue said later, after the police had come again to the Mythology Fair with their cameras and their questions. "We were outside that door all the time and no one entered or left. The killer might have been hiding behind the desk when Dolliman entered the room, but how did he get out?"

"The window?"

He walked over to examine it again, but he knew no one could have left that way. Though the window itself had been raised a few inches, the wire-mesh grille was firmly bolted in place and intact. Sebastian could barely fit two fingers through the openings. The window faced the back lawn, with a cobblestone walk about five feet below. Obviously the grille was to keep out thieves.

"Nothing here," Sebastian decided. "It's an impossible crime—a locked room, except that the room wasn't actually locked."

"You must have had those at Scotland Yard all the time."

"Only in books, my dear." He frowned at the floor where the body had rested, then looked up at the mocking statue of Neptune.

"An arrow could pass through this grillework," Laura remarked, still studying the window. "And they use arrows in the Ulysses skit."

"But he wasn't killed with an arrow," Sebastian reminded her. "He was killed with a trident, and it was right here in the room with him." He'd examined the weapon at some length before the police took it away, and had found nothing except a slight scratch along its shaft. There were no fingerprints, which ruled out the remote possibility of suicide.

"A device of some sort," she suggested next. "An infernal machine rigged up to kill him as soon as he entered the office."

"A giant rubber band?" Sebastian said with a dry chuckle. "But he was in there for a few minutes before the murderer struck, remember? And besides, what happened to this machine of yours? There's no trace of it now."

"A secret passage? We know there are trap doors in the floors around here."

"The police went over every square inch. No, it's nothing like that."

"Then how was it done?"

Sebastian was staring up at Neptune's placid face. "Unless that statue came alive long enough to kill him, I don't see any solution." He turned and headed for the door. "But one person I intend to speak to is Toby Marchant."

They found Toby talking with Frederick and Hilda and some of the others in a downstairs dressing room. While Laura still tried to keep up the pretense that Sebastian Blue had merely been questioning her, he turned his attention to Toby, calling him aside.

"All right, Toby, it's time to quit playing games. Two people are dead now, and with Dolliman gone chances are you'll be out of a job anyway. What do you know about this?"

"Nothing, I swear!"

"But you were looking for Dolliman just before he was killed. You told him something that sent him hurrying to his office to make a phone call."

Toby Marchant hesitated. "Yes," he said finally. "I suppose I'll have to tell you about that, Mr. Blue. You see, I came across some information regarding Gretchen's death—information I thought he should know."

"And now he's dead, so should I know it."

Another hesitation. "It's about Hilda Aarons. I caught her going through some of Gretchen's things, apparently looking for something."

Sebastian glanced past his shoulder toward the tall redhead. She was watching them intently. "And you told Otto Dolliman about this?"

Toby nodded. "He asked us to watch out for anything suspicious. What I told him about Hilda seemed to confirm some information he already had. He said he had to make a phone call at once."

"But not to the police, apparently. He walked right by me and went into his office.

"He may not have trusted an outsider. Sometimes he acted as if he trusted only his wife."

"Have you seen Helen Dolliman recently?" Sebastian asked. He'd had only a few words with her before the police arrived.

"She's probably up in her room. Second floor, the far wing."

Sebastian found Helen Dolliman alone in her room, busy packing a single suitcase. Her eyes were red, as if from tears.

"You're leaving?"

"Do I have anything to stay here for?" she countered. "The police will shut us down now. And even if they don't, I have no intention of spending another night in the same house with a double murderer. He killed Otto and I'm probably next on his list."

"Do you have any idea why your husband was murdered?"

The little woman swept a wisp of hair from her eyes. "I suppose for the same reason the girl was."

"Which was?"

"The gold."

"Yes, the gold. What do you know about it?"

"About a year ago Otto caught a man with some small gold bars. He fired him on the spot, but we've always suspected there were others involved."

"Gretchen Spengler?"

"Yes. Before she died she told Otto she was getting out of it."

"Toby says he caught Hilda Aarons going through Gretchen's things after she was killed. He told Otto about it."

She nodded. "My husband discussed it with me. We were going to fire Hilda."

"Might that have caused her to kill him?"

"It might have, if she's a desperate person."

"Apparently he was trying to call someone about it just before he was killed."

"Perhaps," she said with a shrug, subsiding into a sort of willing acceptance.

He could see there was no more to be learned from her. He excused himself and went back down in search of Laura.

She was talking with Frederick Braun at the foot of the stairs, but the blond tour guide excused himself as Sebastian approached. "What was all that?"

"He's still after me," she said with a shrug. "I really think he's a frustrated Pan, speaking in mythological terms."

Sebastian frowned at the young man's retreating back, watching him go out the rear door of the house. Then he said, "We're going to have to move fast. Helen Dolliman is preparing to close the place and leave. Once everybody scatters we'll never get to the bottom of this thing."

"How can we get to the bottom of it anyway, Sebastian? We've got two murders, one of them an impossibility."

"But we've got a lead, too. Gretchen was killed and the smuggling by aircraft apparently ended. Yet the murderer has stayed on here at the Mythology Fair. We know that because he killed Dolliman, too. I reject for the moment the idea of two independent killers. So what have we? The gold smugglers still at work, but not using aircraft. They have found a new route for their gold, and we must find it, too."

"Let me work on it," Laura Charme said. Staring at an approaching group of tourists, she suddenly got an idea.

NIGHT CAME EARLY at this time of year, with the evening sun vanishing behind the distant Alps by a little after six. One of the tour groups was still inside the big house when Laura slipped out the rear door and moved around the cobblestone walk past the window to Dolliman's office. She came out at the far end of the paved parking area, near the single green tour bus that still waited there.

If the Mythology Fair was really closing down, she knew the smuggler should have to move fast to dispose of any remaining gold. And if she'd guessed right about these tour buses, she might see something very interesting as darkness fell.

She'd been standing in the shadows for about twenty minutes when the bus driver appeared from the corner of the building, carrying something heavy in both hands. He paused by the side of the vehicle and opened one of the luggage compartments. But he wasn't stowing luggage. Instead he seemed to be lifting up a portion of the compartment floor, shifting baggage out of the way.

Laura stepped quickly from the shadows and moved up behind him. "What do you have there?" she asked.

The man whirled at the sound of her voice. He cursed softly and grabbed an iron bar that was holding open the luggage compartment door. As the door slammed shut she saw him coming at her with the bar, raising it high overhead. She dipped, butting him in the stomach, and grabbed his wrist for a quick judo topple that sent him into the bushes by the house.

As he tried to untangle himself and catch his breath, she ripped the wrapper from the object he'd been carrying. Even in the near-darkness she could see the glint of gold.

Then she heard footsteps, and another man rounded the corner of the building. It was Toby Marchant. She rose to her feet and hurried to meet him. "Toby, that bus driver had a bar of gold. He was trying to hide it beneath the luggage compartment."

"What's this?" He hurried over to the bushes with her.

"Toby, I'll keep him here. You go find that Englishman, Sebastian Blue."

Toby turned partly away from her as the bus driver struggled to his feet. "Oh, I don't think we need Blue."

"Of course we need him! He's from Interpol, and so am I."

"That's interesting to know," Toby said. "But I already suspected it." He turned back toward her and now she saw the gun in his hand. "Don't make a sound, my dear, or you'll end up the way Gretchen and Otto did."

"I—"

"Tie her up, Gunter," he told the driver. "And gag her. We'll stow her in the luggage compartment and take her along for security."

Laura felt rough hands yank her wrists behind her. Then, suddenly, the parking area was flooded with light from overhead. Toby whirled and fired a shot without aiming. There was an answering shot as the bus driver dropped her wrists and started to run. He staggered and went down hard.

"Drop the gun, Toby," Sebastian called out from beyond the spotlights. "We want you alive."

Toby Marchant hesitated, weighing his chances, and then let the gun fall from his fingers.

———

IT WAS SOME time later before Laura could get all the facts out of Sebastian Blue. They were driving back to the airport, after Toby Marchant had been turned over to the local police and the bus driver rushed to the hospital.

"How did you manage to get there in the nick of time?" she asked him. "I didn't tell you of my suspicions about the tour buses."

"No, but you didn't have to. I had my own suspicions of Toby, and I was watching him. I saw him meet the driver and get the gold bar from its hiding place. When I saw him point the gun at you, I switched on the overhead lights and then the shooting started. Luckily for us both, Toby had no idea how many guns were against him, so he chose to surrender."

"But how did you know Toby was involved in the smuggling?"

"I didn't, but I was pretty sure he'd committed both murders, which made him the most likely candidate."

"He killed Otto Dolliman in that locked room? But how?"

"There's only one way it could have been done, ruling out secret passages and invisible men. Remember that scratch along the shaft of the trident? Toby entered the office prior to Dolliman's arrival, removed the trident from the statue of Neptune, and thrust the shaft of it through the wire grating on the window. Remember, the window itself was open a few inches. Thus, the pronged head of the trident was inside the office, but the shaft was sticking out the window.

"Toby then got Otto to enter the office on some pretext—probably telling him to phone for urgent supplies of some sort—left the house, walked around the cobblestone path just outside, and positioned himself at the window. Perhaps Dolliman saw the trident sticking through the grillework and walked over to investigate. Or perhaps Toby called him to the window, pretending to find it like that. In either event, as Dolliman reached the window, Toby drove the trident into his stomach, killing him. He then pushed the shaft all the way through the wire grillework, so the trident remained in Dolliman's body and made it appear that the killer must have been in the room with him."

"But why did he want to kill him in a locked room?"

"He didn't. He was just setting up an alibi for himself, since we saw him leave Dolliman alive. He couldn't foresee that we'd remain outside the door and hear Dolliman's dying gasps. You see, once I figured out the method, Toby had to be the killer. We'd seen him come out of that office ourselves. And the killer had to be in the office prior to the killing to push the trident through the screen. He couldn't have it sticking out the window for long, risking discovery, so he had to lure Dolliman back to his office.

"That was where Toby made his big mistake. When we surprised him coming out of the office, he had to act as if he was frantically seeking Dolliman to tell him something. Later, when I asked what it was all about, he had to come up with a good lie. He said he'd told Dolliman he caught Hilda going through Gretchen's things. I suspect that was true, and that it involved your friend Frederick, the guide, *but*—Helen Dolliman later told me her husband had discussed the matter with her."

"Which meant," Laura said, "he must have told Dolliman about it much earlier."

"Exactly. Early enough for Dolliman to discuss it with his wife. And if Toby lied about the reason for luring Dolliman to his office, it figured that he also prepared the trident and killed him with it."

"What about Gretchen?"

"She wanted out of the gold smuggling, so he had to kill her—she knew too much. I suppose Dolliman was suspicious that Toby killed her, so Dolliman had to die, too. Either that, or Dolliman discovered that Toby was now using the tour buses to smuggle the gold out of Switzerland."

"But I thought we decided Toby couldn't have done it because he was still on stage when Gretchen went through the trap door to her death. Don't tell me we have another impossible crime?"

Sebastian shook his head. "Not really. Our mistake was in jumping to the conclusion that the killer was waiting for her. Actually, Toby went downstairs after the act was over and killed her then. I suppose he swung the sword at her in jest, just as he did on stage, only this time it was for real. She wouldn't even have screamed when she saw it coming at her."

"How awful!"

"But what about you? How did you tumble to the fact the tour buses were being used?"

Laura shrugged. "Partly intuition, I suppose. We figured the gold was still leaving the country, and not by plane. It just seemed a likely method. Tour buses cross boundary lines all the time, and they're not usually searched too carefully."

They came in sight of the airport and Sebastian said, "I imagine Paris will look good to you after this. Or did you enjoy playing Medusa?"

She grinned and held up the wig with its writhing snakes. "I brought it along as a souvenir. Just so we'll know the whole thing wasn't a myth."

QUITTERS, INC.

Stephen King

There are certain things that are almost always mentioned when the name Stephen King comes up. How many books he's sold. What he's doing in and for literature today. And (recently) the terrible accident he suffered while walking down a road near his home in Maine. One thing almost never mentioned—and not generally perceived—is that he single-handedly made popular fiction grow up. While there were many good best-selling writers before him, King, more than anybody since John D. MacDonald, brought reality to genre novels. He's often remarked that *Salem's Lot* (1977) was *"Peyton Place* Meets *Dracula."* And so it was. The rich characterization, the careful and caring social eye, the interplay of story line and character development announced that writers could take worn themes such as vampirism and make them fresh again. Before King, many popular writers found their efforts to make their books serious blue-penciled by their editors. Stuff like that gets in the way of the story, they were told. Well, it's stuff like that that has made King so popular, and helped free the popular name from the shackles of simple genre writing. He is a master of masters.

MORRISON WAS WAITING for someone who was hung up in the air traffic jam over Kennedy International when he saw a familiar face at the end of the bar and walked down.

"Jimmy? Jimmy McCann?"

It was. A little heavier than when Morrison had seen him at the Atlanta Exhibition the year before, but otherwise he looked awesomely fit. In college he had been a little thin, pallid chain smoker buried behind huge horn-rimmed glasses. He had apparently switched to contact lenses.

"Dick Morrison?"

"Yeah. You look great." He extended his hand and they shook.

"So do you," McCann said, but Morrison knew it was a lie. He had been overworking, overeating, and smoking too much. "What are you drinking?"

"Bourbon and bitters," Morrison said. He hooked his feet around a bar stool and lighted a cigarette. "Meeting someone, Jimmy?"

"No. Going to Miami for a conference. A heavy client. Bills six million. I'm supposed to hold his hand because we lost out on a big special next spring."

"Are you still with Crager and Barton?"

"Executive veep now."

"Fantastic! Congratulations! When did all this happen?" He tried to tell himself that the little worm of jealousy in his stomach was just acid indigestion. He pulled out a roll of antacid pills and crunched one in his mouth.

"Last August. Something happened that changed my life." He looked speculatively at Morrison and sipped his drink. "You might be interested."

My God, Morrison thought with an inner wince. Jimmy McCann's got religion.

"Sure," he said, and gulped at his drink when it came.

"I wasn't in very good shape," McCann said. "Personal problems with Sharon, my dad died—heart attack—and I'd developed this hacking cough. Bobby Crager dropped by my office one day and gave me a fatherly little pep talk. Do you remember what those are like?"

"Yeah." He had worked at Crager and Barton for eighteen months before joining the Morton Agency. "Get your butt in gear or get your butt out."

McCann laughed. "You know it. Well, to put the capper on it, the doc told me I had an incipient ulcer. He told me to quit smoking." McCann grimaced. "Might as well tell me to quit breathing."

Morrison nodded in perfect understanding. Nonsmokers could afford to be smug. He looked at his own cigarette with distaste and stubbed it out, knowing he would be lighting another in five minutes.

"Did you quit?" he asked.

"Yes, I did. At first I didn't think I'd be able to—I was cheating like hell. Then I met a guy who told me about an outfit over on Forty-sixth Street. Specialists. I said what do I have to lose and went over. I haven't smoked since."

Morrison's eyes widened. "What did they do? Fill you full of some drug?"

"No." He had taken out his wallet and was rummaging through it. "Here it is. I knew I had one kicking around." He laid a plain white business card on the bar between them.

QUITTERS, INC.

Stop Going Up in Smoke!

237 East 46th Street

Treatments by Appointment

"Keep it, if you want," McCann said. "They'll cure you. Guaranteed."

"How?"

"I can't tell you," McCann said.

"Huh? Why not?"

"It's part of the contract they make you sign. Anyway, they tell you how it works when they interview you."

"You signed a *contract*?"

McCann nodded.

"And on the basis of that—"

"Yep." He smiled at Morrison, who thought: Well, it's happened. Jim McCann has joined the smug bastards.

"Why the great secrecy if this outfit is so fantastic? How come I've never seen any spots on TV, billboards, magazine ads—"

"They get all the clients they can handle by word of mouth."

"You're an advertising man, Jimmy. You can't believe that."

"I do," McCann said. "They have a ninety-eight percent cure rate."

"Wait a second," Morrison said. He motioned for another drink and lit a cigarette. "Do these guys strap you down and make you smoke until you throw up?"

"No."

"Give you something so that you get sick every time you light—"

"No, it's nothing like that. Go and see for yourself." He gestured at Morrison's cigarette. "You don't really like that, do you?"

"Nooo, but—"

"Stopping really changed things for me," McCann said. "I don't suppose it's the same for everyone, but with me it was just like dominoes falling over. I felt better and my relationship with Sharon improved. I had more energy, and my job performance picked up."

"Look, you've got my curiosity aroused. Can't you just—"

"I'm sorry, Dick. I really can't talk about it." His voice was firm.

"Did you put on any weight?"

For a moment he thought Jimmy McCann looked almost grim. "Yes. A little too much, in fact. But I took it off again. I'm about right now. I was skinny before."

"Flight 206 now boarding at Gate 9," the loudspeaker announced.

"That's me," McCann said, getting up. He tossed a five on the bar. "Have another, if you like. And think about what I said, Dick. Really." And then he was gone, making his way through the crowd to the escalators. Morrison picked up the card, looked at it thoughtfully, then tucked it away in his wallet and forgot it.

THE CARD FELL out of his wallet and onto another bar a month later. He had left the office early and had come here to drink the afternoon away. Things had not been going well at the Morton Agency. In fact, things were bloody horrible.

He gave Henry a ten to pay for his drink, then picked up the small card and reread it—237 East Forty-sixth Street was only two blocks over; it was a cool, sunny October day outside, and maybe, just for chuckles—

When Henry brought his change, he finished his drink and then went for a walk.

QUITTERS, INC., WAS in a new building where the monthly rent on the office space was probably close to Morrison's yearly salary. From the directory in the lobby, it looked to him like their offices took up one whole floor, and that spelled money. Lots of it.

He took the elevator up and stepped off into a lushly carpeted foyer and from there into a gracefully appointed reception room with a wide window that looked out on the scurrying bugs below. Three men and one woman sat in the chairs along the walls, reading magazines. Business types, all of them. Morrison went to the desk.

"A friend gave me this," he said, passing the card to the receptionist. "I guess you'd say he's an alumnus."

She smiled and rolled a form into her typewriter. "What is your name, sir?"

"Richard Morrison."

Clack-clackety-clack. But very muted clacks; the typewriter was an IBM.

"Your address?"

"Twenty-nine Maple Lane, Clinton, New York."

"Married?"

"Yes."

"Children?"

"One." He thought of Alvin and frowned slightly. "One" was the wrong word. "A half" might be better. His son was mentally retarded and lived at a special school in New Jersey.

"Who recommended us to you, Mr. Morrison?"

"An old school friend. James McCann."

"Very good. Will you have a seat? It's been a very busy day."

"All right."

He sat between the woman, who was wearing a severe blue suit, and a young executive type wearing a herringbone jacket and modish sideburns. He took out his pack of cigarettes, looked around, and saw there were no ashtrays.

He put the pack away again. That was all right. He would see this little game through and then light up while he was leaving. He might even tap some ashes on their maroon shag rug if they made him wait long enough. He picked up a copy of *Time* and began to leaf through it.

He was called a quarter of an hour later, after the woman in the blue suit. His nicotine center was speaking quite loudly now. A man who had come in after him took out a cigarette case, snapped it open, saw there were no ashtrays, and put it away—looking a little guilty, Morrison thought. It made him feel better.

At last the receptionist gave him a sunny smile and said, "Go right in, Mr. Morrison."

Morrison walked through the door beyond her desk and found himself in an indirectly lit hallway. A heavyset man with white hair that looked phony shook his hand, smiled affably, and said, "Follow me, Mr. Morrison."

He led Morrison past a number of closed, unmarked doors and then opened one of them about halfway down the hall with a key. Beyond the door was an austere little room walled with drilled white cork panels. The only furnishings were a desk with a chair on either side. There was what appeared to be a small oblong window in the wall behind the desk, but it was covered with a short green curtain. There was a picture on the wall to Morrison's left—a tall man with iron-gray hair. He was holding a sheet of paper in one hand. He looked vaguely familiar.

"I'm Vic Donatti," the heavyset man said. "If you decide to go ahead with our program, I'll be in charge of your case."

"Pleased to know you," Morrison said. He wanted a cigarette very badly.

"Have a seat."

Donatti put the receptionist's form on the desk, and then drew another form from the desk drawer. He looked directly into Morrison's eyes. "Do you want to quit smoking?"

Morrison cleared his throat, crossed his legs, and tried to think of a way to equivocate. He couldn't. "Yes," he said.

"Will you sign this?" He gave Morrison the form. He scanned it quickly. The undersigned agrees not to divulge the methods or techniques or et cetera, et cetera.

"Sure," he said, and Donatti put a pen in his hand. He scratched his name, and Donatti signed below it. A moment later the paper disappeared back into the desk drawer. Well, he thought ironically, I've taken the pledge. He had taken it before. Once it had lasted for two whole days.

"Good," Donatti said. "We don't bother with propaganda here, Mr. Morrison. Questions of health or expense or social grace. We have no interest in why you want to stop smoking. We are pragmatists."

"Good," Morrison said blankly.

"We employ no drugs. We employ no Dale Carnegie people to sermonize you. We recommend no special diet. And we accept no payment until you have stopped smoking for one year."

"My God," Morrison said.

"Mr. McCann didn't tell you that?"

"No."

"How is Mr. McCann, by the way? Is he well?"

"He's fine."

"Wonderful. Excellent. Now . . . just a few questions, Mr. Morrison. These are somewhat personal, but I assure you that your answers will be held in strictest confidence."

"Yes?" Morrison asked noncommittally.

"What is your wife's name?"

"Lucinda Morrison. Her maiden name was Ramsey."

"Do you love her?"

Morrison looked up sharply, but Donatti was looking at him blandly. "Yes, of course," he said.

"Have you ever had marital problems? A separation, perhaps?"

"What has that got to do with kicking the habit?" Morrison asked. He sounded a little angrier than he had intended, but he wanted—hell, he *needed*—a cigarette.

"A great deal," Donatti said. "Just bear with me."

"No. Nothing like that." Although things *had* been a little tense just lately.

"You just have the one child?"

"Yes. Alvin. He's in a private school."

"And which school is it?"

"That," Morrison said grimly, "I'm not going to tell you."

"All right," Donatti said agreeably. He smiled disarmingly at Morrison. "All your questions will be answered tomorrow at your first treatment."

"How nice," Morrison said, and stood.

"One final question," Donatti said. "You haven't had a cigarette for over an hour. How do you feel?"

"Fine," Morrison lied. "Just fine."

"Good for you!" Donatti exclaimed. He stepped around the desk and opened the door. "Enjoy them tonight. After tomorrow, you'll never smoke again."

"Is that right?"

"Mr. Morrison," Donatti said solemnly, "we guarantee it."

HE WAS SITTING in the outer office of Quitters, Inc., the next day promptly at three. He had spent most of the day swinging between skipping the appointment the receptionist had made for him on the way out and going in a spirit of mulish cooperation—*Throw your best pitch at me, buster.*

In the end, something Jimmy McCann had said convinced him to keep the appointment—*It changed my whole life.* God knew his own life could do with some changing. And then there was his own curiosity. Before going up in the elevator, he smoked a cigarette down to the filter. Too damn bad if it's the last one, he thought. It tasted horrible.

The wait in the outer office was shorter this time. When the receptionist told him to go in, Donatti was waiting. He offered his hand and smiled, and to Morrison the smile looked almost predatory. He began to feel a little tense, and that made him want a cigarette.

"Come with me," Donatti said, and led the way down to the small room. He sat behind the desk again, and Morrison took the other chair.

"I'm very glad you came," Donatti said. "A great many prospective clients never show up again after the initial interview. They discover they don't want to quit as badly as they thought. It's going to be a pleasure to work with you on this."

"When does the treatment start?" Hypnosis, he was thinking. It must be hypnosis.

"Oh, it already has. It started when we shook hands in the hall. Do you have cigarettes with you, Mr. Morrison?"

"Yes."

"May I have them, please?"

Shrugging, Morrison handed Donatti his pack. There were only two or three left in it, anyway.

Donatti put the pack on the desk. Then, smiling into Morrison's eyes, he curled his right hand into a fist and began to hammer it down on the pack of cigarettes, which twisted and flattened. A broken cigarette end flew out. Tobacco crumbs spilled. The sound of Donatti's fist was very loud in the closed room. The smile remained on his face in spite of the force of the blows, and Morrison was chilled by it. Probably just the effect they want to inspire, he thought.

At last Donatti ceased pounding. He picked up the pack, a twisted and battered ruin. "You wouldn't believe the pleasure that gives me," he said, and dropped the pack into the wastebasket. "Even after three years in the business, it still pleases me."

"As a treatment, it leaves something to be desired," Morrison said mildly. "There's a newsstand in the lobby of this very building. And they sell all brands."

"As you say," Donatti said. He folded his hands. "Your son, Alvin Dawes Morrison, is in the Paterson School for Handicapped Children. Born with cranial brain damage. Tested IQ of 46. Not quite in the educable retarded category. Your wife—"

"How did you find that out?" Morrison barked. He was startled and angry. "You've got no goddamn right to go poking around my—"

"We know a lot about you," Donatti said smoothly. "But, as I said, it will all be held in strictest confidence."

"I'm getting out of here," Morrison said thinly. He stood up.

"Stay a bit longer."

Morrison looked at him closely. Donatti wasn't upset. In fact, he looked a little amused. The face of a man who has seen this reaction scores of times—maybe hundreds.

"All right. But it better be good."

"Oh, it is." Donatti leaned back. "I told you we were pragmatists here.

As pragmatists, we have to start by realizing how difficult it is to cure an addiction to tobacco. The relapse rate is almost eighty-five percent. The relapse rate for heroin addicts is lower than that. It is an extraordinary problem. *Extraordinary.*"

Morrison glanced into the wastebasket. One of the cigarettes, although twisted, still looked smokeable. Donatti laughed good-naturedly, reached into the wastebasket, and broke it between his fingers.

"State legislatures sometimes hear a request that the prison systems do away with the weekly cigarette ration. Such proposals are invariably defeated. In a few cases where they have passed, there have been fierce prison riots. *Riots*, Mr. Morrison. Imagine it."

"I," Morrison said, "am not surprised."

"But consider the implications. When you put a man in prison you take away any normal sex life, you take away his liquor, his politics, his freedom of movement. No riots—or few in comparison to the number of prisons. But when you take away his *cigarettes*—wham! bam!" He slammed his fist on the desk for emphasis.

"During World War I, when no one on the German home front could get cigarettes, the sight of German aristocrats picking butts out of the gutter was a common one. During World War II, many American women turned to pipes when they were unable to obtain cigarettes. A fascinating problem for the true pragmatist, Mr. Morrison."

"Could we get to the treatment?"

"Momentarily. Step over here, please." Donatti had risen and was standing by the green curtains Morrison had noticed yesterday. Donatti drew the curtains, discovering a rectangular window that looked into a bare room. No, not quite bare. There was a rabbit on the floor, eating pellets out of a dish.

"Pretty bunny," Morrison commented.

"Indeed. Watch him." Donatti pressed a button by the windowsill. The rabbit stopped eating and began to hop about crazily. It seemed to leap higher each time its feet struck the floor. Its fur stood out spikily in all directions. Its eyes were wild.

"Stop that! You're electrocuting him!"

Donatti released the button. "Far from it. There's a very low-yield charge in the floor. Watch the rabbit, Mr. Morrison!"

The rabbit was crouched about ten feet away from the dish of pellets. His nose wriggled. All at once he hopped away into a corner.

"If the rabbit gets a jolt often enough while he's eating," Donatti said, "he makes the association very quickly. Eating causes pain. Therefore, he won't eat. A few more shocks, and the rabbit will starve to death in front of his food. It's called aversion training."

Light dawned in Morrison's head.

"No, thanks." He started for the door.

"Wait, please, Mr. Morrison."

Morrison didn't pause. He grasped the doorknob . . . and felt it slip solidly through his hand. "Unlock this."

"Mr. Morrison, if you'll just sit down—"

"Unlock this door or I'll have the cops on you before you can say Marlboro Man."

"*Sit down.*" The voice was cold as shaved ice.

Morrison looked at Donatti. His brown eyes were muddy and frightening. My God, he thought, I'm locked in here with a psycho. He licked his lips. He wanted a cigarette more than he ever had in his life.

"Let me explain the treatment in more detail," Donatti said.

"You don't understand," Morrison said with counterfeit patience. "I don't want the treatment. I've decided against it."

"No, Mr. Morrison. *You're* the one who doesn't understand. You don't have any choice. When I told you the treatment had already begun, I was speaking the literal truth. I would have thought you'd tipped to that by now."

"You're crazy," Morrison said wonderingly.

"No. Only a pragmatist. Let me tell you all about the treatment."

"Sure," Morrison said. "As long as you understand that as soon as I get out of here I'm going to buy five packs of cigarettes and smoke them all the way to the police station." He suddenly realized he was biting his thumbnail, sucking on it, and made himself stop.

"As you wish. But I think you'll change your mind when you see the whole picture."

Morrison said nothing. He sat down again and folded his hands.

"For the first month of the treatment, our operatives will have you under constant supervision," Donatti said. "You'll be able to spot some of them. Not all. But they'll always be with you. *Always.* If they see you smoke a cigarette, I get a call."

"And I suppose you bring me here and do the old rabbit trick," Morrison said. He tried to sound cold and sarcastic, but he suddenly felt horribly frightened. This was a nightmare.

"Oh, no," Donatti said. "Your wife gets the rabbit trick, not you."

Morrison looked at him dumbly.

Donatti smiled. "You," he said, "get to watch."

AFTER DONATTI LET him out, Morrison walked for over two hours in a complete daze. It was another fine day, but he didn't notice. The monstrousness of Donatti's smiling face blotted out all else.

"You see," he had said, "a pragmatic problem demands pragmatic solutions. You must realize we have your best interests at heart."

Quitters, Inc., according to Donatti, was a sort of foundation—a nonprofit organization begun by the man in the wall portrait. The gentleman had been extremely successful in several family businesses—including slot machines, massage parlors, numbers, and a brisk (although clandestine) trade between New York and Turkey. Mort "Three-Fingers" Minelli had been a heavy smoker—up in the three-pack-a-day range. The paper he was holding in the picture was a doctor's diagnosis: lung cancer. Mort had died in 1970, after endowing Quitters, Inc., with family funds.

"We try to keep as close to breaking even as possible," Donatti had said. "But we're more interested in helping our fellow man. And of course, it's a great tax angle."

The treatment was chillingly simple. A first offense and Cindy would be brought to what Donatti called "the rabbit room." A second offense, and Morrison would get the dose. On a third offense, both of them would be brought in together. A fourth offense would show grave cooperation problems and would require sterner measures. An operative would be sent to Alvin's school to work the boy over.

"Imagine," Donatti said, smiling, "how horrible it will be for the boy. He wouldn't understand it even if someone explained. He'll only know someone is hurting him because Daddy was bad. He'll be very frightened."

"You bastard," Morrison said helplessly. He felt close to tears. "You dirty, filthy bastard."

"Don't misunderstand," Donatti said. He was smiling sympathetically. "I'm sure it won't happen. Forty percent of our clients never have more than three falls from grace. Those are reassuring figures, aren't they?"

Morrison didn't find them reassuring. He found them terrifying.

"Of course, if you transgress a *fifth* time—"

"What do you mean?"

Donatti beamed. "The room for you and your wife, a second beating for your son, and a beating for your wife."

Morrison, driven beyond the point of rational consideration, lunged over the desk at Donatti. Donatti moved with amazing speed for a man who had apparently been completely relaxed. He shoved the chair backward and drove both of his feet over the desk and into Morrison's belly. Gagging and coughing, Morrison staggered backward.

"Sit down, Mr. Morrison," Donatti said benignly. "Let's talk this over like rational men."

When he could catch his breath, Morrison did as he was told. Nightmares had to end sometime, didn't they?

QUITTERS, INC., DONATTI had explained further, operated on a ten-step punishment scale. Steps six, seven, and eight consisted of further trips to the rabbit room (and increased voltage) and more serious beating. The ninth step would be the breaking of his son's arms.

"And the tenth?" Morrison asked, his mouth dry.

Donatti shook his head sadly. "Then we give up, Mr. Morrison. You become part of the unregenerate two percent."

"You really give up?"

"In a manner of speaking." He opened one of the desk drawers and laid a silenced .45 on the desk. He smiled into Morrison's eyes. "But even the unregenerate two percent never smoke again. We guarantee it."

THE FRIDAY NIGHT Movie was *Bullitt*, one of Cindy's favorites, but after an hour of Morrison's mutterings and fidgetings, her concentration was broken.

"What's the matter with you?" she asked during station identification.

"Nothing . . . everything," he growled. "I'm giving up smoking."

She laughed. "Since when? Five minutes ago?"

"Since three o'clock this afternoon."

"You really haven't had a cigarette since then?"

"No," he said, and began to gnaw his thumbnail. It was ragged, down to the quick.

"That's wonderful! What ever made you decide to quit?"

"You," he said. "And . . . and Alvin."

Her eyes widened, and when the movie came back on, she didn't notice. Dick rarely mentioned their retarded son. She came over, looked at the empty ashtray by his right hand, and then into his eyes. "Are you really trying to quit, Dick?"

"Really." And if I go to the cops, he added mentally, the local goon squad will be around to rearrange your face, Cindy.

"I'm glad. Even if you don't make it, we both thank you for the thought, Dick."

"Oh, I think I'll make it," he said, thinking of the muddy, homicidal look that had come into Donatti's eyes when he kicked him in the stomach.

HE SLEPT BADLY that night, dozing in and out of sleep. Around three o'clock he woke up completely. His craving for a cigarette was like a low-grade fever. He went downstairs and to his study. The room was in the middle of the house. No windows. He slid open the top drawer of his desk and looked in, fascinated by the cigarette box. He looked around and licked his lips.

Constant supervision during the first month, Donatti had said. Eighteen hours a day during the next two—but he would never know *which* eighteen. During the fourth month, the month when most clients backslid; the "service" would return to twenty-four hours a day. Then twelve hours of broken surveillance each day for the rest of the year. After that? Random surveillance for the rest of the client's life.

For the rest of his life.

"We may audit you every other month," Donatti said. "Or every other day. Or constantly for one week two years from now. The point is, *you won't know*. If you smoke, you'll be gambling with loaded dice. Are they watching? Are they picking up my wife or sending a man after my son right now? Beautiful, isn't it? And if you do sneak a smoke, it'll taste awful. It will taste like your son's blood."

But they couldn't be watching now, in the dead of night, in his own study. The house was grave-quiet.

He looked at the cigarettes in the box for almost two minutes, unable to tear his gaze away. Then he went to the study door, peered out into the empty hall, and went back to look at the cigarettes some more. A horrible picture came: his life stretching before him and not a cigarette to be found. How in the name of God was he ever going to be able to make another tough presentation to a wary client, without that cigarette burning nonchalantly between his fingers as he approached the charts and layouts? How would he be able to endure Cindy's endless garden shows without a cigarette? How could he even get up in the morning and face the day without a cigarette to smoke as he drank his coffee and read the paper?

He cursed himself for getting into this. He cursed Donatti. And most of all, he cursed Jimmy McCann. How could he have done it? The son of a bitch had *known*. His hands trembled in their desire to get hold of Jimmy Judas McCann.

Stealthily, he glanced around the study again. He reached into the drawer and brought out a cigarette. He caressed it, fondled it. What was the old slogan? *So round, so firm, so fully packed.* Truer words had never been spoken. He put the cigarette in his mouth and then paused, cocking his head.

Had there been the slightest noise from the closet? A faint shifting? Surely not. But—

Another mental image—that rabbit hopping crazily in the grip of electricity. The thought of Cindy in that room—

He listened desperately and heard nothing. He told himself that all he had to do was to go to the closet door and yank it open. But he was too afraid of what he might find. He went back to bed but didn't sleep for a long time.

———

IN SPITE OF how lousy he felt in the morning, breakfast tasted good. After a moment's hesitation, he followed his customary bowl of corn-flakes with scrambled eggs. He was grumpily washing out the pan when Cindy came downstairs in her robe.

"Richard Morrison! You haven't eaten an egg for breakfast since Hec-tor was a pup."

Morrison grunted. He considered *since Hector was a pup* to be one of Cindy's stupider sayings, on a par with *I should smile and kiss a pig.*

"Have you smoked yet?" she asked, pouring orange juice.

"No."

"You'll be back on them by noon," she proclaimed airily.

"Lot of goddamn help you are!" he rasped, rounding on her. "You and anyone else who doesn't smoke, you all think . . . ah, never mind."

He expected her to be angry, but she was looking at him with some-thing like wonder. "You're really serious," she said. "You really are."

"You bet I am." *You'll never know* how *serious. I hope.*

"Poor baby," she said, going to him. "You look like death warmed over. But I'm very proud."

Morrison held her tightly.

———

SCENES FROM THE life of Richard Morrison, October–November: Morrison and a crony from Larkin Studios at Jack Dempsey's bar. Crony offers a cigarette. Morrison grips his glass a little more tightly and says: *I'm quitting.* Crony laughs and says: *I give you a week.*

Morrison waiting for the morning train, looking over the top of the *Times* at a young man in a blue suit. He sees the young man almost every morning now, and sometimes at other places. At Onde's, where he is meeting a client. Looking at 45s in Sam Goody's, where Morrison is looking for a Sam Cooke album. Once in a foursome behind Morrison's group at the local golf course.

Morrison getting drunk at a party, wanting a cigarette—but not quite drunk enough to take one.

Morrison visiting his son, bringing him a large ball that squeaked when you squeezed it. His son's slobbering, delighted kiss. Somehow not as repulsive as before. Hugging his son tightly, realizing what Donatti and his colleagues had so cynically realized before him: love is the most pernicious drug of all. Let the romantics debate its existence. Pragmatists accept it and use it.

Morrison losing the physical compulsion to smoke little by little, but never quite losing the psychological craving, or the need to have something in his mouth—cough drops, Life Savers, a toothpick. Poor substitutes, all of them.

And finally, Morrison hung up in a colossal traffic jam in the Midtown Tunnel. Darkness. Horns blaring. Air stinking. Traffic hopelessly snarled. And suddenly, thumbing open the glove compartment and seeing the half-open pack of cigarettes in there. He looked at them for a moment, then snatched one and lit it with the dashboard lighter. If anything happens, it's Cindy's fault, he told himself defiantly. I told her to get rid of all the damn cigarettes.

The first drag made him cough smoke out furiously. The second made his eyes water. The third made him feel lightheaded and swoony. It tastes awful, he thought.

And on the heels of that: My God, what am I doing?

Horns blatted impatiently behind him. Ahead, the traffic had begun to move again. He stubbed the cigarette out in the ashtray, opened both front windows, opened the vents, and then fanned the air helplessly like a kid who had just flushed his first butt down the john.

He joined the traffic flow jerkily and drove home.

" CINDY?" HE CALLED. "I'm home."

No answer.

"Cindy? Where are you, hon?"

The phone rang, and he pounced on it. "Hello? Cindy?"

"Hello, Mr. Morrison," Donatti said. He sounded pleasantly brisk and businesslike. "It seems we have a small business matter to attend to. Would five o'clock be convenient?"

"Have you got my wife?"

"Yes, indeed." Donatti chuckled indulgently.

"Look, let her go," Morrison babbled. "It won't happen again. It was a slip, just a slip, that's all. I only had three drags and for God's sake *it didn't even taste good!*"

"That's a shame. I'll count on you for five then, shall I?"

"Please," Morrison said, close to tears. "Please—"

He was speaking to a dead line.

AT 5 P.M. the reception room was empty except for the secretary, who gave him a twinkly smile that ignored Morrison's pallor and disheveled appearance. "Mr. Donatti?" she said into the intercom. "Mr. Morrison to see you." She nodded to Morrison. "Go right in."

Donatti was waiting outside the unmarked room with a man who was wearing a SMILE sweatshirt and carrying a .38. He was built like an ape.

"Listen," Morrison said to Donatti. "We can work something out, can't we? I'll pay you. I'll—"

"Shaddap," the man in the SMILE sweatshirt said.

"It's good to see you," Donatti said. "Sorry it has to be under such adverse circumstances. Will you come with me? We'll make this as brief as possible. I can assure you your wife won't be hurt . . . this time."

Morrison tensed himself to leap at Donatti.

"Come, come," Donatti said, looking annoyed. "If you do that, Junk here is going to pistol-whip you and your wife is still going to get it. Now where's the percentage in that?"

"I hope you rot in hell," he told Donatti.

Donatti sighed. "If I had a nickel for every time someone expressed a similar sentiment, I could retire. Let it be a lesson to you, Mr. Morrison. When a romantic tries to do a good thing and fails they give him a medal. When a pragmatist succeeds, they wish him in hell. Shall we go?"

Junk motioned with the pistol.

Morrison preceded them into the room. He felt numb. The small green curtain had been pulled. Junk prodded him with the gun. This is what being a witness at the gas chamber must have been like, he thought.

He looked in. Cindy was there, looking around bewilderedly.

"Cindy!" Morrison called miserably. "Cindy, they—"

"She can't hear or see you," Donatti said. "One-way glass. Well, let's get it over with. It really was a very small slip. I believe thirty seconds should be enough. Junk?"

Junk pressed the button with one hand and kept the pistol jammed firmly into Morrison's back with the other.

It was the longest thirty seconds of his life.

When it was over, Donatti put a hand on Morrison's shoulder and said, "Are you going to throw up?"

"No," Morrison said weakly. His forehead was against the glass. His legs were jelly. "I don't think so." He turned around and saw that Junk was gone.

"Come with me," Donatti said.

"Where?" Morrison asked apathetically.

"I think you have a few things to explain, don't you?"

"How can I face her? How can I tell her that I . . . I . . ."

"I think you're going to be surprised," Donatti said.

THE ROOM WAS empty except for a sofa. Cindy was on it, sobbing helplessly.

"Cindy?" he said gently.

She looked up, her eyes magnified by tears. "Dick?" she whispered. "Dick? Oh . . . Oh God . . ." He held her tightly. "Two men," she said against his chest. "In the house and at first I thought they were burglars and then I thought they were going to rape me and then they took me someplace with a blindfold over my eyes and . . . and . . . oh it was *h-horrible*—"

"Shhh," he said. "Shhh."

"But why?" she asked, looking up at him. "Why would they—"

"Because of me," he said. "I have to tell you a story, Cindy—"

WHEN HE HAD finished he was silent a moment and then said, "I suppose you hate me. I wouldn't blame you."

He was looking at the floor, and she took his face in both hands and turned it to hers. "No," she said. "I don't hate you."

He looked at her in mute surprise.

"It was worth it," she said. "God bless these people. They've let you out of prison."

"Do you mean that?"

"Yes," she said, and kissed him. "Can we go home now? I feel much better. Ever so much."

THE PHONE RANG one evening a week later, and when Morrison recognized Donatti's voice, he said, "Your boys have got it wrong. I haven't even been near a cigarette."

"We know that. We have a final matter to talk over. Can you stop by tomorrow afternoon?"

"Is it—"

"No, nothing serious. Bookkeeping really. By the way, congratulations on your promotion."

"How did you know about that?"

"We're keeping tabs," Donatti said noncommittally, and hung up.

WHEN THEY ENTERED the small room, Donatti said, "Don't look so nervous. No one's going to bite you. Step over here, please."

Morrison saw an ordinary bathroom scale. "Listen, I've gained a little weight, but—"

"Yes, seventy-three percent of our clients do. Step up, please."

Morrison did, and tipped the scales at one-seventy-four.

"Okay, fine. You can step off. How tall are you, Mr. Morrison?"

"Five-eleven."

"Okay, let's see." He pulled a small card laminated in plastic from his breast pocket. "Well, that's not too bad. I'm going to write you a prescrip for some highly illegal diet pills. Use them sparingly and according to directions. And I'm going to set your maximum weight at . . . let's see . . ." He consulted the card again. "One-eighty-two, how does that sound? And since this is December first, I'll expect you the first of every month for a weigh-in. No problem if you can't make it, as long as you call in advance."

"And what happens if I go over one-eighty-two?"

Donatti smiled. "We'll send someone out to your house to cut off your wife's little finger," he said. "You can leave through this door, Mr. Morrison. Have a nice day."

E IGHT MONTHS LATER:
  Morrison runs into the crony from the Larkin Studios at Dempsey's bar. Morrison is down to what Cindy proudly calls his fighting weight: one-sixty-seven. He works out three times a week and looks as fit as whipcord. The crony from Larkin, by comparison, looks like something the cat dragged in.

Crony: Lord, how'd you ever stop? I'm locked into this damn habit tighter than Tillie. The crony stubs his cigarette out with real revulsion and drains his scotch.

Morrison looks at him speculatively and then takes a small white business card out of his wallet. He puts it on the bar between them. You know, he says, these guys changed my life.

T WELVE MONTHS LATER:
  Morrison receives a bill in the mail. The bill says:
QUITTERS, INC.
237 East 46th Street
New York, N.Y. 10017

1 Treatment	$2500.00
Counselor (Victor Donatti)	$2500.00
Electricity	$ .50
Total (Please pay this amount)	**$5000.50**

Those sons of bitches! he explodes. They charged me for the electricity they used to . . . to . . .

Just pay it, she says, and kisses him.

———

TWENTY MONTHS LATER:

Quite by accident, Morrison and his wife meet the Jimmy McCanns at the Helen Hayes Theatre. Introductions are made all around. Jimmy looks as good, if not better, than he did on that day in the airport terminal so long ago. Morrison has never met his wife. She is pretty in the radiant way plain girls sometimes have when they are very, very happy.

She offers her hand and Morrison shakes it. There is something odd about her grip, and halfway through the second act, he realizes what it was. The little finger on her right hand is missing.

SO YOUNG, SO FAIR, SO DEAD

John Lutz

The old-fashioned private eye just plumb wore out back in the seventies. The trench coat was frayed, the constant boozing had become a serious medical problem, and there were so many dollies a guy needed Viagra, which, alas, hadn't been invented yet. It was at this time that a few gifted writers, such as John Lutz, took a look at the genre and said, "This has got to change." Alo Nudger was Lutz's first entry in the neo-private-eye sweepstakes, and boy, was he a good one. Alo doesn't try to conquer life's vicissitudes with swill and swagger; he simply hopes to survive them—with a lot of help from his endless supply of Tums. Fred Carver came along after that. Fred is a kind of James Joycean P.I., a *Portrait of a Middle-Aged Shamus*. He is all the things a private eye isn't supposed to be: generally confused; frequently unnerved; and unfailingly in need of donuts, sympathy, and various kinds of medication for his various physical ailments. All this is rendered in very nice prose, and with a worldview that occasionally reads like St. Francis of Assisi with a hangover. Lutz is also a true short-story master. He has an Edgar to prove it, and even if he didn't, this story, like dozens of others, would say it just as clearly.

YOU CAN LIVE your life through and try hard to be a decent sort, but trouble might still come to you. That's the way it seems to have been with me. My trouble was never the direct result of what I did, but the product of others, Neighbors especially. My advice is, don't ever get too friendly with your neighbors. I had to learn that the hard way.

Adelaide and I finished moving into our new house on a Sunday. That Monday I managed to stay away from the office and helped her sort the contents of cardboard boxes and move furniture about. We were both very happy that day, for we'd worked and saved for a long time to be able to afford our own home built here in the beautiful rolling hills south of the smoke-palled city. Here the air was clear as crystal and the view was the best nature had to offer.

And the house itself was what we'd always wanted. Though not large, it was well built with excellent materials and designed with a tasteful touch of miniature elegance. Adelaide and I took a walk around our green property before dark that evening and admired the way the wood shingled house seemed to blend so well with the forest-like setting.

Of course the best thing about the house and the property was that it was ours. I'd worked hard to build up my own mail order business, Smathers Enterprises, and Mr. and Mrs. Will Smathers were comparatively well heeled for a couple in their early thirties who'd started married life on practically nothing.

Adelaide stopped strolling and gazed down the narrow blacktop road that fronted our property. I stood off and admired her delicate features and shining blonde hair, the weight of her lithe, graceful body resting on one slender leg. Adelaide, too, blended well with the natural surroundings. She was a natural beauty, the type makeup couldn't improve.

"I wonder about our neighbor," she said.

I moved next to her, slipping my arm about her waist. From where we stood we could see the nearest home through a break in the heavy green of the trees. A large brick home with a swimming pool behind it, it was the only house within a mile of us in either direction. I could just see the top of a small beach house near the pool. Within plain view near the attached two car garage was a long, expensive blue convertible.

"Whoever our neighbor is," I said, "he has money."

"It certainly looks that way."

"On the other hand, he may be mortgaged up to his neck."

We stood for a moment longer looking down at the big house before going back inside. I say looking down because our home was situated high on one of the hills, and the blacktop road snaked sharply downward for the next two or three miles as it meandered like a still tributary to the Red Fox River.

I suppose I had no business saying anything about how our neighbor might have his property mortgaged. We'd gone into debt heavily to buy our own home. But the business was going well, and promised to continue to do so, and there was no reason we shouldn't be happy now and pay as we went along.

And in a way owing on the house could be a good thing. Once we were in it I knew we'd never give it up unless we absolutely had to, and it might serve as a spur to help make me work even harder.

But all the house motivated me to do that day was leave the office early so I could get home to enjoy living there with Adelaide. As I drove up the winding driveway I wondered when I'd get over the feeling that this was someone else's charming home I was approaching and not my own.

Adelaide knew I was coming home early and had dinner in the oven. She fixed us each a drink while we were waiting and we sat in the disarranged living room.

"I don't know when we'll ever get things the way we want them," Adelaide said, glancing around at the mess.

I grinned at her and took a sip of my Scotch and water, admiring her fresh good looks in the plain housedress she did so much for. "There's plenty of time."

"I suppose so." She sighed with contentment and settled back in her chair. "I saw our neighbor today," she said.

"Did he drop by to introduce himself?"

"No, but you can see the house from our bedroom window upstairs. When I looked out this afternoon I noticed a man swimming in the pool. He had a guest, a girl in a purple bikini who stayed there most of the day, then drove away in a little sports car."

I had to laugh. If Adelaide had any faults at all, one of them would be that she was a trifle nosy. "Are you going to stare a dossier on them?" I asked jokingly.

"Not yet," she said with a smile. "And it's not 'them,' it's 'him.' The man seems to live there alone."

"Big house for a single man," I remarked, "though it sounds like he has his fun there."

A timer bell sounded in the kitchen and Adelaide put down her drink and stood. I walked behind her as she hurried into the kitchen to check on the dinner.

"You keep an eye on him and keep me posted," I said, rubbing the back of my hand playfully up the nape of her neck. She didn't answer and I kept quiet. Experience had taught me to joke only so far about Adelaide's feminine curiosity.

Though without any prompting she had another tidbit of information for me the next evening when I returned home.

"Our neighbor seems to be something of a swinger," she said. "There was a girl in a red bikini there today."

"Same girl, different bikini," I speculated.

Adelaide shook her head. "The first one was a tall brunette. Today it was a short blonde."

I smiled and shrugged. "His sister?"

"I doubt it," Adelaide said, and drew a miniature bronze rooster from the carton.

"I'm sure we'll find out more about him," I said. "He'll probably turn up at our door one of these days soon to introduce himself. Could be he doesn't even realize there's anybody living here yet." Silently I wondered if he'd plant a shade tree between us and his pool when he did find out. Then for the next few hours I was busy helping Adelaide finish the job of unpacking and thought about little else.

But that night my own curiosity about our neighbor was aroused when I walked across the bedroom to close the drapes.

As my hand reached for the pull cord my eye caught the flash of a revolving red light in the distance. I leaned forward and squinted into the darkness, and I saw that a police car was parked in our neighbor's driveway beside his long blue convertible.

As I watched another car pulled up behind that one. In the reflection of its headlights I could see that it was a plain gray sedan. Two men got out of it and went into the house without knocking.

A hand touched my shoulder and Adelaide was standing beside me.

"Now who's nosy?" she asked.

I didn't answer, and we stood there for a while and watched shadows cross the distant draped windows. Then the two men and a uniformed policeman came out of the house. They got into their respective cars, the red light on the patrol car was turned off, and both cars left together. A few minutes later the windows of the house went black and Adelaide and I were staring at nothing.

"What do you think?" Adelaide asked as we turned away from the window.

"It could have been a lot of things," I said. "Maybe the police were called because somebody was sick. Maybe the two men in the plain car were doctors. Maybe our neighbor thought he saw a prowler. I guess if we really wanted to find out the thing to do would be to ask him."

THE NEXT EVENING I got in the car and drove down the road to do just that.

"It's because I'm a burglar," our neighbor answered me amiably.

I stood there and blinked, twice. I'd introduced myself when he'd answered the door, and he'd introduced himself as Jack Hogan and invited

me inside and offered me a drink. After a few minutes' exploratory conversation with the tanned and handsome man, I'd gotten around to asking
him about the commotion at his house we'd witnessed last night, offering
our help if anything was wrong.

"The police were here to harass me," Jack Hogan went on. "Lieutenant Faber and his friends. I humor the lieutenant because I understand
he acts out of frustration."

"But if you're innocent—" I said in a rather dumbfounded way.

"But I'm not innocent," Hogan said freely, his gray eyes as sincere as
his voice. "Though if you tell anyone I said so I'll deny it. Lieutenant Faber
knows I'm guilty, but he can't do anything about it because I'm too smart
for him. That's the fun of it."

I didn't know if Hogan was joking or not. When I took a sip of my
drink some of it spilled on my hand.

"A burglary was committed a few nights ago," Hogan said, offering
me his neatly folded handkerchief to dry my fingers. "They know I did it
but they don't know how, or what I did with the loot. Oh, they come and
search here every now and then, but we both know they won't find anything. And if a young lady is prepared to testify that I spent the time of
the robbery in her presence, where does it all leave poor Lieutenant
Faber?"

"Where I am, I suppose," I said. "Confused."

"Well, no need to be confused. I say what's the sense of getting away
with something if nobody knows about it? Surely you can understand that.
Then too, there's the profit. Burglary is a thriving business. How else could
I afford all this, living alone in a ten-room house with a pool, nights on the
town, flashy women, flashy cars? A wonderful life. I admit to you, I need
all that."

"Then, in a way, it's all a game," I said slowly.

"Of course it's a game. Everybody plays his own game. I just admit
mine because I'm good enough to get by with it even though it is illegal."

"But it's wrong," I said, trying to bat down his clearly stated logic.

"Sure, it's wrong," Hogan said, "but so's cheating on your income tax,
overcharging the public if you're a big corporation, leaving a penny for a
paper when you don't have a dime. To tell you the truth, I don't worry
about right or wrong."

"I guess you don't."

"You see," Hogan explained earnestly, "it's the challenge, I like nice
things; I indulge myself. When I see something of value I take it. I guess I
have to take it."

"Kleptomania on a grand scale, huh?"

"Hey, you might say that!" He raised his glass and grinned.

I finished my drink and got up to leave, Hogan walked with me to the door. On the porch I noticed that the long blue, convertible was gone, replaced by an even longer and more expensive tan convertible. Hogan saw me looking at the car.

"Don't worry," he said. "It's not stolen and it doesn't belong to a girl I have hidden in the house. You didn't interrupt anything and I can afford to trade cars any time I feel like it. Say," he said, pointing at the long car, "how do you like it?"

"Beautiful," I said.

"Sure, and it cost a hunk of cash. Well, drop by again, why don't you? Bring the wife and we'll take a dip in the pool."

I walked down the driveway to where my car was parked. I didn't know what to think of our new neighbor. I was sure he wasn't joking, and I must admit I reacted as a lot of people would react. There was a sense of resentment in me that the things I worked so hard for, this man simply went out and took. And yet I found that I couldn't really dislike Jack Hogan. I waved to him as I started the engine and drove away.

When I told Adelaide about the visit she didn't believe me. I didn't blame her.

"You'd have to talk to him to understand how he thinks," I told her. "You might describe him as an honest crook."

"An honest crook?"

"Well, honest about being crooked, anyway."

That confused Adelaide almost as much as I was confused, so I had a snack, went over some work I'd brought home then went to bed.

Neither Adelaide or myself mentioned our neighbor for a while as we busied ourselves about our new home. Though I noticed that Adelaide kept a pair of binoculars in the bedroom now, and she often left the house to drive past the Hogan residence and look more closely at it, I suppose to check for bikini clad guests and sports cars. Still, I don't think she really completely believed what I'd told her about Jack Hogan until Lieutenant Faber called on us one Saturday afternoon.

Adelaide and I were working in the garden she'd planted when the lieutenant drove up in his gray sedan. I stood leaning on my hoe and watched him approach. He was a harried looking man who appeared to be in his mid-forties. His straight graying hair was combed to the side over his forehead and the breeze mussed it as his lined face broke into its emotionless, professional smile. Even before he introduced himself I knew who he was.

"I hope we haven't done anything wrong," Adelaide said, returning the bland smile with one that shone.

"Wrong? No," Lieutenant Faber said. "Actually I'm a city detective and have no authority out here in the county anyway."

"And yet you drove out here to talk to us," I said thoughtfully.

"I don't speak officially, Mr. Smathers," Faber said in his tired, hoarse voice. "Anything I say to you folks is off the record." He got out a cigar and lit it expertly against the breeze. "How you getting along with your neighbor down the road?"

"You mean the burglar?" I'd decided it was time to stop circling.

"You said it, not me," Lieutenant Faber said.

"Actually Mr. Hogan said it. He didn't seem to mind admitting that fact to me at all."

"Oh, he admits it, all right," the lieutenant said in a voice suddenly filled with frustration, "but not to anybody who can do anything about it or prove he even said it. I could tell you some things about your neighbor that would really surprise you."

"You mean he really *is* a burglar?" Adelaide asked suddenly.

"Ask him," Lieutenant Faber said. "He'll tell you. Not that we can get anything on him. We know but we can't prove."

"He told me he was clever," I said.

Lieutenant Faber nodded bitterly. "He's been clever enough so far. We know exactly how he operates—in fact, he always seems to go to some trouble to let us know he's the one who pulled his jobs, but pinning him down's another thing. He gets rid of the loot so fast and secretly we can't get him there, and usually he knows where to find big sums of cash that can't be traced. As far as alibis are concerned, there's always some girl who's willing to testify that he was with her at his house or her apartment or some motel. We can't watch him twenty-four hours a day." The lieutenant added with an undeniable touch of envy, "He seems to have an endless supply of girls."

"He is rather handsome," Adelaide said, and when we looked at her she blushed slightly. "I mean, he would be to a certain type of woman."

"The type he's handsome to will lie for him," Faber said, "that's for sure. He must have something working for him."

"Money," I said. "If used properly money will buy almost anything, and Hogan strikes me as the kind who knows how to use his wealth."

"That'd be okay," Lieutenant Faber said, "only it's other people's wealth. Just last week we know—off the record, of course—that he burglarized over three thousand in cash and five thousand in loot from the home of J. Grestom, president of Grestom Chemical."

"Isn't that the plant about four miles from here?" Adelaide asked. "The one that dumps all that sludge into the Red Fox River?"

"The same," Lieutenant Faber said, "one of the biggest operations of its kind in the state."

"Sounds like Robin Hood," I remarked.

"Yeah," the lieutenant said without amusement, "Hogan steals from the rich, only he doesn't give to anybody."

"From talking to him," I said, "my impression is that it's all a big game to him."

"A game where other people get hurt, and a game I'm tired of playing. Hogan's a crook like all crooks. He's one of the world's takers. He's a kid and the world's one big candy shop with a dumb proprietor."

I thought good manners dictated me not pointing out who that dumb proprieter must be in Hogan's mind.

"Do you think you ever will catch him?" Adelaide asked.

Lieutenant Faber nodded. "We always do in the end. He'll make a mistake, and we'll be there to notice when he does."

"He seemed awfully confident," I said.

"Confident?" Faber snorted with disgust. "Confident's not the word. Brass is more like it! About six months ago he burglarized the payroll office of a company downtown when their safe was full—"

"You mean he's a safe-cracker too?" I interrupted.

"No, he stole the whole blasted safe. It was one of those little boxes that should have been bolted to the floor from the inside but wasn't. The worst thing is that two nights later the safe turned up empty in the middle of a place that manufactures burglar alarms—bolted to the floor!"

"It really is a game with him, isn't it?" I said.

Adelaide was laughing quietly. "You must admit he's good at his game."

"And we're good at ours!" The lieutenant's face was flushed.

"I'm sure you didn't drive up here just to inform us that we're living next to a police character," I said. By that time I was certain I'd figured out the reason for Lieutenant Faber's visit. I was right.

"What I'd like," he said, "is for you to sort of keep an eye on Hogan's house. Not spy, mind you, just keep an eye on." He drew on his cigar and awaited an answer.

I took a lazy swat at the earth with the edge of the hoe blade. "I don't see anything wrong with us telling you if anything odd goes on there," I said, "under the circumstances."

Faber exhaled smoke and handed me a white card with his name and telephone extension number. "Hogan's not used to having neighbors," he said. "That's why he bought the house he's in. He might forget about you and make a slip. Do you have a pair of binoculars or a telescope?"

I looked at Adelaide and winked so the lieutenant couldn't see me. "I think I have an old pair somewhere." That somewhere was on the edge of Adelaide's dresser, where the powerful field glasses could be used by her at a moment's notice.

"Well, it's been nice to meet you folks," Lieutenant Faber said, "and it's good of you to help. Your police department thanks you." Again he shot us his mechanical smile then turned and walked toward his car.

Adelaide and I stood and watched until he'd turned from the driveway and was gone from sight.

"Now you can really play Mata Hari," I said, going back to my hoeing.

Adelaide didn't answer as she bent down and applied the spade to the broken ground.

I LEFT THE spying—as I'd come to think of it—pretty much up to Adelaide. She spent a lot of time sitting at the bedroom window, her elbows resting on the sill as she peered intently through the field glasses. But at the end of two weeks she hadn't noticed anything really noteworthy, just the comings and goings of a high living young bachelor of wealth.

She was sitting concentrating through the glasses one afternoon when the doorbell chimed. I rose from where I was lying on the bed reading and went downstairs to answer it.

When the door swung open there was Jack Hogan, dressed in swimming trunks and smiling, with a brightly colored striped towel slung about his neck.

"How about taking me up on that swimming invitation now?" he asked. "The temperature's over ninety, so I thought it'd be a good time."

I was a little surprised to see him, a little off balance. "Uh, sure, if it's okay with Adelaide," I stepped back. "Come on in and I'll ask her."

When I went upstairs Adelaide was still at the window with her eyes pressed to the binoculars.

"Jack Hogan's downstairs," I said. "He wants to know if we'll go swimming with him in his pool."

Adelaide turned abruptly and looked up at me, her eyes wide and appearing even wider due to the red circles about them left by the binoculars. "But I thought he was in his beach house! I've been waiting for him to come out!"

"You'll wait a long time, darling. He's in our living room. Do you want to go?"

"Swimming? Do you?"

"I don't see why we shouldn't. It is a hot day." I changed quickly into my swimming trunks and went downstairs to tell Jack Hogan we'd be ready to go as soon as Adelaide had changed.

Adelaide had on her skimpiest black bikini when she came downstairs. I saw Hogan look with something like momentary shock at her tanned and shapely body.

This was the first time they'd met, at least close up. After introductions we drove to Hogan's house in his long tan convertible. Seated beside him was an amply proportioned blonde who looked as if she might have been used to model the car on TV. He introduced her as Prudence, which I didn't think fitted, and we were on our way.

As we splashed around, drank highballs and got better acquainted, I found that I liked Jack Hogan, thought I must still admit to some jealousy and distaste that he could come by all he had so easily while I worked so hard for less. What surprised me was that Adelaide seemed to like Hogan too. Adelaide had had a father who'd deserted her, who'd been much like Hogan, free spending and dishonest. She had hated him until the day he died, perhaps still hated his memory. And yet from time to time I could see some of her father in Adelaide, under the surface of the careful, thrifty and loving woman she really was. I saw some of that wildness and daring now as she stood on Hogan's tanned shoulders and let him flip her out and into the deep water.

When we got out of the pool and went inside for snacks I noticed an expensive looking, lewd silver statuette of Bacchus on a low table in the entrance hall. It could hardly escape my attention because Jack Hogan flicked it with his finger as we walked past.

"I stole that earlier this year," he said, "or rather one just like it. The stolen one had the owner's name engraved on the bottom, so I sold it and used the proceeds to buy this exact duplicate. Lieutenant Faber really thought he had me when he discovered that statue sitting there, but when we checked for the owner's engraving it wasn't there, and I could hardly have removed it without any trace. It drove the lieutenant almost wild." Hogan chuckled as he led us into the large kitchen with an attached dining area.

"I don't think I've ever met anyone like you," Adelaide said to Hogan with a bewildered little laugh.

Prudence, the busty blonde, popped a potato chip with cheese dip into her mouth. "Oh, there isn't anyone else like Jackie!"

I could only agree as I mixed myself another highball.

From the time of the little impromptu swimming party on, I began to notice things. It seemed to me that Adelaide spent more and more time spying from the window for Lieutenant Faber. And she found excuses to drive into the city more and more often. And on occasions when I came home from work I noticed that her hair near the base of her skull appeared damp. Did I only imagine the faint scent of chlorine those evenings as she served dinner?

It seemed, too, that Adelaide and I were caught up in more and more domestic quarrels, and we'd seldom quarreled before. She accused me of having ignored her through the years, spending all my free time and weekends working.

It didn't take long for me to be ninety percent sure that Adelaide and Jack Hogan were conducting an affair behind my back. But would I ever be more than ninety percent sure? Hogan managed his love life as he did his burglaries, with such practiced skill that the victims of his callousness could only suspect but never prove, maybe not even to themselves. For a long time I deliberated before taking any action.

There was never any doubt in my mind that I would take some sort of action. I couldn't allow things to go on as they were, and I felt confident that I could do something about them. A man who's hard to best in business is hard to best in any other phase of life.

What I finally did was go to see Lieutenant Faber.

The lieutenant's office was small, littered and dirty. There were no windows, and dented gray file cabinets stood behind the cluttered desk where Lieutenant Faber sat. As I entered he glanced up with his uneasy, weary look—then managed to smile at me.

"Have a seat, Mr. Smathers," he said, motioning toward a chair with a tooth-marked yellow pencil. "I take it you've come here because you know something about Jack Hogan." I couldn't help but notice the hope in his voice.

"In a way that's why I'm here," I said, and watched the wariness creep into the lieutenant's narrow eyes as he settled back in his desk chair.

"What is it that you observed?" he asked.

"Nothing that really pertains to his burglaries, Lieutenant. In fact, nothing of use to you at all."

Faber let the pencil drop onto the desk top with a resonant little clatter. "Why don't we talk straight to each other, Mr. Smathers? Save time, yours as well as mine."

"All right, I came here to ask you for a favor."

"Favor?" His gray eyebrows rose slowly.

"Yes," I said, "I wonder if you could arrange for me to have some in-frared binoculars. I think most of what goes on at Hogan's house happens after dark, and it would help if I could see through that darkness."

Lieutenant Faber rolled his tongue to one side of his mouth and looked thoughtful. "Seems like a good idea," he said. "I can get you the field glasses within a few days."

"Fine. Should I pick them up here?"

"If you'd like." Lieutenant Faber looked even more thoughtful. "What is it you think you're going to see at night?" he asked.

I shrugged. "Who knows? That's why I want the infrared binoculars." I stood to leave.

"I'll give you a telephone call when you can pick them up," the lieu-tenant said, standing behind his desk.

"Call me at my office," I told him, "anytime during the day."

"Why not your home?"

"Because my office would be more convenient."

He came from around the desk and walked with me to the door. "Mr. Smathers," he said in a confidential voice, "I want Jack Hogan any way I can get him. Do you understand?"

"I thought you wanted him that badly," I said as I went out.

THAT VERY EVENING, when I awoke after dozing off while watching television, I found a gold cigarette lighter beneath the sofa cushions. During my sleep my hand had gotten itself wedged between the cushions, and when I freed it my fingertips had just brushed the hard, smooth surface.

When I rolled back the cushion I saw the lighter, with the initials J. H.

engraved on it. I knew it would also have J. H.'s fingerprints on it, so I lifted it gently by the corners and slipped it into my breast pocket before Adelaide came into the room.

Lieutenant Faber telephoned my office in the middle of the week to say I could drop by headquarters and pick up the infrared binoculars. So I wouldn't waste any valuable working time, I drove to see him on my lunch hour.

The binoculars were in a small case sitting on the edge of his desk. I sat down and examined them and he shoved a receipt across the desk top for me to sign.

"You suspect Jack Hogan is seeing your wife, don't you?" he said in a testing voice.

I didn't look at him as I hastily scrawled my signature on the pink receipt. "Yes, and I want to know for sure."

"And what happens if you do find out they're seeing each other?"

I handed the receipt back to him and rested the binoculars in my lap. "What would happen if a burglary was committed and evidence pointing to Hogan was found at the scene?"

"Then all we'd have to worry about would be breaking down his customary alibi."

"And if he had no alibi? If he was actually home alone at the time of the burglary but couldn't prove it because of a witness's testimony that he saw him leave then return?"

Lieutenant Faber ran his tongue over his dry lips. "That's what I've been waiting for, only Hogan has never dropped a clue in his life."

Gingerly I reached into my pocket and dropped the gold cigarette lighter with Jack Hogan's initials onto Faber's desk. As he reached for it I grabbed his hand.

"I think you'll find it has Hogan's fingerprints on it."

Lieutenant Faber leaned back away from the cigarette lighter as if it were something that might explode. I saw his glance dart to his office door to make sure it was closed, and at that moment I was very sure of him.

"Where did you get it?" he asked.

"Under the sofa cushions in my home."

"And you're giving it to me?"

I nodded. "And I don't require a receipt."

Lieutenant Faber slowly unwrapped the cellophane wrapper from one of his cigars. As he held a match to the cigar he looked at me over the rising and falling flame. Then he flattened the cellophane wrapper, slid it deftly beneath the gold lighter and placed both lighter and cellophane in his desk drawer.

"For the next three weekends," I said, "I plan to tell my wife I have to leave town on business from Thursday evening until Monday morning. Instead I'll stay at a motel outside of town, and I'll spend my nights on a hillside watching Hogan's house."

"From Thursday night to Monday morning," Lieutenant Faber repeated slowly.

"When you find the right burglary case, call me at the motel, and I'll tell you if Hogan was home alone that night. Then you 'discover' the lighter at the scene of the crime and I testify that I saw Hogan drive away and that he was gone during the time the robbery was committed."

"One thing," Lieutenant Faber said. "What if . . . ?"

"That's possible," I told him, "but Adelaide will hardly be in a position to say she was at Hogan's house all night, will she? Especially considering the fact that she knows he's a burglar anyway and deserve to be caught. She can't afford to be like his swinging single alibis."

Lieutenant Faber nodded and I stood and carefully tucked the binocular case beneath my arm.

"I'll let you know what motel I'll be staying at," I said to him as I started to leave.

"Smathers." He stopped me. "I want you to know I'm doing this because of what I think of Hogan. He's a—"

And the lieutenant told me in the purplest language I'd ever heard just what he thought of Jack Hogan.

I will say Adelaide put on a good act. When I told her about my upcoming business trips she acted convincingly upset by the idea of being left alone. She even stood in the doorway and waved wistfully after me as I got into a cab for the drive to the airport.

Only I didn't go to the airport. I had the cabbie drive me to a car rental agency where I rented a compact sedan. Then I drove to Sleepy Dan's Motel and checked in. If I worked it right, I could write all this off as business expenses. And I was smart enough to have set up a plan that would require me to miss only three days, Fridays, in three weeks at the office. I could even sneak in and do some work on Sunday when no one was there if need be. I congratulated myself on my cleverness as I lay down to get a little sleep before sunset.

The spot I'd picked was perfect, a small clearing on the side of a hill from where I could look directly down at Hogan's large house and grounds. The powerful binoculars brought everything near to me, and the infrared lenses eliminated the darkness as a problem. The night was warm, and I unbuttoned my shirt and settled back to watch until morning.

There were no results that first week. Lieutenant Faber sounded disappointed when I told him on the phone of Jack Hogan's activities. A burglary had been committed that would have been perfect for our purposes, but I had to tell him that at the time Hogan wasn't home and I didn't know where he'd gone. Lieutenant Faber suggested hopefully that he might have gone to my house, but I quickly told him he could rule that out. My house was in view from where I watched also. We decided to wait for an opportunity we could be absolutely sure of.

The second week that I stationed myself on the hillside something did happen. My wife's affair with Jack Hogan was confirmed beyond even the slightest doubt.

It was about midnight when I saw the headlights turn from the road into Hogan's driveway. As I pressed the binoculars to my eyes and adjusted the focus dial, I saw that it was Adelaide's car that had pulled into Hogan's big double garage to park alongside his convertible. He stepped out onto the porch and met her, and they kissed for an embarrassingly long time before going inside. A few hours later I saw them emerge from the house and go for a late night swim. I didn't want to watch that, so I lowered the binoculars and sat feeling the numbness in me give way to a smoldering rage.

The next night nothing happened. Hogan spent the entire night alone, going to bed about ten o'clock. I suppose he was tired.

That afternoon Lieutenant Faber called me at the motel. A residence in the west end had been burglarized the night before, smoothly and professionally. There were no clues of any kind.

I told him that Hogan had spent the night home alone. The burglary had to have taken place during the early morning hours, so we agreed that I would say I saw Hogan leave in his convertible at two-thirty a.m. and return at five. Tomorrow morning, when Lieutenant Faber returned to question the victim and re-examine the scene of the crime, he would "find" the gold lighter, and the frame around Jack Hogan would be complete.

There was really no reason to go back that third night, but the silent rage had grown in me along with my curiosity. And I suppose it gave me some small sense of power, to be able to watch them without them knowing. It kept me from being a complete fool, and while Hogan didn't know it, he had only one more night of freedom.

ALL THAT DARK, hot night Adelaide didn't arrive at Hogan's home. The windows of the big ranch house were dark, the grounds silent. Around me the crickets chirped madly as if protesting the heat as I sat staring intently through the binoculars.

Then a light came on in one of the windows, the window I knew to be Jack Hogan's bedroom. After a while a downstairs light came on too, and both lights stayed on. I looked at my watch. Four-thirty.

He must have telephoned her. At twenty to five Adelaide turned her car into Hogan's driveway. This time after she pulled her car into the garage Hogan came out and lowered the door, for the sun would soon rise. I watched as he put his arm around her and they went into the house.

The sun came up amid orange streaks on the horizon, turning the heat of night into an even more intense heat.

Then I heard a door slam off in the distance, and I scanned, then focused the binoculars on Adelaide in her skimpy black bikini. Hogan was beside her with a towel draped over his shoulder. He flicked her playfully with the towel and she laughed and dived into the pool, and he laughed and jumped in after her.

I watched them for about twenty minutes before I came to my decision. Jack Hogan had always freely admitted being a burglar. Now I intended to play his game, to tell him openly what was going to happen to him, so that he'd know he'd been outsmarted. Let the knowledge that he couldn't prove his innocence torment him. Let him suffer as he'd made Lieutenant Faber suffer, as he'd made his burglary victims suffer. As he'd made me suffer. I placed the binoculars in their case, stood and clambered down the hillside to where the car was parked.

Then it occurred to me that Hogan might give me a rough time once he realized he was cornered, so I drove by my house first and got my forty-five caliber revolver from my dresser drawer.

They were sitting in lounge chairs alongside the pool when I approached, Adelaide leaning forward and Hogan rubbing suntan lotion onto her back.

"How's the water?" I asked calmly.

They whirled, surprised, then Hogan smiled. "It's great," he said jauntily. "I've invited Adelaide over here before for an early morning swim, but this is the first time she's come."

"I know better," I said, watching Adelaide trying to control the fear and guilt that marked her features. At last she managed a facsimile of a poker face.

"Know better?" Hogan was still playing innocent.

"Yes, and now there are a few things I want you to know. There was a burglary committed night before last in the west end. No clues yet."

Hogan appeared puzzled. "So what? I was home in bed all that night."

"For the last several weekends I've been spying on you from that hillside," I said. "Lieutenant Faber gave me infrared binoculars to use at night. I'm going to swear that I saw you leave and return at the time that burglary took place."

"You can't!" Adelaide said in a high voice.

"Quiet, dear." I looked again at Hogan. He was grinning.

"Your word against mine, old pal. I've beat that one before."

"I believe you lost your initialed gold cigarette lighter," I said. "It has your fingerprints on it and it's going to be found at the scene of the crime."

Now anger showed on Hogan's handsome face. "By Lieutenant Faber, would be my guess."

"Your guess is correct. We're framing you and sending you to prison, to put it plainly."

"As I've always put it, huh?"

I nodded and couldn't help a faint, gloating smile. Hogan's game and he was getting beat at it. "Lieutenant Faber told me you were one of the world's takers," I said. "Well, I'm one of the world's keepers. I don't give up what I have easily."

"Faber was right about that," Hogan said frankly. "I'm a taker. I can't see something of value without taking it."

"Something like Adelaide?"

"Exactly."

"Your mistake," I said tauntingly, "was in trying to take something from me. I'll think of you from time to time when you're in prison." I turned to go home, leaving Adelaide to return when she felt like it.

"It won't work," her voice said behind me.

I turned around and saw that the fear and surprise had left Adelaide's face completely to be replaced by a look of determination.

"And why won't it work?" I asked.

"Because I'll swear in court that I spent that entire night with Jack."

I started to laugh incredulously at her, but the laugh wouldn't come out. "But you were at home."

"Alone," Adelaide said. "You could never prove it. I'll swear I was here instead."

"You'd swear to that in a courtroom, under oath?" I stared at her, feeling the sun on the back of my moist shirt. "But why?"

"I don't think you'd understand."

"Now listen!"

"Nothing more to listen to, or say," Adelaide said, and as a pretense for getting away from me she turned and walked toward the diving board.

Hogan lowered himself into the shallow water with an infuriating smile. "Nothing more to say, old pal. Sorry." And he actually looked as if he might be sorry, the gracious winner.

The sun seemed to grow hotter, unbearably hot, sending beads of sweat darting down my flesh inside my shirt. I looked up and saw Adelaide poised gracefully on the end of the diving board, tanned and beautiful in her tiny swimming suit as she carefully avoided a glance in my direction.

How the revolver got from my pocket into my hand I honestly don't know. I have no recollection of it, a magician's trick. And I don't remember pulling the trigger.

Adelaide was raising her arms, preparing to dive, when the gun roared in my hand as if of its own will. I saw Adelaide's body jerk, saw the spray of blood, heard the scream as she half fell–half jumped awkwardly from the diving board, arms and legs thrashing as she struck the water. Then there was a choking sound and she stopped thrashing and floated motionless face up.

Hogan stroked toward the ladder, a look not of shock or horror on his face, but an expression that suggested he might be very sick. "Oh, God, Smathers!" he said as he started to climb the chrome ladder. I let him get to the second step before blasting him back into the pool.

I stood there then, pulling the trigger automatically, emptying the revolver into their bodies.

Considering how large the pool was, it was amazing how quickly all the water turned red.

So now I'm sitting here awaiting trial, writing this to kill time, though I'm sure the hour will come when I'll pray I had this time back. There isn't any doubt in my mind that I'll be convicted. They have my full confession, and now they'll have this.

What concerns me is that all my life I've tried to be a decent sort of man, hard working, industrious. I'm not very religious, but I have tried to live by the ten commandments, breaking them every now and then, of course, like everybody else. And yet if you went back and read over this again you could put your finger on spot after spot until you'd realize that between the four of us, me, Adelaide, Jack Hogan and Lieutenant Faber, in one way or another we've broken every single commandment.

Evil spreads, I suppose, like the red through the water in Hogan's swimming pool.

NOR IRON BARS

John D. MacDonald

Sometimes novelists achieve fame for the wrong books. The Travis McGee novels by John D. MacDonald (1916–1986) are exemplary adventure books of their type, that being an updating and derivation on the private-eye formulas and mechanisms of the thirties and forties. They contain wisdom, grace, and more than a little droll manly humor. But for many they are not MacDonald's most accomplished work. His novels *Cry Hard, Cry Fast* (1955), *Murdering the Wind* (1956), *Slam the Big Door* (1960), *A Flash of Green* (1962), and the astonishingly good *The End of the Night* (1960) were among his finest work. There were also an imposing number of other paperback originals that were also first-rate crime stories—among them *Dead, Low Tide* (1953) and *One Monday We Killed Them All* (1961)—that were never done in hardcover in the United States. His best work bore the stamp of John O'Hara and John P. Marquand. He knew that crime was an essential part of the American Century (whether it was crime in corporate boardrooms or crime in a Charles Starkweather–like murder spree) and he made it a point to let his readers know how crime really worked. He was the greatest storyteller of his time.

THE APPEARANCE OF Sheriff Commer's hand as he sat in the office of the jail told as much about him as most people who had lived in that little Southern city all their lives had learned. It was a square heavy hand with a thatch of brown curling hair on the back and short knobbed powerful fingers, tanned by the sun and wind, yellowed by the constant cigarette. He sat listening to the angry crowd noises, yelling for Burton, roaring from the park across from the jail, his thumb and first finger clenched so tightly on the short butt of his cigarette that the damp end of it was only a thin brown line.

He glanced down at his hand propped against the side of the oak desk and marveled that his finger didn't tremble; secretly he always wondered at it. He respected and admired the independent nervelessness of his body, the way his brain could whirl in a mad haze of fear, his throat knotted, his heart thumping, and still his body, huge, ponderous and powerful, would go about its appointed tasks, with steady hands, calm eyes, quiet voice.

He kept safely tucked back on a secret shelf of his mind the thought that one day the body would break, the frenzied mind would have its way; and he would collapse into a quivering hulk, moaning over the imminence of pain and death.

The swelling roar of the lynching crowd faded from his conscious mind as he remembered the bright afternoon long ago when he had walked out of the group surrounding the Otis barn, walked steadily across the dark timbered floor, climbed slowly and heavily up the ladder until his head was above the floor of the loft, turned slowly and looked with chill impassivity into the crazed eyes of Danny Reneta. The only objects he saw in the dim hay-fragrant loft were those two shining eyes and the round vacant eye of the rifle which stared at him with infinite menace.

The room seemed to swing around him in a dizzy cycle of remembered fear as he recalled how he had calmly said, "Now, Danny. Better give me the gun," had slowly reached out with a hand as firm as a rock and grasped the muzzle of the rifle.

The two insane eyes had stared into the two calm ones for measureless silent seconds until Commer thought he would drop screaming down the ladder.

Then a great rasping sob had come from Danny's throat and Commer had pulled the rifle out of the nerveless fingers.

Now he dropped his cigarette butt on the stained floor and ground it out with his heavy heel while that incident faded with the others from the dark place in his soul.

He rose slowly to his feet, walked over to the window, stood and looked out into the park, saw dimly the shifting, growing crowd, heard the increased roar as they saw his bulky silhouette against the office light. He half-sneered as he realized who they must be: The drug-store commandos. The pool room Lotharios. The city's amateur Cagneys.

But he felt also the slow certain growth of fear, an ember threatening to ignite the ready tinder of his mind. He realized what a lynching would mean to him and to the city. It would kill his pride and self-respect more certainly than the impact of lead would kill his stubborn body.

He sighed, trying to shrug off his fear, walked to the desk and brought out two large official thirty-eights. He held one in each hand and looked at them then tossed them back into the drawer, slamming it shut with his chunky knee. He fumbled in the wall locker and brought out a submachine gun. He held it and looked down at it, looked at its shining, oiled efficiency, fingered the compensator, tested the slide and then stood silently, testing his strength against the smoldering ember of fear.

He grunted as he stooped and hauled two heavy drums of fifty shells each out of the bottom of the locker. He snapped one onto the gun and then walked back toward the cells, the gun dangling from one blunt hand, the drum clenched in the other.

At the door of Burton's cell he laid the gun and drum on the floor, unlocked the cell and walked in. The hanging bulb made harsh light and blocky shadows in the cell. Burton slid off the cot and made quick short steps backward until he was pressed against the far wall, his huge black hands pressed palm-flat, fingers spread, against the whitewashed concrete, his face a shining impassive mask except for the wide eyes, dark iris rimmed with white. He was straight and tall, broad-shouldered and slim-hipped, a graceful and living creature, shocked and helpless under the pressure of the threat of sudden, violent death.

Commer stood for a few minutes looking at him, expression calm, eyes friendly. "Got a feeling you didn't do it, Burton," he said. "You look like a good boy to me."

Burton licked his lips, the glaze of fear fading slightly from his eyes as he answered, "I swear to God, Sheriff, I didn't do it. I ain't a killin' man. I hear 'em yellin' out there like they goin' to come in and get me any minute. Don't let 'em do it. Don't let 'em do it!" The last few words were a sob.

"Whether they come in or not depends on you, Burton."

"On me, sir? On me?" His tone was incredulous.

"That's right. Can I trust you?"

"Yes, sir. I do anything you tell me."

"Would you run away if you had the chance and knew I didn't want you to?"

Burton stood silently. Then he said, "No, sir." Commer believed him, believed him because of the pause, the weighing of loyalty against the fear that he could almost see in Burton's eyes. The man hadn't answered too fast.

Commer walked out, picked up the gun and drum and went back into the cell. He threw the drum onto the cot and poked the gun toward Burton. The big man stared in silent wonder and then reached out and took the gun in shaking hands.

"Careful, now! This-here thing is the safety. I've set the gun so that each time you pull the trigger you get a shot. The drum comes off like this. See? When it's empty the slide stays back and then you stick on the other drum like this."

"Yessir, but . . ."

"Now I'm going to leave you with your cell door open so you can sight down the hall here. If they come in, they'll come through that door there, the door to my office. Shoot first into the ceiling. If they keep coming put a few in the floor. If they still keep coming, lock yourself in quick. Here's the key. Then drop behind the corner of the cot and shoot low through the bars at their legs. Understand?"

"Yessir." Burton stood holding the gun, a glow of hope in his eyes, his face full of a gratitude so deep that tears formed along his lower lids. "I'll do just like you tell me, sir. I couldn't let you down after this, Sheriff." And he held the gun out, cradled in his arms as though it were the present of kings.

Commer grunted, turned on his heel and walked out, leaving the cell door open, walking steadily and slowly down the corridor, through his office, out the front door and onto the porch. There he stopped and watched the crowd, listening to their animal growling, every fiber of his mind screaming to him to turn and run for shelter. But he stood and held his arms up, a travesty of a benediction, calling for silence. For long minutes there was no response, then the shouting died to a murmuring. He heard a few last shouts of "We want Burton" and "Bring him out or we're a-comin' in after him!"

In his deep slow voice Commer bellowed into the darkness, "You all can come in after him right now. I just give him a submachine gun and plenty of ammunition. He's in there a-waitin' for you. Come ahead, boys! He's all yours!"

There was an angry mutter from the crowd. Commer imagined that those who had bolstered their frail courage with corn liquor now felt a sudden sobering chill. He was glad that he had always backed up his statements, never bluffed. Yet he could hardly see because of the dizzy spin of fear in his head.

Then a top-heavy man with a shock of light hair came striding out of the shadows into the dim glow of the street lamp. Commer walked heavily down the steps to meet him, recognizing him as Ham Alberts, itinerant handyman, loud-mouth and trouble-maker. But he was a bull in the strength of his youth.

They stared at each other. Commer saw through his film of fear that Ham was quivering with outraged righteous indignation. The offended honor of a taxpayer who had never paid a tax.

"Commer," he said hoarsely, "you got no call to arm a killer. You're paid to stay on the side of the law. What the hell you doin?"

"Just saving a man from a bunch of corner loafers. Why?" Commer's voice sounded flat and disinterested, but he wondered if Alberts could hear the beating of his heart.

"If any of us gets kilt goin' in after him, it's gonna be your fault!"

"Do I looked worried, sonny? I do my duty my own way. No call for you to try to tell me how to do it. Now go on in and get him. What you waiting for? Yellow maybe?"

"Why, you tin-shield copper . . ." and Alberts lifted a beefy fist back and poised it two feet from Commer's jaw. In spite of the roaring in his ears, Commer looked calmly at the fist and then into Alberts' narrowed eyes.

"Don't know as that there is one of your best ideas, sonny. I'm going down to the corner for some coffee while you boys take care a this little matter." He turned away from Alberts, jiggling a cigarette out of a crumpled pack as he walked away.

Inside he writhed with terror, but there was room in his mind to wonder at the sober, quiet way his thick legs carried him along down the street. He stopped at the corner and lit his cigarette, his fingers strong and steady, the flare of the wooden match lighting up his stolid cheek bones, his mild brow.

Then he glanced back and saw Ham Alberts under the light, hollering into the shadows, his arms spread wide in a beseeching gesture. Commer couldn't hear the words, but he could see in the distance the vague forms of the men who had been clustered in the park melting back away from the jail, away from the deadly Burton, ignoring the furious Alberts.

Then Alberts dropped his arms helplessly and wandered after them.

Commer sucked in a deep lungful of smoke and expelled it in a long, blue column into the soft night air. He turned and headed for his coffee, knowing in his heart that the strong body had defeated the fear demons of the mind, this time.

But the next time. . . .

GUILT-EDGED BLONDE

Ross Macdonald

The mystery field had long needed a Proust, and it got in it Kenneth Millar (1915–1983), who wrote under the pseudonym Ross Macdonald. Here was a writer who believed that most truths about the present could be found in the past, and he revealed that idea with incredible grace and style in his novels. His private eye Lew Archer was an antiques dealer of sorts, though instead of objects he dealt in souls. Macdonald's version of Southern California of the fifties and sixties is comparable to what Nathaniel West and Horace McCoy achieved in the thirties. Archer was a refined man in a vulgar time, and yet one sensed that for all his surface calm, he was just as deeply troubled as the people he pursued. *The Way Some People Die* (1951), *The Ivory Grin* (1952), and *The Far Side of the Dollar* (1965) are particularly good novels. *The Chill* (1964) is most likely his masterpiece. Tom Nolan's biography *Ross Macdonald* is heartily recommended if you want to know more about this intriguing author.

A MAN WAS waiting for me at the gate at the edge of the runway. He didn't look like the man I expected to meet. He wore a stained tan windbreaker, baggy slacks, a hat as squashed and dubious as his face. He must have been forty years old, to judge by the gray in his hair and the lines around his eyes. His eyes were dark and evasive, moving here and there as if to avoid getting hurt. He had been hurt often and badly, I guessed.

"You Archer?"

I said I was. I offered him my hand. He didn't know what to do with it. He regarded it suspiciously, as if I was planning to try a Judo hold on him. He kept his hands in the pockets of his windbreaker.

"I'm Harry Nemo." His voice was a grudging whine. It cost him an effort to give his name away. "My brother told me to come and pick you up. You ready to go?"

"As soon as I get my luggage."

I collected my overnight bag at the counter in the empty waiting room.

The bag was very heavy for its size. It contained, besides a toothbrush and spare linen, two guns and the ammunition for them. A .38 special for sudden work, and a .32 automatic as a spare.

Harry Nemo took me outside to his car. It was a new seven-passenger custom job, as long and black as death. The windshield and side windows were very thick, and they had the yellowish tinge of bulletproof glass.

"Are you expecting to be shot at?"

"Not me." His smile was dismal. "This is Nick's car."

"Why didn't Nick come himself?"

He looked around the deserted field. The plane I had arrived on was a flashing speck in the sky above the red sun. The only human being in sight was the operator in the control tower. But Nemo leaned towards me in the seat, and spoke in a whisper:

"Nick's a scared pigeon. He's scared to leave the house. Ever since this morning."

"What happened this morning?"

"Didn't he tell you? You talked to him on the phone."

"He didn't say very much. He told me he wanted to hire a bodyguard for six days, until his boat sails. He didn't tell me why."

"They're gunning for him, that's why. He went to the beach this morning. He has a private beach along the back of his ranch, and he went down there by himself for his morning dip. Somebody took a shot at him from the top of the bluff. Five or six shots. He was in the water, see, with no gun handy. He told me the slugs were splashing around him like hailstones. He ducked and swam under water out to sea. Lucky for him he's a good swimmer, or he wouldn't of got away. It's no wonder he's scared. It means they caught up with him, see."

"Who are 'they,' or is that a family secret?"

Nemo turned from the wheel to peer into my face. His breath was sour, his look incredulous. "Christ, don't you know who Nick is? Didn't he tell you?"

"He's a lemon-grower, isn't he?"

"He is now."

"What did he used to be?"

The bitter beaten face closed on itself. "I oughtn't to be flapping at the mouth. He can tell you himself if he wants to."

Two hundred horses yanked us away from the curb. I rode with my heavy leather bag on my knees. Nemo drove as if driving was the one thing in life he enjoyed, rapt in silent communion with the engine. It whisked us along the highway, then down a gradual incline between geometrically planted lemon groves. The sunset sea glimmered red at the foot of the slope.

Before we reached it, we turned off the blacktop into a private lane which ran like a straight hair-parting between the dark green trees. Straight for half a mile or more to a low house in a clearing.

The house was flat-roofed, made of concrete and fieldstone, with an attached garage. All of its windows were blinded with heavy draperies. It was surrounded with well-kept shrubbery and lawn, the lawn with a ten-foot wire fence surmounted by barbed wire.

Nemo stopped in front of the closed and padlocked gate, and honked the horn. There was no response. He honked the horn again.

About halfway between the house and the gate, a crawling thing came out of the shrubbery. It was a man, moving very slowly on hands and knees. His head hung down almost to the ground. One side of his head was bright red, as if he had fallen in paint. He left a jagged red trail in the gravel of the driveway.

Harry Nemo said, "Nick!" He scrambled out of the car. "What happened, Nick?"

The crawling man lifted his heavy head and looked at us. Cumbrously, he rose to his feet. He came forward with his legs spraddled and loose, like a huge infant learning to walk. He breathed loudly and horribly, looking at us with a dreadful hopefulness. Then he died on his feet, still walking. I saw the change in his face before it struck the gravel.

Harry Nemo went over the fence like a weary monkey, snagging his slacks on the barbed wire. He knelt beside his brother and turned him over and palmed his chest. He stood up shaking his head.

I had my bag unzipped and my hand on the revolver. I went to the gate. "Open up, Harry."

Harry was saying, "They got him," over and over. He crossed himself several times. "The dirty bastards."

"Open up," I said.

He found a key ring in the dead man's pocket and opened the padlocked gate. Our dragging footsteps crunched the gravel. I looked down at the specks of gravel in Nicky Nemo's eyes, the bullet hole in the temple.

"Who got him, Harry?"

"I dunno. Fats Jordan, or Artie Castola, or Faronese. It must have been one of them."

"The Purple Gang."

"You called it. Nicky was their treasurer back in the thirties. He was the one that didn't get into the papers. He handled the payoff, see. When the heat went on and the gang got busted up, he had some money in a safe deposit box. He was the only one that got away."

"How much money?"

"Nicky never told me. All I know, he come out here before the war and bought a thousand acres of lemon land. It took them fifteen years to catch up with him. He always knew they were gonna, though. He knew it."

"Artie Castola got off the Rock last spring."

"You're telling me. That's when Nicky bought himself the bulletproof car and put up the fence."

"Are they gunning for you?"

He looked around at the darkening groves and the sky. The sky was streaked with running red, as if the sun had died a violent death.

"I dunno," he answered nervously. "They got no reason to. I'm as clean as soap. I never been in the rackets. Not since I was young, anyway. The wife made me go straight, see?"

I said: "We better get into the house and call the police."

The front door was standing a few inches ajar. I could see at the edge that it was sheathed with quarter-inch steel plate. Harry put my thoughts into words.

"Why in hell would he go outside? He was safe as houses as long as he stayed inside."

"Did he live alone?"

"More or less alone."

"What does that mean?"

He pretended not to hear me, but I got some kind of an answer. Looking through the doorless arch into the living room, I saw a leopardskin coat folded across the back of the chesterfield. There were redtipped cigarette butts mingled with cigar butts in the ash trays.

"Nicky was married?"

"Not exactly."

"You know the woman?"

"Naw." But he was lying.

Somewhere behind the thick walls of the house, there was a creak of springs, a crashing bump, the broken roar of a cold engine, grinding of tires in gravel. I got to the door in time to see a cerise convertible hurtling down the driveway. The top was down, and a yellow-haired girl was small and intent at the wheel. She swerved around Nick's body and got through the gate somehow, with her tires screaming. I aimed at the right rear tire,

and missed. Harry came up behind me. He pushed my gun-arm down before I could fire again. The convertible disappeared in the direction of the
highway.

"Let her go," he said.

"Who is she?"

He thought about it, his slow brain clicking almost audibly. "I dunno.
Some pig that Nicky picked up some place. Her name is Flossie or Florrie
or something. She didn't shoot him, if that's what you're worried about."

"You know her pretty well, do you?"

"The hell I do. I don't mess with Nicky's dames." He tried to work up
a rage to go with the strong words, but he didn't have the makings. The
best he could produce was petulance: "Listen, mister, why should you hang
around? The guy that hired you is dead."

"I haven't been paid, for one thing."

"I'll fix that."

He trotted across the lawn to the body and came back with an alligator billfold. It was thick with money.

"How much?"

"A hundred will do it."

He handed me a hundred-dollar bill. "Now how about you amscray,
bud, before the law gets here?"

"I need transportation."

"Take Nicky's car. He won't be using it. You can park it at the airport
and leave the key with the agent."

"I can, eh?"

"Sure. I'm telling you you can."

"Aren't you getting a little free with your brother's property?"

"It's my property now, bud." A bright thought struck him, disorganiz-
ing his face. "Incidentally, how would you like to get off my land?"

"I'm staying, Harry. I like this place. I always say it's people that make
a place."

The gun was still in my hand. He looked down at it.

"Get on the telephone, Harry. Call the police."

"Who do you think you are, ordering me around? I took my last order
from anybody, see?" He glanced over his shoulder at the dark and shapeless object on the gravel, and spat venomously.

"I'm a citizen, working for Nicky. Not for you."

He changed his tune very suddenly. "How much to go to work for me?"

"Depends on the line of work."

He manipulated the alligator wallet. "Here's another hundred. If you got to hang around, keep the lip buttoned down about the dame, eh? Is it a deal?"

I didn't answer, but I took the money. I put it in a separate pocket by itself: Harry telephoned the county sheriff.

He emptied the ash trays before the sheriff's men arrived, and stuffed the leopardskin coat into the woodbox. I sat and watched him.

WE SPENT THE next two hours with loud-mouthed deputies. They were angry with the dead man for having the kind of past that attracted bullets. They were angry with Harry for being his brother. They were secretly angry with themselves for being inexperienced and incompetent. They didn't even uncover the leopardskin coat.

Harry Nemo left for the courthouse first. I waited for him to leave, and followed him home, on foot.

Where a leaning palm tree reared its ragged head above the pavements, there was a court lined with jerry-built frame cottages. Harry turned up the walk between them and entered the first cottage. Light flashed on his face from inside. I heard a woman's voice say something to him. Then light and sound were cut off by the closing door.

An old gabled house with boarded-up windows stood opposite the court. I crossed the street and settled down in the shadows of its veranda to watch Harry Nemo's cottage. Three cigarettes later, a tall woman in a dark hat and a light coat came out of the cottage and walked briskly to the corner and out of sight. Two cigarettes after that, she reappeared at the corner on my side of the street, still walking briskly. I noticed that she had a large straw handbag under her arm. Her face was long and stony under the streetlight.

Leaving the street, she marched up the broken sidewalk to the veranda where I was leaning against the shadowed wall. The stairs groaned under her decisive footsteps. I put my hand on the gun in my pocket, and waited. With the rigid assurance of a WAC corporal marching at the head of her platoon, she crossed the veranda to me, a thin high-shouldered silhouette against the light from the corner. Her hand was in her straw bag, and the end of the bag was pointed at my stomach. Her shadowed face was a gleam of eyes, a glint of teeth.

"I wouldn't try it if I were you," she said. "I have a gun here, and the safety is off, and I know how to shoot it, mister."

"Congratulations."

"I'm not joking." Her deep contralto rose a notch. "Rapid fire used to be my specialty. So you better take your hands out of your pockets."

I showed her my hands, empty. Moving very quickly, she relieved my pocket of the weight of my gun, and frisked me for other weapons.

"Who are you, mister?" she said as she stepped back. "You can't be Arturo Castola, you're not old enough."

"Are you a policewoman?"

"I'll ask the questions. What are you doing here?"

"Waiting for a friend."

"You're a liar. You've been watching my house for an hour and a half. I tabbed you through the window."

"So you went and bought yourself a gun?"

"I did. You followed Harry home. I'm Mrs. Nemo, and I want to know why."

"Harry's the friend I'm waiting for."

"You're a double liar. Harry's afraid of you. You're no friend of his."

"That depends on Harry. I'm a detective."

She snorted. "Very likely. Where's your buzzer?"

"I'm a private detective," I said. "I have identification in my wallet."

"Show me. And don't try any tricks."

I produced my photostat. She held it up to the light from the street, and handed it back to me. "So you're a detective. You better do something about your tailing technique. It's obvious."

"I didn't know I was dealing with a cop."

"I was a cop," she said. "Not any more."

"Then give me back my .38. It cost me seventy dollars."

"First tell me, what's your interest in my husband? Who hired you?"

"Nick, your brother-in-law. He called me in Los Angeles today, said he needed a bodyguard for a week. Didn't Harry tell you?"

She didn't answer.

"By the time I got to Nick, he didn't need a bodyguard, or anything. But I thought I'd stick around and see what I could find out about his death. He was a client, after all."

"You should pick your clients more carefully."

"What about picking brothers-in-law?"

She shook her head stiffly. The hair that escaped from under her hat was almost white. "I'm not responsible for Nick or anything about him. Harry is my responsibility. I met him in the line of duty and I straightened him out, understand? I tore him loose from Detroit and the rackets, and I brought him out here. I couldn't cut him off from his brother entirely. But he hasn't been in trouble since I married him. Not once."

"Until now."

"Harry isn't in trouble now."

"Not yet. Not officially."

"What do you mean?"

"Give me my gun, and put yours down. I can't talk into iron."

She hesitated, a grim and anxious woman under pressure. I wondered what quirk of fate or psychology had married her to a hood, and decided it must have been love. Only love would send a woman across a dark street to face down an unknown gunman. Mrs. Nemo was horsefaced and aging and not pretty, but she had courage.

She handed me my gun. Its butt was soothing to the palm of my hand. I dropped it into my pocket. A gang of Negro boys at loose ends went by in the street, hooting and whistling purposelessly.

She leaned towards me, almost as tall as I was. Her voice was a low sibilance forced between her teeth:

"Harry had nothing to do with his brother's death. You're crazy if you think so."

"What makes you so sure, Mrs. Nemo?"

"Harry couldn't, that's all. I know Harry, I can read him like a book. Even if he had the guts, which he hasn't, he wouldn't dare to think of killing Nick. Nick was his older brother, understand, the successful one in the family." Her voice rasped contemptuously. "In spite of everything I could do or say, Harry worshipped Nick right up to the end."

"Those brotherly feelings sometimes cut two ways. And Harry had a lot to gain."

"Not a cent. Nothing."

"He's Nick's heir, isn't he?"

"Not as long as he stays married to me. I wouldn't let him touch a cent of Nick Nemo's filthy money. Is that clear?"

"It's clear to me. But is it clear to Harry?"

"I made it clear to him, many times. Anyway, this is ridiculous. Harry wouldn't lay a finger on that precious brother of his."

"Maybe he didn't do it himself. He could have had it done for him. I know he's covering for somebody."

"Who?"

"A blonde girl left the house after we arrived. She got away in a cherry-colored convertible. Harry recognized her."

"A cherry-colored convertible?"

"Yes. Does that mean something to you?"

"No. Nothing in particular. She must have been one of Nick's girls. He always had girls."

"Why would Harry cover for her?"

"What do you mean, cover for her?"

"She left a leopardskin coat behind. Harry hid it, and paid me not to tell the police."

"Harry did that?"

"Unless I'm having delusions."

"Maybe you are at that. If you think that Harry paid that girl to shoot Nick, or had anything—"

"I know. Don't say it. I'm crazy."

Mrs. Nemo laid a thin hand on my arm. "Anyway, lay off Harry. Please. I have a hard enough time handling him as it is. He's worse than my first husband. The first one was a drunk, believe it or not." She glanced at the lighted cottage across the street, and I saw one half of her bitter smile. "I wonder what makes a woman go for the lame ducks the way I did."

"I wouldn't know, Mrs. Nemo. Okay, I lay off Harry."

But I had no intention of laying off Harry. When she went back to her cottage, I walked around three-quarters of the block and took up a new position in the doorway of a dry-cleaning establishment. This time I didn't smoke. I didn't even move, except to look at my watch from time to time.

Around eleven o'clock, the lights went out behind the blinds in the Nemo cottage. Shortly before midnight the front door opened and Harry slipped out. He looked up and down the street and began to walk. He passed within six feet of my dark doorway, hustling along in a kind of furtive shuffle.

Working very cautiously, at a distance, I tailed him downtown. He disappeared into the lighted cavern of an all night garage. He came out of the garage a few minutes later, driving a prewar Chevrolet.

My money also talked to the attendant. I drew a prewar Buick which would still do seventy-five. I proved that it would, as soon as I hit the highway. I reached the entrance to Nick Nemo's private lane in time to see Harry's lights approaching the dark ranch house.

I cut my lights and parked at the roadside a hundred yards below the entrance to the lane, and facing it. The Chevrolet reappeared in a few minutes. Harry was still alone in the front seat. I followed it blind as far as the highway before I risked my lights. Then down the highway to the edge of town.

In the middle of the motel and drive-in district he turned off onto a side road and in under a neon sign which spelled out TRAILER COURT across the darkness. The trailers stood along the bank of a dry creek. The Chevrolet stopped in front of one of them, which had a light in the window. Harry got out with a spotted bundle under his arm. He knocked on the door of the trailer.

I U-turned at the next corner and put in more waiting time. The Chevrolet rolled out under the neon sign and turned towards the highway. I let it go.

Leaving my car, I walked along the creek bank to the lighted trailer. The windows were curtained. The cerise convertible was parked on its far side. I tapped on the aluminum door.

"Harry?" a girl's voice said. "Is that you, Harry?"

I muttered something indistinguishable. The door opened, and the yellow-haired girl looked out. She was very young, but her round blue eyes were heavy and sick with hangover, or remorse. She had on a nylon slip, nothing else.

"What is this?"

She tried to shut the door. I held it open.

"Get away from here. Leave me alone. I'll scream."

"All right. Scream."

She opened her mouth. No sound came out. She closed her mouth again. It was small and fleshy and defiant. "Who are you? Law?"

"Close enough. I'm coming in."

"Come in then, damn you. I got nothing to hide."

"I can see that."

I brushed in past her. There were dead Martinis on her breath. The little room was a jumble of feminine clothes, silk and cashmere and tweed and gossamer nylon, some of them flung on the floor, others hung up to dry. The leopardskin coat lay on the bunk bed, staring with innumerable bold eyes. She picked it up and covered her shoulders with it. Unconsciously, her nervous hands began to pick the woodchips out of the fur. I said:

"Harry did you a favor, didn't he?"

"Maybe he did."

"Have you been doing any favors for Harry?"

"Such as?"

"Such as knocking off his brother."

"You're way off the beam, mister. I was very fond of Uncle Nick."

"Why run out on the killing then?"

"I panicked," she said. "It would happen to any girl. I was asleep when he got it, see, passed out if you want the truth. I heard the gun go off. It woke me up, but it took me quite a while to bring myself to and sober up enough to put my clothes on. By the time I made it to the bedroom window, Harry was back, with some guy." She peered into my face. "Were you the guy?"

I nodded.

"I thought so. I thought you were the law at the time. I saw Nick lying there in the driveway, all bloody, and I put two and two together and got trouble. Bad trouble for me, unless I got out. So I got out. It wasn't nice to do, after what Nick meant to me, but it was the only sensible thing. I got my career to think of."

"What career is that?"

"Modeling. Acting. Uncle Nick was gonna send me to school."

"Unless you talk, you'll finish your education at Corona. Who shot Nick?"

A thin edge of terror entered her voice. "I don't know, I tell you. I was passed out in the bedroom. I didn't see nothing."

"Why did Harry bring you your coat?"

"He didn't want me to get involved. He's my father, after all."

"Harry Nemo is your father?"

"Yes."

"You'll have to do better than that. What's your name?"

"Jeannine. Jeannine Larue."

"Why isn't your name Nemo if Harry is your father? Why do you call him Harry?"

"He's my stepfather, I mean."

"Sure," I said. "And Nick was really your uncle, and you were having a family reunion with him."

"He wasn't any blood relation to me. I always called him uncle, though."

"If Harry's your father, why don't you live with him?"

"I used to. Honest. This is the truth I'm telling you. I had to get out on account of the old lady. The old lady hates my guts. She's a real creep, a square. She can't stand for a girl to have any fun. Just because my old man was a rummy—"

"What's your idea of fun, Jeannine?"

She shook her feathercut hair at me. It exhaled a heavy perfume which was worth its weight in blood. She bared one pearly shoulder and smiled an artificial hustler's smile. "What's yours? Maybe we can get together."

"You mean the way you got together with Nick?"

"You're prettier than him."

"I'm also smarter, I hope. Is Harry really your stepfather?"

"Ask him if you don't believe me. Ask him. He lives in a place on Tule Street—I don't remember the number."

"I know where he lives."

But Harry wasn't at home. I knocked on the door of the frame cottage and got no answer. I turned the knob and found that the door was unlocked. There was a light behind it. The other cottages in the court were dark. It was long past midnight, and the street was deserted. I went into the cottage, preceded by my gun.

A ceiling bulb glared down on sparse and threadbare furniture, a time-eaten rug. Besides the living room, the house contained a cubbyhole of a bedroom and a closet kitchenette. Everything in the poverty-stricken place was pathetically clean. There were moral mottoes on the walls, and one picture. It was a photograph of a tow-headed girl in a teen-age party dress. Jeannine, before she learned that a pretty face and a sleek body could buy her the things she wanted. The things she thought she wanted.

For some reason, I felt sick. I went outside. Somewhere out of sight, an old car-engine muttered. Its muttering grew on the night. Harry Nemo's rented Chevrolet turned the corner under the streetlight. Its front wheels were weaving. One of the wheels climbed the curb in front of the cottage. The Chevrolet came to a halt at a drunken angle.

I crossed the sidewalk and opened the car door. Harry was at the wheel, clinging to it desperately as if he needed it to hold him up. His chest was bloody. His mouth was bright with blood. He spoke through it thickly:

"She got me."

"Who got you, Harry? Jeannine?"

"No. Not her. She was the reason for it, though. We had it coming."

Those were his final words. I caught his body as it fell sideways out of the seat. I laid it out on the sidewalk and left it for the cop on the beat to find.

I drove across town to the trailer court. Jeannine's trailer still had light in it, filtered through the curtains over the windows. I pushed the door open.

The girl was packing a suitcase on the bunk bed. She looked at me over her shoulder, and froze. Her blonde head was cocked like a frightened bird's, hypnotized by my gun.

"Where are you off to, kid?"

"Out of this town. I'm getting out."

"You have some talking to do first."

She straightened up. "I told you all I know. You didn't believe me. What's the matter, didn't you get to see Harry?"

"I saw him. Harry's dead. Your whole family is dying like flies."

She half-turned and sat down limply on the disordered bed. "Dead? You think I did it?"

"I think you know who did. Harry said before he died that you were the reason for it all."

"Me the reason for it?" Her eyes widened in false naiveté, but there was thought behind them, quick and desperate thought. "You mean that Harry got killed on account of me?"

"Harry and Nick both. It was a woman who shot them."

"God," she said. The desperate thought behind her eyes crystallized into knowledge. Which I shared.

The aching silence was broken by a big diesel rolling by on the highway. She said above its roar:

"That crazy old bat. So *she* killed Nick."

"You're talking about your mother. Mrs. Nemo."

"Yeah."

"Did you see her shoot him?"

"No. I was blotto like I told you. But I saw her out there this week, keeping an eye on the house. She's always watched me like a hawk."

"Is that why you were getting out of town? Because you knew she killed Nick?"

"Maybe it was. I don't know. I wouldn't let myself think about it."

Her blue gaze shifted from my face to something behind me. I turned. Mrs. Nemo was in the doorway. She was hugging the straw bag to her thin chest.

Her right hand dove into the bag. I shot her in the right arm. She leaned against the doorframe and held her dangling arm with her left hand. Her face was granite in whose crevices her eyes were like live things caught.

The gun she dropped was a cheap .32 revolver, its nickel plating worn and corroded. I spun the cylinder. One shot had been fired from it.

"This accounts for Harry," I said. "You didn't shoot Nick with this gun, not at that distance."

"No." She was looking down at her dripping hand. "I used my old police gun on Nick Nemo. After I killed him, I threw the gun into the sea. I didn't know I'd have further use for a gun. I bought that little suicide gun tonight."

"To use on Harry?"

"To use on you. I thought you were on to me. I didn't know until you told me that Harry knew about Nick and Jeannine."

"Jeannine is your daughter by your first husband?"

"My only daughter." She said to the girl: "I did it for you, Jeannine. I've seen too much—the awful things that can happen."

The girl didn't answer. I said:

"I can understand why you shot Nick. But why did Harry have to die?"

"Nick paid him," she said. "Nick paid him for Jeannine. I found Harry in a bar an hour ago, and he admitted it. I hope I killed him."

"You killed him, Mrs. Nemo. What brought you here? Was Jeannine the third on your list?"

"No. No. She's my own girl. I came to tell her what I did for her. I wanted her to know."

She looked at the girl on the bed. Her eyes were terrible with pain and love. The girl said in a stunned voice:

"Mother. You're hurt. I'm sorry."

"Let's go, Mrs. Nemo," I said.

RED CLAY

Michael Malone

Dingley Falls, *Handling Sin*, *Uncivil Seasons*, and *Time's Witness* are novels that endure in popularity and acclaim. Author Michael Malone has demonstrated that literary fiction can both appeal to its basic audience and find favor with readers of popular novels as well, including those most often found in the mystery sections of bookstores. The story reprinted here, winner of the 1996 Edgar award for short fiction, is a sample of Malone's writing at its finest.

U P ON ITS short slope the columned front of our courthouse was wavy in the August sun, like a courthouse in lake water. The leaves hung from maples, and the flag of North Carolina wilted flat against its metal pole. Heat sat sodden over Devereux County week by relentless week; they called the weather "dog days," after the star, Sirius, but none of us knew that. We thought they meant no dog would leave shade for street on such days—no dog except a mad one. I was ten that late August in 1959; I remembered the summer because of the long heat wave, and because of Stella Doyle.

When they pushed open the doors, the policemen and lawyers flung their arms up to their faces to block the sun and stopped there in the doorway as if the hot light were shoving them back inside. Stella Doyle came out last, a deputy on either side to walk her down to where the patrol car, orange as Halloween candles, waited to take her away until the jury could make up its mind about what had happened two months earlier out at Red Hills. It was the only house in the county big enough to have a name. It was where Stella Doyle had, maybe, shot her husband, Hugh Doyle, to death.

Excitement over Doyle's murder had swarmed through the town and stung us alive. No thrill would replace it until the assassination of John F. Kennedy. Outside the courthouse, sidewalk heat steaming up through our shoes, we stood patiently waiting to hear Mrs. Doyle found guilty. The news stood waiting, too, for she was, after all, not merely the murderer of the wealthiest man we knew; she was Stella Doyle. She was the movie star.

Papa's hand squeezed down on my shoulder and there was a tight line to his mouth as he pulled me into the crowd and said, "Listen now, Buddy, if anybody ever asks you, when you're grown, 'Did you ever see the most beautiful woman God made in your lifetime,' son, you say 'Yes, I had that luck, and her name was Stella Dora Doyle.' " His voice got louder, right there in the crowd for everybody to hear. "You tell them how her beauty was so bright, it burned back the shame they tried to heap on her head, burned it right on back to scorch their faces."

Papa spoke these strange words looking up the steps at the almost plump woman in black the deputies were holding. His arms were folded over his seersucker vest, his fingers tight on the sleeves of his shirt. People around us had turned to stare and somebody snickered.

Embarrassed for him, I whispered, "Oh, Papa, she's nothing but an old murderer. Everybody knows how she got drunk and killed Mr. Doyle. She shot him right through the head with a gun."

Papa frowned. "You don't know that."

I kept on. "Everybody says she was so bad and drunk all the time, she wouldn't let his folks even live in the same house with her. She made him throw out his own mama and papa."

Papa shook his head at me. "I don't like to hear ugly gossip coming out of your mouth, all right, Buddy?"

"Yes, sir."

"She didn't kill Hugh Doyle."

"Yes, sir."

His frown scared me; it was so rare. I stepped closer and took his hand, took his stand against the rest. I had no loyalty to this woman Papa thought so beautiful. I just could never bear to be cut loose from the safety of his good opinion. I suppose that from that moment on, I felt toward Stella Doyle something of what my father felt, though in the end perhaps she meant less to me, and stood for more. Papa never had my habit of symbolizing.

The courthouse steps were wide, uneven stone slabs. As Mrs. Doyle came down, the buzzing of the crowd hushed. All together, like trained dancers, people stepped back to clear a half-circle around the orange patrol car. Newsmen shoved their cameras to the front. She was rushed down so fast that her shoe caught in the crumbling stone and she fell against one of the deputies.

"She's drunk!" hooted a woman near me, a country woman in a flowered dress belted with a strip of painted rope. She and the child she jiggled against her shoulder were puffy with the fat of poverty. "Look'it her"—the woman pointed—"look at that dress. She thinks she's still out there in Hollywood." The woman beside her nodded, squinting out from under the visor of the kind of hat pier fishermen wear. "I went and killed my husband, wouldn't no rich lawyers come running to weasel me out of the law." She slapped at a fly's buzz.

Then they were quiet and everybody else was quiet and our circle of sun-stunned eyes fixed on the woman in black, stared at the wonder of one as high as Mrs. Doyle about to be brought so low.

Holding to the stiff, tan arm of the young deputy, Mrs. Doyle reached down to check the heel of her shoe. Black shoes, black suit and purse, wide black hat—they all sinned against us by their fashionableness, blazing wealth as well as death. She stood there, arrested a moment in the hot immobility of the air, then she hurried down, rushing the two big deputies down with her, to the open door of the orange patrol car. Papa stepped forward so quickly that the gap filled with people before I could follow him. I squeezed through, fighting with my elbows, and I saw that he was holding his straw hat in one hand, and offering the other hand out to the murderer. "Stella, how are you? Clayton Hayes."

As she turned, I saw the strawberry gold hair beneath the hat; then her hand, bright with a big diamond, took away the dark glasses. I saw what Papa meant. She was beautiful. Her eyes were the color of lilacs, but darker than lilacs. And her skin held the light like the inside of a shell. She was not like other pretty women, because the difference was not one of degree. I have never seen anyone else of her kind.

"Why, Clayton! God Almighty, it's been years."

"Well, yes, a long time now, I guess," he said, and shook her hand.

She took the hand in both of hers. "You look the same as ever. Is this your boy?" she said. The violet eyes turned to me.

"Yes, this is Buddy. Ada and I have six so far, three of each."

"Six? Are we that old, Clayton?" She smiled. "They said you'd married Ada Hackney."

A deputy cleared his throat. "Sorry, Clayton, we're going to have to get going."

"Just a minute, Lonnie. Listen, Stella, I just wanted you to know I'm sorry as I can be about your losing Hugh."

Tears welled in her eyes. "He did it himself, Clayton," she said.

"I know that. I know you didn't do this." Papa nodded slowly again and again, the way he did when he was listening. "I know that. Good luck to you."

She swatted tears away. "Thank you."

"I'm telling everybody I'm sure of that."

"Clayton, thank you."

Papa nodded again, then tilted his head back to give her his slow, peaceful smile. "You call Ada and me if there's ever something we can do to help you, you hear?" She kissed his cheek and he stepped back with me into the crowd of hostile, avid faces as she entered the police car. It moved slow as the sun through the sightseers. Cameras pushed against its windows.

A sallow man biting a pipe skipped down the steps to join some other reporters next to us. "Jury sent out for food," he told them. "No telling with these yokels. Could go either way." He pulled off his jacket and balled it under his arm. "Jesus, it's hot."

A younger reporter with thin, wet hair disagreed. "They all think Hollywood's Babylon and she's the whore. Hugh Doyle was the local prince, his daddy kept the mills open in the bad times, quote unquote half the rednecks in the county. They'll fry her. For that hat if nothing else."

"Could go either way," grinned the man with the pipe. "She was born in a shack six miles from here. Hat or no hat, that makes her one of them. So what if she did shoot the guy, he was dying of cancer anyhow, for Christ's sake. Well, she never could act worth the price of a bag of popcorn, but Jesus damn she was something to look at!"

Now that Stella Doyle was gone, people felt the heat again and went back to where they could sit still in the shade until the evening breeze and wait for the jury's decision. Papa and I walked back down Main Street to our furniture store. Papa owned a butcher shop, too, but he didn't like the meat business and wasn't very good at it, so my oldest brother ran it while Papa sat among the mahogany bedroom suites and red maple dining-room sets in a big rocking chair and read, or talked to friends who dropped by. The rocker was actually for sale, but he had sat in it for so long now that it was just Papa's chair. Three ceiling fans stirred against the quiet, shady air while he answered my questions about Stella Doyle.

He said that she grew up Stella Dora Hibble on Route 19, in a three-room, tin-roofed little house propped off the red clay by concrete blocks— the kind of saggy-porched, pinewood house whose owners leave on display in their dirt yard, like sculptures, the broken artifacts of their aspirations and the debris of their unmendable lives: the doorless refrigerator and the rusting car, the pyre of metal and plastic that tells drivers along the highway, "Dreams don't last."

Stella's mother, Dora Hibble, had believed in dreams anyhow. Dora had been a pretty girl who'd married a farmer and worked harder than she had the health for, because hard work was necessary just to keep from going under. But in the evenings Mrs. Hibble had looked at movie magazines. She had believed the romance was out there and she wanted it, if not for her, for her children. At twenty-seven, Dora Hibble died during her fifth labor. Stella was eight when she watched from the door of the bedroom as they covered her mother's face with a thin blanket. When Stella was fourteen, her father died when a machine jammed at Doyle Mills. When Stella was sixteen, Hugh Doyle, Jr., who was her age, my father's age, fell in love with her.

"Did you love her, too, Papa?"

"Oh, yes. All us boys in town were crazy about Stella Dora, one time or another. I had my attack of it, same as the rest. We were sweethearts in seventh grade. I bought a big-size Whitman's Sampler on Valentine's. I remember it cost every cent I had."

"Why were y'all crazy about her?"

"I guess you'd have to worry you'd missed out on being alive if you didn't feel that way about Stella, one time or another."

I was feeling a terrible emotion I later defined as jealousy. "But didn't you love Mama?"

"Well, now, this was before it was my luck to meet your mama."

"And you met her coming to town along the railroad track and you told your friends 'That's the girl for me and I'm going to marry her,' didn't you?"

"Yes, sir, and I was right on both counts." Papa rocked back in the big chair, his hands peaceful on the armrests.

"Was Stella Dora still crazy about you after you met Mama?"

His face crinkled into the lines of his ready laughter. "No, sir, she wasn't. She loved Hugh Doyle, minute she laid eyes on him, and he felt the same. But Stella had this notion about going off to get to be somebody in the movies. And Hugh couldn't hold her back, and I guess she couldn't get him to see what it was made her want to go off so bad either."

"What was it made her want to go?"

Papa smiled at me. "Well, I don't know, son. What makes you want to go off so bad? You're always saying you're going here, and there, 'cross the world, up to the moon. I reckon you're more like Stella than I am."

"Do you think she was wrong to want to go be in the movies?"

"No."

"You don't think she killed him?"

"No, sir, I don't."

"Somebody killed him."

"Well, Buddy, sometimes people lose hope and heart, and feel like they can't go on living."

"Yeah, I know. Suicide."

Papa's shoes tapped the floor as the rocker creaked back and forth. "That's right. Now you tell me, why're you sitting in here? Why don't you ride your bike on over to the ballpark and see who's there?"

"I want to hear about Stella Doyle."

"You want to hear. Well. Let's go get us a Coca-Cola, then. I don't guess somebody's planning to show up in this heat to buy a chest of drawers they got to haul home."

"You ought to sell air conditioners, Papa. People would buy air conditioners."

"I guess so."

So Papa told me the story. Or at least his version of it. He said Hugh and Stella were meant for each other. From the beginning it seemed to the whole town a fact as natural as harvest that so much money and so much beauty belonged together, and only Hugh Doyle with his long, free, easy stride was rich enough to match the looks of Stella Dora. But even Hugh Doyle couldn't hold her. He was only halfway through the state university, where his father had told him he'd have to go before he married Stella, if he wanted a home to bring her to, when she quit her job at Coldsteam's beauty parlor and took the bus to California. She was out there for six years before Hugh broke down and went after her.

By then every girl in the county was cutting Stella's pictures out of the movie magazines and reading how she got her lucky break, how she married a big director, and divorced him, and married a big star, and how that marriage broke up even quicker. Photographers traveled all the way to Thermopylae to take pictures of where she was born. People tried to tell them her house was gone, had fallen down and been used for firewood, but they just took photographs of Reverend Ballister's house instead and said Stella had grown up in it. Before long, even local girls would go stand in front of the Ballister house like a shrine, sometimes they'd steal flowers out of the yard. The year that *Fever*, her best movie, came to the Grand Theater on Main Street, Hugh Doyle flew out to Los Angeles and won her back. He took her down to Mexico to divorce the baseball player she'd married after the big star. Then Hugh married her himself and put her on an ocean liner and took her all over the world. For a whole two years, they didn't come home to Thermopylae. Everybody in the county talked about this two-year honeymoon, and Hugh's father confessed to some friends that he was disgusted by his son's way of life.

But when the couple did come home, Hugh walked right into the mills and turned a profit. His father confessed to the same friends that he was flabbergasted Hugh had it in him. But after the father died Hugh started drinking and Stella joined him. The parties got a little wild. The fights got loud. People talked. They said he had other women. They said Stella'd been locked up in a sanitorium. They said the Doyles were breaking up.

And then one June day a maid at Red Hills, walking to work before the morning heat, fell over something that lay across a path to the stables. And it was Hugh Doyle in riding clothes with a hole torn in the side of his head. Not far from his gloved hand, the police found Stella's pistol, already too hot from the sun to touch. The cook testified that the Doyles had been fighting like cats and dogs all night long the night before, and Hugh's mother testified that he wanted to divorce Stella but she wouldn't let him, and so Stella was arrested. She said she was innocent, but it was her gun, she was his heir, and she had no alibi. Her trial lasted almost as long as that August heat wave.

———

A NEIGHBOR STROLLED past the porch, where we sat out the evening heat, waiting for the air to lift. "Jury's still out," he said. Mama waved her hand at him. She pushed herself and me in the big green wood swing that hung from two chains to the porch roof, and answered my questions about Stella Doyle. She said, "Oh, yes, they all said Stella was specially pretty. I never knew her to talk to myself."

"But if Papa liked her so much, why didn't y'all get invited out to their house and everything?"

"Her and your papa just went to school together, that's all. That was a long time back. The Doyles wouldn't ask folks like us over to Red Hills."

"Why not? Papa's family used to have a *whole* lot of money. That's what you said. And Papa went right up to Mrs. Doyle at the courthouse today, right in front of everybody. He told her, You let us know if there's anything we can do."

Mama chuckled the way she always did about Papa, a low ripple like a pigeon nesting, a little exasperated at having to sit still so long. "You know your papa'd offer to help out anybody he figured might be in trouble, white or black. That's just him; that's not any Stella Dora Doyle. Your papa's just a good man. You remember that, Buddy."

Goodness was Papa's stock-in-trade; it was what he had instead of money or ambition, and Mama often reminded us of it. In him she kept safe all the kindness she had never felt she could afford for herself. She, who could neither read nor write, who had stood all day in a cigarette factory from the age of nine until the morning Papa married her, was a fighter. She wanted her children to go farther than Papa had. Still, for years after he died, she would carry down from the attic the yellow mildewed ledgers where his value was recorded in more than $75,000 of out-of-date bills he had been unwilling to force people in trouble to pay. Running her sun-spotted finger down the brown wisps of names and the money they'd owed, she would sigh that proud, exasperated ripple, and shake her head over foolish, generous Papa.

Through the front parlor window I could hear my sisters practicing the theme from *The Apartment* on the piano. Someone across the street turned on a light. Then we heard the sound of Papa's shoes coming a little faster than usual down the sidewalk. He turned at the hedge carrying the package of shiny butcher's paper in which he brought meat home every evening. "Verdict just came in!" he called out happily. "Not guilty! Jury came back about forty minutes ago. They already took her home."

Mama took the package and sat Papa down in the swing next to her. "Well, well," she said. "They let her off."

"Never ought to have come up for trial in the first place, Ada, like I told everybody all along. It's like her lawyers showed. Hugh went down to Atlanta, saw that doctor, found out he had cancer, and he took his own life. Stella never even knew he was sick."

Mama patted his knee. "Not guilty; well, well."

Papa made a noise of disgust. "Can you believe some folks out on Main Street tonight are all fired up *because* Stella got off! Adele Simpson acted downright indignant!"

Mama said, "And you're surprised?" And she shook her head with me at Papa's innocence.

Talking of the trial, my parents made one shadow along the wood floor of the porch, while inside my sisters played endless variations of "Chopsticks," the notes handed down by ghostly creators long passed away.

A few weeks later, Papa was invited to Red Hills, and he let me come along; we brought a basket of sausage biscuits Mama had made for Mrs. Doyle.

As soon as Papa drove past the wide white gate, I learned how money could change even weather. It was cooler at Red Hills, and the grass was the greenest grass in the county. A black man in a black suit let us into the house, then led us down a wide hallway of pale yellow wood into a big room shuttered against the heat. She was there in an armchair almost the color of her eyes. She wore loose-legged pants and was pouring whiskey from a bottle into a glass.

"Clayton, thanks for coming. Hello there, little Buddy. Look, I hope I didn't drag you from business."

Papa laughed. "Stella, I could stay gone a week and never miss a customer." It embarrassed me to hear him admit such failure to her.

She said she could tell I liked books, so maybe I wouldn't mind if they left me there to read while she borrowed my daddy for a little bit. There were white shelves in the room, full of books. I said I didn't mind, but I did; I wanted to keep on seeing her. Even with the loose shirt soiled and rumpled over a waist she tried to hide, even with her face swollen from heat and drink and grief, she was something you wanted to look at as long as possible.

They left me alone. On the white piano were dozens of photographs of Stella Doyle in silver frames. From a big painting over the mantelpiece her remarkable eyes followed me around the room. I looked at that painting as sun deepened across it, until finally she and Papa came back. She had a tissue to her nose, a new drink in her hand. "I'm sorry, honey," she said to me. "Your daddy's been sweet letting me run on. I just needed somebody to talk to for a while about what happened to me." She kissed the top of my head and I could feel her warm lips at the part in my hair.

We followed her down the wide hall out onto the porch. "Clayton, you'll forgive a fat old souse talking your ear off and bawling like a jackass."

"No such thing, Stella."

"And you *never* thought I killed him, even when you first heard. My God, thank you."

Papa took her hand again. "You take care now," he said.

Then suddenly she was hugging herself, rocking from side to side. Words burst from her like a door flung open by wind. "I could kick him in the ass, that bastard! Why didn't he tell me? To quit, to *quit*, and use *my* gun, and just about get me strapped in the gas chamber, that goddamn bastard, and never say a word!" Her profanity must have shocked Papa as much as it did me. He never used it, much less ever heard it from a woman.

But he nodded and said, "Well, good-bye, I guess, Stella. Probably won't be seeing you again."

"Oh, Lord, Clayton, I'll be back. The world's so goddamn little."

She stood at the top of the porch, tears wet in those violet eyes that the movie magazines had loved to talk about. On her cheek a mosquito bite flamed like a slap. Holding to the big white column, she waved as we drove off into the dusty heat. Ice flew from the glass in her hand like diamonds.

PAPA WAS RIGHT; they never met again. Papa lost his legs from diabetes, but he'd never gone much of anywhere even before that. And afterward, he was one of two places—home or the store. He'd sit in his big wood wheelchair in the furniture store, with his hands peaceful on the armrests, talking with whoever came by.

I did see Stella Doyle again; the first time in Belgium, twelve years later. I went farther than Papa.

In Bruges there are small restaurants that lean like elegant elbows on the canals and glance down at passing pleasure boats. Stella Doyle was sitting, one evening, at a table in the crook of the elbow of one of them, against an iron railing that curved its reflection in the water. She was alone there when I saw her. She stood, leaned over the rail, and slipped the ice cubes from her glass into the canal. I was in a motor launch full of tourists passing below. She waved with a smile at us and we waved back. It had been a lot of years since her last picture, but probably she waved out of habit. For the tourists motoring past, Stella in white against the dark restaurant was another snapshot of Bruges. For me, she was home and memory. I craned to look back as long as I could, and leapt from the boat at the next possible stop.

When I found the restaurant, she was yelling at a well-dressed young man who was leaning across the table, trying to soothe her in French. They appeared to be quarreling over his late arrival. All at once she hit him, her diamond flashing into his face. He filled the air with angry gestures, then turned and left, a white napkin to his cheek. I was made very shy by what I'd seen—the young man was scarcely older than I was. I stood unable to speak until her staring at me jarred me forward. I said, "Mrs. Doyle? I'm Buddy Hayes. I came out to see you at Red Hills with my father Clayton Hayes one time. You let me look at your books."

She sat back down and poured herself a glass of wine. "You're *that* little boy? God Almighty, how old am I? Am I a hundred yet?" Her laugh had been loosened by the wine. "Well, a Red Clay rambler, like me. How 'bout that. Sit down. What are *you* doing over here?"

I told her, as nonchalantly as I could manage, that I was traveling on college prize money, a journalism award. I wrote a prize essay about a murder trial.

"Mine?" she asked, and laughed.

A waiter, plump and flushed in his neat black suit, trotted to her side. He shook his head at the untouched plates of food. "Madame, your friend has left, then?"

Stella said, "Mister, I helped him along. And turns out, he was no friend."

The waiter then turned his eyes, sad and reproachful, to the trout on the plate.

"How about another bottle of that wine and a great big bucket of ice?" Stella asked.

The waiter kept flapping his fat quick hands around his head, entreating us to come inside. *"Les moustiques, madame!"*

"I just let them bite," she said. He went away grieved.

She was slender now, and elegantly dressed. And while her hands and throat were older, the eyes hadn't changed, nor the red-gold hair. She was still the most beautiful woman God had made in my lifetime, the woman of whom my father had said that any man who had not desired her had missed out on being alive, the one for whose honor my father had turned his back on the whole town of Thermopylae. Because of Papa, I had entered my adolescence daydreaming about fighting for Stella Doyle's honor; we had starred together in a dozen of her movies: I dazzled her jury; I cured Hugh Doyle while hiding my own noble love for his wife. And now here I sat drinking wine with her on a veranda in Bruges; me, the first Hayes ever to win a college prize, ever to get to college. Here I sat with a movie star.

She finished her cigarette, dropped it spinning down into the black canal. "You look like him," she said. "Your papa. I'm sorry to hear that about the diabetes."

"I look like him, but I don't think like him," I told her.

She tipped the wine bottle upside down in the bucket. "You want the world," she said. "Go get it, honey."

"That's what my father doesn't understand."

"He's a good man," she answered. She stood up slowly. "And I think Clayton would want me to get you to your hotel."

All the fenders of her Mercedes were crushed. She said, "When I've had a few drinks, I need a strong car between me and the rest of the cock-eyed world."

The big car bounced over the moon-white street. "You know what, Buddy? Hugh Doyle gave me my first Mercedes, one morning in Paris. At breakfast. He held the keys out in his hand like a damn daffodil he'd picked in the yard. He gave me *this* goddamn thing." She waved her finger with its huge diamond. "This damn thing was tied to my big toe one Christmas morning!" And she smiled up at the stars as if Hugh Doyle were up there tying diamonds on them. "He had a beautiful grin, Buddy, but he was a son of a bitch."

The car bumped to a stop on the curb outside my little hotel. "Don't miss your train tomorrow," she said. "And you listen to me, don't go back home; go on to Rome."

"I'm not sure I have time."

She looked at me. "*Take* time. Just take it. Don't get scared, honey."

Then she put her hand in my jacket pocket and the moon came around her hair, and my heart panicked crazily, thudding against my shirt, think-ing she might kiss me. But her hand went away, and all she said was, "Say hi to Clayton when you get home, all right? Even losing his legs and all, your daddy's lucky, you know that?"

I said, "I don't see how."

"Oh, I didn't either till I was a lot older than you. And had my damn in-laws trying to throw me into the gas chamber. Go to bed. So long, Red Clay."

Her silver car floated away. In my pocket, I found a large wad of French money, enough to take me to Rome, and a little ribboned box, clearly a gift she had decided not to give the angry young man in the beau-tiful suit who'd arrived too late. On black velvet lay a man's wristwatch, reddish gold.

It's an extremely handsome watch, and it still tells me the time.

———

I ONLY WENT home to Thermopylae for the funerals. It was the worst of the August dog days when Papa died in the hospital bed they'd set up next to his and Mama's big four-poster in their bedroom. At his grave, the clots of red clay had already dried to a dusty dull color by the time we shoveled them down upon him, friend after friend taking a turn at the shovel. The petals that fell from roses fell limp to the red earth, wilted like the crowd who stood by the grave while Reverend Ballister told us that Clayton Hayes was "a good man." Behind a cluster of Mama's family, I saw a woman in black turn away and walk down the grassy incline to a car, a Mercedes.

After the services I went driving, but I couldn't out-travel Papa in Devereux County. The man at the gas pump listed Papa's virtues as he cleaned my windshield. The woman who sold me the bottle of bourbon said she'd owed Papa $215.00 since 1944, and when she'd paid him back in 1966 he'd forgotten all about it. I drove along the highway where the foundations of tin-roofed shacks were covered now by the parking lots of mini-malls; beneath the asphalt, somewhere, was Stella Doyle's birthplace. Stella Dora Hibble, Papa's first love.

Past the white gates, the Red Hills lawn was as parched as the rest of the county. Paint blistered and peeled on the big white columns. I waited a long time before the elderly black man I'd met twenty years before opened the door irritably.

I heard her voice from the shadowy hall yelling, "Jonas! Let him in."

On the white shelves the books were the same. The photos on the piano as young as ever. She frowned so strangely when I came into the room, I thought she must have been expecting someone else and didn't recognize me.

"I'm Buddy Hayes, Clayton's—"

"I know who you are."

"I saw you leaving the cemetery. . . ."

"I know you did."

I held out the bottle.

Together we finished the bourbon in memory of Papa, while shutters beat back the sun, hid some of the dirty glasses scattered on the floor, hid Stella Doyle in her lilac armchair. Cigarette burns scarred the armrests, left their marks on the oak floor. Behind her the big portrait showed Time up for the heartless bastard he is. Her hair was cropped short, and gray. Only the color of her eyes had stayed the same; they looked as remarkable as ever in the swollen face.

"I came out here to bring you something."

"What?"

I gave her the thin, cheap, yellowed envelope I'd found in Papa's desk with his special letters and papers. It was addressed in neat, cursive pencil to "Clayton." Inside was a silly Valentine card. Betty Boop popping bonbons in her pouty lips, exclaiming "Ooooh, I'm sweet on you." It was childish and lascivious at the same time, and it was signed with a lipstick blot, now brown with age, and with the name "Stella," surrounded by a heart.

I said, "He must have kept this since the seventh grade."

She nodded. "Clayton was a good man." Her cigarette fell from her ashtray onto the floor. When I came over to pick it up, she said, "Goodness is luck; like money, like looks. Clayton was lucky that way." She went to the piano and took more ice from the bucket there; one piece she rubbed around the back of her neck, then dropped into her glass. She turned, the eyes wet, like lilac stars. "You know, in Hollywood, they said, '*Hibble?!* What kind of hick name is that, we can't use that!' So I said, 'Use Doyle, then.' I mean, I took Hugh's name six years before he ever came out to get me. Because I knew he'd come. The day I left Thermopylae he kept yelling at me, 'You can't have both!' He kept yelling it while the bus was pulling out. 'You can't have me and it both!' He wanted to rip my heart out for leaving, for *wanting* to go." Stella moved along the curve of the white piano to a photograph of Hugh Doyle in a white open shirt, grinning straight out at the sun. She said, "But I could have both. There were only two things I *had* to have in this little world, and one was the lead in a movie called *Fever*, and the other one was Hugh Doyle." She put the photograph down carefully. "I didn't know about the cancer till my lawyers found out he'd been to see that doctor in Atlanta. Then it was easy to get the jury to go for suicide." She smiled at me. "Well, not easy. But we turned them around. I think your papa was the only man in town who *never* thought I was guilty."

It took me a while to take it in. "Well, he sure convinced me," I said.

"I expect he convinced a lot of people. Everybody thought so much of Clayton."

"You killed your husband."

We looked at each other. I shook my head. "Why?"

She shrugged. "We had a fight. We were drunk. He was sleeping with my fucking maid. I was crazy. Lots of reasons, no reason. I sure didn't plan it."

"You sure didn't confess it either."

"What good would that have done? Hugh was dead. I wasn't about to let his snooty-assed mother shove me in the gas chamber and pocket the money."

I shook my head. "Jesus. And you've never felt a day's guilt, have you?"

Her head tilted back, smoothing her throat. The shuttered sun had fallen down the room onto the floor, and evening light did a movie fade and turned Stella Doyle into the star in the painting behind her. "Ah, baby, don't believe it," she said. The room stayed quiet.

I stood up and dropped the empty bottle in the wastebasket. I said, "Papa told me how he was in love with you."

Her laugh came warmly through the shuttered dusk. "Yes, and I guess I was sweet on him, too, boop boop dedoo."

"Yeah, Papa said no man could say he'd been alive if he'd seen you and not felt that way. I just wanted to tell you I know what he meant." I raised my hand to wave good-bye.

"Come over here," she said, and I went to her chair and she reached up and brought my head down to her and kissed me full and long on the mouth. "So long, Buddy." Slowly her hand moved down my face, the huge diamond radiant.

NEWS CAME OVER the wire. The tabloids played with it for a few days on back pages. They had some pictures. They dug up the Hugh Doyle trial photos to put beside the old studio glossies. The dramatic death of an old movie star was worth sending a news camera down to Thermopylae, North Carolina, to get a shot of the charred ruin that had once been Red Hills. A shot of the funeral parlor and the flowers on the casket.

My sister phoned me that there was even a crowd at the coroner's inquest at the courthouse. They said Stella Doyle had died in her sleep after a cigarette set fire to her mattress. But rumors started that her body had been found at the foot of the stairs, as if she'd been trying to escape the fire, but had fallen. They said she was drunk. They buried her beside Hugh Doyle in the family plot, the fanciest tomb in the Methodist cemetery, not far from where my parents were buried. Not long after she died, one of the cable networks did a night of her movies. I stayed up to watch *Fever* again.

My wife said, "Buddy, I'm sorry, but this is the biggest bunch of sentimental slop I ever saw. The whore'll sell her jewels and get the medicine and they'll beat the epidemic but she'll die to pay for her past and then the town'll see she was really a saint. Am I right?"

"You're right."

She sat down to watch awhile. "You know, I can't decide if she's a really lousy actress or a really good one. It's weird."

I said, "Actually, I think she was a much better actress than anyone gave her credit for."

My wife went to bed, but I watched through the night. I sat in Papa's old rocking chair that I'd brought north with me after his death. Finally at dawn I turned off the set, and Stella's face disappeared into a star, and went out. The reception was awful and the screen too small. Besides, the last movie was in black-and-white; I couldn't see her eyes as well as I could remember the shock of their color, when she first turned toward me at the foot of the courthouse steps, that hot August day when I was ten, when my father stepped forward out of the crowd to take her hand, when her eyes were lilacs turned up to his face, and his straw hat in the summer sun was shining like a knight's helmet.

POETIC JUSTICE

Steve Martini

Legal fiction has become one of the most popular forms of entertainment these days. Lawyer-writers are everywhere, it seems. Certainly one of the most formidable is Steve Martini, whose bestsellers *Compelling Evidence* (1992) and *Undue Influence* (1994) launched a long run on various lists across the country. Martini is a solid constructor of complicated tales and his particular approach to his material has been much imitated, but in vain. He works in his own way, and writes fiction like no one else. His most recent work is *The Jury*.

> *Harvey was a lazy lawyer,*
> *a cynic, and an ethics destroyer.*
> *He learned his vices at an early age,*
> *practicing to be the devil's sage.*
> *In school he copied homework before class,*
> *and peeked over shoulders on tests to pass.*
>
> *He wondered where he'd gotten his scruples,*
> *for after all, he was not a bad pupil.*
>
> *But somewhere in his distant gene pool,*
> *Harvey found a miraculous tool.*
> *He'd inherited a knack to cheat,*
> *a phenomenal gift he couldn't beat.*
> *Way down in that murky depth,*
> *a serious streak of dishonesty crept.*
> *It didn't come from his father or mother,*
> *his aunt or uncle, or any other.*
> *His relatives were working drones,*
> *civil servants worn to the bone.*

They worried about bills and had
low-paying jobs.
To Harvey they were just working slobs.
He was different. He was no fool.
He knew how the world worked,
he'd learn to be cool.

THE CLIMB

B Y THE TIME he was twelve, Harvey had taken on the primal good
looks of a predator—tall and handsome with chiseled features—so
that by high school the girls were waiting for him. When it came to the
fairer sex, Harvey always went for brains. A good body and a beautiful
face were consolations if they could be found. But a good mind allowed
Harvey to copy a girl's assignments, and look over her shoulder on exams
with no complaint. Like a sailor in every port, Harvey had a girl in every
class.

He followed the pattern through college and into law school, where it
became more difficult. Now the exams were not simple true-false or multi-
ple choice questions. Now they required the originality of an essay, something in Harvey's own words and sufficiently different from others so that
he would not be caught.

But Harvey didn't panic. Harvey never panicked. He relied on old talents and an innate genius for deception that seemed to come so naturally,
from somewhere deep down inside.

Harvey struck up a relationship with the dean's secretary. She was
Harvey's age, but without the prospects of a law school education. The girl
became quite fond of him, and Harvey of her. After all, she possessed the
combination to the dean's safe. The safe possessed the questions to every
exam, along with the model answers prepared by the professors. With no
need to study, Harvey loaded up on units. Why waste time? In less than
three years he graduated with honors, said good-bye to the secretary, and
was on his way.

Now Harvey had to hurdle the bar examination. This was no mean
feat for someone who had never studied in school or earned an honest
grade. He had considered the problem for a long time, long before he ever
left law school. What good was a law degree if he couldn't use it to make
money? Only 50 percent of the applicants who took the bar usually passed
it on the first shot. Harvey had no intention of wasting time by taking the

exam more than once. Besides, bar review courses were long and tedious. They cost money and offered no guarantees of a passing score. Harvey wanted a sure thing.

To this end he hired a private investigator, a slime-bucket named Jersey Joe Janis. Jersey Joe had skinny legs, a beer belly, and triple jowls. It was a physique that amused Harvey, something on the order of Ichabod Crane, only with a spotted tie and a tidy gut that hung over his belt.

Jersey Joe's specialty was following married men to sleazy motels and taking pictures for anxious wives. His services cost Harvey only a small part of the price for a bar review course, and it guaranteed him a lock on the exam.

Janis posed as a gas company employee, uniform and all. He visited a small printing plant in the center of town and told the owner that the gas company had reports of a dangerous leak. The printer and his employees would have to vacate the building, but just for a few minutes. The leak was probably down the street. But still, to be safe . . .

It took Jersey Joe just ten minutes to collect a complete set of the bar exam questions, along with the model answers to each one. Harvey had discovered the state bar's soft underbelly. They used the same printer every year, a relative of one of their executives. After all, isn't that how everybody got ahead?

Harvey maxed the bar exam on his first shot. He set up practice in the city center, and specialized in a field for which he seemed to have a natural aptitude—the criminal law. Harvey never really understood why, but for some strange reason he seemed to empathize with, and gravitate toward, those accused of crimes. He grasped perfectly their perverse motivations and skewed logic, even as he scoffed at the slipshod practices that got them caught. Of course, that was why they hired Harvey.

Jersey Joe had stood him well, and so Harvey found other areas in which to employ the man's talents. To be specific, in the offices of the county district attorney.

The law provided Harvey with what it called formal "discovery." This required the state to disclose all of the documents and evidence they intended to use against Harvey's clients in any criminal case. But Harvey wanted more. He wanted an edge, something that his competitors in the criminal bar didn't get. He wanted access to the prosecutor's theory of the case, privileged information that was the product of the other side's work. He wanted copies of their notes and confidential correspondence, and the names of their witnesses before their recollection of events became locked in stone, while Harvey could still *reach them*, so to speak.

Jersey Joe played janitor at night. He planted listening devices in the offices of the deputy prosecutors and used good-looking young men to seduce secretaries in the D.A.'s office. With husky voices on overheated couches and steaming shag carpets, they plumbed the depths for office secrets, and compromised the D.A.'s staff to obtain confidential information.

Within a short time, Harvey knew what prosecutors were thinking before they did. He quickly developed an uncanny record of courtroom victories, outflanking the state on points of evidence, and slamming its witnesses with earlier inconsistent statements.

Prosecutors who could not beat him started dealing with him, giving up cases, rolling over like trained dogs on a stage. Harvey became a principal player in the criminal courts, and soon branched out. He began taking high-dollar civil cases. Other lawyers took heed of him. Some took his measure, but didn't like the odds. Using Jersey Joe, and unknown to his adversaries, Harvey was plucking their files and tapping their phones.

Aware of Harvey's talents but mostly of his amazing intuition at trials, judges began to cut him more slack in the courtroom, as if he needed a further edge. Harvey learned that in the practice of law, a reputation for winning goes a long way. That and a little bluster, which he had in abundance, drove most of his opponents to their knees early. Harvey became known as a man who did his homework. What others didn't know is that it was being done by Jersey Joe.

Harvey joined the silk-sock set. Invited to become a partner in a major downtown law firm, he found a whole new set of clients, upper-crust, waiting for him in the tony skyscraper on K Street. Suddenly he was surrounded by powerful lobbyists and corporate high-rollers. Harvey had made it to Gucci Gulch.

> *He met with Jersey Joe out on the sly,*
> *out of the office and out of the eye.*
> *The man didn't fit with Harvey's new digs,*
> *among high-tone clients and partners*
> *who were prigs.*

> *Janis wondered why Harvey had*
> *become so distant.*
> *Though his feelings were hurt*
> *he wasn't persistent.*
> *Jersey Joe was a man who bided his time,*
> *smart as a whip though he looked nickel-dime.*

For seven years Harvey led a charmed life, vacationing in the best resorts, running with the chic crowd. He counted among his friends the powerful and wealthy, an elite cadre of celebrities and a growing number of influential politicians. He was courted on television talk shows, where he boosted Harvey-authored books touting his legal prowess, never revealing that the words between the covers were ghostwritten by others.

Harvey was appointed to corporate boards, and joined the best clubs. The law school from which he graduated *magnum cum cheatum* named Harvey as an honorary regent. He received an offer, an appointment to the bench, a tribute that he magnanimously declined. After all, what good would Jersey Joe be there?

In any gathering, Harvey's repute as a top-gun lawyer preceded him, until one evening he climbed the highest peak.

After shaking loose with some coin come election time, Harvey met the top couple, and one night found himself sawing wood in the Lincoln Bedroom—*a friend of the family.*

Now he numbered among his patrons the most powerful man in the land. Harvey was appointed to high commissions and became an advisor to the mighty. Such was his celebrity that he was asked to add his name to the list of partners in an even more powerful law firm, where retired cabinet members hung their spurs of state to turn a profit in the practice of law. He had arrived, and on the door it read:

HARVEY OF COUNSEL

He appeared in only important cases
where the stakes were high and the clients aces.
These were all people of the high repute,
corporate high-rollers with golden parachute.
Yet in all of the cases that Harvey tried,
it was Jersey Joe on whose skills he relied.

THE CRIME

THE WORLD CAME crashing down because of a missing tag from a Chinese laundry.

It was early on a Sunday afternoon when Harvey received the call. There was an urgent problem. It was the White House. It seemed the President needed Harvey's help.

They met beyond the black iron fence with its spear-tipped points, over the manicured lawn long dead beneath a blanket of snow. In that great white house they stood toe to toe, Harvey and the great man. He was ushered to the inner sanctum and offered a seat on a couch before a crackling fire in that grand elliptical room.

"Some coffee or tea?"

Harvey politely declined.

"Perhaps something stronger?" asked the President.

Harvey shook his head. He wanted to cut to the chase.

The presidential problems were no mystery to any who followed the national scene. The man's troubles had begun not with a single act but a series of events. Any one of these taken alone might be almost laughable, but together they eroded presidential credibility in the way that glacial grinding carves canyons.

By the time Harvey was called, there were those in Congress who were talking of "high crimes and misdemeanors," the language of impeachment.

Some claimed he used the IRS
to pursue political ends,
specifically to audit
those who were not his friends.

Others claimed he was snooping
through stacks of personal files,
and wondered what their own were doing
on the White House floor in piles.

There were rumors of campaign abuses,
and the laundering of money,
such an incredible list of scandals
the President dismissed them as funny.

But as months turned into years
it didn't take a sleuth
to figure out the President
had a problem with the truth.

But now he had another scandal.
This latest was a whopper.
And what he wanted most of all
was a good lawyer to be the stopper.

All things considered, the man was in deep trouble. Still there were compensating advantages. The President was the repository of power in the mightiest nation on earth. Not a bad friend to have, thought Harvey. No doubt he would have been in jail, except for the fact that he deftly controlled all the levers of power.

He had an attorney general who provided cover by the hour. Whenever scandal got too close, and there was fear he might be nailed, a friendly government lawyer popped up, and some other goat would be unveiled.

> *They offered up business kings*
> *and megabucks tycoons,*
> *and had the gall to tell us all*
> *they were saving children from these goons.*

> *They announced programs every hour*
> *and stories for the press.*
> *They would serve up anything*
> *to distract the people from this mess.*

To Harvey, if the ability to thwart the law wasn't enough, the President had personal strengths to boot. He was the very soul of affability. He possessed the hail bluster of a fellow well met, a disarming smile and the wily mind of one who had weathered many a political storm. Harvey had always been struck by the man's uncanny ability to wiggle away from scandal, usually over the bodies of others, and always with moves befitting a belly dancer.

Harvey admired him greatly! In fact they looked a lot alike, same size and build, brothers under the skin. An affinity that had been planted in their very first meeting, a crowded reception at which the President seemed to notice only Harvey. It was as if there were no one else in the room.

Harvey assumed it must have been his natural magnetism.

The President was tall and handsome, with the generous motions of practiced greatness about him. He possessed the fluid animation of a pope, except that when he committed sin, he offered absolution to others.

No matter the accusation, his poll numbers kept rising. Public sympathy for the man flowed like a babbling spring.

Standing in that great house, Harvey incisively appraised the man's situation.

A lifetime in office develops good spin,
variations on the truth like a violin.

He could deal with scandal, whether
fact or fiction,
and even when dissembling never
tripped on his diction.

When cornered he could slip into
the passive tense:
"Nothing going on here, just some negligence."

"Mistakes were made, but no laws were broken."
Even if it wasn't credible, it was
very well-spoken.

"We cleared it with our lawyers, they said
it was fine.
We may have come close, but we didn't
cross the line."

Invented by his spin doctors, these evasions had become the mottoes of his administration, like *E Pluribus Unum* and *In God We Trust*. What was even more mystifying to Harvey was that the public bought it. As he listened to the chief of state, excuses flowed like silken mercury from the man's tongue. Harvey realized why it was that the people ate from his hands like pigeons in a park.

The President's face could assume the full flush of humor as if even the most serious charge was a matter of mere amusement. When things heated up and necessity required, he could work up a healthy head of righteous indignation, a variation on the theme:

"Mistakes were made, but
no laws were violated."
Those responsible would be annihilated.

Lawyers and staffers wore sackcloth and ashes,
and were regularly featured in
"Breaking News Flashes."

> *There wasn't any question;*
> *Harvey had his doubts.*
> *Still the President swore*
> *'twas the truth—or thereabouts.*

"How about a cigar?" The President opened a humidor and offered one to Harvey.

"Cuban made and rolled. I get 'em from Guantánamo. Under the fence, as they say."

"Wouldn't mind," said Harvey as he reached into the box and took one.

"Take a few. They're small."

Harvey helped himself. The President already had one; he lit up and blew. This was the man who had only recently stood on the stump and eviscerated the tobacco industry. He looked at Harvey as if he could read minds.

"Cigars don't count," he said.

They laughed to one another, the way great men do. Just a couple of power people.

Two smoke rings settled like halos over the President's head before they slowly dissipated. This might have been a premonition of things to come, had Harvey been paying attention.

They settled down to business. The President puffed and blew.

"With all of my current problems, I don't need any more. By the way, do we have attorney-client privilege?" He said it as if it were an afterthought, before cleansing his soul.

Harvey assured him that they did.

"Fine. That's fine. I just wanted to be sure. I didn't want to use government lawyers. I didn't know who to trust. It's a serious matter, national security and all."

Harvey's eyebrows arched as he lit up.

"It will require a great deal of discretion. Total secrecy," said the President.

"I understand," said Harvey.

After a long pause and some serious puffs of dense blue smoke, evidence of considerable distress, the President spoke.

"I suspect that one of my cabinet members is selling state secrets. Which one, I can't be sure. I need somebody on the outside who can be my eyes and ears. Someone I can trust to get to the bottom of this thing quickly. I don't know if you've heard, but the FBI is a mess."

"I know." If the agency were up to snuff, the man talking to Harvey probably would have been in jail.

"Why me?" asked Harvey.

"You seem to have a knack at trials to get the evidence you need to win your case. That's the kind of thing I need now. You know. Someone who can fill in all the blanks with the right information."

Harvey couldn't be sure, but he thought for a second that the President had actually winked at him. Perhaps it was some mythic secret sign used by the powerful, like the Masonic handshake or rapper talk. Then again, maybe it was just a nervous twitch. Still, Harvey didn't want to be thought of as a hick. He did the natural thing. He winked back, and then quickly rubbed his eye, as if he had an itch.

Immediately the President smiled. It was a sign. Harvey had been initiated into the fold.

"Then you'll help me."

As a lawyer Harvey'd spent a lifetime building up his name. How could he refuse without diminishing his fame?

"I'm glad to find a man who understands duty." The President rose from his chair and put his left hand firmly on Harvey's shoulder. Then, with his right, he pumped Harvey's hand three or four times with enthusiasm, like he was trying to bring up water out on the prairie.

"Together you and I, we'll find this spy. And if you are successful," said the President, "you can write your own ticket."

That word seemed to bring the great man back down to earth, to the crisis at hand. It was what had caused the predicament in the first place—a missing Chinese laundry ticket.

It all started on a summer day, the kind of day that made the capital famous, hot and humid. It began in the commercial laundry of Too Fu Waun.

A thousand-dollar suit, pinstripes and worsted wool, had somehow become separated from its laundry ticket. The man doing the pressing saw one on the floor and assumed the obvious, pinning it on the coat's lapel.

The suit in turn was shipped to its owner in accordance with the ticket, and received by a sergeant-at-arms at the Capitol, where it was promptly hung on a hook in the senate cloakroom. At the end of the day it was collected without question by one Senator Smooch. He took it home and hung it in his closet. It wasn't until two weeks later when he tried it on that he discovered the suit didn't fit. The pants were too tight and the arms too long. What troubled him most was what he found in the suit coat pocket;

a signed check, made out for two million dollars, drawn against a bank in Hong Kong. It was stapled to a note:

> MAKE THE DEPOSIT, AFTER FILLING
> IN THE RIGHT NAME.
> I DECIDED TO LEAVE IT BLANK SO
> YOU COULD AVOID BLAME.

Senator Smooch tried on the coat again, but no matter how hard he tried, he couldn't make it fit.

> *He pulled so hard that he ripped one sleeve,*
> *buttoned the pants but found*
> *he couldn't breathe.*
> *He pulled and grunted and made funny faces.*
> *It just wouldn't fit, even with corset and laces.*
>
> *But what Smooch found next was*
> *the real bombshell,*
> *a shiny gold pin under the coat's left lapel.*
> *He fingered the check and tried not to fall.*
> *Then rushed to the phone and*
> *promptly placed a call.*
>
> *He buckled up his dignity,*
> *refused to be the pawn.*
> *Smooch had found a spy nest at Too Fu Waun.*
> *They were selling out the country in*
> *a sleazy deal,*
> *for there on the pin was the Presidential Seal.*

The President indeed had a Teflon coating, for Smooch as it turned out was a friend. The call he placed was to the White House. After getting agreement from the President not to veto the senator's heartfelt bill for a deepwater port in Smooch's home state—Nebraska—the senator turned the pants, the coat, the lapel pin, and the check over to the White House.

Now the President and his people were going to get to the bottom of it. Harvey was assured that he would get full cooperation.

"I don't understand one thing," said Harvey. "How did the pin get there?"

"Presidential pins are given out as favors to friends and supporters. But those particular pins," said the President, "they were only given to members of my cabinet."

"Ahh." Suddenly Harvey understood.

"Too Fu Waun is an agent for a foreign government," said the President.

"How do you know that?"

"Trust me," said the chief, and winked at him again.

This time Harvey got it. It was national security. Details were being parceled out on a need-to-know basis. The President figured Harvey didn't need to know. In fact he said he didn't know himself. It was better that way. Then, if he was called before a federal grand jury, said the President, he couldn't be expected to remember what he never knew. To Harvey it all seemed very confusing. Still, he really didn't care.

What Harvey had in mind was
a pivotal maneuver
to find out where the bodies were,
like J. Edgar Hoover.
While some might believe this was
highly reprehensible,
one thing Harvey knew: it would
make him indispensable.

"We know that the suit belongs to one of my cabinet members. The problem is, we don't know which one. You can see my problem," said the President. "I can't exactly go around the table and ask which one of them's been committing treason."

"It would be a start," said Harvey.

"They'd lie to me."

"All of them?"

The President ignored the question and played his trump card. "If the press finds out, they'll have a field day."

"There you've got a point," said Harvey.

"What I need is for you to use your skills, your discretion, to find out who that suit belongs to." He pointed to a chair in the corner behind Harvey. There on a hanger covered in dark plastic hung the dreaded garment.

He shook Harvey's hand one final time, and led him to the door.

"This should be no problem for a top-notch lawyer like you. Like a walk in the park," said the President. "All in a day's work."

The man was very smooth, thought Harvey. He used your own pride like a crowbar for leverage.

As Harvey left the mansion, he realized too late
he didn't have a thing to prove
he'd met the chief of state.
Still, upon leaving he wasted no time.
He called Jersey Joe to help solve the crime.

THE SLIME

As Harvey assessed it, the matter was plain.
He'd turn it over to Jersey and avoid all the pain.
Joe was nimble and quick of mind;
why should Harvey waste his time?

In this case Jersey was up and running so fast that even Harvey was surprised. Within hours he had a plan, and was ready to go. It was almost as if he'd been waiting for Harvey to show up. But then this was no surprise. Jersey had a deceitful mind, the kind that always seemed to work overtime.

The plan was ingenious in its simplicity, artfully thought out and filled with duplicity. In short, it was a gem.

Jersey pretended to be a photographer doing a layout for *Gentlemen's Quarterly*. It was a piece on "The People of Power," something politicians couldn't resist. Dropping the names of a few movie stars who were also going to be in the piece as bait (Jersey found this opened doors), he began to work his way through the cabinet, visiting their homes and offices with cameras slung about his neck.

Of course he came armed with the ultimate "power suit." Every major world leader was wearing it. Hadn't they heard? The ripped sleeve was the latest thing from Italy.

Even if it didn't fit he wanted to see if the colors worked on them. As soon as it became a stretch to get on the coat, Jersey would move out, claiming he'd left his film behind, or needed better light. He would call another day, and bring his crew next time.

Two weeks went by and Harvey didn't hear a word from Jersey Joe. He was getting a little nervous, so he called. There was no answer from the man, so he left a message on his tape. Jersey had never failed him. Why would he start now?

Days went by and no call came back. Now he was getting worried. Harvey continued to pursue him for days, leaving messages and trying all of Jersey's haunts. He was becoming increasingly anxious. After all, the President was expecting results. It wouldn't do to keep him waiting.

> *Finally on a Friday night, he reached*
> *the man at home.*
> *Jersey was busy stretching his mind,*
> *working on a poem.*
> *Harvey peppered him with questions,*
> *and probed to get the news.*
> *Jersey put him off; he still had*
> *cabinet members to schmooze.*
> *Two of them were women, attractive*
> *and quite slinky.*
> *Maybe they wore men's suits sometimes,*
> *thinking it was kinky.*

Harvey had learned never to question Jersey Joe's tactics. The man was a master of deceit, well trained in the various forms of low ethics. Besides, he had a good point. It could indeed be a member of the fairer sex. After all, espionage was one of those crimes more in keeping with the female mind, not something manly and aboveboard—like embezzlement.

Even though he trusted Jersey, something prompted Harvey to poke around a little on his own. In later years he would often wonder what caused him to go to the laundry of Too Fu Waun. Maybe it was a sudden flash of mental telepathy. Harvey himself wasn't sure. Perhaps it was just that little nagging voice inside that told him something was wrong, not ethically wrong, but some detail out of place.

Waun's laundry was a dark place, and real steamy. It reminded Harvey of his last date at a drive-in as a teenager. As with the face of the girl he'd taken out, he could make out only faint images of the person on the other side of the counter. It was that hazy.

Harvey introduced himself and said he was checking on a missing piece of laundry. Then he described the pinstriped suit to a tee. He did everything but produce a picture.

"I get boss," said the man across the counter. He was obviously not the owner.

A moment later the steam evaporated as someone turned off a noisy piece of equipment in the back of the shop. Harvey was surprised. The man who approached did not appear to be Asian. Harvey wanted to see the man Waun himself. This guy was tall, a big man, and light-skinned like Harvey. He propped himself against the other side of the counter, looked over at Harvey, and smiled.

"Hi. I'm Harry Tool. Maybe I can help you."

Harvey looked him up and down, and refused to play the fool. "I'm looking for a missing suit. I'd like to talk to Mr. Waun."

The man smiled. "There is no Mr. Waun."

"If he's out, I can come back," said Harvey.

The guy looked at him. Now he was getting a little mean around the eyes. "I told you, there's no Mr. Waun."

"Right," said Harvey. "That's why his name is all over your window. And the plastic clothing covers." He picked one up off the counter, as if to make his point.

"I told you there's no Mr. Waun. Now if you got clothes to clean, fine. If not, there's the door."

Harvey'd spent a lifetime in court. He knew when someone was lying.

"Listen. All I'm looking for is a little information. Get rid of your help here and I can make it worth your while." Harvey nodded toward the Asian standing behind Tool.

Tool looked at his helper, but made no move to dismiss him.

Harvey lifted his wallet from his inside coat pocket and slid three twenty-dollar bills across the counter as a show of good faith.

Tool seemed mystified, but he still didn't dismiss the Asian. "I don't know what you want. What do you think I can tell you?"

"I simply want a couple of minutes with Mr. Waun."

Tool took the three bills and just like that slid them into his shirt pocket. All of this was done brazenly, right in front of the Asian help.

"Now what do you want to know?"

Harvey didn't want to talk in front of the help. After all, blood was thicker than water. Tool might sell out his boss. Harvey wasn't so sure about the Asian.

Tool didn't give him a choice. "You got two minutes of my time."

"You're telling me you're Mr. Waun?"

"No. But for sixty bucks I'll pretend."

"I paid you good money to see Mr. Waun."

"And I told you there is no Mr. Waun."

"Then what's his name doing . . . ?"

"It's a sales gimmick. Don't you get it?" said the man. "Too Fu Waun." Harvey still didn't understand.

"Two for one," said the man. "You get two suits cleaned and pressed for the price of one."

Harvey forced a smile, but there was a sinking feeling in his stomach, like there was something sick deep down inside. For a second he thought Tool might be lying. But "two for one"? That was too lame to be made up. He swallowed hard, and tried to look cool. Then he did the only thing he could think of. He described the pinstriped suit one more time in hopes that Tool would remember it.

"We get a lot of pinstriped suits," said Tool. "You'd have to be more specific."

Suddenly there was a glow of recognition, not from the man Tool, but instead from his assistant:

"Ah, yes belong to President you know,
Secret Service come looking for it,
the day after it go."

Harvey's eyes got wide and his throat got dry. An electric charge flashed through him like the confusion of a deer when the lights hit him, in that instant before the bumper arrives.

Without another word, he left the shop of Too Fu Waun and in a panic started running down the street toward his car. Harvey had to get away. He had to find Jersey Joe.

Before he could get to his car, two men stepped out of a side alley. One of them flashed credentials in a wallet.

"FBI. You're under arrest. You have a right to remain silent. Anything you say can be used against you . . ."

While the one man read Harvey his rights, the other cuffed Harvey's hands behind his back. Instantly a dark car pulled up at the curb, and the two men pushed him roughly into the backseat.

Harvey's brain struggled to take it all in. He sat in the back of the car in a daze, and stared out the window at the crowd that was assembling to gawk at the caged criminal the FBI had just arrested.

It was like an out-of-body experience, as if he were floating somewhere in space over the dark unmarked car. Harvey couldn't believe that this was happening to him.

IN HARVEY'S CASE, justice was swift and the trial very quick. Because it involved espionage and national security, it was closed to the public and the press.

In deference to his high office, the President was allowed to testify on a special closed-circuit television hookup. He was a very busy man. The fate of the nation was in his hands.

His cross-examination was televised from Camp David and lasted only twenty-five minutes. On the big screen, as Harvey watched, the President explained that he had a pressing engagement.

To Harvey it seemed that he emitted an almost sinister smile as he said the word *pressing*. He was meeting with the Premier of China and some Asian business leaders for an important round of golf. And afterward they were going to discuss a number of important foreign-trade issues.

Harvey knew what kind of "trading" was going on. He had everything but the evidence.

The government's case against Harvey was straightforward and clear. The FBI claimed they caught him in the act, exiting the forbidden Chinese laundry where the infamous suit with the check in the pocket had been laundered. According to the government, he was trying to cover his tracks. Harvey, they said, was the leader of an infamous spy ring.

The President filled in the last missing piece of this puzzle: the notorious lapel pin bearing the Presidential Seal. Yes, he did recall it. It was truly a collector's item. You see, there were only four of them in this style that had ever been made, at the President's own personal expense, of course.

They'd been given only to generous campaign contributors, people who had slept in the Lincoln Bedroom. The other three were all accounted for. The only one that was missing was the pin given to Harvey.

Of course this was a lie. Harvey knew the truth, but how could he prove it? The President had carefully laid the trap and covered all the tracks. It was the reason he'd seized on Harvey in that very first reception. It wasn't because of Harvey's generosity, or the fact that they were spirits of a kind. It was because of Harvey's size and build. The President realized that his suit, the one his valet had stupidly delivered to the laundry with the check still in the pocket, and which had mistakenly been returned to the senate cloakroom, would fit Harvey perfectly.

The President had found his pigeon—and just like the public, he had Harvey eating out of his hands. Now Harvey would pay the price.

The final insult came when the defense put on its case. Harvey called Jersey Joe to the stand. It was his only chance. After all, Jersey was the one person who knew the truth—that Harvey had been framed by the President.

Jersey took the stand, put his hand on the Bible, and swore he'd tell the truth.

"Have you ever seen this suit before?" The lawyer held it up in a clear plastic bag.

"Nope." Just like that. Without hesitation.

Harvey's lawyer was flabbergasted. Harvey was stunned.

"You do know this man?" The lawyer pointed to Harvey sitting at the counsel table.

Jersey squinted from the stand, lifted his glasses to look closely at Harvey.

"He looks like somebody who might have invited me to his office once a long time ago, but I can't be sure."

Jersey hesitated for a moment.

"No. On second thought, I don't think I've ever seen him before. In fact I'm sure of it."

Harvey's head fell into his hands at the table. He was lost.

It wouldn't be until months later, long after Harvey was sentenced, that he finally discovered what happened. Jersey Joe had been named Commissioner of the Internal Revenue Service.

It was a new twist on an old story—"The Emperor's New Clothes." Only in this case it was Harvey who'd been caught in his BVD's.

Espionage carries a lifetime term,
so Harvey had time to sit and squirm.
The cell was cold and the other cons were scary.
Harvey wasn't getting out until
the 30th of February.
The President had gotten to Jersey Joe.
Harvey'd been betrayed; a very low blow.
He had many years to think about ethics.
The age-old question: was it social or genetics?

Harvey and the President were the same size.
They shared a lot of other things,
the same color eyes.

If Harvey knew the truth,
he wouldn't be so bitter.
He was made of sterner stuff. He was no quitter.

He and the President both had been adopted.
It wasn't through bad friends that
they'd been co-opted.
They shared one feature that neither
man could know;
they'd inherited their morals from
their dad, Jersey Joe.

A VERY MERRY CHRISTMAS

Ed McBain

The word "prolific" has been used to describe Ed McBain so many times you might think it was part of his name. Mr. Ed "Prolific" McBain. But there's no denying that McBain—aka Evan Hunter—has amassed a body of work that stuns the senses when one sits down to reckon with it. That so much of it is excellent, and that some of it is possessed of true genius, and that every single piece of it makes for enjoyable reading is a testament to the man's prowess as an author. He is like watching a world-class boxer at his peak; he knows all the moves. Because of such bestsellers as *The Blackboard Jungle* and *A Matter of Conviction*, his early fame was for his mainstream novels. But over the years he became better known for the 87th Precinct series. It's impossible to choose the "best" of the 87th books—there are just too many good ones—but one might suggest a peek at *He Who Hesitates* (1965), *Blood Relatives* (1975), *Long Time No See* (1977) and *The Big Bad City* (1999). He wrote the screenplay of *The Birds* for Alfred Hitchcock and his powerful novel *Last Summer* became one of the seminal films of the seventies. His recent novels include another 87th Precinct book, *The Last Dance*.

SITTING AT THE bar, Pete Charpens looked at his own reflection in the mirror, grinned, and said, "Merry Christmas."

It was not Christmas yet, true enough, but he said it anyway, and the words sounded good, and he grinned foolishly and lifted his drink and sipped a little of it and said again, "Merry Christmas," feeling very good, feeling very warm, feeling in excellent high spirits. Tonight, the city was his. Tonight, for the first time since he'd arrived from Whiting Center eight months ago, he felt like a part of the city. Tonight, the city enveloped him like a warm bath, and he lounged back and allowed the undulating waters to cover him. It was Christmas Eve, and all was right with the world, and Pete Charpens loved every mother's son who roamed the face of the earth because he felt as if he'd finally come home, finally found the place, finally found himself.

It was a good feeling.

This afternoon, as soon as the office party was over, he'd gone into the streets. The shop windows had gleamed like pot-bellied stoves, cherry hot against the sharp bite of the air. There was a promise of snow in the sky, and Pete had walked the tinseled streets of New York with his tweed coat collar against the back of his neck, and he had felt warm and happy. There were shoppers in the streets, and Santa Clauses with bells, and giant wreaths and giant trees, and music coming from speakers, the timeless carols of the holiday season. But more than that, he had felt the pulse beat of the city. For the first time in eight months, he had felt the pulse beat of the city, the people, the noise, the clutter, the rush, and above all the warmth. The warmth had engulfed him, surprising him. He had watched it with the foolish smile of a spectator and then, with sudden realization, he had known he was a part of it. In the short space of eight months, he had become a part of the city—and the city had become a part of him. He had found a home.

"Bartender," he said.

The bartender ambled over. He was a big red-headed man with freckles all over his face. He moved with economy and grace. He seemed like a very nice guy who probably had a very nice wife and family decorating a Christmas tree somewhere in Queens.

"Yes, sir?" he asked.

"Pete. Call me Pete."

"Okay, Pete."

"I'm not drunk," Pete said, "believe me. I know all drunks say that, but I mean it. I'm just so damn happy I could bust. Did you ever feel that way?"

"Sure," the bartender said, smiling.

"Let me buy you a drink."

"I don't drink."

"Bartenders never drink, I know, but let me buy you one. Please. Look, I want to thank people, you know? I want to thank everybody in this city. I want to thank them for being here, for making it a city. Do I sound nuts?"

"Yes," the bartender said.

"Okay. Okay then, I'm nuts. But I'm a hick, do you know? I came here from Whiting Center eight months ago. Straw sticking out of my ears. The confusion here almost killed me. But I got a job, a good job, and I met a lot of wonderful people, and I learned how to dress, and I . . . I found a home. That's corny. I know it. That's the hick in me talking. But I love this damn city, I *love* it. I want to go around kissing girls in the streets. I want to shake hands with every guy I meet. I want to tell them I feel like a person, a human being, I'm alive, alive! For Christ's sake, I'm alive!"

"That's a good way to be," the bartender agreed.

"I know it. Oh, my friend, do I know it! I was dead in Whiting Center, and now I'm here and alive and . . . look, let me buy you a drink, huh?"

"I don't drink," the bartender insisted.

"Okay. Okay, I won't argue. I wouldn't argue with anyone tonight. Gee, it's gonna be a great Christmas, do you know? Gee, I'm so damn happy I could bust." He laughed aloud, and the bartender laughed with him. The laugh trailed off into a chuckle, and then a smile. Pete looked into the mirror, lifted his glass again, and again said, "Merry Christmas. Merry Christmas."

He was still smiling when the man came into the bar and sat down next to him. The man was very tall, his body bulging with power beneath the suit he wore. Coatless, hatless, he came into the bar and sat alongside Pete, signaling for the bartender with a slight flick of his hand. The bartender walked over.

"Rye neat," the man said.

The bartender nodded and walked away. The man reached for his wallet.

"Let me pay for it." Pete said.

The man turned. He had a wide face with a thick nose and small brown eyes. The eyes came as a surprise in his otherwise large body. He studied Pete for a moment and then said, "You a queer or something?"

Pete laughed. "Hell, no," he said. "I'm just happy. It's Christmas Eve, and I feel like buying you a drink."

The man pulled out his wallet, put a five dollar bill on the bar top and said, "I'll buy my own drink." He paused. "What's the matter? Don't I look as if I can afford a drink?"

"Sure you do," Pete said. "I just wanted to . . . look, I'm happy. I want to share it, that's all."

The man grunted and said nothing. The bartender brought his drink. He tossed off the shot and asked for another.

"My name's Pete Charpens," Pete said, extending his hand.

"So what?" the man said.

"Well . . . what's your name?"

"Frank."

"Glad to know you, Frank." He thrust his hand closer to the man.

"Get lost, Happy," Frank said.

Pete grinned, undismayed. "You ought to relax," he said, "I mean it. You know, you've got to stop . . ."

"Don't tell me what I've got to stop. Who the hell are you, anyway?"

"Pete Charpens. I told you."

"Take a walk, Pete Charpens. I got worries of my own."

"Want to tell me about them?"

"No, I don't want to tell you about them."

"Why not? Make you feel better."

"Go to hell, and stop bothering me," Frank said.

The bartender brought the second drink. He sipped at it, and then put the shot glass on the bar top.

"Do I look like a hick?" Pete asked.

"You look like a goddamn queer," Frank said.

"No, I mean it."

"You asked me, and I told you."

"What's troubling you, Frank?"

"You a priest or something?"

"No, but I thought . . ."

"Look, I come in here to have a drink. I didn't come to see the chaplain."

"You an ex-Army man?"

"Yeah."

"I was in the Navy," Pete said. "Glad to be out of that, all right. Glad to be right here where I am, in the most wonderful city in the whole damn world."

"Go down to Union Square and get a soap box," Frank said.

"Can't I help you, Frank?" Pete asked. "Can't I buy you a drink, lend you an ear, do something? You're so damn sad, I feel like . . ."

"I'm not sad."

"You sure look sad. What happened? Did you lose your job?"

"No, I didn't lose my job."

"What do you do, Frank?"

"Right now, I'm a truck driver. I used to be a fighter."

"Really? You mean a boxer? No kidding?"

"Why would I kid you?"

"What's your last name?"

"Blake."

"Frank Blake? I don't think I've heard it before. Of course, I didn't follow the fights much."

"Tiger Blake, they called me. That was my ring name."

"Tiger Blake. Well, we didn't have fights in Whiting Center. Had to go over to Waterloo if we wanted to see a bout. I guess that's why I never heard of you."

"Sure," Frank said.

"Why'd you quit fighting?"

"They made me."

"Why?"

"I killed a guy in 1947."

Pete's eyes widened. "In the ring?"

"Of course in the ring. What the hell kind of a moron are you, anyway? You think I'd be walking around if it wasn't in the ring? Jesus!"

"Is that what's troubling you?"

"There ain't nothing troubling me. I'm fine."

"Are you going home for Christmas?"

"I got no home."

"You must have a home," Pete said gently. "*Everybody's* got a home."

"Yeah? Where's your home? Whiting Center or wherever the hell you said?"

"Nope. This is my home now. New York City. New York, New York. The greatest goddamn city in the whole world."

"Sure," Frank said sourly.

"My folks are dead," Pete said. "I'm an only child. Nothing for me in Whiting Center anymore. But in New York, well, I get the feeling that I'm here to stay. That I'll meet a nice girl here, and marry her, and raise a family here and . . . and this'll be home."

"Great," Frank said sourly.

"How'd you happen to kill this fellow?" Pete asked suddenly.

"I hit him."

"And killed him?"

"I hit him on the Adam's apple. Accidentally."

"Were you sore at him?"

"We were in the ring. I already told you that."

"Sure, but were you sore?"

"A fighter don't have to be sore. He's paid to fight."

"Did you like fighting?"

"I loved it," Frank said flatly.

"How about the night you killed that fellow?"

Frank was silent for a long time. Then he said, "Get lost, huh?"

"I could never fight for money," Pete said. "I got a quick temper, and I get mad as hell, but I could never do it for money. Besides, I'm too happy right now to . . ."

"Get lost," Frank said again, and he turned his back. Pete sat silently for a moment.

"Frank?" he said at last.

"You back again?"

"I'm sorry. I shouldn't have talked to you about something that's painful to you. Look, it's Christmas Eve. Let's . . ."

"Forget it."

"Can I buy you a drink?"

"No. I told you no a hundred times. I buy my own damn drinks!"

"This is Christmas E . . ."

"I don't care what it is. You happy jokers give me the creeps. Get off my back, will you?"

"I'm sorry. I just . . ."

"Happy, happy, happy. Grinning like a damn fool. What the hell is there to be so happy about? You got an oil well someplace? A gold mine? What is it with you?"

"I'm just . . ."

"You're just a jerk! I probably pegged you right the minute I laid eyes on you. You're probably a damn queer."

"No, no," Pete said mildly. "You're mistaken, Frank. Honestly, I just feel . . ."

"Your old man was probably a queer, too. Your old lady probably took on every sailor in town."

The smile left Pete's face, and then tentatively reappeared. "You don't mean that, Frank," he said.

"I mean everything I ever say," Frank said. There was a strange gleam in his eyes. He studied Pete carefully.

"About my mother, I meant," Pete said.

"I know what you're talking about. And I'll say it again. She probably took on every sailor in town."

"Don't say that, Frank," Pete said, the smile gone now, a perplexed frown teasing his forehead, appearing, vanishing, reappearing.

"You're a queer, and your old lady was a . . ."

"Stop it, Frank."

"Stop what? If your old lady was . . ."

Pete leaped off the bar stool. "Cut it out!" he yelled.

From the end of the bar, the bartender turned. Frank caught the movement with the corner of his eye. In a cold whisper, he said, "Your mother was a slut," and Pete swung at him.

Frank ducked, and the blow grazed the top of his head. The bartender was coming towards them now. He could not see the strange light in Frank's eyes, nor did he hear Frank whisper again, "A slut, a slut."

Pete pushed himself off the bar wildly. He saw the beer bottle then, picked it up, and lunged at Frank.

THE PATROLMAN KNELT near his body.

"He's dead, all right," he said. He stood up and dusted off his trousers. "What happened?"

Frank looked bewildered and dazed. "He went berserk," he said. "We were sitting and talking. Quiet. All of a sudden, he swings at me." He turned to the bartender. "Am I right?"

"He was drinking," the bartender said. "Maybe he was drunk."

"I didn't even swing back," Frank said, "not until he picked up the beer bottle. Hell, this is Christmas Eve. I didn't want no trouble."

"What happened when he picked up the bottle?"

"He swung it at me. So I . . . I put up my hands to defend myself. I only gave him a push, so help me."

"Where'd you hit him?"

Frank paused. "In . . . in the throat, I think." He paused again. "It was self-defense, believe me. This guy just went berserk. He musta been a maniac."

"He *was* talking kind of queer," the bartender agreed.

The patrolman nodded sympathetically. "There's more nuts outside than there is in," he said. He turned to Frank. "Don't take this so bad, Mac. You'll get off. It looks open and shut to me. Just tell them the story downtown, that's all."

"Berserk," Frank said. "He just went berserk."

"Well . . ." The patrolman shrugged. "My partner'll take care of the meat wagon when it gets here. You and me better get downtown. I'm sorry I got to ruin your Christmas, but . . ."

"It's *him* that ruined it," Frank said, shaking his head and looking down at the body on the floor.

Together, they started out of the bar. At the door, the patrolman waved to the bartender and said, "Merry Christmas, Mac."

AMONG MY SOUVENIRS

Sharyn McCrumb

Sharyn McCrumb, who holds degrees from the University of North Carolina and Virginia Tech, lives in Virginia's Blue Ridge Mountains but travels the United States and the world lecturing on her work, most recently leading a writers' workshop in Paris in the summer of 2001.

McCrumb's Ballad series, beginning with *If I Ever Return, Pretty Peggy-O* (1990), has won her numerous honors, including the Appalachian Writers Association's Award for Outstanding Contribution to Appalachian Literature and several listings as the *New York Times* and the *Los Angeles Times* notable books. In the introduction to her short-story collection *Foggy Mountain Breakdown and Other Stories* (1997), she details the family history in North Carolina and Tennessee that contributed to her Appalachian fiction. One of the continuing characters, Sheriff Spencer Arrowood, takes his surname from ancestors on her father's side, while Frankie Silver ("the first woman hanged for murder in the state of North Carolina"), whose story McCrumb would incorporate in *The Ballad of Frankie Silver* (1998), was a distant cousin. "My books are like Appalachian quilts," she writes. "I take brightly colored scraps of legends, ballads, fragments of rural life, and local tragedy, and I place them together into a complex whole that tells not only a story, but also a deeper truth about the nature of the mountain south." The sixth and most recent title in the series, *The Songcatcher*, appeared in the summer of 2001.

THE FACE WAS a little blurry, but she was used to seeing it that way. She must have looked at it a thousand times in old magazines—grainy black-and-white shots, snapped by a magazine photographer at a nightclub; amateurish candid photos on the back of record albums; misty publicity stills that erased even the pores of his skin. She knew that face. A poster-size version of it had stared down at her from beneath the high school banner on her bedroom wall—twenty-odd years ago. God, had it been that long? Now the face was blurry with booze, fatigue, and the sagging of a jawline that was no longer boyish. But it was still him, sitting in the bar, big as life.

Maggie used to wonder what she would do if she met him in the flesh. In the tenth grade she and Kathy Ryan used to philosophize about such things at slumber parties: "Why don't you fix your hair like Connie Stevens'?"—"Which Man From U.N.C.L.E. do you like best?"—"What would you do if you met Devlin Robey?" Then they'd collapse in giggles, unable even to fantasize meeting a real, live rock 'n' roll singer. He lived a glamorous life of limousines and penthouse suites while they suffered through gym class, and algebra with Mrs. Cady. Growing up seemed a hundred years away.

When Maggie was a senior, she did get to see Devlin Robey—when you live on Long Island, sooner or later your prince will come. Everybody comes to the Big Apple. But the encounter was as distant and unreal as the airbrushed poster on her closet door. Devlin Robey was a shining blur glimpsed on a distant stage, and Maggie was a tiny speck in a sea of scream-ing adolescents. She and Kathy squealed and cried and threw paper roses at the stage, but it didn't really feel like *seeing* him. He was a lot clearer on the television screen when she watched *American Bandstand*. After the concert, they had fought their way through a horde of fans to reach the stage door, only to be driven off by three thugs in overcoats—Mr. Robey's "handlers," while Devlin himself plowed his way through the throng to a waiting lim-ousine, oblivious to the screams of protest in his wake.

They cried all the way home.

Maggie was so disillusioned by her idol's callous behavior that she wrote him a letter, in care of his record company, complaining about how he let his fans be treated. She enclosed her ticket stub from the concert, and one of her wallet-size class pictures. A few weeks later, she received an au-tographed eight by ten of Devlin Robey, a copy of his latest album, and a handwritten apology on Epic Records notepaper. He said he was sorry to rush past them like that, but that he'd had to hurry back to the hotel to call his mother, who had been ill that night. He hoped that Maggie would for-give him for his thoughtlessness, and he promised to visit with his fans af-ter concerts whenever he possibly could.

That letter was enough magic to keep Maggie going for weeks, and she played the album until it was scarred from wear, but eventually the wonder of it faded, and the memory, like the albums and fan magazines, was packed away in tissue paper in the closet of her youth, while Maggie got on with her life.

She took business courses, and made mostly B's. She thought she'd probably end up as a secretary somewhere after high school. It was no use thinking about college: her parents didn't have that kind of money, and if they had, they wouldn't have spent it sending her off to get more educated. Since she'd just end up getting married anyway, her father reasoned, wasting her time and their savings on a fancy education made no sense. Maggie wished she could have taken shop or auto mechanics like the guys did, but the guidance counselor had smiled and vetoed the suggestion. Home economics and typing: that's what girls took. He was sure that Maggie would be happier in one of those courses, where she belonged. Now, sometimes, when the plumbing needed fixing or the toaster wouldn't work, Maggie wished she had insisted on being allowed to take practical courses, so that she wouldn't have to use the grocery money to pay repair bills, but it was no use looking back, she figured. What's done was done.

The summer after high school, Maggie married Leon Holtz, who wasn't as handsome as Devlin Robey, but he was real. He said he loved her, and he rented a sky-blue tux and bought her a white gardenia corsage when he took her to the senior prom. There wasn't any reason not to get married, that Maggie could see. Leon had a construction job in his uncle's business, and she was a clerk at the Ford dealership, which meant nearly six hundred a month in take-home pay after taxes. They could afford a small apartment, and some furniture from Sofa City, so why wait? If Maggie had any flashes of prewedding jitters about happily-ever-after with Leon, or any lingering regrets at relinquishing dreams of some other existence, where one could actually know people like Devlin Robey—if she had misgivings about any of it, she gave no sign.

Richie was born fourteen months later. The marriage lasted until he was two. He was a round-faced, solemn child with his mother's brown eyes, but he had scoliosis—which is doctor talk for a crook-back—so there were medical bills on top of everything else, and finally, Leon, fed up with the confinement of wedded poverty, took off. Maggie moved to Manhattan, because she figured the pay would be better, especially if she forgot about being a clerk. She was just twenty-one, then, and her looks were still okay.

After a couple of false starts, she got a job as a cocktail waitress in the Red Lion Lounge. She didn't like the red velvet uniform that came to the top of her thighs, or the black net stockings she had to wear with it, but the tips were good, and Maggie supposed that the outfit had a lot to do with that. She was twenty-seven now. Sometimes, when her feet throbbed from spending six hours in spike heels and her face ached from smiling at jerks who like to put the make on waitresses, she'd think about the high school shop classes, wondering what life would have been like if she'd learned how to fix cars.

"You want to bring me a drink?" He smiled up at her lazily. The ladies man who is sure of his magnetism. *You want to bring me a drink?* Like he was conferring a privilege on her. Well, maybe he was. Maggie looked down at Devlin Robey's blurring middle-aged features, and thought with surprise that once she would have been honored to serve this man. Would have fought for the chance to do it. But that was half a lifetime ago. Now she was just tired, trying to get through the shift with enough money to pay the phone bill. She'd been up most of the night before with one of Richie's back aches, and now she felt as if she were sleepwalking. She stared at the graying curls of chest hair at the top of his purple shirt, the pouches under his eyes that were darker than his fading tan, and the plastic smile. What the hell.

"Sure," she said with no more than her customary brightness, "A drink. What do you want?"

When she brought back the Dewar's-rocks, he was reading the racing news, but as she approached, he set the page aside and smiled up at her. "Thanks," he said, and then after a beat: "You know who I am?"

It struck her as kind of sad the way he asked it. Hesitant, like he had heard "no" too many times lately, as if each denial of his fame cut the lines deeper into his face. She felt sorry for him. Wished it were twenty years ago. But it wasn't. "Yeah," said Maggie, smoothing out the napkin as she set down his drink. "Yeah, I remember. You're Devlin Robey. I seen you sing once."

The lines smoothed out and his eyes widened: you could just see the teen idol somewhere in there. "No kiddin'!" he said, with a laugh that sounded like sheer relief. "Well, here . . ." That ought to be good for a twenty, Maggie was thinking, but as she watched, Devlin Robey pulled the cocktail napkin out from under his drink and signed his name with a flourish.

"Thanks," said Maggie, slipping the napkin into her pocket with the tips. Maybe the twenty would come later. At least it would be something to tell Kathy Ryan if she ever saw her again. She started to move away to another table, but he touched her arm. "Don't leave yet. So, you heard me sing, huh? At Paradise Alley?"

She told him where the concert had been, and for a moment she thought of mentioning her letter to him, but the two suits at table nine were waving like their tongues might shrivel up, so she eased out of his grasp. "I'll check on you in a few," she promised, summoning her smile for the thirsting suits.

For the rest of her shift, Maggie alternated between real customers and the wistful face of Devlin Robey, who ordered drinks just for the small talk that came with them. "Which one of my songs did you like best?"

" 'I'm Afraid to Go Home,' " said Maggie instantly, and when he looked puzzled, she reminded him, "It was the B side to 'Tiger Lily.' "

"Yeah! Yeah! I almost got an award for that one." His eyes crinkled with pleasure.

Another round he wanted to know if she'd seen him in the beach movie he made for Buena Vista. She remembered the movie, and didn't say that she couldn't place him in it. It had been a bit part, leading nowhere. After that he went back to singing, mostly in Vegas. Now in Atlantic City. "They love me in the casinos," he told her. "The folks from the 'burbs go wild over me—makes 'em remember the good times, they tell me."

Maggie tried to remember some good times, but all she found was stills of her and Kathy Ryan listening to records and talking about the future. She was going to be a fashion model and live in Paris. Kathy would be a vet in an African Wildlife Preserve. They would spend holidays together in the Bahamas. "You want some peanuts to go with that drink?" Maggie asked.

At two o'clock the Red Lion was closing, but Devlin Robey had not budged. He kept nursing a Dewar's that was more water than Scotch, hunched down like a stray dog who didn't want to be thrown out in the street. Maggie wondered what was wrong with the guy. He was rich and famous, right?

"Are you about finished with that drink? Boss says it's quittin' time."

"Yeah, yeah. I'm a night owl, I guess. All those years of doing casino shows at eleven. Seems like the shank of the evening to me." He glanced at his watch, and then at her: the red velvet tunic, the black fishnet stockings, the cleavage. "You're getting off work now?"

The smile never wavered but inside she groaned. Tonight had seemed about two days long, and all that kept her going was the thought of a hot bubble bath to soak her feet and the softness of clean sheets to sink into before she passed out from sheer weariness. So now—twenty years too late to be an answer to prayer—Devlin Robey wants to take her out. Where was he when it would have mattered?

"I'm sorry," she said. "Thanks anyway, but not tonight." *Maybe ten years ago, but not tonight.*

The one answer she wouldn't have made back when she was Devlin Robey's vestal virgin turned out to be the only one that worked the charm.

Suddenly his halfhearted invitation became urgent. "I'll be straight with you," he said, with eyes like stained glass. "I'm feeling kind of down tonight, and I thought it might help to spend some time with an old friend."

Is that what we were? Maggie thought. *I was twenty-five rows back at the concert; I was on the other side of the speakers when WABC's Cousin Brucie played your records; and while you were airbrushed and glossy, I was wearing Clearasil and holding the fan magazine. We were friends?* She didn't say it, though. If Maggie had learned anything in seven years as a cocktail waitress, it was not to reply to outrageous statements. She shrugged. "I'm sorry," thinking that would be the end of it. Wondering if she'd even bother to tell anybody about it. It wouldn't be any fun to talk about if you had to explain to the other waitresses, bunch of kids, who Devlin Robey was.

"At least give me your phone number—uh—Maggie." Her name was signed with a flourish on his check: *Thank you! Maggie.* "I get to the city every so often. Maybe I could call you, give you more notice. We could set something up. You're all right. You ever think about the business?"

No. Show business offered the same hours as nightclub waitressing, and besides she couldn't sing or dance. But Lana Turner had been discovered in a drugstore, so maybe . . . After all, who was Maggie Holtz to slap the hand of fate? She tore off the business expense tab from the Red Lion check, and scribbled her name and phone number across it. "Sure. Why not," she said. "Call me sometime."

She patted the autographed cocktail napkin folded in the pocket with her tips, wondering if Richie would like to have it for his scrapbook. Or maybe she should put it in his baby book: *the guy I was pretending to make it with the night you were conceived.* Two scraps of paper; one for each of them to toss. She figured that would be the end of it.

It wasn't, though. Four nights later—four a.m.—the Advil had finally kicked in, allowing her to plunge into sleep, when the phone screamed, dragging her back. She'd forgotten to turn on the damned answering machine. She grabbed for the receiver, only to reinstate the silence, but his voice came through to her, a little swacked, crooning, "I'm Afraid to Go Home," and she knew it was him.

"Devlin Robey," she said, wondering why wishes got granted only when you no longer wanted them.

"Maggie doll." He slurred her name. "I just wanted a friendly voice. I got the blues so bad."

"Hangover?"

"No. That'll be after I wake up—if I ever get to sleep, that is. Thought I might get sleepy talking about old times, you know?"

"Old times."

"I lost big tonight at the tables. I played seventeen in roulette a dozen times and it wouldn't come up for me. Seventeen—my number!"

She caught herself nodding forward, and forced the number seventeen to roll around in her memories. Oh, yeah. " 'Seventeen, My Heaven Teen,' " she murmured. "That was your big hit, wasn't it?"

"I got a Cashbox Award for that one. S'in the den at my place in Vegas. Maybe I'll show it to you some time."

"Wouldn't your wife object?"

She heard him sigh. "Jeez, Trina. What a cow. She was a showgirl when I married her. Ninety-five pounds of blonde. Now she acts like giving me a blow job is a major act of charity, and she's in the tanning salon so much she looks like a leather Barbie doll. Not that I'm home much. I'm on the road a lot."

"Yeah. It's a tough life." She pictured him in a suite the size of her apartment. Maybe one of those sunken tubs in a black marble bathroom.

"It's not like I'm too keen to go home, you know? I have a daughter, Claudia, but jeez it breaks my heart to see her. She was born premature. Probably 'cause Trina was always trying to barf up her dinner to stay skinny. She's never been right, Claudia hasn't. Brain damage at birth. But she always smiles so big when she sees me, and throws her little arms out."

"How old is she?"

"Twelve, I guess. I always picture her when she was little. She was beautiful when she was three all over. Now she's just three inside. Her birthday is the seventeenth of June. My lucky number. Seventeen."

"Not tonight, though, huh?"

"No. Tonight it cost me plenty. I shouldn't bet when I'm loaded. Loaded drunk, I mean; the other kind is never an issue. I like to be with people, though. I'd like to be with you. You don't have an ax to grind. You're not like these glitter tarts here, running around in feathers, can't remember past nineteen-seventy-five. You're good people, Maggie. Look, can I come over some time?"

"I bet you get lotsa offers," said Maggie, hoping somebody else would take the heat.

"I like you," he said. "You're real. Like my kid. Not just some hardass in the chorus line with a Pepsodent smile and an angle. I've had a bellyful of them."

She shouldn't have let him tell her about his kid. It made her think of

Richie, and made her think that maybe Devlin Robey hadn't had it all his way like she'd figured. All of a sudden, he wasn't just some glossy poster that she could toss when she tired of it. He was a regular guy with feelings. And maybe she owed him. After all, she had used him as her fantasy all those years ago. Maybe it was time to pay up.

"Okay, like Tuesday? That's when I'm off." She could send Richie to her folks in Rockaway. They kept talking until his voice slurred into unconsciousness.

"**Y**OUR MONOGAMOUS JOHN is here," said Cap the bartender, nodding toward table seven.

"Yeah," said Maggie. She'd already seen Devlin Robey come in, trying to look casual. He came three days a month now, whenever he could get away from his casino gig. Sometimes it was her night off, and if it wasn't, he'd sit at number seven until closing time, nursing a Dewar's-water, and trying to keep a conversation going as Maggie edged her way past to wait on the paying customers.

On her nights off, they'd eat Italian, which meant mostly vino for Devlin Robey, and then go back to her place for sex. Robey was only good for once a night, so he liked to prolong it with kinky stuff, strip shows, and listening to Maggie talk dirty, which she found she could do while her mind focused on planning her grocery list for the coming week, and thinking what she needed to take to the cleaners. She felt sorry for Robey, because he had been famous once, and the coddling he received as a star had crippled him for life. He couldn't get used to people not being kind anymore; to being ignored by all the regular folks who used to envy him. Whereas she'd had a lifetime of getting used to the world's indifference. But he had been her idol, and he had once stooped down to be kind to her, a nobody, with a beautiful, sincere handwritten letter. So now he needed somebody, so it was Payback. And Payback is a Mother. She thought about how famous he was while he grunted and strained on top of her. She pictured that airbrushed poster on her wall.

"Maybe you should charge him," said Cap, as she was about to walk away.

"I ain't on the game," said Maggie.

"Didn't say you were. But you're providing a service. Shrinks charge, don't they? And they got more money than you, Maggie dearest."

She shrugged. "Some things aren't about money."

"Well, if money is no object with you, you can leave early tonight. You might as well. It's dead in here."

He said it too loud. Devlin Robey heard him, and she saw his face light up. No use telling him she was stuck here now. Thanks a heap, Cap. At least Richie was gone—sleeping over at Kevin's tonight. Devlin Robey was already putting his coat on by the time she reached his table. "Boy, am I glad we can get outta here! I'm afraid I might have company tonight."

His face was even more like a fish belly than usual, and his eyes sagged into dark pouches. "What do you mean, company?" asked Maggie, glancing toward the door.

"Tell you later."

They went to a different Italian restaurant, but it had the same oilcloth table covers, and the same vino, which he drank in equal quantities to the usual stuff, and she had the angel hair pasta, less rubbery than that of the old place. He wouldn't talk about *company*, while they were eating, but he kept looking around, and he whispered, even when he was just talking to her. She had to get him back to her place—in a cab, because he was scared to walk—and get two cups of black decaf down him, before he'd open up.

"Tell me," she said, and she wasn't being Fantasy Girl this time.

"It's okay." He took a thick brown envelope out of the breast pocket of his suit, and laid it on top of the stack of *Redbook* and *Enquirers*. "I got it covered, see? Most of it anyhow. I think it's enough to call the dogs off."

"You've been gambling again," she said.

"Hey, sooner or later 'Seventeen' will sing for me again, right?"

"So you owe some pretty heavy people, I guess."

He shrugged, palms up. "It's Atlantic City. They're not Boy Scouts. I was supposed to meet them tonight with the cash, but I was a little short. Had to come up here, hock some things. Borrow what I could from a home boy, and hope I got it together before they came looking for me. Now I'm okay. I can take the meeting. It's not all there, but it's enough to keep me going. I wrote a note with it, promising more next week. I got record royalties coming."

Maggie's eyes narrowed. "Why'd you want to see me?"

"Not for money!" He laughed a little. "Maggie, this is way out of your league, doll. You just keep your stash in that cookie jar of yours, and let me worry about these gentlemen. I just came to see you 'cause I love you."

He probably does, Maggie thought sadly as she led him to the bedroom. He can see the reflection of the record album poster in my eyes.

IT WAS PAST two when she got up to take a leak. Robey had been asleep for hours, sated with sweat and swear words. She saw the envelope lying on the coffee table, and scooped it up as she passed. Might as well see how deep he's in, she thought. Was saving a fallen idol part of the deal? Maybe she could talk him into getting counseling. Gamblers Anonymous, or something. She wondered why dead and famous were the only two choices some people seemed to want.

She didn't go back to bed. When Robey woke up at nine, she gave him aspirin and Bloody Mary Mix for his hangover, and a plastic cup of decaf for the road, but no kiss. He was headed back to Atlantic City, still too sleepy and hung over for pleasantries. Devlin Robey was not a morning person. Neither was Maggie Holtz, but this morning she was wide awake. She sat in front of the television, listening to the game shows, but watching the phone. It rang at five past noon. The answering machine kicked in, and after it said its piece, she heard Devlin Robey's famous, not-so-velvet voice, now shrill in the speaker. "Maggie! Are you there? Pick up! It's me. Listen, you know that envelope I told you about? The one with the cash in it. Listen, I must have left it at your place. There are some gentlemen here who need to know I had it. Could you just pick up, Maggie? Could you tell them about the cash in the envelope, please? It's important."

She heard another voice say, "Real important."

Maggie picked up the phone. "I never saw any envelope, Devlin," she said. "Can't you just stall those guys like you said you would? Till you get some money?"

She heard him cry out as she was replacing the receiver. She set the brown envelope back on the table. There were a lot of hundreds inside it, but that wasn't the point. Some things aren't about money. It was the letter that mattered, the one he wrote to the gamblers asking for more time to pay in full. That wasn't anything like the handwriting she'd seen on his other letter, the one she'd received so long ago containing an apology from "Devlin Robey." So she really didn't owe him anything. She owed herself a lot of years. She wondered how much it would cost to go to trade school, and if the bills in the brown envelope would cover it. Maggie wanted to learn to fix things.

THE PEOPLE ACROSS THE CANYON

Margaret Millar

The novel *How Like an Angel* (1962) shows an eerie prescience: many of its characters are early versions of the hippies who came to dominate the Southern California social landscape in just a few years. *Angel* is Margaret Millar's (1915–1994) darkest and most complex novel, but it is only one of her many masterpieces, which include *An Air that Kills* (1957), *A Stranger in my Grave* (1960), and *The Murder of Miranda* (1979). Some critics suggested that she was a more accomplished writer than her husband, Ross Macdonald (Ken Millar), a contention she always angrily denied. But her humility to the contrary, many argue that she was the single best writer of mysteries ever. The shame was that she never had a huge hit. She was somewhere between a cult and a coterie writer. Her vengeance is that her books are fresh as ever—brooding, frightening, and frequently hilarious right in the middle of all the terror. Her social eye was merciless and she delighted in lynching pomposity in all its forms. She is one of those rare writers of any stripe whose prose can be read aloud to great effect. Just open one of her books at random and start reading. You'll find something quotable soon enough.

THE FIRST TIME the Bortons realized that someone had moved into the new house across the canyon was one night in May when they saw the rectangular light of a television set shining in the picture window. Marion Borton knew it had to happen eventually, but that didn't make it any easier to accept the idea of neighbors in a part of the country she and Paul had come to consider exclusively their own.

They had discovered the site, had bought six acres, and built the house over the objections of the bank, which didn't like to lend money on unimproved property, and of their friends who thought the Bortons were foolish to move so far out of town. Now other people were discovering the spot, and here and there through the eucalyptus trees and the live oaks, Marion could see half-finished houses.

But it was the house directly across the canyon that bothered her most;

she had been dreading this moment ever since the site had been bulldozed the previous summer.

"There goes our privacy." Marion went over and snapped off the television set, a sign to Paul that she had something on her mind which she wanted to transfer to his. The transference, intended to halve the problem, often merely doubled it.

"Well, let's have it," Paul said, trying to conceal his annoyance.

"Have what?"

"Stop kidding around. You don't usually cut off Perry Mason in the middle of a sentence."

"All I said was, there goes our privacy."

"We have plenty left," Paul said.

"You know how sounds carry across the canyon."

"I don't hear any sounds."

"You will. They probably have ten or twelve children and a howling dog and a sports car."

"A couple of children wouldn't be so bad—at least, Cathy would have someone to play with."

Cathy was eight, in bed now, and ostensibly asleep, with the night light on and her bedroom door open just a crack.

"She has plenty of playmates at school," Marion said, pulling the drapes across the window so that she wouldn't have to look at the exasperating rectangle of light across the canyon. "Her teacher tells me Cathy gets along with everyone and never causes any trouble. You talk as if she's deprived or something."

"It would be nice if she had more interests, more children of her own age around."

"A lot of things would be nice *if*. I've done my best."

Paul knew it was true. He'd heard her issue dozens of weekend invitations to Cathy's schoolmates. Few of them came to anything. The mothers offered various excuses: poison oak, snakes, mosquitoes in the creek at the bottom of the canyon, the distance of the house from town in case something happened and a doctor was needed in a hurry . . . these excuses, sincere and valid as they were, embittered Marion. *"For heaven's sake, you'd think we lived on the moon or in the middle of a jungle."*

"I guess a couple of children would be all right," Marion said. "But please, no sports car."

"I'm afraid that's out of our hands."

"Actually, they might even be quite *nice* people."

"Why not? Most people are."

Both Marion and Paul had the comfortable feeling that something had been settled, though neither was quite sure what. Paul went over and turned the television set back on. As he had suspected, it was the doorman who'd killed the nightclub owner with a baseball bat, not the blonde dancer or her young husband or the jealous singer.

It was the following Monday that Cathy started to run away.

Marion, ironing in the kitchen and watching a quiz program on the portable set Paul had given her for Christmas, heard the school bus groan to a stop at the top of the driveway. She waited for the front door to open and Cathy to announce in her high thin voice, "I'm home, Mommy."

The door didn't open.

From the kitchen window Marion saw the yellow bus round the sharp curve of the hill like a circus cage full of wild captive children screaming for release.

Marion waited until the end of the program, trying to convince herself that another bus had been added to the route and would come along shortly, or that Cathy had decided to stop off at a friend's house and would telephone any minute. But no other bus appeared, and the telephone remained silent.

Marion changed into her hiking boots and started off down the canyon, avoiding the scratchy clumps of chapparal and the creepers of poison oak that looked like loganberry vines.

She found Cathy sitting in the middle of the little bridge that Paul had made across the creek out of two fallen eucalyptus trees. Cathy's short plump legs hung over the logs until they almost touched the water. She was absolutely motionless, her face hidden by a straw curtain of hair. Then a single frog croaked a warning of Marion's presence and Cathy responded to the sound as if she were more intimate with nature than adults were, and more alert to its subtle communications of danger.

She stood up quickly, brushing off the back of her dress and drawing aside the curtain of hair to reveal eyes as blue as the periwinkles that hugged the banks of the creek.

"Cathy."

"I was only counting waterbugs while I was waiting. Forty-one."

"Waiting for what?"

"The ten or twelve children, and the dog."

"What ten or twelve chil—" Marion stopped. "I see. You were listening the other night when we thought you were asleep."

"I wasn't listening," Cathy said righteously. "My ears were hearing."

Marion restrained a smile. "Then I wish you'd tell those ears of yours to hear properly. I didn't say the new neighbors had ten or twelve children, I said they *might* have. Actually, it's very unlikely. Not many families are that big these days."

"Do you have to be old to have a big family?"

"Well, you certainly can't be very young."

"I bet people with big families have station wagons so they have room for all the children."

"The lucky ones do."

Cathy stared down at the thin flow of water carrying fat little minnows down to the sea. Finally she said, "They're too young, and their car is too small."

In spite of her aversion to having new neighbors, Marion felt a quickening of interest. "Have you seen them?"

But the little girl seemed deaf, lost in a water world of minnows and dragonflies and tadpoles.

"I asked you a question, Cathy. Did you see the people who just moved in?"

"Yes."

"When?"

"Before you came. Their name is Smith."

"How do you know that?"

"I went up to the house to look at things and they said, hello, little girl, what's your name? And I said, Cathy, what's yours? And they said Smith. Then they drove off in the little car."

"You're not supposed to go poking around other people's houses," Marion said brusquely. "And while we're at it, you're not supposed to go anywhere after school without first telling me where you're going and when you'll be back. You know that perfectly well. Now why didn't you come in and report to me after you got off the school bus?"

"I didn't want to."

"That's not a satisfactory answer."

Satisfactory or not, it was the only answer Cathy had. She looked at her mother in silence, then she turned and darted back up the hill to her own house.

After a time Marion followed her, exasperated and a little confused. She hated to punish the child, but she knew she couldn't ignore the matter entirely—it was much too serious. While she gave Cathy her graham crackers and orange juice, she told her, reasonably and kindly, that she would have to stay in her room the following day after school by way of learning a lesson.

That night, after Cathy had been tucked in bed, Marion related the incident to Paul. He seemed to take a less serious view of it than Marion, a fact of which the listening child became well aware.

"I'm glad she's getting acquainted with the new people," Paul said. "It shows a certain degree of poise I didn't think she had. She's always been so shy."

"You're surely not condoning her running off without telling me?"

"She didn't run far. All kids do things like that once in a while."

"We don't want to spoil her."

"Cathy's always been so obedient I think she has *us* spoiled. Who knows, she might even teach us a thing or two about going out and making new friends." He realized, from past experience, that this was a very touchy subject. Marion had her house, her garden, her television sets; she didn't seem to want any more of the world than these, and she resented any implication that they were not enough. To ward off an argument he added, "You've done a good job with Cathy. Stop worrying . . . Smith, their name is?"

"Yes."

"Actually, I think it's an excellent sign that Cathy's getting acquainted."

At three the next afternoon the yellow circus cage arrived, released one captive, and rumbled on its way.

"I'm home, Mommy."

"Good girl."

Marion felt guilty at the sight of her: the child had been cooped up in school all day, the weather was so warm and lovely, and besides Paul hadn't thought the incident of the previous afternoon too important.

"I know what," Marion suggested, "let's you and I go down to the creek and count waterbugs."

The offer was a sacrifice for Marion because her favorite quiz program was on and she liked to answer the questions along with the contestants. "How about that?"

Cathy knew all about the quiz program; she'd seen it a hundred times, had watched the moving mouths claim her mother's eyes and ears and mind. "I counted the waterbugs yesterday."

"Well, minnows, then."

"You'll scare them away."

"Oh, will I?" Marion laughed self-consciously, rather relieved that Cathy had refused her offer and was clearly and definitely a little guilty about the relief. "Don't you scare them?"

"No. They think I'm another minnow because they're used to me."

"Maybe they could get used to me, too."

"I don't think so."

When Cathy went off down the canyon by herself Marion realized, in a vaguely disturbing way, that the child had politely but firmly rejected her mother's company. It wasn't until dinner time that she found out the reason why.

"The Smiths," Cathy said, "have an Austin-Healey."

Cathy, like most girls, had never shown any interest in cars, and her glib use of the name moved her parents to laughter.

The laughter encouraged Cathy to elaborate. "An Austin-Healey makes a lot of noise—like Daddy's lawn mower."

"I don't think the company would appreciate a commercial from you, young lady," Paul said. "Are the Smiths all moved in?"

"Oh, yes. I helped them."

"Is that a fact? And how did you help them?"

"I sang two songs. And then we danced and danced."

Paul looked half pleased, half puzzled. It wasn't like Cathy to perform willingly in front of people. During the last Christmas concert at the school she'd left the stage in tears and hidden in the cloak room . . . Well, maybe her shyness was only a phase and she was finally getting over it.

"They must be very nice people," he said, "to take time out from getting settled in a new house to play games with a little girl."

Cathy shook her head. "It wasn't games. It was real dancing—like on Ed Sullivan."

"As good as that, eh?" Paul said, smiling. "Tell me about it."

"Mrs. Smith is a nightclub dancer."

Paul's smile faded, and a pulse began to beat in his left temple like a small misplaced heart. "Oh? You're sure about that, Cathy?"

"Yes."

"And what does Mr. Smith do?"

"He's a baseball player."

"You mean that's what he does for a living?" Marion asked. "He doesn't work in an office like Daddy?"

"No, he just plays baseball. He always wears a baseball cap."

"I see. What position does he play on the team?" Paul's voice was low. Cathy looked blank.

"Everybody on a ball team has a special thing to do. What does Mr. Smith do?"

"He's a batter."

"A batter, eh? Well, that's nice. Did he tell you this?"

"Yes."

"Cathy," Paul said, "I know you wouldn't deliberately lie to me, but sometimes you get your facts a little mixed up."

He went on in this vein for some time but Cathy's story remained unshaken: Mrs. Smith was a nightclub dancer, Mr. Smith a professional baseball player, they loved children, and they never watched television.

"That, at least, must be a lie," Marion said to Paul later when she saw the rectangular light of the television set shining in the Smiths' picture window. "As for the rest of it, there isn't a nightclub within fifty miles, or a professional ball club within two hundred."

"She probably misunderstood. It's quite possible that at one time Mrs. Smith was a dancer of sorts and that he played a little baseball."

Cathy, in bed and teetering dizzily on the brink of sleep, wondered if she should tell her parents about the Smiths' child—the one who didn't go to school.

She didn't tell them; Marion found out for herself the next morning after Paul and Cathy had gone. When she pulled back the drapes in the living room and opened the windows she heard the sharp slam of a screen door from across the canyon and saw a small child come out on the patio of the new house. At that distance she couldn't tell whether it was a boy or a girl. Whichever it was, the child was quiet and well behaved; only the occasional slam of the door shook the warm, windless day.

The presence of the child, and the fact that Cathy hadn't mentioned it, gnawed at Marion's mind all day. She questioned Cathy about it as soon as she came home.

"You didn't tell me the Smiths have a child."

"No."

"Why not?"

"I don't know why not."

"Is it a boy or a girl?"

"Girl."

"How old?"

Cathy thought it over carefully, frowning up at the ceiling. "About ten."

"Doesn't she go to school?"

"No."

"Why not?"

"She doesn't want to."

"That's not a very good reason."

"It is her reason," Cathy said flatly. "Can I go out to play now?"

"I'm not sure you should. You look a little feverish. Come here and let me feel your forehead."

Cathy's forehead was cool and moist, but her cheeks and the bridge of her nose were very pink, almost as if she'd been sunburned.

"You'd better stay inside," Marion said, "and watch some cartoons."

"I don't like cartoons."

"You used to."

"I like real people."

She means the Smiths, of course, Marion thought as her mouth tightened. "People who dance and play baseball all the time?"

If the sarcasm had any effect on Cathy she didn't show it. After waiting until Marion had become engrossed in her quiz program, Cathy lined up all her dolls in her room and gave a concert for them, to thunderous applause.

"Where are your old Navy binoculars?" Marion asked Paul when she was getting ready for bed.

"Oh, somewhere in the sea chest, I imagine. Why?"

"I want them."

"Not thinking of spying on the neighbors, are you?"

"I'm thinking of just that," Marion said grimly.

The next morning, as soon as she saw the Smith child come out on the patio, Marion went downstairs to the storage room to search through the sea chest. She located the binoculars and was in the act of dusting them off when the telephone started to ring in the living room. She hurried upstairs and said breathlessly, "Hello?"

"Mrs. Borton?"

"Yes."

"This is Miss Park speaking, Cathy's teacher."

Marion had met Miss Park several times at P.T.A. meetings and report-card conferences. She was a large, ruddy-faced, and unfailingly cheerful young woman—the kind, as Paul said, you wouldn't want to live with but who'd be nice to have around in an emergency. "How are you, Miss Park?"

"Oh, fine, thank you, Mrs. Borton. I meant to call you yesterday but things were a bit out of hand around here, and I knew there was no great hurry to check on Cathy; she's such a well-behaved little girl."

Even Miss Park's loud, jovial voice couldn't cover up the ominous sound of the word *check*. "I don't think I quite understand. Why should you check on Cathy?"

"Purely routine. The school doctor and the health department like to keep records of how many cases of measles or flu or chicken pox are going the rounds. Right now it looks like the season for mumps. Is Cathy all right?"

"She seemed a little feverish yesterday afternoon when she got home from school, but she acted perfectly normal when she left this morning."

Miss Park's silence was so protracted that Marion became painfully conscious of things she wouldn't otherwise have noticed—the weight of the binoculars in her lap, the thud of her own heartbeat in her ears. Across the canyon the Smith child was playing quietly and alone on the patio. *There is definitely something the matter with that girl*, Marion thought. *Perhaps I'd better not let Cathy go over there any more, she's so imitative.* "Miss Park, are you still on the line? Hello? Hello—"

"I'm here," Miss Park's voice seemed fainter than usual, and less positive. "What time did Cathy leave the house this morning?"

"Eight, as usual."

"Did she take the school bus?"

"Of course. She always does."

"Did you see her get on?"

"I kissed her goodbye at the front door," Marion said. "What's this all about, Miss Park?"

"Cathy hasn't been at school for two days, Mrs. Borton."

"Why, that's absurd, impossible! You must be mistaken." But even as she was speaking the words, Marion was raising the binoculars to her eyes: the little girl on the Smiths' patio had a straw curtain of hair and eyes as blue as the periwinkles along the creek banks.

"Mrs. Borton, I'm not likely to be mistaken about which of my children are in class or not."

"No. No, you're—you're not mistaken, Miss Park. I can see Cathy from here—she's over at the neighbor's house."

"Good. That's a load off my mind."

"Off yours, yes," Marion said. "Not mine."

"Now we mustn't become excited, Mrs. Borton. Don't make too much of this incident before we've had a chance to confer. Suppose you come and talk to me during my lunch hour and bring Cathy along. We'll all have a friendly chat."

But it soon became apparent, even to the optimistic Miss Park, that Cathy didn't intend to take part in any friendly chat. She stood by the window in the classroom, blank-eyed, mute, unresponsive to the simplest questions, refusing to be drawn into any conversation even about her favorite topic, the Smiths. Miss Park finally decided to send Cathy out to play in the schoolyard while she talked to Marion alone.

"Obviously," Miss Park said, enunciating the word very distinctly because it was one of her favorites, "obviously, Cathy's got a crush on this young couple and has concocted a fantasy about belonging to them."

"It's not so obvious what my husband and I are going to do about it."

"Live through it, the same as other parents. Crushes like this are common at Cathy's age. Sometimes the object is a person, a whole family, even a horse. And, of course, to Cathy a nightclub dancer and a baseball player must seem very glamorous indeed. Tell me, Mrs. Borton, does she watch television a great deal?"

Marion stiffened. "No more than any other child."

Oh, dear, Miss Park thought sadly, *they all do it; the most confirmed addicts are always the most defensive.* "I just wondered," she said. "Cathy likes to sing to herself and I've never heard such a repertoire of television commercials."

"She picks things up very fast."

"Yes. Yes, she does indeed." Miss Park studied her hands, which were always a little pale from chalk dust and were even paler now because she was angry—at the child for deceiving her, at Mrs. Borton for brushing aside the television issue, at herself for not preventing, or at least anticipating, the current situation, and perhaps most of all at the Smiths who ought to have known better than to allow a child to hang around their house when she should obviously be in school.

"Don't put too much pressure on Cathy about this," she said finally, "until I talk the matter over with the school psychologist. By the way, have you met the Smiths, Mrs. Borton?"

"Not yet," Marion said grimly. "But believe me, I intend to."

"Yes, I think it would be a good idea for you to talk to them and make it clear that they're not to encourage Cathy in this fantasy."

The meeting came sooner than Marion expected.

She waited at the school until classes were dismissed, then she took Cathy into town to do some shopping. She had parked the car and she and Cathy were standing hand in hand at a corner waiting for a traffic light to change; Marion was worried and impatient, Cathy still silent, unresisting, inert, as she had been ever since Marion had called her home from the Smiths' patio.

Suddenly Marion felt the child's hand tighten in a spasm of excitement. Cathy's face had turned so pink it looked ready to explode and with her free hand she was waving violently at two people in a small cream-colored sports car—a very pretty young woman with blonde hair in the driver's seat, and beside her a young man wearing a wide friendly grin and a baseball cap. They both waved back at Cathy just before the lights changed and then the car roared through the intersection.

"The Smiths," Cathy shouted, jumping up and down in a frenzy. "That was the Smiths."

"Sssh, not so loud. People will—"

"But it was the *Smiths*!"

"Hurry up before the light changes."

The child didn't hear. She stood as if rooted to the curb, staring after the cream-colored car.

With a little grunt of impatience Marion picked her up, carried her across the road, and let her down quite roughly on the other side. "There. If you're going to act like a baby, I'll carry you like a baby."

"I saw the Smiths!"

"All right. What are you so excited about? It's not very unusual to meet someone in town whom you know."

"It's unusual to meet *them*."

"Why?"

"Because it is." The color was fading from Cathy's cheeks, but her eyes still looked bedazzled, quite as if they'd seen a miracle.

"I'm sure they're very unique people," Marion said coldly. "Nevertheless they must stop for groceries like everyone else."

Cathy's answer was a slight shake of her head and a whisper heard only by herself: "No, they don't, never."

When Paul came home from work Cathy was sent to play in the front yard while Marion explained matters to him. He listened with increasing irritation—not so much at Cathy's actions but at the manner in which Marion and Miss Park had handled things. There was too much talking, he said, and too little acting.

"The way you women beat around the bush instead of tackling the situation directly, meeting it head-on—fantasy life. Fantasy life, my foot! Now we're going over to the Smiths right this minute and talk to them and that will be that. End of fantasy. Period."

"We'd better wait until after dinner. Cathy missed her lunch."

Throughout the meal Cathy was pale and quiet. She ate nothing and spoke only when asked a direct question; but inside herself the conversation was very lively, the dinner a banquet with dancing, and afterward a wild, windy ride in the roofless car . . .

Although the footpath through the canyon provided a shorter route to the Smiths' house, the Bortons decided to go more formally, by car, and to take Cathy with them. Cathy, told to comb her hair and wash her face, protested: "I don't want to go over there."

"Why not?" Paul said. "You were so anxious to spend time with them that you played hooky for two days. Why don't you want to see them now?"

"Because they're not there."

"How do you know?"

"Mrs. Smith told me this morning that they wouldn't be home tonight because she's putting on a show."

"Indeed?" Paul said grim faced. "Just where does she put on these shows of hers?"

"And Mr. Smith has to play baseball. And after that they're going to see a friend in the hospital who has leukemia."

"Leukemia, eh?" He didn't have to ask how Cathy had found out about such a thing; he'd watched a semidocumentary dealing with it a couple of nights ago. Cathy was supposed to have been sleeping.

"I wonder," he said to Marion when Cathy went to comb her hair, "just how many 'facts' about the Smiths have been borrowed from television."

"Well, I know for myself that they drive a sports car, and Mr. Smith was wearing a baseball cap. And they're both young and good-looking. Young and good-looking enough," she added wryly, "to make me feel— well, a little jealous."

"Jealous?"

"Cathy would rather belong to them than to us. It makes me wonder if it's something the Smiths have or something the Bortons don't have."

"Ask her."

"I can't very well—"

"Then I will, dammit," Paul said. And he did.

Cathy merely looked at him innocently. "I don't know. I don't know what you mean."

"Then listen again. Why did you pretend that you were the Smiths' little girl?"

"They asked me to be. They asked me to go with them."

"They actually said, Cathy, will you be our little girl?"

"Yes."

"Well, by heaven, I'll put an end to this nonsense," Paul said, and strode out to the car.

It was twilight when they reached the Smiths' house by way of the narrow, hilly road. The moon, just appearing above the horizon, was on the wane, a chunk bitten out of its side by some giant jaw. A warm dry wind, blowing down the mountain from the desert beyond, carried the sweet scent of pittosporum.

The Smiths' house was dark, and both the front door and the garage were locked. Out of defiance or desperation, Paul pressed the door chime anyway, several times. All three of them could hear it ringing inside, and it seemed to Marion to echo very curiously—as if the carpets and drapes were too thin to muffle the sound vibrations. She would have liked to peer in through the windows and see for herself, but the venetian blinds were closed.

"What's their furniture like?" she asked Cathy.

"Like everybody's."

"I mean, is it new? Does Mrs. Smith tell you not to put your feet on it?"

"No, she never tells me that," Cathy said truthfully. "I want to go home now. I'm tired."

It was while she was putting Cathy to bed that Marion heard Paul call to her from the living room in an urgent voice, "Marion, come here a minute."

She found him standing motionless in the middle of the room, staring across the canyon at the Smiths' place. The rectangular light of the Smiths' television set was shining in the picture window of the room that opened onto the patio at the back of the Smiths' house.

"Either they've come home within the past few minutes," he said, "or they were there all the time. My guess is that they were home when we went over, but they didn't want to see us, so they just doused the lights and pretended to be out. Well, it won't work! Come on, we're going back."

"I can't leave Cathy alone. She's already got her pajamas on."

"Put a bathrobe on her and bring her along. This has gone beyond the point of observing such niceties as correct attire."

"Don't you think we should wait until tomorrow?"

"Hurry up and stop arguing with me."

Cathy, protesting that she was tired and that the Smiths weren't home anyway, was bundled into a bathrobe and carried to the car.

"They're home all right," Paul said. "And by heaven they'd better answer the door this time or I'll break it down."

"That's an absurd way to talk in front of a child," Marion said coldly. "She has enough ideas without hearing—"

"Absurd is it? Wait and see."

Cathy, listening from the back seat, smiled sleepily. She knew how to get in without breaking anything: ever since the house had been built, the real estate man who'd been trying to sell it always hid the key on a nail underneath the window box.

The second trip seemed a nightmarish imitation of the first: the same moon hung in the sky but it looked smaller now, and paler. The scent of pittosporum was funereally sweet, and the hollow sound of the chimes from inside the house was like the echo in an empty tomb.

"They must be crazy to think they can get away with a trick like this twice in one night," Paul shouted. "Come on, we're going around to the back."

Marion looked a little frightened. "I don't like trespassing on someone else's property."

"They trespassed on our property first."

He glanced down at Cathy. Her eyes were half closed and her face was pearly in the moonlight. He pressed her hand to reassure her that everything was going to be all right and that his anger wasn't directed at her, but she drew away from him and started down the path that led to the back of the house.

Paul clicked on his flashlight and followed her, moving slowly along the unfamiliar terrain. By the time he turned the corner of the house and reached the patio, Cathy was out of sight.

"Cathy," he called. "Where are you? Come back here!"

Marion was looking at him accusingly. "You upset her with that silly threat about breaking down the door. She's probably on her way home through the canyon."

"I'd better go after her."

"She's less likely to get hurt than you are. She knows every inch of the way. Besides, you came here to break down the doors. All right, start breaking."

But there was no need to break down anything. The back door opened as soon as Paul rapped on it with his knuckles, and he almost fell into the room.

It was empty except for a small girl wearing a blue bathrobe that matched her eyes.

Paul said, "Cathy. Cathy, what are you doing here?"

Marion stood with her hand pressed to her mouth to stifle the scream that was rising in her throat. There were no Smiths. The people in the sports car whom Cathy had waved at were just strangers responding to the friendly greeting of a child—had Cathy seen them before, on a previous trip to town? The television set was no more than a contraption rigged up by Cathy herself—an orange crate and an old mirror that caught and reflected the rays of the moon.

In front of it Cathy was standing, facing her own image. "Hello, Mrs. Smith. Here I am, all ready to go."

"Cathy," Marion said in a voice that sounded torn by claws. "What do you see in that mirror?"

"It's not a mirror. It's a television set."

"What—what program are you watching?"

"It's not a program, silly. It's real. It's the Smiths. I'm going away with them to dance and play baseball."

"There are no Smiths," Paul bellowed. "Will you get that through your head? *There are no Smiths!*"

"Yes, there are. I see them."

Marion knelt on the floor beside the child. "Listen to me, Cathy. This is a mirror—only a mirror. It came from Daddy's old bureau and I had it put away in the storage room. That's where you found it, isn't it? And you brought it here and decided to pretend it was a television set, isn't that right? But it's really just a mirror, and the people in it are us—you and Mommy and Daddy."

But even as she looked at her own reflection, Marion saw it beginning to change. She was growing younger, prettier; her hair was becoming lighter and her cotton suit was changing into a dancing dress. And beside her in the mirror, Paul was turning into a stranger, a laughing-eyed young man wearing a baseball cap.

"I'm ready to go now, Mr. Smith," Cathy said, and suddenly all three of them, the Smiths and their little girl, began walking away in the mirror. In a few moments they were no bigger than matchsticks—and then the three of them disappeared, and there was only the moonlight in the glass.

"Cathy," Marion cried. "Come back, Cathy! Please come back!"

Propped up against the door like a dummy, Paul imagined he could hear above his wife's cries the mocking muted roar of a sports car.

BENNY'S SPACE

Marcia Muller

Female private eyes date back to at least the pulps. They were always "gals," saucy versions of guys, whose stories were told with a wink and a smirk. Marcia Muller reinvented the female private investigator, giving her pith, dignity, intelligence, and the kind of social sensitivity that had oddly been limited to the male P.I.s. All of her books about Sharon McCone, investigator for the All Souls Legal Cooperative in San Francisco, were sound and professional from the start. But Muller has proved to be one of those writers who constantly push themselves to do more challenging work. *A Wild and Lonely Place* (1994) and *The Broken Promise Land* (1996) signaled the start of longer and even more powerful McCone mysteries. And her audience was eager to accompany her on these journeys, turning Muller into a mystery genre brand name. Her most recent work is *Listen to the Silence*.

AMORFINA ANGELES WAS terrified, and I could fully empathize with her. Merely living in the neighborhood would have terrified me—all the more so had I been harassed by members of one of its many street gangs.

Hers was a rundown side street in the extreme southeast of San Francisco, only blocks from the drug- and crime-infested Sunnydale public housing projects. There were bars over the windows and grilles on the doors of the small stucco houses; dead and vandalized cars stood at the broken curbs; in the weed-choked yard next door, a mangy guard dog of indeterminate breed paced and snarled. Fear was written on this street as plainly as the graffiti on the walls and fences. Fear and hopelessness and a dull resignation to a life that none of its residents would willingly have opted to lead.

I watched Mrs. Angeles as she crossed her tiny living room to the front window, pulled the edge of the curtain aside a fraction, and peered out at the street. She was no more than five feet tall, with rounded shoulders, sallow skin, and graying black hair that curled in short, unruly ringlets. Her shapeless flower-printed dress did little to conceal a body made soft and fleshy by bad food and too much childbearing. Although she was only forty, she moved like a much older woman.

Her attorney and my colleague, Jack Stuart of All Souls Legal Cooperative, had given me a brief history of his client when he'd asked me to undertake an investigation on her behalf. She was a Filipina who had emigrated to the states with her husband in search of their own piece of the good life that was reputed to be had here. But as with many of their countrymen and -women, things hadn't worked out as the Angeleses had envisioned: first Amorfina's husband had gone into the import-export business with a friend from Manila; the friend absconded two years later with Joe Angeles's life savings. Then, a year after that, Joe was killed in a freak accident at a construction site where he was working. Amorfina and their six children were left with no means of support, and in the years since Joe's death their circumstances had gradually been reduced to this two-bedroom rental cottage in one of the worst areas of the city.

Mrs. Angeles, Jack told me, had done the best she could for her family, keeping them off the welfare rolls with a daytime job at a Mission district sewing factory and nighttime work doing alterations. As they grew older, the children helped with part-time jobs. Now there were only two left at home: sixteen-year-old Alex and fourteen-year-old Isabel. It was typical of their mother, Jack said, that in the current crisis she was more concerned for them than for herself.

She turned from the window now, her face taut with fear, deep lines bracketing her full lips. I asked, "Is someone out there?"

She shook her head and walked wearily to the worn recliner opposite me. I occupied the place of honor on a red brocade sofa encased in the same plastic that doubtless had protected it long ago upon delivery from the store. "I never see anybody," she said. "Not till it's too late."

"Mrs. Angeles, Jack Stuart told me about your problem, but I'd like to hear it in your own words—from the beginning, if you would."

She nodded, smoothing her bright dress over her plump thighs. "It goes back a long time, to when Benny Crespo was . . . they called him the Prince of Omega Street, you know."

Hearing the name of her street spoken made me aware of its ironic appropriateness: the last letter of the Greek alphabet is symbolic of endings, and for most of the people living here, Omega Street was the end of a steady decline into poverty.

Mrs. Angeles went on, "Benny Crespo was Filipino. His gang controlled the drugs here. A lot of people looked up to him; he had power, and that don't happen much with our people. Once I caught Alex and one of my older boys calling him a hero. I let them have it pretty good, you bet, and there wasn't any more of *that* kind of talk around this house. I got no use for the gangs—Filipino or otherwise."

"What was the name of Benny Crespo's gang?"

"The *Kabalyeros*. That's Tagalog for Knights."

"Okay—what happened to Benny?"

"The house next door, the one with the dog—that was where Benny lived. He always parked his fancy Corvette out front, and people knew better than to mess with it. Late one night he was getting out of the car and somebody shot him. A drug burn, they say. After that the *Kabalyeros* decided to make the parking space a shrine to Benny. They roped it off, put flowers there every week. On All Saints Day and the other fiestas, it was something to see."

"And that brings us to last March thirteenth," I said.

Mrs. Angeles bit her lower lip and smoothed her dress again.

When she didn't speak, I prompted her. "You'd just come home from work."

"Yeah. It was late, dark. Isabel wasn't here, and I got worried. I kept looking out the window, like a mother does."

"And you saw . . . ?"

"The guy who moved into the house next door after Benny got shot, Reg Dawson. He was black, one of a gang called the Victors. They say he moved into that house to show the *Kabalyeros* that the Victors were taking over their turf. Anyway, he drives up and stops a little way down the block. Waits there, revving his engine. People start showing up; the word's been put out that something's gonna go down. And when there's a big crowd, Reg Dawson guns his car and drives right into Benny's space, over the rope and the flowers.

"Well, that started one hell of a fight—Victors and *Kabalyeros* and folks from the neighborhood. And while it's going on, Reg Dawson just stands there in Benny's space acting macho. That's when it happened, what I saw."

"And what was that?"

She hesitated, wet her lips. "The leader of the *Kabalyeros*, Tommy Dragón—the Dragon, they call him—was over by the fence in front of Reg Dawson's house, where you couldn't see him unless you were really looking. I was, 'cause I was trying to see if Isabel was anyplace out there. And I saw Tommy Dragón point this gun at Reg Dawson and shoot him dead."

"What did you do then?"

"Ran and hid in the bathroom. That's where I was when the cops came to the door. Somebody'd told them I was in the window when it all went down and then ran away when Reg got shot. Well, what was I supposed to do? I got no use for the *Kabalyeros* or the Victors, so I told the truth. And now here I am in this mess."

Mrs. Angeles had been slated to be the chief prosecution witness at Tommy Dragón's trial this week. But a month ago the threats had started: anonymous letters and phone calls warning her against testifying. As the trial date approached, this had escalated into blatant intimidation: a fire was set in her trash can; someone shot out her kitchen window; a dead dog turned up on her doorstep. The previous Friday, Isabel had been accosted on her way home from the bus stop by two masked men with guns. And that had finally made Mrs. Angeles capitulate; in court yesterday, she'd refused to take the stand against Dragón.

The state needed her testimony; there were no other witnesses, Dragón insisted on his innocence, and the murder gun had not been found. The judge had tried to reason with Mrs. Angeles, then cited her for contempt—reluctantly, he said. "The court is aware that there have been threats made against you and your family," he told her, "but it is unable to guarantee your protection." Then he gave her forty-eight hours to reconsider her decision.

As it turned out, Mrs. Angeles had a champion in her employer. The owner of the sewing factory was unwilling to allow one of his long-term workers to go to jail or to risk her own and her family's safety. He brought her to All Souls, where he held a membership in our legal-services plan, and this morning Jack Stuart had asked me to do something for her.

What? I'd asked. What could I do that the SFPD couldn't to stop vicious harassment by a street gang?

Well, he said, get proof against whoever was threatening her so they could be arrested and she'd feel free to testify.

Sure, Jack, I said. And exactly why *hadn't* the police been able to do anything about the situation?

His answer was not surprising: lack of funds. Intimidation of prosecution witnesses in cases relating to gang violence was becoming more and more prevalent and open in San Francisco, but the city did not have the resources to protect them. An old story nowadays—not enough money to go around.

Mrs. Angeles was watching my face, her eyes tentative. As I looked back at her, her gaze began to waver. She'd experienced too much disappointment in her life to expect much in the way of help from me.

I said, "Yes, you certainly are in a mess. Let's see if we can get you out of it."

WE TALKED FOR a while longer, and I soon realized that Amor— as she asked me to call her—held the misconception that there was some way I could get the contempt citation dropped. I asked her if she'd known beforehand that a balky witness could be sent to jail. She shook her head. A person had a right to change her mind, didn't she? When I set her straight on that, she seemed to lose interest in the conversation; it was difficult to get her to focus long enough to compile a list of people I should talk with. I settled for enough names to keep me occupied for the rest of the afternoon.

I was ready to leave when angry voices came from the front steps. A young man and woman entered. They stopped speaking when they saw the room was occupied, but their faces remained set in lines of contention. Amor hastened to introduce them as her son and daughter, Alex and Isabel. To them she explained that I was a detective "helping with the trouble with the judge."

Alex, a stocky youth with a tracery of moustache on his upper lip, seemed disinterested. He shrugged out of his high school letter jacket and vanished through a door to the rear of the house. Isabel studied me with frank curiosity. She was a slender beauty, with black hair that fell in soft curls to her shoulders; her features had a delicacy lacking in those of her mother and brother. Unfortunately, bright blue eyeshadow and garish orange lipstick detracted from her natural good looks, and she wore an imitation leather outfit in a particularly gaudy shade of purple. However, she was polite and well-spoken as she questioned me about what I could do to help her mother. Then, after a comment to Amor about an assignment that was due the next day, she left through the door her brother had used.

I turned to Amor, who was fingering the leaves of a philodendron plant that stood on a stand near the front window. Her posture was stiff, and when I spoke to her she didn't meet my eyes. Now I was aware of a tension in her that hadn't been there before her children returned home. Anxiety, because of the danger her witnessing the shooting had placed them in? Or something else? It might have had to do with the quarrel they'd been having, but weren't arguments between siblings fairly common? They certainly had been in my childhood home in San Diego.

I told Amor I'd be back to check on her in a couple of hours. Then, after a few precautionary and probably unnecessary reminders about locking doors and staying clear of windows, I went out into the chill November afternoon.

The first name on my list was Madeline Dawson, the slain gang leader's widow. I glanced at the house next door and saw with some relief that the guard dog no longer paced in its yard. When I pushed through the gate in the chain link fence, the creature's whereabouts quickly became apparent: a bellowing emanated from the small, shabby cottage. I went up a broken walk bordered by weeds, climbed the sagging front steps, and pressed the bell. A woman's voice yelled for the dog to shut up, then a door slammed somewhere within, muffling the barking. Footsteps approached, and the woman called, "Yes, who is it?"

"My name's Sharon McCone, from All Souls Legal Cooperative. I'm investigating the threats your neighbor, Mrs. Angeles, has been receiving."

A couple of locks turned and the door opened on its chain. The face that peered out at me was very thin and pale, with wisps of red hair straggling over the high forehead; the Dawson marriage had been an interracial one, then. The woman stared at me for a moment before she asked, "What threats?"

"You don't know that Mrs. Angeles and her children have been threatened because she's to testify against the man who shot your husband?"

She shook her head and stepped back, shivering slightly—whether from the cold outside or the memory of the murder, I couldn't tell. "I . . . don't get out much these days."

"May I come in, talk with you about the shooting?"

She shrugged, unhooked the chain, and opened the door. "I don't know what good it will do. Amor's a damned fool for saying she'd testify in the first place."

"Aren't you glad she did? The man killed your husband."

She shrugged again and motioned me into a living room the same size as that in the Angeles house. All resemblance stopped there, however. Dirty glasses and dishes, full ashtrays, piles of newspapers and magazines covered every surface; dust balls the size of rats lurked under the shabby Danish modern furniture. Madeline Dawson picked up a heap of tabloids from the couch and dumped it on the floor, then indicated I should sit there and took a hassock for herself.

I said, "You *are* glad that Mrs. Angeles was willing to testify, aren't you?"

"Not particularly."

"You don't care if your husband's killer is convicted or not?"

"Reg was asking to be killed. Not that I wouldn't mind seeing the Dragon get the gas chamber—he may not have killed Reg, but he killed plenty of other people—"

"What did you say?" I spoke sharply, and Madeline Dawson blinked in surprise. It made me pay closer attention to her eyes; they were glassy, their pupils dilated. The woman, I realized, was high.

"I said the Dragon killed plenty of other people."

"No, about him not killing Reg."

"Did I say that?"

"Yes."

"I can't imagine why. I mean, Amor must know. She was up there in the window watching for sweet Isabel like always."

"You don't sound as if you like Isabel Angeles."

"I'm not fond of flips in general. Look at the way they're taking over this area. Daly City's turning into another Manila. All they do is buy, buy, buy—houses, cars, stuff by the truckload. You know, there's a joke that the first three words their babies learn are 'Mama, Papa, and Serramonte.' " Serramonte was a large shopping mall south of San Francisco.

The roots of the resentment she voiced were clear to me. One of our largest immigrant groups today, the Filipinos are highly westernized and by and large better educated and more affluent than other recently arrived Asians—or many of their neighbors, black or white. Isabel Angeles, for all her bright, cheap clothing and excessive makeup, had behind her a tradition of industriousness and upward mobility that might help her to secure a better place in the world than Madeline Dawson could aspire to.

I wasn't going to allow Madeline's biases to interfere with my line of questioning. I said, "About Dragón not having shot your husband—"

"Hey, who knows? Or cares? The bastard's dead, and good riddance."

"Why good riddance?"

"The man was a pig. A pusher who cheated and gouged people—people like me who need the stuff to get through. You think I was always like this, lady? No way. I was a nice Irish Catholic girl from the Avenues when Reg got his hands on me. Turned me on to coke and a lot of other things when I was only thirteen. Liked his pussy young, Reg did. But then I got old—I'm all of nineteen now—and I needed more and more stuff just to keep going, and all of a sudden Reg didn't even *see* me anymore. Yeah, the man was a pig, and I'm glad he's dead."

"But you don't think Dragón killed him."

She sighed in exasperation. "I don't know what I think. It's just that I always supposed that when Reg got it it would be for something more personal than driving his car into a stupid shrine in a parking space. You know what I mean? But what does it matter who killed him, anyway?"

"It matters to Tommy Dragón, for one."

She dismissed the accused man's life with a flick of her hand. "Like I said, the Dragon's a killer. He might as well die for Reg's murder as for any of the others. In a way it'd be the one good thing Reg did for the world."

Perhaps in a certain primitive sense she was right, but her offhandedness made me uncomfortable. I changed the subject. "About the threats to Mrs. Angeles—which of the *Kabalyeros* would be behind them?"

"All of them. The guys in the gangs, they work together."

But I knew enough about the structure of street gangs—my degree in sociology from UC Berkeley hadn't been totally worthless—to be reasonably sure that wasn't so. There is usually one dominant personality, supported by two or three lieutenants; take away these leaders, and the followers become ineffectual, purposeless. If I could turn up enough evidence against the leaders of the *Kabalyeros* to have them arrested, the harassment would stop.

I asked, "Who took over the *Kabalyeros* after Dragón went to jail?"

"Hector Bulis."

It was a name that didn't appear on my list; Amor had claimed not to know who was the current head of the Filipino gang. "Where can I find him?"

"There's a fast-food joint over on Geneva, near the Cow Palace. Fat Robbie's. That's where the *Kabalyeros* hang out."

The second person I'd intended to talk with was the young man who had reportedly taken over the leadership of the Victors after Dawson's death, Jimmy Willis. Willis could generally be found at a bowling alley, also on Geneva Avenue near the Cow Palace. I thanked Madeline for taking the time to talk with me and headed for the Daly City line.

THE FIRST OF the two establishments that I spotted was Fat Robbie's, a cinderblock-and-glass relic of the early sixties whose specialties appeared to be burgers and chicken-in-a-basket. I turned into a parking lot that was half-full of mostly shabby cars and left my MG beside one of the defunct drive-in speaker poles.

The interior of the restaurant took me back to my high school days: orange leatherette booths beside the plate glass windows; a long Formica counter with stools; laminated color pictures of disgusting-looking food on the wall above the pass-through counter from the kitchen. Instead of a jukebox there was a bank of video games along one wall. Three Filipino youths in jeans and denim jackets gathered around one called "Invader!" The *Kabalyeros*, I assumed.

I crossed to the counter with only a cursory glance at the trio, sat, and ordered coffee from a young waitress who looked to be Eurasian. The *Kabalyeros* didn't conceal their interest in me; they stared openly, and after a moment one of them said something that sounded like "tick-tick," and they all laughed nastily. Some sort of Tagalog obscenity, I supposed. I ignored them, sipping the dishwater-weak coffee, and after a bit they went back to their game.

I took out the paperback that I keep in my bag for protective coloration and pretended to read, listening to the few snatches of conversation that drifted over from the three. I caught the names of two: Sal and Hector—the latter presumably Bulis, the gang's leader. When I glanced covertly at him, I saw he was tallish and thin, with long hair caught back in a ponytail; his features were razor-sharp and slightly skewed, creating the impression of a perpetual sneer. The trio kept their voices low, and although I strained to hear, I could make out nothing of what they were saying. After about five minutes Hector turned away from the video machine. With a final glance at me he motioned to his companions, and they all left the restaurant.

I waited until they'd driven away in an old green Pontiac before I called the waitress over and showed her my identification. "The three men who just left," I said. "Is the tall one Hector Bulis?"

Her lips formed a little "O" as she stared at the ID. Finally she nodded.

"May I talk with you about them?"

She glanced toward the pass-through to the kitchen. "My boss, he don't like me talking with the customers when I'm supposed to be working."

"Take a break. Just five minutes."

Now she looked nervously around the restaurant. "I shouldn't—"

I slipped a twenty-dollar bill from my wallet and showed it to her. "Just five minutes."

She still seemed edgy, but fear lost out to greed. "Okay, but I don't want anybody to see me talking to you. Go back to the restroom—it's through that door by the video games. I'll meet you there as soon as I can."

I got up and found the ladies room. It was tiny, dimly lit, with a badly cracked mirror. The walls were covered with a mass of graffiti; some of it looked as if it had been painted over and had later worked its way back into view through the fading layers of enamel. The air in there was redolent of grease, cheap perfume, and stale cigarette and marijuana smoke. I leaned against the sink as I waited.

The young Eurasian woman appeared a few minutes later. "Bastard gave me a hard time," she said. "Tried to tell me I'd already taken my break."

"What's your name?"

"Anna Smith."

"Anna, the three men who just left—do they come in here often?"

"Uh-huh."

"Keep pretty much to themselves, don't they?"

"It's more like other people stay away from them." She hesitated. "They're from one of the gangs; you don't mess with them. That's why I wanted to talk with you back here."

"Have you ever heard them say anything about Tommy Dragón?"

"The Dragon? Sure. He's in jail; they say he was framed."

Of course they would claim that. "What about a Mrs. Angeles— Amorfina Angeles?"

". . . Not that one, no."

"What about trying to intimidate someone? Setting fires, going after someone with a gun?"

"Uh-uh. That's gang business; they keep it pretty close. But it wouldn't surprise me. Filipinos—I'm part Filipina myself, my mom met my dad when he was stationed at Subic Bay—they've got this saying, *kumukuló ang dugó*. It means 'the blood is boiling.' They can get pretty damn mad, 'specially the men. So stuff like what you said—sure they do it."

"Do you work on Fridays?"

"Yeah, two to ten."

"Did you see any of the *Kabalyeros* in here last Friday around six?" That was the time when Isabel had been accosted.

Anna Smith scrunched up her face in concentration. "Last Friday . . . oh, yeah, sure. That was when they had the big meeting, all of them."

"*All* of them?"

"Uh-huh. Started around five thirty, went on a couple of hours. My boss, he was worried something heavy was gonna go down, but the way it turned out, all he did was sell a lot of food."

"What was this meeting about?"

"Had to do with the Dragon, who was gonna be character witnesses at the trial, what they'd say."

The image of the three I'd seen earlier—or any of their ilk—as character witnesses was somewhat ludicrous, but I supposed in Tommy Dragón's position you took what you could get. "Are you sure they were all there?"

"Uh-huh."

"And no one at the meeting said anything about trying to keep Mrs. Angeles from testifying?"

"No. That lawyer the Dragon's got, he was there too."

Now that was odd. Why had Dragón's public defender chosen to meet with his witnesses in a public place? I could think of one good reason: he was afraid of them, didn't want them in his office. But what if the *Kabalyeros* had set the time and place—as an alibi for when Isabel was to be assaulted?

"I better get back to work," Anna Smith said. "Before the boss comes looking for me."

I gave her the twenty dollars. "Thanks for your time."

"Sure." Halfway out the door she paused, frowning. "I hope I didn't get any of the *Kabalyeros* in trouble."

"You didn't."

"Good. I kind of like them. I mean, they push dope and all, but these days, who doesn't?"

These days, who doesn't? I thought. *Good Lord. . . .*

⸻

THE STARLIGHT LANES was an old-fashioned bowling alley girded by a rough cliff face and an auto dismantler's yard. The parking lot was crowded, so I left the MG around back by the garbage cans. Inside, the lanes were brightly lit and noisy with the sound of crashing pins, rumbling balls, shouts, and groans. I paused by the front counter and asked where I might find Jimmy Willis. The woman behind it directed me to a lane at the far end.

Bowling alleys—or lanes, as the new upscale bowler prefers to call them—are familiar territory to me. Up until a few years ago my favorite uncle Jim was a top player on the pro tour. The Starlight Lanes reminded me of the ones where Jim used to practice in San Diego—from the racks full of tired-looking rental shoes to the greasy-spoon coffeeshop smells to the molded plastic chairs and cigarette-burned score-keeping consoles. I walked along, soaking up the ambience—some people would say the lack of it—until I came to lane 32 and spotted an agile young black man bowling alone. Jimmy Willis was a left-hander, and his ball hooked back with deadly precision. I waited in the spectator area, admiring his accuracy and graceful form. His concentration was so great that he didn't notice me until he'd finished the last frame and retrieved his ball.

"You're quite a bowler," I said. "What's your average?"

He gave me a long look before he replied. "Two hundred."

"Almost good enough to turn pro."

"That's what I'm looking to do."

Odd, for the head of a street gang that dealt in drugs and death. "You ever hear of Jim McCone?" I asked.

"Sure. Damned good in his day."

"He's my uncle."

"No kidding." Willis studied me again, now as if looking for a resemblance.

Rapport established, I showed him my ID and explained that I wanted to talk about Reg Dawson's murder. He frowned, hesitated, then nodded. "Okay, since you're Jim McCone's niece, but you'll have to buy me a beer."

"Deal."

Willis toweled off his ball, stowed it and his shoes in their bag, and led me to a typical smoke-filled, murkily lighted bowling alley bar. He took one of the booths while I fetched us a pair of Buds.

As I slid into the booth I said, "What can you tell me about the murder?"

"The way I see it, Dawson was asking for it."

So he and Dawson's wife were of a mind about that. "I can understand what you mean, but it seems strange, coming from you. I hear you were his friend, that you took over the Victors after his death."

"You heard wrong on both counts. Yeah, I was in the Victors, and when Dawson bought it, they tried to get me to take over. But by then I'd figured out—never mind how, doesn't matter—that I wanted out of that life. Ain't nothing in it but what happened to Benny Crespo and Dawson— or what's gonna happen to the Dragon. So I decided to put my hand to something with a future." He patted the bowling bag that sat on the banquette beside him. "Got a job here now—not much, but my bowling's free and I'm on my way."

"Good for you. What about Dragón—do you think he's guilty?"

Willis hesitated, looking thoughtful. "Why you ask?"

"Just wondering."

". . . Well, to tell you the truth, I never did believe the Dragon shot Reg."

"Who did, then?"

He shrugged.

I asked him if he'd heard about the *Kabalyeros* trying to intimidate the chief prosecution witness. When he nodded, I said, "They also threatened the life of her daughter last Friday."

He laughed mirthlessly. "Wish I could of seen that. Kind of surprises me, though. That lawyer of Dragón's, he found out what the *Kabalyeros* were up to, read them the riot act. Said they'd put Dragón in the gas chamber for sure. So they called it off."

"When was this?"

"Week, ten days ago."

Long before Isabel had been accosted. Before the dead dog and shooting incidents, too. "Are you sure?"

"It's what I hear. You know, in a way I'm surprised that they'd go after Mrs. Angeles at all."

"Why?"

"The Filipinos have this macho tradition. 'Specially when it comes to their women. They don't like them messed with, 'specially by non-Filipinos. So how come they'd turn around and mess with one of their own?"

"Well, her testimony *would* jeopardize the life of one of their fellow gang members. It's an extreme situation."

"Can't argue with that."

Jimmy Willis and I talked a bit more, but he couldn't—or wouldn't—offer any further information. I bought him a second beer, then went out to where I'd left my car.

And came face-to-face with Hector Bulis and the man called Sal.

Sal grabbed me by the arm, twisted it behind me, and forced me up against the latticework fence surrounding the garbage cans. The stench from them filled my nostrils; Sal's breath rivaled it in foulness. I struggled, but he got hold of my other arm and pinned me tighter. I looked around, saw no one, nothing but the cliff face and the high board fence of the auto dismantler's yard. Bulis approached, flicking open a switchblade, his twisty face intense. I stiffened, went very still, eyes on the knife.

Bulis placed the tip of the knife against my jawbone, then traced a line across my cheek. "Don't want to hurt you, bitch," he said. "You do what I say, I won't have to mess you up."

The Tagalog phrase that Anna Smith had translated for me—*kumukuló ang dugó*—flashed through my mind. *The blood is boiling.* I sensed Bulis's was—and dangerously high.

I wet my dry lips, tried to keep my voice from shaking as I said, "What do you want me to do?"

"We hear you're asking around about Dawson's murder, trying to prove the Dragon did it."

"That's not—"

"We want you to quit. Go back to your own part of town and leave our business alone."

"Whoever told you that is lying. I'm only trying to help the Angeles family."

"They wouldn't lie." He moved the knife's tip to the hollow at the base of my throat. I felt it pierce my skin—a mere pinprick, but frightening enough.

When I could speak, I did so slowly, phrasing my words carefully. "What I hear is that Dragón is innocent. And that the *Kabalyeros* aren't behind the harassment of the Angeleses—at least not for a week or ten days."

Bulis exchanged a look with his companion—quick, unreadable.

"Someone's trying to frame you." I added, "Just like they did Dragón."

Bulis continued to hold the knife to my throat, his hand firm. His gaze wavered, however, as if he was considering what I'd said. After a moment he asked, "All right—who?"

"I'm not sure, but I think I can find out."

He thought a bit longer, then let his arm drop and snapped the knife shut. "I'll give you till this time tomorrow," he said. Then he stuffed the knife into his pocket, motioned for Sal to let go of me, and the two quickly walked away.

I sagged against the latticework fence, feeling my throat where the knife had pricked it. It had bled a little, but the flow already was clotting. My knees were weak and my breath came fast, but I was too caught up in the possibilities to panic. There were plenty of them—and the most likely was the most unpleasant.

Kumukuló ang dugó. The blood is boiling. . . .

TWO HOURS LATER I was back at the Angeles house on Omega Street. When Amor admitted me, the tension I'd felt in her earlier had drained. Her body sagged, as if the extra weight she carried had finally proved to be too much for her frail bones; the skin of her face looked flaccid, like melting putty; her eyes were sunken and vague. After she shut the door and motioned for me to sit, she sank into the recliner, expelling a sigh. The house was quiet—too quiet.

"I have a question for you," I said. "What does 'tick-tick' mean in Tagalog?"

Her eyes flickered with dull interest. "*Tiktík.*" She corrected my pronunciation. "It's a word for detective."

Ever since Hector Bulis and Sal had accosted me I'd suspected as much.

"Where did you hear that?" Amor asked.

"One of the *Kabalyeros* said it when I went to Fat Robbie's earlier. Someone had told them I was a detective, probably described me. Whoever it was said I was trying to prove Tommy Dragón killed Reg Dawson."

"Why would—"

"More to the point, *who* would? At the time, only four people knew that I'm a detective."

She wet her lips, but remained silent.

"Amor, the night of the shooting, you were standing in your front window, watching for Isabel."

"Yes."

"Do you do that often?"

". . . Yes."

"Because Isabel is often late coming home. Because you're afraid she may have gotten into trouble."

"A mother worries—"

"Especially when she's given good cause. Isabel is running out of control, isn't she?"

"No, she—"

"Amor, when I spoke with Madeline Dawson, she said you were standing in the window watching for 'sweet Isabel, like always.' She didn't say 'sweet' in a pleasant way. Later, Jimmy Willis implied that your daughter is not . . . exactly a vulnerable young girl."

Amor's eyes sparked. "The Dawson woman is jealous."

"Of course she is. There's something else: when I asked the waitress at Fat Robbie's if she'd ever overheard the *Kabalyeros* discussing you, she said, 'No, not that one.' It didn't register at the time, but when I talked to her again a little while ago, she told me Isabel is the member of your family they discuss. They say she's wild, runs around with the men in the gangs. You know that, so does Alex. And so does Madeline Dawson. She just told me the first man Isabel became involved with was her husband."

Amor seemed to shrivel. She gripped the arms of the chair, white-knuckled.

"It's true, isn't it?" I asked more gently.

She lowered her eyes, nodding. When she spoke her voice was ragged. "I don't know what to do with her anymore. Ever since that Reg Dawson got to her, she's been different, not my girl at all."

"Is she on drugs?"

"Alex says no, but I'm not so sure."

I let it go; it didn't really matter. "When she came home earlier," I said, "Isabel seemed very interested in me. She asked questions, looked me over carefully enough to be able to describe me to the *Kabalyeros*. She was afraid of what I might find out. For instance, that she wasn't accosted by any men with guns last Friday."

"She was!"

"No, Amor. That was just a story, to make it look as if your life—and your children's—were in danger if you testified. In spite of what you said early on, you haven't wanted to testify against Tommy Dragón from the very beginning.

"When the *Kabalyeros* began harassing you a month ago, you saw that as the perfect excuse not to take the stand. But you didn't foresee that Dragón's lawyer would convince the gang to stop the harassment. When that happened, you and Isabel, and probably Alex, too, manufactured incidents—the shot-out window, the dead dog on the doorstep, the men with the guns—to make it look as if the harassment was still going on."

"Why would I? They're going to put me in jail."

"But at the time you didn't know they could do that—or that your employer would hire me. My investigating poses yet another danger to you and your family."

"This is . . . why would I do all that?"

"Because basically you're an honest woman, a good woman. You didn't want to testify because you knew Dragón didn't shoot Dawson. It's my guess you gave the police his name because it was the first one that came to mind."

"I had no reason to—"

"You had the best reason in the world: a mother's desire to protect her child."

She was silent, sunken eyes registering despair and defeat.

I kept on, even though I hated to inflict further pain on her. "The day he died, Dawson had let the word out that he was going to desecrate

Benny's space. The person who shot him knew there would be fighting and confusion, counted on that as a cover. The killer hated Dawson—"

"Lots of people did."

"But only one person you'd want to protect so badly that you'd accuse an innocent man."

"Leave my mother alone. She's suffered enough on account of what I did."

I turned. Alex had come into the room so quietly I hadn't noticed. Now he moved midway between Amor and me, a Saturday night special clutched in his right hand.

The missing murder weapon.

I tensed, but one look at his face told me he didn't intend to use it. Instead he raised his arm and extended the gun, grip first.

"Take this," he said. "I never should of bought it. Never should of used it. I hated Dawson on account of what he did to my sister. But killing him wasn't worth what we've all gone through since."

I glanced at Amor; tears were trickling down her face.

Alex said, "Mama, don't cry. I'm not worth it."

When she spoke, it was to me. "What will happen to him?"

"Nothing like what might have happened to Dragón; Alex is a juvenile. You, however—"

"I don't care about myself, only my children."

Maybe that was the trouble. She was the archetypal selfless mother: living only for her children, sheltering them from the consequences of their actions—and in the end doing them irreparable harm.

There were times when I felt thankful that I had no children. And there were times when I was thankful that Jack Stuart was a very good criminal lawyer. This was a time when I was thankful on both counts. I went to the phone, called Jack, and asked him to come over here. At least I could leave the Angeles family in good legal hands.

After he arrived, I went out into the gathering dusk. An old yellow VW was pulling out of Benny's space. I walked down there and stood on the curb. Nothing remained of the shrine to Benny Crespo. Nothing remained to show that blood had boiled and been shed here. It was merely a stretch of cracked asphalt, splotched with oil drippings, littered with the detritus of urban life. I stared at it for close to a minute, then turned away from the bleak landscape of Omega Street.

HEARTBREAK HOUSE

Sara Paretsky

Sara Paretsky is regularly reviewed in places where other mystery writers are never mentioned. Her novels, dealing as they do with the lives of contemporary women, have found an audience outside genre. She appeals to people who rarely if ever read mystery stories. And she appeals to that generation known as boomers who have learned the hard way that despite some major advances for women, there is still a substantial way to go before we reach anything like parity between the sexes. Here is Paretsky at the top of her game, much as she is in her latest novel, *Total Recall*.

N ATASHA'S HAIR, AS *sleek and black as a raven's wing, framed the delicate oval of her face. Raoul thought she had never looked more desirable than now, with her dark, doelike eyes filled with tears, and a longing beyond tears.*

"It's no good, darling," she whispered, summoning a valiant smile. "Papa has lost all his money. I must go to India with the Crawfords to mind their children."

"Darling—for you to be a nanny—how utterly absurd. And in that climate. You must not!" His square, manly face suffused with color, betraying the strength of his feeling.

"You haven't even mentioned marriage," Natasha whispered, looking at the bracelets on her slender wrist, wondering if they, too, must be sold, along with Mama's diamonds.

Raoul flushed more deeply. "We're engaged. Even if our families don't know about it. But how can I marry you now, when I have no prospects and your papa cannot give you a dowry. . . ."

A MY LOOKED UP. "Wonderful, Roxanne. Your strongest effort yet. Do Raoul and Natasha get married in the end?"

"No, no." Roxanne took the manuscript back. "They're just the first generation. Natasha marries a planter, not that she can ever give her heart to him, and Raoul dies of blackwater fever in the jungle during the Boer War, with Natasha's name on his writhen lips. It's their grandchildren who finally get together. That's the significance of the last page."

She turned the manuscript over and read aloud to Amy, *"Natalie had never met Granny Natasha, but she recognized the face smiling at the head of the bed as she embraced Ralph. It seemed to say 'Godspeed and God bless,' and even, in the brief glimpse she caught before surrendering herself to love, to wink."*

"Yes, yes, I see," Amy agreed, wondering if there were another person in New York—in the world—who could use *writhen* with Roxanne's sincere intensity. "Very much in the spirit of Isabel Allende or Laura Esquivel."

Roxanne looked haughtily at her editor. She didn't know the names and didn't care to learn them. If Amy thought the star of Gaudy Press needed to copy someone, it was time for her to have a conversation with Lila Trumbull, Roxanne's agent.

Amy, an expert on Roxanne Craybourne's own doelike glances, leaned forward. "All the South American writers who've been winning Nobel prizes lately have ghosts haunting their work. I thought it was a nice touch, to show *The New York Times* and some of these other snobs in the most delicate way imaginable that you are fully aware of contemporary literary conventions, but you only choose to use them when you can enhance them."

Roxanne smiled. Amy really was quite nice. She'd proved it the weekend she'd stayed at the Taos house, after all. It was terrible to be so suspicious of everyone that you couldn't trust their lightest comments. But then, when she thought how badly Kenny had betrayed her . . .

Amy, watching the shift from complacency to tragedy on her star's face, wondered what nerve-storm she now had to deflect. "Is everything all right, Roxanne?" she asked in a gentle, caring voice that would have astounded her own children and grandchildren.

Roxanne gave a little sniff, brushing the hint of a tear from her left eye. "I was just thinking of Kenny, and how badly he treated me. And then to see it written up in the *Star* and the *Sun*. It's too much to suffer tragedy, without having it plastered around the supermarkets where all one's friends see it, and badger one forever. Not to mention Mother's insufferable mah-jongg club."

"Kenny? What—did his embezzling habits not die at the end of his parole?" Amy was startled out of maternal concern into her normal sardonic speech. She cursed herself as soon as the words were out, but Roxanne, in as full a dramatic flight as one of her own heroines, hadn't noticed.

"I thought he was trying." She fluttered tapered, manicured fingers, muscular from the weight of the rings they held up. "Mother kept telling me he was just taking advantage, but it's the kind of thing she's always saying about my boyfriends, ever since high school, jealous because she never had half as many when she was young. And when he hit me the first time and said he was *truly* sorry of course I believed him. Anyone would have. But when he walked off with a million in bearer bonds it was just too much. What else could I do? And then, well, you know I had to spend *months* in the hospital."

Amy did know. There had been dreadful late-night meetings at Gaudy Press over the news that Roxanne Craybourne might have suffered permanent brain damage when Kenny Coleman beat her up for the last time. Even Roxanne, on checking out of the rehabilitation clinic where she'd spent two months after leaving the hospital, had decided she couldn't forgive Kenny that. She divorced him, changed her security system, and moved the twenty-four-year-old gardener who'd brought her flowers every day into the master suite.

And then, in eleven weeks, gone on to write the thrilling tale of Natasha, the heiress victimized by her papa's trusted henchman, who embezzled all his money. "Poured white-hot from her molten pen" was the copy Gaudy would run in the national ad campaign.

"And I'm terrified that she'll marry that damned gardener next," Amy told her boss the next morning. "First it was the dreadful surgeon who slept with his women patients, then Kenny, and now some gardener who needs a green card."

Clay Rossiter grinned. "Send her a wedding present. She thrives on that kind of situation."

"I'm the one who has to hold her hand through all these trials," Amy snapped. "She doesn't thrive: she trembles on the verge of a nervous breakdown."

"But, Amy, sweetie, don't you see—that's what makes her such a phenomenal success. She's the helpless waif who crops up in *A Clean Wound*, *Embarrassment of Riches*, and the rest. She believes in the agonies of all those idiotic Glendas and Corinnes and—who did you say the latest was—Natasha? Did you persuade her she couldn't call it *A Passage to India?*"

"It was tough," Amy said. "Of course she'd never heard of E. M.

Forster—I finally had to show her the video of *A Passage to India* before she listened to me. And even then she only agreed to a title change when I persuaded her that Forster's estate would make money from her because her fans would buy the video thinking it was her story. And no, I haven't got a clue whether he's got an estate or if it would get royalties, and don't go talking to Lila Trumbull about it, either, for pity's sake. We're calling Natasha's misery *Broken Covenant*. Oh, by the way, *A Clean Wound* hit the paperback list at number two. We're printing another five hundred thousand."

Rossiter smiled. "Just keep feeding her herbal tea. Send her roses. Let her know we're her best friends. See if you can engender some kind of vicious streak in the gardener, assuming he hasn't got one already."

"*You* do that," Amy said, getting to her feet. "I've got a meeting with one of our few real writers—Gary Blanchard has done a beautiful book, a kind of modern-day quest set in the Dakotas. It'll sell around eight thousand, ten if we're lucky. *Broken Covenant* should make it possible to give him an advance."

After Amy left, Clay went back to the fax he'd received from Jambon et Cie PLC, his corporate masters in Brussels. They were very disappointed in Gaudy's third-quarter performance. It's true they'd made a profit, thanks to the strong showing of *Embarrassment of Riches* in hardcover, but Gaudy needed several more bankable stars. They were too dependent on Roxanne Craybourne—if they lost her they'd be dribbling along with the nickel-and-dime stuff, the so-called literary writers which Jambon was doing its best to discard. If Clay Rossiter didn't want to be looking for a new job in six months, Jambon expected a marketing plan and sales numbers to show the list was acquiring market flexibility.

Clay curled his lip. Eighteen pages of numbers followed, a demented outburst of someone's spreadsheet program. Title by title Brussels had gone through Gaudy's list, with projections of sales based on changing the number of copies in Wal-Mart, the amount of bus-side advertising, the weight of paper used in dust jackets, the number of trips each sales rep made to key accounts. And Clay was expected—ordered, really—to give a written response to all these projections by the end of the month.

"The curse of modern business is not tight capital, bad management, low productivity, or poor education, but the personal computer," he snarled.

His secretary poked her head through the door. "Did you say something, Clay?"

"Yes. Idiotic boys—and girls—who've never held a book think they can run the book industry from three thousand miles away because they have a microchip that lets them conjure up scenarios. If they'd ever ridden a truck from a warehouse into Wal-Mart they'd know you can't even tell how many copies the store took, let alone—oh, well. What's the use. Send a note down to Amy that she cannot give her new literary pet—what's his name? Gary Blanchard?—more than twenty thousand. If he wants to walk, let him. If I see Farrar or Knopf on the spine when the book comes out it will not make me weep with frustration."

ISABELLA TREMBLED IN his arms. "I must not. You know I must not. Your mama, if she saw me—"

Her raven hair, enhancing the milky purity of her skin, cascaded over his shoulders as Albion pulled her to him more tightly. "She will learn to love you as I do, my beautiful Mexican flower. Ah, how could I ever have thought I was in love before?"

Albion Whittley thought distastefully of all the spoiled debutantes he'd squired around New York City. He wasn't just Albion Whittley—there was that damned "IV" after his name, meaning his parents expected him to marry someone in their set. How could he expect them to believe that the gardener's daughter stood head and shoulders above all the Bennington girls he'd had to date? The purity of her heart, the nobility of her impulses—every penny she earned going back to Guadalupe to her crippled grandmother.

"Albion, darling, are you enjoying your little holiday? Isabella, I left my gloves on my dressing table. Fetch them for me while my son and I have a talk."

Mrs. Albion Whittley the Third had appeared on the terrace. Her tinkling laugh and light sarcastic manner made both young people blush. Albion dropped Isabella's hand as though it had turned to molten lava. The girl fled inside the mansion. . . .

"BEAUTIFUL," AMY GUSHED, marveling at her own acting ability. "They triumph over every obstacle in the end? Or is it like Natasha, only able to experience happiness through her granddaughter?"

Roxanne looked reproachful. "I never tell the same story twice. My readers wouldn't stand for it. Albion joins the CIA to prove his manliness to Mama. He's sent on a secret mission to Central America, where he has to take on a drug lord. When he's wounded Isabella finds him in the jungle and nurses him back to health, but the drug lord is smitten by her beauty. Since she knows Albion's mother is implacable she agrees to become the drug lord's mistress. This leads her to a jet-setting career in Brazil and Spain, and she meets Mrs. Whittley as an equal in Majorca. In the end the CIA kills the drug lord, and Albion, who's never forgotten her, rescues her from the fortress where she's been incarcerated."

"Wonderful," Amy said. "Only I don't think we can call it *The Trail of Tears*."

She tried explaining how disrespectful this might seem to the American Indian community, but gave up when her star's eyes flashed fury.

"Everyone knows how good I am to the Indians who live on my estate in Taos. I'm not having them wreck my book because of some hundred-year-old battle they can't forget. And after the way Gerardo treated me—he was half Indian, and always bragging about it—I think they owe me some consideration for a change."

"It's the libraries," Amy said hastily. "*So* ignorant. But we don't want your book shelved with Indian literature, do we? Your loyal fans will want to see it prominently displayed with new fiction."

They agreed in the end on *Fool's Gold*, with a Central American pyramid to be shown in jagged pieces around a single rose. Roxanne settled her jacket around her shoulders and held out her cup for more tea. She wasn't sure she even wanted a Central American pyramid. Wouldn't it always remind her of the misery she'd felt when Gerardo betrayed her? Her mother had warned her, but then Mother was positively lying in wait to watch her misery.

Amy, alert to the quiver in Roxanne's chin, asked if the cover decision troubled her. "We'll get Peter to do a series of layouts. You know we're not tied to what we decide today."

Roxanne held out a hand. Amy tried hard, but she wasn't sensitive—she wasn't an artist, after all—she lived in the world of sales and bottom lines.

"This whole discussion overwhelms me with memories of Gerardo. People said he only wanted me for my money. And to get a green card. But it's not impossible for love to flourish between a man of twenty-four and a woman my age. Just think of Cher. And despite all those ridiculous exercise videos she isn't any better looking than I am."

That much was true. Adolescent passion kept Roxanne young. Her own skin could indeed be described as milky, her dark eyes lustrous, child-like, confiding. Her auburn hair was perhaps hand tinted to keep its youthful shades of color, but if you didn't know she was forty-six you'd assume the rich browns and reds were natural.

"When I found him in bed with my maid I believed Gerardo, that she was homesick and he was comforting her. My mother ridiculed me, but how can you possibly live so cynically and ever be happy?"

Roxanne held her hands out in mute appeal—two poignant doves, Amy thought, murmuring, "Yes, indeed."

"But then, the night I got back from Cannes, I found them together at the swimming pool. He wouldn't come to Cannes with me—he said he shouldn't leave the country until his immigrant status was straightened out, so I raced home a day early just to be with him, but then even I had to realize—and he'd paid for her abortion, with money I'd given him."

"You poor child," Amy said, patting her hand. "You're far too trusting."

Roxanne lifted her doelike eyes in mute gratitude. Amy was so warm, a true friend, unlike the hangers-on who only wanted to sponge off her success.

"Someone in Santa Fe suggested I talk to a psychiatrist. As if I were sick!"

"How dreadful." Amy sounded shocked. "And yet, the right psychiatrist—a sympathetic woman, perhaps—could listen to you impartially. Unlike your mother, or your friends, who are always judging you and scolding you."

"Is that what psychiatrists do?" Roxanne opened her eyes wide. "Listen?"

"The good ones do," Amy said.

"YOU DID WHAT?" Clay Rossiter screamed. "You're the one who needs a psychiatrist. We can't have her getting over her neuroses. They're what drive her books. Look, fifteen weeks after finding Raoul in bed with her maid she produces a bestseller for us. We can do an initial run of a million five. That's our paychecks for the entire year, Amy."

"Raoul was the hero of Broken Covenant. Gerardo was her gardener. You're not the one who has to feed her tea and bolster her after the cad has been found out. Not to mention take her to Lutèce and listen to the storm of passion while it's at gale force."

Clay bared his teeth at her. "That's what we pay you to do, Amy.

You're the goddamn star's goddamn editor. She likes you. We even had to write it into her last contract that she will only work with you."

"Don't lose sleep over it. The chances are against Roxanne entering therapy. She's more likely to pick some New Age guru and have a deep mystical experience with him." Amy got up. "You know Gary Blanchard signed with Ticknor & Fields? I'm really annoyed, Clay. We could have kept him for twenty-five thousand: he's very humble in his needs and it makes me sick to lose a talented writer."

"He's humble because he knows no one wants to read artistic work. Let Ticknor & Fields have him. They don't have Jambon et Cie breathing down their necks." Clay picked up his latest fax from Brussels and waved it at her.

Amy skimmed it. Jambon was disappointed that Clay had rejected all of their previous marketing proposals, but pleased he had let Gary Blanchard go. All of the scenarios they had run on Quattro showed that every dollar spent on advertising would lose them thirty cents on revenue from Blanchard's work. They definitely did not want anyone on the Gaudy list who sold fewer than twenty-seven thousand in hardcover.

"This isn't publishing," she said, tossing it back at him. "They ought to go into breakfast cereal. It's more suited to their mentality."

"Yes, Amy, but they own us. So unless you want to look for a job right before Christmas, don't go signing any more literary lights. We can't afford them."

"*I DREAMED I went to the airport to catch my flight to Paris, but they wouldn't let me in first class. They said I was dirty, and badly dressed, and I had to fly coach. But all the coach seats were taken so I had to go by Greyhound, and the bus got lost and ended up in this dreary farmhouse in the middle of Kansas.*"

The eminent psychiatrist, his kindly gray eyes moved to tears by the beautiful girl on the couch in front of him, sighed and stirred in his chair. How could he ever persuade her that she was clean enough, good enough, for first class?

AMY CHOKED. "ROXANNE. Dear. Where's the story?"
"It's here. In front of you. Have you forgotten how to read?"

"But your readers expect passion, romance. Nothing happens. The doctor doesn't even fall in love with Clarissa."

"Well, he does of course, but he keeps it to himself." Roxanne picked up the manuscript and thumbed through it. She began reading aloud, clicking her rings against the chair arm for emphasis.

CLARISSA PUT HER hand trustingly in the older man's. "You don't know how much this means to me, Doctor. To finally find someone who understands what I've been through."

Dr. Friedrich felt his flesh stir. His professional calm had never been pierced by any of his patients before, but this gaminelike waif, abused by father, abandoned by mother, so in need of trust and guidance, was different.

He longed to be able to say "My dear, I wish you would not think of me as your doctor, but your dearest friend as well. I long for nothing more than to protect you from the blasts of the stormy world beyond these walls." But if he spoke he would lose her precious trust forever.

ROXANNE DROPPED THE pages with a thump, as though that settled the point.

"Well, why can't he marry her?" Amy asked.

"Amy, you didn't read it, did you? He's already got a wife, only she's in an institution for the criminally insane. But his compassion is so great he can't bring himself to divorce her. Then the Nazi-hunters confuse him with a man who was a prison-camp guard who looked like him, and he gets arrested. It turns out that the wife has turned him in—that her criminal insanity has given her a persecution complex and she blames him for all her troubles. So Clarissa has to find him, behind the Iron Curtain—this takes place in 1983—where he's been put into a gulag—and rescue him. And the wife has a brainstorm when she finds out he's been rescued. That kills her. But Clarissa has already become a nun. They sometimes dream about each other, but they die without seeing one another again."

Amy blinked. "It seems a little downbeat for your readers, Roxanne. I wonder if—"

"Don't wonder at me, Amy," Roxanne snapped, her luminous eyes flashing magnificently. "Dr. Reindorf says happy endings are difficult to find. My readers need to learn that just as much as I do. If they keep expecting every book to be a panacea they'll be just as badly off as me, expecting every man I fall in love with to solve all my problems."

———

"I WARNED YOU," Clay snarled. "Send her off to the fucking shrinks and what happens? We get cheap psychology about her readers and a book no one will buy. The woman can't write, for Christ sake. If she loses her adolescent fantasy about true love she loses her audience."

"Maybe Dr. Reindorf will betray her as badly as Gerardo and Kenny, and that surgeon, her first husband, who gave us *A Clean Wound*."

"We can't take that chance," Clay said. "You've got to do something."

"I'm sixty," Amy said. "I can take early retirement. You're the one who's worried about it. You do something. Get the publicity department to plant a story in the *National Enquirer* that Roxanne is getting therapy from a child molester."

She meant it as a joke, but Clay thought it was worth an effort. His publicity staff turned him down.

"We can't plant stories about our own writers. Publishing is a community of gossips. Someone will know, they'll leak it to someone else who hates you, and the next thing you know Roxanne will be at Putnam and you'll be eating wiener-water soup."

Clay began to lose sleep. *Final Analysis*, done in silver with a suggestive couch on the cover, came well out of the gate, but word of mouth began killing it before the second printing was ready. It jumped onto the *Times* list in third place but stayed there only a week before plummeting to ninth. After five short weeks *Final Analysis* dropped off the list into the black hole of overstock and remainders.

The faxes from Brussels were hot enough to scorch the veneer from Clay Rossiter's desktop, while Roxanne's agent, Lila Trumbull, called daily to blame Clay for not marketing the book properly.

"But you can't market long, dull dreams and their interpretation," Clay howled to his secretary. "As I told Amy."

Clay fired Amy, to relieve his feelings, then had to rehire her the next morning: Roxanne had an editor clause in her contract. She could leave Gaudy if Amy did.

"Only, if she's going to keep turning out cheap psychology it won't matter. Pretty soon even Harlequin won't touch her. And, by the way, we won't be able to afford you. How long has she been seeing this damned shrink?"

"About nine months. And the last time she was in New York she only stayed overnight so as not to miss a session. So it doesn't seem to be following the course of her usual infatuations."

"He's not in New York? Where is he?"

"Santa Fe. This isn't the only town with psychiatrists in it, Clay."

"Yeah, they're like rats: wherever you find a human population, there they'll be, eating the garbage," Clay grumbled. "Maybe he can fall off a mesa."

When Amy left he stared at the clock. It was eleven in New York. Nine A.M. in New Mexico. He got up abruptly and took his coat from behind the door.

"I have the flu," he told his secretary. "If some moron calls from Brussels tell him I'm running a high fever and can't talk."

"You look healthy to me," she said.

"It's the hectic flush of fever."

He was out of the office before she could chide him further. He flagged a cab, then changed his mind. The cops were forever questioning cabdrivers. He took the long, slow subway ride to Queens.

On the flight to Albuquerque he wondered what he should do about renting a car. He'd paid cash for his ticket so that he could use an assumed name, but he'd need a driver's license and credit card to rent a car. When the man next to him got up to use the bathroom Clay went through his breastpocket. They didn't look anything alike, but no one ever inspected those photos. And fortunately the man's home was in New Mexico. He wouldn't miss his license until after Clay mailed it back to him, with cash for the price of the rental, of course.

It turned out to be easy, Pathetically easy. He called Dr. Reindorf and told him the truth, that he was Roxanne's publisher, that they were all worried about her, and could he have a word in confidence. Someplace quiet, remote, where they wouldn't run the risk of Roxanne seeing Clay and feeling spied upon. Reindorf suggested a mesa with a view of Santa Fe below it when he'd finished seeing patients for the day.

Clay made the red-eye back to New York with an hour to spare. The next morning Amy stuck her head around his door. She started to ask him something, but decided he really did have the flu, his eyes were so puffy. It wasn't until later in the day that Roxanne called her, distraught at Reindorf's death.

"She somehow ended up going to the morgue to look at the body, don't ask me why," Amy told Clay's secretary, since Clay had gone home sick again. "It had been run over by a car several times before being thrown from the mesa. The cops hauled her ex-gardener in for questioning, but they don't seem to have any suspects."

"The news should revive Clay," his secretary said.

---

*A*NCILLA'S HANDS FLUTTERED *at her sides like captive birds. "You don't understand, Karl. Papa is dead. His work—I never valued it properly, but I must try to carry it on."*

"But, darling girl, it's too heavy a burden for you. It's just not a suitable job for a woman."

"Ah, if you knew what I felt, when I saw him—had to identify his body after the jackals had been at it—no burden could be too big for me now."

Karl felt pride stir within him. He had loved Ancilla when she had been a beautiful, willful girl, the toast of Vienna. But now, prepared to assume a woman's role in life—to shoulder a load most men would turn from—the spoiled child lines dropped from her cherry lips, giving her the mouth of a woman, firm, ripe, desirable.

"I LOVE IT," Clay said. "I'm ecstatic. And you're calling it *Life's Work*? You got her to change it from *An Unsuitable Job for a Woman*? Good going. It's been only seventeen weeks since that shrink died and she's already cured. We ought to be able to print a million, a million two, easy. I'll fax Brussels. We'll go out to celebrate."

"I'd rather celebrate right here." Amy shut his office door. "We have a chance to sign a really brilliant new writer. Her name is Lisa Ferguson and she's written an extraordinary novel about life in western Kansas during the sixties. She's going to be the next Eudora Welty."

"No, Amy. Hispanic experience is good. African is possible. But rural Kansas is of no interest to anyone these days except you. I'm certainly not going to pitch it to Brussels."

Amy leaned over the desk. "Clay, Lila Trumbull called me seventeen weeks ago. The day after you went home sick with the flu."

"She's always calling. How can you know what day it was?"

"Because that was when Roxanne's shrink's body was found." Amy smiled and spoke softly, as if to Roxanne herself. "Lila thought she saw you in the Albuquerque airport the day before. She was stopping to see Roxanne on her way back to New York from L.A. and was sure you were renting a car when she was picking up her bags. She'd called to you, but you were in such a hurry you didn't hear her."

Clay shifted in his chair. When he spoke his voice came out in a croak.

"I—she—she should have asked at the rental counter. They could've told her no one rented a car in my name that day. Anyway, I couldn't have been there. I was home with the flu."

"That's what I told her, Clay. You were home sick—she must have been mistaken. And that's what I'll tell anyone else who asks. . . . I'll call Lisa Ferguson's agent and tell her thirty, okay?"

Clay stared at her glassily, like a stuffed owl. "Sure, Amy. You do that."

Amy stood up. "Oh—and, Clay, in case you're thinking how good I'd look at the bottom of a mesa—or under the IRT—I hope you remember Roxanne has an editor clause in her contract. And she's made it clear a dozen different ways that she won't work with you."

Clay's secretary came down to Amy's office a few minutes later. "Can you talk to old Mr. Jambon in Brussels? Clay's gone home sick again. I hope there isn't anything serious wrong with him."

Amy smiled. "He's fine. He just got a little overexcited this morning about Roxanne's new book."

STACKED DECK

Bill Pronzini

While the Nameless Detective series is very well written, cleverly plotted, and steeped with fascinating characters, it is also, one senses, a kind of diary for its author. Stretching over several decades now, the series spotlights both San Francisco and an unnamed detective, and charts how both have changed over this period of time. *Shackles* (1988) and *Sentinels* (1996) are two of the series highlights. And author Bill Pronzini has proved he can write nonseries novels, too—*Blue Lonesome* (1995) and *A Wasteland of Strangers* (1997) being among the most creative and moving novels of the 1990s, in or out of crime fiction. Nameless makes his most recent appearances in *Illusions* and *Crazybone*. Also, as you are about to discover, Pronzini is a master of the short story.

ONE

FROM WHERE HE stood in the shadow of a split-bole Douglas fir, Deighan had a clear view of the cabin down below. Big harvest moon tonight, and only a few streaky clouds scudding past now and then to dim its hard yellow shine. The hard yellow glistened off the surface of Lake Tahoe beyond, softened into a long silverish stripe out toward the middle. The rest of the water shone like polished black metal. All of it was empty as far as he could see, except for the red-and-green running lights of a boat well away to the south, pointed toward the neon shimmer that marked the South Shore gambling casinos.

The cabin was big, made of cut pine logs and red-wood shakes. It had a railed redwood deck that overlooked the lake, mostly invisible from where Deighan was. A flat concrete pier jutted out into the moonstruck water, a pair of short wooden floats making a T at its outer end. The boat tied up there was a thirty-foot Chris-Craft with sleeping accommodations for four. Nothing but the finer things for the Shooter.

Deighan watched the cabin. He'd been watching it for three hours now, from this same vantage point. His legs bothered him a little, standing around like this, and his eyes hurt from squinting. Time was, he'd had the night vision of an owl. Not anymore. What he had now, that he hadn't had when he was younger, was patience. He'd learned that in the last three years, along with a lot of other things—patience most of all.

On all sides the cabin was dark, but that was because they'd put the blackout curtains up. The six of them had been inside for better than two hours now, the same five-man nucleus as on every Thursday night except during the winter months, plus the one newcomer. The Shooter went to Hawaii when it started to snow. Or Florida or the Bahamas—someplace warm. Mannlicher and Brandt stayed home in the winter. Deighan didn't know what the others did, and he didn't care.

A match flared in the darkness between the carport, where the Shooter's Caddy Eldorado was slotted, and the parking area back among the trees. That was the lookout—Mannlicher's boy. Some lookout: he smoked a cigarette every five minutes, like clockwork, so you always knew where he was. Deighan watched him smoke this one. When he was done, he threw the butt away in a shower of sparks, and then seemed to remember that he was surrounded by dry timber and went after it and stamped it out with his shoe. *Some* lookout.

Deighan held his watch up close to his eyes, pushed the little button that lighted its dial. Ten-nineteen. Just about time. The lookout was moving again, down toward the lake. Pretty soon he would walk out on the pier and smoke another cigarette and admire the view for a few minutes. He apparently did that at least twice every Thursday night—that had been his pattern on each of the last two—and he hadn't gone through the ritual yet tonight. He was bored, that was the thing. He'd been at his job a long time and it was always the same; there wasn't anything for him to do except walk around and smoke cigarettes and look at three hundred square miles of lake. Nothing ever happened. In three years nothing had ever happened.

Tonight something was going to happen.

Deighan took the gun out of the clamshell holster at his belt. It was a Smith & Wesson .38, light-weight, compact—a good piece, one of the best he'd ever owned. He held it in his hand, watching as the lookout performed as if on cue—walked to the pier, stopped, then moved out along its flat surface. When the guy had gone halfway, Deighan came out of the shadows and went down the slope at an angle across the driveway, to the rear of the cabin. His shoes made little sliding sounds on the needled ground, but they weren't sounds that carried.

He'd been over this ground three times before, dry runs the last two Thursday nights and once during the day when nobody was around; he knew just where and how to go. The lookout was lighting up again, his back to the cabin, when Deighan reached the rear wall. He eased along it to the spare-bedroom window. The sash went up easily, noiselessly. He could hear them then, in the rec room—voices, ice against glass, the click and rattle of the chips. He got the ski mask from his jacket pocket, slipped it over his head, snugged it down. Then he climbed through the window, put his penlight on just long enough to orient himself, went straight across to the door that led into the rec room.

It didn't make a sound, either, when he opened it. He went in with the revolver extended, elbow locked. Sturgess saw him first. He said, "Jesus Christ!" and his body went as stiff as if he were suffering a stroke. The others turned in their chairs, gawking. The Shooter started up out of his.

Deighan said, fast and hard, "Sit still if you don't want to die. Hands on the table where I can see them—all of you. Do it!"

They weren't stupid; they did what they were told. Deighan watched them through a thin haze of tobacco smoke. Six men around the hexagonal poker table, hands flat on its green baize, heads lifted or twisted to stare at him. He knew five of them. Mannlicher, the fat owner of the Nevornia Club; he had Family ties, even though he was a Prussian, because he'd once done some favors for an east-coast *capo*. Brandt, Mannlicher's cousin and private enforcer, who doubled as the Nevornia's floor boss. Bellah, the quasi-legitimate real-estate developer and high roller. Sturgess, the bankroll behind the Jackpot Lounge up at North Shore. And the Shooter— hired muscle, hired gun, part-time coke runner, whose real name was Dennis D'Allesandro. The sixth man was the pigeon they'd lured in for this particular game, a lean guy in his fifties with Texas oil money written all over him and his fancy clothes—Donley or Donavan, something like that.

Mannlicher was the bank tonight; the table behind his chair was covered with stacks of dead presidents—fifties and hundreds, mostly. Deighan took out the folded-up flour sack, tossed it on top of the poker chips that littered the baize in front of Mannlicher. "All right. Fill it."

The fat man didn't move. He was no pushover; he was hard, tough, mean. And he didn't like being ripped off. Veins bulged in his neck, throbbed in his temples. The violence in him was close to the surface now, held thinly in check.

"You know who we are?" he said. "Who I am?"

"Fill it."

"You dumb bastard. You'll never live to spend it."

"Fill the sack. *Now.*"

Deighan's eyes, more than his gun, made up Mannlicher's mind for him. He picked up the sack, pushed around in his chair, began to savagely feed in the stacks of bills.

"The rest of you," Deighan said, "put your wallets, watches, jewelry on the table. Everything of value. Hurry it up."

The Texan said, "Listen heah—" and Deighan pointed the .38 at his head and said, "One more word, you're a dead man." The Texan made an effort to stare him down, but it was just to save face; after two or three seconds he lowered his gaze and began stripping the rings off his fingers.

The rest of them didn't make any fuss. Bellah was sweating; he kept swiping it out of his eyes, his hands moving in little jerks and twitches. Brandt's eyes were like dull knives, cutting away at Deighan's masked face. D'Allesandro showed no emotion of any kind. That was his trademark; he was your original iceman. They might have called him that, maybe, if he'd been like one of those old-timers who used an ice pick or a blade. As it was, with his preferences, the Shooter was the right name for him.

Mannlicher had the sack full now. The platinum ring on his left hand, with its circle of fat diamonds, made little gleams and glints in the shine from the low-hanging droplight. The idea of losing that bothered him even more than losing his money; he kept running the fingers of his other hand over the stones.

"The ring," Deighan said to him. "Take it off."

"Go to hell."

"Take it off or I'll put a third eye in the middle of your forehead. Your choice."

Mannlicher hesitated, tried to stare him down, didn't have any better luck at it than the Texan. There was a tense moment; then, because he didn't want to die over a piece of jewelry, he yanked the ring off, slammed it down hard in the middle of the table.

Deighan said, "Put it in the sack. The wallets and the rest of the stuff too."

This time Mannlicher didn't hesitate. He did as he'd been told.

"All right," Deighan said. "Now get up and go over by the bar. Lie down on the floor on your belly."

Mannlicher got up slowly, his jaw set and his teeth clenched as if to keep the violence from spewing out like vomit. He lay down on the floor. Deighan gestured at Brandt, said, "You next. Then the rest of you, one at a time."

When they were all on the floor he moved to the table, caught up the sack. "Stay where you are for ten minutes," he told them. "You move before that, or call to the guy outside, I'll blow the place up. I got a grenade in my pocket, the fragmentation kind. Anybody doubt it?"

None of them said anything.

Deighan backed up into the spare bedroom, leaving the door open so he could watch them all the way to the window. He put his head out, saw no sign of the lookout. Still down by the lake somewhere. The whole thing had taken just a few minutes.

He swung out through the window, hurried away in the shadows—but in the opposite direction from the driveway and the road above. On the far side of the cabin there was a path that angled through the pine forest to the north; he found it, followed it at a trot. Enough moonlight penetrated through the branches overhead to let him see where he was going.

He was almost to the lakefront when the commotion started back there: voices, angry and pulsing in the night, Mannlicher's the loudest of them. They hadn't waited the full ten minutes, but then he hadn't expected them to. It didn't matter. The Shooter's cabin was invisible from here, cut off by a wooded finger of land a hundred yards wide. And they wouldn't be looking for him along the water, anyway. They'd be up on the road, combing that area; they'd figure automatically that his transportation was a car.

The hard yellow-and-black gleam of the lake was just ahead, the rushes and ferns where he'd tied up the rented Beachcraft inboard. He moved across the sandy strip of beach, waded out to his calves, dropped the loaded flour sack into the boat, then eased the craft free of the rushes before he lifted himself over the gunwale. The engine caught with a quiet rumble the first time he turned the key.

They were still making noise back at the cabin, blundering around like fools, as he eased away into the night.

TWO

THE MOTEL WAS called the Whispering Pines. It was back off Highway 28 below Crystal Bay, a good half mile from the lake, tucked up in a grove of pines and Douglas fir. Deighan's cabin was the farthest from the office, detached from its nearest neighbor by thirty feet of open ground.

Inside he sat in darkness except for flickering light from the television. The set was an old one; the picture was riddled with snow and kept jumping every few seconds. But he didn't care; he wasn't watching it. Or listening to it: he had the sound turned off. It was on only because he didn't like waiting in the dark.

It had been after midnight when he came in—too late to make the ritual call to Fran, even though he'd felt a compulsion to do so. She went to bed at eleven-thirty; she didn't like the phone to ring after that. How could he blame her? When he was home and she was away at Sheila's or her sister's, he never wanted it to ring that late either.

It was one-ten now. He was tired, but not too tired. The evening was still in his blood, warming him, like liquor or drugs that hadn't quite worn off yet. Mannlicher's face . . . that was an image he'd never forget. The Shooter's, too, and Brandt's, but especially Mannlicher's.

Outside, a car's headlamps made a sweep of light across the curtained window as it swung in through the motel courtyard. When it stopped nearby and the lights went out, Deighan thought: It's about time.

Footsteps made faint crunching sounds on gravel. Soft knock on the door. Soft voice following: "Prince? You in there?"

"Door's open."

A wedge of moonlight widened across the floor, not quite reaching to where Deighan sat in the lone chair with the .38 in his hand. The man who stood silhouetted in the opening made a perfect target—just a damned airhead, any way you looked at him.

"Prince?"

"I'm over here. Come on in, shut the door."

"Why don't you turn on a light?"

"There's a switch by the door."

The man entered, shut the door. There was a click and the ceiling globe came on. Deighan stayed where he was, but reached over with his left hand to turn off the TV.

Bellah stood blinking at him, running his palms along the sides of his expensive cashmere jacket. He said nervously, "For God's sake, put the gun away. What's the idea?"

"I'm the cautious type."

"Well, put it away. I don't like it."

Deighan got to his feet, slid the revolver into his belt holster. "How'd it go?"

"Hairy, damned hairy. Mannlicher was like a madman." Bellah took a handkerchief out of his pocket, wiped his forehead. His angular face was pale, shiny-damp. "I didn't think he'd take it this hard. Christ."

That's the trouble with people like you, Deighan thought. You never think. He pinched a cigarette out of his shirt pocket, lit it with the Zippo

Fran had given him fifteen years ago. Fifteen years, and it still worked. Like their marriage, even with all the trouble. How long was it now? Twenty-two years in May? Twenty-three?

Bellah said, "He started screaming at D'Allesandro. I thought he was going to choke him."

"Who? Mannlicher?"

"Yeah. About the window in the spare bedroom."

"What'd D'Allesandro say?"

"He said he always keeps it locked, you must have jimmied it some way that didn't leave any traces. Mannlicher didn't believe him. He thinks D'Allesandro forgot to lock it."

"Nobody got the idea it was an inside job?"

"No."

"Okay then. Relax, Mr. Bellah. You're in the clear."

Bellah wiped his face again. "Where's the money?"

"Other side of the bed. On the floor."

"You count it?"

"No. I figured you'd want to do that."

Bellah went over there, picked up the flour sack, emptied it on the bed. His eyes were bright and hot as he looked at all the loose green. Then he frowned, gnawed at his lower lip, and poked at Mannlicher's diamond ring. "What'd you take this for? Mannlicher is more pissed about the ring than anything else. He said his mother gave it to him. It's worth ten thousand."

"That's why I took it," Deighan said. "Fifteen percent of the cash isn't a hell of a lot."

Bellah stiffened. "I set it all up, didn't I? Why shouldn't I get the lion's share?"

"I'm not arguing, Mr. Bellah. We agreed on a price; okay, that's the way it is. I'm only saying I got a right to a little something extra."

"All right, all right." Bellah was looking at the money again. "Must be at least two hundred thousand," he said. "That Texan, Donley, brought fifty grand alone."

"Plenty in his wallet too, then."

"Yeah."

Deighan smoked and watched Bellah count the loose bills and what was in the wallets and billfolds. There was an expression on the developer's face like a man has when he's fondling a naked woman. Greed, pure and simple. Greed was what drove Lawrence Bellah; money was his best friend, his lover, his god. He didn't have enough ready cash to buy the lakefront property down near Emerald Bay—property he stood to make three to four million on, with a string of condos—and he couldn't raise it fast enough any legitimate way; so he'd arranged to get it by knocking over his own weekly poker game, even if it meant crossing some hard people. He had balls, you had to give him that. He was stupid as hell, and one of these days he was liable to end up in pieces at the bottom of the lake, but he did have balls.

He was also lucky, at least for the time being, because the man he'd picked to do his strong-arm work was Bob Prince. He had no idea the name was a phony, no idea the whole package on Bob Prince was the result of three years of careful manipulation. All he knew was that Prince had a reputation as dependable, easy to work with, not too smart or money-hungry, and that he was willing to do any kind of muscle work. Bellah didn't have an inkling of what he'd really done by hiring Bob Prince. If he kept on being lucky, he never would.

Bellah was sweating by the time he finished adding up the take. "Two hundred and thirty-three thousand and change," he said. "More than we figured on."

"My cut's thirty-five thousand," Deighan said.

"You divide fast." Bellah counted out two stacks, hundreds and fifties, to one side of the flowered bed-spread. Then he said, "Count it? Or do you trust me?"

Deighan grinned. He rubbed out his cigarette, went to the bed, and took his time shuffling through the stacks. "On the nose," he said when he was done.

Bellah stuffed the rest of the cash back into the flour sack, leaving the watches and jewelry where they lay. He was still nervous, still sweating; he wasn't going to sleep much tonight, Deighan thought.

"That's it, then," Bellah said. "You going back to Chicago tomorrow?"

"Not right away. Thought I'd do a little gambling first."

"Around here? Christ, Prince . . ."

"No. Reno, maybe. I might even go down to Vegas."

"Just get away from Tahoe."

"Sure," Deighan said. "First thing in the morning."

Bellah went to the door. He paused there to tuck the flour sack under his jacket; it made him look as if he had a tumor on his left side. "Don't do anything with that jewelry in Nevada. Wait until you get back to Chicago."

"Whatever you say, Mr. Bellah."

"Maybe I'll need you again sometime," Bellah said. "You'll hear from me if I do."

"Any time. Any old time."

When Bellah was gone, Deighan put five thousand dollars into his suitcase and the other thirty thousand into a knapsack he'd bought two days before at a South Shore sporting goods store. Mannlicher's diamond ring went into the knapsack, too, along with the better pieces among the rest of the jewelry. The watches and the other stuff were no good to him; he bundled those up in a hand towel from the bathroom, stuffed the bundle into the pocket of his down jacket. Then he had one more cigarette, set his portable alarm clock for six a.m., double-locked the door, and went to bed on the left side, with the revolver under the pillow near his right hand.

THREE

IN THE DAWN light the lake was like smoky blue glass, empty except for a few optimistic fishermen anchored close to the eastern shoreline. The morning was cold, autumn-crisp, but there was no wind. The sun was just beginning to rise, painting the sky and its scattered cloudstreaks in pinks and golds. There was old snow on the upper reaches of Mount Tallac, on some of the other Sierra peaks that ringed the lake.

Deighan took the Beachcraft out half a mile before he dropped the bundle of watches and worthless jewelry overboard. Then he cut off at a long diagonal to the north that brought him to within a few hundred yards of the Shooter's cabin. He had his fishing gear out by then, fiddling with the glass rod and tackle—just another angler looking for rainbow, Mackinaw, and cutthroat trout.

There wasn't anybody out and around at the Shooter's place. Deighan glided past at two knots, angled into shore a couple of hundred yards beyond, where there were rushes and some heavy brush and trees overhanging the water. From there he had a pretty good view of the cabin, its front entrance, the Shooter's Caddy parked inside the carport.

It was eight o'clock, and the sun was all the way up, when he switched off the engine and tied up at the bole of the collapsed pine. It was a few minutes past nine-thirty when D'Allesandro came out and walked around to the Caddy. He was alone. No chippies from the casino this morning, not after what had gone down last night. He might be going to the store for cigarettes, groceries, or to a café somewhere for breakfast. He might be going to see somebody, do some business. The important thing was, how long would he be gone?

Deighan watched him back his Caddy out of the carport, drive it away and out of sight on the road above. He stayed where he was, fishing, waiting. At the end of an hour, when the Shooter still hadn't come back, he started the boat's engine and took his time maneuvering around the wooded finger of land to the north and then into the cove where he'd anchored last night. He nosed the boat into the reeds and ferns, swung overboard, and pushed it farther in, out of sight. Then he caught up the knapsack and set off through the woods to the Shooter's cabin.

He made a slow half circle of the place, keeping to the trees. The carport was still empty. Nothing moved anywhere within the range of his vision. Finally he made his way down to the rear wall, around it and along the side until he reached the front door. He didn't like standing out here for even a little while because there was no cover; but this door was the only one into the house, except for sliding doors on the terrace and a porch on the other side, and you couldn't jimmy sliding doors easily and without leaving marks. The same was true of windows. The Shooter would have made sure they were all secure anyway.

Deighan had one pocket of the knapsack open, the pick gun in his hand, when he reached the door. He'd got the pick gun from a housebreaker named Caldwell, an old-timer who was retired now; he'd also got some other tools and lessons in how to use them on the various kinds of locks. The lock on the Shooter's door was a flush-mounted, five-pin cylinder lock, with a steel lip on the door frame to protect the bolt and strike plate. That meant it was a lock you couldn't loid with a piece of plastic or a shim. It also meant that with a pick gun you could probably have it open in a couple of minutes.

Bending, squinting, he slid the gun into the lock. Set it, working the little knob on top to adjust the spring tension. Then he pulled the trigger—and all the pins bounced free at once and the door opened under his hand.

He slipped inside, nudged the door shut behind him, put the pick gun away inside the knapsack, and drew on a pair of thin plastic gloves. The place smelled of stale tobacco smoke and stale liquor. They hadn't been doing all that much drinking last night; maybe the Shooter had nibbled a few too many after the rest of them finally left. He didn't like losing money and valuables any more than Mannlicher did.

Deighan went through the front room. Somebody'd decorated the place for D'Allesandro: leather furniture, deer and antelope heads on the walls, Indian rugs on the floors, tasteful paintings. Cocaine deals had paid for part of it; contract work, including two hits on greedy Oakland and San Francisco drug dealers, had paid for the rest. But the Shooter was still small-time. He wasn't bright enough to be anything else. Cards and dice and whores-in-training were all he really cared about.

The front room was no good; Deighan prowled quickly through the other rooms. D'Allesandro wasn't the kind to have an office or a den, but there was a big old-fashioned rolltop desk in a room with a TV set and one of those big movie-type screens. None of the desk drawers were locked. Deighan pulled out the biggest one, saw that it was loaded with Danish porn magazines, took the magazines out and set them on the floor. He opened the knapsack and transferred the thirty thousand dollars into the back of the drawer. He put Mannlicher's ring in there, too, along with the other rings and a couple of gold chains the Texan had been wearing. Then he stuffed the porn magazines in at the front and pushed the drawer shut.

On his way back to the front room he rolled the knapsack tight around the pick gun and stuffed them into his jacket pocket. He opened the door, stepped out. He'd just finished resetting the lock when he heard the car approaching on the road above.

He froze for a second, looking up there. He couldn't see the car because of a screen of trees; but then he heard its automatic transmission gear down as it slowed for the turn into the Shooter's driveway. He pulled the door shut and ran toward the lake, the only direction he could go. Fifty feet away the log-railed terrace began, raised up off the sloping ground on redwood pillars. Deighan caught one of the railings, hauled himself up and half-rolled through the gap between them. The sound of the oncoming car was loud in his ears as he landed, off balance, on the deck.

He went to one knee, came up again. The only way to tell if he'd been seen was to stop and look, but that was a fool's move. Instead he ran across the deck, climbed through the railing on the other side, dropped down, and tried to keep from making noise as he plunged into the woods. He stopped moving after thirty yards, where ferns and a deadfall formed a thick concealing wall. From behind it, with the .38 in his hand, he watched the house and the deck, catching his breath, waiting.

Nobody came up or out on the deck. Nobody showed himself anywhere. The car's engine had been shut off sometime during his flight; it was quiet now, except for birds and the faint hum of a powerboat out on the lake.

Deighan waited ten minutes. When there was still nothing to see or hear, he transcribed a slow curl through the trees to where he could see the front of the cabin. The Shooter's Caddy was back inside the carport, no sign of haste in the way it had been neatly slotted. The cabin door was shut. The whole area seemed deserted.

But he waited another ten minutes before he was satisfied. Even then, he didn't holster his weapon until he'd made his way around to the cove where the Beachcraft was hidden. And he didn't relax until he was well out on the lake, headed back toward Crystal Bay.

FOUR

THE NEVORNIA WAS one of South Shore's older clubs, but it had undergone some recent modernizing. Outside, it had been given a glass and gaudy-neon face-lift. Inside, they'd used more glass, some cut crystal, and a wine-red decor that included carpeting, upholstery, and gaming tables.

When Deighan walked in a few minutes before two, the banks of slots and the blackjack tables were getting moderately heavy play. That was because it was Friday; some of the small-time gamblers liked to get a jump on the weekend crowds. The craps and roulette layouts were quiet. The high rollers were like vampires: they couldn't stand the daylight, so they only came out after dark.

Deighan bought a roll of quarters at one of the change booths. There were a couple of dozen rows of slots in the main casino—flashy new ones, mostly, with a few of the old scrolled nickel-plated jobs mixed in for the sake of nostalgia. He stopped at one of the old quarter machines, fed in three dollars' worth. Lemons and oranges. He couldn't even line up two cherries for a three-coin drop. He smiled crookedly to himself, went away from the slots and into the long concourse that connected the main casino with the new, smaller addition at the rear.

There were telephone booths along one side of the concourse. Deighan shut himself inside one of them, put a quarter in the slot, pushed 0 and then the digits of his home number in San Francisco. When the operator came on he said it was a collect call; that was to save himself the trouble of having to feed in a handful of quarters. He let the circuit make exactly five burrs in his ear before he hung up. If Fran was home, she'd know now that he was all right. If she wasn't home, then she'd know it later when he made another five-ring call. He always tried to call at least twice a day, at different times, because sometimes she went out shopping or to a movie or to visit with Sheila and the kids.

It'd be easier if she just answered the phone, talked to him, but she never did when he was away. Never. Sheila or anybody else wanted to get hold of her, they had to call one of the neighbors or come over in person. She didn't want anything to do with him when he was away, didn't want to know what he was doing or even when he'd be back. "Suppose I picked up the phone and it wasn't you?" she'd said. "Suppose it was somebody telling me you were dead? I couldn't stand that." That part of it didn't make sense to him. If he were dead, somebody'd come by and tell it to her face; dead was dead, and what difference did it make how she got the news? But he didn't argue with her. He didn't like to argue with her, and it didn't cost him anything to do it her way.

He slotted the quarter again and called the Shooter's number. Four rings, five, and D'Allesandro's voice said, "Yeah?"

"Mr. Carson?"

"Who?"

"Isn't this Paul Carson?"

"No. You got the wrong number."

"Oh, sorry," Deighan said, and rang off.

Another quarter in the slot. This time the number he punched out was the Nevornia's business line. A woman's voice answered, crisp and professional. He said, "Mr. Mannlicher. Tell him it's urgent."

"Whom shall I say is calling?"

"Never mind that. Just tell him it's about what happened last night."

"Sir, I'm afraid I can't—"

"Tell him last night's poker game, damn it. He'll talk to me."

There was a click and some canned music began to play in his ear. He lit a cigarette. He was on his fourth drag when the canned music quit and the fat man's voice said, "Frank Mannlicher. Who's this?"

"No names. Is it all right to talk on this line?"

"Go ahead, talk."

"I'm the guy who hit your game last night."

Silence for four or five seconds. Then Mannlicher said, "Is that so?" in a flat, wary voice.

"Ski mask, Smith & Wesson .38, grenade in my jacket pocket. The take was better than two hundred thousand. I got your ring—platinum with a circle of diamonds."

Another pause, shorter this time. "So why call me today?"

"How'd you like to get it all back—the money and the ring?"

"How?"

"Go pick it up. I'll tell you where."

"Yeah? Why should you do me a favor?"

"I didn't know who you were last night. I wasn't told. If I had been, I wouldn't of gone through with it. I don't mess with people like you, people with your connections."

"Somebody hired you, that it?"

"That's it."

"Who?"

"D'Allesandro."

"*What?*"

"The Shooter. D'Allesandro."

". . . Bullshit."

"You don't have to believe me. But I'm telling you—he's the one. He didn't tell me who'd be at the game, and now he's trying to screw me on the money. He says there was less than a hundred and fifty thousand in the sack; I know better."

"So now you want to screw him."

"That's right. Besides, I don't like the idea of you pushing to find out who I am, maybe sending somebody to pay me a visit someday. I figure if I give you the Shooter, you'll lose interest in me."

More silence. "Why'd he do it?" Mannlicher said in a different voice— harder, with the edge of violence it had held last night. "Hit the game like that?"

"He needs some big money, fast. He's into some kind of scam back east; he wouldn't say what it is."

"Where's the money and the rest of the stuff?"

"At his cabin. We had a drop arranged in the woods; I put the sack there last night, he picked it up this morning when nobody was around. The money's in his desk—the big rolltop. Your ring, too. That's where it was an hour ago, anyhow, when I walked out."

Mannlicher said, "In his desk," as if he were biting the words off something bitter.

"Go out there, see for yourself."

"If you're telling this straight, you got nothing to worry about from me. Maybe I'll fix you up with a reward or something. Where can I get in touch?"

"You can't," Deighan said. "I'm long gone as soon as I hang up this phone."

"I'll make it five thousand. Just tell me where you—"

Deighan broke the connection.

His cigarette had burned down to the filter; he dropped it on the floor, put his shoe on it before he left the booth. On his way out of the casino he paused long enough to push another quarter into the same slot machine he'd played before. More lemons and oranges. This time he didn't smile as he moved away.

FIVE

NARROW AND TWISTY, hemmed in by trees, Old Lake Road branched off Highway 50 on the Nevada side and took two miles to get all the way to the lake. But it wasn't a dead-end; another road picked it up at the lakefront and looped back out to the highway. There were several nice homes hidden away in the area—it was called Pine Acres—with plenty of space between them. The Shooter's cabin was a mile and a half from the highway, off an even narrower lane called Little Cove Road. The only other cabin within five hundred yards was a summer place that the owners had already closed up for the year.

Deighan drove past the intersection with Little Cove, went two-tenths of a mile, parked on the turnout at that point. There wasn't anybody else around when he got out, nothing to see except trees and little winks of blue that marked the nearness of the lake. If anybody came along they wouldn't pay any attention to the car. For one thing, it was a '75 Ford Galaxy with nothing distinctive about it except the antenna for the GTE mobile phone. It was his—he'd driven it up from San Francisco—but the papers on it said it belonged to Bob Prince. For another thing, Old Lake Road was only a hundred yards or so from the water here, and there was a path through the trees to a strip of rocky beach. Local kids used it in the summer; he'd found that out from Bellah. Kids might have decided to stop here on a sunny autumn day as well. No reason for anybody to think otherwise.

He found the path, went along it a short way to where it crossed a little creek, dry now and so narrow it was nothing more than a natural drainage ditch. He followed the creek to the north, on a course he'd taken three days ago. It led him to a shelflike overhang topped by two chunks of granite outcrop that leaned against each other like a pair of old drunks. Below the shelf, the land fell away sharply to the Shooter's driveway some sixty yards distant. Off to the right, where the incline wasn't so steep and the trees grew in a pack, was the split-bole Douglas fir where he'd stood waiting last night. The trees were fewer and more widely spaced apart between here and the cabin, so that from behind the two outcrops you had a good look at the Shooter's property, Little Cove Road, the concrete pier, and the lake shimmering under the late afternoon sun.

The Caddy Eldorado was still slotted inside the carport. It was the only car in sight. Deighan knelt behind where the outcrops came together to form a notch, rubbed tension out of his neck and shoulders while he waited.

He didn't have to wait long. Less than ten minutes had passed when the car appeared on Little Cove Road, slowed, turned down the Shooter's driveway. It wasn't Mannlicher's fancy limo; it was a two-year-old Chrysler—Brandt's, maybe. Brandt was driving it: Deighan had a clear view of him through the side window as the Chrysler pulled up and stopped near the cabin's front door. He could also see that the lone passenger was Mannlicher.

Brandt got out, opened the passenger door for the fat man, and the two of them went to the cabin. It took D'Allesandro ten seconds to answer Brandt's knock. There was some talk, not much; then Mannlicher and Brandt went in, and the door shut behind them.

All right, Deighan thought. He'd stacked the deck as well as he could; pretty soon he'd know how the hand—and the game—played out.

Nothing happened for maybe five minutes. Then he thought he heard some muffled sounds down there, loud voices that went on for a while, something that might have been a bang, but the distance was too great for him to be sure that he wasn't imagining them. Another four or five minutes went by. And then the door opened and Brandt came out alone, looked around, called something back inside that Deighan didn't understand. If there was an answer, it wasn't audible. Brandt shut the door, hurried down to the lake, went out onto the pier. The Chris-Craft was still tied up there. Brandt climbed on board, disappeared for thirty seconds or so, reappeared carrying a square of something gray and heavy. Tarpaulin, Deighan saw when Brandt came back up the driveway. Big piece of it—big enough for a shroud.

The Shooter's hand had been folded. That left three of them still in the game.

When Brandt had gone back inside with the tarp, Deighan stood and half ran along the creek and through the trees to where he'd left the Ford. Old Lake Road was deserted. He yanked open the passenger door, leaned in, caught up the mobile phone, and punched out the emergency number for the county sheriff's office. An efficient-sounding male voice answered.

"Something's going on on Little Cove Road," Deighan said, making himself sound excited. "That's in Pine Acres, you know? It's the cabin at the end, down on the lake. I heard shots—people shooting at each other down there. It sounds like a war."

"What's the address?"

"I don't know the address, it's the cabin right on the lake. People *shooting* at each other. You better get right out there."

"Your name, sir?"

"I don't want to get involved. Just hurry, will you?"

Deighan put the receiver down, shut the car door, ran back along the path and along the creek to the shelf. Mannlicher and Brandt were still inside the cabin. He went to one knee again behind the outcrops, drew the .38, held it on his thigh.

It was another two minutes before the door opened down there. Brandt came out, looked around as he had before, went back inside—and then he and Mannlicher both appeared, one at each end of a big, tarp-wrapped bundle. They started to carry it down the driveway toward the lake. Going to put it on the boat, Deighan thought, take it out now or later on, when it's dark. Lake Tahoe was sixteen hundred feet deep in the middle. The bundle wouldn't have been the first somebody'd dumped out there.

He let them get clear of the Chrysler, partway down the drive, before he poked the gun into the notch, sighted, and fired twice. The shots went where he'd intended them to, wide by ten feet and into the roadbed so they kicked up gravel. Mannlicher and Brandt froze for an instant, confused. Deighan fired a third round, putting the slug closer this time, and that one panicked them: they let go of the bundle and began scrambling.

There was no cover anywhere close by; they both ran for the Chrysler. Brandt had a gun in his hand when he reached it, and he dropped down behind the rear deck, trying to locate Deighan's position. Mannlicher kept on scrambling around to the passenger door, pulled it open, pushed himself across the seat inside.

Deighan blew out the Chrysler's near front tire. Sighted, and blew out the rear tire. Brandt threw an answering shot his way, but it wasn't even close. The Chrysler was tilting in Deighan's direction as the tires flattened. Mannlicher pushed himself out of the car, tried to make a run for the cabin door with his arms flailing, his fat jiggling. Deighan put a bullet into the wall beside the door. Mannlicher reversed himself, fell in his frantic haste, crawled back behind the Chrysler.

Reloading the .38, Deighan could hear the sound of cars coming up fast on Little Cove Road. No sirens, but revolving lights made faint blood-red flashes through the trees.

From behind the Chrysler Brandt fired again, wildly. Beyond him, on the driveway, one corner of the tarp-wrapped bundle had come loose and was flapping in the wind off the lake.

A county sheriff's cruiser, its roof light slashing the air, made the turn off Little Cove onto the driveway. Another one was right behind it. In his panic, Brandt straightened up when he saw them and fired once, blindly, at the first in line.

Deighan was on his feet by then, hurrying away from the outcrops, holstering his weapon. Behind him he heard brakes squeal, another shot, voices yelling, two more shots. All the sounds faded as he neared the turnout and the Ford. By the time he pulled out onto the deserted road, there was nothing to hear but the sound of his engine, the screeching of a jay somewhere nearby.

Brandt had thrown in his hand by now; so had Mannlicher.

This pot belonged to him.

S I X

FRAN WAS IN the back yard, weeding her garden, when he got home late the following afternoon. He called to her from the doorway, and she glanced around and then got up, unsmiling, and came over to him. She was wearing jeans and one of his old shirts and a pair of gardening gloves, and her hair was tied in a long ponytail. Used to be a light, silky brown, her hair; now it was mostly gray. His fault. She was only forty-six. A woman of forty-six shouldn't be so gray.

She said, "So you're back." She didn't sound glad to see him, didn't kiss him or touch him at all. But her eyes were gentle on his face.

"I'm back."

"You all right? You look tired."

"Long drive. I'm fine; it was a good trip."

She didn't say anything. She didn't want to hear about it, not any of it. She just didn't want to know.

"How about you?" he asked. "Everything been okay?"

"Sheila's pregnant again."

"Christ. What's the matter with her? Why don't she get herself fixed? Or get Hank fixed?"

"She likes kids."

"I like kids too, but four's too many at her age. She's only twenty-seven."

"She wants eight."

"She's crazy," Deighan said. "What's she want to bring all those kids into a world like this for?"

There was an awkward moment. It was always awkward at first when he came back. Then Fran said, "You hungry?"

"You know me. I can always eat." Fact was, he was starved. He hadn't eaten much up in Nevada, never did when he was away. And he hadn't had anything today except an English muffin and some coffee for breakfast in Truckee.

"Come into the kitchen," Fran said. "I'll fix you something."

They went inside. He got a beer out of the refrigerator; she waited and then took out some covered dishes, some vegetables. He wanted to say something to her, talk a little, but he couldn't think of anything. His mind was blank at times like this. He carried his beer into the living room.

The goddamn trophy case was the first thing he saw. He hated that trophy case; but Fran wouldn't get rid of it, no matter what he said. For her it was like some kind of shrine to the dead past. All the mementoes of his years on the force—twenty-two years, from beat patrolman in North Beach all the way up to inspector on the narcotics squad. The certificate he'd won in marksmanship competition at the police academy, the two citations from the mayor for bravery, other crap like that. Bones, that's all they were to him. Pieces of a rotting skeleton. What was the sense in keeping them around, reminding both of them of what he'd been, what he'd lost.

His fault he'd lost it, sure. But it was their fault too, goddamn them. The laws, the lawyers, the judges, the *system*. No convictions on half of all the arrests he'd ever made—half! Turning the ones like Mannlicher and Brandt and D'Allesandro loose, putting them right back on the street, letting them make their deals and their hits, letting them screw up innocent lives. Sheila's kids, his grandkids—lives like that. How could they blame him for being bitter? How could they blame him for taking too many drinks now and then?

He sat down on the couch, drank some of his beer, lit a cigarette. Ah Christ, he thought, it's not them. You know it wasn't them. It was *you*, you dumb bastard. They warned you twice about drinking on duty. And you kept on doing it, you were hog-drunk the night you plowed the departmental sedan into that vanload of teenagers. What if one of *those* kids had died? You were lucky, by God. You got off easy.

Sure, he thought. Sure. But he'd been a good cop, damn it, a cop inside and out; it was all he knew how to be. What was he supposed to do after they threw him off the force? Live on his half-pension? Get a job as a part-time security guard? Forty-four years old, no skills, no friends outside the department—what the hell was he supposed to do?

He'd invented Bob Prince, that was what he'd done. He'd gone into business for himself.

Fran didn't understand. "You'll get killed one of these days," she'd said in the beginning. "It's vigilante justice," she'd said. "You think you're Rambo, is that it?" she'd said. She just didn't understand. To him it was the same job he'd always done, the only one he was any good at, only now *he* made up some of the rules. He was no Rambo, one man up against thousands, a mindless killing machine; he hated that kind of phony flag-waving crap. It wasn't real. What he was doing, that was real. It meant something. But a hero? No. Hell, no. He was a sniper, that was all, picking off a weak or vulnerable enemy here and there, now and then. Snipers weren't heroes, for Christ's sake. Snipers were snipers, just like cops were cops.

He finished his beer and his cigarette, got up, went into Fran's sewing room. The five thousand he'd held out of the poker-game take was in his pocket—money he felt he was entitled to because his expenses ran high sometimes, and they had to eat, they had to live. He put the roll into her sewing cabinet, where he always put whatever money he made as Bob Prince. She'd spend it when she had to, parcel it out, but she'd never mention it to him or anyone else. She'd told Sheila once that he had a sales job, he got paid in cash a lot, that was why he was away from home for such long periods of time.

When he walked back into the kitchen she was at the sink, peeling potatoes. He went over and touched her shoulder, kissed the top of her head. She didn't look at him; stood there stiffly until he moved away from her. But she'd be all right in a day or two. She'd be fine until the next time Bob Prince made the right kind of connection.

He wished it didn't have to be this way. He wished he could roll back the clock three years, do things differently, take the gray out of her hair and the pain out of her eyes. But he couldn't. It was just too late.

You had to play the cards you were dealt, no matter how lousy they were. The only thing that made it tolerable was that sometimes, on certain hands, you could find ways to stack the damn deck.

THE ADVENTURE OF THE DAUPHIN DOLL

Ellery Queen

Ellery Queen was the joint pen name of first cousins Frederic Dannay and Manfred B. Lee. Their enormous and enduring contributions to the modern mystery came in three ways—through their Ellery Queen novels; through their founding and editing of *Ellery Queen Mystery Magazine*; and through the untold number of careers their magazine started. Their run as writers lasted from roughly 1929 to the late 1960s, and they led the pack every year. While a number of paperback originals bearing their name were ghosted by other writers, their own earlier novels revived the pure detective story (Golden Age if you will) with a popularity that surpassed that of even S. S. Van Dine. Movies, radio shows, and—later—TV series also blossomed. While their novels are not much read today, their legacy lives on in the pages of the monthly *EQ* magazine, which continues to prosper and publish stories of import and entertainment, an all-too-rare accomplishment in this day and age.

THERE IS A law among story-tellers, originally passed by Editors at the cries (they say) of their constituents, which states that stories about Christmas shall have children in them. This Christmas story is no exception; indeed, misopedists will complain that we have overdone it. And we confess in advance that this is also a story about Dolls, and that Santa Claus comes into it, and even a Thief; though as to this last, whoever he was—and that was one of the questions—he was certainly not Barabbas, even parabolically.

Another section of the statute governing Christmas stories provides that they shall incline toward Sweetness and Light. The first arises, of course, from the orphans and the never-souring savor of the annual Miracle; as for Light, it will be provided at the end, as usual, by that luminous prodigy, Ellery Queen. The reader of gloomier temper will also find a large measure of Darkness, in the person and works of one who, at least in Inspector Queen's harassed view, was surely the winged Prince of that region. His name, by the way, was not Satan, it was Comus; and this is paradox enow, since the original Comus, as everyone knows, was the god of festive joy and mirth, emotions not commonly associated with the Underworld. As Ellery struggled to embrace his phantom foe, he puzzled over this *non sequitur* in vain; in vain, that is, until Nikki Porter, no scorner of the obvious, suggested that he *might* seek the answer where any ordinary mortal would go at once. And there, to the great man's mortification, it was indeed to be found: On page 262b of Volume 6, *Coleb to Damasci*, of the 175th Anniversary edition of the *Encyclopaedia Britannica*. A French conjuror of that name, performing in London in the year 1789, caused his wife to vanish from the top of a table—the very first time, it appeared, that this feat, uxorial or otherwise, had been accomplished without the aid of mirrors. To track his dark adversary's *nom de nuit* to its historic lair gave Ellery his only glint of satisfaction until that blessed moment when light burst all around him and exorcised the darkness, Prince and all.

But this is chaos.

Our story properly begins not with our invisible character but with our dead one.

Miss Ypson had not always been dead; *au contraire*. She had lived for seventy-eight years, for most of them breathing hard. As her father used to remark, 'She was a very active little verb.' Miss Ypson's father was a professor of Greek at a small Mid-western university. He had conjugated his daughter with the rather bewildered assistance of one of his brawnier students, an Iowa poultry heiress.

Professor Ypson was a man of distinction. Unlike most professors of Greek, he was a Greek professor of Greek, having been born Gerasymos Aghamos Ypsilonomon in Polykhnitos, on the island of Mytilini, 'where,' he was fond of recalling on certain occasions, 'burning Sappho loved and sung'—a quotation he found unfailingly useful in his extracurricular activities; and, the Hellenic ideal notwithstanding, Professor Ypson believed wholeheartedly in immoderation in all things. This hereditary and cultural background explains the professor's interest in fatherhood—to his wife's chagrin, for Mrs. Ypson's own breeding prowess was confined almost exclusively to the barnyards on which her income was based; he held their daughter to be nothing less than a biological miracle.

The professor's mental processes also tended to confuse Mrs. Ypson. She never ceased to wonder why, instead of shortening his name to Ypson, her husband had not sensibly changed it to Jones. 'My dear,' the professor once replied, 'you are an Iowa snob.' 'But nobody,' Mrs. Ypson cried, 'can spell it or pronounce it!' 'This is a cross,' murmured Professor Ypson, 'which we must bear with Ypsilanti.' 'Oh,' said Mrs. Ypson.

There was invariably something Sibylline about his conversation. His favorite adjective for his wife was 'ypsiliform,' a term, he explained, which referred to the germinal spot at one of the fecundation stages in a ripening egg and which was, therefore, exquisitely à propos. Mrs. Ypson continued to look bewildered; she died at an early age.

And the professor ran off with a Kansas City variety girl of considerable talent, leaving his baptized chick to be reared by an eggish relative of her mother's named Jukes.

The only time Miss Ypson heard from her father—except when he wrote charming and erudite little notes requesting, as he termed it, *lucrum*—was in the fourth decade of his Odyssey, when he sent her a handsome addition to her collection, a terracotta play doll of Greek origin over three thousand years old which, unhappily, Miss Ypson felt duty-bound to return to the Brooklyn museum from which it had unaccountably vanished. The note accompanying her father's gift had said, whimsically: *'Timeo Danaos et dona ferentes.'*

There was poetry behind Miss Ypson's dolls. At her birth the professor, ever harmonious, signalized his devotion to fecundity by naming her Cytherea. This proved the Olympian irony. For, it turned out, her father's philoprogenitiveness throbbed frustrate in her mother's stony womb: even though Miss Ypson interred five husbands of quite adequate vigor, she remained infertile to the end of her days. Hence it is classically tragic to find her, when all passion was spent, a sweet little old lady with a vague if eager smile who, under the name of her father, pattered about a vast and echoing New York apartment playing enthusiastically with dolls.

In the beginning they were dolls of common clay: a Billiken, a kewpie, a Kathe Kruse, a Patsy, a Foxy Grandpa, and so forth. But then, as her need increased, Miss Ypson began her fierce sack of the past.

Down into the land of Pharaoh she went for two pieces of thin desiccated board, carved and painted and with hair of strung beads, and legless—so that they might not run away—which any connoisseur will tell you are the most superb specimens of ancient Egyptian paddle doll extant, far superior to those in the British Museum, although this fact will be denied in certain quarters.

Miss Ypson unearthed a foremother of 'Letitia Penn,' until her discovery held to be the oldest doll in America, having been brought to Philadelphia from England in 1699 by William Penn as a gift for a playmate of his small daughter's. Miss Ypson's find was a wooden-hearted 'little lady' in brocade and velvet which had been sent by Sir Walter Raleigh to the first

English child born in the New World. Since Virginia Dare had been born in 1587, not even the Smithsonian dared impugn Miss Ypson's triumph.

On the old lady's racks, in her plate-glass cases, might be seen the wealth of a thousand childhoods, and some riches—for such is the genetics of dolls—possessed by children grown. Here could be found 'fashion babies' from fourteenth-century France, sacred dolls of the Orange Free State Fingo tribe, Satsuma paper dolls and court dolls from old Japan, beady-eyed 'Kalifa' dolls of the Egyptian Sudan, Swedish birchbark dolls, 'Katcina' dolls of the Hopis, mammoth-tooth dolls of the Eskimos, feather dolls of the Chippewa, tumble dolls of the ancient Chinese, Coptic bone dolls, Roman dolls dedicated to Diana, *pantin* dolls which had been the street toys of Parisian exquisites before Madame Guillotine swept the boulevards, early Christian dolls in their crèches representing the Holy Family—to specify the merest handful of Miss Ypson's Briarean collection. She possessed dolls of pasteboard, dolls of animal skin, spool dolls, crab-claw dolls, eggshell dolls, cornhusk dolls, rag dolls, pine-cone dolls with moss hair, stocking dolls, dolls of bisque, dolls of palm leaf, dolls of papier mâché, even dolls made of seed pods. There were dolls forty inches tall, and there were dolls so little Miss Ypson could hide them in her gold thimble.

Cytherea Ypson's collection bestrode the centuries and took tribute of history. There was no greater—not the fabled playthings of Montezuma, or Victoria's, or Eugene Field's; not the collection at the Metropolitan, or the South Kensington, or the royal palace in old Bucharest, or anywhere outside the enchantment of little girls' dreams.

It was made of Iowan eggs and the Attic shore, corn-fed and myrtle-clothed; and it brings us at last to Attorney John Somerset Bondling and his visit to the Queen residence one December twenty-third not so very long ago.

DECEMBER THE TWENTY-THIRD is ordinarily not a good time to seek the Queens. Inspector Richard Queen likes his Christmas old-fashioned; his turkey stuffing, for instance, calls for twenty-two hours of over-all preparation and some of its ingredients are not readily found at the corner grocer's. And Ellery is a frustrated gift-wrapper. For a month before Christmas he turns his sleuthing genius to tracking down unusual wrapping papers, fine ribbons, and artistic stickers; and he spends the last two days creating beauty.

So it was that when Attorney John S. Bondling called, Inspector Queen was in his kitchen, swathed in a barbecue apron, up to his elbows in *fines herbes*, while Ellery, behind the locked door of his study, composed a secret symphony in glittering fuchsia metallic paper, forest-green moiré ribbon, and pine cones.

'It's almost useless,' shrugged Nikki, studying Attorney Bondling's card, which was as crackly-looking as Attorney Bondling. 'You say you know the Inspector personally, Mr. Bondling?'

'Just tell him Bondling the estate lawyer,' said Bondling neurotically. 'Park Row. He'll know.'

'Don't blame me,' said Nikki, 'if you wind up in his stuffing. Goodness knows he's used everything else.' And she went for Inspector Queen.

While she was gone, the study door opened noiselessly for one inch. A suspicious eye reconnoitered from the crack.

'Don't be alarmed,' said the owner of the eye, slipping through the crack and locking the door hastily behind him. 'Can't trust them, you know. Children, just children.'

'Children!' Attorney Bondling snarled. 'You're Ellery Queen, aren't you?'

'Yes.'

'Interested in youth? Christmas? Orphans, dolls, that sort of thing?' Mr. Bondling went on in a remarkably nasty way.

'I suppose so.'

'The more fool you. Ah, here's your father. Inspector Queen—!'

'Oh, that Bondling,' said the old gentleman absently, shaking his visitor's hand. 'My office called to say someone was coming up. Here, use my handkerchief; that's a bit of turkey liver. Know my son? His secretary, Miss Porter? What's on your mind, Mr. Bondling?'

'Inspector, I'm in charge of handling the Cytherea Ypson estate, and—'

'Cytherea Ypson,' frowned the Inspector. 'Oh, yes. She died only recently.'

'Leaving me with the headache,' said Mr. Bondling bitterly, 'of disposing of her Dollection.'

'Her what?' asked Ellery.

'Dolls—collection. Dollection. She coined the word.'

Ellery strolled over to his armchair.

'Do I take this down?' sighed Nikki.

'Dollection,' said Ellery.

'Spent about thirty years at it. Dolls!'

'Yes, Nikki, take it down.'

'Well, well, Mr. Bondling,' said Inspector Queen. 'What's the problem? Christmas comes but once a year, you know.'

'Will provides the Dollection be sold at auction,' grated the attorney, 'and the proceeds used to set up a fund for orphan children. I'm holding the public sale right after New Year's.'

'Dolls and orphans, eh?' said the Inspector, thinking of Javanese black pepper and Country Gentleman Seasoning Salt.

'That's *nice*,' beamed Nikki.

'Oh, is it?' said Mr. Bondling softly. 'Apparently, young woman, you've never tried to satisfy a Surrogate. I've administered estates for nineteen years without a whisper against me, but let an estate involve the interests of just one little fatherless child, and you'd think from the Surrogate's attitude I was Bill Sikes himself!'

'My stuffing,' began the Inspector.

'I've had those dolls catalogued. The result is ominous! Did you know there's no set market for the damnable things? And aside from a few personal possessions, the Dollection constitutes the old lady's entire estate. Sank every nickel she had in it.'

'But it should be worth a fortune,' remarked Ellery.

'To whom, Mr. Queen? Museums always want such things as free and unencumbered gifts. I tell you, except for one item, those hypothetical orphans won't realize enough from that sale to keep them in—in bubble gum for two days!'

'Which item would that be, Mr. Bondling?'

'Number Six-seventy-four,' the lawyer snapped. 'This one.'

'Number Six-seventy-four,' read Inspector Queen from the fat catalogue Bondling had fished out of a large greatcoat pocket. 'The Dauphin's Doll. Unique. Ivory figure of a boy Prince eight inches tall, clad in court dress, genuine ermine, brocade, velvet. Court sword in gold strapped to waist. Gold circlet crown surmounted by single blue brilliant diamond of finest water, weight approximately forty-nine carats—'

'How many carats?' exclaimed Nikki.

'Larger than the Hope and the Star of South Africa,' said Ellery, with a certain excitement.

'—appraised,' continued his father, 'at one hundred and ten thousand dollars.'

'Expensive dollie.'

'Indecent!' said Nikki.

'This indecent—I mean exquisite royal doll,' the Inspector read on, 'was a birthday gift from King Louis XVI of France to Louis Charles, his second son, who became dauphin at the death of his elder brother in 1789. The little dauphin was proclaimed Louis XVII by the royalists during the French Revolution while in custody of the *sans-culottes*. His fate is shrouded in mystery. Romantic, historic item.'

'*Le prince perdu*. I'll say,' muttered Ellery. 'Mr. Bondling, is this on the level?'

'I'm an attorney, not an antiquarian,' snapped their visitor. 'There are documents attached, one of them a sworn statement—holograph—by Lady Charlotte Atkyns, the English actress-friend of the Capet family—she was in France during the Revolution—or purporting to be in Lady Atkyns's hand. It doesn't matter, Mr. Queen. Even if the history is bad, the diamond's good!'

'I take it this hundred-and-ten-thousand-dollar dollie constitutes the bone, as it were, or that therein lies the rub?'

'You said it!' cried Mr. Bondling, cracking his knuckles in a sort of agony. 'For my money the Dauphin's Doll is the only negotiable asset of that collection. And what's the old lady do? She provides by will that on the day preceding Christmas the Cytherea Ypson Dollection is to be publicly displayed . . . on the main floor of Nash's Department Store! *The day before Christmas, gentlemen!* Think of it!'

'But why?' asked Nikki, puzzled.

'Why? Who knows why? For the entertainment of New York's army of little beggars, I suppose! Have you any notion how many peasants pass through Nash's on the day before Christmas? My cook tells me—she's a very religious woman—it's like Armageddon.'

'Day before Christmas,' frowned Ellery. 'That's tomorrow.'

'It does sound chancy,' said Nikki anxiously. Then she brightened. 'Oh, well, maybe Nash's won't cooperate, Mr. Bondling.'

'Oh, won't they!' howled Mr. Bondling. 'Why, old lady Ypson had this stunt cooked up with that gang of peasant-purveyors for years! They've been snapping at my heels ever since the day she was put away!'

'It'll draw every crook in New York,' said the Inspector, his gaze on the kitchen door.

'Orphans,' said Nikki. 'The orphans' interests *must* be protected.' She looked at her employer accusingly.

'Special measures, dad,' he said.

'Sure, sure,' said the Inspector, rising. 'Don't you worry about this, Mr. Bondling. Now if you'll be kind enough to excu—'

'Inspector Queen,' hissed Mr. Bondling, leaning forward tensely, 'that is not all.'

'Ah,' said Ellery briskly, lighting a cigarette. 'There's a specific villain in this piece, Mr. Bondling, and you know who he is.'

'I do,' said the lawyer hollowly, 'and then again I don't. I mean, it's Comus.'

'*Comus!*' the Inspector screamed.

'Comus?' said Ellery slowly.

'Comus?' said Nikki. 'Who dat?'

'Comus,' nodded Mr. Bondling. 'First thing this morning. Marched right into my office, bold as day—must have followed me, I hadn't got my coat off, my secretary wasn't even in. Marched in and tossed this card on my desk.'

Ellery seized it. 'The usual, dad.'

'His trademark,' growled the Inspector, his lips working.

'But the card just says "Comus," ' complained Nikki. 'Who—?'

'Go on, Mr. Bondling!' thundered the Inspector.

'And he calmly announced to me,' said Bondling, blotting his cheeks with an exhausted handkerchief, 'that he's going to steal the Dauphin's Doll tomorrow, in Nash's.'

'Oh, a maniac,' said Nikki.

'Mr. Bondling,' said the old gentleman in a terrible voice, 'just what did this fellow look like?'

'Foreigner—black beard—spoke with a European accent of some sort. To tell you the truth, I was so thunderstruck I didn't notice details. Didn't even chase him till it was too late.'

The Queens shrugged at each other, Gallically.

'The old story,' said the Inspector; the corners of his nostrils were greenish. 'The brass of the colonel's monkey and when he does show himself nobody remembers anything but beards and foreign accents. Well, Mr. Bondling, with Comus in the game it's serious business. Where's the collection right now?'

'In the vaults of the Life Bank and Trust, Forty-third Street branch.'

'What time are you to move it over to Nash's?'

'They wanted it this evening. I said nothing doing. I've made special arrangements with the bank, and the collection's to be moved at seven thirty tomorrow morning.'

'Won't be much time to set up,' said Ellery thoughtfully, 'before the store opens its doors.' He glanced at his father.

'You leave Operation Dollie to us, Mr. Bondling,' said the Inspector grimly. 'Better give me a buzz this afternoon.'

'I can't tell you, Inspector, how relieved I am—'

'Are you?' said the old gentleman sourly. 'What makes you think he won't get it?'

───────

WHEN ATTORNEY BONDLING had left, the Queens put their heads together, Ellery doing most of the talking, as usual. Finally, the Inspector went into the bedroom for a session with his direct line to headquarters.

'Anybody would think,' sniffed Nikki, 'you two were planning the defense of the Bastille. Who on earth is this Comus, anyway?'

'We don't know, Nikki,' said Ellery slowly. 'Might be anybody. Began his criminal career about five years ago. He's in the grand tradition of Lupin—a saucy, highly intelligent rascal who's made stealing an art. He seems to take a special delight in stealing valuable things under virtually impossible conditions. Master of make-up—he's appeared in a dozen different disguises. And he's an uncanny mimic. Never been caught, photographed, or fingerprinted. Imaginative, daring—I'd say he's the most dangerous thief operating right now in the United States.'

'If he's never been caught,' said Nikki skeptically, 'how do you know he commits these crimes?'

'You mean and not someone else?' Ellery smiled pallidly. 'The techniques mark the thefts as his work. And then, like Arsène, he leaves a card—with the name "Comus" on it—on the scene of each visit.'

'Does he usually announce in advance that he's going to swipe the crown jewels?'

'No.' Ellery frowned. 'To my knowledge, this is the first such instance. Since he's never done anything without a reason, that visit to Bondling's office this morning must be part of his greater plan. I wonder if—'

The telephone in the living room rang clear and loud.

Nikki looked at Ellery. Ellery looked at the telephone.

'Do you suppose—?' began Nikki. But then she said, 'Oh, it's too absurd.'

'Where Comus is involved,' said Ellery wildly, 'nothing is too absurd!' and he leaped for the phone. 'Hello!'

'A call from an old friend,' announced a deep and hollowish male voice. 'Comus.'

'Well,' said Ellery. 'Hello again.'

'Did Mr. Bondling,' asked the voice jovially, 'persuade you to "prevent" me from stealing the Dauphin's Doll in Nash's tomorrow?'

'So you know Bondling's been here.'

'No miracle involved, Queen. I followed him. Are you taking the case?'

'See here, Comus,' said Ellery. 'Under ordinary circumstances I'd welcome the sporting chance to put you where you belong. But these circumstances are not ordinary. That doll represents the major asset of a future fund for orphaned children. I'd rather we didn't play catch with it. Comus, what do you say we call this one off?'

'Shall we say,' asked the voice gently, 'Nash's Department Store—tomorrow?'

THUS THE EARLY morning of December twenty-fourth finds Messrs. Queen and Bondling, and Nikki Porter, huddled on the iron sidewalk of Forty-third Street before the holly-decked windows of the Life Bank & Trust Company, just outside a double line of armed guards. The guards form a channel between the bank entrance and an armored truck, down which Cytherea Ypson's Dollection flows swiftly. And all about gapes New York, stamping callously on the aged, icy face of the street against the uncharitable Christmas wind.

Now is the winter of his discontent, and Mr. Queen curses.

'I don't know what you're beefing about,' moans Miss Porter. 'You and Mr. Bondling are bundled up like Yukon prospectors. Look at *me*.'

'It's that rat-hearted public relations tripe from Nash's,' says Mr. Queen murderously. 'They all swore themselves to secrecy, Brother Rat included. Honor! Spirit of Christmas!'

'It was all over the radio last night,' whimpers Mr. Bondling. 'And in this morning's papers.'

'I'll cut his creep's heart out. Here! Velie, keep those people away!'

Sergeant Velie says good-naturedly from the doorway of the bank, 'You jerks stand back.' Little does the Sergeant know the fate in store for him.

'Armored trucks,' says Miss Porter bluishly. 'Shotguns.'

'Nikki, Comus made a point of informing us in advance that he meant to steal the Dauphin's Doll in Nash's Department Store. It would be just like him to have said that in order to make it easier to steal the doll en route.'

'Why don't they hurry?' shivers Mr. Bondling. 'Ah!' Inspector Queen appears suddenly in the doorway. His hands clasp treasure.

'Oh!' cries Nikki.

New York whistles.

It is magnificence, an affront to democracy. But street mobs, like children, are royalists at heart.

New York whistles, and Sergeant Thomas Velie steps menacingly before Inspector Queen, Police Positive drawn, and Inspector Queen dashes across the sidewalk between the bristling lines of guards.

Queen the Younger vanishes, to materialize an instant later at the door of the armored truck.

'It's just immorally, hideously beautiful, Mr. Bondling,' breathes Miss Porter, sparkly-eyed.

Mr. Bondling cranes, thinly.

ENTER *Santa Claus, with bell.*

Santa. Oyez, oyez. Peace, good will. Is that the dollie the radio's been yappin' about, folks?

Mr. B. Scram.

Miss P. Why, Mr. Bondling.

Mr. B. Well, he's got no business here. Stand back, er, Santa. Back!

Santa. What eateth you, my lean and angry friend? Have you no compassion at this season of the year?

Mr. B. Oh . . . Here! (*Clink.*) Now will you kindly . . . ?

Santa. Mighty pretty dollie. Where they takin' it, girlie?

Miss P. Over to Nash's, Santa.

Mr. B. You asked for it. Officer!!!

Santa. (*Hurriedly*) Little present for you, girlie. Compliments of old Santy. Merry, merry.

Miss P. For *me?* (EXIT *Santa, rapidly, with bell.*) Really, Mr. Bondling, was it necessary to . . . ?

Mr. B. Opium for the masses! What did that flatulent faker hand you, Miss Porter? What's in that unmentionable envelope?

Miss P. I'm sure I don't know, but isn't it the most touching idea? Why, it's addressed to *Ellery.* Oh! Elleryyyyyy!

Mr. B. (EXIT *excitedly*) Where is he? You—! Officer! Where did that baby-deceiver disappear to? A Santa Claus . . .

Mr. Q. (Entering on the run) Yes? Nikki, what is it? What's happened?

Miss P. A man dressed as Santa Claus just handed me this envelope. It's addressed to you.

Mr. Q. Note? (*He snatches it, withdraws a miserable slice of paper from it on which is block-lettered in pencil a message which he reads aloud with considerable expression.*) 'Dear Ellery, Don't you trust me? I said I'd steal the Dauphin in Nash's emporium today and that's exactly where I'm going to do it. Yours—' Signed . . .

Miss P. *(Craning)* 'Comus.' That Santa?

Mr. Q. *(Sets his manly lips. An icy wind blows)*

E VEN THE MASTER had to acknowledge that their defenses against Comus were ingenious.

From the Display Department of Nash's they had requisitioned four miter-jointed counters of uniform length. These they had fitted together, and in the center of the hollow square thus formed they had erected a platform six feet high. On the counters, in plastic tiers, stretched the long lines of Miss Ypson's babies. Atop the platform, dominant, stood a great chair of hand-carved oak, filched from the Swedish Modern section of the Fine Furniture Department; and on this Valhalla-like throne, a huge and rosy rotundity, sat Sergeant Thomas Velie of police headquarters, morosely grateful for the anonymity endowed by the scarlet suit and the jolly mask and whiskers of his appointed role.

Nor was this all. At a distance of six feet outside the counters shimmered a surrounding rampart of plate glass, borrowed in its various elements from *The Glass Home of the Future* display on the sixth floor rear, and assembled to shape an eight-foot wall quoined with chrome, its glistening surfaces flawless except at one point, where a thick glass door had been installed. But the edges fitted intimately and there was a formidable lock in the door, the key to which lay buried in Mr. Queen's right trouser pocket.

It was 8:54 a.m. The Queens, Nikki Porter, and Attorney Bondling stood among store officials and an army of plain-clothesmen on Nash's main floor surveying the product of their labors.

'I think that about does it,' muttered Inspector Queen at last. 'Men! Positions around the glass partition.'

Twenty-four assorted gendarmes in mufti jostled one another. They took marked places about the wall, facing it and grinning up at Sergeant Velie. Sergeant Velie, from his throne, glared back.

'Hagstrom and Piggott—the door.'

Two detectives detached themselves from a group of reserves. As they marched to the glass door, Mr. Bondling plucked at the Inspector's overcoat sleeve. 'Can all these men be trusted, Inspector Queen?' he whispered. 'I mean, this fellow Comus—'

'Mr. Bondling,' replied the old gentleman coldly, 'you do your job and let me do mine.'

'But—'

'Picked men, Mr. Bondling! I picked 'em myself.'

'Yes, yes, Inspector. I merely thought I'd—'

'Lieutenant Farber.'

A little man with watery eyes stepped forward.

'Mr. Bondling, this is Lieutenant Geronimo Farber, headquarters jewelry expert. Ellery?'

Ellery took the Dauphin's Doll from his greatcoat pocket, but he said, 'If you don't mind, dad, I'll keep holding on to it.'

Somebody said, 'Wow,' and then there was silence.

'Lieutenant, this doll in my son's hand is the famous Dauphin's Doll with the diamond crown that—'

'Don't touch it, Lieutenant, please,' said Ellery. 'I'd rather nobody touched it.'

'The doll,' continued the Inspector, 'has just been brought here from a bank vault which it ought never to have left, and Mr. Bondling, who's handling the Ypson estate, claims it's the genuine article. Lieutenant, examine the diamond and give us your opinion.'

Lieutenant Farber produced a loupe. Ellery held the dauphin securely, and Farber did not touch it.

Finally, the expert said: 'I can't pass an opinion about the doll itself, of course, but the diamond's a beauty. Easily worth a hundred thousand dollars at the present state of the market—maybe more. Looks like a very strong setting, by the way.'

'Thanks, Lieutenant. Okay, son,' said the Inspector. 'Go into your waltz.'

Clutching the dauphin, Ellery strode over to the glass gate and unlocked it.

'This fellow Farber,' whispered Attorney Bondling in the Inspector's hairy ear. 'Inspector, are you absolutely sure he's—?'

'He's really Lieutenant Farber?' The Inspector controlled himself. 'Mr. Bondling, I've known Gerry Farber for eighteen years. Calm yourself.'

Ellery was crawling perilously over the nearest counter. Then, bearing the dauphin aloft, he hurried across the floor of the enclosure to the platform.

Sergeant Velie whined, 'Maestro, how in hell am I going to sit here all day without washin' my hands?'

But Mr. Queen merely stooped and lifted from the floor a heavy little structure faced with black velvet consisting of a floor and a backdrop, with a two-armed chromium support. This object he placed on the platform directly between Sergeant Velie's massive legs.

Carefully, he stood the Dauphin's Doll in the velvet niche. Then he clambered back across the counter, went through the glass door, locked it with the key, and turned to examine his handiwork.

Proudly the prince's plaything stood, the jewel in his little golden crown darting 'on pale electric streams' under the concentrated tide of a dozen of the most powerful floodlights in the possession of the great store.

'Velie,' said Inspector Queen, 'you're not to touch that doll. Don't lay a finger on it.'

The sergeant said, 'Gaaaaa.'

'You men on duty. Don't worry about the crowds. Your job is to keep watching that doll. You're not to take your eyes off it all day. Mr. Bondling, are you satisfied?' Mr. Bondling seemed about to say something, but then he hastily nodded. 'Ellery?'

The great man smiled. 'The only way he can get that bawbie,' he said, 'is by spells and incantations. Raise the portcullis!'

THEN BEGAN THE interminable day, *dies irae*, the last shopping day before Christmas. This is traditionally the day of the inert, the procrastinating, the undecided, and the forgetful, sucked at last into the mercantile machine by the perpetual pump of Time. If there is peace upon earth, it descends only afterward; and at no time, on the part of anyone embroiled, is there good will toward men. As Miss Porter expresses it, a cat fight in a bird cage would be more Christian.

But on this December twenty-fourth, in Nash's the normal bedlam was augmented by the vast shrilling of thousands of Children. It may be, as the Psalmist insists, that happy is the man that hath his quiver full of them; but no bowmen surrounded Miss Ypson's darlings this day, only detectives carrying revolvers, not a few of whom forbore to use same only by the most heroic self-discipline. In the black floods of humanity overflowing the main floor little folks darted about like electrically charged minnows, pursued by exasperated maternal shrieks and the imprecations of those whose shins and rumps and toes were at the mercy of hot, happy little limbs; indeed, nothing was sacred, and Attorney Bondling was seen to quail and wrap his greatcoat defensively about him against the savage innocence of childhood. But the guardians of the law, having been ordered to simulate store employees, possessed no such armor; and many a man earned his citation that day for unique cause. They stood in the very millrace of the tide; it churned about them, shouting, 'Dollies! *Dollies!*' until the very word lost its familiar meaning and became the insensate scream of a thousand Loreleis beckoning strong men to destruction below the eye-level of their diamond Light.

But they stood fast.

And Comus was thwarted. Oh, he tried. At 11:18 a.m. a tottering old man holding fast to the hand of a small boy tried to wheedle Detective Hagstrom into unlocking the glass door 'so my grandson here—he's terrible nearsighted—can get a closer look at the pretty dollies.' Detective Hagstrom roared, 'Rube!' and the old gentleman dropped the little boy's hand violently and with remarkable agility lost himself in the crowd. A spot investigation revealed that, coming upon the boy, who had been crying for his mommy, the old gentleman had promised to find her. The little boy, whose name—he said—was Lance Morganstern, was removed to the Lost and Found Department; and everyone was satisfied that the great thief had finally launched his attack. Everyone, that is, but Ellery Queen. He seemed puzzled. When Nikki asked him why, he merely said: 'Stupidity, Nikki. It's not in character.'

At 1:46 p.m., Sergeant Velie sent up a distress signal. Inspector Queen read the message aright and signaled back: 'O.K. Fifteen minutes.' Sergeant Santa C. Velie scrambled off his perch, clawed his way over the counter, and pounded urgently on the inner side of the glass door. Ellery let him out, relocking the door immediately, and the Sergeant's red-clad figure disappeared on the double in the general direction of the main-floor gentlemen's relief station, leaving the dauphin in solitary possession of the dais.

During the Sergeant's recess Inspector Queen circulated among his men repeating the order of the day.

The episode of Velie's response to the summons of Nature caused a temporary crisis. For at the end of the specified fifteen minutes he had not returned. Nor was there a sign of him at the end of a half-hour. An aide dispatched to the relief station reported back that the Sergeant was not there. Fears of foul play were voiced at an emergency staff conference held then and there and countermeasures were being planned even as, at 2:35 p.m. the familiar Santa-clad bulk of the Sergeant was observed battling through the lines, pawing at his mask.

'Velie,' snarled Inspector Queen, 'where have you been?'

'Eating my lunch,' growled the Sergeant's voice, defensively. 'I been taking my punishment like a good soldier all day, Inspector, but I draw the line at starvin' to death even in line of duty.'

'Velie—!' choked the Inspector; but then he waved his hand feebly and said, 'Ellery, let him back in there.'

And that was very nearly all. The only other incident of note occurred at 4:22 p.m. A well-upholstered woman with a red face yelled, 'Stop! Thief! He grabbed my pocketbook! Police!' about fifty feet from the Ypson exhibit. Ellery instantly shouted, *'It's a trick! Men, don't take your eyes off that doll!'*

'It's Comus disguised as a woman,' exclaimed Attorney Bondling, as Inspector Queen and Detective Hesse wrestled the female figure through the mob. She was now a wonderful shade of magenta. 'What are you *doing?*' she screamed. 'Don't arrest *me!*—catch that crook who stole my pocketbook!' 'No dice, Comus,' said the Inspector. 'Wipe off that makeup.' 'McComas?' said the woman loudly. 'My name is Rafferty, and all these folks saw it. He was a fat man with a mustache.' 'Inspector,' said Nikki Porter, making a surreptitious scientific test. 'This is a female. Believe me.' And so, indeed, it proved. All agreed that the mustachioed fat man had been Comus, creating a diversion in the desperate hope that the resulting confusion would give him an opportunity to steal the little dauphin.

'Stupid, stupid,' muttered Ellery, gnawing his fingernails.

'Sure,' grinned the Inspector. 'We've got him nibbling his tail, Ellery. This was his do-or-die pitch. He's through.'

'Frankly,' sniffed Nikki, 'I'm a little disappointed.'

'Worried,' said Ellery, 'would be the word for me.'

INSPECTOR QUEEN WAS too case-hardened a sinner's nemesis to lower his guard at his most vulnerable moment. When the 5:30 bells bonged and the crowds began struggling toward the exits, he barked: 'Men, stay at your posts. Keep watching that doll!' So all hands were on the *qui vive* even as the store emptied. The reserves kept hustling people out. Ellery, standing on an information booth, spotted bottlenecks and waved his arms.

At 5:50 p.m. the main floor was declared out of the battle zone. All stragglers had been herded out. The only persons visible were the refugees trapped by the closing bell on the upper floors, and these were pouring out of elevators and funneled by a solid line of detectives and accredited store personnel to the doors. By 6:05 they were a trickle; by 6:10 even the trickle had dried up. And the personnel itself began to disperse.

'No, men!' called Ellery sharply from his observation post. 'Stay where you are till all the store employees are out!' The counter clerks had long since disappeared.

Sergeant Velie's plaintive voice called from the other side of the glass door. 'I got to get home and decorate my tree. Maestro, make with the key.'

Ellery jumped down and hurried over to release him. Detective Piggott jeered, 'Going to play Santa to your kids tomorrow morning, Velie?' at which the Sergeant managed even through his mask to project a four-letter word distinctly, forgetful of Miss Porter's presence, and stamped off toward the gentlemen's relief station.

'Where you going, Velie?' asked the Inspector, smiling.

'I got to get out of these x-and-dash Santy clothes somewheres, don't I?' came back the Sergeant's mask-muffled tones, and he vanished in a thunderclap of his fellow-officers' laughter.

'Still worried, Mr. Queen?' chuckled the Inspector.

'I don't understand it.' Ellery shook his head. 'Well, Mr. Bondling, there's your dauphin, untouched by human hands.'

'Yes. Well!' Attorney Bondling wiped his forehead happily. 'I don't profess to understand it, either, Mr. Queen. Unless it's simply another case of an inflated reputation . . .' He clutched the Inspector suddenly. 'Those men!' he whispered. '*Who are they?*'

'Relax, Mr. Bondling,' said the Inspector good-naturedly. 'It's just the men to move the dolls back to the bank. Wait a minute, you men! Perhaps, Mr. Bondling, we'd better see the dauphin back to the vaults ourselves.'

'Keep those fellows back,' said Ellery to the headquarters men, quietly, and he followed the Inspector and Mr. Bondling into the enclosure. They pulled two of the counters apart at one corner and strolled over to the platform. The dauphin was winking at them in a friendly way. They stood looking at him.

'Cute little devil,' said the Inspector.

'Seems silly now,' beamed Attorney Bondling. 'Being so worried all day.'

'Comus must have had *some* plan,' mumbled Ellery.

'Sure,' said the Inspector. 'That old man disguise. And that purse-snatching act.'

'No, no, dad. Something clever. He's always pulled something clever.'

'Well, there's the diamond,' said the lawyer comfortably. 'He didn't.'

'Disguise . . . ' muttered Ellery. 'It's always been a disguise. Santa Claus costume—he used that once—this morning in front of the bank. . . . Did we see a Santa Claus around here today?'

'Just Velie,' said the Inspector, grinning. 'And I hardly think—'

'Wait a moment, please,' said Attorney Bondling in a very odd voice. He was staring at the Dauphin's Doll.

'Wait for what, Mr. Bondling?'

'What's the matter?' said Ellery, also in a very odd voice.

'But . . . not possible . . . ' stammered Bondling. He snatched the doll from its black velvet repository. '*No!*' he howled. '*This isn't the dauphin! It's a fake—a copy!*'

Something happened in Mr. Queen's head—a little *click!* like the sound of a switch. And there was light.

'Some of you men!' he roared. '*After Santa Claus!*'

'After who, Ellery?' gasped Inspector Queen.

'Don't stand here! *Get him!*' screamed Ellery, dancing up and down. 'The man I just let out of here! The Santa who made for the men's room!'

Detectives started running, wildly.

'But Ellery,' said a small voice, and Nikki found that it was her own, 'that was Sergeant Velie.'

'It was *not* Velie, Nikki! When Velie ducked out just before two o'-clock, *Comus waylaid him!* It was Comus who came back in Velie's Santa Claus rig, wearing Velie's whiskers and mask! *Comus has been on this platform all afternoon!*' He tore the dauphin from Attorney Bondling's grasp. 'Copy . . . He did it, he did it!'

'But Mr. Queen,' whispered Attorney Bondling, 'his voice. He spoke to us . . . in Sergeant Velie's voice.'

'Yes, Ellery,' Nikki heard herself saying.

'I told you yesterday Comus is a great mimic, Nikki. Lieutenant Far-ber! Is Farber still here?'

The jewelry expert, who had been gaping from a distance, shook his head and shuffled into the enclosure.

'Lieutenant,' said Ellery in a strangled voice. 'Examine this dia-mond . . . I mean, *is* it a diamond?'

Inspector Queen removed his hands from his face and said froggily, 'Well, Gerry?'

Lieutenant Farber squinted once through his loupe. 'The hell you say. It's strass—'

'It's what?' said the Inspector piteously.

'Strass, Dick—lead glass—paste. Beautiful job of imitation—as nice as I've ever seen.'

'Lead me to that Santa Claus,' whispered Inspector Queen.

But Santa Claus was being led to him. Struggling in the grip of a dozen detectives, his red coat ripped off, his red pants around his ankles, but his whiskery mask still on his face, came a large shouting man.

'But I tell you,' he was roaring, 'I'm Sergeant Tom Velie! Just take the mask off—that's all!'

'It's a pleasure,' growled Detective Hagstrom, trying to break their prisoner's arm, 'we're reservin' for the Inspector.'

'Hold him, boys,' whispered the Inspector. He struck like a cobra. His hand came away with Santa's face.

And there, indeed, was Sergeant Velie.

'Why, it's Velie,' said the Inspector wonderingly.

'I only told you that a thousand times,' said the Sergeant, folding his great hairy arms across his great hairy chest. 'Now who's the so-and-so who tried to bust my arm?' Then he said, 'My pants!' and as Miss Porter turned delicately away, Detective Hagstrom humbly stooped and raised Sergeant Velie's pants.

'Never mind that,' said a cold, remote voice.

It was the master, himself.

'Yeah?' said Sergeant Velie.

'Velie, weren't you attacked when you went to the men's room just before two?'

'Do I look like the attackable type?'

'You did go to lunch?—in person?'

'And a lousy lunch it was.'

'It was *you* up here among the dolls all afternoon?'

'Nobody else, Maestro. Now, my friends, I want action. Fast patter. What's this all about? Before,' said Sergeant Velie softly, 'I lose my temper.'

While divers headquarters orators delivered impromptu periods before the silent Sergeant, Inspector Richard Queen spoke.

'Ellery. Son. How in the name of the second sin did he do it?'

'Pa,' replied the master, 'you got me.'

DECK THE HALL with boughs of holly, but not if your name is Queen on the evening of a certain December twenty-fourth. If your name is Queen on that lamentable evening you are seated in the living room of a New York apartment uttering no falalas but staring miserably into a somber fire. And you have company. The guest list is short, but select. It numbers two, a Miss Porter and a Sergeant Velie, and they are no comfort.

No, no ancient Yuletide carol is being trolled; only the silence sings.

Wail in your crypt, Cytherea Ypson; all was for nought; your little dauphin's treasure lies not in the empty coffers of the orphans but in the hot clutch of one who took his evil inspiration from a long-crumbled specialist in vanishments.

Fact: Lieutenant Geronimo Farber of police headquarters had examined the diamond in the genuine dauphin's crown a matter of seconds before it was conveyed to its sanctuary in the enclosure. Lieutenant Farber had pronounced the diamond a diamond, and not merely a diamond, but a diamond worth in his opinion over one hundred thousand dollars.

Fact: It was this genuine diamond and this genuine Dauphin's Doll which Ellery with his own hands had carried into the glass-enclosed fortress and deposited between the authenticated Sergeant Velie's verified feet.

Fact: All day—specifically, between the moment the dauphin had been deposited in his niche until the moment he was discovered to be a fraud; that is, during the total period in which a theft-and-substitution was even theoretically possible—no person whatsoever, male or female, adult or child, had set foot within the enclosure except Sergeant Thomas Velie, alias Santa Claus; and some dozens of persons with police training and specific instructions, not to mention the Queens themselves, Miss Porter, and Attorney Bondling, testified unqualifiedly that Sergeant Velie had not touched the doll, at any time, all day.

Fact: All those deputized to watch the doll swore that they had done so without lapse or hindrance the everlasting day; moreover, that at no time had anything touched the doll—human or mechanical—either from inside or outside the enclosure.

Fact: Despite all the foregoing, at the end of the day they had found the real dauphin gone and a worthless copy in its place.

'It's brilliantly, unthinkably clever,' said Ellery at last. 'A master illusion. For, of course, it *was* an illusion. . . . '

'Witchcraft,' groaned the Inspector.

'Mass mesmerism,' suggested Nikki Porter.

'Mass bird gravel,' growled the Sergeant.

Two hours later Ellery spoke again.

'So Comus had a worthless copy of the dauphin all ready for the switch,' he muttered. 'It's a world-famous dollie, been illustrated countless times, minutely described, photographed. . . . All ready for the switch, but how did he make it? How? How?'

'You said that,' said the Sergeant, 'once or forty-two times.'

'The bells are tolling,' sighed Nikki, 'but for whom? Not for us.' And indeed, while they slumped there, Time, which Seneca named father of truth, had crossed the threshold of Christmas; and Nikki looked alarmed, for as that glorious song of old came upon the midnight clear, a great light spread from Ellery's eyes and beatified the whole contorted countenance, so that peace sat there, the peace that approximateth understanding; and he threw back that noble head and laughed with the merriment of an innocent child.

'Hey,' said Sergeant Velie, staring.

'Son,' began Inspector Queen, half-rising from his armchair; when the telephone rang.

'Beautiful!' roared Ellery. 'Oh, exquisite! How did Comus make the switch, eh? Nikki—'

'From somewhere,' said Nikki, handing him the telephone receiver, 'a voice is calling, and if you ask me it's saying "Comus." Why not ask him?'

'Comus,' whispered the Inspector, shrinking.

'Comus,' echoed the Sergeant, baffled.

'Comus?' said Ellery heartily. 'How nice. Hello there! Congratulations.'

'Why, thank you,' said the familiar deep and hollow voice. 'I called to express my appreciation for a wonderful day's sport and to wish you the merriest kind of Yuletide.'

'You anticipate a rather merry Christmas yourself, I take it.'

'*Laeti triumphantes,*' said Comus jovially.

'And the orphans?'

'They have my best wishes. But I won't detain you, Ellery. If you'll look at the doormat outside your apartment door, you'll find on it—in the spirit

of the season—a little gift, with the compliments of Comus. Will you remember me to Inspector Queen and to Attorney Bondling?'

Ellery hung up, smiling.

On the doormat he found the true Dauphin's Doll, intact except for a
contemptible detail. The jewel in the little golden crown was missing.

'IT WAS,' SAID Ellery later, over pastrami sandwiches, 'a fundamen-
tally simple problem. All great illusions are. A valuable object is placed
in full view in the heart of an impenetrable enclosure, it is watched hawk-
ishly by dozens of thoroughly screened and reliable trained persons, it is
never out of their view, it is not once touched by human hand or any other
agency, and yet, at the expiration of the danger period, it is gone—exchanged for a worthless copy. Wonderful. Amazing. It defies the imagination. Actually, it's susceptible—like all magical hocus-pocus—to immediate
solution if only one is able—as I was not—to ignore the wonder and stick
to the fact. But then, the wonder is there for precisely that purpose: to
stand in the way of the fact.

'What is the fact?' continued Ellery, helping himself to a dill pickle.
'The fact is that between the time the doll was placed on the exhibit platform and the time the theft was discovered no one and no thing touched it.
Therefore between the time the doll was placed on the platform and the
time the theft was discovered *the dauphin could not have been stolen.* It
follows, simply and inevitably, that the dauphin must have been stolen *outside that period.*

'Before the period began? No. I placed the authentic dauphin inside the
enclosure with my own hands; at or about the beginning of the period,
then, no hand but mine had touched the doll—not even, you'll recall, Lieutenant Farber's.

'Then the dauphin must have been stolen after the period closed.'

Ellery brandished half the pickle. 'And who,' he demanded solemnly,
'is the only one besides myself who handled that doll after the period
closed and before Lieutenant Farber pronounced the diamond to be paste?
The only one?'

The Inspector and the Sergeant exchanged puzzled glances, and Nikki
looked blank.

'Why, Mr. Bondling,' said Nikki, 'and he doesn't count.'

'He counts very much, Nikki,' said Ellery, reaching for the mustard,
'because the facts say Bondling stole the dauphin at that time.'

'Bondling!' The Inspector paled.

'I don't get it,' complained Sergeant Velie.

'Ellery, you must be wrong,' said Nikki. 'At the time Mr. Bondling grabbed the doll off the platform, the theft had already taken place. It was the worthless copy he picked up.'

'That,' said Ellery, reaching for another sandwich, 'was the focal point of his illusion. How do we know it was the worthless copy he picked up? Why, he said so. Simple, eh? He said so and like the dumb bunnies we were, we took his unsupported word as gospel.'

'That's right!' mumbled his father. 'We didn't actually examine the doll till quite a few seconds later.'

'Exactly,' said Ellery in a munchy voice. 'There was a short period of beautiful confusion, as Bondling knew there would be. I yelled to the boys to follow and grab Santa Claus—I mean, the Sergeant here. The detectives were momentarily demoralized. You, dad, were stunned. Nikki looked as if the roof had fallen in. I essayed an excited explanation. Some detectives ran; others milled around. And while all this was happening—during those few moments when nobody was watching the genuine doll in Bondling's hand because everyone thought it was a fake—Bondling calmly slipped it into one of his greatcoat pockets and from the other produced the worthless copy which he'd been carrying there all day. When I did turn back to him, it was the copy I grabbed from his hand. And his illusion was complete.

'I know,' said Ellery dryly, 'it's rather on the let-down side. That's why illusionists guard their professional secrets so closely; knowledge is disenchantment. No doubt the incredulous amazement aroused in his periwigged London audience by Comus the French conjuror's dematerialization of his wife from the top of a table would have suffered the same fate if he'd revealed the trapdoor through which she had dropped. A good trick, like a good woman, is best in the dark. Sergeant, have another pastrami.'

'Seems like funny chow to be eating early Christmas morning,' said the Sergeant, reaching. Then he stopped. Then he said, 'Bondling,' and shook his head.

'Now that we know it was Bondling,' said the Inspector, who had recovered a little, 'it's a cinch to get that diamond back. He hasn't had time to dispose of it yet. I'll just give downtown a buzz—'

'Wait, dad,' said Ellery.

'Wait for what?'

'Whom are you going to sic the hounds on?'

'What?'

'You're going to call headquarters, get a warrant, and so on. Who's your man?'

The Inspector felt his head. 'Why . . . Bondling, didn't you say?'

'It might be wise,' said Ellery, thoughtfully searching with his tongue for a pickle seed, 'to specify his alias.'

'Alias?' said Nikki. 'Does he have one?'

'What alias, son?'

'Comus.'

'*Comus!*'

'*Comus?*'

'Oh, come off it,' said Nikki, pouring herself a shot of coffee, straight, for she was in training for the Inspector's Christmas dinner. 'How could Bondling be Comus when Bondling was with us all day?—and Comus kept making disguised appearances all over the place . . . that Santa who gave me the note in front of the bank—the old man who kidnapped Lance Morganstern—the fat man with the mustache who snatched Mrs. Rafferty's purse.'

'Yeah,' said the Sergeant. 'How?'

'These illusions die hard,' said Ellery. 'Wasn't it Comus who phoned a few minutes ago to rag me about the theft? Wasn't it Comus who said he'd left the stolen dauphin—minus the diamond—on our doormat? Therefore Comus is Bondling.

'I told you Comus never does anything without a good reason,' said Ellery. 'Why did "Comus" announce to "Bondling," that he was *going* to steal the Dauphin's Doll? Bondling told us that—putting the finger on his *alter ego*—because he wanted us to believe he and Comus were separate individuals. He wanted us to watch for *Comus* and take *Bondling* for granted. In tactical execution of this strategy Bondling provided us with three "Comus" appearances during the day—obviously, confederates.

'Yes,' said Ellery, 'I think, dad, you'll find on backtracking that the great thief you've been trying to catch for five years has been respectable estate attorney on Park Row all the time, shedding his quiddities and his quillets at night in favor of the soft shoe and the dark lantern. And now he'll have to exchange them all for a number and a grilled door. Well, well, it couldn't have happened at a more appropriate season; there's an old English proverb that says the Devil makes his Christmas pie of lawyers' tongues. Nikki, pass the pastrami.'

BURNING END

Ruth Rendell

Ruth Rendell is generally recognized as one of a handful of writers whose work has profoundly changed the crime genre. Whether with her psychological novels or her Inspector Wexford books, her style, insight, quiet but frequently tart wit, and constant confrontation with our modern moral dilemmas has elevated her books to their very own niche far above the average mystery effort. Her most recent novel is *Harm Done*. It has been argued that her short stories are even better than her novels. An enjoyable argument, really, because you have the pleasure of reading both and deciding for yourself.

AFTER SHE HAD been doing it for a year, it occurred to Linda that looking after Betty fell to her lot because she was a woman. Betty was Brian's mother, not hers, and Betty had two other children, both sons, both unmarried men. No one had ever suggested that either of them should take a hand in looking after their mother. Betty had never much liked Linda, had sometimes hinted that Brian had married beneath him, and once, in the heat of temper, said that Linda was "not good enough" for her son, but still it was Linda who cared for her now. Linda felt a fool for not having thought of it in these terms before.

But she knew she would not get very far talking about it to Brian. Brian would say—and did say—that this was women's work. A man couldn't perform intimate tasks for an old woman, it wasn't fitting. When Linda asked why not, he told her not to be silly, everyone knew why not.

"Suppose it had been your dad that was left, suppose he'd been bedridden, would I have looked after him?"

Brian looked over the top of his evening paper. He was holding the remote in his hand but he didn't turn down the sound. "He wasn't left, was he?"

"No, but if he had been?"

"I reckon you would have. There isn't anyone else, is there? It's not as if the boys were married."

Every morning after Brian had gone out into the farmyard and before she left for work, Linda drove down the road, turned left at the church into the lane, and after a mile came to the very small cottage on the very large piece of land where Betty had lived since the death of her husband twelve years before. Betty slept downstairs in the room at the back. She was always awake when Linda got there, although that was invariably before seven-thirty, and she always said she had been awake since five.

Linda got her up and changed the incontinence pad. Most mornings she had to change the sheets as well. She washed Betty, put her into a clean nightgown and clean bedjacket, socks, and slippers, and while Betty shouted and moaned, lifted and shoved her as best she could into the armchair she would remain in all day. Then it was breakfast. Sweet milky tea and bread and butter and jam. Betty wouldn't use the feeding cup with the spout. What did Linda think she was, a baby? She drank from a cup, and unless Linda had remembered to cover her up with the muslin squares that had indeed once had their use for babies, the tea would go all down the clean nightgown and Betty would have to be changed again.

After Linda had left her and gone off to work, the district nurse would come, though not every day, not for certain. The Meals-on-Wheels lady would come and give Betty her midday dinner, bits and pieces in foil containers, all labelled with the names of their contents. At some point Brian would come. Brian would "look in." Not to *do* anything, not to clear anything away or give his mother something to eat or make her a cup of tea or run the vacuum cleaner around—Linda did that on Saturdays—but to sit in Betty's bedroom for ten minutes smoking a cigarette and watching whatever was on television. Very occasionally, perhaps once a month, the brother who lived two miles away would come for ten minutes and watch television with Brian. The other brother, the one who lived ten miles away, never came at all except at Christmas.

Linda always knew if Brian had been there by the smell of smoke and the cigarette end stubbed out in the ashtray. But even if there had been no smell and no stub she would have known because Betty always told her. Betty thought Brian was a saint and an angel to spare a moment away from the farm to visit his old mother. She could no longer speak distinctly, but she was positively articulate on the subject of Brian, the most perfect son any woman ever had.

It was about five when Linda got back there. Usually the incontinence pad needed changing again and often the nightdress too. Considering how ill she was, and partially paralysed, Betty ate a great deal. Linda made her scrambled egg or sardines on toast. She brought pastries with her from the cakeshop or, in the summer, strawberries and cream. She made more tea for Betty, and when the meal was over, somehow heaved Betty back into that bed.

The bedroom window was never opened. Betty wouldn't have it. The room smelt of urine and lavender, camphor and Meals-on-Wheels, so every day on her way to work Linda opened the window in the front room and left the doors open. It didn't make much difference but she went on doing it. When she had got Betty to bed she washed up the day's teacups, emptied the ashtray and washed it, and put all the soiled linen into a plastic bag to take home. The question she asked Betty before she left had become meaningless because Betty always said no, and she hadn't asked it once since having that conversation with Brian about whose job it was to look after his mother, but she asked it now.

"Wouldn't it be better if we moved you in with us, Mum?"

Betty's hearing was erratic. This was one of her deaf days.

"What?"

"Wouldn't you be better off coming to live with us?"

"I'm not leaving my home till they carry me out feet first. How many times do I have to tell you?"

Linda said all right and she was off now and she would see her in the morning. Looking rather pleased at the prospect, Betty said she would be dead by the morning.

"Not you," said Linda, which was what she always said, and so far she had always been right.

She went into the front room and closed the window. The room was furnished in a way which must have been old-fashioned even when Betty was young. In the center of it was a square dining table, around which stood six chairs with seats of faded green silk. There was a large, elaborately carved sideboard but no armchairs, no small tables, no books, and no lamps but the central light which, enveloped in a shade of parchment panels stitched together with leather thongs, was suspended directly over the glass vase that stood on a lace mat in the absolute center of the table.

For some reason, ever since the second stroke had incapacitated Betty two years before, all the post, all the junk mail, and every freebie newssheet that was delivered to the cottage ended up on this table. Every few months it was cleared away, but this hadn't been done for some time, and Linda noticed that only about four inches of the glass vase now showed above the sea of paper. The lace mat was not visible at all. She noticed something else as well.

It had been a warm sunny day, very warm for April. The cottage faced south and all afternoon the sunshine had poured through the window, was still pouring through the window, striking at the neck of the vase so that the glass was too bright to look at. Where the sun-struck glass touched a sheet of paper a burning had begun. The burning glass was making a dark charred channel through the sheet of thin printed paper.

Linda screwed up her eyes. They had not deceived her. That was smoke she could see. And now she could smell burning paper. For a moment she stood there, fascinated, marvelling at this phenomenon which she had heard of but had never believed in. A magnifying glass to make boy scout's fires, she thought, and somewhere she had read of a forest burnt down through a piece of broken glass left in a sunlit glade.

There was nowhere to put the piles of paper, so she found another plastic bag and filled that. Betty called out something but it was only to know why she was still there. Linda dusted the table, replaced the lace mat and the glass vase, and, with a bag of washing in one hand and a bag of wastepaper in the other, went home to do the washing and get an evening meal for Brian and herself and the children.

THE INCIDENT OF the glass vase, the sun, and the burning paper had been so interesting that Linda meant to tell Brian and Andrew and Gemma all about it while they were eating. But they were also watching the finals of a quiz game on television and hushed her when she started to speak. The opportunity went by and somehow there was no other until the next day. But by that time the sun and the glass setting the paper on fire no longer seemed so remarkable and Linda decided not to mention it.

Several times in the weeks that followed Brian asked his mother if it wasn't time she came to live with them at the farm. He always told Linda of these attempts, as if in issuing this invitation he had been particularly magnanimous and self-denying. Perhaps this was because Betty responded very differently from when Linda asked her. Brian and his children, Betty said, shouldn't have to have a useless old woman under their roof, age and youth were not meant to live together, though nobody appreciated her son's generosity in asking her more than she did. Meanwhile Linda went on going to the cottage and looking after Betty for an hour every morning and an hour and a half every evening and cleaning the place on Saturdays and doing Betty's washing.

One afternoon while Brian was sitting with his mother smoking a cigarette and watching television, the doctor dropped in to pay his twice-yearly visit. He beamed at Betty, said how nice it was for her to have her devoted family around her, and on his way out told Brian it was best for the old folks to end their days at home whenever possible. If he said anything about the cigarette, Brian didn't mention it when he recounted this to Linda.

He must have picked up a pile of junk mail from the doormat and the new phone book from outside the door, for all this was lying on the table in the front room when Linda arrived at ten to five. The paper had accumulated during the past weeks, but when Linda went to look for a plastic bag she saw that the entire stock had been used up. She made a mental note to buy some more and in the meantime had to put the soiled sheets and Betty's two wet nightdresses into a pillowcase to take them home. The sun wasn't shining; it had been a dull day and the forecast was for rain, so there was no danger from the conjunction of glass vase with the piles of paper. It could safely remain where it was.

On her way home it occurred to Linda that the simplest solution was to remove not the paper but the vase. Yet, when she went back next day, she didn't remove the vase. It was a strange feeling she had, that if she moved the vase to the mantelpiece, say, or the top of the sideboard, she would somehow have closed a door or missed a chance. Once she had moved it she would never be able to move it back again, for though she could easily have explained to anyone why she had moved it from the table, she would never be able to say why she had put it back. These thoughts frightened her and she put them from her mind.

Linda bought a pack of fifty black plastic sacks. Betty said it was a wicked waste of money. When she was up and about she had been in the habit of burning all paper waste. All leftover food and cans and bottles got mixed up together and went out for the dustman. Betty had never heard of the environment. When Linda insisted, one hot day in July, on opening the bedroom windows, Betty said she was freezing, Linda was trying to kill her, and she would tell her son his wife was an evil woman. Linda took the curtains home and washed them but she didn't open the bedroom window again, it wasn't worth it, it caused too much trouble.

But when Brian's brother Michael got engaged, she did ask if Suzanne would take her turn looking after Betty once they were back from their honeymoon.

"You couldn't expect it of a young girl like her," Brian said.

"She's twenty-eight," said Linda.

"She doesn't look it." Brian switched on the television. "Did I tell you Geoff's been made redundant?"

"Then maybe he could help out with Betty if he hasn't got a job to go to."

Brian looked at her and shook his head gently. "He's feeling low enough as it is. It's a blow to a man's pride, that is, going on the dole. I couldn't ask him."

Why does he have to be asked, Linda thought. It's his mother. The sun was already high in the sky when she got to the cottage at seven-thirty next morning, already edging round the house to penetrate the front-room window by ten. Linda put the junk mail on the table and took the letter and the postcard into the bedroom. Betty wouldn't look at them. She was wet through and the bed was wet. Linda got her up and stripped off the wet clothes, wrapping Betty in a clean blanket because she said she was freezing. When she was washed and in her clean nightdress, she wanted to talk about Michael's fiancée. It was one of her articulate days.

"Dirty little trollop," said Betty. "I remember her when she was fifteen. Go with anyone, she would. There's no knowing how many abortions she's had, messed all her insides up, I shouldn't wonder."

"She's very pretty, in my opinion," said Linda, "and a nice nature."

"Handsome is as handsome does. It's all that makeup and hair dye as has entrapped my poor boy. One thing, she won't set foot in this house while I'm alive."

Linda opened the window in the front room. It was going to be a hot day, but breezy. The house could do with a good draught of air blowing through to freshen it. She thought: I wonder why no one ever put flowers in that vase, there's no point in a vase without flowers. The letters and envelopes and newsprint surrounded it so that it no longer looked like a vase but like a glass tube inexplicably poking out between a stack of paper and a telephone directory.

Brian didn't visit that day. He had started harvesting. When Linda came back at five, Betty told her Michael had been in. She showed Linda the box of chocolates that was his gift, his way of "soft-soaping" her, Betty said. Not that a few violet creams had stopped her speaking her mind on the subject of that trollop.

The chocolates had gone soft and sticky in the heat. Linda said she would put them in the fridge but Betty clutched the box to her chest, saying she knew Linda, she knew her sweet tooth, if she let that box out of her sight she'd never see it again. Linda washed Betty and changed her. While she was doing Betty's feet, rubbing cream round her toes and powdering them, Betty struck her on the head with the bedside clock, the only weapon she had to hand.

"You hurt me," said Betty. "You hurt me on purpose."

"No, I didn't, Mum. I think you've broken that clock."

"You hurt me on purpose because I wouldn't give you my chocolates my son brought me."

Brian said he was going to cut the field behind the cottage next day. Fifty acres of barley, and he'd be done by midafternoon if the heat didn't kill him. He could have seen to his mother's needs, he'd be practically on the spot, but he didn't offer. Linda wouldn't have believed her ears if she'd heard him offer.

It was hotter than ever. It was even hot at seven-thirty. Linda washed Betty and changed the sheets. She gave her cereal for breakfast and a boiled egg and toast. From her bed Betty could see Brian going round the barley field on the combine, and this seemed to bring her enormous pleasure, though her enjoyment was tempered with pity.

"He knows what hard work is," Betty said, "he doesn't spare himself when there's a job to be done," as if Brian were cutting the fifty acres with a scythe instead of sitting up there in a cabin with twenty kingsize and a can of Coke and the Walkman on his head playing Beatles songs from his youth.

Linda opened the window in the front room very wide. The sun would be round in a couple of hours to stream through that window. She adjusted an envelope on the top of the pile, moving the torn edge of its flap to brush against the glass vase. Then she moved it away again. She stood, looking at the table and the papers and the vase. A brisk draught of air made the thinner sheets of paper flutter a little. From the bedroom she heard Betty call out, through closed windows, to a man on a combine a quarter of a mile away, "Hallo, Brian, you all right then, are you? You keep at it, son, that's right, you got the weather on your side."

One finger stretched out, Linda lightly poked at the torn edge of the envelope flap. She didn't really move it at all. She turned her back quickly. She marched out of the room, out of the house, to the car.

THE FIRE MUST have started somewhere around four in the afternoon, the hottest part of that hot day. Brian had been in to see his mother when he had finished cutting the field at two. He had watched television with her and then she said she wanted to have a sleep. Those who know about these things said she had very likely died from suffocation without ever waking. That was why she hadn't phoned for help, though the phone was by her bed.

A builder driving down the lane, on his way to a barn conversion his firm was working on, called the fire brigade. They were volunteers whose headquarters was five miles away, and they took twenty minutes to get to the fire. By then Betty was dead and half the cottage destroyed. Nobody told Linda, there was hardly time, and when she got to Betty's at five it was all over. Brian and the firemen were standing about, poking at the wet black ashes with sticks, and Andrew and Gemma were in Brian's estate car outside the gate, eating potato crisps.

The will was a surprise. Betty had lived in that cottage for twelve years without a washing machine or a freezer and her television set was rented by Brian. The bed she slept in was her marriage bed, new in 1939, the cottage hadn't been painted since she moved there, and the kitchen had last been refitted just after the war. But she left what seemed an enormous sum of money. Linda could hardly believe it. A third was for Geoff, a third for Michael, and the remaining third as well as the cottage, or what was left of it, for Brian.

The insurance company paid up. It was impossible to discover the cause of the fire. Something to do with the great heat, no doubt, and the thatched roof, and the ancient electrical wiring which hadn't been renewed for sixty or seventy years. Linda, of course, knew better, but she said nothing. She kept what she knew and let it fester inside her, giving her sleepless nights and taking away her appetite.

Brian cried noisily at the funeral. All the brothers showed excessive grief, and no one told Brian to pull himself together or be a man, but put their arms round his shoulders and told him what a marvellous son he'd been and how he'd nothing to reproach himself with. Linda didn't cry but soon after went into a black depression from which nothing could rouse her, not the doctor's tranquillizers, nor Brian's promise of a slap-up holiday somewhere, even abroad if she liked, nor people telling her Betty hadn't felt any pain but had just slipped away in her smoky sleep.

An application to build a new house on the site of the cottage was favourably received by the planning authority, and permission was granted. Why shouldn't they live in it, Brian said, he and Linda and the children? The farmhouse was ancient and awkward, difficult to keep clean, just the sort of place Londoners would like for a second home. How about moving, he said, how about a modern house, with everything you want, two bathrooms, say, and a laundry room, and a sun lounge? Design it yourself and don't worry about the cost, he said, for he was concerned for his wife, who had always been so practical and efficient as well as easygoing and tractable, but was now a miserable, silent woman.

Linda refused to move. She didn't want a new house, especially a new house on the site of that cottage. She didn't want a holiday or money to buy clothes. She refused to touch Betty's money. Depression had forced her to give up her job but, although she was at home all day and there was no old woman to look after every morning and every evening, she did nothing in the house and Brian was obliged to get a woman in to clean. Brian could build his house and sell it, if that was what he wanted, but she wouldn't touch the money and no one could make her.

"She must have been a lot fonder of Mum than I thought," Brian said to his brother Michael. "She's always been one to keep her feelings all bottled up, but that's the only explanation. Mum must have meant a lot more to her than I ever knew."

"Or else it's guilt," said Michael, whose fiancée's sister was married to a man whose brother was a psychotherapist.

"Guilt? You have to be joking. What's she got to be guilty about? She couldn't have done more if she'd been Mum's own daughter."

"Yeah, but folks feel guilt over nothing when someone dies, it's a well-known fact."

"It is, is it? Is that what it is, doctor? Well, let me tell you something. If anyone ought to feel guilt, it's me. I've never said a word about this to a soul. Well, I couldn't, could I? Not if I wanted to collect the insurance; but the fact is it was me set that place on fire."

"You what?" said Michael.

"It was an accident. I don't mean on purpose. Come on, what do you take me for, my own brother? And I don't feel guilty, I can tell you, I don't feel a scrap of guilt, accidents will happen and there's not a thing you can do about it. But when I went in to see Mum that afternoon, I left my cigarette burning on the side of the chest of drawers. You know how you put them down, with the burning end stuck out. Linda'd taken away the damned ashtray and washed it or something. When I saw Mum was asleep, I just crept out. Just crept out and left that fag end burning. Without a backward glance."

Awed, Michael asked in a small voice, "When did you realise?"

"Soon as I saw the smoke; soon as I saw the fire brigade. Too late then, wasn't it? I'd crept out of there without a backward glance."

CARRYING CONCEALED

Lisa Scottoline

Some reviewers have noted that Lisa Scottoline has brought back the Jean Arthur kind of female protagonist, Arthur being the bright, comely, sardonic heroine of some of Hollywood's best screwball romances. There is at least one other similarity between Scottoline's heroines and Jean Arthur's characters. Despite the surface humor, they manage to convey an undercurrent of very real feelings. Without resorting to sentimentality, the Scottoline-Arthur heroine adds real emotional power to the sometimes frothy story lines. No small feat. Scottoline brings her own charms and talents to the legal thriller.

IT WAS ALMOST seven o'clock in the morning and Assistant District Attorney Tom Moran was late for court. He shaved lethally fast, slipped into his suitpants, and pinwheeled into his pinstriped jacket, all the time rehearsing his cross-examination in a continuous loop. If Tom didn't break this witness today, he'd lose for sure. He jumped into his wingtips and sprinted downstairs, his tie flying behind him.

Tom hit the hardwood running and snatched his briefcase from the floor like it was a baton on the final leg. He had perfected his handoff at St. Joe's Prep and could still hear the roar of the crowd cheering him toward the tape. WEEEAAAH! Then Tom realized that it wasn't cheering he heard, it was one of the twins crying in the kitchen. At three months old, the babies cried a lot. *Gastric reflux*, Marie called it, but Tom didn't think these two words should ever appear together.

He stopped in his tracks at the front door, his hand on the brass knob. The crying from the kitchen intensified. Tom checked his watch. 7:12 A.M. A tsunami of guilt washed over him. He had worked all night at the office, and Marie had been alone with the twins. He couldn't leave without checking on her. Tom dropped his briefcase and dashed into the kitchen, where he froze in disbelief. Marie was asleep standing up, rocking the crying infant in sagging arms. "Honey, wake up!" he shouted.

Marie's eyelids fluttered open. "Does it come in navy?" she asked, drowsy.

"Marie, wake up, wake up." Tom rushed across the room and grabbed the wailing baby. It was Ashley, who was his favorite of the twins, even though Marie made him swear not to have a favorite. "You were sleeping."

"No, I was shopping," she said. Marie leaned against the kitchen counter, dark shadows encircling her blue eyes and her strawberry-blonde hair uncombed. She hadn't lost the weight from the babies yet and wore a tentlike chenille robe over her Eagles T-shirt. She wasn't the girl he married, but Tom was too sensitive a guy to expect that. It would be nice to have sex again, however.

"Sit down, you look exhausted," Tom said. "Did you get any sleep last night?"

"I'm fine. Fine, really. I slept a little. Really." Marie sank into a chair, bumping into the kitchen table. Pink pacifiers rocked on its pine surface and an empty plastic bottle rolled onto the floor. In the middle of the table like a human centerpiece was the other twin, Brittany, slumbering through the ruckus in a quilted baby chair. Marie raked her fingers through her hair. "Ashley's cold is worse, she's coughing and wheezing. I had her on the nebulizer three times last night."

"What's a nebulizer?"

"That thing." Marie waved a hand at a grayish machine on the counter. A clear plastic tube snaked from the machine, and at the end of the tube was a small plastic cup like a doll's oxygen mask. "Got it yesterday from the pediatrician, but it didn't help. I have to take her in again, and the pediatrician's in his Cherry Hill office tomorrow. I mean, today."

"Cherry Hill?" Tom felt terrible for her. "How will you get two babies to Cherry Hill? You're beat."

"I'll do it somehow, I have to. Ashley's not really a problem, if I could find someone to sit with Brittany."

"What about your mom? Can't she help?"

"On Tuesday? Her golf day?"

Tom bit his tongue. His bitchy mother-in-law, St. Teresa of the Perpetual Cigarette. "How about your sister?"

"Out of town."

"Again?" His sister-in-law was never around when she wasn't borrowing money. Damn. Tom jiggled Ashley and winced against the racket. The baby was so loud he couldn't hear himself think. "I wish I could help you,"

Tom said, and suddenly Marie looked up at him, her eyes full of adoration. It was the way she used to look at him. Back when they had sex.

"You can?" Marie asked, with a relieved smile. "But you're on trial."

"What?" Tom said, confused. Brittany was screaming full-throttle, and he still had his mind on the sex part.

"Tom, how can you take Brittany if you're on trial?"

"Take *who?*"

"Brittany." Marie was still giving him the love face, and Tom swallowed hard.

"Me take Brittany?"

"I thought that was what you said." Marie's love face dropped like a mask. "You'd take Brittany for the day so I could take Ashley to the pediatrician. Isn't that what you said?"

What? Was she insane? "Right. Absolutely. Sure." How could Tom say no? He didn't have time to think about it. He'd figure something out. The D.A.'s office had 34,350 secretaries. One of them had to be lactating.

"This is so wonderful of you, Tom. I'm at my wit's end. You sure you can do this?"

"Don't worry about it. It's not a problem. Nothing is a problem." Tom felt sick inside. He didn't want to think about how much time an infant would add to his trip downtown. It took an hour to get one strapped like a paratrooper into the car seat.

"But you have your big case today, don't you?"

"Don't worry, you take care of Ashley. I'm late. I have to go," Tom said. He off-loaded Ashley into Marie's lap and unhooked Brittany from her baby chair. Her head flopped to one side and her non-skid feet drooped in her fuzzy pink sleeper. He boosted her onto his shoulder and kissed his wife on the cheek. "Am I a hero or what?"

"Take the diaper bag."

"Heroes don't need diaper bags," Tom said, and hurried out of the kitchen with the baby, trying not to get slobber on his suit.

"Take my car!" Marie called after him. "The keys are on the hall table!"

"Gotcha!" Tom called back, and scurried into the hall, genuflecting to pick up his briefcase and Marie's keys. He bolted out the door into the sun, running in a cramped position so Brittany's head wouldn't bump around. Lucky it was spring, a warm morning, and Brittany was warm enough in her sleeper, the body bag for babies.

Tom dashed across the lawn to Marie's huge Ford Expedition, the only car larger than their home, chirped it unlocked, and threw his briefcase in ahead of him. Then he popped the baby off his shoulder and into her car seat, facing backward in the passenger seat. Her head bobbled slightly but her eyes didn't open as he fumbled with the woven straps, then ended up tying them in a knot. He didn't have time to get fancy.

Tom jumped in beside the baby, started the ignition, and roared out of the driveway, his hand on Brittany's tummy. Her minuscule chest rose and fell with a reassuring regularity. Her fleecy sleeper felt warm and soft. She smelled milky and sweet. She slept, well, like a baby.

Tom smiled. This was going to be a piece of cake.

"WWWWAAAAAAAHH!" Brittany wailed, and a thoroughly shaken Tom Moran skidded to a stop at the NO PARK-ING–TOW ZONE sign in front of the Office of the District Attorney. "WWWWAAAAAAAHH!" Shock waves of sound bounced around the Ford, reverberating off the windshield and walls. Tom thought his eardrums would explode.

"Shh, honey, don't cry, shhh," he said, struggling with the knot on the car seat. His fingers shook. His skull pounded. His brain hurt. "It's okay, quiet now, please be quiet." Tom couldn't hear himself speak, but he saw his lips moving in the rearview mirror.

"WWWAAAHHHH!" Brittany cried. She squeezed her eyes shut. Her face had gone dangerously red. Her mouth was a wet trumpet of sound, blasting like Gabriel's horn.

Tom broke into a sweat. He glanced at the car's digital clock. 8:21. He had to be in court by 9:00. He couldn't take her into the office hysterical. He didn't have time to wait. What's a lawyer to do?

"WWWAAAHHH!"

Tom looked frantically around the car. Wasn't there anything here to amuse her? Baby toys, plastic links, things that squeaked? Tom checked everywhere, covering his ears. Nothing. Damn! Marie was too damn neat. His gaze fell on the ignition. Keys! The babies loved their Fisher-Price keys. Tom yanked his keys out of the ignition and jingled them in front of Brittany's face like a mobile from Pep Boys. "Keys! Keys, Brit!" he yelped.

"WAAH!" The baby kept crying, and Tom jingled harder.

"Keys! Look, Brit! Keys! You love keys! These are the real thing! The others are knockoffs!"

"Waah!" Brittany cried, but her heart wasn't in it anymore. She was watching the keys, her eyes brimming with unspilled tears.

"Look! Genuine keys! Supply limited! Order now!" Tom bounced the keys around, and the baby finally made a kitten's swipe at them. "Yes!" Tom exclaimed and handed her the keys. Her lower lip buckled as she struggled to hold them, cross-eyed with absorption. Tom looped a baby finger through the keychain to hold them on, and her crying ceased as quickly as it had started. "Thank you, Jesus," Tom said.

He slipped Brittany from the car seat, grabbed his briefcase, and jumped out of the car. He didn't bother to lock it, he couldn't risk taking the keys from Brittany. Let the punks steal the car; let the cops tow it. He was only one man. Tom whirled through the revolving door, babe in arms, and got the hoped-for response from Luz Diaz, the knockout receptionist.

"A baby! You brought one of the babies!" she squealed, her lipsticked lips parting in delight. Luz had a black mane of oiled curls and a body that had never borne children, which was undoubtedly why she was so happy to see this one.

"Luz, this is Brittany! Say hello!" Tom hurried past the packed waiting area and thrust Brittany in the arms of a startled Luz. Possession was nine tenths of the law.

"Oooh, she's so pretty, so pretty." Luz smiled down at the pink bundle, then her face fell. "Tom, she's eating car keys."

"She loves car keys." Tom glanced at the big clock on the wall. Its hand ticked onto 8:29. "Don't touch her car keys."

"But she's got them in her mouth," Luz said, horrified, and Tom looked down. Brittany was sucking on an ignition key. So what? When he was little, he ate worms.

"Listen, Luz, you gotta help me. I have to go to court and I need you to take Brittany, just for the day."

"What?" Luz looked at Tom like he was nuts. "I'm at the front desk. I can't do that."

"Then give her to somebody who can."

"Who?"

"Somebody you trust. One of the other secretaries. Just not Janine." Tom knew all about Janine. She kept sex toys in the drawer.

"I can't do that." Luz pushed Brittany back into Tom's arms. "I need this job. Ask one of the girls in your unit, upstairs."

"Okay, okay, fine. Thanks anyway." He hustled Brittany from the front desk and hurried down the corridor, flying past his colleagues who were going in the opposite direction. To court, childless.

"Moran, aren't you supposed to be trying *Ranelle?*" Stan Kullman asked, squeezing past him with two trial bags.

"I do it all," Tom called back, on his way to the staircase. He was running out of time. Maybe one of the girls in the Major Trials Unit could help. His secretary was on vacation this week, since he was on trial. Tom bounded up the stairs two-by-two, cradling Brittany's head. She was starting to whimper again. The jingling had vanished. God knew where the car keys were.

Tom reached the second floor and scurried past the secretaries' desks, which were empty. Everybody was in the coffee room, where he'd be if he didn't have a murder case to win and a baby to unload. Tom took a hard left into the tiny room, fragrant with the aromas of coffee and perfume. "It's a girl!" Tom said to the group, who flocked around Brittany, cooing.

"She's so little!" Rachel said.

"She's so cute!" Sandy said.

"She's so good!" Franca said.

"She's the best baby in the world," Tom said, smiling. "She's little and cute and sweet. She sleeps a lot. She loves keys. Can anybody baby-sit her today?"

The secretaries looked at Tom like he was nuts. "Tom, we *work* here," Rachel said. She was an older woman, and her tone was kind yet stern. "We can't just drop everything and baby-sit for the day."

"Maybe you could take turns, an hour for each of you? I'll pay, I swear. I'll pay anything. Each of you. Overtime."

Rachel shook her graying head. "She's an infant, Tom. She needs complete attention. I can't type with her on my lap, you know." Behind her, Sandy and Franca and Judy nodded in agreement, which panicked Tom. They were all turning against him.

"But it's an emergency. I need help, and she's no trouble. She sleeps all the time. Well, a lot, anyway."

"My boss is away," chirped a voice from the back, and Tom's heart leapt with hope.

"Who said that?" he asked, on tiptoe, and the crowd parted, revealing a black leather minidress and a pair of spike heels. Janine. Our Lady of the Handcuffs. Tom's mouth went dry. He looked from the black leather to the pink fleece. "Uh, no thanks, maybe I can handle this," he said, and fled the coffee room.

Brittany whined as Tom ran down the corridor, his mind working furiously. The wall clock was a blur. 8:42. Tom had to think of something fast. He ducked into his office, slammed his door closed with his heel, dropped his briefcase on the floor, and set Brittany down on a soft pile of correspondence, which was when he smelled it. Babypoop. No wonder Brittany was fussing. She was knee-deep in shit. Now she knew what it was like to be an assistant district attorney.

Tom unzipped her sleeper and took her feet out, exposing her Pampers diaper. The stench was assault and battery. The sight was cruel and unusual. Brittany would need a new diaper and new clothes. Tom reached for the diaper bag, but there was none. "God help me," he murmured, but he didn't have time to think, only to react.

Tom took off the soggy diaper and sleeper, ripped some legal paper from a pad to wipe the baby clean, and rolled the mess into a basketball and shot it into the wastebasket. Brittany, smooth as a cherub, kicked her feet and calmed instantly, which almost made her his new favorite.

But she was naked. How could Tom palm off a naked baby, still a little sticky? He needed a diaper. He'd have to make one. Go! He grabbed a suppression motion, good for nothing anyway, and ripped it into four strips, lengthwise. Then he took one of the strips and stuck it between the baby's legs like a loincloth. "Well, it's a brief, isn't it?" he said to Brittany, who smiled even though she'd heard that one.

But how to hold the diaper up? A rubber band was too small. Eureka! Tom grabbed his tape dispenser, yanked out an endless strip of Scotch tape, and wrapped it around Brittany's waist. She kicked happily all the while, then shivered visibly. "You cold?" Tom asked and frowned. There wasn't anything on the baby's legs.

Tom kicked off his shoes, tore off his black socks, and slipped one over Brittany's left leg and one over her right. Then he stapled the socks to the briefs and checked his desk clock. 8:47. The courthouse was fifteen minutes away. He sweated bullets, and Brittany wriggled on the correspondence, making her legal diaper crackle. Her tiny face squinched into a frown, and her mouth opened and closed like a puppy. Uh-oh. Tom knew what that meant. She was hungry.

Damn it! Some things couldn't be improvised. Nursing, for one, and maybe that was it in toto. Tom thought a minute. Brittany was too young for solid food. The only liquid around was half-&-half. That was no good. What did Marie give her when they were out of breast milk? Tea. Tom was a tea drinker, he had plenty of tea around.

He scooted behind his desk, splashed some water from a plastic pitcher into a Styrofoam cup, and plopped his immersion coil inside with a Lipton's teabag. Tom put on his shoes as the clock hand moved to 9:01. *Come on.* He tested the water with a fingertip. Not too hot, not too cold. Perfect! And he cooks, too!

Tom plucked the coil and teabag from the cup and scurried with the brew back to Brittany, whose bow-shaped lips were making sucking sounds. He scooped up the baby and raised the cup, then stopped stupidly in midair. What was he thinking? Tom had fed the twins enough times to know they weren't drinking from Styrofoam yet. Hmm. Another hurdle, but Tom had been quite a hurdler in his day.

"Got it!" he said. Tom grabbed a brown coffee stirrer from his desk, wiped it clean on his pants, and dipped it in the tea. He held his finger over the top until the skinny straw was full, then he brought the straw over to Brittany, cradled in the crook of his arm.

"Down the hatch, honey," Tom said. He removed his finger from the top of the straw and released the tea into her mouth. The baby's face contorted almost immediately and she looked about to cry, then her lips latched onto the coffee stirrer as easily as a nipple.

"That's my girl," Tom cooed, then went down for another strawful and let it trickle into the baby's mouth. She took it, sucking eagerly, and was on her third helping when the phone rang. Tom let it ring, then reconsidered. Maybe it was one of the secretaries, regretting her professionalism. He hit the speakerphone button.

"Moran, you there?" bellowed a man's powerful voice, and Tom jumped, leaking Lipton's all over Brittany's briefs. On the telephone was Bill Masterson, the district attorney himself. *Jesus, Mary, and Joseph.* Tom would have dropped to his knees but he had a baby to feed. "Moran, you there?" Masterson boomed.

"Yes, sire. I mean, sir."

"You there, Moran? You in your office, Moran?"

"I am, sir."

"What the fuck are you doing there? You're not supposed to be there. You're supposed to be in court. You, in your office? What the fuck, Moran?"

"I, uh, had to get some exhibits."

"I don't care. You think I care? I don't get it. You're trying the case but you're in your office. I'm at the courthouse. You're not here."

Gulp. "*You're* at the courthouse, sir?"

"I'm here but you're there. I'm at the courthouse but you're at the office. Why does this always happen with you, Moran?"

"I'll be leaving right away, sir."

"What the fuck are you doing in your office? You're supposed to be in court, not in your office. I'm not trying the case but I'm in court. You're trying the case but you're at the office. I don't get it, do you? Moran? Why?"

"I'll be right over, sir. I'm on my way."

"What the fuck, Moran?" Masterson said, without further elaboration, then hung up.

Tom punched the Off button in a panic. Masterson would be watching the trial today. Holy Shit. Tom had to get to court. Now. He looked helplessly at Brittany, nestled in a manger of correspondence, dressed in black socks and a losing brief. He couldn't leave her here. He couldn't park her with anybody. He was her father. She was gurgling happily, her tummy temporarily full.

There was only one choice.

TOM APPROACHED THE reception area carrying his briefcase in one hand and a large black trial bag in the other. The lawyer's bag was as wide as a salesman's sample case, which wasn't a bad analogy, and stuffed with shredded exhibits had proved an ample crib for Brittany, who rested quietly on its flat bottom. A careful observer would have noticed the airholes punched in the top of the briefcase, but none of the people seated in the waiting room were careful observers. They were Commonwealth witnesses, after all. They saw what they were told to see.

"Tom, where's the baby?" Luz asked, as Tom walked by.

"All taken care of," he answered. He whirled out the revolving door and hit the pavement just in time to see Marie's Ford Expedition being towed down the street in traffic. Tom closed his eyes in prayer, then squared his shoulders. He'd lost the keys anyway. He hailed a cab.

"Yo!" Tom shouted, and a Yellow cab pulled up. Tom and his bags got in. "Criminal Justice Center," he said, closing the door.

"Weee," came a sound from the trial bag.

"What was 'at?" the cabbie asked. He was a squat older man in need of a shave, with a soiled Phillies cap pulled low on his forehead.

"Nothing."

"I heard something. I heard like a squeak."

"It's my shoes, they're new," Tom said, but he knew it would happen again. Brittany would never last through the day in the trial bag. But Tom was an experienced father. He knew what to do. "Stop at that store and wait for me," he said, pointing, and the cab pulled up at the curbside.

Tom jumped out with the trial bag and burst into the store, squinting at his watch on the run. 9:11. Where was the goddamn aisle? Tom forced himself to think. It was a chain, and the layout was the same in every store.

He ran to 4D, grabbed the package from the shelf, and hustled to the cashier, where he forked over a ten-dollar bill. "Keep the change," Tom said.

"Weee," said the bag. And they both fled the store.

Tom leapt back into the cab, set the trial bag on the floor, unlatched its brass locks, and plucked Brittany from its bottom.

She emerged writhing, looking vaguely colicky. Tom was just in the nick of time.

"Your shoes, huh?" said the cabbie.

"It's not what it looks like."

"Sure it is."

"Drive."

The cab lurched off, and Tom set the baby on his lap. He grabbed his bag and reached inside for his purchase, then tore off the cellophane with his teeth and shoved a spare finger through the thin cardboard top. IN-FANTS' TYLENOL, read the pink pastel carton, and underneath, "Suspension Drops."

Tom ripped the safety seal off the bottle with his teeth, then did the same to the tiny plastic dropper. One dropper of Tylenol would buy him three hours of slumbering baby. Tom felt a pang of conscience, but it was a necessity. It wouldn't hurt her, it would just make her sleep. With one dose now and one at lunch, Brittany wouldn't wake up until the jury came back with a conviction.

"Where'd you get the baby?" asked the driver, a wary eye on the rearview.

"It's mine."

"What are you doin' with her in the suitcase?"

"None of your business."

"No man is an island, buddy."

"Talk to me when you have twins, professor." Tom took the dropper, plunged it into the bottle, and extracted a dropper of Day-Glo-pink sleeping potion. The fill line on the dropper read .8 milliliters, but Tom had no idea how much a milliliter was. He just knew it was what Marie gave them.

"So what'sa matter with the baby, she sick?" the cabbie asked.

"No, just sleepy."

"Baby don't look sleepy."

"Well, she is," Tom shot back, defensive. He squirted a dropperful of cherry-flavored syrup into the baby's mouth, and Brittany swallowed, apparently happily. "Good girl," Tom said. What a kid! He gave her a quick good-night kiss and stuck her back in the bag just as the cab pulled up in front of the Criminal Justice Center. Tom dug for a ten and handed it to the driver. "Keep the change," he said, but the cabbie turned and scowled at him.

"It's blood money," he snarled, so Tom threw the bill in the front seat, leapt out with the bags, and slammed the door behind him.

The sidewalk in front of the Criminal Justice Center was thick with cops in blue uniforms, talking and smoking, waiting to testify. Tom normally felt welcome among them, but things were different now that he'd become a borderline child abuser. One of the uniforms waved at him, and Tom acknowledged him with a jittery nod, then escaped inside the courthouse with his living luggage.

The lobby was jammed, with long lines leading to the metal detectors. The courthouse clock read 9:14. Oh, no. He was late. Tom barreled through the crowd as politely as possible. If he didn't get his ass upstairs, he'd be held in contempt. Fined. Fired.

He picked up his pace and hurried to the lawyers' entrance on the far side of the security desk. As a member of the bar, Tom could bypass the detectors and the security personnel, which was the only way he could smuggle his own offspring into a courtroom. No security officer had planned for that contingency, probably because no lawyer would be boneheaded enough to try it. Overestimating lawyers was not a smart thing to do.

Tom crossed the marble floor to the elevators. A throng of three-piece suits waited in front of the modern brass-lacquered doors, and Tom got bumped by a defense lawyer. "Hey, watch it," Tom said.

"It's not his fault," said the defense lawyer, and Tom turned away as the elevator doors opened. To protect his cargo, he let the others rush into the cab and stepped inside last. The doors closed almost on Tom's nose, so he got a good look at himself in the mirrored insides of the doors. A tall, lanky Irishman with rumpled dark hair and blue eyes as guilty as a felon's, carrying a briefcase of exhibits and a trial bag of baby. What kind of father was he? Stuffing his kid in a bag? Drugging her with cherry gunk? Having a favorite in the first place? Tom had a lot of confessing to do.

Ping! went the elevator, and Tom got off into an even bigger mob. Second floor, the *Ranelle* case. Tom used to think of it as his "baby" until now. He wedged his way into the crowd of reporters, lawyers, witnesses, and spectators who didn't get a seat in the morning's lottery. On the far side of the throng was Masterson, standing above the crowd like the power forward he used to be at Bishop Neumann.

Tom's stomach churned. His hands sweated. He was going to lose, he was going to be disbarred, and his child would have memories of being locked in darkness. Also he'd lost Marie's car keys. Tom shuddered, then shook it off.

"Fashionably late, eh, Moran?" Masterson boomed, his hail-fellow manner disguising how furious he must be. Tom, for once grateful for Masterson's phoniness, made his way over to his boss as casually as if he were at a cocktail party.

"Shall we go?" Tom said, with ersatz confidence.

"Sure," the district attorney said, surprised, and Tom threaded his way to Courtroom 206, ducking reporters and their questions. He wasn't the grandstanding type, which meant he'd eventually wash out as an A.D.A. Tom was one of those guys who became a prosecutor because he wanted to do good. Several were still left. In the world.

"Any comment, Mr. Moran?" the reporters asked, notebooks at the ready. "What will you do today, Tom?" "What's your strategy for Hammer, Mr. Moran?" "Think you can get a conviction?"

"No comment," Tom said, holding his trial bag close to his side. None of the investigative reporters seemed to notice the airholes in the bag. Not a Geraldo among them.

"Of course he'll get a conviction, friends," Masterson boomed, spreading his arms as the reporters swarmed to him. "How can you doubt one of our best and brightest?"

Tom left them behind and entered the courtroom, where his trials were just beginning.

———

TOM HATED EVERY sterile inch of Courtroom 206, which looked just like all the other courtrooms in the new Criminal Justice Center. It was sleek, modern, and spacious, with muted gray fabric covering the walls, and a dais, jury box, and gallery pews of gleaming rosewood. Tom preferred the old courtrooms in City Hall, a creaky Victorian dowager of a building, with grimy brass sconces and dusty radiators that rattled. Tom liked things to stay the same. He wished they still held mass in Latin.

He shifted unhappily in his slippery chair at the prosecution table. His trial bag snoozed next to him, and Tom kept the toe of his wingtip protectively near the end with the baby's head. He had already determined he wouldn't travel far from the table during his cross, even if he had to sacrifice the theatrics. Brittany's cerebellum was more important. Tom had some priorities.

He tried to compose himself during the defense examination of the witness. In the morning's confusion, his careful preparation of the night before had flown from his head and he'd accidentally left his notes under Brittany in the trial bag. Tom sighed. At least the baby was asleep. He forced himself to forget about Brittany and focus on the direct examination by the defense.

"That's right, I work part-time in the rifle range," the witness was saying. The witness, Elwood "Elvis" Fahey, was a low-rent punk with a coke-white pallor and jet-black hair. He looked scrawny on the stand in a black windbreaker that said MEMBERS ONLY on the pocket. Tom wondered what club Elvis was a member of, and made a mental note not to join.

"What do you do in the rifle range, sir?" asked defense counsel Dan Harrison. Harrison was a trim forty, on the short side but natty in a tan Italian suit, no vent, that draped just right on the shoulders and broke on the instep. Lawyers who defended drug dealers always wore Italian. It was like MEMBERS ONLY with a law degree. MEMBERS OF THE BAR ONLY.

"At the shootin' range? I clean up, hand out the earphones, help out, stuff like that."

Harrison nodded. "This is a steady, gainful employment for you, sir?"

"Sure. For three years. Three days a week. Regular."

"And you met the decedent, Guillermo Juarez, at the rifle range, did you not?"

"Yeah. We got to be friends, me and Chicken Bill."

Harrison winced. "By 'Chicken Bill' are you referring to the decedent, Guillermo Juarez?"

"Yeah. Guillermo is the de-, the dece-, the dead guy." Elvis answered, laughing with a deep-throated *huh huh huh*.

The jurors didn't find this amusing, though their hearts weren't bleeding for the decedent either. A conscientious group of nine women and three men, the jury had already heard testimony that Chicken Bill had been a crack dealer. Nobody was crying over his demise, least of all the defendant, James Ranelle, who listened quietly, his sweet face covered with freckles and his cropped hair the color of barbecued potato chips. Ranelle looked more altar boy than drug dealer, but Tom wasn't fooled. He was a better Catholic than most.

"Now, sir," Harrison continued, "would you tell the jury, in your own words, what happened to Chicken Bill on the night of August 12, at around eleven o'clock in the evening?"

"Well," Elvis began, and grabbed the microphone like his namesake. He had been in and out of prison, and his many court appearances had sharpened his skills as an entertainer. "I hear a gunshot downstairs, and I wake up and run down the stairs."

"Where were you at the time, sir?"

"In the bedroom, sleepin'. I hear the noise and I run downstairs and all hell's breaking loose. Everything's real bright. There's big flames everywhere. I see smoke. I smell gasoline. It's all orange and real hot. I know right off it's a fire."

Tom made a note. The genius club.

"And what were the other inhabitants of the house doing, sir?"

"They're shoutin', yellin', runnin' out the door." Elvis waved his hands, to add courtroom drama. "Sammy and his girl Raytel, then Jamal. They all get out in a hurry, so they don't get a hotfoot."

"When did you see Chicken Bill, sir?"

"Right when I come down. He was just lying on the floor. I went up to him to see if he was okay, but he was half dead."

"And what did you do, sir, when you found Chicken Bill dying on the floor?"

"I lifted him up, like, and held him in my arms. Like a cradle."

"And did you say anything to him, sir?"

"I sure did. I axed him, 'Who did this fire, Chicken? Did you see who did this fire?' "

"And did Chicken Bill answer you?"

Tom sprung to his wingtips. "Objection, hearsay, Your Honor," he said, and Harrison did a custom-tailored half-turn toward the bench.

"Your Honor," Harrison argued, "I believe this testimony falls within the dying-declaration exception to the hearsay rule. Chicken Bill—Mr. Juarez—was clearly in extremis at the time he made the statement."

A dying declaration? Tom couldn't believe his ears. He hadn't seen a case with a dying declaration since evidence class. You didn't have to be a member of anything to think up this whopper. It was so absurd, all Tom could say was, *"A dying declaration. Your Honor?"*

"A dying declaration, Mr. Harrison?" Judge Amelio Canova repeated, only slower. Canova was a short, sluggish sixty-five, and his smooth bald head stretched from his robe like a turtle's, craning over his papers on the dais.

"Yes, Your Honor," Harrison said. "Our experts yesterday testified as to his approximate time of death, if you recall. Mr. Juarez perished from third-degree burns at or about 11 P.M. Any statement he made to the witness falls squarely within this well-accepted exception to the hearsay rule."

Judge Canova blinked, heavy-lidded. "I'll permit it," he said wearily, and Tom sank into his chair.

Harrison turned back to his witness. "Now, sir, before the prosecutor interrupted you, you were about to tell the jury what Chicken Bill said, as he lay dying."

"Yes, I was." Elvis straightened at the microphone. "It's like this, Chicken can barely talk, his throat is all burned up, and he's, like, whispering. He says to me, 'Cowboy Ron did this to me, Elvis. Cowboy Ron did this fire.' "

The jurors reacted, shifting in their seats and sneaking glances at each other. They didn't like Elvis but Tom knew they'd find it difficult to completely discount his testimony later. Elvis was the only witness, and the defense had put up a chorus line of experts. Tom had seen expert witnesses seduce even the smartest juries. They were like hookers in lab coats.

It made Tom's blood boil. He knew the way the murder went down, he just had to prove it; Ranelle had torched a competing crackhouse, run by Chicken Bill. Chicken Bill got dead as desired, and everybody else got out alive, including Elvis, who instantly perceived that the murder of his friend was the opportunity of a lifetime. If Elvis helped Ranelle beat the murder rap, he'd have a new job with Ranelle's organization. One man's ceiling is another man's floor, even in crackhouses.

Harrison leaned on the witness box. "Did you know who Chicken Bill meant by Cowboy Ron, sir?"

"Yes, he meant the dude wore a cowboy hat, a brown cowboy hat. Lived a block away."

"And, to the best of your knowledge, is this Cowboy Ron known to be a drug dealer?"

"Yes, far as I know. Cowboy Ron competed with Chicken Bill."

"Is Cowboy Ron in the courtroom this morning, sir?"

Elvis's bedroom eyes swept the courtroom, for show. "No, sir."

"Is the defendant James Ranelle also known as Cowboy Ron?"

"No. The defendant ain't Cowboy Ron. Cowboy Ron is somebody else. Cowboy Ron ain't here today."

"I see." Harrison lingered with a frown before the jury box. He was pretending to think, but Tom knew he was only pausing to let the testimony sink in. Harrison hadn't had an unrehearsed moment in his life. It made him a superb defense lawyer. "I have no further questions," Harrison said. "Thank you, sir."

Tom rose quickly to his feet. "If I may cross-examine, Your Honor," he said, then stopped as the law clerk murmured in the judge's ear.

Judge Canova peered down from the dais, waving a wrinkled hand. "Not quite yet, Mr. Moran. Sit down, please."

Tom resettled in his chair and glanced over at Harrison, who looked pleased at the defense table. Any interruption would only give the testimony time to set, like concrete.

"Ladies and gentlemen of the jury," Judge Canova said, turning to them, "please excuse me for just a minute or two. I have a brief matter to attend to in chambers, and since I'll be gone but a minute, I won't put you to the trouble of dismissing you and bringing you back in again. Please stand by, as they say on the television." The jury smiled, and the judge shuffled from the dais and out the side door.

The jurors relaxed when Judge Canova left, but Tom didn't. As long as they were in the box, he was on show. Harrison turned to make fake-conversation with Ranelle, who stayed in character as a candidate for the priesthood. Tom struggled to remember his outline of the night before. He was grateful for the recess, but worried, too. He didn't have much time left on the Tylenol, did he? He snuck a peek at his watch. 10:15.

Tom told himself to relax. He wouldn't start to worry until 11:45. And that was a long way off.

B UT AT 11:45, the judge was still out. The jury was dozing in the jury box. The bailiff was reading the sports page. The courtroom reporter was cleaning the black keys of her steno machine with a Q-tip. The gallery conversed quietly among themselves. The courtroom was in a state of suspended animation.

Except for Tom, who was in a state of panic. His shirt was soaked under his jacket. His legal pad was full of scribbles. He crossed and uncrossed his legs. Suddenly he heard a rustling in the trial bag. Holy Christ. Was Brittany waking up?

Tom bent over and unlocked the trial bag as casually as possible. A square of fluorescent light fell on the baby's face. She squirmed in the sudden brightness and her blue eyes flared open. Tom snapped the lid closed. Oh, no. What was he going to do? Where was the judge?

Tom looked around in desperation. Masterson, sitting in the front row of the gallery, leaned over the bar of the court and handed him a note. Tom read it with a shaking hand:

What the fuck is the matter with you, Moran?

Tom shoved the note into his pocket and closed his eyes in pain. *Father, forgive me, for I have sinned. I lost my notes. I locked my baby in a briefcase. I don't know how much a milliliter is.* He opened his eyes just as Judge Canova entered the courtroom, his face etched with contrition.

"Ladies and gentlemen," the judge said, even before he reached his leather chair, "I must beg your forgiveness. I was detained on an emergency administrative matter and kept thinking it would be over in just five minutes. Well, you know how that is," he said, sitting down with a red face. The jurors smiled indulgently, and Judge Canova gestured to Tom. "Mr. Moran, please pick up where we left off. I'd like to get something accomplished before we dismiss for lunch, at twelve-thirty."

"Of course, Your Honor." Tom edged forward on his seat, unsteady. He had to come up with a killer cross-examination before Brittany exploded. "Now, uh, Mr. Fahey, you were at the home of Chicken Bill on the night in question, is that right?"

"Yes."

"Did you live at that home?"

"No. I just visited."

"Why did you visit there?"

Elvis glanced at Harrison, who didn't object. "Just because."

"Because why?" Tom rose, finding his footing next to the trial bag, which rustled softly again. It must have been Brittany's briefs, crackling around her legs. His heart raced in his chest.

"I just kind of hung at Chicken Bill's."

"By 'hung,' you mean smoked crack, don't you?"

"Objection!" Harrison yelped, leaping to his Gucci loafers.

"Your Honor," Tom said, "defense counsel opened the door on this testimony yesterday. The witness is an admitted crack user, and the prosecution is entitled to impeach."

"Sustained," Judge Canova said. He banged his gavel halfheartedly, but the sound provoked more rustling from the trial bag and a quiet, though unmistakable, baby yawn. Tom glanced around nervously. No one seemed to notice the sound. He was the only one close enough to hear it. How long would his luck hold out? And his baby?

"Uh, Mr. Fahey," Tom said, wiping his forehead, "you said you ran down the stairs when you heard the gunshot, and you smelled gasoline."

"Yeah."

"Did you see where the gasoline came from?"

"No, it was all on the floor, on fire."

"Did you see anyone throw the gasoline in the house?"

"No."

"Did you see anyone shoot the gasoline to ignite it?"

"No."

"So the only way you know who the perpetrator of this crime is, is because Chicken Bill told you?"

"Yeah, he told me hisself."

"Weee," said the trial bag softly, and Tom gulped. Harrison looked over at the sound, and Tom coughed twice.

"Mr. Fahey," he continued, clearing his throat, "you testified that people were running out the door, isn't that right?"

"Yeah. They're runnin', screamin', crying."

"Weee," repeated the trial bag, and Tom started hacking away like he had tuberculosis.

Judge Canova stretched out his neck in concern. "Mr. Moran, perhaps you should pause for some water."

"No, sure, well," Tom stammered. "Actually, Your Honor, if we broke for lunch, I could compose myself."

Judge Canova shook his head slowly. "I'd rather not, counsel. Let's do as much as we can. Please proceed. Perhaps some water will help."

"Yes, Your Honor," Tom said, a sickening feeling at the pit of his stomach. He choked down his water and glanced at the trial bag, which began to wobble slightly on the carpet. Tom froze. Brittany was awake, squirming inside the bag. She was hungry. She was thirsty. She was wearing an evidentiary motion.

"Please proceed, Mr. Moran," Judge Canova repeated.

"Yes, sir." Tom said, setting down his glass. "Mr. Fahey, you were downstairs with the screaming and the crying, correct?"

"Yeah. Everybody was yellin', runnin' for their lives."

"Weee," insisted the bag, and Harrison looked over again, arching an eyebrow.

"Mr. Fahey," Tom said loudly, to mask the sound, "you ran down the stairs to Chicken Bill's side, is that correct?"

"Yeah, he's lying there, all messed up. All burnt up, yeah."

"Weee," said the bag, and Tom coughed again. Out of the corner of his eye, he could see the courtroom sketch artist stop her drawing. A reporter blinked, holding his steno pad. The front pew of the gallery was looking in the direction of the trial bag. Soon Masterson would hear. *Jesus, Mary, and Joseph.*

"And you asked Chicken Bill who started the fire?"

"Yeah."

"Weeaah," said the bag, slightly louder than before, and Tom watched helplessly as the court reporter startled at the sound. Two of the jurors in the front row exchanged puzzled looks. Tom's heart jumped to his throat. What was he going to do? His coughing fit didn't work. Maybe if he just ignored it. He walked away from the bag to distance himself from it.

"Mr. Fahey," Tom asked, standing before the witness, "is it your testimony that Chicken Bill named Cowboy Ron as the perpetrator?"

"Yeah. That's what he said. Cowboy Ron did the crime." Elvis nodded in the direction of his new employer, but Ranelle was staring at the trial bag.

"Weeah, weeah," said the bag, but Tom pretended not to hear. Behind him, he glimpsed Masterson shifting angrily in his pew.

"And while he was telling you who set the fire, the others were yelling and screaming?"

"Yes."

"WeeAh, weeAHHH," said the bag, getting hungrier, and the bailiff cocked his head at the noise. Next to him, the law clerk giggled, and the jurors in the back row were looking around, their heads swiveling toward the fussing.

Tom plowed ahead, apparently oblivious. "And they were running out the door, Mr. Fahey?"

"Yeah."

"WeeeeeAHHH," the bag said, a decibel louder. The jury was completely distracted by the noise, and even Judge Canova was adjusting his hearing aid. Then Tom realized something. Everybody could hear Brittany but Elvis.

"How did you hear what Chicken Bill said, with all that noise?" Tom said quickly, following a hunch.

"I heard him just fine."

"You heard him just fine, despite the screaming and yelling?"

"Yeah."

"Over the noise of the fire? The panic? The confusion?"

"Yeah."

"Weeeaaahhhh," fussed the trial bag, and only Elvis didn't react.

"Even though Chicken Bill was injured, near death, and speaking in a whisper?"

"I heard him," Elvis insisted, though he didn't flinch at the wailing that set the entire jury looking from the trial bag to Elvis and back again. Judge Canova craned over the dais and signaled to the bailiff. Suddenly Tom knew what to do.

"Don't you work in a firing range, Mr. Fahey?" he asked.

"Yeah, for three years. I clean up."

"You work while gunshots are being fired, correct?"

"Sure." Elvis snickered. "That's why they call it a firin' range."

"You don't wear earphones when you clean up, do you, Mr. Fahey?"

"No way. Them things are for wussies." Elvis *huh huh huh*ed at the jury, but again, they weren't laughing. They were grave, beginning to understand. Tom was giving them a reason to reject Elvis's testimony and they were going to take it. The gallery murmured among themselves. Masterson broke into a grin.

"Objection!" Harrison said, loud enough for Elvis to hear, but Judge Canova waved the defense lawyer into his seat.

"Mr. Fahey, isn't it a fact that your hearing has been impaired from your job at the firing range, so much so that you couldn't hear what Chicken Bill was saying to you?"

"Whut?" Elvis said, and just then the trial bag broke into an earsplitting cry.

"I have no further questions." Tom said, and rushed to rescue his co-counsel.

LATER, TOM AND Marie dozed on the patchwork quilt over their bed, completely dressed. The babies had finally stopped fussing, and snuggled between them. Ashley snored slightly as she slept, her breathing still congested. Brittany slumbered quietly. A golden glow emanated from a porcelain lamp on the night table. The alarm clock read 2:13 A.M. It was so late. Tom wanted to turn off the light but he was too exhausted to do even that.

"You sure you won't get fired, hon?" Marie murmured, half asleep.

"Nah. I'm a hero."

"I knew that already," she said, and stretched her toe to touch his, still barefoot.

"Is this sex?" Tom asked.

"Yes."

"Funny. I remember it differently," Tom said, and Marie burst into laughter. Tom closed his eyes, listening to his wife laughing and his children snoring, and realized suddenly that heaven itself was only a slight variation on this scene, with somebody to turn out the light for you.

Then he fell soundly asleep.

THE LITTLE HOUSE
AT CROIX-ROUSSE

Georges Simenon

(Translated by Anthony Boucher)

Sometimes the writer is more famous than his work. This was almost the case with Georges Simenon (1903–1989). His autobiography genuinely shocked many reviewers—he openly discussed the thousands (yes, thousands) of women he claimed to have slept with—and his prolific career genuinely stunned his literary rivals. Depending on whose estimate you believe, Simenon wrote between 500 and 700 novels and many, many short stories. He started out in the French pulps and just kept writing. He brought true sophistication to the crime novel, both in his Maigret whodunits and his straight psychological novels. In many respects, he is without peer. While not at the level of Balzac, he certainly gave us both first-rank watercolors and mug shots of Paris over a fifty-year span. The following story will help explain his huge international success.

I HAD NEVER seen Joseph Leborgne at work before. I received something of a shock when I entered his room that day.

His blond hair, usually plastered down, was in complete disorder. The individual hairs, stiffened by brilliantine, stuck out all over his head. His face was pale and worn. Nervous twitches distorted his features.

He threw a grudging glare at me which almost drove me from the room. But since I could see that he was hunched over a diagram, my curiosity was stronger than my sensitivity. I advanced into the room and took off my hat and coat.

"A fine time you've picked!" he grumbled.

This was hardly encouraging. I stammered, "A tricky case?"

"That's putting it mildly. Look at that paper."

"It's the plan of a house? A small house?"

"The subtlety of your mind! A child of four could guess that. You know the Croix-Rousse district in Lyons?"

"I've passed through there."

"Good! This little house lies in one of the most deserted sections of the district—not a district, I might add, which is distinguished by its liveli-ness."

"What do these black crosses mean, in the garden and on the street?"

"Policemen."

"Good Lord! And the crosses mark where they've been killed?"

"Who said anything about dead policemen? The crosses indicate po-licemen who were on duty at these several spots on the night of the eighth-to-ninth. The cross that's heavier than the others is Corporal Manchard."

I dared not utter a word or move a muscle. It felt wisest not to inter-rupt Leborgne, who was favoring the plan with the same furious glares which he had bestowed upon me.

"Well? Aren't you going to ask me *why* policemen were stationed there—six of them, no less—on the night of the eighth-to-ninth? Or maybe you're going to pretend that you've figured it out?"

I said nothing.

"They were there because the Lyons police had received, the day be-fore, the following letter:

*"Dr. Luigi Ceccioni will be murdered, at his home,
on the night of the eighth-to-ninth instant."*

"And the doctor had been warned?" I asked at last.

"No! Since Ceccioni was an Italian exile and it seemed more than likely that the affair had political aspects, the police preferred to take their precautions without warning the party involved."

"And he was murdered anyway?"

"Patience! Dr. Ceccioni, fifty years of age, lived alone in this wretched little hovel. He kept house for himself and ate his evening meal every day in an Italian restaurant nearby. On the eighth he left home at seven o'clock, as usual, for the restaurant. And Corporal Manchard, one of the best po-lice officers in France and a pupil, to boot, of the great Lyons criminologist Dr. Eugene Locard, searched the house from basement to attic. He proved to himself that no one was hidden there and that it was impossible to get in by any other means than the ordinary doors and windows visible from the outside. No subterranean passages nor any such hocus-pocus. Nothing out of a mystery novel . . . You understand?"

I was careful to say nothing, but Leborgne's vindictive tone seemed to accuse me of willfully interpolating hocus-pocus.

"No one in the house! Nothing to watch but two doors and three win-dows! A lesser man than Corporal Manchard would have been content to set up the watch with only himself and one policeman. But Manchard requisitioned five, one for each entrance, with himself to watch the watchers. At nine p.m. the shadow of the doctor appeared in the street. He re-entered his house, *absolutely alone*. His room was upstairs; a light went on in there promptly. And then the police vigil began. Not one of them dozed! Not one of them deserted his post! Not one of them lost sight of the precise point which he had been delegated to watch!

"Every fifteen minutes Manchard made the round of the group. Around three a.m. the petroleum lamp upstairs went out slowly, as though it had run out of fuel. The corporal hesitated. At last he decided to use his lock-picking gadget and go in. Upstairs, in the bedroom, seated—or rather half lying—on the edge of the bed was Dr. Luigi Ceccioni. His hands were clutched to his chest and he was dead. He was completely dressed, even to the cape which still hung over his shoulders. His hat had fallen to the floor. His underclothing and suit were saturated with blood and his hands were soaked in it. One bullet from a six-millimeter Browning had penetrated less than a centimeter above his heart."

I gazed at Joseph Leborgne with awe. I saw his lip tremble.

"No one had entered the house! No one had left!" he groaned. "I'll swear to that as though I'd stood guard myself: I know my Corporal Manchard. And don't go thinking that they found the revolver in the house. *There wasn't any revolver!* Not in sight and not hidden. Not in the fireplace, or even in the roof gutter. Not in the garden—not anywhere at all! In other words, a bullet was fired in a place where there was no one save the victim himself and where there was no firearm!

"As for the windows, they were closed and undamaged; a bullet fired from outside would have shattered the panes. Besides, a revolver doesn't carry far enough to have been fired from outside the range covered by the cordon of policemen. Look at the plan! Eat it up with your eyes! And you may restore some hope of life to poor Corporal Manchard, who has given up sleeping and looks upon himself virtually as a murderer."

I timidly ventured, "What do you know about Ceccioni?"

"That he used to be rich. That he's hardly practiced medicine at all, but rather devoted himself to politics—which made it healthier for him to leave Italy."

"Married? Bachelor?"

"Widower. One child, a son, at present studying in Argentina."

"What did he live on in Lyons?"

"A little of everything and nothing. Indefinite subsidies from his political colleagues. Occasional consultations, but those chiefly *gratis* among the poor of the Italian colony."

"Was anything stolen from the house?"

"Not a trace of any larcenous entry or of anything stolen."

I don't know why, but at this moment I wanted to laugh. It suddenly seemed to me that some master of mystification had amused himself by presenting Joseph Leborgne with a totally impossible problem, simply to give him a needed lesson in modesty.

He noticed the broadening of my lips. Seizing the plan, he crossed the room to plunge himself angrily into his armchair.

"Let me know when you've solved it!" he snapped.

"I can certainly solve nothing before you," I said tactfully.

"Thanks," he observed.

I began to fill my pipe. I lit it, disregarding my companion's rage which was reaching the point of paroxysm.

"All I ask of you is that you sit quietly," he pronounced. "And don't breathe so loudly," he added.

Ten minutes passed as unpleasantly as possible. Despite myself, I called up the image of the plan, with the six black crosses marking the policemen.

And the impossibility of this story, which had at first so amused me, began to seem curiously disquieting.

After all, this was not a matter of psychology or of detective *flair*, but of pure geometry.

"This Manchard," I asked suddenly. "Has he ever served as a subject for hypnotism?"

Joseph Leborgne did not even deign to answer that one.

"Did Ceccioni have any political enemies in Lyons?"

Leborgne shrugged.

"And it's been proved that the son is in Argentina?"

This time he merely took the pipe out of my mouth and tossed it on the mantelpiece.

"You have the names of all the policemen?"

He handed me a sheet of paper:

> *Jérôme Pallois, 28, married*
> *Jean-Joseph Stockman, 31, single*
> *Armand Dubois, 26, married*
> *Hubert Trajanu, 43, divorced*
> *Germain Garros, 32, married*

I reread these lines three times. The names were in the order in which the men had been stationed around the building, starting from the left.

I was ready to accept the craziest notions. Desperately I exclaimed at last, "It *is* impossible!"

And I looked at Joseph Leborgne. A moment before his face had been pale, his eyes encircled, his lips bitter. Now, to my astonishment, I saw him smilingly head for a pot of jam.

As he passed a mirror he noticed himself and seemed scandalized by the incongruous contortions of his hair. He combed it meticulously. He adjusted the knot of his cravat.

Once again Joseph Leborgne was his habitual self. As he looked for a spoon with which to consume his horrible jam of leaves-of-God-knows-what, he favored me with a sarcastic smile.

"How simple it would always be to reach the truth if preconceived ideas did not falsify our judgment!" he sighed. "You have just said, 'It *is* impossible!' So therefore . . ."

I waited for him to contradict me. I'm used to that.

"So, therefore," he went on, "it *is* impossible. Just so. And all that we needed to do from the very beginning was simply to admit that fact. There was no revolver in the house, no murderer hidden there. Very well: then there was no shot fired there."

"But then . . . ?"

"Then, very simply, Luigi Ceccioni arrived *with the bullet already in his chest.* I've every reason to believe that he fired the bullet himself. He was a doctor; he knew just where to aim—'less than a centimeter above the heart,' you'll recall—so that the wound would not be *instantly* fatal, but would allow him to move about for a short time."

Joseph Leborgne closed his eyes.

"Imagine this poor hopeless man. He has only one son. The boy is studying abroad, but the father no longer has any money to send him. Ceccioni insures his life with the boy as beneficiary. His next step is to die—but somehow to die with no suspicion of suicide, or the insurance company will refuse to pay.

"By means of an anonymous letter he summons the police themselves as witnesses. They see him enter his house where there is no weapon and they find him dead several hours later.

"It was enough, once he was seated on his bed, to massage his chest, forcing the bullet to penetrate more deeply, at last to touch the heart . . ."

I let out an involuntary cry of pain. But Leborgne did not stir. He was no longer concerned with me.

IT WAS NOT until a week later that he showed me a telegram from Corporal Manchard:

AUTOPSY REVEALS ECCHYMOSIS AROUND WOUNDS AND TRACES FINGER PRESSURE STOP DOCTOR AND SELF PUZ-ZLED POSSIBLE CAUSE STOP REQUEST YOUR ADVICE IM-MEDIATELY

"You answered?"

He looked at me reproachfully. "It requires both great courage and great imagination to massage oneself to death. Why should the poor man have done that in vain? The insurance company has a capital of four hundred million . . ."

THE GIRL BEHIND THE HEDGE

Mickey Spillane

Back in the 1950s, when Americans were exulting in winning the war and moving into houses their parents could never have afforded, Mickey Spillane took it upon himself to tell us that there was a darkness upon the land (see the opening page of *One Lonely Night* to see how well he describes this darkness) and that it had to be dealt with. While his critics savaged him for the violence in his books, and for his angry anti-Communism, they seemed to overlook the fact that most of Spillane's crime stories dealt with municipal corruption and thugs hired by quite respectable people. This was at a time when a record number of midsized cities were mobbed up. Only Spillane and a few others seemed concerned about this. His critics—who were sometimes embarrassingly overwrought—didn't seem to care. Well, Spillane easily survived his critics (his most recent novels are *Golden Girl* and *The Snake*) and is acknowledged today as one of the true masters of the hard-boiled crime story. As here.

THE STOCKY MAN handed his coat and hat to the attendant and went through the foyer to the main lounge of the club. He stood in the doorway for a scant second, but in that time his eyes had seen all that was to be seen; the chess game beside the windows, the foursome at cards and the lone man at the rear of the room sipping a drink.

He crossed between the tables, nodding briefly to the card players, and went directly to the back of the room. The other man looked up from his drink with a smile. "Afternoon, Inspector. Sit down. Drink?"

"Hello, Dunc. Same as you're drinking."

Almost languidly, the fellow made a motion with his hand. The waiter nodded and left. The inspector settled himself in his chair with a sigh. He was a big man, heavy without being given to fat. Only his high shoes proclaimed him for what he was. When he looked at Chester Duncan he grimaced inwardly, envying him his poise and manner, yet not willing to trade him for anything.

Here, he thought smugly, *is a man who should have everything yet has nothing. True, he has money and position, but the finest of all things, a family life, was denied him.* And with a brood of five in all stages of growth at home, the inspector felt that he had achieved his purpose in life.

The drink came and the inspector took his, sipping it gratefully. When he put it down he said, "I came to thank you for that, er . . . tip. You know, that was the first time I've ever played the market."

"Glad to do it," Duncan said. His hands played with the glass, rolling it around in his palms. He eyebrows shot up suddenly, as though he was amused at something. "I suppose you heard all the ugly rumors."

A flush reddened the inspector's face. "In an offhand way, yes. Some of them were downright ugly." He sipped his drink again and tapped a cigarette on the side table. "You know," he said. "If Walter Harrison's death hadn't been so definitely a suicide, you might be standing an investigation right now."

Duncan smiled slowly. "Come now, Inspector. The market didn't budge until after his death, you know."

"True enough. But rumor has it that you engineered it in some manner." He paused long enough to study Duncan's face. "Tell me, did you?"

"Why should I incriminate myself?"

"It's over and done with. Harrison leaped to his death from the window of a hotel room. The door was locked and there was no possible way anyone could have gotten in that room to give him a push. No, we're quite satisfied that it was suicide, and everybody that ever came in contact with Harrison agrees that he did the world a favor when he died. However, there's still some speculation about you having a hand in things."

"Tell me, Inspector, do you really think I had the courage or the brains to oppose a man like Harrison, and force him to kill himself?"

The inspector frowned, then nodded. "As a matter of fact, yes. You *did* profit by his death."

"So did *you*," Duncan laughed.

"Ummmm."

"Though it's nothing to be ashamed about," Duncan added. "When Harrison died the financial world naturally expected that the stocks he financed were no good and tried to unload. It so happened that I was one of the few who knew they were as good as gold and bought while I could. And, of course, I passed the word on to my friends. Somebody had might as well profit by the death of a . . . a rat."

Through the haze of the smoke Inspector Early saw his face tighten around the mouth. He scowled again, leaning forward in his chair. "Duncan, we've been friends quite a while. I'm just cop enough to be curious and I'm thinking that our late Walter Harrison was cursing you just before he died."

Duncan twirled his glass around. "I've no doubt of it," he said. His eyes met the inspector's. "Would you really like to hear about it?"

"Not if it means your confessing to murder. If that has to happen I'd much rather you spoke directly to the DA."

"Oh, it's nothing like that at all. No, not a bit, Inspector. No matter how hard they tried, they couldn't do a thing that would impair either my honor or reputation. You see, Walter Harrison went to his death through his own greediness."

The inspector settled back in his chair. The waiter came with drinks to replace the empties and the two men toasted each other silently.

"Some of this you probably know already, Inspector," Duncan said . . .

"NEVERTHELESS, I'LL START at the beginning and tell you everything that happened. Walter Harrison and I met in law school. We were both young and not too studious. We had one thing in common and only one. Both of us were the products of wealthy parents who tried their best to spoil their children. Since we were the only ones who could afford certain—er—pleasures, we naturally gravitated to each other, though when I think back, even at that time, there was little true friendship involved.

It so happened that I had a flair for my studies whereas Walter didn't give a damn. At examination time, I had to carry him. It seemed like a big joke at the time, but actually I was doing all the work while he was having his fling around town. Nor was I the only one he imposed upon in such a way. Many students, impressed with having his friendship, gladly took over his papers. Walter could charm the devil himself if he had to.

And quite often he had to. Many's the time he's talked his way out of spending a week end in jail for some minor offense—and I've even seen him twist the dean around his little finger, so to speak. Oh, but I remained his loyal friend. I shared everything I had with him, including my women, and even thought it amusing when I went out on a date and met him, only to have him take my girl home.

In the last year of school the crash came. It meant little to me because my father had seen it coming and got out with his fortune increased. Walter's father tried to stick it out and went under. He was one of the ones who killed himself that day.

Walter was quite stricken, of course. He was in a blue funk and got stinking drunk. We had quite a talk and he was for quitting school at once, but I talked him into accepting the money from me and graduating. Come to think of it, he never did pay me back that money. However, it really doesn't matter.

After we left school I went into business with my father and took over the firm when he died. It was that same month that Walter showed up. He stopped in for a visit, and wound up with a position, though at no time did he deceive me as to the real intent of his visit. He got what he came after and in a way it was a good thing for me. Walter was a shrewd businessman.

His rise in the financial world was slightly less than meteoric. He was much too astute to remain in anyone's employ for long, and with the Street talking about Harrison, the Boy Wonder of Wall Street, in every other breath, it was inevitable that he open up his own office. In a sense, we became competitors after that, but always friends.

Pardon me, Inspector, let's say that I was his friend, he never was mine. His ruthlessness was appalling at times, but even then he managed to charm his victims into accepting their lot with a smile. I for one know that he managed the market to make himself a cool million on a deal that left me gasping. More than once he almost cut the bottom out of my business, yet he was always in with a grin and a big hello the next day as if it had been only a tennis match he had won.

If you've followed his rise then you're familiar with the social side of his life. Walter cut quite a swath for himself. Twice, he was almost killed by irate husbands, and if he had been, no jury on earth would have convicted his murderer. There was the time a young girl killed herself rather than let her parents know that she had been having an affair with Walter and had been trapped. He was very generous about it. He offered her money to travel, her choice of doctors and anything she wanted . . . except his name for her child. No, he wasn't ready to give his name away then. That came a few weeks later.

I was engaged to be married at the time. Adrianne was a girl I had loved from the moment I saw her and there aren't words enough to tell how happy I was when she said she'd marry me. We spent most of our waking hours poring over plans for the future. We even selected a site for our house out on the Island and began construction. We were timing the wedding to coincide with the completion of the house and if ever I was a man living in a dream world, it was then. My happiness was complete, as was Adrianne's, or so I thought. Fortune seemed to favor me with more than one smile at the time. For some reason my own career took a sudden spurt and whatever I touched turned to gold, and in no time the Street had taken to following me rather than Walter Harrison. Without realizing it, I turned several deals that had him on his knees, though I doubt if many ever realized it. Walter would never give up the amazing front he affected.

A T THIS POINT Duncan paused to study his glass, his eyes narrowing. Inspector Early remained motionless, waiting for him to go on.

"WALTER CAME TO see me," Duncan said. "It was a day I shall never forget. I had a dinner engagement with Adrianne and invited him along. Now I know that what he did was done out of sheer spite, nothing else. At first I believed that it was my fault, or hers, never giving Walter a thought . . .

Forgive me if I pass over the details lightly, Inspector. They aren't very pleasant to recall. I had to sit there and watch Adrianne captivated by this charming rat to the point where I was merely a decoration in the chair opposite her. I had to see him join us day after day, night after night, then hear the rumors that they were seeing each other without me, then discover for myself that she was in love with him.

Yes, it was quite an experience. I had the idea of killing them both, then killing myself. When I saw that that could never solve the problem I gave it up.

Adrianne came to me one night. She sat and told me how much she hated to hurt me, but she had fallen in love with Walter Harrison and wanted to marry him. What else was there to do? Naturally, I acted the part of a good loser and called off the engagement. They didn't wait long. A week later they were married and I was the laughing stock of the Street.

Perhaps time might have cured everything if things hadn't turned out the way they did. It wasn't very long afterwards that I learned of a break in their marriage. Word came that Adrianne had changed and I knew for a fact that Walter was far from being true to her.

You see, now I realized the truth. Walter never loved her. He never loved anybody but himself. He married Adrianne because he wanted to hurt me more than anything else in the world. He hated me because I had something he lacked . . . happiness. It was something he searched after desperately himself and always found just out of reach.

In December of that year Adrianne took sick. She wasted away for a month and died. In the final moments she called for me, asking me to forgive her; this much I learned from a servant of hers. Walter, by the way, was enjoying himself at a party when she died. He came home for the funeral and took off immediately for a sojourn in Florida with some attractive showgirl.

God, how I hated that man! I used to dream of killing him! Do you know, if ever my mind drifted from the work I was doing I always pictured myself standing over his corpse with a knife in my hand, laughing my head off.

Every so often I would get word of Walter's various escapades, and they seemed to follow a definite pattern. I made it my business to learn more about him and before long I realized that Walter was almost frenzied in his search to find a woman he could really love. Since he was a fabulously wealthy man he was always suspicious of a woman wanting him more than his wealth, and this very suspicion always was the thing that drove a woman away from him.

It may seem strange to you, but regardless of my attitude, I saw him quite regularly. And equally strange, he never realized that I hated him so. He realized, of course, that he was far from popular in any quarter, but he never suspected me of anything else save a stupid idea of friendship. But having learned my lesson the hard way, he never got the chance to impose upon me again, though he never really had need to.

It was a curious thing, the solution I saw to my problem. It had been there all the time, I was aware of it being there, yet using the circumstances never occurred to me until the day I was sitting on my veranda reading a memo from my office manager. The note stated that Walter had pulled another coup in the market and had the Street rocking on its heels. It was one of those times when any variation in Wall Street reflected the economy of the country, and what he did was undermine the entire economic structure of the United States. It was with the greatest effort that we got back to normal without toppling, but in doing so a lot of places had to close up. Walter Harrison, however, had doubled the wealth he could never hope to spend, anyway.

As I said, I was sitting there reading the note when I saw her behind the window in the house across the way. The sun was streaming in, reflecting the gold in her hair, making a picture of beauty so exquisite as to be unbelievable. A servant came and brought her a tray, and as she sat down to lunch I lost sight of her behind the hedges and the thought came to me of how simple it would all be.

I met Walter for lunch the next day. He was quite exuberant over his latest adventure, treating it like a joke.

I said, "Say, you've never been out to my place on the Island, have you?"

He laughed, and I noticed a little guilt in his eyes. "To tell you the truth," he said, "I would have dropped in if you hadn't built the place for Adrianne. After all . . ."

"Don't be ridiculous, Walter. What's done is done. Look, until things get back to normal, how about staying with me a few days. You need a rest after your little deal."

"Fine, Duncan, fine! Anytime you say."

"All right, I'll pick you up tonight."

We had quite a ride out, stopping at a few places for drinks and hashing over the old days at school. At any other time I might have laughed, but all those reminiscences had taken on an unpleasant air. When we reached the house I had a few friends in to meet the fabulous Walter Harrison, left him accepting their plaudits and went to bed.

We had breakfast on the veranda. Walter ate with relish, breathing deeply of the sea air with animal-like pleasure. At exactly nine o'clock the sunlight flashed off the windows of the house behind mine as the servant threw them open to the morning breeze.

Then she was there. I waved and she waved back. Walter's head turned to look and I heard his breath catch in his throat. She was lovely, her hair a golden cascade that tumbled around her shoulders. Her blouse was a radiant white that enhanced the swell of her breasts, a gleaming contrast to the smooth tanned flesh of her shoulders.

Walter looked like a man in a dream. "Lord, she's lovely!" he said. "Who is she, Dunc?"

I sipped my coffee. "A neighbor," I said lightly.

"Do you . . . do you think I could get to meet her?"

"Perhaps. She's quite young and just a little bit shy and it would be better to have her see me with you a few times before introductions are in order."

He sounded hoarse. His face had taken on an avid, hungry look. "Anything you say, but I have to meet her." He turned around with a grin. "By golly, I'll stay here until I do, too!"

We laughed over that and went back to our cigarettes, but every so often I caught him glancing back toward the hedge with that desperate expression creasing his face.

Being familiar with her schedule, I knew that we wouldn't see her

again that day, but Walter knew nothing of this. He tried to keep away
from the subject, yet it persisted in coming back. Finally he said, "Incidentally, just who is she?"

"Her name is Evelyn Vaughn. Comes from quite a well-to-do family."

"She here alone?"

"No, besides the servants she has a nurse and a doctor in attendance.
She hasn't been quite well."

"Hell, she looks the picture of health."

"Oh, she is now," I agreed. I walked over and turned on the television
and we watched the fights. For the sixth time a call came in for Walter, but
his reply was the same. He wasn't going back to New York. I felt the anticipation in his voice, knowing why he was staying, and had to concentrate on the screen to keep from smiling.

Evelyn was there the next day and the next. Walter had taken to waving when I did and when she waved back his face seemed to light up until
it looked almost boyish. The sun had tanned him nicely and he pranced
around like a colt, especially when she could see him. He pestered me with
questions and received evasive answers. Somehow he got the idea that his
importance warranted a visit from the house across the way. When I told
him that to Evelyn neither wealth nor position meant a thing he looked at
me sharply to see if I was telling the truth. To have become what he was he
had to be a good reader of faces and he knew that it *was* the truth beyond
the shadow of a doubt.

So I sat there day after day watching Walter Harrison fall helplessly in
love with a woman he hadn't met yet. He fell in love with the way she
waved until each movement of her hand seemed to be for him alone. He
fell in love with the luxuriant beauty of her body, letting his eyes follow her
as she walked to the water from the house, aching to be close to her. She
would turn sometimes and see us watching, and wave.

At night he would stand by the window not hearing what I said because he was watching her windows, hoping for just one glimpse of her,
and often I would hear him repeating her name slowly, letting it roll off his
tongue like a precious thing.

It couldn't go on that way. I knew it and he knew it. She had just come
up from the beach and the water glistened on her skin. She laughed at
something the woman said who was with her and shook her head back so
that her hair flowed down her back.

Walter shouted and waved and she laughed again, waving back. The
wind brought her voice to him and Walter stood there, his breath hot in my
face. "Look here, Duncan, I'm going over and meet her. I can't stand this

waiting. Good Lord, what does a guy have to go through to meet a woman?"

"You've never had any trouble before, have you?"

"Never like this!" he said. "Usually they're dropping at my feet. I haven't changed, have I? There's nothing repulsive about me, is there?"

I wanted to tell the truth, but I laughed instead. "You're the same as ever. It wouldn't surprise me if she was dying to meet you, too. I can tell you this . . . she's never been outside as much as since you've been here."

His eyes lit up boyishly. "Really, Dunc. Do you think so?"

"I think so. I can assure you of this, too. If she does seem to like you it's certainly for yourself alone."

As crudely as the barb was placed, it went home. Walter never so much as glanced at me. He was lost in thought for a long time, then: "I'm going over there now, Duncan. I'm crazy about that girl. By God, I'll marry her if it's the last thing I do."

"Don't spoil it, Walter. Tomorrow, I promise you. I'll go over with you."

His eagerness was pathetic. I don't think he slept a wink that night. Long before breakfast he was waiting for me on the veranda. We ate in silence, each minute an eternity for him. He turned repeatedly to look over the hedge and I caught a flash of worry when she didn't appear.

Tight little lines had appeared at the corner of his eyes and he said, "Where is she, Dunc? She should be there by now, shouldn't she?"

"I don't know," I said. "It does seem strange. Just a moment." I rang the bell on the table and my housekeeper came to the door. "Have you seen the Vaughns, Martha?" I asked her.

She nodded sagely. "Oh, yes, sir. They left very early this morning to go back to the city."

Walter turned to me. "Hell!"

"Well, she'll be back," I assured him.

"Damn it, Dunc, that isn't the point!" He stood up and threw his napkin on the seat. "Can't you realize that I'm in love with the girl? I can't wait for her to get back!"

His face flushed with frustration. There was no anger, only the crazy hunger for the woman. I held back my smile. It happened. It happened the way I planned for it to happen. Walter Harrison had fallen so deeply in love, so truly in love that he couldn't control himself. I might have felt sorry for him at that moment if I hadn't asked him, "Walter, as I told you, I know very little about her. Supposing she is already married."

He answered my question with a nasty grimace. "Then she'll get a divorce if I have to break the guy in pieces. I'll break anything that stands in my way, Duncan. I'm going to have her if it's the last thing I do!"

He stalked off to his room. Later I heard the car roar down the road. I let myself laugh then.

I went back to New York and was there a week when my contacts told me of Walter's fruitless search. He used every means at his disposal, but he couldn't locate the girl. I gave him seven days, exactly seven days. You see, that seventh day was the anniversary of the date I introduced him to Adrianne. I'll never forget it. Wherever Walter is now, neither will he.

When I called him I was amazed at the change in his voice. He sounded weak and lost. We exchanged the usual formalities; then I said, "Walter, have you found Evelyn yet?"

He took a long time to answer. "No, she's disappeared completely."

"Oh, I wouldn't say that," I said.

He didn't get it at first. It was almost too much to hope for. "You . . . mean you know where she is?"

"Exactly."

"Where? Please, Dunc . . . where is she?" In a split second he became a vital being again. He was bursting with life and energy, demanding that I tell him.

I laughed and told him to let me get a word in and I would. The silence was ominous then. "She's not very far from here, Walter, in a small hotel right off Fifth Avenue." I gave him the address and had hardly finished when I heard his phone slam against the desk. He was in such a hurry he hadn't bothered to hang up . . .

DUNCAN STOPPED AND drained his glass, then stared at it remorsefully. The inspector coughed lightly to attract his attention, his curiosity prompting him to speak. "He found her?" he asked eagerly.

"Oh yes, he found her. He burst right in over all protests, expecting to sweep her off her feet."

This time the inspector fidgeted nervously. "Well, go on."

Duncan motioned for the waiter and lifted a fresh glass in a toast. The Inspector did the same. Duncan smiled gently. "When she saw him she laughed and waved. Walter Harrison died an hour later . . . from a window in the same hotel."

It was too much for the inspector. He leaned forward in his chair, his forehead knotted in a frown. "But what happened? Who was she? Damn it, Duncan . . ."

Duncan took a deep breath, then gulped the drink down.

"Evelyn Vaughn was a hopeless imbecile," he said.

"She had the beauty of a goddess and the mentality of a two-year-old. They kept her well tended and dressed so she wouldn't be an object of curiosity. But the only habit she ever learned was to wave bye-bye . . ."

FOURTH OF JULY PICNIC

Rex Stout

The classical British mysteries are still fun to read precisely because they are, in virtually every sense, a kind of science fiction—an extrapolation on common reality. Not only were the puzzles outrageous (my God, some of those murder methods!), but they also employed the aristocracy to solve crimes. Lords were always running about foggy London in top hats and hansom cabs figuring out locked-room puzzles. Rex Stout's (1886–1975) wonderful world of Nero Wolfe wasn't much more reliable on the reality scale. But, as least for Yankee tastes, he was a lot more palatable. Here was a Great Detective you could laugh at—on purpose. He created a world as hermetically sealed and delightfully peopled as P. G. Wodehouse's. And he even threw in a wry and relentlessly suave and horny private-detective-narrator to boot. Something for everyone, including gardeners and gourmets. Stout was also an enjoyable writer line-by-line. He was a polished craftsman who had fun with his work. As you will too.

ONE

FLORA KORBY SWIVELED her head, with no hat hiding any of her dark brown hair, to face me with her dark brown eyes. She spoke.

"I guess I should have brought my car and led the way."

"I'm doing fine," I assured her. "I could shut one eye too."

"Please don't," she begged. "I'm stupefied as it is. May I have your autograph—I mean when we stop?"

Since she was highly presentable I didn't mind her assuming that I was driving with one hand because my right arm wanted to stretch across her shoulders, though she was wrong. I had left the cradle long ago. But there was no point in explaining to her that Nero Wolfe, who was in the back seat, had a deep distrust of moving vehicles and hated to ride in one unless

I drove it, and therefore I was glad to have an excuse to drive with one hand because that would make it more thrilling for him.

Anyway, she might have guessed it. The only outside interest that Wolfe permits to interfere with his personal routine of comfort, not to mention luxury, is Rusterman's restaurant. Its founder, Marko Vukcic, was Wolfe's oldest and closest friend; and when Vukcic died, leaving the restaurant to members of the staff and making Wolfe executor of his estate, he also left a letter asking Wolfe to see to it that the restaurant's standards and reputation were maintained; and Wolfe had done so, making unannounced visits there once or twice a week, and sometimes even oftener, without ever grumbling—well, hardly ever. But he sure did grumble when Felix, the maître d'hôtel, asked him to make a speech at the Independence Day picnic of the United Restaurant Workers of America. Hereafter I'll make it URWA.

He not only grumbled, he refused. But Felix kept after him, and Wolfe finally gave in when Felix came to the office one day with reinforcements: Paul Rago, the sauce chef at the Churchill; James Korby, the president of URWA; H. L. Griffin, a food and wine importer who supplied hard-to-get items not only for Rusterman's but also for Wolfe's own table; and Philip Holt, URWA's director of organization. They also were to be on the program at the picnic, and their main appeal was that they simply had to have the man who was responsible for keeping Rusterman's the best restaurant in New York after the death of Marko Vukcic. Since Wolfe is only as vain as three peacocks, and since he had loved Marko if he ever loved anyone, that got him. There had been another inducement: Philip Holt had agreed to lay off of Fritz, Wolfe's chef and housekeeper. For three years Fritz had been visiting the kitchen at Rusterman's off and on as a consultant, and Holt had been pestering him, insisting that he had to join URWA. You can guess how Wolfe liked that.

Since I do everything that has to be done in connection with Wolfe's business and his rare social activities, except that he thinks he does all the thinking, and we won't go into that now, it would be up to me to get him to the scene of the picnic, Culp's Meadows on Long Island, on the Fourth of July. Around the end of June James Korby phoned and introduced his daughter Flora. She told me that the directions to Culp's Meadows were very complicated, and I said that all directions on Long Island were very complicated, and she said she had better drive us out in her car.

I liked her voice, that is true, but also I have a lot of foresight, and it occurred to me immediately that it would be a new and exciting experience for my employer to watch me drive with one hand, so I told her that, while it must be Wolfe's car and I must drive, I would deeply appreciate it if she would come along and tell me the way. That was how it happened, and that was why, when we finally rolled through the gate at Culp's Meadows, after some thirty miles of Long Island parkways and another ten of grade intersections and trick turns, Wolfe's lips were pressed so tight he didn't have any. He had spoken only once, around the fourth or fifth mile, when I had swept around a slowpoke.

"Archie. You know quite well."

"Yes, sir." Of course I kept my eyes straight ahead. "But it's an impulse, having my arm like this, and I'm afraid to take it away because if I fight an impulse it makes me nervous, and driving when you're nervous is bad."

A glance in the mirror showed me his lips tightening, and they stayed tight.

Passing through the gate at Culp's Meadows, and winding around as directed by Flora Korby, I used both hands. It was a quarter to three, so we were on time, since the speeches were scheduled for three o'clock. Flora was sure a space would have been saved for us back of the tent, and after threading through a few acres of parked cars I found she was right, and rolled to a stop with the radiator only a couple of yards from the canvas. She hopped out and opened the rear door on her side, and I did likewise on mine. Wolfe's eyes went right to her, and then left to me. He was torn. He didn't want to favor a woman, even a young and pretty one, but he absolutely had to show me what he thought of one-hand driving. His eyes went right again, the whole seventh of a ton of him moved, and he climbed out on her side.

TWO

THE TENT, ON a wooden platform raised three feet above the ground, not much bigger than Wolfe's office, was crowded with people, and I wormed through to the front entrance and on out, where the platform extended into the open air. There was plenty of air, with a breeze dancing in from the direction of the ocean, and plenty of sunshine. A fine day for the Fourth of July. The platform extension was crammed with chairs, most of them empty. I can't report on the condition of the meadow's grass because my view was obstructed by ten thousand restaurant workers and their guests, maybe more. A crowd of a thousand of them were in a solid mass facing the platform, presumably those who wanted to be up front for the speeches, and the rest were sprayed around all over, clear across to a fringe of trees and a row of sheds.

Flora's voice came from behind my shoulder. "They're coming out, so if there's a chair you like, grab it. Except the six up front; they're for the speakers."

Naturally I started to tell her I wanted the one next to hers, but didn't get it out because people came jostling out of the tent onto the extension. Thinking I had better warn Wolfe that the chair he was about to occupy for an hour or so was about half as wide as his fanny, to give him time to fight his impulses, I worked past to the edge of the entrance, and when the exodus had thinned out I entered the tent. Five men were standing grouped beside a cot which was touching the canvas of the far side, and a man was lying on the cot. To my left Nero Wolfe was bending over to peer at the contents of a metal box there on a table with its lid open. I stepped over for a look and saw a collection of bone-handled knives, eight of them, with blades varying in length from six inches up to twelve. They weren't shiny, but they looked sharp, worn narrow by a lot of use for a lot of years. I asked Wolfe whose throat he was going to cut.

"They are Dubois," he said. "Real old Dubois. The best. They belong to Mr. Korby. He brought them to use in a carving contest, and he won, as he should. I would gladly steal them." He turned. "Why don't they let that man alone?"

I turned too, and through a gap in the group saw that the man on the cot was Philip Holt, URWA's director of organization. "What's the matter with him?" I asked.

"Something he ate. They think snails. Probably the wrong kind of snails. A doctor gave him something to help his bowels handle them. Why don't they leave him alone with his bowels?"

"I'll go ask," I said, and moved.

As I approached the cot James Korby was speaking. "I say he should be taken to a hospital, in spite of what the doctor said. Look at his color!"

Korby, short, pudgy, and bald, looked more like a restaurant customer than a restaurant worker, which may have been one reason he was president of URWA.

"I agree," Dick Vetter said emphatically. I had never seen Dick Vetter in person, but I had seen him often enough on his TV show—in fact, a little too often. If I quit dialing his channel he wouldn't miss me, since twenty million Americans, mostly female, were convinced that he was the youngest and handsomest MC on the waves. Flora Korby had told me he would be there, and why. His father had been a bus boy in a Broadway restaurant for thirty years, and still was because he wouldn't quit.

Paul Rago did not agree, and said so. "It would be a pity," he declared.

He made it "peety," his accent having tapered off enough not to make it "peetee." With his broad shoulders and six feet, his slick black hair going gray, and his mustache with pointed tips that was still all black, he looked more like an ambassador from below the border than a sauce chef. He was going on. "He is the most important man in the union—except, of course, the president—and he should make an appearance on the platform. Perhaps he can before we are through."

"I hope you will pardon me." That was H. L. Griffin, the food and wine importer. He was a skinny little runt, with a long narrow chin and something wrong with one eye, but he spoke with the authority of a man whose firm occupied a whole floor in one of the midtown hives. "I may have no right to an opinion, since I am not a member of your great organization, but you have done me the honor of inviting me to take part in your celebration of our country's independence, and I do know of Phil Holt's high standing and wide popularity among your members. I would merely say that I feel that Mr. Rago is right, that they will be disappointed not to see him on the platform. I hope I am not being presumptuous."

From outside the tent, from the loudspeakers at the corners of the platform, a booming voice had been calling to the picnickers scattered over the meadow to close in and prepare to listen. As the group by the cot went on arguing, a state trooper in uniform, who had been standing politely aside, came over and joined them and took a look at Philip Holt, but offered no advice. Wolfe also approached for a look. Myself, I would have said that the place for him was a good bed with an attractive nurse smoothing his brow. I saw him shiver all over at least three times. He decided it himself, finally, by muttering at them to let him alone and turning on his side to face the canvas. Flora Korby had come in, and she put a blanket over him, and I noticed that Dick Vetter made a point of helping her. The breeze was sweeping through and one of them said he shouldn't be in a draft, and Wolfe told me to lower the flap of the rear entrance, and I did so. The flap didn't want to stay down, so I tied the plastic tape fastening to hold it, in a single bowknot. Then they all marched out through the front entrance to the platform, including the state trooper, and I brought up the rear. As Korby passed the table he stopped to lower the lid on the box of knives, real old Dubois.

The speeches lasted an hour and eight minutes, and the ten thousand URWA members and guests took them standing like ladies and gentlemen. You are probably hoping I will report them word for word, but I didn't take them down and I didn't listen hard enough to engrave them on my memory. At that, the eagle didn't scream as much or as loud as I had expected. From my seat in the back row I could see most of the audience, and it was quite a sight.

The first speaker was a stranger, evidently the one who had been calling on them to gather around while we were in the tent, and after a few fitting remarks he introduced James Korby. While Korby was orating, Paul Rago left his seat, passed down the aisle in the center, and entered the tent. Since he had plugged for an appearance by Philip Holt I though his purpose might be to drag him out alive or dead, but it wasn't. In a minute he was back again, and just in time, for he had just sat down when Korby finished and Rago was introduced.

The faces out front had all been serious for Korby, but Rago's accent through the loudspeakers had most of them grinning by the time he warmed up. When Korby left his chair and started down the aisle I suspected him of walking out on Rago because Rago had walked out on him, but maybe not, since his visit in the tent was even shorter than Rago's had been. He came back out and returned to his chair, and listened attentively to the accent.

Next came H. L. Griffin, the importer, and the chairman had to lower the mike for him. His voice took the loudspeakers better than any of the others, and in fact he was darned good. It was only fair, I thought, to have the runt of the bunch take the cake, and I was all for the cheers from the throng that kept him on his feet a full minute after he finished. He really woke them up, and they were still yelling when he turned and went down the aisle to the tent, and it took the chairman a while to calm them down. Then, just as he started to introduce Dick Vetter, the TV star suddenly bounced up and started down the aisle with a determined look on his face, and it was easy to guess why. He thought Griffin was going to take advantage of the enthusiasm he had aroused by hauling Philip Holt out to the platform, and he was going to stop him. But he didn't have to. He was still two steps short of the tent entrance when Griffin emerged alone. Vetter moved aside to let him pass and then disappeared into the tent. As Griffin proceeded to his chair in the front row there were some scattered cheers from the crowd, and the chairman had to quiet them again before he could go on. Then he introduced Dick Vetter, who came out of the tent and along to the mike, which had to be raised again, at just the right moment.

As Vetter started to speak, Nero Wolfe arose and headed for the tent, and I raised my brows. Surely, I thought, he's not going to involve himself in the Holt problem; and then, seeing the look on his face, I caught on. The edges of the wooden chair seat had been cutting into his fanny for nearly an hour and he was in a tantrum, and he wanted to cool off a little before he was called to the mike. I grinned at him sympathetically as he passed and then gave my ear to Vetter. His soapy voice (I say soapy) came through the loudspeakers in a flow of lather, and after a couple of minutes of it I was thinking that it was only fair for Griffin, the runt, to sound like a man, and for Vetter, the handsome young idol of millions, to sound like whipped cream, when my attention was called. Wolfe was at the tent entrance, crooking a finger at me. As I got up and approached he backed into the tent, and I followed. He crossed to the rear entrance, lifted the flap, maneuvered his bulk through the hole, and held the flap for me. When I had made it he descended the five steps to the ground, walked to the car, grabbed the handle of the rear door, and pulled. Nothing doing. He turned to me.

"Unlock it."

I stood. "Do you want something?"

"Unlock it and get in and get the thing started. We're going."

"We are like hell. You've got a speech to make."

He glared at me. He knows my tones of voice as well as I know his. "Archie," he said, "I am not being eccentric. There is a sound and cogent reason and I'll explain on the way. Unlock this door."

I shook my head. "Not till I hear the reason. I admit it's your car." I took the keys from my pocket and offered them. "Here. I resign."

"Very well." He was grim. "That man on the cot is dead. I lifted the blanket to adjust it. One of those knives is in his back, clear to the handle. He is dead. If we are still here when the discovery is made you know what will happen. We will be here all day, all night, a week, indefinitely. That is intolerable. We can answer questions at home as well as here. Confound it, unlock the door!"

"How dead is he?"

"I have told you he is dead."

"Okay. You ought to know better. You do know better. We're stuck. They wouldn't ask us questions at home, they'd haul us back out here. They'd be waiting for us on the stoop and you wouldn't even get inside the house." I returned the keys to my pocket. "Running out when you're next on the program, that would be nice. The only question is do we report it now or do you make your speech and let someone else find it, and you can answer that."

He had stopped glaring. He took in a long, deep breath, and when it was out again he said, "I'll make my speech."

"Fine. It'd be a shame to waste it. A question. Just now when you lifted the flap to come out I didn't see you untie the tape fastening. Was it already untied?"

"Yes."

"The makes it nice." I turned and went to the steps, mounted, raised the flap for him, and followed him into the tent. He crossed to the front and on out, and I stepped to the cot. Philip Holt lay facing the wall, with the blanket up to his neck, and I pulled it down far enough to see the handle of the knife, an inch to the right of the point of the shoulder blade. The knife blade was all buried. I lowered the blanket some more to get at a hand, pinched a fingertip hard for ten seconds, released it, and saw it stay white. I picked some fluff from the blanket and dangled it against his nostrils for half a minute. No movement. I put the blanket back as I had found it, went to the metal box on the table and lifted the lid, and saw that the shortest knife, the one with the six-inch blade, wasn't there.

As I went to the rear entrance and raised the flap, Dick Vetter's lather or whipped cream, whichever you prefer, came to an end through the loudspeakers, and as I descended the five steps the meadowful of picnickers was cheering.

Our sedan was the third car on the right from the foot of the steps. The second car to the left of the steps was a 1955 Plymouth, and I was pleased to see that it still had an occupant, having previously noticed her—a woman with careless gray hair topping a wide face and a square chin, in the front seat but not behind the wheel.

I circled around to her side and spoke through the open window. "I beg your pardon. May I introduce myself?"

"You don't have to, young man. Your name's Archie Goodwin, and you work for Nero Wolfe, the detective." She had tired gray eyes. "You were just out here with him."

"Right. I hope you won't mind if I ask you something. How long have you been sitting here?"

"Long enough. But it's all right, I can hear the speeches. Nero Wolfe is just starting to speak now."

"Have you been here since the speeches started?"

"Yes, I have. I ate too much of the picnic stuff and I didn't feel like standing up in that crowd, so I came to sit in the car."

"Then you've been here all the time since the speeches began?"

"That's what I said. Why do you want to know?"

"I'm just checking on something. If you don't mind. Has anyone gone into the tent or come out of it while you've been here?"

Her tired eyes woke up a little. "Ha," she said, "so something's missing. I'm not surprised. What's missing?"

"Nothing, as far as I know. I'm just checking a certain fact. Of course you saw Mr. Wolfe and me come out and go back in. Anyone else, either going or coming?"

"You're not fooling me, young man. Something's missing, and you're a detective."

I grinned at her. "All right, have it your way. But I do want to know, if you don't object."

"I don't object. As I told you, I've been right here ever since the speeches started, I got here before that. And nobody has gone into the tent, nobody but you and Nero Wolfe, and I haven't either. I've been right here. If you want to know about me, my name is Anna Banau, Mrs. Alexander Banau, and my husband is a captain at Zoller's—"

A scream came from inside the tent, an all-out scream from a good pair of lungs. I moved, to the steps, up, and past the flap into the tent. Flora Korby was standing near the cot with her back to it, her hand covering her mouth. I was disappointed in her. Granting that a woman has a right to scream when she finds a corpse, she might have kept it down until Wolfe had finished his speech.

THREE

IT WAS A little after four o'clock when Flora Korby screamed. It was 4:34 when a glance outside through a crack past the flap of the tent's rear entrance, the third such glance I had managed to make, showed me that the Plymouth containing Mrs. Alexander Banau was gone. It was 4:39 when the medical examiner arrived with his bag and found that Philip Holt was still dead. It was 4:48 when the scientists came, with cameras and fingerprint kits and other items of equipment, and Wolfe and I and the others were herded out to the extension, under guard. It was 5:16 when I counted a total of seventeen cops, state and county, in uniform and out, on the job. It was 5:30 when Wolfe muttered at me bitterly that it would certainly be all night. It was 5:52 when a chief of detectives named Baxter got so personal with me that I decided, finally and definitely, not to play. It was 6:21 when we all left Culp's Meadows for an official destination. There were four in our car: one in uniform with Wolfe in the back seat, and one in his own clothes with me in front. Again I had someone beside me to tell me the way, but I didn't put my arm across his shoulders.

There had been some conversing with us separately, but most of it had been a panel discussion, open air, out on the platform extension, so I knew pretty well how things stood. Nobody was accusing anybody. Three of them—Korby, Rago, and Griffin—gave approximately the same reason for their visits to the tent during the speechmaking: that they were concerned about Philip Holt and wanted to see if he was all right. The fourth, Dick Vetter, gave the reason I had guessed, that he thought Griffin might bring Holt out to the platform, and he intended to stop him. Vetter, by the way, was the only one who raised a fuss about being detained. He said that it hadn't been easy to get away from his duties that afternoon, and he had a studio rehearsal scheduled for six o'clock, and he absolutely had to be there. At 6:21, when we all left for the official destination, he was fit to be tied.

None of them claimed to know for sure that Holt had been alive at the time he visited the tent; they all had supposed he had fallen asleep. All except Vetter said they had gone to the cot and looked at him, at his face, and had suspected nothing wrong. None of them had spoken to him. To the question, "Who do you think did it and why?" they all gave the same answer: someone must have entered the tent by the rear entrance, stabbed him, and departed. The fact that the URWA director of organization had got his stomach into trouble and had been attended by a doctor in the tent had been no secret, anything but.

I have been leaving Flora out, since I knew and you know she was clear, but the cops didn't. I overheard one of them tell another one it was probably her, because stabbing a sick man was more like something a woman would do than a man.

Of course the theory that someone had entered by the back door made the fastening of the tent flap an important item. I said I had tied the tape before we left the tent, and they all agreed that they had seen me do so except Dick Vetter, who said he hadn't noticed because he had been helping to arrange the blanket over Holt; and Wolfe and I both testified that the tape was hanging loose when we had entered the tent while Vetter was speaking. Under this theory the point wasn't who had untied it, since the murderer could have easily reached through the crack from the outside and jerked the knot loose; the question was when. On that none of them was any help. All four said they hadn't noticed whether the tape was tied or not when they went inside the tent.

That was how it stood, as far as I knew, when we left Culp's Meadows. The official destination turned out to be a building I had been in before a time or two, not as a murder suspect—a county courthouse back of a smooth green lawn with a couple of big trees. First we were collected in a room on the ground floor, and, after a long wait, were escorted up one flight and through a door that was inscribed DISTRICT ATTORNEY.

At least 91.2 per cent of the district attorneys in the State of New York think they would make fine tenants of the governor's mansion at Albany, and that should be kept in mind in considering the conduct of DA James R. Delaney. To him at least four of that bunch, and possibly all five, were upright, important citizens in positions to influence segments of the electorate. His attitude as he attacked the problem implied that he was merely chairing a meeting of a community council called to deal with a grave and difficult emergency—except, I noticed, when he was looking at or speaking to Wolfe or me. Then his smile quit working, his tone sharpened, and his eyes had a different look.

With a stenographer at a side table taking it down, he spent an hour going over it with us, or rather with them, with scattered contributions from Chief of Detectives Baxter and others who had been at the scene, and then spoke his mind.

"It seems," he said, "to be the consensus that some person unknown entered the tent from the rear, stabbed him, and departed. There is the question, how could such a person have known the knife would be there at hand? but he need not have known. He might have decided to murder only when he saw the knives, or he might have had some other weapon with him, and, seeing the knives, thought one of them would better serve his purpose and used it instead. Either is plausible. It must be admitted that the whole theory is plausible, and none of the facts now known are in contradiction to it. You agree, Chief?"

"Right," Baxter conceded. "Up to now. As long as the known facts are facts."

Delaney nodded. "Certainly. They have to be checked." His eyes took in the audience. "You gentlemen, and you, Miss Korby, you understand that you are to remain in this jurisdiction, the State of New York, until further notice, and you are to be available. With that understood, it seems unnecessary at present to put you under bond as material witnesses. We have your addresses and know where to find you."

He focused on Wolfe, and his tone changed. "With you, Wolfe, the situation is somewhat different. You're a licensed private detective, and so is Goodwin, and the record of your high-handed performances does not inspire confidence in your—uh—candor. There may be some complicated

and subtle reasons why the New York City authorities have stood for your
tricks, but out here in the suburbs we're more simple-minded. We don't
like tricks."

He lowered his chin, which made his eyes slant up under his heavy
brows. "Let's see if I've got your story right. You say that as Vetter started
to speak you felt in your pocket for a paper on which you had made notes
for your speech, found it wasn't there, thought you had left it in your car,
went to get it, and when, after you had entered the tent, it occurred to you
that the car was locked and Goodwin had the keys, you summoned him
and you and he went out to the car. Then Goodwin remembered that the
paper had been left on your desk at your office, and you and he returned to
the tent, and you went out to the platform and resumed your seat. Another
item: when you went to the rear entrance to leave the tent to go out to the
car, the tape fastening of the flap was hanging loose, not tied. Is that your
story?"

Wolfe cleared his throat. "Mr. Delaney. I suppose it is pointless to challenge your remark about my candor or to ask you to phrase your question
less offensively." His shoulders went up an eighth of an inch, and down.
"Yes, that's my story."

"I merely asked you the question."

"I answered it."

"So you did." The DA's eyes came to me. "And of course, Goodwin,
your story is the same. If it needed arranging, there was ample time for that
during the hubbub that followed Miss Korby's scream. But with you
there's more to it. You say that after you and Wolfe re-entered the tent, and
he continued through the front entrance to the platform, it occurred to you
that there was a possibility that he had taken the paper from his desk and
put it in his pocket, and had consulted it during the ride, and had left it in
the car, and you went out back again to look, and you were out there when
Miss Korby screamed. Is that correct?"

As I had long since decided not to play, when Baxter had got too personal, I merely said, "Check."

Delaney returned to Wolfe. "If you object to my being offensive,
Wolfe, I'll put it this way: I find some of this hard to believe. Anyone as
glib as you are needing notes for a little speech like that? And you thinking
you had left the paper in the car, and Goodwin remembering it had been
left at home on your desk and then thinking it might be in the car after all?
Also there are certain facts. You and Goodwin were the last people inside
the tent before Miss Korby entered and found the body. You admit it. The
others all state that they don't know whether the tape was tied or not when

they visited the tent; you and Goodwin can't very well say that, since you went out that way, so you say you found it untied."

He cocked his head. "You admit you had had words with Philip Holt during the past year. You admit he had become obnoxious to you—your word, obnoxious—by his insistence that your personal chef must join his union. The record of your past performances justifies me in saying that a man who renders himself obnoxious to you had better watch his step. I'll say this, if it weren't for the probability that some unknown person entered from the rear, and I concede that it's quite possible, you and Goodwin would be held in custody until a judge could be found to issue a warrant for your arrest as material witnesses. As it is, I'll make it easier for you." He looked at his wristwatch. "It's five minutes to eight. I'll send a man with you to a restaurant down the street, and we'll expect you back here at nine-thirty. I want to cover all the details with you, thoroughly." His eyes moved. "The rest of you may go for the present, but you are to be available."

Wolfe stood up. "Mr. Goodwin and I are going home," he announced. "We will not be back this evening."

Delaney's eyes narrowed. "If that's the way you feel about it, you'll stay. You can send out for sandwiches."

"Are we under arrest?"

The DA opened his mouth, closed it, and opened it again. "No."

"Then we're going." Wolfe was assured but not belligerent. "I understand your annoyance, sir, at this interference with your holiday, and I'm aware that you don't like me—or what you know, or think you know, of my record. But I will not surrender my convenience to your humor. You can detain me only if you charge me, and with what? Mr. Goodwin and I have supplied all the information we have. Your intimation that I am capable of murdering a man, or of inciting Mr. Goodwin to murder him, because he has made a nuisance of himself, is puerile. You concede that the murderer could have been anyone in that throng of thousands. You have no basis whatever for any supposition that Mr. Goodwin and I are concealing any knowledge that would help you. Should such a basis appear, you know where to find us. Come, Archie."

He turned and headed for the door, and I followed. I can't report the reaction because Delaney at his desk was behind me, and it would have been bad tactics to look back over my shoulder. All I knew was that Baxter took two steps and stopped, and none of the other cops moved. We made the hall, and the entrance, and down the path to the sidewalk, without a shot being fired; and half a block to where the car was parked. Wolfe told me to find a phone booth and call Fritz to tell him when we would arrive for dinner, and I steered for the center of town.

As I had holiday traffic to cope with, it was half past nine by the time we got home and washed and seated at the dinner table. A moving car is no place to give Wolfe bad news, or good news either for that matter, and there was no point in spoiling his dinner, so I waited until after we had finished with the poached and truffled broilers and broccoli and stuffed potatoes with herbs, and salad and cheese, and Fritz had brought coffee to us in the office, to open the bag. Wolfe was reaching for the remote-control television gadget, to turn it on so as to have the pleasure of turning it off again, when I said, "Hold a minute. I have a report to make. I don't blame you for feeling self-satisfied, you got us away very neatly, but there's a catch. It wasn't somebody that came in the back way. It was one of them."

"Indeed." He was placid, after-dinner placid, in the comfortable big made-to-order chair back of his desk. "What is this, flummery?"

"No, sir. Nor am I trying to show that I'm smarter than you are for once. It's just that I know more. When you left the tent to go to the car your mind was on a quick getaway, so you may not have noticed that a woman was sitting there in a car to the left, but I did. When we returned to the tent and you went on out front, I had an idea and went out back again and had a talk with her. I'll give it to you verbatim, since it's important."

I did so. That was simple, compared with the three-way and four-way conversations I have been called on to report word for word. When I finished he was scowling at me, as black as the coffee in his cup.

"Confound it," he growled.

"Yes, sir. I was going to tell you, there when we were settling the details of why we went out to the car, the paper with your notes, but as you know we were interrupted, and after that there was no opportunity that I liked, and anyway I had seen that Mrs. Banau and the car were gone, and that baboon named Baxter had hurt my feelings, and I had decided not to play. Of course the main thing was you, your wanting to go home. If they had known it was one of us six, or seven counting Flora, we would all have been held as material witnesses, and you couldn't have got bail on the Fourth of July, and God help you. I can manage in a cell, but you're too big. Also if I got you home you might feel like discussing a raise in pay. Do you?"

"Shut up." He closed his eyes, and after a moment opened them again. "We're in a pickle. They may find that woman any moment, or she may disclose herself. What about her? You have given me her words, but what about her?"

"She's good. They'll believe her. I did. You would. From where she sat the steps and tent entrance were in her minimum field of vision, no obstructions, less than ten yards away."

"If she kept her eyes open."

"She thinks she did, and that will do for the cops when they find her. Anyhow, I think she did too. When she said nobody had gone into the tent but you and me she meant it."

"There's the possibility that she herself, or someone she knew and would protect—No, that's absurd, since she stayed there in the car for some time after the body was found. We're in a fix."

"Yes, sir." Meeting his eyes, I saw no sign of the gratitude I might reasonably have expected, so I went on. "I would like to suggest, in considering the situation don't bother about me. I can't be charged with withholding evidence because I didn't report my talk with her. I can just say I didn't believe her and saw no point in making it tougher for us by dragging it in. The fact that someone might have come in the back way didn't eliminate us. Of course I'll have to account for my questioning her, but that's easy. I can say I discovered that he was dead after you went back out to the platform to make your speech, and, having noticed her there in the car, I went out to question her before reporting the discovery, and was interrupted by the scream in the tent. So don't mind me. Anything you say. I can phone Delaney in the morning, or you can, and spill it, or we can just sit tight and wait for the fireworks."

"Pfui," he said.

"Amen," I said.

He took in air, audibly, and let it out. "That woman may be communicating with them at this moment, or they may be finding her. I don't complain of your performance; indeed, I commend it. If you had reported that conversation we would both be spending tonight in jail." He made a face. "Bah. As it is, at least we can try something. What time is it?"

I looked at my wristwatch. He would have had to turn his head almost to a right angle to glance at the wall clock, which was too much to expect. "Eight after eleven."

"Could you get them here tonight?"

"I doubt it. All five of them?"

"Yes."

"Possibly by sunup. Bring them to your bedroom?"

He rubbed his nose with a fingertip. "Very well. But you can call them now, as many as you can get. Make it eleven in the morning. Tell them I have a disclosure to make and must consult with them."

"That should interest them," I granted, and reached for the phone.

FOUR

BY THE TIME Wolfe came down from the plant rooms to greet the guests, at two minutes past eleven the next morning, there hadn't been a peep out of the Long Island law. Which didn't mean there couldn't be one at three minutes past eleven. According to the morning paper, District Attorney Delaney and Chief of Detectives Baxter had both conceded that anyone could have entered the tent from the back and therefore it was wide open. If Anna Banau read newspapers, and she probably did, she might at any moment be going to the phone to make a call.

I had made several, both the night before and that morning, getting the guests lined up; and one special one. There was an address and phone number for an Alexander Banau in the Manhattan book, but I decided not to dial it. I also decided not to ring Zoller's restaurant on Fifty-second Street. I hadn't eaten at Zoller's more than a couple of times, but I knew a man who had been patronizing it for years, and I called him. Yes, he said, there was a captain at Zoller's named Alex, and yes, his last name was Banau. He liked Alex and hoped that my asking about him didn't mean that he was headed for some kind of trouble. I said no trouble was contemplated, I just might want to check a little detail, and thanked him. Then I sat and looked at the slip on which I had scribbled the Banau home phone number, with my finger itching to dial it, but to say what? No.

I mention that around ten-thirty I got the Marley .38 from the drawer, saw that it was loaded, and put it in my side pocket, not to prepare for bloodshed, but just to show that I was sold on Mrs. Banau. With a murderer for a guest, and an extremely nervy one, there was no telling.

H. L. Griffin, the importer, and Paul Rago, the sauce chef, came alone and separately, but Korby and Flora had Dick Vetter with them. I had intended to let Flora have the red leather chair, but when I showed them to the office, Rago, the six-footer with the mustache and the accent, had copped it, and she took one of the yellow chairs in a row facing Wolfe's desk, with her father on her right and Vetter on her left. Griffin, the runt who had made the best speech, was at the end of the row nearest my desk.

When Wolfe came down from the plant rooms, entered, greeted them, and headed for his desk, Vetter spoke up before he was seated.

"I hope this won't last long, Mr. Wolfe. I asked Mr. Goodwin if it couldn't be earlier, and he said it couldn't. Miss Korby and I must have an early lunch because I have a script conference at one-thirty."

I raised a brow. I had been honored. I had driven a car with my arm across the shoulders of a girl whom Dick Vetter himself thought worthy of a lunch.

Wolfe, adjusted in his chair, said mildly, "I won't prolong it beyond necessity, sir. Are you and Miss Korby friends?"

"What's that got to do with it?"

"Possibly nothing. But now, nothing about any of you is beyond the bounds of my curiosity. It is a distressing thing to have to say, in view of the occasion of our meeting yesterday, the anniversary of the birth of this land of freedom, but I must. One of you is a miscreant. One of you people killed Philip Holt."

The idea is to watch them and see who faints or jumps up and runs. But nobody did. They all stared.

"One of us?" Griffin demanded.

Wolfe nodded. "I thought it best to begin with that bald statement, instead of leading up to it. I thought—"

Korby cut in. "This is funny. This is a joke. After what you said yesterday to that district attorney. It's a *bad* joke."

"It's no joke, Mr. Korby. I wish it were. I thought yesterday I was on solid ground, but I wasn't. I now know that there is a witness, a credible and confident witness, to testify that no one entered the tent from the rear between the time that the speeches began and the discovery of the body. I also know that neither Mr. Goodwin nor I killed him, so it was one of you. So I think we should discuss it."

"You say a witness?" Rago made it "weetnuss."

"Who is he?" Korby wanted to know. "Where is he?"

"It's a woman, and she is available. Mr. Goodwin, who has spoken with her, is completely satisfied of her competence and bona fides, and he is hard to satisfy. It is highly unlikely that she can be impeached. That's all I—"

"I don't get it," Vetter blurted. "If they've got a witness like that why haven't they come for us?"

"Because they haven't got her. They know nothing about her. But they may find her at any moment, or she may go to them. If so you will soon be discussing the matter not with me but with officers of the law—and so will I. Unless you do discuss it with me, and unless the discussion is productive, I shall of course be constrained to tell Mr. Delaney about her. I wouldn't like that and neither would you. After hearing her story his manner with you, and with me, would be quite difference from yesterday. I want to ask you some questions."

"Who is she?" Korby demanded. "Where is she?"

Wolfe shook his head. "I'm not going to identify her or place her for you. I note your expressions—especially yours, Mr. Korby, and yours, Mr. Griffin. You are skeptical. But what conceivable reason could there be for my getting you here to point this weapon at you except the coercion of events? Why would I invent or contrive such a dilemma? I, like you, would vastly prefer to have it as it was, that the murderer came from without, but that's no good now. I concede that you may suspect me too, and Mr. Goodwin, and you may question us as I may question you. But one of us killed Philip Holt, and getting answers to questions is clearly in the interest of all the rest of us."

They exchanged glances. But they were not the kind of glances they would have exchanged five minutes earlier. They were glances of doubt, suspicion, and surmise, and they weren't friendly.

"I don't see," Griffin objected, "what good questions will do. We were all there together and we all know what happened. We all know what everybody said."

Wolfe nodded. "But we were all supporting the theory that excluded us. Now we're not. We can't. One of us has something in his background which, if known, would account for his determination to kill that man. I suggest beginning with autobiographical sketches from each of us, and here is mine. I was born in Montenegro and spent my early boyhood there. At the age of sixteen I decided to move around, and in fourteen years I became acquainted with most of Europe, a little of Africa, and much of Asia, in a variety of roles and activities. Coming to this country in nineteen-thirty, not penniless, I bought this house and entered into practice as a private detective. I am a naturalized American citizen. I first heard of Philip Holt about two years ago when Fritz Brenner, who works for me, came to me with a complaint about him. My only reason for wishing him harm, but not the extremity of death, was removed, as you know, when he agreed to stop annoying Mr. Brenner about joining your union if I would make a speech at your blasted picnic. Mr. Goodwin?"

I turned my face to the audience. "Born in Ohio. Public high school, pretty good at geometry and football, graduated with honor but no honors. Went to college two weeks, decided it was childish, came to New York and got a job guarding a pier, shot and killed two men and was fired, was recommended to Nero Wolfe for a chore he wanted done, did it, was offered a full-time job by Mr. Wolfe, took it, still have it. Personally, was more entertained than bothered by Holt's trying to get union dues out of Fritz Brenner. Otherwise no connection with him or about him."

"You may," Wolfe told them, "question us later if you wish. Miss Korby?"

"Well—" Flora said. She glanced at her father, and, when he nodded, she aimed at Wolfe and went on, "My autobiography doesn't amount to much. I was born in New York and have always lived here. I'm twenty years old. I didn't kill Phil Holt and had no reason to kill him." She turned her palms up. "What else?"

"If I may suggest," H. L. Griffin offered, "if there's a witness as Wolfe says, if there *is* such a witness, they'll dig everything up. For instance, about you and Phil."

She gave him an eye. "What about us, Mr. Griffin?"

"I don't know. I've only heard talk, that's all, and they'll dig up the talk."

"To hell with the talk," Dick Vetter blurted, the whipped cream sounding sour.

Flora looked at Wolfe. "I can't help talk," she said. "It certainly is no secret that Phil Holt was—well, he liked women. And it's no secret that I'm a woman, and I guess it's not a secret that I didn't like Phil. For me he was what you called him, a nuisance. When he wanted something."

Wolfe grunted. "And he wanted you?"

"He thought he did. That's all there was to it. He was a pest, that's all there is to say about it."

"You said you had no reason to kill him."

"Good heavens, I didn't! A girl doesn't kill a man just because he won't believe her when she says no!"

"No to what? A marriage proposal?"

Her father cut in. "Look here," he told Wolfe, "you're barking up the wrong tree. Everybody knows how Phil Holt was about women. He never asked one to marry him and probably he never would. My daughter is old enough and smart enough to take care of herself, and she does, but not by sticking a knife in a man's back." He turned to Griffin. "Much obliged, Harry."

The importer wasn't fazed. "It was bound to come out, Jim, and I thought it ought to be mentioned now."

Wolfe was regarding Korby. "Naturally it raises the question how far a father might go to relieve his daughter of a pest."

Korby snorted. "If you're asking it, the answer is no. My daughter can take care of herself. If you want a reason why I might have killed Phil Holt you'll have to do better than that."

"Then I'll try, Mr. Korby. You are the president of your union, and Mr. Holt was an important figure in it, and at the moment the affairs of unions, especially their financial affairs, are front-page news. Have you any reason to fear an investigation, or had Mr. Holt?"

"No. They can investigate as much as they damn please."

"Have you been summoned?"

"No."

"Had Mr. Holt been summoned?"

"No."

"Have any officials of your union been summoned?"

"No." Korby's pudgy face and bald top were pinking up a little. "You're barking up the wrong tree again."

"But at least another tree. You realize, sir, that if Mr. Delaney starts after us in earnest, the affairs of the United Restaurant Workers of America will be one of his major concerns. For the murder of Philip Holt we all had opportunity, and the means were there at hand; what he will seek is the motive. If there was a vulnerable spot in the operation of your union, financial or otherwise, I suggest that it would be wise for you to disclose it now for discussion."

"There wasn't anything." Korby was pinker. "There's nothing wrong with my union except rumors. That's all it is, rumors, and where's a union that hasn't got rumors with all the stink they've raised? We're not vulnerable to anything or anybody?"

"What kind of rumors?"

"Any kind you want to name. I'm a crook. All the officers are crooks. We've raided the benefit fund. We've sold out to the big operators. We steal lead pencils and paper clips."

"Can you be more specific? What was the most embarrassing rumor?"

Korby was suddenly not listening. He took a folded handkerchief from his pocket, opened it up, wiped his face and his baldness, refolded the handkerchief at the creases, and returned it to his pocket. Then his eyes went back to Wolfe.

"If you want something specific," he said, "it's not a rumor. It's a strictly internal union matter, but it's sure to leak now and it might as well leak here first. There have been some charges made, and they're being looked into, about kickbacks from dealers to union officers and members. Phil Holt had something to do with some of the charges, though that wasn't in his department. He got hot about it."

"Were you the target of any of the charges?"

"I was not. I have the complete trust of my associates and my staff."

"You said 'dealers.' Does that include importers?"

"Sure, importers are dealers."

"Was Mr. Griffin's name mentioned in any of the charges?"

"I'm not giving any names, not without authority from my board. Those things are confidential."

"Much obliged, Jim," H. L. Griffin said, sounding the opposite of obliged. "Even exchange?"

"Excuse me." It was Dick Vetter, on his feet. "It's nearly twelve o'clock and Miss Korby and I have to go. We've got to get some lunch and I can't be late for that conference. Anyway, I think it's a lot of hooey. Come on, Flora."

She hesitated a moment, then left her chair, and he moved. But when Wolfe snapped out his name he turned. "Well?"

Wolfe swiveled his chair. "My apologies. I should have remembered that you are pressed for time. If you can give us, say five minutes?"

The TV star smiled indulgently. "For my autobiography? You can look it up. It's in print—*TV Guide* a couple of months ago, or *Clock* magazine, I don't remember the date. I say this is hooey. If one of us is a murderer, okay, I wish you luck, but this isn't getting you anywhere. Couldn't I just tell you anything I felt like?"

"You could indeed, Mr. Vetter. But if inquiry reveals that you have lied or have omitted something plainly relevant that will be of interest. The magazine articles you mentioned—do they tell of your interest in Miss Korby?"

"Nuts." Many of his twenty million admirers wouldn't have liked either his tone or his diction.

Wolfe shook his head. "If you insist, Mr. Vette, you may of course be disdainful about it with me, but not with the police once they get interested in you. I asked you before if you and Miss Korby are friends, and you asked what that had to do with it, and I said possibly nothing. I now say possibly something, since Philip Holt was hounding her—how savagely I don't know yet. Are you and Miss Korby friends?"

"Certainly we're friends. I'm taking her to lunch."

"Are you devoted to her?"

His smile wasn't quite so indulgent, but it was still a smile. "Now that's a delicate question," he said. "I'll tell you how it is, I'm a public figure and I have to watch my tongue. If I said yes, I'm devoted to Miss Korby, it would be in all the columns tomorrow and I'd get ten thousand telegrams and a million letters. If I said no, I'm not devoted to Miss Korby, that wouldn't be polite with her here at my elbow. So I'll just skip it. Come on, Flora."

"One more question. I understand that your father works in a New York restaurant. Do you know whether he is involved in any of the charges Mr. Korby spoke of?"

"Oh, for God's sake. Talk about hooey." He turned and headed for the door, taking Flora with him. I got up and went to the hall and on to the front door, opened it for them, closed it after them, put the chain-bolt on, and returned to the office. Wolfe was speaking.

". . . and I assure you, Mr. Rago, my interest runs with yours—with all of you except one. You don't want the police crawling over you and neither do I."

The sauce chef had straightened up in the red leather chair, and the points of his mustache seemed to have straightened up too. "Treeks," he said.

"No, sir," Wolfe said. "I have no objection to tricks, if they work, but this is merely a forthright discussion of a lamentable situation. No trick. Do you object to telling us what dealings you had with Philip Holt?"

"I am deesappointed," Rago declared. "Of course I knew you made a living with detective work, everybody knows that, but to me your glory is your great contributions to cuisine—your *sauce printemps,* your oyster pic, your *artichauts drigants,* and others. I know what Pierre Mondor said of you. So it is a deesappointment when I am in your company that the only talk is of the ugliness of murder."

"I don't like it any better than you do, Mr. Rago. I am pleased to know that Pierre Mondor spoke well of me. Now about Philip Holt?"

"If you insist, certainly. But what can I say? Nothing."

"Didn't you know him?"

Rago spread his hands and raised his shoulders and brows. "I had met him. As one meets people. Did I know him? Whom does one know? Do I know you?"

"But you never saw me until two weeks ago. Surely you must have seen something of Mr. Holt. He was an important official of your union, in which you were active."

"I have not been active in the union."

"You were a speaker at its picnic yesterday."

Rago nodded and smiled. "Yes, that is so. But that was because of my activity in the kitchen, not in the union. It may be said, even by me, that in sauces I am supreme. It was for that distinction that it was thought desirable to have me." His head turned. "So, Mr. Korby?"

The president of URWA nodded yes. "That's right," he told Wolfe. "We thought the finest cooking should be represented, and we picked Rago for it. So far as I know, he has never come to a union meeting. We wish he would, and more like him."

"I am a man of the kitchen," Rago declared. "I am an artist. The business I leave to others."

Wolfe was on Korby. "Did Mr. Rago's name appear in any of the charges you spoke of?"

"No. I said I wouldn't give names, but I can say no. No, it didn't."

"You didn't say no when I asked about Mr. Griffin." Wolfe turned to the importer. "Do you wish to comment on that, sir?"

I still hadn't decided exactly what was wrong with Griffin's left eye. There was no sign of an injury, and it seemed to function okay, but it appeared to be a little off center. From an angle, the slant I had from my desk, it looked normal.

He lifted his long narrow chin. "What do you expect?" he demanded.

"My expectations are of no consequence. I merely invite comment."

"On that, I have none. I know nothing about any charges. What I want, I want to see that witness."

Wolfe shook his head. "As I said, I will not produce the witness—for the present. Are you still skeptical?"

"I'm always skeptical." Griffin's voice would have suited a man twice his size. "I want to see that witness and hear what she has to say. I admit I can see no reason why you would invent her—if there is one it's too deep for me, since it puts you in the same boat with us—but I'm not going to believe her until I see her. Maybe I will then, and maybe I won't."

"I think you will. Meanwhile, what about your relations with Philip Holt? How long and how well did you know him?"

"Oh, to hell with this jabber!" Griffin bounced up, not having far to bounce. "If there was anything in my relations with him that made me kill him, would I be telling you?" He flattened his palms on Wolfe's desk. "Are you going to produce that witness? No?" He wheeled. "I've had enough of this! You, Jim? Rago?"

That ended the party. Wolfe could have held Korby and Rago for more jabber, but apparently he didn't think it worth the effort. They asked some questions, what was Wolfe going to do now, and what was the witness going to do, and why couldn't they see her, and why did Wolfe believe her, and was he going to see her and question her, and of course nobody got anything out of that. The atmosphere wasn't very cordial when they left. After letting them out I returned to the office and stood in front of Wolfe's desk. He was leaning back with his arms folded.

"Lunch in twenty minutes," I said cheerfully.

"Not in peace," he growled.

"No, sir. Any instructions?"

"Pfui. It would take an army, and I haven't got one. To go into all of them, to trace all their connections and dealings with the man one of them murdered . . ." He unfolded his arms and put his fists on the desk. "I can't even limit it by assuming that it was an act of urgency, resulting from something that had been said or done that day or in the immediate past. The need or desire to kill him might have dated from a week ago, or a month, or even a year, and it was satisfied yesterday in that tent only because circumstances offered the opportunity. No matter which one it was—Rago, who visited the tent first, or Korby or Griffin or Vetter, who visited it after him in that order—no matter which, the opportunity was tempting. The man was there, recumbent and disabled, and the weapon was there. He had a plausible excuse for entering the tent. To spread the cloud of suspicion to the multitude, all he had to do was untie the tape that held the flap. Even if the body were discovered soon after he left the tent, even seconds after, there would be no question he couldn't answer."

He grunted. "No. Confound it, no. The motive may be buried not only in a complexity of associations but also in history. It might take months. I will have to contrive something."

"Yeah. Any time."

"There may be none. That's the devil of it. Get Saul and Fred and Orrie and have them on call. I have no idea for what, but no matter, get them. And let me alone."

I went to my desk and pulled the phone over.

FIVE

THERE HAVE BEEN only five occasions in my memory when Wolfe has cut short his afternoon session with the orchids in the plant rooms, from four o'clock to six, and that was the fifth.

If there had been any developments inside his skull I hadn't been informed. There had been none outside, unless you count my calling Saul and Fred and Orrie, our three best bets when we needed outside help, and telling them to stand by. Back at his desk after lunch, Wolfe fiddled around with papers on his desk, counted the week's collection of bottle caps in his drawer, rang for Fritz to bring beer and then didn't drink it, and picked up his current book, *The Fall* by Albert Camus, three or four times, and put it down again. In between he brushed specks of dust from his desk with his little finger. When I turned on the radio for the four-o'clock newscast he waited until it was finished to leave for his elevator trip up to the roof.

Later, nearly an hour later, I caught myself brushing a speck of dust off my desk with my little finger, said something I needn't repeat here, and went to the kitchen for a glass of milk.

When the doorbell rang at a quarter past five I jumped up and shot for the hall, realized that was unmanly, and controlled my legs to a normal gait. Through the one-way glass panel of the front door I saw, out on the stoop, a tall lanky guy, narrow from top to bottom, in a brown suit that needed pressing and a brown straw hat. I took a breath, which I needed apparently, and went and opened the door the two inches allowed by the chain-bolt. His appearance was all against it, but there was no telling what kind of a specimen District Attorney Delaney or Chief of Detectives Baxter might have on his staff.

I spoke through the crack. "Yes, sir?"

"I would like to see Mr. Nero Wolfe. My name is Banau, Alexander Banau."

"Yes, sir." I took the bolt off and swung the door open, and he crossed the sill. "Your hat, sir?" He gave it to me and I put it on the shelf. "This way, sir." I waited until I had him in the office and in the red leather chair to say, "Mr. Wolfe is engaged at the moment. I'll tell him you're here."

I went to the hall and on to the kitchen, shutting doors on the way, buzzed the plant rooms on the house phone, and in three seconds, instead of the usual fifteen or twenty, had a growl in my ear. "Yes?"

"Company. Captain Alexander Banau."

Silence, then: "Let him in."

"He's already in. Have you any suggestions how I keep him occupied until six o'clock?"

"No." A longer silence. "I'll be down."

As I said, that was the fifth time in all the years I have been with him. I went back to the office and asked the guest if he would like something to drink, and he said no, and in two minutes there was the sound of Wolfe's elevator descending and stopping, the door opening and shutting, and his tread. He entered, circled around the red leather chair, and offered a hand.

"Mr. Banau? I'm Nero Wolfe. How do you do, sir?"

He was certainly spreading it on. He doesn't like to shake hands, and rarely does. When he adjusted in his chair he gave Banau a look so sociable it was damn close to fawning, for him.

"Well, sir?"

"I fear," Banau said, "that I may have to make myself disagreeable. I don't like to be disagreeable. Is that gentleman"—he nodded at me—"Mr. Archie Goodwin?"

"He is, yes, sir."

"Then it will be doubly disagreeable, but it can't be helped. It concerns the tragic event at Culp's Meadows yesterday. According to the newspaper accounts, the police are proceeding on the probability that the murderer entered the tent from the rear, and left that way after he had performed the deed. Just an hour ago I telephoned to Long Island to ask if they still regard that as probable, and was told that they do."

He stopped to clear his throat. I would have liked to get my fingers around it to help. He resumed.

"It is also reported that you and Mr. Goodwin were among those interviewed, and that compels me to conclude, reluctantly, that Mr. Goodwin has failed to tell you of a conversation he had with my wife as she sat in our car outside the tent. I should explain that I was in the crowd in front, and when your speech was interrupted by the scream, and confusion resulted, I made my way around to the car, with some difficulty, and got in and drove away. I do not like tumult. My wife did not tell me of her conversation with Mr. Goodwin until after we got home. She regards it as unwise to talk while I am driving. What she told me was that Mr. Goodwin approached the car and spoke to her through the open window. He asked her if anyone—"

"If you please." Wolfe wiggled a finger. "Your assumption that he hasn't reported the conversation to me is incorrect. He has."

"What! He has?"

"Yes, sir. If you will—"

"Then you know that my wife is certain that no one entered the tent from the rear while the speeches were being made? No one but you and Mr. Goodwin? Absolutely certain? You know she told him that?"

"I know what she told him, yes. But if you will—"

"And you haven't told the police?"

"No, not yet. I would like—"

"Then she has no choice." Banau was on his feet. "It is even more disagreeable than I feared. She must communicate with them at once. This is terrible, a man of your standing, and the others too. It is terrible, but it must be done. In a country of law the law must be served."

He turned and headed for the door.

I left my chair. Stopping him and wrapping him up would have been no problem, but I was myself stopped by the expression on Wolfe's face. He looked relieved; he even looked pleased. I stared at him, and was still staring when the sound came of the front door closing. I stepped to the hall, saw that he was gone and hadn't forgotten his hat, and returned and stood at Wolfe's desk.

"Goody," I said. "Cream? Give me some."

He took in air, all the way, and let it out. "This is more like it," he declared. "I've had all the humiliation I can stand. Jumping out of my skin every time the phone rang. Did you notice how quickly I answered your ring upstairs? Afraid, by heaven, afraid to go into the tropical room to look over the Renanthera imschootiana! Now we know where we are."

"Yeah. Also where we soon will be. If it had been me I would have kept him at least long enough to tell him—"

"Shut up."

I did so. There are certain times when it is understood that I am not to badger, and the most important is when he leans back in his chair and shuts his eyes and his lips start to work. He pushes them out, pulls them in, out and in, out and in. . . . That means his brain has crashed the sound barrier. I have seen him, dealing with a tough one, go on with that lip action for up to an hour. I sat down at my desk, thinking I might as well be near the phone.

That time he didn't take an hour, not having one. More like eight minutes. He opened his eyes, straightened up, and spoke.

"Archie. Did he tell you where his wife was?"

"No. He told me nothing. He was saving it for you. She could have been in the drugstore at the corner, sitting in the phone booth."

He grunted. "Then we must clear out of here. I am going to find out which of them killed that man before we are all hauled in. The motive and the evidence will have to come later; the thing now is to identify him as a bone to toss to Mr. Delaney. Where is Saul?"

"At home, waiting to hear. Fred and Orrie—"

"We need only Saul. Call him. Tell him we are coming there at once. Where would Mr. Vetter have his conference?"

"I suppose at the MXO studio."

"Get him. And if Miss Korby is there, her also. And the others. You must get them all before they hear from Mr. Delaney. They are all to be at

Saul's place without delay. At the earliest possible moment. Tell them they are to meet and question the witness, and it is desperately urgent. If they balk I'll speak to them and—"

I had the phone, dialing.

S I X

AFTER THEY WERE all there and Wolfe started in, it took him less than fifteen minutes to learn which one was it. I might have managed it in fifteen days, with luck. If you like games you might lean back now, close your eyes and start pushing your lips out and in, and see how long it takes you to decide how you would do it. Fair enough, since you know everything that Wolfe and I knew. But get it straight; don't try to name him or come up with evidence that would nail him; the idea is, how do you use what you now know to put the finger on him? That was what Wolfe did, and I wouldn't expect more of you than of him.

Saul Panzer, below average in size but miles above it in savvy, lived alone on the top floor—living room, bedroom, kitchenette, and bath—of a remodeled house on Thirty-eighth Street between Lexington and Third. The living room was big, lighted with two floor lamps and two table lamps, even at seven o'clock of a July evening, because the blinds were drawn. One wall had windows, another was solid with books, and the other two had pictures and shelves that were cluttered with everything from chunks of minerals to walrus tusks. In the far corner was a grand piano.

Wolfe sent his eyes around and said, "This shouldn't take long."

He was in the biggest chair Saul had, by a floor lamp, almost big enough for him. I was on a stool to his left and front, and Saul was off to his right, on the piano bench. The chairs of the five customers were in an arc facing him. Of course it would have been sensible and desirable to arrange the seating so that the murderer was next to either Saul or me, but that wasn't practical since we had no idea which one it was, and neither did Wolfe.

"Where's the witness?" Griffin demanded. "Goodwin said she'd be here."

Wolfe nodded. "I know. Mr. Goodwin is sometimes careless with his pronouns. The witness is present." He aimed a thumb at the piano bench. "There. Mr. Saul Panzer, who is not only credible and confident but—"

"You said it was a woman!"

"There is another witness who is a woman; doubtless there will be oth-

ers when one of you goes on trial. The urgency Mr. Goodwin spoke of re-
lates to what Mr. Panzer will tell you. Before he does so, some explanation
is required."

"Let him talk first," Dick Vetter said, "and then explain. We've heard
from you already."

"I'll make it brief." Wolfe was unruffled. "It concerns the tape fastening on the flap of the rear entrance of the tent. As you know, Mr. Goodwin
tied it before we left to go to the platform, and when he and I entered the
tent later and left by the rear entrance it had been untied. By whom? Not
by someone entering from the outside, since there is a witness to testify
that no one had—"

James Korby cut in. "That's the witness we want to see. Goodwin said
she'd be here."

"You'll see her, Mr. Korby, in good time. Please bear with me. Therefore the tape had been untied by someone who had entered from the
front—by one of you four men. Why? The presumption is overwhelming
that it was untied by the murderer, to create and support the probability
that Philip Holt had been stabbed by someone who entered from the rear.
It is more than a presumption; it approaches certainty. So it seemed to me
that it was highly desirable, if possible, to learn who had untied the tape;
and I enlisted the services of Mr. Panzer." His head turned. "Saul, if you
please?"

Saul had his hand on a black leather case beside him on the bench.
"Do you want it all, Mr. Wolfe? How I got it?"

"Not at the moment, I think. Later, if they want to know. What you
have is more important than how you got it."

"Yes, sir." He opened the lid of the case and took something from it.
"I'd rather not explain how I got it because it might make trouble for
somebody."

I horned in. "What do you mean 'might'? You know damn well it
would make trouble for somebody."

"Okay, Archie, okay." His eyes went to the audience. "What I've got is
these photographs of fingerprints that were lifted from the tape on the flap
of the rear entrance of the tent. There are some blurry ones, but here are
four good ones. Two of the good ones are Mr. Goodwin's, and that leaves
two unidentified." He turned to the case and took things out. He cocked
his head to the audience. "The idea is, I take your prints and—"

"Not so fast, Saul." Wolfe's eyes went right, and left again. "You see
how it is, and you understand why Mr. Goodwin said it was urgent. Surely
those of you who did *not* untie the tape will not object to having your

prints compared with the photographs. If anyone does object he cannot complain if an inference is made. Of course there is the possibility that none of your prints will match the two unidentified ones in the photographs, and in that case the results will be negative and not conclusive. Mr. Panzer has the equipment to take your prints, and he is an expert. Will you let him?"

Glances were exchanged.

"What the hell," Vetter said. "Mine are on file anyway. Sure."

"Mine also," Griffin said. "I have no objection."

Paul Rago abruptly exploded. "Treeks again!"

All eyes went to him. Wolfe spoke. "No, Mr. Rago, no tricks. Mr. Panzer would prefer not to explain how he got the photographs, but he will if you insist. I assure you—"

"I don't mean treeks how he gets them." The sauce chef uncrossed his legs. "I mean what you said, it was the murderer who untied the tape. That is not necessary. I can say that was a lie! When I entered the tent and looked at him it seemed to me he did not breathe good, there was not enough air, and I went and untied the tape so the air could come through. So if you take my print and find it is like the photograph, what will that prove? Nothing at all. Nuh-theeng! So I say it is treeks again, and in this great land of freedom—"

I wasn't trying to panic him. I wasn't even going to touch him. And I had the Marley .38 in my pocket, and Saul had one too, so if he had tried to start something he would have got stopped quick. But using a gun, especially in a crowd, is always bad management unless you have to, and he was twelve feet away from me, and I got up and moved merely because I wanted to be closer. Saul had the same notion at the same instant, and the sight of us two heading for him, with all that he knew that we didn't know yet, was too much for him. He was out of his chair and plunging toward the door as I took my second step.

Then, of course, we had to touch him. I reached him first, not because I'm faster than Saul but because he was farther off. And the damn fool put up a fight, although I had him wrapped. He kicked Saul where it hurt, and knocked a lamp over, and bumped my nose with his skull. When he sank his teeth in my arm I thought, That will do for you, mister, and jerked the Marley from my pocket and slapped him above the ear, and he went down.

Turning, I saw that Dick Vetter had also wrapped his arms around someone, and she was neither kicking nor biting. In moments of stress people usually show what is really on their minds, even important public figures like TV stars. There wasn't a word about it in the columns next day.

SEVEN

I HAVE OFTEN wondered how Paul Rago felt when, at his trial a couple of months later, no evidence whatever was introduced about fingerprints. He knew then, of course, that it had been a treek and nothing but, that no prints had been lifted from the tape by Saul or anyone else, and that if he had kept his mouth shut and played along he might have been playing yet.

I once asked Wolfe what he would have done if that had happened.

He said, "It didn't happen."

I said, "What if it had?"

He said, "Pfui. The contingency was too remote to consider. It was as good as certain that the murderer had untied the tape. Confronted with the strong probability that it was about to be disclosed that his print was on the tape, he had to say something. He had to explain how it got there, and it was vastly preferable to do so voluntarily instead of waiting until evidence compelled it."

I hung on. "Okay, it was a good trick, but I still say what if?"

"And I still say it is pointless to consider remote contingencies. What if your mother had abandoned you in a tiger's cage at the age of three months? What would you have done?"

I told him I'd think it over and let him know.

As for motive, you can have three guesses if you want them, but you'll never get warm if you dig them out of what I have reported. In all the jabber in Wolfe's office that day, there wasn't one word that had the slightest bearing on why Philip Holt died, which goes to show why detectives get ulcers. No, I'm wrong; it was mentioned that Philip Holt liked women, and certainly that had a bearing. One of the women he had liked was Paul Rago's wife, an attractive blue-eyed number about half as old as her husband, and he was still liking her, and, unlike Flora Korby, she had liked him and proved it.

Paul Rago hadn't liked that.

LADY HILLARY

Janwillem van de Wetering

The Amsterdam mysteries of Janwillem van de Wetering have fascinated international audiences ever since the appearance of 1975's *Outsider in Amsterdam*.
Van de Wetering is still publishing today, his following as devoted as ever for
novels about a small group of Amsterdam cops who change and sometimes
grow because of their collision with the world of crime. The author has talked
about his attachment to Zen Buddhism and makes it clear that his vision of it
is frequently the subtext of his books and stories. Van de Wetering now lives in
Maine, a fact well presented in many of his recent books.

GOOD DAY, MA'AM Tourist Group Leader from America.
Welcome to the Tariand Isles of Niugini.

Your tourist group likes my little Pacific isle? I'm glad. I'm the chief
here, just a little chief. My great-grandfather Waku was a great chief who
became ruler, after much carefully planned and brilliantly executed interis-
land warfare, of all the Tariand Islands here in Pangea Bay on the east
coast of Niugini. Niugini is our name for Papua New Guinea. PNG (we
call it that too) is, next to the immensity of Greenland, this planet's biggest
island. Even so, few people know our country, except experienced travel-
ers, like yourself, ma'am, and your group.

I don't know America, but I did travel to Europe. After Independence,
in 1975, we thought we should introduce ourselves to our former masters,
the British, the Germans, the Dutch, the Portuguese. I was part of the ret-
inue of our prime minister; we wore three-piece suits and headgear made
out of casuari feathers. Everywhere we went we were mistaken for repre-
sentatives of some newborn African nation. We kept saying, "Papua New
Guinea, North of Australia," and a departmental secretary would say, ". . .
Ah . . ." and buy us lunch maybe. Hamburgers. French fries. In Bonn we
were fed sushi; that was nice, actually. We do care for fresh fish.

During the Second World War we were important, though, and even
American warriors admitted that my grandfather, Witu of the Tariand

Crocodile Clan of Niugini, was a great Papuan island chief. Lieutenant James Cosby of the U.S. Marines came back to present my grandfather with a Legion of Merit medal. We keep it in our Long House, it has its own shelf.

The medal came with this beautiful ribbon that I wear on my belt between these parrot feathers. Just one moment, I have to undo its clasp. Here you are, ma'am, you can pass the ribbon along to your fellow tourists. Chief Witu earned the great honor because he kept you Allieds informed about Japanese naval movements. My grandfather once tricked a Japanese destroyer (by observing and copying Japanese light signals) into breaking up on a reef. Chief Witu was also known for his cunning counsel.

My grandfather's wisdom once saved face for your Marine Corps. Shall I tell you what happened or would you rather take your group skin diving?

Your group's itinerary allows for an extra hour to spend on trivial matters? Good. We can all sit in the shade of the banyan tree there. See where the tree's air roots have formed a little cabin? That's where my throne is, I can look down on the people and direct their formal dancing. But there's no need for formality now. Some other time perhaps, maybe some of you would like to learn about our sacred dances, but for now . . . let me tell you. . . .

The Marine Corps face-saving matter was tricky, both personal and political. Lieutenant James Cosby, "Jim Bwana," as he liked us to call him, was accused of raping Leia, my beautiful sister, and cutting her throat afterward. Our murder suspect Jim Bwana was a splendid man, of course, not just a Marine warrior but a graduate of the, ahhh,—I can never say it right, *Havvard*(?) School as well. Do I pronounce that right? *Havvard*, yes? The American school of wizards? Good. Even so, in spite of his qualifications, Jim Bwana, liked and admired by all of us, nearly lost name and fame here but was saved by my father's father, chief Witu.

Isn't war fun?

I was only a boy then but never will I forget the glorious days when your war birds dueled with their Japanese counterparts in our sky, when our giant crocodiles slid into the lagoons looking for parachuted corpses, when dried chicken eggs and other exotic foods were served out of little green cans, when we tore gold braid off Japanese officer tunics and used it in our hairdos together with polished pieces we cut from spent cannon shells. Later the fun improved. There were Japanese landings, brief fights among the sharp eight-feet-high alun-alun grasses—we used our weapons.

I'm sorry, I'll try to be brief. I forget the other items in your program, skin diving, was it? I hope you won't be naked. We hear nakedness is rude in America and we can't abide rudeness. You won't be rude? That's nice. I am glad.

As I said, my mind wanders back sometimes, to throwing spears, or swinging them, like clubs.

We play golf now. Have you seen our course? Japanese tycoons fly their business jets out to Port Moresby on the mainland, then ferry across Pangea Bay in their hydrofoil. When they come ashore here I charge big money for entry and dues. Would any of you like to be a member? The memory of Jim Bwana will warrant a discount. Here is my card, for you, sir. We don't allow ladies on our course. You and your colleagues, when you plan to come out again, can fax me at my office so that I can confirm reservations. Winter months are quite busy.

We, male members of the Crocodile Clan, follow the warrior path. I'm glad to see white hair on your party's gentlemen's heads, it means the gents will remember the great war of the forties. Once in a while the sightseeing schooner out of Port Moresby brings us your anthropology students who need to fill up their lap-top computers. I get paid by the tourist agency to answer their questions. I tell them our war stories. It's all news to them. Sometimes those bright young folks stare at me as if they don't know nothing.

Oh dear . . .

Wearing a pig's tusk through my nose doesn't excuse use of the double negative. If Sister Cissy could hear me she'd rap my knuckles with that *bad* wooden ruler. Sister Cissy was an Australian nun who taught school here, before Independence, of course. The young Papuan sister who met you at the dock is now in charge of the Mission.

Pardon?

Yes, ma'am, when our nation was considered old enough to make its own decisions we, on this island, retained the Roman Catholic faith. We didn't make religious changes, but appearances changed somewhat. We're in the tropics here. You will have noticed the heat. So our sisters go topless, as far as we are concerned we consider that quite polite.

I'm sure Sister Cissy forgives that change, but I'm equally sure my use of the double negative will infuriate her spirit. I apologize to her spirit. You see, ma'am, now that we're seeing modern movies we tend to pick up bad language, but as for me, I do make an effort to practice your Queen's English.

Does America have a queen? I get confused sometimes. I only traveled to Europe, you see. You do have one now, right? The Lady Hillary? No? I thought I read that somewhere. *Time* magazine? No? She was on the cover. A lovely lady.

America, to me, is kind of a dream. Like movies.

What was that, ma'am? You were saying that violence on TV has an unfortunate influence on us native people?

That may be so, but here in Niugini we don't have TV yet. So far the prime minister says we don't need more advertising. He sees TV in Australia in hotel rooms and he says it's repulsive. All dead babies and fast food. We do see movies, though. In the Long House over there, the very tall building with the sloping roofs, I keep a VCR and a large-size monitor that a Japanese group gave us. The old Caterpillar generator Sister Cissy left makes it go. My cousin the schooner captain brings out videotapes that he copies in Port Moresby. Kick-ass movies are great fun, ma'am. The language may be bad, but the action is simply splendid. We particularly like Chief Schwarzenegger, he who married Lady Hillary of the Kennedy tribe.

Oh, I see. Pardon our ignorance, ma'am. We don't get too many newspapers here. Clint? Clint Eastwood? Wrong again? Clint Ton? I see, *Clinton*. Just a president, you say? I'm glad you explained. I'll try to remember.

Shall I tell your group about the time your Marine Corps nearly lost face, about splendid Jim Bwana and my poor sister Leia?

Jim Bwana and his men were dropped off a U.S. Navy motor patrol boat when the Battle of the Coral Sea was going on. As you remember, a flotilla of Japanese invasion vessels, aimed at Australia, was defeated between Guadalcanal and these islands. It is impossible to forget the views we enjoyed then. The first great happening was Japanese warships sailing by in formation. I had never seen anything like it—those big light-gray-colored vessels with their smoothly swiveling guns, the bright flags used for communication, their sea planes being catapulted off their rear decks, scouting everywhere. Whenever the warships came by, theirs or yours, it didn't matter, I ran along our beaches, with the other boys behind me, screaming and waving. We had no idea what we were looking at, but we were so happy it drove us crazy. Like the Speechless One here, but she is always that way. . . .

Then you folks, in Mustangs, suddenly dove out of the sky and bombed us. You thought the Japanese had taken over our village and lands but what you saw were women tilling our fields (they still did that then; now they insist we take turns) and little girls manning bamboo lookout towers, keeping seed-eating birds away. The Mustang pilots must have been nervous, they kept strafing and bombing. Us males happened to have an important ceremony going on, me and some other boys were being prepared for coming of age. Dressed in my creamy white parrot-feather skirt and bright red-clay ghost mask, I was stomping about the village square, and suddenly air devils dove down and the village was burning. Wasn't that an intimidating initiation? I thought I had done something wrong at first. Fortunately you missed our two community temples. Both the Long House and the Boys House are considered as kind of holy. There are treasures inside. Used to elevate our spirits. You didn't miss my father and brother. They both got hit. My brother Masset died instantly, my father took his time, having many helpful hallucinations before he floated off on the turtle shell.

Yes, ma'am, quite a few women and girls were hit too.

Then the Japanese sent a boat ashore, to see why you bombed us.

No, ma'am, Sister Cissy had left us already. She died before the war and the other Australian nuns had fled to their convent in Brisbane. They had been teaching us knitting and Jesus and how to wash hands and relieve ourselves before dinner and be respectful to our masters. I forget how to knit, but we still love Jesus. The Japanese had Buddha. He lives in a little mahogany box, with hinged doors that open; you get to burn incense and clap your hands and sing. I like Buddha too. We keep him in the Long House, in the box that we captured from the Japanese captain. Our holy sisters keep a little Jesus in their church, but we have our own big Jesus in the Long House. My brother Masset carved him long ago, from specially selected pieces of driftwood that he dovetailed together. The big statue is still in service, in spite of the squirrel living in Jesus' stomach. The squirrel has long whiskers, he takes part in some of the ceremonies, running about and squeaking. We also have Elvis Presley, he is a painting done by the Speechless One here. We started with a poster that a sea captain gave us, but the paper wore out. The Speechless One loves him.

Yes, ma'am? How did Sister Cissy die? Unnecessarily, I'm afraid. There is a hill behind the village that we can climb after we have purified ourselves. It's just for sitting, gazing, quietness, that sort of thing. Sister Cissy wanted to grow tomatoes on that hill's slope. We warned her, but she was somewhat strong-minded and started pulling up weeds, tearing the soil, and one of the hill's devil-lizards bit her bottom. Those devil-lizards are quick. They're big too, ten feet long, including the tail of course. They like to eat our goats, but they eat us too if we make ourselves defenseless by not paying attention. Sister Cissy got bitten badly. Afterward she hit the lizard with her rake and he backed off and hid in the bushes. This happened over fifty years ago, before we had penicillin here.

Let me sing you the story while the Speechless One plays her bones. All set?

Go!

Devil-lizard doesn't mind being chased off, he can think. He waits be-hind bushes for Sister Cissy to weaken. My grandfather, Chief Witu, can think too. Devil-lizard concentrates on Sister Cissy and grandfather con-centrates on Devil-lizard, and gets him. We roast Devil-lizard, have a death feast for the sister. Devil-lizard enters by the mouth, Sister Cissy enters by the ear. (Bone music. Bone music.)

Don't let the sacred Speechless One frighten you. She carries the crazi-ness of this island, but we keep her in check. We always have one, you see. Craziness is so useful.

No, the Speechless One is not always female. In fact, I think there is a mistake here, but somehow this generation's Speechless One entered a woman. Could it be the greenhouse effect? Or nuclear carelessness some-where? Worrying, somehow. Very.

Okay, Speechless One, that's enough now. Sit down. Yes, you have lovely legs. Fold them. That's better. Thank you. Please relax, dear.

Where was I? Sister Cissy's bottom? We used herbs on Sister Cissy's wound but couldn't stop the lizard bite's infection. A high fever set in that resulted in death. We buried the body for a while, within view of the Long House, within earshot too. We did a lot of drumming and chanting and so forth, to prepare Sister Cissy's bones.

Yes, sir. It does get a tad chilly here in the evenings, could be the sea breeze. Makes you shiver, doesn't it? I have the same trouble.

Any other questions?

What the Japanese were like?

A little fishy, ma'am, reminded me of that seagull I ate when my canoe broke on a reef during a storm, and I had to wait for my father to find me. We are what we eat. That makes seagulls flying fish. Japanese are walking fish. Australian soldiers, we met quite a few of those too, with those hats that curl up on one side; Australians are sort of muttony and Americans kind of beefy.

Ha ha.

Sorry, ma'am. Just kidding—I beg your pardon. We're not cannibals on the Tariand Isles. We do have some customs, of course—what tribe hasn't?—but for really consuming human flesh I'd have to refer you to the mainland. Foreign rule stopped flesh eating for some time, as you know. We were colonized for, oh, over a hundred years, I should think. There were the Dutch out west side, the Germans up north side, the British/Australians down here, south and east, and roving Portuguese in the past. Your white tribes' customs differ a little but all you folks agreed that we shouldn't catch and eat each other. "Headhunting," as you called our pastime, took up too much time. Instead you had us pick coconuts to make margarine or kill off birds of paradise to stick feathers in your girlfriends' hats. All work, no fun for us, all fun, no work for you. Tribal warfare is our fun, though, and now that we're on our own again it's drifting back on the mainland.

Ancient customs, something to keep us busy.

How about us island people? Well, everything changes so fast—I'm not too sure. I have no way of knowing for certain, but maybe some of our young men still practice a little customs. The young men are very much on their own, you see. We allow our boys some privacy, to grow up in. Adults live rather dull lives, they'll have enough of that later. Eventually they'll be like I am now, like to play a little golf. Some fishing in the afternoon. A nap. Watch Chief Arnold in the Long House. Chief Schwarzenegger, on the big monitor, with the VCR the Japanese gave us—that's right, ma'am.

What kind of customs do our young ones practice?

Our young fellows, from fourteen through seventeen, not an easy age as you may recall, live in the Boys House over there. With the skulls on the veranda. They're plastic, you know. I bought them in London, they came in flat cartons, all broken up in parts, we had to glue the parts together. I had sticky fingers for a week. They do look real, don't they now?

Well, yes, we do train our boys a little, but apart from weekly instruction we pay no attention to what our successors are doing. For instruction the boys join us in our Long House. There's ritual, there's storytelling by the chief—our sorcerer, Mr. Waya, is in charge of ritual. We beat wooden drums and shake lizard-skin tambourines (baby rat skulls are the jingles), and the Speechless One rattles Sister Cissy's thighbones. The Long House is dark but the shadows are dancing. Hollow-eyed images of the ancestors look down from the rafters. There is always a draft in the Long House, even if there is no wind outside. It rustles the ancestors' grass skirts and Leia's coral necklace. Mr. Waya's herbal student burns twigs, roots, and leaves. The wooden Jesus statue, pale white, lifts its arms while Buddha smiles quietly in his box. The foreign chiefs smile too, especially Chief Elvis when we do his "You're Nothing but a Hound Dog." You know the hymn? Big Bart's Marine fighting knife squeaks in its sheath. We don't have Sergeant Big Bart's bones here but the Speechless One made a mask that catches his likeness. Now that you mention it, I haven't seen that mask lately. I hope she didn't take it out of its niche.

Well, never mind.

So our big boys are humming, the younger ones, with the clear high voices, chant "Heartbreak Hotel." We also have our own hymns. After an hour of good chanting and burning there's that strong acrid smell that shows things are beginning to jump a little.

Ha!

Excuse me. I get too enthusiastic.

No, ma'am, girls are not allowed either in the Long House or in the Boys House.

After instruction in the Long House our young men go back to their Boys House.

What do they do there? Play cards, I think. Smoke Benson & Hedges, I imagine, that's a brand of cigarettes that is advertised on billboards here: The pictures show handsome warriors in ceremonial dress impressing attentive, beautiful girls that look like my dead sister Leia. Everybody smokes. Or the boys drink Budweiser maybe. The schooner brings beer once a week, taking wood sculptures in return. We like to chisel palm-wood on this island. Our specialty. Here's an example of our art. See? Big penis on one side, gun butt on the other. The butt side of the art object curves. The Portuguese raiders, a hundred years ago, were armed with that kind of handgun. Portuguese "blackbirders" didn't do too well here, though. We caught some, but most of them died by natural causes. Or so I heard.

Yes. That's true, ma'am. I did live in the Boys House myself and do recall that in my time . . . of course . . . I don't know if such a pastime would still be popular now. Each of our Tariand islands had a custom then, when I was a boy—but, as I said, that's a long time ago now—of "hunting *Her*."

"Hunting *Her*," involved sending scouts to the neighboring islands to look for *Her*, for that island's female principle. My sister Leia, on this island, was a candidate to be the female principle, we knew that, but the custom said that we could only use a *Her* from another island. It meant that we had to protect Leia, for boys from another island would be likely to be attracted.

So, when I was a boy living in our Boys House . . .

What the new building is on the other side of the village? Ah, you noticed, did you? Oh, some newfangled idea we haven't quite dealt with. We may have to pull that building down soon, but please don't interrupt, ma'am. I'm trying to tell this story.

So once our scouts determined what girl *Her* inhabited in one of the other islands, we would carefully note that girl's habits, her timetable, and so forth, when and where she might be alone. Then . . . you really want to hear the story, ma'am? You're sure? Not too rough for your group? I notice it's mostly female. Okay, I continue.

There might be some sick boys who would stay behind in our home island's Boys House to light and tend fires, burn twigs, make the acrid smoke I mentioned. Us others would sneak out in a war canoe shaped like a two-headed crocodile. You saw the canoe boats in our harbor? Tourist display now, but they were all in use once. We kept our paddles razor sharp so that they can also serve as weapons. Us boys, naked, rubbed with oils, honed by all sorts of war games that we used to play all the time, were weapons ourselves. We would have waited for a moonless, windless night. Once on the chosen island (we have six islands here) we would hide in the jungle that surrounds the village, wait for daybreak, for *Her* to show herself, catch the girl, sling her body from a pole, race back to the canoe, wait for nightfall, paddle home.

And then?

Hmmm. I don't know whether your anthropologists ever got that part of our customs right. Eating human flesh is not for sustenance, you know. We keep pigs for that. The "hunting *Her*" custom intends to join spirits, there is no room for the stomach. If boys partake of *Her* it's to harmonize their manhood.

Oh yes, I'm afraid, in those long-bygone days, we did eat *Her*. There were other sacred customs too, that came first.

Pardon? You say "rape"?

How could we? Poor girl? Perhaps. But think of the honor, though, how the chosen one knew that she did represent the highest, the most elevated part of half of what goes on. How she was the essence of what all men are looking for? Forever?

Think of the custom's aftermath too. To us participating boys, the adventure was fraught with danger. If we were caught, we died. There was always revenge when the boys from the other island would notice that their divine one was missing and send their scouts to even things out. If they found us they'd have to kill us. Of course they'd also come to find *Her* on this island. Keep us on our toes, so to speak.

Disgusting, you say?

Remember First Lieutenant James Cosby, "Jim Bwana"?

What was he suspected of doing? How come Leia got raped; then murdered?

Guilty?

Perhaps you'd like to drink some coconut juice first? We serve Heineken too. A Perrier for the ladies?

You are refreshed?

Good.

Leia and I had different mothers. Leia's mother was a *Her* who never got caught. We knew Leia was *Her* too and made an effort to guard her.

You saw our girls when you walked up the ramp from the schooner this morning? Arranged into two rows, facing each other, leaving just enough space so that our visitors can shuffle through? Wearing grass-minis? Perfumed with squirrel secretion? Chanting and bopping while the Speechless One taps her bones to carry the chant? The girls brushing the gentlemen in your party with their breasts? Our new local nuns clapping and smiling?

Leia was many times as attractive.

The American Marines liked to look at Leia but she had eyes for Jim Bwana only. The lieutenant and his men came to set up radio equipment and to train us as spotters, but when the Japanese landed patrols too the Marines stayed on. In order not to attract attention, the Marines killed with their knives.

Later, when the Japanese had left the area and the Marines had little to do, Jim Bwana had a long jetty built into the ocean. The Marines constructed a little thatch-covered hut at the end of the jetty. Jim Bwana liked to sit there quietly for hours on end. I think he was thinking of Leia. He probably knew she was *Her*. Leia kept showing herself to the lieutenant, finding things to do in the yard when he came back from his jetty, smiling, reaching up to pick flowers or fruits.

Even good men are bad sometimes. You have noticed? There was a good/bad man in Lieutenant Jim's war group. His name was Sergeant Big Bart. The sergeant was driven crazy by Leia's smiles and movements, directed at Jim Bwana, who seemed not to notice. Not expecting a raid from a neighboring island—the Great War was still on—us boys weren't paying attention. Big Bart broke into my sister's cabin one night and raped her. That same night Jim Bwana, made bold by my sister's seductive invitations, finally gathered courage and knocked on Leia's door. Inside Leia was about to scream for help. Big Bart, hearing the lieutenant's voice, cut Leia's throat. Big Bart escaped through the window. The lieutenant, perturbed by Leia's throaty death-gurgle, entered the cabin. He tried to help Leia, had her leaning against his chest. There was blood all over his tunic. Big Bart had left his knife. The lieutenant wasn't armed. Seeing Leia was dead, the lieutenant panicked. He left, leaving footprints.

We found Leia's corpse in the morning, the blood, the knife, the footprints that enabled us to track the lieutenant, who was waiting for us in his thatched hut at the end of the jetty.

We liked Jim Bwana fine, and we understood what he had been doing, but custom demanded the intruder's death.

We were all very sorry, but our brothers, the huge lagoon crocodiles, were hungry now. We would have to feed them.

The lieutenant told my grandfather, Chief Witu, that he was innocent, but the evidence (although we didn't understand why he hadn't tried to eat her) was overwhelming. Even the Marines didn't believe their own chief. Chief Witu kept quiet. He just nodded, had the lieutenant locked up in the bamboo cage behind the Long House, and appointed me as a guard. That night I heard my grandfather ask Jim Bwana if his Havvard (I wish I could say it right) training suggested a solution. Jim Bwana said it did not. He had no idea who was the real killer. When he entered Leia's house there was just blood, and the corpse.

Sergeant Big Bart had gone off to check radio equipment on a hill on the other side of our island.

While all this happened word came from the mainland that the Great War was coming to an end, and we knew our friends, the Marines, were waiting to be picked up by a warship.

There were some twenty victorious white Marines and some five thousand of us black, friendly, armed, and war-trained *Fuzzyheads*, that's what we were called then. It was a term of endearment. We had been of use. There were a few million of us in the islands and on the mainland. It was rude to repay us for our wartime help with what a Marine lieutenant had done to Leia, daughter of a chief.

As I said before, the matter was tricky.

The Speechless One of that time played Sister Cissy's thighbones and Mr. Waya, after consulting a cracked tortoise shell in the Long House while my father made the acrid smell, set a date and time for pronouncing a verdict. My grandfather's decision could be predicted. Weren't the facts clear? My sister's dead body on the straw mat? The Marine fighting knife on the floor? A man's seed in her shell? Lieutenant Jim's bloody trail leading out of the house toward the jetty, ending in the thatched hut at the end where we found him crying?

So what to do?

My father said that, as the tortoise shell indicated that his final decision had to be reached late that night, it might be nice to have a knife-throwing match first. All available Marines and quite a few of our warriors entered the contest. The target was a female figure cut from a lizard's skin that was strapped between bamboo poles. Just as the first contestant was about to throw his knife, a heavy rain poured down, as it always did at that time during that part of the rainy season. My father ordered that all knives had to be put on a table while we waited for the downpour to stop. While Mr. Waya beat a drum and the Speechless One danced, I replaced one of the Marines' knives with the one that had killed Leia.

The rain stopped, everybody went to the table to pick up his knife. One Marine said his weapon was missing. I pointed at the sharp flat dagger that was left on the table.

"Not mine."

"Whose?" my grandfather asked.

All the Americans studied the knife. Although Marine knives are standard issue and apparently look alike, they don't stay that way. After a while each Marine knows his own weapon, and those of his friends, by individual dents, stubborn rust spots, blemishes on the handle, or just the feel of the weapon.

Several Marines declared the murderous knife to belong to Sergeant Big Bart. As they were prepared to swear to the truth of their statements, Jim Bwana was released at once.

Beg pardon, ma'am?

Ah, you want to know what happened to Big Bart, the sergeant? He wasn't there. Feeling guilty, Big Bart was wandering all over our island, on all sorts of errands—catching Japanese stragglers, looking for downed pilots, that sort of thing.

Well, we first had a feast. We were ready, of course. Prize pigs were slaughtered, big grouper fish were lanced with skewers to be rotated above coals, a multivegetable stew simmered, crackly tree bugs were being roasted, the girls were lining up for their dance. Us boys were shaking the rain sticks. Leia's image moved in the breeze. We drank captured sake. Big Bart came back in the middle of the party, felt something was wrong, and took off again.

No, ma'am, a lizard got the sergeant. Us boys found Big Bart on the same hill slope as Sister Cissy. Wound fever had almost killed him then. Sergeant Big Bart died as we carried him in. The Marines had left, we sent the metal tag we took off Big Bart's neck to the mainland, by schooner.

The body?

Crocodiles ate the body, ma'am. We are of the Crocodile Clan, as I said.

You have to go now?

Thank you, ma'am. We appreciate presents, but on this island we sometimes do things the other way round. Today we don't accept presents. Here is a cassette for each of you. Mr. Waya composed the music. Here, I'll play one for you on this boombox.

You liked the music?

You heard the thighbones?

Excuse me, ma'am?

The crying in between the Speechless One's percussion? No, that isn't Big Bart, that's just the sound of large bats with flat faces that fly between the palm tops, looking for coconuts. I tried to chase them away when we were making the recording but the Speechless One was unhappy. Yes, the big bats do sound rather guilty. Like little male ghost voices, you say? Sorry for catching all those girls? Well, we only caught one girl once every three years or so. It's a custom, you see, with a very deep meaning. Religious, you might say.

So . . . have a safe journey home and please give my regards to Lady Hillary, do tell her to be careful.

Yes, aren't our girls noisy? The Girls House is having a ceremony again. Preparing for something or other? Yes, it does rather seem so. Why they keep chanting "Abau, Abau"? I don't really know. "Abau" is our word for "male principle." What those war canoes are doing in the cove near their building? Our nuns have been encouraging the girls to learn how to paddle.

Times are changing?

Who that handsome boy is? He is my son Kokoda, isn't he an exceptional fellow? A perfect male. A little fearful maybe.

What is troubling you, Kokoda? The idea that the girls on the other islands, in their newfangled Girls Houses, are chanting "Abau" too?

THIS IS DEATH

Donald E. Westlake

It's an accepted fact that Donald E. Westlake has excelled at every single sub-genre the mystery field has to offer—humorous books (*Scared Monster*); terri-fying books (*The Ax*, about a man who wants vengeance on the company that downsized him out of a job, and probably Westlake's most accomplished novel); and hard-boiled books (the Parker series, a benchmark in the noir world of professional thieves). One learns from his books that Westlake the man is possessed of a remarkable intelligence, and that he can translate that intelli-gence into plot, character, and spiffy prose with what appears to be astonishing ease. He is the sort of writer other writers study endlessly; every Westlake novel has something to teach authors, no matter how long they've been at the word processor. And he seems to have been discovered—at last and long overdue—by a mass audience. He's never written a dull book or a sloppy one. And given his enormous output, that is saying a lot indeed. His most recent novel is *The Hook*, a scathing look at the business of being an author.

IT'S HARD NOT to believe in ghosts when you are one. I hanged my-self in a fit of truculence—stronger than pique, but not so dignified as despair—and regretted it before the thing was well begun. The instant I kicked the chair away I wanted it back, but gravity was turning my former wish to its present command; the chair would not right itself from where it lay on the floor, and my 193 pounds would not cease to urge downward from the rope thick around my neck.

There was pain, of course, quite horrible pain centered in my throat, but the most astounding thing was the way my cheeks seemed to swell. I could barely see over their round red hills, my eyes staring in agony at the door, *willing* someone to come in and rescue me, though I knew there was no one in the house, and in any event the door was carefully locked. My kicking legs caused me to twist and turn, so that sometimes I faced the door and some-times the window, and my shivering hands struggled with the rope so deep in my flesh I could barely find it and most certainly could not pull it loose.

I was frantic and terrified, yet at the same time my brain possessed a cold corner of aloof observation. I seemed now to be everywhere in the room at once, within my writhing body but also without, seeing my frenzied spasms, the thick rope, the heavy beam, the mismatched pair of lit bedside lamps throwing my convulsive double shadow on the walls, the closed locked door, the white-curtained window with its shade drawn all the way down. *This is death*, I thought, and I no longer wanted it, now that the choice was gone forever.

My name is—was—Edward Thornburn, and my dates are 1938–1977. I killed myself just a month before my fortieth birthday, though I don't believe the well-known pangs of that milestone had much if anything to do with my action. I blame it all (as I blamed most of the errors and failures of my life) on my sterility. Had I been able to father children my marriage would have remained strong, Emily would not have been unfaithful to me, and I would not have taken my own life in a final fit of truculence.

The setting was the guestroom of our house in Barnstaple, Connecticut, and the time was just after seven p.m.; deep twilight, at this time of year. I had come home from the office—I was a Realtor, a fairly lucrative occupation in Connecticut, though my income had been falling off recently—shortly before six, to find the note on the kitchen table: "Antiquing with Greg. Afraid you'll have to make your own dinner. Sorry. Love, Emily."

Greg was the one; Emily's lover. He owned an antique shop out on the main road toward New York, and Emily filled a part of her days as his ill-paid assistant. I knew what they did together in the back of the shop on those long midweek afternoons when there were no tourists, no antique collectors to disturb them. I knew, and I'd known for more than three years, but I had never decided how to deal with my knowledge. The fact was, I blamed myself, and therefore I had no way to *behave* if the ugly subject were ever to come into the open.

So I remained silent, but not content. I was discontent, unhappy, angry, resentful—truculent.

I'd tried to kill myself before. At first with the car, by steering it into an oncoming truck (I swerved at the last second, amid howling horns) and by driving it off a cliff into the Connecticut River (I slammed on the brakes at the very brink, and sat covered in perspiration for half an hour before backing away) and finally by stopping athwart one of the few level crossings left in this neighborhood. But no train came for 20 minutes, and my truculence wore off, and I drove home.

Later I tried to slit my wrists, but found it impossible to push sharp metal into my own skin. Impossible. The vision of my naked wrist and that shining steel so close together washed my truculence completely out of my mind. Until the next time.

With the rope; and then I succeeded. Oh, totally, oh, fully I succeeded. My legs kicked at air, my fingernails clawed at my throat, my bulging eyes stared out over my swollen purple cheeks, my tongue thickened and grew bulbous in my mouth, my body jigged and jangled like a toy at the end of a string, and the pain was excruciating, horrible, not to be endured. I can't endure it, I thought, it can't be endured. Much worse than knife slashings was the knotted strangled pain in my throat, and my head ballooned with pain, pressure outward, my face turning black, my eyes no longer human, the pressure in my head building and building as though I would explode. Endless horrible pain, not to be endured, but going on and on.

My legs kicked more feebly. My arms sagged, my hands dropped to my sides, my fingers twitched uselessly against my sopping trouser legs, my head hung at an angle from the rope, I turned more slowly in the air, like a broken windchime on a breezeless day. The pains lessened, in my throat and head, but never entirely stopped.

And now I saw that my distended eyes had become lusterless, gray. The moisture had dried on the eyeballs, they were as dead as stones. And yet I could see them, my own eyes, and when I widened my vision I could see my entire body, turning, hanging, no longer twitching, and with horror I realized I was dead.

But *present*. Dead, but still present, with the scraping ache still in my throat and the bulging pressure still in my head. Present, but no longer in that used-up clay, that hanging meat; I was suffused through the room, like indirect lighting, everywhere present but without a source. What happens now? I wondered, dulled by fear and strangeness and the continuing pains, and I waited, like a hovering mist, for whatever would happen next.

But nothing happened. I waited; the body became utterly still; the double shadow on the wall showed no vibration; the bedside lamps continued to burn; the door remained shut and the window shade drawn; and nothing happened.

What *now*? I craved to scream the question aloud, but I could not. My throat ached, but I had no throat. My mouth burned, but I had no mouth. Every final strain and struggle of my body remained imprinted in my mind, but I had no body and no brain and no *self*, no substance. No power to speak, no power to move myself, no power to remove myself from this room and this suspended corpse. I could only wait here, and wonder, and go on waiting.

There was a digital clock on the dresser opposite the bed, and when it first occurred to me to look at it the numbers were 7:21—perhaps twenty minutes after I'd kicked the chair away, perhaps fifteen minutes since I'd died. Shouldn't something happen, shouldn't some *change* take place?

The clock read 9:11 when I heard Emily's Volkswagen drive around to the back of the house. I had left no note, having nothing I wanted to say to anyone and in any event believing my own dead body would be eloquent enough, but I hadn't thought I would be *present* when Emily found me. I was justified in my action, however much I now regretted having taken it, I was justified, I knew I was justified, but I didn't want to see her face when she came through that door. She had wronged me, she was the cause of it, she would have to know that as well as I, but I didn't want to see her face.

The pains increased, in what had been my throat, in what had been my head. I heard the back door slam, far away downstairs, and I stirred like air currents in the room, but I didn't leave. I couldn't leave.

"Ed? Ed? It's me, hon!"

I know it's you. I must go away now, I can't stay here, I must go away. Is there a God? Is this my soul, this hovering presence? *Hell* would be better than this, take me away to Hell or wherever I'm to go, don't leave me here!

She came up the stairs, calling again, walking past the closed guest-room door. I heard her go into our bedroom, heard her call my name, heard the beginnings of apprehension in her voice. She went by again, out there in the hall, went downstairs, became quiet.

What was she doing? Searching for a note perhaps, some message from me. Looking out the window, seeing again my Chevrolet, knowing I must be home. Moving through the rooms of this old house, the original structure a barn nearly 200 years old, converted by some previous owner just after the Second World War, bought by me twelve years ago, furnished by Emily—and Greg—from their interminable, damnable, awful antiques. Shaker furniture, Colonial furniture, hooked rugs and quilts, the old yellow pine tables, the faint sense always of being in some slightly shabby minor museum, this house that I had bought but never loved. I'd bought it for Emily, I did everything for Emily, because I knew I could never do the one thing for Emily that mattered. I could never give her a child.

She was good about it, of course. Emily *is* good, I never blamed her, never completely blamed *her* instead of myself. In the early days of our marriage she made a few wistful references, but I suppose she saw the effect they had on me, and for a long time she has said nothing. But I have known.

The beam from which I had hanged myself was a part of the original building, a thick hand-hewed length of aged timber eleven inches square, chevroned with the marks of the hatchet that had shaped it. A strong beam, it would support my weight forever. It would support my weight until I was found and cut down. Until I was found.

The clock read 9:23 and Emily had been in the house twelve minutes when she came upstairs again, her steps quick and light on the old wood, approaching, pausing, stopping. "Ed?"

The doorknob turned.

The door was locked, of course, with the key on the inside. She'd have to break it down, have to call someone else to break it down, perhaps she wouldn't be the one to find me after all. Hope rose in me, and the pains receded.

"Ed? Are you in there?" She knocked at the door, rattled the knob, called my name several times more, then abruptly turned and ran away downstairs again, and after a moment I heard her voice, murmuring and unclear. She had called someone, on the phone.

Greg, I thought, and the throat-rasp filled me, and I wanted this to be the end. I wanted to be taken away, dead body and living soul, taken away. I wanted everything to be finished.

She stayed downstairs, waiting for him, and I stayed upstairs, waiting for them both. Perhaps she already knew what she'd find up here, and that's why she waited below.

I didn't mind about Greg, about being present when he came in. I didn't mind about *him*. It was Emily I minded.

The clock read 9:44 when I heard tires on the gravel at the side of the house. He entered, I heard them talking down there, the deeper male voice slow and reassuring, the lighter female voice quick and frightened, and then they came up together, neither speaking. The doorknob turned, jiggled, rattled, and Greg's voice called, "Ed?"

After a little silence Emily said, "He wouldn't—He wouldn't *do* anything, would he?"

"Do anything?" Greg sounded almost annoyed at the question. "What do you mean, do anything?"

"He's been so depressed, he's—Ed!" And forcibly the door was rattled, the door was shaken in its frame.

"Emily, don't. Take it easy."

"I shouldn't have called you," she said. "Ed, *please!*"

"Why not? For heaven's sake, Emily—"

"Ed, *please* come out, don't scare me like this!"

"Why *shouldn't* you call me, Emily?"

"Ed isn't stupid, Greg. He's—"

There was then a brief silence, pregnant with the hint of murmuring. They thought me still alive in here, they didn't want me to hear Emily say, "He *knows*, Greg, he knows about us."

The murmurings sifted and shifted, and then Greg spoke loudly, "That's ridiculous. Ed? Come out, Ed, let's talk this over." And the door-knob rattled and clattered, and he sounded annoyed when he said, "We must get in, that's all. Is there another key?"

"I think all the locks up here are the same. Just a minute."

They were. A simple skeleton key would open any interior door in the house. I waited, listening, knowing Emily had gone off to find another key, knowing they would soon come in together, and I felt such terror and revulsion for Emily's entrance that I could feel myself shimmer in the room, like a reflection in a warped mirror. Oh, can I at least stop seeing? In life I had eyes, but also eyelids, I could shut out the intolerable, but now I was only a presence, a total presence, I *could not* stop my awareness.

The rasp of key in lock was like rough metal edges in my throat; my memory of a throat. The pain flared in me, and through it I heard Emily asking what was wrong, and Greg answering, "The key's in it, on the other side."

"Oh, dear God! Oh, Greg, what has he done?"

"We'll have to take the door off its hinges," he told her. "Call Tony. Tell him to bring the toolbox."

"Can't you push the key through?"

Of course he could, but he said, quite determinedly, "Go *on*, Emily," and I realized then he had no intention of taking the door down. He simply wanted her away when the door was first opened. Oh, very good, *very* good!

"All right," she said doubtfully, and I heard her go away to phone Tony. A beetle-browed young man with great masses of black hair and an olive complexion, Tony lived in Greg's house and was a kind of handyman. He did work around the house and was also (according to Emily) very good at restoration of antique furniture; stripping paint, reassembling broken parts, that sort of thing.

There was now a renewed scraping and rasping at the lock, as Greg struggled to get the door open before Emily's return. I found myself feeling unexpected warmth and liking toward Greg. He wasn't a bad person; an opportunist with my wife, but not in general a bad person. Would he marry her now? They could live in this house, he'd had more to do with its furnishing than I. Or would this room hold too grim a memory, would Emily have to sell the house, live elsewhere? She might have to sell at a low price; as a Realtor, I knew the difficulty in selling a house where a suicide has taken place. No matter how much they may joke about it, people are still afraid of the supernatural. Many of them would believe this room was haunted.

It was then I finally realized the room *was* haunted. With me! *I'm a ghost*, I thought, thinking the word for the first time, in utter blank astonishment. I'm a ghost.

Oh, how dismal! To hover here, to be a boneless fleshless aching *presence* here, to be a kind of ectoplasmic mildew seeping through the days and nights, alone, unending, a stupid pain-racked misery-filled observer of the comings and goings of strangers—she *would* sell the house, she'd have to, I was sure of that. Was this my punishment? The punishment of the suicide, the solitary hell of him who takes his own life. To remain forever a sentient nothing, bound by a force greater than gravity itself to the place of one's finish.

I was distracted from this misery by a sudden agitation in the key on this side of the lock. I saw it quiver and jiggle like something alive, and then it popped out—it seemed to *leap* out, itself a suicide leaping from a cliff—and clattered to the floor, and an instant later the door was pushed open and Greg's ashen face stared at my own purple face, and after the astonishment and horror, his expression shifted to revulsion—and contempt?—and he backed out, slamming the door. Once more the key turned in the lock, and I heard him hurry away downstairs.

The clock read 9:58. *Now* he was telling her. *Now* he was giving her a drink to calm her. *Now* he was phoning the police. *Now* he was talking to her about whether or not to admit their affair to the police; what would they decide?

"Noooooooooo!"

The clock read 10:07. What had taken so long? Hadn't he even called the police yet?

She was coming up the stairs, stumbling and rushing, she was pounding on the door, screaming my name. I shrank into the corners of the room, I *felt* the thuds of her fists against the door, I cowered from her. She can't come in, dear God don't let her in! I don't care what she's done, I don't care about anything, just don't let her see me! *Don't let me see her!*

Greg joined her. She screamed at him, he persuaded her, she raved, he argued, she demanded, he denied. "Give me the key. Give me the key."

Surely he'll hold out, surely he'll take her away, surely he's stronger, more forceful.

He gave her the key.

No. *This* cannot be endured. *This* is the horror beyond all else. She came in, she walked into the room, and the sound she made will always live inside me. That cry wasn't human; it was the howl of every creature that has ever despaired. *Now* I know what despair is, and why I called my own state mere truculence.

Now that it was too late, Greg tried to restrain her, tried to hold her shoulders and draw her from the room, but she pulled away and crossed the room toward . . . not toward *me*. I was everywhere in the room, driven by pain and remorse, and Emily walked toward the carcass. She looked at it almost tenderly, she even reached up and touched its swollen cheek. "Oh, Ed," she murmured.

The pains were as violent now as in the moments before my death. The slashing torment in my throat, the awful distension in my head, they made me squirm in agony all over again; but I *could not* feel her hand on my cheek.

Greg followed her, touched her shoulder again, spoke her name, and immediately her face dissolved, she cried out once more and wrapped her arms around the corpse's legs and clung to it, weeping and gasping and uttering words too quick and broken to understand. Thank *God* they were too quick and broken to understand!

Greg, that fool, did finally force her away, though he had great trouble breaking her clasp on the body. But he succeeded, and pulled her out of the room, and slammed the door, and for a little while the body swayed and turned, until it became still once more.

That was the worst. Nothing could be worse than that. The long days and nights here—how long must a stupid creature like myself *haunt* his death-place before release?—would be horrible, I knew that, but not so bad as this. Emily would survive, would sell the house, would slowly forget. (Even I would slowly forget.) She and Greg could marry. She was only 36, she could still be a mother.

For the rest of the night I heard her wailing, elsewhere in the house. The police did come at last, and a pair of grim silent white-coated men from the morgue entered the room to cut me—it—down. They bundled it like a broken toy into a large oval wicker basket with long wooden handles, and they carried it away.

I had thought I might be forced to stay with the body, I had feared the

possibility of being buried with it, of spending eternity as a thinking nothingness in the black dark of a casket, but the body left the room and I remained behind.

A doctor was called. When the body was carried away the room door
was left open, and now I could plainly hear the voices from downstairs.
Tony was among them now, his characteristic surly monosyllable occasionally rumbling, but the main thing for a while was the doctor. He was
trying to give Emily a sedative, but she kept wailing, she kept speaking
high hurried frantic sentences as though she had too little time to say it all.
"I did it!" she cried, over and over. "I did it! I'm to blame!"

Yes. That was the reaction I'd wanted, and expected, and here it was,
and it was horrible. Everything I had desired in the last moments of my life
had been granted to me, and they were all ghastly beyond belief. I *didn't*
want to die! I *didn't* want to give Emily such misery! And more than all the
rest I didn't want to be here, seeing and hearing it all.

They did quiet her at last, and then a policeman in a rumpled blue suit
came into the room with Greg, and listened while Greg described everything that had happened. While Greg talked, the policeman rather
grumpily stared at the remaining length of rope still knotted around the
beam, and when Greg had finished the policeman said, "You're a close
friend of his?"

"More of his wife. She works for me. I own The Bibelot, an antique
shop out on the New York road."

"Mm. Why on earth did you let her in here?"

Greg smiled; a sheepish embarrassed expression. "She's stronger than I
am," he said. "A more forceful personality. That's always been true."

It was with some surprise I realized it *was* true. Greg was something of
a weakling, and Emily was very strong. (*I* had been something of a weakling, hadn't I? Emily was the strongest of us all.)

The policeman was saying, "Any idea why he'd do it?"

"I think he suspected his wife was having an affair with me." Clearly
Greg had rehearsed this sentence, he'd much earlier come to the decision to
say it and had braced himself for the moment. He blinked all the way
through the statement, as though standing in a harsh glare.

The policeman gave him a quick shrewd look. "Were you?"

"Yes."

"She was getting a divorce?"

"No. She doesn't love me, she loved her husband."

"Then why sleep around?"

"Emily wasn't sleeping *around*," Greg said, showing offense only with that emphasized word. "From time to time, and not very often, she was sleeping with me."

"Why?"

"For comfort." Greg too looked at the rope around the beam, as though it had become me and he was awkward speaking in its presence. "Ed wasn't an easy man to get along with," he said carefully. "He was moody. It was getting worse."

"Cheerful people don't kill themselves," the policeman said.

"Exactly. Ed was depressed most of the time, obscurely angry now and then. It was affecting his business, costing him clients. He made Emily miserable but she wouldn't leave him, she loved him. I don't know what she'll do now."

"You two won't marry?"

"Oh, no." Greg smiled, a bit sadly. "Do you think we murdered him, made it look like suicide so we could marry?"

"Not at all," the policeman said. "But what's the problem? You already married?"

"I am homosexual."

The policeman was no more astonished than I. He said, "I don't get it."

"I live with my friend; that young man downstairs. I am—capable—of a wider range, but my preferences are set. I am very fond of Emily, I felt sorry for her, the life she had with Ed. I told you our physical relationship was infrequent. And often not very successful."

Oh, Emily. Oh, poor Emily.

The policeman said, "Did Thornburn know you were, uh, that way?"

"I have no idea. I don't make a public point of it."

"All right." The policeman gave one more half-angry look around the room, then said, "Let's go."

They left. The door remained open, and I heard them continue to talk as they went downstairs, first the policeman asking, "Is there somebody to stay the night? Mrs. Thornburn shouldn't be alone."

"She has relatives in Great Barrington. I phoned them earlier. Somebody should be arriving within the hour."

"You'll stay until then? The doctor says she'll probably sleep, but just in case—"

"Of course."

That was all I heard. Male voices murmured a while longer from below, and then stopped. I heard cars drive away.

How complicated men and women are. How stupid are simple actions. I had never understood anyone, least of all myself.

The room was visited once more that night, by Greg, shortly after the police left. He entered, looking as offended and repelled as though the body were still here, stood the chair up on its legs, climbed on it, and with some difficulty untied the remnant of rope. This he stuffed partway into his pocket as he stepped down again to the floor, then returned the chair to its usual spot in the corner of the room, picked the key off the floor and put it in the lock, switched off both bedside lamps and left the room, shutting the door behind him.

Now I was in darkness, except for the faint line of light under the door, and the illuminated numerals of the clock. How long one minute is! That clock was my enemy, it dragged out every minute, it paused and waited and paused and waited till I could stand it no more, and then it waited longer, and *then* the next number dropped into place. Sixty times an hour, hour after hour, all night long. I couldn't stand one night of this, how could I stand eternity?

And how could I stand the torment and torture inside my brain? That was much worse now than the physical pain, which never entirely left me. I had been right about Emily and Greg, but at the same time I had been hopelessly brainlessly wrong. I had been right about my life, but wrong; right about my death, but wrong. How *much* I wanted to make amends, and how impossible it was to do anything any more, anything at all. My actions had all tended to this, and ended with this: black remorse, the most dreadful pain of all.

I had all night to think, and to feel the pains, and to wait without knowing what I was waiting for or when—or if—my waiting would ever end. Faintly I heard the arrival of Emily's sister and brother-in-law, the murmured conversation, then the departure of Tony and Greg. Not long afterward the guestroom door opened, but almost immediately closed again, no one having entered, and a bit after that the hall light went out, and now only the illuminated clock broke the darkness.

When next would I see Emily? Would she ever enter this room again? It wouldn't be as horrible as the first time, but it would surely be horror enough.

Dawn grayed the window shade, and gradually the room appeared out of the darkness, dim and silent and morose. Apparently it was a sunless day, which never got very bright. The day went on and on, featureless, each protracted minute marked by the clock. At times I dreaded someone's entering this room, at other times I prayed for something, anything—even the presence of Emily herself—to break this unending boring *absence*. But the day went on with no event, no sound, no activity anywhere—they must be keeping Emily sedated through this first day—and it wasn't until twilight, with the digital clock reading 6:52, that the door again opened and a person entered.

At first I didn't recognize him. An angry-looking man, blunt and determined, he came in with quick ragged steps, switched on both bedside lamps, then shut the door with rather more force than necessary, and turned the key in the lock. Truculent, his manner was, and when he turned from the door I saw with incredulity that he was *me*. Me! I wasn't dead, I was alive! But how could that be?

And what was that he was carrying? He picked up the chair from the corner, carried it to the middle of the room, stood on it—

No! No!

He tied the rope around the beam. The noose was already in the other end, which he slipped over his head and tightened around his neck.

Good God, *don't!*

He kicked the chair away.

The instant I kicked the chair away I wanted it back, but gravity was turning my former wish to its present command; the chair would not right itself from where it lay on the floor, and my 193 pounds would not cease to urge downward from the rope thick around my neck.

There was pain, of course, quite horrible pain centered in my throat, but the most astounding thing was the way my cheeks seemed to swell. I could barely see over their round red hills, my eyes staring in agony at the door, *willing* someone to come in and rescue me, though I knew there was no one in the house, and in any event the door was carefully locked. My kicking legs caused me to twist and turn, so that sometimes I faced the door and sometimes the window, and my shivering hands struggled with the rope so deep in my flesh I could barely find it and most certainly could not pull it loose.

I was frantic and horrified, yet at the same time my brain possessed a cold corner of aloof observation. I seemed now to be everywhere in the room at once, within my writhing body but also without, seeing my frenzied spasms, the thick rope, the heavy beam, the mismatched pair of lit bedside lamps throwing my convulsive double shadow on the walls, the closed locked door, the white-curtained window with its shade drawn all the way down. *This is death.*